D1431697

THE LINCOLN LAWYER NOVELS

Also by Michael Connelly

Fiction

The Black Echo

The Black Ice

The Concrete Blonde

The Last Coyote

The Poet

Trunk Music

Blood Work

Angels Flight

Void Moon

A Darkness More than Night

City of Bones

Chasing the Dime

Lost Light

The Narrows

The Closers

The Lincoln Lawyer

Echo Park

The Overlook

The Brass Verdict

The Scarecrow

Nine Dragons

The Reversal

The Fifth Witness

Nonfiction

Crime Beat

Michael CONNELLY

THE LINCOLN LAWYER NOVELS

The Lincoln Lawyer

The Brass Verdict

The Reversal

LITTLE, BROWN AND COMPANY
NEW YORK BOSTON LONDON

Little, Brown and Company
Hachette Book Group
237 Park Avenue, New York, NY 10017
www.hachettebookgroup.com

First Omnibus Edition: July 2011

Little, Brown and Company is a division of Hachette Book Group, Inc.
The Little, Brown name and logo are trademarks of
Hachette Book Group, Inc.

The author wishes to acknowledge the following, whose lyrics
are quoted in *The Lincoln Lawyer*: "To Live And Die In L.A." Words
and music by Quincy Jones III, Val Young, and Tupac Shakur
copyright © 1996 by Deep Technology Music, Music of Windswept
and Songs of Universal, Inc., and Val Young Publishing. All rights for
Deep Technology Music administered by Music of Windswept. All
rights reserved. Used by permission; "To Live and Die in L.A." by
Tupac Amaru Shakur, Quincy Delight Jones III, Val Young © 1996 by
Music Corporation of America/Joshua's Dream Music. All rights
administered by Songs of Universal, Inc./BMI. Used by permission.
All rights reserved.

ISBN 978-0-316-20344-9
Library of Congress Control Number: 2011929601

10 9 8 7 6 5 4 3 2 1

RRD-C

Printed in the United States of America

Contents

The Lincoln Lawyer

*This is for Daniel F. Daly
and Roger O. Mills*

There is no client as scary as an innocent man.

—J. Michael Haller, criminal defense attorney,
Los Angeles, 1962

PART ONE
— Pretrial Intervention

1

Monday, March 7

The morning air off the Mojave in late winter is as clean and crisp as you'll ever breathe in Los Angeles County. It carries the taste of promise on it. When it starts blowing in like that I like to keep a window open in my office. There are a few people who know this routine of mine, people like Fernando Valenzuela. The bondsman, not the baseball pitcher. He called me as I was coming into Lancaster for a nine o'clock calendar call. He must have heard the wind whistling in my cell phone.

"Mick," he said, "you up north this morning?"

"At the moment," I said as I put the window up to hear him better. "You got something?"

"Yeah, I got something. I think I got a franchise player here. But his first appearance is at eleven. Can you make it back down in time?"

Valenzuela has a storefront office on Van Nuys Boulevard a block from the civic center, which includes two courthouses and the Van Nuys jail. He calls his business Liberty Bail Bonds. His phone number, in red neon on the roof of his establishment, can be seen from the high-power wing on the third floor of the jail. His number is scratched into the paint on the wall next to every pay phone on every other ward in the jail.

You could say his name is also permanently scratched onto my Christmas list. At the end of the year I give a can of salted nuts to everybody on it. Planters holiday mix. Each can has a ribbon and bow on it. But no nuts inside. Just cash. I have a lot of bail bondsmen on my Christmas list. I eat holiday mix out of Tupperware well into spring. Since my last divorce, it is sometimes all I get for dinner.

Before answering Valenzuela's question I thought about the calendar call I was headed to. My client was named Harold Casey. If the docket was handled alphabetically I could make an eleven o'clock hearing down in Van Nuys, no problem. But Judge Orton Powell was in his last term on the bench. He was retiring. That meant he no longer faced reelection pressures, like those from the private bar. To demonstrate his freedom — and possibly as a form of payback to those he had been politically beholden to for twelve years — he liked to mix things up in his courtroom. Sometimes the calendar went alphabetical, sometimes reverse alphabetical, sometimes by filing date. You never knew how the call would go until you got there.

Often lawyers cooled their heels for better than an hour in Powell's courtroom. The judge liked that.

"I think I can make eleven," I said, without knowing for sure. "What's the case?"

"Guy's gotta be big money. Beverly Hills address, family lawyer waltzing in here first thing. This is the real thing, Mick. They booked him on a half mil and his mother's lawyer came in here today ready to sign over property in Malibu to secure it. Didn't even ask about getting it lowered first. I guess they aren't too worried about him running."

"Booked for what?" I asked.

I kept my voice even. The scent of money in the water often leads to a feeding frenzy but I had taken care of Valenzuela on enough Christmases to know I had him on the hook exclusively. I could play it cool.

"The cops booked him for ag-assault, GBI and attempted rape for starters," the bondsman answered. "The DA hasn't filed yet as far as I know."

The police usually overbooked the charges. What mattered was what the prosecutors finally filed and took to court. I always say cases go in like a lion and come out like a lamb. A case going in as attempted rape and aggravated assault with great bodily injury could easily come out as simple battery. It wouldn't surprise me and it wouldn't make for much of a franchise case. Still, if I could get to the client and make a fee agreement based on the announced charges, I could look good when the DA later knocked them down.

"You got any of the details?" I asked.

"He was booked last night. It sounds like a bar pickup gone bad. The family lawyer said the woman's in it for the money. You know, the civil suit to follow the criminal case. But I'm not so sure. She got beat up pretty good from what I heard."

"What's the family lawyer's name?"

"Hold on a sec. I've got his card here somewhere."

I looked out the window while waiting for Valenzuela to find the business card. I was two minutes from the Lancaster courthouse and twelve minutes from calendar call. I needed at least three of those minutes in between to confer with my client and give him the bad news.

"Okay, here it is," Valenzuela said. "Guy's name is Cecil C. Dobbs, Esquire. Out of Century City. See, I told you. Money."

Valenzuela was right. But it wasn't the lawyer's Century City address that said money. It was the name. I knew of C. C. Dobbs by reputation and guessed that there wouldn't be more than one or two names on his entire client list that didn't have a Bel-Air or Holmby Hills address. His kind of client went home to the places where the stars seemed to reach down at night to touch the anointed.

"Give me the client's name," I said.

"That would be Louis Ross Roulet."

He spelled it and I wrote it down on a legal pad.

"Almost like the spinning wheel but you pronounce it Roo-*lay*," he said. "You going to be here, Mick?"

Before responding I wrote the name C. C. Dobbs on the pad. I then answered Valenzuela with a question.

"Why me?" I asked. "Was I asked for? Or did you suggest me?"

I had to be careful with this. I had to assume Dobbs was the kind of lawyer who would go to the California bar in a heartbeat if he came across a criminal defense attorney paying off bondsmen for client referrals. In fact, I started wondering if the whole thing might be a bar sting operation that Valenzuela hadn't picked up on. I wasn't one of the bar's favorite sons. They had come at me before. More than once.

"I asked Roulet if he had a lawyer, you know? A criminal defense lawyer, and he said no. I told him about you. I didn't push it. I just said you were good. Soft sell, you know?"

"Was this before or after Dobbs came into it?"

"No, before. Roulet called me this morning from the jail. They got him up on high power and he saw the sign, I guess. Dobbs showed up after that. I told him you were in, gave him your pedigree, and he was cool with it. He'll be there at eleven. You'll see how he is."

I didn't speak for a long moment. I wondered how truthful Valenzuela was being with me. A guy like Dobbs would have had his own man. If it wasn't his own forte, then he'd have had a criminal specialist in the firm or, at least, on standby. But Valenzuela's story seemed to contradict this. Roulet came to him empty-handed. It told me that there was more to this case I didn't know than what I did.

"Hey, Mick, you there?" Valenzuela prompted.

I made a decision. It was a decision that would eventually lead me back to Jesus Menendez and that I would in many ways come to regret. But at the moment it was made, it was just another choice made of necessity and routine.

"I'll be there," I said into the phone. "I'll see you at eleven."

I was about to close the phone when I heard Valenzuela's voice come back at me.

"And you'll take care of me for this, right, Mick? I mean, you know, if this is the franchise."

It was the first time Valenzuela had ever sought assurance of a payback from me. It played further into my paranoia and I carefully constructed an answer that would satisfy him and the bar — if it was listening.

"Don't worry, Val. You're on my Christmas list."

I closed the phone before he could say anything else and told my driver to drop me off at the employee entrance to the courthouse. The line at the metal detector would be shorter and quicker there and the security men usually didn't mind the lawyers — the regulars — sneaking through so they could make court on time.

As I thought about Louis Ross Roulet and the case and the possible riches and dangers that waited for me, I put the window back down so I could enjoy the morning's last minute of clean, fresh air. It still carried the taste of promise.

2

The courtroom in Department 2A was crowded with lawyers negotiating and socializing on both sides of the bar when I got there. I could tell the session was going to start on time because I saw the bailiff seated at his desk. This meant the judge was close to taking the bench.

In Los Angeles County the bailiffs are actually sworn deputy sheriffs who are assigned to the jail division. I approached the bailiff, whose desk was right next to the bar railing so citizens could come up to ask questions without having to violate the space assigned to the lawyers, defendants and courtroom personnel. I saw the calendar on the clipboard in front of him. I checked the nameplate on his uniform — R. Rodriguez — before speaking.

"Roberto, you got my guy on there? Harold Casey?"

The bailiff used his finger to start down the list on the call sheet but stopped quickly. This meant I was in luck.

"Yeah, Casey. He's second up."

"Alphabetical today, good. Do I have time to go back and see him?"

"No, they're bringing the first group in now. I just called. The judge is coming out. You'll probably have a couple minutes to see your guy in the pen."

"Thank you."

I started to walk toward the gate when he called after me.

"And it's Reynaldo, not Roberto."

"Right, right. I'm sorry about that, Reynaldo."

"Us bailiffs, we all look alike, right?"

I didn't know if that was an attempt at humor or just a dig at me. I didn't answer. I just smiled and went through the gate. I nodded at a couple lawyers I didn't know and a couple that I did. One stopped me to ask how long I was going to be up in front of the judge because he wanted to gauge when to come back for his own client's appearance. I told him I was going to be quick.

During a calendar call incarcerated defendants are brought to the courtroom in groups of four and held in a wood-and-glass enclosure known as the pen. This allows the defendants to confer with their attorneys in the moments before their case is called for whatever matter is before the court.

I got to the side of the pen just as the door from the interior holding cell was opened by a deputy, and the first four defendants on the docket were marched out. The last of the four to step into the pen was Harold Casey, my client. I took a position near the side wall so that we would have privacy on at least one side and signaled him over.

Casey was big and tall, as they tend to recruit them in the Road Saints motorcycle gang—or club, as the membership prefers to be known. While being held in the Lancaster jail he had cut his hair and shaved, as I had requested, and he looked reasonably presentable, except for the tattoos that wrapped both arms and poked up above his collar. But there is only so much you can do. I don't know much about the effect of tattoos on a jury but I suspect it's not overly positive, especially when grinning skulls are involved. I *do* know that jurors in general don't care for ponytails—on either the defendants or the lawyers who represent them.

Casey, or Hard Case, as he was known in the club, was charged with cultivation, possession and sale of marijuana as well as other drug and weapons charges. In a predawn raid on the ranch where he lived and worked, sheriff's deputies found a barn and Quonset hut complex that had been turned into an indoor growing facility. More than two thousand fully mature plants were seized along with sixty-three pounds of harvested marijuana packaged in various weights in plastic bags. Additionally, twelve ounces of crystal meth which the packagers sprinkled on the harvested crop to give it an extra kick were seized, along with a small arsenal of weapons, many of them later determined to be stolen.

It would appear that Hard Case was fucked. The state had him cold. He was actually found asleep on a couch in the barn, five feet from the packaging table. Added to this, he had twice previously been convicted of drug offenses and was currently still on parole for the most recent. In the state of California the third time is the charm. Realistically, Casey was facing at least a decade in prison, even with good time.

But what was unusual about Casey was that he was a defendant who was looking forward to trial and even to the likelihood of conviction. He had refused to waive his right to a speedy trial and now, less than three months after his arrest, eagerly wanted to bring it on. He was eager because it was likely that his only hope lay in an appeal of that likely conviction. Thanks to his attorney, Casey saw a glimmer of hope—that small, twinkling light that only a good attorney can bring to the darkness of a case like this. From this glimmer a case strategy was born that might ultimately work to free Casey. It was daring and would cost Casey time as he waited out the appeal, but he knew as well as I did that it was the only real shot he had.

The crack in the state's case was not in its assumption that Casey was a marijuana grower, packager and seller. The state was absolutely correct in these assumptions and the evidence more than proved it. It was in how the state came to that evidence that the case tottered on an unsteady foundation. It was my job to probe that crack in trial, exploit it, put it on record and then convince an appellate court of what I had not been able to convince Judge Orton Powell of during a pretrial motion to suppress the evidence in the case.

The seed of the prosecution of Harold Casey was planted on a Tuesday in mid-December when Casey walked into a Home Depot in Lancaster and made a number of mundane purchases that included three lightbulbs of the variety used in hydroponic farming. The man behind him in the check-out line happened to be an off-duty sheriff's deputy about to purchase out-door Christmas lights. The deputy recognized some of the artwork on Casey's arms — most notably the skull with halo tattoo that is the emblem-atic signature of the Road Saints — and put two and two together. The off-duty man then dutifully followed Casey's Harley as he rode to the ranch in nearby Pearblossom. This information was passed to the sheriff's drug squad, which arranged for an unmarked helicopter to fly over the ranch with a thermal imaging camera. The subsequent photographs, detailing rich red heat blooms from the barn and Quonset hut, along with the state-ment of the deputy who saw Casey purchase hydroponic lights, were sub-mitted in an affidavit to a judge. The next morning Casey was rousted from sleep on the couch by deputies with a signed search warrant.

In an earlier hearing I argued that all evidence against Casey should be excluded because the probable cause for the search constituted an invasion of Casey's right to privacy. Using an individual's commonplace purchases at a hardware store as a springboard to conduct a further invasion of pri-vacy through surveillance on the ground and in the air and by thermal imag-ing would surely be viewed as excessive by the framers of the Constitution.

Judge Powell rejected my argument and the case moved toward trial or disposition by plea agreement. In the meantime new information came to light that would bolster Casey's appeal of a conviction. Analysis of the photographs taken during the flyover of Casey's house and the focal speci-fications of the thermal camera used by the deputies indicated the helicop-ter was flying no more than two hundred feet off the ground when the photographs were taken. The U.S. Supreme Court has held that a law enforcement observation flight over a suspect's property does not violate an individual's right to privacy so long as the aircraft is in public airspace. I had Raul Levin, my investigator, check with the Federal Aviation Adminis-tration. Casey's ranch was located beneath no airport flight pattern. The floor for public airspace above the ranch was a thousand feet. The deputies had clearly invaded Casey's privacy while gathering the probable cause to raid the ranch.

My job now was to take the case to trial and elicit testimony from the deputies and pilot as to the altitude they were flying when they went over the ranch. If they told the truth, I had them. If they lied, I had them. I don't relish the idea of embarrassing law enforcement officers in open court, but my hope was that they would lie. If a jury sees a cop lie on the witness stand, then the case might as well end right there. You don't have to appeal a not-guilty verdict. The state has no comebacks from a not-guilty verdict.

Either way, I was confident I had a winner. We just had to get to trial and there was only one thing holding us back. That was what I needed to talk to Casey about before the judge took the bench and called the case.

My client sauntered over to the corner of the pen and didn't offer a hello. I didn't, either. He knew what I wanted. We'd had this conversation before.

"Harold, this is calendar call," I said. "This is when I tell the judge if we're ready to go to trial. I already know the state's ready. So today's about us."

"So?"

"So, there's a problem. Last time we were here you told me I'd be getting some money. But here we are, Harold, and no money."

"Don't worry. I have your money."

"That's why I am worried. *You* have my money. I don't have my money."

"It's coming. I talked to my boys yesterday. It's coming."

"You said that last time, too. I don't work for free, Harold. The expert I had go over the photos doesn't work for free, either. Your retainer is long gone. I want some more money or you're going to have to get yourself a new lawyer. A public defender."

"No PD, man. I want you."

"Well, I got expenses and I gotta eat. You know what my nut is each week just to pay for the yellow pages? Take a guess."

Casey said nothing.

"A grand. Averages out a grand a week just to keep my ad in there and that's before I eat or pay the mortgage or the child support or put gas in the Lincoln. I'm not doing this on a promise, Harold. I work on green inspiration."

Casey seemed unimpressed.

"I checked around," he said. "You can't just quit on me. Not now. The judge won't let you."

A hush fell over the courtroom as the judge stepped out of the door to his chambers and took the two steps up to the bench. The bailiff called the courtroom to order. It was showtime. I just looked at Casey for a long moment and stepped away. He had an amateur, jailhouse knowledge of the law and how it worked. He knew more than most. But he was still in for a surprise.

I took a seat against the rail behind the defendant's table. The first case called was a bail reconsideration that was handled quickly. Then the clerk called the case of *California v. Casey* and I stepped up to the table.

"Michael Haller for the defense," I said.

The prosecutor announced his presence as well. He was a young guy named Victor DeVries. He had no idea what was going to hit him when we got to trial. Judge Orton Powell made the usual inquiries about whether a last-minute disposition in the case was possible. Every judge had an overflowing calendar and an overriding mandate to clear cases through disposition. The last thing any judge wanted to hear was that there was no hope of agreement and that a trial was inevitable.

But Powell took the bad news from DeVries and me in stride and asked if we were ready to schedule the trial for later in the week. DeVries said yes. I said no.

"Your Honor," I said, "I would like to carry this over until next week, if possible."

"What is the cause of your delay, Mr. Haller?" the judge asked impatiently. "The prosecution is ready and I want to dispose of this case."

"I want to dispose of it as well, Your Honor. But the defense is having trouble locating a witness who will be necessary to our case. An indispensable witness, Your Honor. I think a one-week carryover should be sufficient. By next week we should be ready to go forward."

As expected, DeVries objected to the delay.

"Your Honor, this is the first the state has heard about a missing witness. Mr. Haller has had almost three months to locate his witnesses. He's the one who wanted the speedy trial and now he wants to wait. I think this is just a delay tactic because he's facing a case that—"

"You can hold on to the rest of that for the jury, Mr. DeVries," the judge said. "Mr. Haller, you think one week will solve your problem?"

"Yes, Your Honor."

"Okay, we'll see you and Mr. Casey next Monday and you will be ready to go. Is that understood?"

"Yes, Your Honor. Thank you."

The clerk called the next case and I stepped away from the defense table. I watched a deputy lead my client out of the pen. Casey glanced back at me, a look on his face that seemed to be equal parts anger and confusion. I went over to Reynaldo Rodriguez and asked if I could be allowed back into the holding area to further confer with my client. It was a professional courtesy allowed to most of the regulars. Rodriguez got up, unlocked a door behind his desk and ushered me through. I made sure to thank him by his correct name.

Casey was in a holding cell with one other defendant, the man whose case had been called ahead of his in the courtroom. The cell was large and had benches running along three sides. The bad thing about getting your case called early in the courtroom is that after the hearing you have to sit in this cage until it fills with enough people to run a full bus back to the county jail. Casey came right up to the bars to speak to me.

"What witness were you talking about in there?" he demanded.

"Mr. Green," I said. "Mr. Green is all we need for this case to go forward."

Casey's face contorted in anger. I tried to cut him off at the pass.

"Look, Harold, I know you want to move this along and get to the trial and then the appeal. But you've got to pay the freight along the way. I know from long, hard experience that it does me no good to chase people for money after the horse is out of the barn. You want to play now, then you pay now."

I nodded and was about to turn back to the door that led to freedom. But then I spoke to him again.

"And don't think the judge in there didn't know what was going on," I said. "You got a young prosecutor who's wet behind the ears and doesn't have to worry about where his next paycheck's coming from. But Orton

Powell spent a lot of years in the defense bar before he got to the bench. He knows about chasing indispensable witnesses like Mr. Green and he probably won't look too kindly upon a defendant who doesn't pay his lawyer. I gave him the wink, Harold. If I want off the case, I'll get off. But what I'd rather do is come in here next Monday and stand up out there and tell him we found our witness and we are ready to go. You understand?"

Casey didn't say anything at first. He walked to the far side of the cell and sat down on the bench. He didn't look at me when he finally spoke.

"As soon as I get to a phone," he said.

"Sounds good, Harold. I'll tell one of the deputies you have to make a call. Make the call, then sit tight and I'll see you next week. We'll get this thing going."

I headed back to the door, my steps quick. I hate being inside a jail. I'm not sure why. I guess it's because sometimes the line seems so thin. The line between being a criminal attorney and a *criminal* attorney. Sometimes I'm not sure which side of the bars I am on. To me it's always a dead-bang miracle that I get to walk out the way I walked in.

3

In the hallway outside the courtroom I turned my cell phone back on and called my driver to tell him I was coming out. I then checked voicemail and found messages from Lorna Taylor and Fernando Valenzuela. I decided to wait until I was in the car to make the callbacks.

Earl Briggs, my driver, had the Lincoln right out front. Earl didn't get out and open the door or anything. His deal was just to drive me while he worked off the fee he owed me for getting him probation on a cocaine sales conviction. I paid him twenty bucks an hour to drive me but then held half of it back to go against the fee. It wasn't quite what he was making dealing crack in the projects but it was safer, legal and something that could go on a résumé. Earl said he wanted to go straight in life and I believed him.

I could hear the sound of hip-hop pulsing behind the closed windows of the Town Car as I approached. But Earl killed the music as soon as I reached for the door handle. I slid into the back and told him to head toward Van Nuys.

"Who was that you were listening to?" I asked him.

"Um, that was Three Six Mafia."

"Dirty south?"

"That's right."

Over the years, I had become knowledgeable in the subtle distinctions, regional and otherwise, in rap and hip-hop. Across the board, most of my clients listened to it, many of them developing their life strategies from it.

I reached over and picked up the shoebox full of cassette tapes from the Boyleston case and chose one at random. I noted the tape number and the time in the little logbook I kept in the shoebox. I handed the tape over the seat to Earl and he slid it into the dashboard stereo. I didn't have to tell him to play it at a volume so low that it would amount to little more than background noise. Earl had been with me for three months. He knew what to do.

Roger Boyleston was one of my few court-appointed clients. He was facing a variety of federal drug-trafficking charges. DEA wiretaps on Boyleston's phones had led to his arrest and the seizure of six kilos of cocaine that he had planned to distribute through a network of dealers. There were numerous tapes — more than fifty hours of recorded phone conversations. Boyleston talked to many people about what was coming and when to expect it. The case was a slam dunk for the government. Boyleston was going to go away for a long time and there was almost nothing I could do but negotiate a deal, trading Boyleston's cooperation for a lower sentence. That didn't matter, though. What mattered to me were the tapes. I took the case because of the tapes. The federal government would pay me to listen to the tapes in preparation for defending my client. That meant I would get a minimum of fifty billable hours out of Boyleston and the government before it was all settled. So I made sure the tapes were in heavy rotation whenever I was riding in the Lincoln. I wanted to make sure that if I ever had to put my hand on the book and swear to tell the truth, I could say in good conscience that I played every one of those tapes I billed Uncle Sugar for.

I called Lorna Taylor back first. Lorna is my case manager. The phone number that runs on my half-page ad in the yellow pages and on thirty-six bus benches scattered through high-crime areas in the south and east county goes directly to the office/second bedroom of her Kings Road condo in West Hollywood. The address the California bar and all the clerks of the courts have for me is the condo as well.

Lorna is the first buffer. To get to me you start with her. My cell number is given out to only a few and Lorna is the gatekeeper. She is tough, smart, professional and beautiful. Lately, though, I only get to verify this last attribute once a month or so when I take her to lunch and sign checks — she's my bookkeeper, too.

"Law office," she said when I called in.

"Sorry, I was still in court," I said, explaining why I didn't get her call. "What's up?"

"You talked to Val, right?"

"Yeah. I'm heading down to Van Nuys now. I got that at eleven."

"He called here to make sure. He sounds nervous."

"He thinks this guy is the golden goose, wants to make sure he's along for the ride. I'll call him back to reassure him."

"I did some preliminary checking on the name Louis Ross Roulet. Credit check is excellent. The name in the *Times* archive comes up with a few hits. All real estate transactions. Looks like he works for a real estate firm in Beverly Hills. It's called Windsor Residential Estates. Looks like they handle all exclusive pocket listings—not the sort of properties where they put a sign out front."

"That's good. Anything else?"

"Not on that. And just the usual so far on the phone."

Which meant that she had fielded the usual number of calls drawn by the bus benches and the yellow pages, all from people who wanted a lawyer. Before the callers hit my radar they had to convince Lorna that they could pay for what they wanted. She was sort of like the nurse behind the desk in the emergency room. You have to convince her you have valid insurance before she sends you back to see the doc. Next to Lorna's phone she keeps a rate schedule that starts with a $5,000 flat fee to handle a DUI and ranges to the hourly fees I charge for felony trials. She makes sure every potential client is a paying client and knows the costs of the crime they have been charged with. There's that saying, Don't do the crime if you can't do the time. Lorna likes to say that with me, it's Don't do the crime if you can't pay for my time. She accepts MasterCard and Visa and will get purchase approval before a client ever gets to me.

"Nobody we know?" I asked.

"Gloria Dayton called from Twin Towers."

I groaned. The Twin Towers was the county's main lockup in downtown. It housed women in one tower and men in the other. Gloria Dayton was a high-priced prostitute who needed my legal services from time to time. The first time I represented her was at least ten years earlier, when she was young and drug-free and still had life in her eyes. Now she was a pro bono client. I never charged her. I just tried to convince her to quit the life.

"When did she get popped?"

"Last night. Or rather, this morning. Her first appearance is after lunch."

"I don't know if I can make that with this Van Nuys thing."

"There's also a complication. Cocaine possession as well as the usual."

I knew that Gloria worked exclusively through contacts made on the Internet, where she billed herself on a variety of websites as Glory Days. She was no streetwalker or barroom troller. When she got popped, it was usually after an undercover vice officer was able to penetrate her check system and set up a date. The fact that she had cocaine on her person when they met sounded like an unusual lapse on her part or a plant from the cop.

"All right, if she calls back tell her I will try to be there and if I'm not there I will have somebody take it. Will you call the court and firm up the hearing?"

"I'm on it. But, Mickey, when are you going to tell her this is the last time?"

"I don't know. Maybe today. What else?"

"Isn't that enough for one day?"

"It'll do, I guess."

We talked a little more about my schedule for the rest of the week and I opened my laptop on the fold-down table so I could check my calendar against hers. I had a couple hearings set for each morning and a one-day trial on Thursday. It was all South side drug stuff. My meat and potatoes. At the end of the conversation I told her that I would call her after the Van Nuys hearing to let her know if and how the Roulet case would impact things.

"One last thing," I said. "You said the place Roulet works handles pretty exclusive real estate deals, right?"

"Yeah. Every deal his name was attached to in the archives was in seven figures. A couple got up into the eights. Holmby Hills, Bel-Air, places like that."

I nodded, thinking that Roulet's status might make him a person of interest to the media.

"Then why don't you tip Sticks to it," I said.

"You sure?"

"Yeah, we might be able to work something there."

"Will do."

"Talk to you later."

By the time I closed the phone, Earl had us back on the Antelope Valley Freeway heading south. We were making good time and getting to Van Nuys for Roulet's first appearance wasn't going to be a problem. I called Fernando Valenzuela to tell him.

"That's real good," the bondsman said. "I'll be waiting."

As he spoke I watched two motorcycles glide by my window. Each rider wore a black leather vest with the skull and halo patch sewn on the back.

"Anything else?" I asked.

"Yeah, one other thing I should probably tell you," Valenzuela said. "I was double-checking with the court on when his first appearance was going to be and I found out the case was assigned to Maggie McFierce. I don't know if that's going to be a problem for you or not."

Maggie McFierce as in Margaret McPherson, who happened to be one of the toughest and, yes, fiercest deputy district attorneys assigned to the Van Nuys courthouse. She also happened to be my first ex-wife.

"It won't be a problem for me," I said without hesitation. "She's the one who'll have the problem."

The defendant has the right to his choice of counsel. If there is a conflict of interest between the defense lawyer and the prosecutor, then it is the prosecutor who must bow out. I knew Maggie would hold me personally responsible for her losing the reins on what might be a big case but I couldn't help that. It had happened before. In my laptop I still had a motion to disqualify from the last case in which we had crossed paths. If necessary, I would just have to change the name of the defendant and print it out. I'd be good to go and she'd be as good as gone.

The two motorcycles had now moved in front of us. I turned and looked out the back window. There were three more Harleys behind us.

"You know what that means, though," I said.

"No, what?"

"She'll go for no bail. She always does with crimes against women."

"Shit, can she get it? I'm looking at a nice chunk of change on this, man."

"I don't know. You said the guy's got family and C. C. Dobbs. I can make something out of that. We'll see."

"Shit."

Valenzuela was seeing his major payday disappear.

"I'll see you there, Val."

I closed the phone and looked over the seat at Earl.

"How long have we had the escort?" I asked.

"Just came up on us," Earl said. "You want me to do something?"

"Let's see what they—"

I didn't have to wait until the end of my sentence. One of the riders from the rear came up alongside the Lincoln and signaled us toward the upcoming exit for the Vasquez Rocks County Park. I recognized him as Teddy Vogel, a former client and the highest-ranked Road Saint not incarcerated. He might have been the largest Saint as well. He went at least 350 pounds and he gave the impression of a fat kid riding his little brother's bike.

"Pull off, Earl," I said. "Let's see what he's got."

We pulled into the parking lot next to the jagged rock formation named after an outlaw who had hid in them a century before. I saw two people sitting and having a picnic on the edge of one of the highest ledges. I didn't think I would feel comfortable eating a sandwich in such a dangerous spot and position.

I lowered my window as Teddy Vogel approached on foot. The other four Saints had killed their engines but remained on their bikes. Vogel leaned down to the window and put one of his giant forearms on the sill. I could feel the car tilt down a few inches.

"Counselor, how's it hanging?" he said.

"Just fine, Ted," I said, not wanting to call him by his obvious gang sobriquet of Teddy Bear. "What's up with you?"

"What happened to the ponytail?"

"Some people objected to it, so I cut it off."

"A jury, huh? Must've been a collection of stiffs from up this way."

"What's up, Ted?"

"I got a call from Hard Case over there in the Lancaster pen. He said I might catch you heading south. Said you were stalling his case till you got some green. That right, Counselor?"

It was said as routine conversation. No threat in his voice or words. And I didn't feel threatened. Two years ago I got an abduction and aggravated assault case against Vogel knocked down to a disturbing the peace. He ran a Saints-owned strip club on Sepulveda in Van Nuys. His arrest came after he learned that one of his most productive dancers had quit and crossed the street to work at a competing club. Vogel had crossed the street after her, grabbed her off the stage and carried her back to his club. She was naked. A passing motorist called the police. Knocking the case down was one of my better plays and Vogel knew this. He had a soft spot for me.

"He's pretty much got it right," I said. "I work for a living. If he wants me to work for him he's gotta pay me."

"We gave you five grand in December," Vogel said.

"That's long gone, Ted. More than half went to the expert who is going to blow the case up. The rest went to me and I already worked off those hours. If I'm going to take it to trial, then I need to refill the tank."

"You want another five?"

"No, I need ten and I told Hard Case that last week. It's a three-day trial and I'll need to bring my expert in from Kodak in New York. I've got his fee to cover and he wants first class in the air and the Chateau Marmont on the ground. Thinks he's going to be drinking at the bar with movie stars or something. That place is four hundred a night just for the cheap rooms."

"You're killing me, Counselor. Whatever happened to that slogan you had in the yellow pages? 'Reasonable doubt for a reasonable fee.' You call ten grand reasonable?"

"I liked that slogan. It brought in a lot of clients. But the California bar wasn't so pleased with it, made me get rid of it. Ten is the price and it is reasonable, Ted. If you can't or don't want to pay it, I'll file the paperwork today. I'll drop out and he can go with a PD. I'll turn everything I have over. But the PD probably won't have the budget to fly in the photo expert."

Vogel shifted his position on the window sill and the car shuddered under the weight.

"No, no, we want you. Hard Case is important to us, you know what I mean? I want him out and back to work."

I watched him reach inside his vest with a hand that was so fleshy that the knuckles were indented. It came out with a thick envelope that he passed into the car to me.

"Is this cash?" I asked.

"That's right. What's wrong with cash?"

"Nothing. But I have to give you a receipt. It's an IRS reporting requirement. This is the whole ten?"

"It's all there."

I took the top off of a cardboard file box I keep on the seat next to me. My receipt book was behind the current case files. I started writing out the receipt. Most lawyers who get disbarred go down because of financial violations. The mishandling or misappropriation of client fees. I kept meticulous records and receipts. I would never let the bar get to me that way.

"So you had it all along," I said as I wrote. "What if I had backed down to five? What would you have done then?"

Vogel smiled. He was missing one of his front teeth on the bottom. Had to have been a fight at the club. He patted the other side of his vest.

"I got another envelope with five in it right here, Counselor," he said. "I was ready for you."

"Damn, now I feel bad, leaving you with money in your pocket."

I tore out his copy of the receipt and handed it out the window.

"I receipted it to Casey. He's the client."

"Fine with me."

He took the receipt and dropped his arm off the window sill as he stood up straight. The car returned to a normal level. I wanted to ask him where the money came from, which of the Saints' criminal enterprises had earned it, whether a hundred girls had danced a hundred hours for him to pay me, but that was a question I was better off not knowing the answer to. I watched Vogel saunter back to his Harley and struggle to swing a trash can–thick leg over the seat. For the first time I noticed the double shocks on the back wheel. I told Earl to get back on the freeway and get going to Van Nuys, where I now needed to make a stop at the bank before hitting the courthouse to meet my new client.

As we drove I opened the envelope and counted out the money, twenties, fifties and hundred-dollar bills. It was all there. The tank was refilled and I was good to go with Harold Casey. I would go to trial and teach his young prosecutor a lesson. I would win, if not in trial, then certainly on appeal. Casey would return to the family and work of the Road Saints. His guilt in the crime he was charged with was not something I even considered as I filled out a deposit slip for my client fees account.

"Mr. Haller?" Earl said after a while.

"What, Earl?"

"That man you told him was coming in from New York to be the expert? Will I be picking him up at the airport?"

I shook my head.

"There is no expert coming in from New York, Earl. The best camera and photo experts in the world are right here in Hollywood."

Now Earl nodded and his eyes held mine for a moment in the rearview mirror. Then he looked back at the road ahead.

"I see," he said, nodding again.

And I nodded to myself. No hesitation in what I had done or said. That was my job. That was how it worked. After fifteen years of practicing law I had come to think of it in very simple terms. The law was a large, rusting machine that sucked up people and lives and money. I was just a mechanic. I had become expert at going into the machine and fixing things and extracting what I needed from it in return.

There was nothing about the law that I cherished anymore. The law school notions about the virtue of the adversarial system, of the system's checks and balances, of the search for truth, had long since eroded like the faces of statues from other civilizations. The law was not about truth. It was about negotiation, amelioration, manipulation. I didn't deal in guilt and innocence, because everybody was guilty. Of something. But it didn't matter, because every case I took on was a house built on a foundation poured by overworked and underpaid laborers. They cut corners. They made mistakes. And then they painted over the mistakes with lies. My job was to peel away the paint and find the cracks. To work my fingers and tools into those cracks and widen them. To make them so big that either the house fell down or, failing that, my client slipped through.

Much of society thought of me as the devil but they were wrong. I was a greasy angel. I was the true road saint. I was needed and wanted. By both sides. I was the oil in the machine. I allowed the gears to crank and turn. I helped keep the engine of the system running.

But all of that would change with the Roulet case. For me. For him. And certainly for Jesus Menendez.

4

Louis Ross Roulet was in a holding tank with seven other men who had made the half-block bus ride from the Van Nuys jail to the Van Nuys court-house. There were only two white men in the cell and they sat next to each other on a bench while the six black men took the other side of the cell. It was a form of Darwinian segregation. They were all strangers but there was strength in numbers.

Since Roulet supposedly came from Beverly Hills money, I looked at the two white men and it was easy to choose between them. One was rail thin with the desperate wet eyes of a hype who was long past fix time. The other looked like the proverbial deer in the headlights. I chose him.

"Mr. Roulet?" I said, pronouncing the name the way Valenzuela had told me to.

The deer nodded. I signaled him over to the bars so I could talk quietly.

"My name is Michael Haller. People call me Mickey. I will be representing you during your first appearance today."

We were in the holding area behind the arraignment court, where attorneys are routinely allowed access to confer with clients before court begins. There is a blue line painted on the floor outside the cells. The three-foot line. I had to keep that distance from my client.

Roulet grasped the bars in front of me. Like the others in the cage, he had on ankle, wrist and belly chains. They wouldn't come off until he was taken into the courtroom. He was in his early thirties and, though at least six feet tall and 180 pounds, he seemed slight. Jail will do that to you. His eyes were pale blue and it was rare for me to see the kind of panic that was so clearly set in them. Most of the time my clients have been in lockup before and they have the stone-cold look of the predator. It's how they get by in jail.

But Roulet was different. He looked like prey. He was scared and he didn't care who saw it and knew it.

"This is a setup," he said urgently and loudly. "You have to get me out of here. I made a mistake with that woman, that's all. She's trying to set me up and—"

I put my hands up to stop him.

"Be careful what you say in here," I said in a low voice. "In fact, be careful what you say until we get you out of here and can talk in private."

He looked around, seemingly not understanding.

"You never know who is listening," I said. "And you never know who will say he heard you say something, even if you didn't say anything. Best thing is to not talk about the case at all. You understand? Best thing is not to talk to anyone about anything, period."

He nodded and I signaled him down to the bench next to the bars. There was a bench against the opposite wall and I sat down.

"I am really here just to meet you and tell you who I am," I said. "We'll talk about the case after we get you out. I already spoke to your family lawyer, Mr. Dobbs, out there and we will tell the judge that we are prepared to post bail. Do I have all of that right?"

I opened a leather Mont Blanc folder and prepared to take notes on a legal pad. Roulet nodded. He was learning.

"Good," I said. "Tell me about yourself. How old you are, whether you're married, what ties you have to the community."

"Um, I'm thirty-two. I've lived here my whole life—even went to school here. UCLA. Not married. No kids. I work—"

"Divorced?"

"No, never married. I work for my family's business. Windsor Residential Estates. It's named after my mother's second husband. It's real estate. We sell real estate."

I was writing notes. Without looking up at him, I quietly asked, "How much money did you make last year?"

When Roulet didn't answer I looked up at him.

"Why do you need to know that?" he asked.

"Because I am going to get you out of here before the sun goes down today. To do that, I need to know everything about your standing in the community. That includes your financial standing."

"I don't know exactly what I made. A lot of it was shares in the company."

"You didn't file taxes?"

Roulet looked over his shoulder at the others in the cell and then whispered his answer.

"Yes, I did. On that my income was a quarter million."

"But what you're saying is that with the shares you earned in the company you really made more."

"Right."

One of Roulet's cellmates came up to the bars next to him. The other white man. He had an agitated manner, his hands in constant motion, moving from hips to pockets to each other in desperate grasps.

"Hey, man, I need a lawyer, too. You got a card?"

"Not for you, pal. They'll have a lawyer out there for you."

I looked back at Roulet and waited a moment for the hype to move away. He didn't. I looked back at him.

"Look, this is private. Could you leave us alone?"

The hype made some kind of motion with his hands and shuffled back to the corner he had come from. I looked back at Roulet.

"What about charitable organizations?" I asked.

"What do you mean?" Roulet responded.

"Are you involved in any charities? Do you give to any charities?"

"Yeah, the company does. We give to Make a Wish and a runaway shelter in Hollywood. I think it's called My Friend's Place or something like that."

"Okay, good."

"Are you going to get me out?"

"I'm going to try. You've got some heavy charges on you — I checked before coming back here — and I have a feeling the DA is going to request no bail, but this is good stuff. I can work with it."

I indicated my notes.

"No bail?" he said in a loud, panicked voice.

The others in the cell looked in his direction because what he had said was their collective nightmare. No bail.

"Calm down," I said. "I said that is what she is going to go for. I didn't say she would get it. When was the last time you were arrested?"

I always threw that in out of the blue so I could watch their eyes and see if there was going to be a surprise thrown at me in court.

"Never. I've never been arrested. This whole thing is —"

"I know, I know, but we don't want to talk about that here, remember?"

He nodded. I looked at my watch. Court was about to start and I still needed to talk to Maggie McFierce.

"I'm going to go now," I said. "I'll see you out there in a few minutes and we'll see about getting you out of here. When we are out there, don't say anything until you check with me. If the judge asks you how you are doing, you check with me. Okay?"

"Well, don't I say 'not guilty' to the charges?"

"No, they're not going to even ask you that. Today all they do is read you the charges, talk about bail and set a date for an arraignment. That's when we say 'not guilty.' So today you say nothing. No outbursts, nothing. Got that?"

He nodded and frowned.

"Are you going to be all right, Louis?"

He nodded glumly.

"Just so you know," I said. "I charge twenty-five hundred dollars for a first appearance and bail hearing like this. Is that going to be a problem?"

He shook his head no. I liked that he wasn't talking. Most of my clients talk way too much. Usually they talk themselves right into prison.

"Good. We can talk about the rest of it after you are out of here and we can get together in private."

I closed my leather folder, hoping he had noticed it and was impressed, then stood up.

"One last thing," I said. "Why'd you pick me? There's a lot of lawyers out there, why me?"

It was a question that didn't matter to our relationship but I wanted to test Valenzuela's veracity.

Roulet shrugged.

"I don't know," he said. "I remembered your name from something I read in the paper."

"What did you read about me?"

"It was a story about a case where the evidence got thrown out against some guy. I think it was drugs or something. You won the case because they had no evidence after that."

"The Hendricks case?"

It was the only one I could think of that had made the papers in recent months. Hendricks was another Road Saint client and the sheriff's department had put a GPS bug on his Harley to track his deliveries. Doing that on public roads was fine. But when he parked his bike in the kitchen of his home at night, that bug constituted unlawful entry by the cops. The case was tossed by a judge during the preliminary hearing. It made a decent splash in the *Times*.

"I can't remember the name of the client," Roulet said. "I just remembered your name. Your last name, actually. When I called the bail bondsman today I gave him the name Haller and asked him to get you and to call my own attorney. Why?"

"No reason. Just curious. I appreciate the call. I'll see you in the courtroom."

I put the differences between what Roulet had said about my hiring and what Valenzuela had told me into the bank for later consideration and made my way back into the arraignment court. I saw Maggie McFierce sitting at one end of the prosecution table. She was there along with five other prosecutors. The table was large and L-shaped so it could accommodate an endlessly revolving number of lawyers who could sit and still face the bench. A prosecutor assigned to the courtroom handled most of the routine appearances and arraignments that were paraded through each day. But special cases brought the big guns out of the district attorney's office on the second floor of the courthouse next door. TV cameras did that, too.

As I stepped through the bar I saw a man setting up a video camera on a tripod next to the bailiff's desk. There was no network symbol on the camera or the man's clothes. The man was a freelancer who had gotten wind of the case and would shoot the hearing and then try to sell it to one of the local stations whose news director needed a thirty-second story. When I had checked with the bailiff earlier about Roulet's place on the calendar, he told me the judge had already authorized the filming.

I walked up to my ex-wife from behind and bent down to whisper into her ear. She was looking at photographs in a file. She was wearing a navy suit with a thin gray stripe. Her raven-colored hair was tied back with a matching gray ribbon. I loved her hair when it was back like that.

"Are you the one who used to have the Roulet case?"

She looked up, not recognizing the whisper. Her face was involuntarily forming a smile but then it turned into a frown when she saw it was me. She knew exactly what I had meant by using the past tense and she slapped the file closed.

"Don't tell me," she said.

"Sorry. He liked what I did on Hendricks and gave me a call."

"Son of a bitch. I wanted this case, Haller. This is the second time you've done this to me."

"I guess this town ain't big enough for the both of us," I said in a poor Cagney imitation.

She groaned.

"All right," she said in quick surrender. "I'll go peacefully after this hearing. Unless you object to even that."

"I might. You going for a no-bail hold?"

"That's right. But that won't change with the prosecutor. That was a directive from the second floor."

I nodded. That meant a case supervisor must have called for the no-bail hold.

"He's connected in the community. And has never been arrested."

I studied her reaction, not having had the time to make sure Roulet's denial of ever being previously arrested was the truth. It's always amazing how many clients lie about previous engagements with the machine, when it is a lie that has no hope of going the distance.

But Maggie gave no indication that she knew otherwise. Maybe it was true. Maybe I had an honest-to-goodness first-time offender for a client.

"It doesn't matter whether he's done anything before," Maggie said. "What matters is what he did last night."

She opened the file and quickly checked through the photos until she saw the one she liked and snatched it out.

"Here's what your pillar of the community did last night. So I don't really care what he did before. I'm just going to make sure he doesn't get out to do this again."

The photo was an 8 × 10 close-up of a woman's face. The swelling around the right eye was so extensive that the eye was completely and tightly closed. The nose was broken and pushed off center. Blood-soaked gauze protruded from each nostril. There was a deep gash over the right eyebrow that had been closed with nine butterfly stitches. The lower lip was cut and had a marble-size swelling as well. The worst thing about the photo was the eye that was undamaged. The woman looked at the camera with fear, pain and humiliation undeniably expressed in that one tearful eye.

"If he did it," I said, because that is what I would be expected to say.

"Right," Maggie said. "Sure, if he did it. He was only arrested in her home with her blood on him, but you're right, that's a valid question."

"I like it when you're sarcastic. Do you have the arrest report there? I'd like to get a copy of it."

"You can get it from whoever takes the case over from me. No favors, Haller. Not this time."

I waited, expecting more banter, more indignation, maybe another shot across the bow, but that was all she said. I decided that getting more out of her on the case was a lost cause. I changed the subject.

"So," I said. "How is she?"

"She's scared shitless and hurting like hell. How else would she be?"

She looked up at me and I saw the immediate recognition and then judgment in her eyes.

"You weren't even asking about the victim, were you?"

I didn't answer. I didn't want to lie to her.

"Your daughter is doing fine," she said perfunctorily. "She likes the things you send her but she would rather *you* show up a little more often."

That wasn't a shot across the bow. That was a direct hit and it was deserved. It seemed as though I was always chasing cases, even on weekends. Deep down inside I knew I needed to start chasing my daughter around the backyard more often. The time to do it was going by.

"I will," I said. "Starting right now. What about this weekend?"

"Fine. You want me to tell her tonight?"

"Uh, maybe wait until tomorrow so I know for sure."

She gave me one of those knowing nods. We had been through this before.

"Great. Let me know tomorrow."

This time I didn't enjoy the sarcasm.

"What does she need?" I asked, trying to stumble back to just being even.

"I just told you what she needs. More of you in her life."

"Okay, I promise. I will do that."

She didn't respond.

"I really mean that, Maggie. I'll call you tomorrow."

She looked up at me and was ready to hit me with both barrels. She had done it before, saying I was all talk and no action when it came to fatherhood. But I was saved by the start of the court session. The judge came out of chambers and bounded up the steps to the bench. The bailiff called the courtroom to order. Without another word to Maggie I left the prosecution table and went back to one of the seats along the bar.

The judge asked his clerk if there was any business to be discussed before the custodies were brought out. There was none, so the judge ordered the first group out. As with the courtroom in Lancaster, there was a large holding area for in-custody defendants. I got up and moved to the opening in the glass. When I saw Roulet come through the door I signaled him over.

"You're going first," I told him. "I asked the judge to take you out of order as a favor. I want to try to get you out of here."

This was not the truth. I hadn't asked the judge anything, and even if I had, the judge would do no such thing for me as a favor. Roulet was going first because of the media presence in the courtroom. It was a general practice to deal with the media cases first. This was a courtesy to the cameramen who supposedly had other assignments to get to. But it also made for less tension in the courtroom when lawyers, defendants and even the judge could operate without a television camera on them.

"Why's that camera here?" Roulet asked in a panicked whisper. "Is that for me?"

"Yes, it's for you. Somebody tipped him to the case. If you don't want to be filmed, try to use me as a shield."

Roulet shifted his position so I was blocking the view of him from the camera across the courtroom. This lowered the chances that the cameraman would be able to sell the story and film to a local news program. That was good. It also meant that if he was able to sell the story, I would be the focal point of the images that went with it. This was also good.

The Roulet case was called, his name mispronounced by the clerk, and Maggie announced her presence for the prosecution and then I announced mine. Maggie had upped the charges, as was her usual MO as Maggie McFierce. Roulet now faced attempted murder along with the attempted rape count. It would make it easier for her to argue for a no-bail hold.

The judge informed Roulet of his constitutional rights and set an arraignment date for March 21. Speaking for Roulet, I asked to address the no-bail hold. This set off a spirited back-and-forth between Maggie and me, all of which was refereed by the judge, who knew we were formerly married because he had attended our wedding. While Maggie listed the atrocities committed upon the victim, I in turn listed Roulet's ties to the community and charitable efforts and pointed to C. C. Dobbs in the gallery and offered to put him on the stand to further discuss Roulet's good standing. Dobbs was my ace in the hole. His stature in the legal community would supersede Roulet's standing and certainly be influential with the judge, who held his position on the bench at the behest of the voters — and campaign contributors.

"The bottom line, Judge, is that the state cannot make a case for this man being a flight risk or a danger to the community," I said in closing. "Mr. Roulet is anchored in this community and intends to do nothing other than vigorously attack the false charges that have been leveled against him."

I used the word *attack* purposely in case the statement got on the air and happened to be watched by the woman who had leveled the charges.

"Your Honor," Maggie responded, "all grandstanding aside, what should not be forgotten is that the victim in this case was brutally—"

"Ms. McPherson," the judge interrupted. "I think we have gone back and forth on this enough. I am aware of the victim's injuries as well as Mr. Roulet's standing. I also have a busy calendar today. I am going to set bail at one million dollars. I am also going to require Mr. Roulet to be supervised by the court with weekly check-ins. If he misses one, he forfeits his freedom."

I quickly glanced out into the gallery, where Dobbs was sitting next to Fernando Valenzuela. Dobbs was a thin man who shaved his head to hide male-pattern balding. His thinness was exaggerated by Valenzuela's girth. I waited for a signal as to whether I should take the judge's bail order or try to argue for a lower amount. Sometimes, when a judge thinks he is giving you a gift, it can backfire to press for more—or in this case less.

Dobbs was sitting in the first seat in the first row. He simply got up and started to walk out of the courtroom, leaving Valenzuela behind. I took that to mean that I should leave well enough alone, that the Roulet family could handle the million. I turned back to the bench.

"Thank you, Your Honor," I said.

The clerk immediately called the next case. I glanced at Maggie as she was closing the file on the case she would no longer prosecute. She then stood up and walked out through the bar and down the center aisle of the courtroom. She spoke to no one and she did not look back at me.

"Mr. Haller?"

I turned to my client. Behind him I saw a deputy coming to take him back into holding. He'd be bused the half block back to jail and then, depending on how fast Dobbs and Valenzuela worked, released later in the day.

"I'll work with Mr. Dobbs and get you out," I said. "Then we'll sit down and talk about the case."

"Thank you," Roulet said as he was led away. "Thank you for being here."

"Remember what I said. Don't talk to strangers. Don't talk to anybody."

"Yes, sir."

After he was gone I walked to the bar. Valenzuela was waiting at the gate for me with a big smile on his face. Roulet's bail was likely the highest he had ever secured. That meant his cut would be the highest he'd ever received. He clapped me on the arm as I came through the gate.

"What'd I tell you?" he said. "We got ourselves a franchise here, boss."

"We'll see, Val," I said. "We'll see."

5

Every attorney who works the machine has two fee schedules. There is schedule A, which lists the fees the attorney would like to get for certain services rendered. And there is schedule B, the fees he is willing to take because that is all the client can afford. A franchise client is a defendant who wants to go to trial and has the money to pay his lawyer's schedule A rates. From first appearance to arraignment to preliminary hearing and on to trial and then appeal, the franchise client demands hundreds if not thousands of billable hours. He can keep gas in the tank for two to three years. From where I hunt, they are the rarest and most highly sought beast in the jungle.

And it was beginning to look like Valenzuela had been on the money. Louis Roulet was looking more and more like a franchise client. It had been a dry spell for me. It had been almost two years since I'd had anything even approaching a franchise case or client. I'm talking about a case earning six figures. There were many that started out looking like they might reach that rare plateau but they never went the distance.

C. C. Dobbs was waiting in the hallway outside the arraignment court when I got out. He was standing next to the wall of glass windows that looked down upon the civic center plaza below. I walked up to him quickly. I had a few seconds' lead on Valenzuela coming out of the court and I wanted some private time with Dobbs.

"Sorry," Dobbs said before I could speak. "I didn't want to stay in there another minute. It was so depressing to see the boy caught up in that cattle call."

"The boy?"

"Louis. I've represented the family for twenty-five years. I guess I still think of him as a boy."

"Are you going to be able to get him out?"

"It won't be a problem. I have a call in to Louis's mother to see how she wants to handle it, whether to put up property or go with a bond."

To put up property to cover a million-dollar bail would mean that at least a million dollars in the property's value could not be encumbered by a mortgage. Additionally, the court might require a current appraisal of the property, which could take days and keep Roulet waiting in jail. Conversely, a bond could be purchased through Valenzuela for a ten percent premium. The difference was that the ten percent was never returned. That stayed with Valenzuela for his risks and trouble and was the reason for his broad smile in the courtroom. After paying his insurance premium on the million-dollar bail, he'd end up clearing close to ninety grand. And he was worried about me taking care of *him*.

"Can I make a suggestion?" I asked.

"Please do."

"Louis looked a little frail when I saw him back in the lockup. If I were you I would get him out of there as soon as possible. To do that you should have Valenzuela write a bond. It will cost you a hundred grand but the boy will be out and safe, you know what I mean?"

Dobbs turned to the window and leaned on the railing that ran along the glass. I looked down and saw that the plaza was filling up with people from the government buildings on lunch break. I could see many people with the red-and-white name tags I knew were given to jurors.

"I know what you mean."

"The other thing is that cases like this tend to bring the rats out of the walls."

"What do you mean?"

"I mean other inmates who will say they heard somebody say something. Especially a case that gets on the news or into the newspapers. They'll take that info off the tube and make it sound like our guy was talking."

"That's criminal," Dobbs said indignantly. "That shouldn't be allowed."

"Yeah, I know, but it happens. And the longer he stays in there, the wider the window of opportunity is for one of these guys."

Valenzuela joined us at the railing. He didn't say anything.

"I will suggest we go with the bond," Dobbs said. "I already called and she was in a meeting. As soon as she calls me back we will move on this."

His words prompted something that had bothered me during the hearing.

"She couldn't come out of a meeting to talk about her son in jail? I was wondering why she wasn't in court today if this boy, as you call him, is so clean and upstanding."

Dobbs looked at me like I hadn't used mouthwash in a month.

"Mrs. Windsor is a very busy and powerful woman. I am sure that if I had stated it was an emergency concerning her son, she would have been on the phone immediately."

"Mrs. Windsor?"

"She remarried after she and Louis's father divorced. That was a long time ago."

I nodded, then realized that there was more to talk about with Dobbs but nothing I wanted to discuss in front of Valenzuela.

"Val, why don't you go check on when Louis will be back at Van Nuys jail so you can get him out."

"That's easy," Valenzuela said. "He'll go on the first bus back after lunch."

"Yeah, well, go double-check that while I finish with Mr. Dobbs."

Valenzuela was about to protest that he didn't need to double-check it when he realized what I was telling him.

"Okay," he said. "I'll go do it."

After he was gone I studied Dobbs for a moment before speaking. Dobbs looked to be in his late fifties. He had a deferential presence that probably came from thirty years of taking care of rich people. My guess was that he had become rich in the process himself but it hadn't changed his public demeanor.

"If we're going to be working together, I guess I should ask what you want to be called. Cecil? C.C.? Mr. Dobbs?"

"Cecil will be fine."

"Well, my first question, Cecil, is whether we are going to be working together. Do I have the job?"

"Mr. Roulet made it clear to me he wanted you on the case. To be honest, you would not have been my first choice. You may not have been any choice, because frankly I had never heard of you. But you are Mr. Roulet's first choice, and that is acceptable to me. In fact, I thought you acquitted yourself quite well in the courtroom, especially considering how hostile that prosecutor was toward Mr. Roulet."

I noticed that the boy had become "Mr. Roulet" now. I wondered what had happened to advance him in Dobbs's view.

"Yeah, well, they call her Maggie McFierce. She's pretty dedicated."

"I thought she was a bit overboard. Do you think there is any way to get her removed from the case, maybe get someone a little more...grounded?"

"I don't know. Trying to shop prosecutors can be dangerous. But if you think she needs to go, I can get it done."

"That's good to hear. Maybe I should have known about you before today."

"Maybe. Do you want to talk about fees now and get it out of the way?"

"If you would like."

I looked around the hallway to make sure there were no other lawyers hanging around in earshot. I was going to go schedule A all the way on this.

"I get twenty-five hundred for today and Louis already approved that. If you want to go hourly from here, I get three hundred an hour and that gets bumped to five in trial because I can't do anything else. If you'd rather go with a flat rate, I'll want sixty thousand to take it from here through a preliminary hearing. If we end it with a plea, I'll take twelve more on top of that. If we go to trial instead, I need another sixty on the day we decide that and twenty-five more when we start picking a jury. This case doesn't look like more than a week, including jury selection, but if it goes past a week, I get twenty-five-a-week extra. We can talk about an appeal if and when it becomes necessary."

I hesitated a moment to see how Dobbs was reacting. He showed nothing so I pressed on.

"I'll need thirty thousand for a retainer and another ten for an investigator by the end of the day. I don't want to waste time on this. I want to get an investigator out and about on this thing before it hits the media and maybe before the cops talk to some of the people involved."

Dobbs slowly nodded.

"Are those your standard fees?"

"When I can get them. I'm worth it. What are you charging the family, Cecil?"

I was sure he wouldn't walk away from this little episode hungry.

"That's between me and my client. But don't worry. I will include your fees in my discussion with Mrs. Windsor."

"I appreciate it. And remember, I need that investigator to start today."

I gave him a business card I pulled from the right pocket of my suit coat. The cards in the right pocket had my cell number. The cards in my left pocket had the number that went to Lorna Taylor.

"I have another hearing downtown," I said. "When you get him out call me and we'll set up a meeting. Let's make it as soon as possible. I should be available later today and tonight."

"Perfect," Dobbs said, pocketing the card without looking at it. "Should we come to you?"

"No, I'll come to you. I'd like to see how the other half lives in those high-rises in Century City."

Dobbs smiled glibly.

"It is obvious by your suit that you know and practice the adage that a trial lawyer should never dress too well. You want the jury to like you, not to be jealous of you. Well, Michael, a Century City lawyer can't have an office that is nicer than the offices his clients come from. And so I can assure you that our offices are very modest."

I nodded in agreement. But I was insulted just the same. I was wearing my best suit. I always did on Mondays.

"That's good to know," I said.

The courtroom door opened and the videographer walked out, lugging his camera and folded tripod with him. Dobbs saw him and immediately tensed.

"The media," he said. "How can we control this? Mrs. Windsor won't—"

"Hold on a sec."

I called to the cameraman and he walked over. I immediately put my hand out. He had to put his tripod down to take it.

"I'm Michael Haller. I saw you in there filming my client's appearance."

Using my formal name was a code.

"Robert Gillen," the cameraman said. "People call me Sticks."

He gestured to his tripod in explanation. His use of his formal name was a return code. He was letting me know he understood that I had a play working here.

"Are you freelancing or on assignment?" I asked.

"Just freelancing today."

"How'd you hear about this thing?"

He shrugged as though he was reluctant to answer.

"A source. A cop."

I nodded. Gillen was locked in and playing along.

"What do you get for that if you sell it to a news station?"

"Depends. I take seven-fifty for an exclusive and five for a nonexclusive."

Nonexclusive meant that any news director who bought the tape from him knew that he might sell the footage to a competing news station. Gillen had doubled the fees he actually got. It was a good move. He must have been listening to what had been said in the courtroom while he shot it.

"Tell you what," I said. "How about we take it off your hands right now for an exclusive?"

Gillen was perfect. He hesitated like he was unsure of the ethics involved in the proposition.

"In fact, make it a grand," I said.

"Okay," he said. "You got a deal."

While Gillen put the camera on the floor and took the tape out of it, I pulled a wad of cash from my pocket. I had kept twelve hundred from the Saints cash Teddy Vogel had given me on the way down. I turned to Dobbs.

"I can expense this, right?"

"Absolutely," he said. He was beaming.

I exchanged the cash for the tape and thanked Gillen. He pocketed the money and moved toward the elevators a happy man.

"That was brilliant," Dobbs said. "We have to contain this. It could literally destroy the family's business if this — in fact, I think that is one reason Mrs. Windsor was not here today. She didn't want to be recognized."

"Well, we'll have to talk about that if this thing goes the distance. Meantime, I'll do my best to keep it off the radar."

"Thank you."

A cell phone began to play a classical number by Bach or Beethoven or some other dead guy with no copyright and Dobbs reached inside his jacket, retrieved the device and checked the small screen on it.

"This is she," he said.

"Then I'll leave you to it."

As I walked off I heard Dobbs saying, "Mary, everything is under control. We need now to concentrate on getting him out. We are going to need some money..."

While the elevator made its way up to me, I was thinking that I was pretty sure that I was dealing with a client and family for which "some money" meant more than I had ever seen. My mind moved back to the sartorial comment Dobbs had made about me. It still stung. The truth was, I didn't have a suit in my closet that cost less than six hundred dollars and I always felt good and confident in any one of them. I wondered if he had intended to insult me or he had intended something else, maybe trying at this early stage of the game to imprint his control over me and the case. I decided I would need to watch my back with Dobbs. I would keep him close but not that close.

6

Traffic heading downtown bottlenecked in the Cahuenga Pass. I spent the time in the car working the phone and trying not to think about the conversation I'd had with Maggie McPherson about my parenting skills. My ex-wife had been right about me, and that's what hurt. For a long time I had put my law practice ahead of my parenting practice. It was something I promised myself to change. I just needed the time and the money to slow down. I thought that maybe Louis Roulet would provide both.

In the back of the Lincoln I first called Raul Levin, my investigator, to put him on alert about the potential meeting with Roulet. I asked him to do a preliminary run on the case to see what he could find out. Levin had retired early from the LAPD and still had contacts and friends who did him favors from time to time. He probably had his own Christmas list. I told him not to spend a lot of time on it until I was sure I had Roulet locked down as a paying client. It didn't matter what C. C. Dobbs had said to me face-to-face in the courthouse hallway. I wouldn't believe I had the case until I got the first payment.

Next I checked on the status of a few cases and then called Lorna Taylor again. I knew the mail was delivered at her place most days right before noon. But she told me nothing of importance had come in. No checks and no correspondence I had to pay immediate attention to from the courts.

"Did you check on Gloria Dayton's arraignment?" I asked her.

"Yes. It looks like they might hold her over until tomorrow on a medical."

I groaned. The state has forty-eight hours to charge an individual after arrest and bring them before a judge. Holding Gloria Dayton's first appearance over until the next day because of medical reasons meant that she was probably drug sick. This would help explain why she had been holding cocaine when she was arrested. I had not seen or spoken to her in at least seven months. Her slide must have been quick and steep. The thin line between controlling the drugs and the drugs controlling her had been crossed.

"Did you find out who filed it?" I asked.

"Leslie Faire," she said.

I groaned again.

"That's just great. Okay, well, I'm going to go down and see what I can do. I've got nothing going until I hear about Roulet."

Leslie Faire was a misnamed prosecutor whose idea of giving a defendant a break or the benefit of the doubt was to offer extended parole supervision on top of prison time.

"Mick, when are you going to learn with this woman?" Lorna said about Gloria Dayton.

"Learn what?" I asked, although I knew exactly what Lorna would say.

"She drags you down every time you have to deal with her. She's never going to get out of the life, and now you can bet she's never going to be anything less than a twofer every time she calls. That would be fine, except you never charge her."

What she meant by *twofer* was that Gloria Dayton's cases would from now on be more complicated and time-consuming because it was likely that drug charges would always accompany solicitation or prostitution charges. What bothered Lorna was that this meant more work for me but no more income in the process.

"Well, the bar requires that all lawyers practice some pro bono work, Lorna. You know —"

"You don't listen to me, Mick," she said dismissively. "That's exactly why we couldn't stay married."

I closed my eyes. What a day. I had managed to get both my ex-wives angry with me.

"What does this woman have on you?" she asked. "Why don't you charge even a basic fee with her?"

"Look, she doesn't have anything on me, okay?" I said. "Can we sort of change the subject now?"

I didn't tell her that years earlier when I had looked through the dusty old account books from my father's law practice, I had found that he'd had a soft spot for the so-called women of the night. He defended many and charged few. Maybe I was just continuing a family tradition.

"Fine," Lorna said. "How did it go with Roulet?"

"You mean, did I get the job? I think so. Val's probably getting him out right now. We'll set up a meeting after that. I already asked Raul to sniff around on it."

"Did you get a check?"

"Not yet."

"Get the check, Mick."

"I'm working on it."

"How's the case look?"

"I've only seen the pictures but it looks bad. I'll know more after I see what Raul comes up with."

"And what about Roulet?"

I knew what she was asking. How was he as a client? Would a jury, if it came to a jury, like him or despise him? Cases could be won or lost based on jurors' impressions of the defendant.

"He looks like a babe in the woods."

"He's a virgin?"

"Never been inside the iron house."

"Well, did he do it?"

She always asked the irrelevant question. It didn't matter in terms of the strategy of the case whether the defendant "did it" or not. What mattered was the evidence against him—the proof—and if and how it could be neutralized. My job was to bury the proof, to color the proof a shade of gray. Gray was the color of reasonable doubt.

But the question of did he or didn't he always seemed to matter to her.

"Who knows, Lorna? That's not the question. The question is whether or not he's a paying customer. The answer is, I think so."

"Well, let me know if you need any—oh, there's one other thing."

"What?"

"Sticks called and said he owes you four hundred dollars next time he sees you."

"Yeah, he does."

"You're doing pretty good today."

"I'm not complaining."

We said our good-byes on a friendly note, the dispute over Gloria Dayton seemingly forgotten for the moment. Probably the security that comes with knowing money is coming in and a high-paying client is on the hook made Lorna feel a bit better about my working some cases for free. I wondered, though, if she'd have minded so much if I was defending a drug dealer for free instead of a prostitute. Lorna and I had shared a short and sweet marriage, with both of us quickly finding out that we had moved too quickly while rebounding from divorces. We ended it, remained friends, and she continued to work with me, not for me. The only time I felt uncomfortable about the arrangement was when she acted like a wife again and second-guessed my choice of client and who and what I charged or didn't charge.

Feeling confident in the way I had handled Lorna, I called the DA's office in Van Nuys next. I asked for Margaret McPherson and caught her eating at her desk.

"I just wanted to say I'm sorry about this morning. I know you wanted the case."

"Well, you probably need it more than me. He must be a paying customer if he's got C. C. Dobbs carrying the roll behind him."

By that she was referring to a roll of toilet paper. High-priced family lawyers were usually seen by prosecutors as nothing more than ass wipers for the rich and famous.

"Yeah, I could use one like him—the paying client, not the wiper. It's been a while since I had a franchise."

"Well, you didn't get as lucky a few minutes ago," she whispered into the phone. "The case was reassigned to Ted Minton."

"Never heard of him."

"He's one of Smithson's young guns. Just brought him in from downtown, where he was filing simple possession cases. He didn't see the inside of a courtroom until he came up here."

John Smithson was the ambitious head deputy in charge of the Van Nuys Division. He was a better politician than a prosecutor and had parlayed that skill into a quick climb over other more experienced deputies to the division chief's post. Maggie McPherson was among those he'd passed by. Once he was in the slot, he started building a staff of young prosecutors who did not feel slighted and were loyal to him for giving them a shot.

"This guy's never been in court?" I asked, not understanding how going up against a trial rookie could be unlucky, as Maggie had indicated.

"He's had a few trials up here but always with a babysitter. Roulet will be his first time flying solo. Smithson thinks he's giving him a slam dunk."

I imagined her sitting in her cubicle, probably not far from where my new opponent was sitting in his.

"I don't get it, Mags. If this guy's green, why wasn't I lucky?"

"Because these guys Smithson picks are all cracked out of the same mold. They're arrogant assholes. They think they can do no wrong and what's more..."

She lowered her voice even more.

"They don't play fair. And the word on Minton is that he's a cheater. Watch yourself, Haller. Better yet, watch him."

"Well, thanks for the heads-up."

But she wasn't finished.

"A lot of these new people just don't get it. They don't see it as a calling. To them it's not about justice. It's just a game — a batting average. They like to keep score and to see how far it will get them in the office. In fact, they're all just like junior Smithsons."

A calling. It was her sense of calling that ultimately cost us our marriage. On an intellectual level she could deal with being married to a man who worked the other side of the aisle. But when it came down to the reality of what we did, we were lucky to have lasted the eight years we had managed. *Honey, how was your day? Oh, I got a guy who murdered his roommate with an ice pick a seven-year deal. And you? Oh, I put a guy away for five years because he stole a car stereo to feed his habit...* It just didn't work. Four years in, a daughter arrived, but through no fault of her own, she only kept us going another four years.

Still, I didn't regret a thing about it. I cherished my daughter. She was the only thing that was really good about my life, that I could be proud of. I think deep down, the reason I didn't see her enough — that I was chasing cases instead of her — was because I felt unworthy of her. Her mother was a hero. She put bad people in jail. What could I tell her was good and holy about what I did, when I had long ago lost the thread of it myself?

"Hey, Haller, are you there?"

"Yeah, Mags, I'm here. What are you eating today?"

"Just the oriental salad from downstairs. Nothing special. Where are you?"

"Heading downtown. Listen, tell Hayley I'll see her this Saturday. I'll make a plan. We'll do something special."

"You really mean that? I don't want to get her hopes up."

I felt something lift inside me, the idea that my daughter would get her hopes up about seeing me. The one thing Maggie never did was run me down with Hayley. She wasn't the kind that would do that. I always admired that.

"Yes, I'm sure," I said.

"Great, I'll tell her. Let me know when you're coming or if I can drop her off."

"Okay."

I hesitated. I wanted to talk to her longer but there was nothing else to say. I finally said good-bye and closed the phone. In a few minutes we broke free of the bottleneck. I looked out the window and saw no accident. I saw nobody with a flat tire and no highway patrol cruiser parked on the shoulder. I saw nothing that explained what had caused the traffic tie-up. It was often like that. Freeway traffic in Los Angeles was as mysterious as marriage. It moved and flowed, then stalled and stopped for no easily explainable reason.

I am from a family of attorneys. My father, my half brother, a niece and a nephew. My father was a famous lawyer in a time when there was no cable television and no Court TV. He was the dean of criminal law in L.A. for almost three decades. From Mickey Cohen to the Manson girls, his clients always made the headlines. I was just an afterthought in his life, a surprise visitor to his second marriage to a B-level movie actress known for her exotic Latin looks but not her acting skills. The mix gave me my black Irish looks. My father was old when I came, so he was gone before I was old enough to really know him or talk to him about the calling of the law. He only left me his name. Mickey Haller, the legal legend. It still opened doors.

But my older brother—the half brother from the first marriage—told me that my father used to talk to him about the practice of law and criminal defense. He used to say he would defend the devil himself just as long as he could cover the fee. The only big-time case and client he ever turned down was Sirhan Sirhan. He told my brother that he had liked Bobby Kennedy too much to defend his killer, no matter how much he believed in the ideal that the accused deserved the best and most vigorous defense possible.

Growing up I read all the books about my father and his cases. I admired the skill and vigor and strategies he brought to the defense table. He was damn good and it made me proud to carry his name. But the law was different now. It was grayer. Ideals had long been downgraded to notions. Notions were optional.

My cell phone rang and I checked the screen before answering.

"What's up, Val?"

"We're getting him out. They already took him back to the jail and we're processing him out now."

"Dobbs went with the bond?"

"You got it."

I could hear the delight in his voice.

"Don't be so giddy. You sure he's not a runner?"

"I'm never sure. I'm going to make him wear a bracelet. I lose him, I lose my house."

I realized that what I had taken as delight at the windfall that a million-dollar bond would bring to Valenzuela was actually nervous energy. Valenzuela would be taut as a wire until this one was over, one way or the other. Even if the court had not ordered it, Valenzuela was going to put an electronic tracking bracelet on Roulet's ankle. He was taking no chances with this guy.

"Where's Dobbs?"

"Back at my office, waiting. I'll bring Roulet over as soon as he's out. Shouldn't be too much longer."

"Is Maisy over there?"

"Yeah, she's there."

"Okay, I'm going to call over."

I ended the call and hit the speed-dial combo for Liberty Bail Bonds. Valenzuela's receptionist and assistant answered.

"Maisy, it's Mick. Can you put Mr. Dobbs on the line?"

"Sure thing, Mick."

A few seconds later Dobbs got on the line. He seemed put out by something. Just in the way he said, "This is Cecil Dobbs."

"This is Mickey Haller. How is it going over there?"

"Well, if you consider I am letting my duties to other clients slide while I sit here and read year-old magazines, not good."

"You don't carry a cell phone to do business?"

"I do. But that's not the point. My clients aren't cell phone people. They're face-to-face people."

"I see. Well, the good news is, I hear our boy is about to be released."

"Our boy?"

"Mr. Roulet. Valenzuela should have him out inside the hour. I am about to go into a client conference, but as I said before, I am free in the afternoon. Do you want to meet to go over the case with our mutual client or do you want me to take it from here?"

"No, Mrs. Windsor has insisted that I monitor this closely. In fact, she may choose to be there as well."

"I don't mind the meet-and-greet with Mrs. Windsor, but when it comes down to talking about the case, it's just going to be the defense team. That can include you but not the mother. Okay?"

"I understand. Let's say four o'clock at my office. I will have Louis there."

"I'll be there."

"My firm employs a crack investigator. I'll ask him to join us."

"That won't be necessary, Cecil. I have my own and he's already on the job. We'll see you at four."

I ended the call before Dobbs could start a debate about which investigator to use. I had to be careful that Dobbs didn't control the investigation, preparation and strategy of the case. Monitoring was one thing. But I was Louis Roulet's attorney now. Not him.

When I called Raul Levin next, he told me he was already on his way to the LAPD Van Nuys Division to pick up a copy of the arrest report.

"Just like that?" I asked.

"No, not just like that. In a way, you could say it took me twenty years to get this report."

I understood. Levin's connections, procured over time and experience, traded over trust and favors, had come through for him. No wonder he charged five hundred dollars a day when he could get it. I told him about the meeting at four and he said he would be there and would be ready to furnish us with the law enforcement view of the case.

The Lincoln pulled to a stop when I closed the phone. We were in front of the Twin Towers jail facility. It wasn't even ten years old but the smog was beginning to permanently stain its sand-colored walls a dreary gray. It was a sad and forbidding place that I spent too much time in. I opened the car door and got out to go inside once again.

7

There was an attorney's check-in window that allowed me to bypass the long line of visitors waiting to get in to see loved ones incarcerated in one of the towers. When I told the window deputy whom I wanted to see, he tapped the name into the computer and never said anything about Gloria Dayton being in medical and unavailable. He printed out a visitor's pass which he slid into the plastic frame of a clip-on badge and told me to put it on and wear it at all times in the jail. He then told me to step away from the window and wait for an attorney escort.

"It will be a few minutes," he said.

I knew from prior experience that my cell phone did not get a signal inside the jail and that if I stepped outside to use it, I might miss my escort and then have to go through the whole sign-in process again. So I stayed put and watched the faces of the people who came to visit those being held inside. Most were black and brown. Most had the look of routine on their faces. They all probably knew the ropes here much better than I.

After twenty minutes a large woman in a deputy's uniform came into the waiting area and collected me. I knew that she had not gotten into the sheriff's department with her current dimensions. She was at least a hundred pounds overweight and seemed to struggle just to carry it while walking. But I also knew that once somebody was in, it was hard to get them out. About the best this one could do if there was a jail break was lean up against a door to keep it closed.

"Sorry it took so long," she told me as we waited between the double steel doors of a mantrap in the women's tower. "I had to go find her, make sure we still had her."

She signaled that everything was all right to a camera above the next door and its lock clacked open. She pushed through.

"She was up in medical getting fixed up," she said.

"Fixed up?"

I wasn't aware of the jail having a drug-treatment program that included "fixing up" addicts.

"Yeah, she got hurt," the deputy said. "Got a little banged up in a scuffle. She can tell you."

I let the questions go at that. In a way, I was relieved that the medical delay was not due — not directly, at least — to drug ingestion or addiction.

The deputy led me to the attorney room, which I had been in many times before with many different clients. The vast majority of my clients were men and I didn't discriminate, but the truth was I hated representing women who were incarcerated. From prostitutes to murderers — and I had defended them all — there was something pitiful about a woman in jail. I had found that almost all of the time, their crimes could be traced back to men. Men who took advantage of them, abused them, deserted them, hurt them. This is not to say they were not responsible for their actions or that some of them did not deserve the punishments they received. There were predators among the female ranks that easily rivaled those among the males. But, even still, the women I saw in jail seemed so different from the men in the other tower. The men still lived by wiles and strength. The women had nothing left by the time they locked the door on them.

The visiting area was a row of booths in which an attorney could sit on one side and confer with a client who sat on the other side, separated by an eighteen-inch sheet of clear Plexiglas. A deputy sat in a glassed-in booth at the end of the room and observed but supposedly didn't listen. If paper-work needed to be passed to the client, it was held up for the booth deputy to see and approve.

I was led to a booth and my escort left me. I then waited another ten minutes before the same deputy appeared on the other side of the Plexiglas with Gloria Dayton. Immediately, I saw that my client had a swelling around her left eye and a single butterfly stitch over a small laceration just below her widow's peak. Gloria Dayton had jet-black hair and olive skin. She had once been beautiful. The first time I represented her, seven or eight years before, she was beautiful. The kind of beauty that leaves you stunned at the fact she was selling it, that she had decided that selling herself to strangers was her best or only option. Now she just looked hard to me. The lines of her face were taut. She had visited surgeons who were not the best, and anyway, there was nothing they could do about eyes that had seen too much.

"Mickey Mantle," she said. "You're going to bat for me again?"

She said it in her little girl's voice that I suppose her regular clients enjoyed and responded to. It just sounded strange to me, coming from that tightly drawn mouth and face with eyes that were as hard and had as much life in them as marbles.

She always called me Mickey Mantle, even though she was born after the great slugger had long retired and probably knew little about him or the game he played. It was just a name to her. I guess the alternative would have been to call me Mickey Mouse, and I probably wouldn't have liked it much.

"I'm going to try, Gloria," I told her. "What happened to your face? How'd you get hurt?"

She made a dismissive gesture with her hand.

"There was a little disagreement with some of the girls in my dorm."

"About what?"

"Just girl stuff."

"Are you getting high in there?"

She looked indignant and then she tried putting a pouting look on her face. "No, I'm not."

I studied her. She seemed straight. Maybe she wasn't getting high and that was not what the fight had been about.

"I don't want to stay in here, Mickey," she said in her real voice.

"I don't blame you. I don't like being in here myself and I get to leave."

I immediately regretted saying the last part and reminding her of her situation. She didn't seem to notice.

"You think maybe you could get me into one of those pretrial whatchamacallits where I can get myself right?"

I thought it was interesting how addicts call both getting high and getting sober the same thing — *getting right.*

"The problem is, Gloria, we got into a pretrial intervention program last time, remember? And it obviously didn't work. So this time I don't know. They only have so many spaces in those things and the judges and prosecutors don't like sending people back when they didn't take advantage of it in the first place."

"What do you mean?" she protested. "I took advantage. I went the whole damn time."

"That's right. That was good. But then after it was over, you went right back to doing what you do and here we are again. They wouldn't call that a success, Gloria. I have to be honest with you. I don't think I can get you into a program this time. I think you have to be ready for them to be tougher this time."

Her eyes drooped.

"I can't do it," she said in a small voice.

"Look, they have programs in the jail. You'll get straight and come out with another chance to start again clean."

She shook her head; she looked lost.

"You've had a long run but it can't go on," I said. "If I were you I'd think about getting out of this place. L.A., I mean. Go somewhere and start again."

She looked up at me with anger in her eyes.

"Start over and do what? Look at me. What am I going to do? Get married, have kids and plant flowers?"

I didn't have an answer and neither did she.

"Let's talk about that when the time comes. For now, let's worry about your case. Tell me what happened."

"What always happens. I screened the guy and it all checked out. He looked legit. But he was a cop and that was that."

"You went to him?"

She nodded.

"The Mondrian. He had a suite—that's another thing. The cops usually don't have suites. They don't have the budget."

"Didn't I tell you how stupid it would be to take coke with you when you work? And if a guy even asks you to bring coke with you, then you know he's a cop."

"I know all of that and he didn't ask me to bring it. I forgot I had it, okay? I got it from a guy I went to see right before him. What was I supposed to do, leave it in the car for the Mondrian valets to take?"

"What guy did you get it from?"

"A guy at the Travelodge on Santa Monica. I did him earlier and he offered it to me, you know, instead of cash. Then after I left I checked my messages and I had the call from the guy at the Mondrian. So I called him back, set it up and went straight there. I forgot I had the stuff in my purse."

Nodding, I leaned forward. I was seeing a glimmer on this one, a possibility.

"This guy in the Travelodge, who was he?"

"I don't know, just some guy who saw my ad on the site."

She arranged her liaisons through a website which carried photos, phone numbers and e-mail addresses of escorts.

"Did he say where he was from?"

"No. He was Mexican or Cuban or something. He was sweaty from using."

"When he gave you the coke, did you see if he had any more?"

"Yeah, he had some. I was hoping for a call back...but I don't think I was what he was expecting."

Last time I had checked her ad on LA-Darlings.com to see if she was still in the life, the photos she'd put up were at least five years old and looked ten. I imagined that it could lead to some disappointment when her clients opened their hotel room doors.

"How much did he have?"

"I don't know. I just knew he had to have more because if it was all he had left, he wouldn't have given it to me."

It was a good point. The glimmer was getting brighter.

"Did you screen him?"

"'Course."

"What, his driver's license?"

"No, his passport. He said he didn't have a license."

"What was his name?"

"Hector something."

"Come on, Gloria, Hector what? Try to re—"

"Hector something Moya. It was three names. But I remember 'Moya' because I said 'Hector give me Moya' when he brought out the coke."

"Okay, that's good."

"You think it's something you can use to help me?"

"Maybe, depending on who this guy is. If he's a trade-up."

"I want to get out."

"Okay, listen, Gloria. I'm going to go see the prosecutor and see what she's thinking and see what I can do for you. They've got you in here on twenty-five thousand dollars' bail."

"What?"

"It's higher than usual because of the drugs. You don't have twenty-five hundred for the bond, do you?"

She shook her head. I could see the muscles in her face constricting. I knew what was coming.

"Could you front it to me, Mickey? I promise I'd—"

"I can't do that, Gloria. That's a rule and I could get in trouble if I broke it. You're going to have to be in here overnight and they'll take you over to arraignment in the morning."

"No," she said, more like a moan than a word.

"I know it's going to be tough but you have to nut it out. And you have to be straight in the morning when you come into court or I'll have no shot at lowering your bond and getting you out. So none of that shit they trade in here. You got that?"

She raised her arms over her head, almost as if she was protecting herself from falling debris. She squeezed her hands into tight fists of dread. It would be a long night ahead.

"You've got to get me out tomorrow."

"I'll do my best."

I waved to the deputy in the observation booth. I was ready to go.

"One last thing," I said. "Do you remember what room the guy at the Travelodge was in?"

She thought a moment before answering.

"Yeah, it's an easy one. Three thirty-three."

"Okay, thanks. I'm going to see what I can do."

She stayed sitting when I stood up. Soon the escort deputy came back and told me I would have to wait while she first took Gloria back to her dorm. I checked my watch. It was almost two. I hadn't eaten and was getting a headache. I also had only two hours to get to Leslie Faire in the DA's office to talk about Gloria and then out to Century City for the case meeting with Roulet and Dobbs.

"Isn't there somebody else who can take me out of here?" I said irritably. "I need to get to court."

"Sorry, sir, that's how it works."

"Well, please hurry."

"I always do."

Fifteen minutes later I realized that my complaining to the deputy had only succeeded in her making sure she left me waiting even longer than had I just kept my mouth shut. Like a restaurant customer who gets the cold soup he sent back to the kitchen returned hot with the piquant taste of saliva in it, I should have known better.

On the quick drive over to the Criminal Courts Building I called Raul Levin. He was back at his home office in Glendale, looking through the police reports on the Roulet investigation and arrest. I asked him to put it aside to make some calls. I wanted to see what he could find out about the man in room 333 at the Travelodge on Santa Monica. I told him I needed the information yesterday. I knew he had sources and ways of running the name Hector Moya. I just didn't want to know who or what they were. I was only interested in what he got.

As Earl pulled to a stop in front of the CCB, I told him that while I was inside he should take a run over to Philippe's to get us roast beef sandwiches. I'd eat mine on my way out to Century City. I passed a twenty-dollar bill over the seat to him and got out.

While waiting for an elevator in the always crowded lobby of the CCB, I popped a Tylenol from my briefcase and hoped it would head off the migraine I felt coming on from lack of food. It took me ten minutes to get to the ninth floor and another fifteen waiting for Leslie Faire to grant me an audience. I didn't mind the wait, though, because Raul Levin called back just before I was allowed entrance. If Faire had seen me right away, I wouldn't have gone in with the added ammunition.

Levin had told me that the man in room 333 at the Travelodge had checked in under the name Gilberto Garcia. The motel did not require identification, since he paid cash in advance for a week and put a fifty-dollar deposit on phone charges. Levin had also run a trace on the name I had given him and came up with Hector Arrande Moya, a Colombian wanted on a fugitive warrant issued after he fled San Diego when a federal grand jury handed down an indictment for drug trafficking. It added up to real good stuff and I planned to put it to use with the prosecutor.

Faire was in an office shared with three other prosecutors. Each had a desk in a corner. Two were gone, probably in court, but a man I didn't know sat at the desk in the corner opposite Faire. I had to speak to her with him in earshot. I hated doing this because I found that the prosecutor I was dealing with in these situations would often play to the others in the room, trying to sound tough and shrewd, sometimes at the expense of my client.

I pulled a chair away from one of the empty desks and brought it over to sit down. I skipped the pleasantries because there weren't any and got right to the point because I was hungry and didn't have a lot of time.

"You filed on Gloria Dayton this morning," I said. "She's mine. I want to see what we can do about it."

"Well, we can plead her guilty and she can do one to three years at Frontera."

She said it matter-of-factly with a smile that was more of a smirk.

"I was thinking of PTI."

"I was thinking she already got a bite out of that apple and she spit it out. No way."

"Look, how much coke did she have on her, a couple grams?"

"It's still illegal, no matter how much she had. Gloria Dayton has had numerous opportunities to rehabilitate herself and avoid prison. But she's run out of chances."

She turned to her desk, opened a file and glanced at the top sheet.

"Nine arrests in just the last five years," she said. "This is her third drug charge and she's never spent more than three days in jail. Forget PTI. She's got to learn sometime and this is that time. I'm not open to discussion on this. If she pleads, I'll give her one to three. If she doesn't, I'll go get a verdict and she takes her chances with the judge at sentencing. I will ask for the max on it."

I nodded. It was going about the way I thought it would with Faire. A one-to-three-year sentence would likely result in a nine-month stay in the slam. I knew Gloria Dayton could do it and maybe should do it. But I still had a card to play.

"What if she had something to trade?"

Faire snorted like it was a joke.

"Like what?"

"A hotel room number where a major dealer is doing business."

"Sounds a little vague."

It was vague but I could tell by the change in her voice she was interested. Every prosecutor likes to trade up.

"Call your drug guys. Ask them to run the name Hector Arrande Moya on the box. He's a Colombian. I can wait."

She hesitated. She clearly didn't like being manipulated by a defense attorney, especially when another prosecutor was in earshot. But the hook was already set.

She turned again to her desk and made a call. I listened to one side of the conversation, her telling someone to give her a background check on Moya.

She waited awhile and then listened to the response. She thanked whoever it was she had called and hung up. She took her time turning back to me.

"Okay," she said. "What does she want?"

I had it ready.

"She wants a PTI slot. All charges dropped upon successful completion. She doesn't testify against the guy and her name is on no documents. She simply gives the hotel and room number where he's at and your people do the rest."

"They'll need to make a case. She's got to testify. I take it the two grams she had came from this guy. Then she has to tell us about it."

"No, she doesn't. Whoever you just talked to told you there's already a warrant. You can take him down for that."

She worked it over for a few moments, moving her jaw back and forth as if tasting the deal and deciding whether to eat more. I knew what the stumble was. The deal was a trade-up but it was a trade-up to a federal case. That meant that they would bust the guy and the feds would take over. No prosecutorial glory for Leslie Faire — unless she had designs on jumping over to the U.S. Attorney's Office one day.

"The feds will love you for this," I said, trying to wedge into her conscience. "He's a bad guy and he'll probably check out soon and the chance to get him will be lost."

She looked at me like I was a bug.

"Don't try that with me, Haller."

"Sorry."

She went back to her thinking. I tried again.

"Once you have his location, you could always try to set up a buy."

"Would you be quiet, please? I can't think."

I raised my hands in surrender and shut up.

"All right," she finally said. "Let me talk to my boss. Give me your number and I'll call you later. But I'll tell you right now, if we go for it, she'll have to go to a lockdown program. Something at County-USC. We're not going to waste a residency slot on her."

I thought about it and nodded. County-USC was a hospital with a jail wing where injured, sick, and addicted inmates were treated. What she was offering was a program where Gloria Dayton could be treated for her addiction and released upon completion. She would not face any charges or further time in jail or prison.

"Fine with me," I said.

I looked at my watch. I had to get going.

"Our offer is good until first appearance tomorrow," I said. "After that I'll call the DEA and see if they want to deal directly. Then it will be taken out of your hands."

She looked indignantly at me. She knew that if I got a deal with the feds, they would squash her. Head to head, the feds always trumped the state. I stood up to go and put a business card down on her desk.

"Don't try to back-door me, Haller," she said. "If it goes sideways on you, I'll take it out on your client."

I didn't respond. I pushed the chair I had borrowed back to its desk. She then dropped the threat with her next line.

"Anyway, I'm sure we can handle this on a level that makes everybody happy."

I looked back at her as I got to the office door.

"Everybody except for Hector Moya," I said.

The law offices of Dobbs and Delgado were on the twenty-ninth floor of one of the twin towers that created the signature skyline of Century City. I was right on time but everyone was already gathered in a conference room with a long polished wood table and a wall of glass that framed a western exposure stretching across Santa Monica to the Pacific and the charter islands beyond. It was a clear day and I could see Catalina and Anacapa out there at the very edge of the world. Because the sun was going down and seemed to be almost at eye level, a film had been rolled down over the window to cut the glare. It was like the room had sunglasses on.

And so did my client. Louis Roulet sat at the head of the table with a pair of black-framed Ray-Bans on. Out of his gray jail jumpsuit, he now wore a dark brown suit over a pale silk T-shirt. He looked like a confident and cool young real estate executive, not the scared boy I saw in the holding pen in the courthouse.

To Roulet's left sat Cecil Dobbs and next to him was a well-preserved, well-coiffed and bejeweled woman I assumed to be Roulet's mother. I also assumed that Dobbs hadn't told her that the meeting would not include her.

To Roulet's right the first seat was empty and waiting for me. In the seat next to it sat my investigator, Raul Levin, with a closed file in front of him on the table.

Dobbs introduced Mary Alice Windsor to me. She shook my hand with a strong grip. I sat down and Dobbs explained that she would be paying for her son's defense and had agreed to the terms I had outlined earlier. He slid an envelope across the table to me. I looked inside and saw a check for sixty thousand dollars with my name on it. It was the retainer I had asked for, but I had expected only half of it in the initial payment. I had made more in total on cases before but it was still the largest single check I had ever received.

The check was drawn on the account of Mary Alice Windsor. The bank was solid gold—First National of Beverly Hills. I closed the envelope and slid it back across the table.

"I'm going to need that to come from Louis," I said, looking at Mrs. Windsor. "I don't care if you give him the money and then he gives it to me. But I want the check I get to come from Louis. I work for him and that's got to be clear from the start."

I knew this was different from even my practice of that morning—accepting payment from a third party. But it was a control issue. One look across the table at Mary Alice Windsor and C. C. Dobbs and I knew I had to make sure that they knew this was my case to manage, to win or to lose.

I wouldn't have thought it could happen but Mary Windsor's face hardened. For some reason she reminded me of an old grandfather clock, her face flat and square.

"Mother," Roulet said, heading something off before it started. "It's all right. I will write him a check. I should be able to cover it until you give me the money."

She looked from me to her son and then back to me.

"Very well," she said.

"Mrs. Windsor," I said. "Your support for your son is very important. And I don't mean just the financial end of things. If we are not successful in getting these charges dropped and we choose the alternative of trial, it will be very important for you to show your support in public ways."

"Don't be silly," she said. "I will back him come hell or high water. These ridiculous charges must be removed, and that woman...she isn't going to get a penny from us."

"Thank you, Mother," Roulet said.

"Yes, thank you," I said. "I will be sure to inform you, probably through Mr. Dobbs, where and when you are needed. It's good to know you will be there for your son."

I said nothing else and waited. It didn't take her long to realize she had been dismissed.

"But you don't want me here right now, is that it?"

"That's right. We need to discuss the case and it is best and most appropriate for Louis to do this only with his defense team. The attorney-client privilege does not cover anyone else. You could be compelled to testify against your son."

"But if I leave, how will Louis get home?"

"I have a driver. I will get him home."

She looked at Dobbs, hoping he might have higher standing and be able to overrule me. Dobbs smiled and stood up so he could pull her chair back. She finally let him and stood up to go.

"Very well," she said. "Louis, I will see you at dinner."

Dobbs walked her through the door of the conference room and I saw them exchange conversation in the hallway. I couldn't hear what was said. Then she left and Dobbs came back, closing the door.

I went through some preliminaries with Roulet, telling him he would have to be arraigned in two weeks and submit a plea. He would have the opportunity at that time to put the state on notice that he was not waiving his right to a speedy trial.

"That's the first choice we have to make," I said. "Whether you want this thing to drag out or you want to move quickly and put the pressure on the state."

"What are the options?" Dobbs asked.

I looked at him and then back at Roulet.

"I'll be very honest with you," I said. "When I have a client who is not incarcerated, my inclination is to drag it out. It's the client's freedom that is on the line—why not get the most of it before the hammer comes down."

"You're talking about a guilty client," Roulet said.

"On the other hand," I said, "if the state's case is weak, then delaying things only gives them time to strengthen their hand. You see, time is our only leverage at this point. If we refuse to waive our right to a speedy trial, it puts a lot of pressure on the prosecutor."

"I didn't do what they are saying I did," Roulet said. "I don't want to waste any time. I want this shit behind me."

"If we refuse to waive, then theoretically they must put you on trial within sixty days of arraignment. The reality is that it gets pushed back when they move to a preliminary hearing. In a prelim a judge hears the evidence and decides if there is enough there to warrant a trial. It's a rubber-stamp process. The judge will hold you over for trial, you will be arraigned again and the clock is reset to sixty days."

"I can't believe this," Roulet said. "This is going to last forever."

"We could always waive the prelim, too. It would really force their hand. The case has been reassigned to a young prosecutor. He's pretty new to felonies. It may be the way to go."

"Wait a minute," Dobbs said. "Isn't a preliminary hearing useful in terms of seeing what the state's evidence is?"

"Not really," I said. "Not anymore. The legislature tried to streamline things a while back and they turned the prelim into a rubber stamp because they relaxed hearsay rules. Now you usually just get the case cop on the stand and he tells the judge what everybody said. The defense usually doesn't get a look at any witnesses other than the cop. If you ask me, the best strategy is to force the prosecution to put up or shut up. Make them go sixty days from first arraignment."

"I like that idea," Roulet said. "I want this over with as soon as possible."

I nodded. He had said it as though a not-guilty verdict was a foregone conclusion.

"Well, maybe it doesn't even get to a trial," Dobbs said. "If these charges don't hold muster—"

"The DA is not going to drop this," I said, cutting him off. "Usually, the cops overcharge and then the DA cuts the charges back. That didn't happen here. Instead, the DA upped the charges. That tells me two things. One is that they believe the case is solid and, two, they upped the charges so that when we start to negotiate they will deal from a higher ground."

"You're talking about a plea bargain?" Roulet asked.

"Yeah, a disposition."

"Forget it, no plea bargain. I'm not going to jail for something I didn't do."

"It might not mean going to jail. You have a clean rec—"

"I don't care if it means I could walk. I'm not going to plead guilty to something I didn't do. If that is going to be a problem for you, then we need to part company right here."

I looked closely at him. Almost all of my clients make protestations of innocence at one point along the way. Especially if it is our first case together. But Roulet's words came with a fervor and directness I hadn't seen in a long time. Liars falter. They look away. Roulet's eyes were holding mine like magnets.

"There is also the civil liability to consider," Dobbs added. "A guilty plea will allow this woman to—"

"I understand all of that," I said, cutting him off again. "I think we're all getting ahead of ourselves here. I only wanted to give Louis a general idea of the way this was going to go. We don't have to make any moves or any hard-and-fast decisions for at least a couple of weeks. We just need to know at the arraignment how we are going to play it."

"Louis took a year of law at UCLA," Dobbs said. "I think he has baseline knowledge of the situation."

Roulet nodded.

"Okay, good," I said. "Then let's just get to it. Louis, let's start with you. Your mother said she expects to see you at dinner. Do you live at home? I mean at her home?"

"I live in the guesthouse. She lives in the main house."

"Anyone else live on the premises?"

"The maid. In the main house."

"No siblings, boyfriends, girlfriends?"

"That's it."

"And you work at your mother's firm?"

"More like I run it. She's not there too much anymore."

"Where were you Saturday night?"

"Satur—you mean last night, don't you?"

"No, I mean Saturday night. Start there."

"Saturday night I didn't do anything. I stayed home and watched television."

"By yourself?"

"That's right."

"What did you watch?"

"A DVD. An old movie called *The Conversation*. Coppola."

"So nobody was with you or saw you. You just watched the movie and then went to bed."

"Basically."

"Basically. Okay. That brings us to Sunday morning. What did you do yesterday during the day?"

"I played golf at Riviera, my usual foursome. Started at ten and finished at four. I came home, showered and changed, had dinner at my mother's house — you want to know what we had?"

"That won't be necessary. But later on I probably will need the names of the guys you played golf with. What happened after dinner?"

"I told my mother I was going to my place but instead I went out."

I noticed that Levin had started taking notes on a small notebook he had taken out of a pocket.

"What kind of car do you drive?"

"I have two, an oh-four Range Rover I use for taking clients around in and an oh-one Carrera I use for myself."

"You used the Porsche last night, then?"

"That's right."

"Where'd you go?"

"I went over the hill and down into the Valley."

He said it as though it was a risky move for a Beverly Hills boy to descend into the working-class neighborhoods of the San Fernando Valley.

"Where did you go?" I asked.

"Ventura Boulevard. I had a drink at Nat's North and then I went down the street a ways to Morgan's and I had a drink there, too."

"Those places are pickup bars, wouldn't you say?"

"Yes. That's why I went to them."

He was matter-of-fact about it and I appreciated his honesty.

"So you were looking for someone. A woman. Anyone in particular, someone you knew?"

"No one in particular. I was looking to get laid, pure and simple."

"What happened at Nat's North?"

"What happened was that it was a slow night, so I left. I didn't even finish my drink."

"You go there often? Do the bartenders know you?"

"Yeah, they know me. A girl named Paula was working last night."

"Okay, so it wasn't working for you there and you left. You drove down to Morgan's. Why Morgan's?"

"It's just another place I go."

"They know you there?"

"They should. I'm a good tipper. Last night Denise and Janice were behind the bar. They know me."

I turned to Levin.

"Raul, what is the victim's name?"

Levin opened his file to pull out a police report but answered before having to look it up.

"Regina Campo. Friends call her Reggie. Twenty-six years old. She told police she's an actress working as a telephone solicitor."

"And hoping to retire soon," Dobbs said.

I ignored him.

"Louis, did you know Reggie Campo before last night?" I asked.

Roulet shrugged.

"Sort of. I'd seen her around the bar scene. But I had never been with her before. I'd never even spoken to her."

"Had you ever tried?"

"No, I never could really get to her. She always seemed to be with someone or more than one person. I don't like to have to penetrate the crowd, you know? My style is to look for the singles."

"What was different last night?"

"Last night she came to me, that was what was different."

"Tell us about it."

"Nothing to tell. I was at the bar at Morgan's, minding my own business, having a look at the possibilities, and she was at the other end and she was with some guy. So she wasn't even on my radar because she looked like she was already taken, you know?"

"Uh-huh, so what happened?"

"Well, after a while the guy she was with gets up to go take a leak or go outside for a smoke, and as soon as he's gone she gets up and slides on down the bar to me and asks if I'm interested. I said I was but what about the guy she's already with? She says don't worry about him, he'll be out the door by ten and then she's free the rest of the night. She wrote her address down for me and said to come by after ten. I told her I'd be there."

"What did she write the address down on?"

"A napkin, but the answer to your next question is no, I don't still have it. I memorized the address and threw out the napkin. I work in real estate. I can remember addresses."

"About what time was this?"

"I don't know."

"Well, she said come by at ten. Did you look at your watch at any point to see how long you would have to wait until then?"

"I think it was between eight and nine. As soon as the guy came back in they left."

"When did you leave the bar?"

"I stayed for a few minutes and then I left. I made one more stop before I went to her place."

"Where was that?"

"Well, she lived in an apartment in Tarzana so I went up to the Lamplighter. It was on the way."

"Why?"

"Well, you know, I wanted to see what the possibilities were. You know, see if there was something better out there, something I didn't have to wait around for or..."

"Or what?"

He still didn't finish the thought.

"Take seconds on?"

He nodded.

"Okay, so who'd you talk to at the Lamplighter? Where is that, by the way?"

It was the only place so far I was unfamiliar with.

"It's on Ventura near White Oak. I didn't really talk to anybody. It was crowded but there really wasn't anybody I was interested in there."

"The bartenders know you there?"

"No, not really. I don't go there all that much."

"You usually get lucky before you hit the third option?"

"Nah, I usually just give up after two."

I nodded just to buy a little time to think about what else to ask before we got to what happened at the victim's house.

"How long were you at the Lamplighter?"

"About an hour, I'd say. Maybe a little less."

"At the bar? How many drinks?"

"Yeah, two drinks at the bar."

"How many drinks in all did you have last night before getting to Reggie Campo's apartment?"

"Um, four at the most. Over two, two and a half, hours. I left one drink untouched at Morgan's."

"What were you drinking?"

"Martinis. Gray Goose."

"Did you pay for any of these drinks in any of these places with a credit card?" Levin asked, offering his first question of the interview.

"No," Roulet said. "When I go out, I pay cash."

I looked at Levin and waited to see if he had anything else to ask. He knew more about the case than I did at this moment. I wanted to give him free rein to ask what he wanted. He looked at me and nodded. He was good to go.

"Okay," I said. "What time was it when you got to Reggie's place?"

"It was twelve minutes to ten. I looked at my watch. I wanted to make sure I didn't knock on her door early."

"So what did you do?"

"I waited in the parking lot. She said ten so I waited till ten."

"Did you see the guy she left Morgan's with come out?"

"Yeah, I saw him. He came out and left, then I went up."

"What kind of car was he driving?" Levin asked.

"A yellow Corvette," Roulet said. "It was a nineties version. I don't know the exact year."

Levin nodded. He was finished. I knew he was just trying to get a line on the man who had been in Campo's apartment before Roulet. I took the questioning back.

"So he leaves and you go in. What happens?"

"I go in the building and her place is on the second floor. I go up and knock and she answers and I walk in."

"Hold on a second. I don't want the shorthand. You went up? How? Stairs, elevator, what? Give us the details."

"Elevator."

"Anybody else on it? Anybody see you?"

Roulet shook his head. I signaled him to continue.

"She opened the door a crack, saw it was me and told me to come in. There was a hallway by the front door so it was kind of a tight space. I walked by her so she could close the door. That's how come she was behind me. And so I didn't see it coming. She had something. She hit me with something and I went down. It got black real fast."

I was silent while I thought about this, tried to picture it in my mind.

"So before a single thing happened, she just knocked you out? She didn't say anything, yell anything, just sort of came up behind and *bang*."

"That's right."

"Okay, then what? What do you remember next?"

"It's still pretty foggy. I remember waking up and these two guys are sitting on me. Holding me down. And then the police came. And the paramedics. I was sitting up against the wall and my hands were cuffed and the paramedic put that ammonia or something under my nose and that's when I really came out of it."

"You were still in the apartment?"

"Yeah."

"Where was Reggie Campo?"

"She was sitting on the couch and another paramedic was working on her face and she was crying and telling the other cop that I had attacked her. All these lies. That I had surprised her at the door and punched her, that I said I was going to rape her and then kill her, all these things I didn't do. And I moved my arms so I could look down at my hands behind my back. I saw they had my hand in like a plastic bag and I could see blood on my hand, and that's when I knew the whole thing was a setup."

"What do you mean by that?"

"She put blood on my hand to make it look like I did it. But it was my left hand. I'm not left-handed. If I was going to punch somebody, I'd use my right hand."

He made a punching gesture with his right hand to illustrate this for me in case I didn't get it. I got up from my spot and paced over to the window. It now seemed like I was higher than the sun. I was looking down at the sunset. I felt uneasy about Roulet's story. It seemed so far-fetched that it might actually be true. And that bothered me. I was always worried that I might not recognize innocence. The possibility of it in my job was so rare that I operated with the fear that I wouldn't be ready for it when it came. That I would miss it.

"Okay, let's talk about this for a second," I said, still facing the sun. "You're saying that she puts blood on your hand to set you up. And she puts it on your left. But if she was going to set you up, wouldn't she put the blood on your right, since the vast majority of people out there are right-handed? Wouldn't she go with the numbers?"

I turned back to the table and got blank stares from everyone.

"You said she opened the door a crack and then let you in," I said. "Could you see her face?"

"Not all of it."

"What could you see?"

"Her eye. Her left eye."

"So did you ever see the right side of her face? Like when you walked in."

"No, she was behind the door."

"That's it!" Levin said excitedly. "She already had the injuries when he got there. She hid it from him, then he steps in and she clocks him. All the injuries were to the right side of her face and that dictated that she put the blood on his left hand."

I nodded as I thought about the logic of this. It seemed to make sense.

"Okay," I said, turning back to the window and continuing to pace. "I think that'll work. Now, Louis, you've told us you had seen this woman around the bar scene before but had never been with her. So, she was a stranger. Why would she do this, Louis? Why would she set you up like you say she did?"

"Money."

But it wasn't Roulet who answered. It had been Dobbs. I turned from the window and looked at him. He knew he had spoken out of turn but didn't seem to care.

"It's obvious," Dobbs said. "She wants money from him, from the family. The civil suit is probably being filed as we speak. The criminal charges are just the prelude to the suit, the demand for money. That's what she's really after."

I sat back down and looked at Levin, exchanging eye contact.

"I saw a picture of this woman in court today," I said. "Half her face was pulped. You are saying that's our defense, that she did that to herself?"

Levin opened his file and took out a piece of paper. It was a black-and-white photocopy of the evidence photograph Maggie McPherson had showed me in court. Reggie Campo's swollen face. Levin's source was good but not good enough to get him actual photos. He slid the photocopy across the table to Dobbs and Roulet.

"We'll get the real photos in discovery," I said. "They look worse, a lot worse, and if we go with your story, then the jury—that is, if this gets to a jury—is going to have to buy that she did that to herself."

I watched Roulet study the photocopy. If it had been he who attacked Reggie Campo, he showed no tell while studying his handiwork. He showed nothing at all.

"You know what?" I said. "I like to think I'm a good lawyer and a good persuader when it comes to juries. But even I'm having trouble believing myself with that story."

9

≋

It was now Raul Levin's turn in the conference room. We'd spoken while I had been riding into Century City and eating bites of roast beef sandwich. I had plugged my cell into the car's speaker phone and told my driver to put his earbuds in. I'd bought him an iPod his first week on the job. Levin had given me the basics of the case, just enough to get me through the initial questioning of my client. Now Levin would take command of the room and go through the case, using the police and evidence reports to tear Louis Roulet's version of events to shreds, to show us what the prosecution would have on its side. At least initially I wanted Levin to be the one to do this because if there was going to be a good guy/bad guy aspect to the defense, I wanted to be the one Roulet would like and trust. I wanted to be the good guy.

Levin had his own notes in addition to the copies of the police reports he had gotten through his source. It was all material the defense was certainly entitled to and would receive through the discovery process, but usually it took weeks to get it through court channels instead of the hours it had taken Levin. As he spoke he held his eyes down on these documents.

"At ten-eleven last night the LAPD communications center received a nine-one-one emergency call from Regina Campo of seventeen-sixty White Oak Boulevard, apartment two-eleven. She reported an intruder had entered her home and attacked her. Patrol officers responded and arrived on the premises at ten-seventeen. Slow night, I guess, because that was pretty quick. Better than average response to a hot shot. Anyway, the patrol officers were met in the parking lot by Ms. Campo, who said she had fled the apartment after the attack. She informed the officers that two neighbors named Edward Turner and Ronald Atkins were in her apartment, holding the intruder. Officer Santos proceeded to the apartment, where he found the suspect intruder, later identified as Mr. Roulet, lying on the floor and in the command and control of Turner and Atkins."

"They were the two faggots who were sitting on me," Roulet said.

I looked at Roulet and saw the flash of anger quickly fade.

"The officers took custody of the suspect," Levin continued, as if he had not been interrupted. "Mr. Atkins—"

"Wait a minute," I said. "Where was he found on the floor? What room?"

"Doesn't say."

I looked at Roulet.

"It was the living room. It wasn't far from the front door. I never got that far in."

Levin wrote a note to himself before continuing.

"Mr. Atkins produced a folding knife with the blade open, which he said had been found on the floor next to the intruder. The officers handcuffed the suspect, and paramedics were called to treat both Campo and Roulet, who had a head laceration and slight concussion. Campo was transported to Holy Cross Medical Center for continued treatment and to be photographed by an evidence technician. Roulet was taken into custody and booked into Van Nuys jail. The premises of Ms. Campo's apartment were sealed for crime scene processing and the case was assigned to Detective Martin Booker of Valley Bureau detectives."

Levin spread more photocopies of the police photos of Regina Campo's injuries out on the table. There were front and profile shots of her face and two close-ups of bruising around her neck and a small puncture mark under her jaw. The copy quality was poor and I knew the photocopies weren't worthy of serious study. But I did notice that all the facial injuries were on the right side of Campo's face. Roulet had been correct about that. She had either been repeatedly punched by someone's left hand—or possibly her own right hand.

"These were taken at the hospital, where Ms. Campo also gave a statement to Detective Booker. In summary, she said she came home about eight-thirty Sunday night and was home alone when there was a knock at her door at about ten o'clock. Mr. Roulet represented himself as someone Ms. Campo knew and so she opened the door. Upon opening the door she was immediately struck by the intruder's fist and driven backwards into the apartment. The intruder entered and closed and locked the door. Ms. Campo attempted to defend herself but was struck at least twice more and driven to the floor."

"This is such bullshit!" Roulet yelled.

He slammed his fists down on the table and stood up, his seat rolling backwards and banging loudly into the glass window behind him.

"Hey, easy now!" Dobbs cautioned. "You break the window and it's like a plane. We all get sucked out of here and go down."

No one smiled at his attempt at levity.

"Louis, sit back down," I said calmly. "These are police reports, nothing more or less. They are not supposed to be the truth. They are one person's view of the truth. All we are doing here is getting a first look at the case, seeing what we are up against."

Roulet rolled his chair back to the table and sat down without further protest. I nodded to Levin and he continued. I noted that Roulet had long stopped acting like the meek prey I had seen earlier in the day in lockup.

"Ms. Campo reported that the man who attacked her had his fist wrapped in a white cloth when he punched her."

I looked across the table at Roulet's hands and saw no swelling or bruising on the knuckles or fingers. Wrapping his fist could have allowed him to avoid such telltale injuries.

"Was it taken into evidence?" I asked.

"Yes," Levin said. "In the evidence report it is described as a cloth dinner napkin with blood on it. The blood and the cloth are being analyzed."

I nodded and looked at Roulet.

"Did the police look at or photograph your hands?"

Roulet nodded.

"The detective looked at my hands but nobody took pictures."

I nodded and told Levin to continue.

"The intruder straddled Ms. Campo on the floor and grasped one hand around her neck," he said. "The intruder told Ms. Campo that he was going to rape her and that it didn't matter to him whether she was alive or dead when he did it. She could not respond because the suspect was choking her with his hand. When he released pressure she said she told him that she would cooperate."

Levin slid another photocopy onto the table. It was a photo of a black-handled folding knife that was sharpened to a deadly point. It explained the earlier photo of the wound under the victim's neck.

Roulet slid the photocopy over to look at it more closely. He slowly shook his head.

"This is not my knife," he said.

I didn't respond and Levin continued.

"The suspect and the victim stood up and he told her to lead the way to the bedroom. The suspect maintained a position behind the victim and pressed the point of the knife against the left side of her throat. As Ms. Campo entered a short hallway that led to the apartment's two bedrooms she turned in the confined space and pushed her attacker backwards into a large floor vase. As he stumbled backwards over the vase, she made a break for the front door. Realizing that her attacker would recover and catch her at the front door, she ducked into the kitchen and grabbed a bottle of vodka off the counter. When the intruder passed by the kitchen on his way to the front door to catch her, Ms. Campo stepped out of the blind and struck him on the back of the head, knocking him to the floor. Ms. Campo then stepped over the fallen man and unlocked the front door. She ran out the door and called the police from the first-floor apartment shared by Turner and Atkins. Turner and Atkins returned to the apartment, where they found the intruder unconscious on the floor. They maintained control of him as he started to regain consciousness and remained in the apartment until police arrived."

"This is incredible," Roulet said. "To have to sit here and listen to this. I can't believe what has happened to me. I DID NOT do this. This is like a dream. She is lying! She —"

"If it is all lies, then this will be the easiest case I ever had," I said. "I will tear her apart and throw her entrails into the sea. But we have to know what she has put on the record before we can construct traps and go after her. And if you think this is hard to sit through, wait until we get to trial and it's stretched out over days instead of minutes. You have to control yourself, Louis. You have to remember that you will get your turn. The defense always gets its turn."

Dobbs reached over and patted Roulet on the forearm, a nice fatherly gesture. Roulet pulled his arm away.

"Damn right you are going to go after her," Roulet said, pointing a finger across the table at my chest. "I want you to go after her with everything we've got."

"That's what I am here for, and you have my promise I will. Now, let me ask my associate a few questions before we finish up here."

I waited to see if Roulet had anything else to say. He didn't. He leaned back into his chair and clasped his hands together.

"You finished, Raul?" I asked.

"For now. I'm still working on all the reports. I should have a transcript of the nine-one-one call tomorrow morning and there will be more stuff coming in."

"Good. What about a rape kit?"

"There wasn't one. Booker's report said she declined, since it never got to that."

"What's a rape kit?" Roulet asked.

"It's a hospital procedure where bodily fluids, hair and fibers are collected from the body of a rape victim," Levin said.

"There was no rape!" Roulet exclaimed. "I never touched —"

"We know that," I said. "That's not why I asked. I am looking for cracks in the state's case. The victim said she was not raped but was reporting what was certainly a sex crime. Usually, the police insist on a rape kit, even when a victim claims there was no sexual assault. They do this just in case the victim actually has been raped and is just too humiliated to say so or might be trying to keep the full extent of the crime from a husband or family member. It's standard procedure, and the fact that she was able to talk her way out of it might be significant to us."

"She didn't want the first guy's DNA showing up in her," Dobbs said.

"Maybe," I said. "It might mean any number of things. But it might be a crack. Let's move on. Raul, is there any mention anywhere about this guy who Louis saw her with?"

"No, none. He's not in the file."

"And what did crime scene find?"

"I don't have the report but I am told that no evidence of any significant nature was located during the crime scene evaluation of the apartment."

"That's good. No surprises. What about the knife?"

"Blood and prints on the knife. But nothing back on that yet. Tracing ownership will be unlikely. You can buy those folding knives in any fishing or camping store around."

"I'm telling you, that is not my knife," Roulet interjected.

"We have to assume the fingerprints will be from the man who turned it in," I said.

"Atkins," Levin responded.

"Right, Atkins," I said, turning to Louis. "But it would not surprise me to find prints from you on it as well. There is no telling what occurred while you were unconscious. If she put blood on your hand, then she probably put your prints on the knife."

Roulet nodded his agreement and was about to say something, but I didn't wait for him.

"Is there any statement from her about being at Morgan's earlier in the evening?" I asked Levin.

He shook his head.

"No, the interview with the victim was in the ER and not formal. It was basic and they didn't go back with her to the early part of the evening. She didn't mention the guy and she didn't mention Morgan's. She just said she had been home since eight-thirty. They asked about what happened at ten. They didn't really get into what she had been doing before. I'm sure that will all be covered in the follow-up investigation."

"Okay, if and when they go back to her for a formal, I want that transcript."

"I'm on it. It will be a sit-down on video when they do it."

"And if crime scene does a video, I want that, too. I want to see her place."

Levin nodded. He knew I was putting on a show for the client and Dobbs, giving them a sense of my command of the case and all the irons that were going into the fire. The reality was I didn't need to tell Raul Levin any of this. He already knew what to do and what to get for me.

"Okay, what else?" I asked. "Do you have any questions, Cecil?"

Dobbs seemed surprised by the focus suddenly shifting to him. He quickly shook his head.

"No, no, I'm fine. This is all good. We're making good progress."

I had no idea what he meant by "progress," but I let it go by without question.

"So what do you think?" Roulet asked.

I looked at him and waited a long moment before answering.

"I think the state has got a strong case against you. They have you in her home, they have a knife and they have her injuries. They also have what I am assuming is her blood on your hands. Added to that, the photos are powerful. And, of course, they will have her testimony. Having never seen or spoken to the woman, I don't know how impressive she will be."

I stopped again and milked the silence even longer before continuing.

"But there is a lot they don't have — evidence of break-in, DNA from the suspect, a motive or even a suspect with a past record of this or any sort of crime. There are a lot of reasons — legitimate reasons — for you to have been in that apartment. Plus..."

I looked past Roulet and Dobbs and out the window. The sun was dropping behind Anacapa and turning the sky pink and purple. It beat anything I ever saw from the windows of my office.

"Plus what?" Roulet asked, too anxious to wait on me.

"Plus you have me. I got Maggie McFierce off the case. The new prosecutor is good but he's green and he'll have never come up against someone like me before."

"So what's our next step?" Roulet asked.

"The next step is for Raul to keep doing his thing, finding out what he can about this alleged victim and why she lied about being alone. We need to find out who she is and who her mystery man is and to see how that plays into our case."

"And what will you do?"

"I'll be dealing with the prosecutor. I'll set something up with him, try to see where he's going and we'll make our choice on which way to go. I have no doubt that I'll be able to go to the DA and knock all of this down to something you can plea to and get behind you. But it will require a concession. You —"

"I told you. I will not —"

"I know what you said but you have to hear me out. I may be able to get a no-contest plea so that you don't actually ever say the word 'guilty,' but I am not seeing the state completely dropping this. You will have to concede responsibility in some regard. It is possible to avoid jail time but you will likely have to perform community service of some sort. There, I've said it. That is the first recitation. There will be more. I am obligated as your attorney to tell you and make sure you understand your options. I know it's not what you want or are willing to do but it is my duty to educate you on the choices. Okay?"

"Fine. Okay."

"Of course, as you know, any concession on your part will pretty much make any civil action Ms. Campo takes against you a slam dunk. So, as you can guess, disposing of the criminal case quickly will probably end up costing you a lot more than my fee."

Roulet shook his head. The plea bargain was already not an option.

"I understand my choices," he said. "You have fulfilled your duty. But I'm not going to pay her a cent for something I didn't do. I'm not going to plead guilty or no contest to something I didn't do. If we go to trial, can you win?"

I held his gaze for a moment before answering.

"Well, you understand that I don't know what will come up between now and then and that I can't guarantee anything...but, yes, based on what I see now, I can win this case. I'm confident of that."

I nodded to Roulet and I think I saw a look of hope enter his eyes. He saw the glimmer.

"There is a third option," Dobbs said.

I looked from Roulet to Dobbs, wondering what wrench he was about to throw into the franchise machine.

"And what's that?" I asked.

"We investigate the hell out of her and this case. Maybe help Mr. Levin out with some of our people. We investigate six ways from Sunday and establish our own credible theory and evidence and present it to the DA. We head this off before it ever gets to trial. We show this greenhorn prosecutor where he will definitely lose the case and get him to drop all charges before he suffers that professional embarrassment. Added to this, I am sure this man works for a man who runs that office and is susceptible, shall we say, to political pressures. We apply it until things turn our way."

I felt like kicking Dobbs under the table. Not only did his plan involve cutting my biggest fee ever by more than half, not only did it see the lion's share of client money going to the investigators, including his own, but it could only have come from a lawyer who had never defended a criminal case in his entire career.

"That's an idea but it is very risky," I said calmly. "If you can blow their case out of the water and you go in before trial to show them how, you are also giving them a blueprint for what to do and what to avoid in trial. I don't like to do that."

Roulet nodded his agreement and Dobbs looked a bit taken aback. I decided to leave it at that and to address Dobbs further on it when I could do it without the client present.

"What about the media?" Levin asked, thankfully changing the subject.

"That's right," Dobbs said, anxious to change it himself now. "My secretary says I have messages from two newspapers and two television stations."

"I probably do as well," I said.

What I didn't mention was that the messages left with Dobbs were left by Lorna Taylor at my direction. The case had not attracted the media yet, other than the freelance videographer who showed up at the first appearance. But I wanted Dobbs and Roulet and his mother to believe they all could be splashed across the papers at any moment.

"We don't want publicity on this," Dobbs said. "This is the worst kind of publicity to get."

He seemed to be adept at stating the obvious.

"All media should be directed to me," I said. "I will handle the media and the best way to do that is to ignore it."

"But we have to say something to defend him," Dobbs said.

"No, we don't have to say anything. Talking about the case legitimizes it. If you get into a game of talking to the media, you keep the story alive. Information is oxygen. Without it they die. As far as I am concerned, let 'em die. Or at least wait until there is no avoiding them. If that happens, only one person speaks for Louis. That's me."

Dobbs reluctantly nodded his agreement. I pointed a finger at Roulet.

"Under no circumstances do you talk to a reporter, even to deny the charges. If they contact you, you send them to me. Got it?"

"I got it."

"Good."

I decided that we had said enough for a first meeting. I stood up.

"Louis, I'll take you home now."

But Dobbs wasn't going to release his grasp on his client so quickly.

"Actually, I've been invited to dinner by Louis's mother," he said. "I could take him, since I am going there."

I nodded my approval. The criminal defense attorney never seemed to get invited to dinner.

"Fine," I said. "But we'll meet you there. I want Raul to see his place and Louis needs to give me that check we spoke about earlier."

If they thought I had forgotten about the money, they had a lot to learn about me. Dobbs looked at Roulet and got an approving nod. Dobbs then nodded to me.

"Sounds like a plan," he said. "We'll meet again there."

Fifteen minutes later I was riding in the back of the Lincoln with Levin. We were following a silver Mercedes carrying Dobbs and Roulet. I was checking with Lorna on the phone. The only message of importance had come from Gloria Dayton's prosecutor, Leslie Faire. The message was we had a deal.

"So," Levin said when I closed the phone. "What do you really think?"

"I think there is a lot of money to be made on this case and we're about to go get the first installment. Sorry I'm dragging you over there. I didn't want it to seem like it was all about the check."

Levin nodded but didn't say anything. After a few moments I continued.

"I'm not sure what to think yet," I said. "Whatever happened in that apartment happened quick. That's a break for us. No actual rape, no DNA. That gives us a glimmer of hope."

"It sort of reminds me of Jesus Menendez, only without DNA. Remember him?"

"Yeah, but I don't want to."

I tried not to think about clients who were in prison without appellate hopes or anything else left but years of time in front of them to nut out. I do what I can with each case but sometimes there is nothing that can be done. Jesus Menendez's case was one of those.

"How's your time on this?" I asked, putting us back on course.

"I've got a few things but I can move them around."

"You are going to have to work nights on this. I need you to go into those bars. I want to know everything about him and everything about her. This case looks simple at this point. We knock her down and we knock the case down."

Levin nodded. He had his briefcase on his lap.

"You got your camera in there?"

"Always."

"When we get to the house take some pictures of Roulet. I don't want you showing his mug shot in the bars. It'll taint things. Can you get a picture of the woman without her face being all messed up?"

"I got her driver's license photo. It's recent."

"Good. Run them down. If we find a witness who saw her come over to him at the bar in Morgan's last night, then we're gold."

"That's where I was thinking I'd start. Give me a week or so. I'll come back to you before the arraignment."

I nodded. We drove in silence for a few minutes, thinking about the case. We were moving through the flats of Beverly Hills, heading up into the neighborhoods where the real money was hidden and waiting.

"And you know what else I think?" I said. "Money and everything aside, I think there's a chance he isn't lying. His story is just quirky enough to be true."

Levin whistled softly between his teeth.

"You think you might have found the innocent man?" he said.

"That would be a first," I said. "If I had only known it this morning, I would have charged him the innocent man premium. If you're innocent you pay more because you're a hell of a lot more trouble to defend."

"Ain't that the truth."

I thought about the idea of having an innocent client and the dangers involved.

"You know what my father said about innocent clients?"

"I thought your father died when you were like six years old."

"Five, actually. They didn't even take me to the funeral."

"And he was talking to you about innocent clients when you were five?"

"No, I read it in a book long after he was gone. He said the scariest client a lawyer will ever have is an innocent client. Because if you fuck up and he goes to prison, it'll scar you for life."

"He said it like that?"

"Words to that effect. He said there is no in-between with an innocent client. No negotiation, no plea bargaining, no middle ground. There's only one verdict. You have to put an NG up on the scoreboard. There's no other verdict but not guilty."

Levin nodded thoughtfully.

"The bottom line was my old man was a damn good lawyer and he didn't like having innocent clients," I said. "I'm not sure I do, either."

10

Thursday, March 17

The first ad I ever put in the yellow pages said "Any Case, Anytime, Anywhere" but I changed it after a few years. Not because the bar objected to it, but because *I* objected to it. I got more particular. Los Angeles County is a wrinkled blanket that covers four thousand square miles from the desert to the Pacific. There are more than ten million people fighting for space on the blanket and a considerable number of them engage in criminal activity as a lifestyle choice. The latest crime stats show almost a hundred thousand violent crimes are reported each year in the county. Last year there were 140,000 felony arrests and then another 50,000 high-end misdemeanor arrests for drug and sex offenses. Add in the DUIs and every year you could fill the Rose Bowl twice over with potential clients. The thing to remember is that you don't want clients from the cheap seats. You want the ones sitting on the fifty-yard line. The ones with money in their pockets.

When the criminals get caught they get funneled into a justice system that has more than forty courthouses spread across the county like Burger Kings ready to serve them — as in serve them up on a plate. These stone fortresses are the watering holes where the legal lions come to hunt and to feed. And the smart hunter learns quickly where the most bountiful locations are, where the paying clients graze. The hunt can be deceptive. The client base of each courthouse does not necessarily reflect the socioeconomic structure of the surrounding environs. Courthouses in Compton, Downey and East Los Angeles have produced a steady line of paying clients for me. These clients are usually accused of being drug dealers but their money is just as green as a Beverly Hills stock swindler's.

On the morning of the seventeenth I was in the Compton courthouse representing Darius McGinley at his sentencing. Repeat offenders mean repeat customers and McGinley was both, as many of my clients tend to be. For the sixth time since I had known him, he had been arrested and charged with dealing crack cocaine. This time it was in Nickerson Gardens, a housing project known by most of its residents as Nixon Gardens. No one I ever asked knew whether this was an abbreviation of the true name of the place or a name bestowed in honor of the president who held office when the vast apartment complex and drug market was built. McGinley was arrested after making a direct hand-to-hand sale of a balloon containing a dozen rocks to an undercover narcotics officer. At the time, he had been out on bail after being arrested for the exact same offense two months earlier. He also had four prior convictions for drug sales on his record.

Things didn't look good for McGinley, who was only twenty-three years old. After he'd taken so many previous swings at the system, the system had now run out of patience with him. The hammer was coming down. Though McGinley had been coddled previously with sentences of probation and county jail time, the prosecutor set the bar at the prison level this time. Any negotiation of a plea agreement would begin and end with a prison sentence. Otherwise, no deal. The prosecutor was happy to take the two outstanding cases to trial and go for a conviction and a double-digit prison sentence.

The choice was hard but simple. The state held all of the cards. They had him cold on two hand-to-hand sales with quantity. The reality was that a trial would be an exercise in futility. McGinley knew this. The reality was that his selling of three hundred dollars in rock cocaine to a cop was going to cost him at least three years of his life.

As with many of my young male clients from the south side of the city, prison was an anticipated part of life for McGinley. He grew up knowing he was going. The only questions were when and for how long and whether he would live long enough to make it there. In my many jailhouse meetings with him over the years, I had learned that McGinley carried a personal philosophy inspired by the life and death and rap music of Tupac Shakur, the thug poet whose rhymes carried the hope and hopelessness of the desolate streets McGinley called home. Tupac correctly prophesied his own violent death. South L.A. teemed with young men who carried the exact same vision.

McGinley was one of them. He would recite to me long riffs from Tupac's CDs. He would translate the meanings of the ghetto lyrics for me. It was an education I valued because McGinley was only one of many clients with a shared belief in a final destiny that was "Thug Mansion," the place between heaven and earth where all gangsters ended up. To McGinley, prison was only a rite of passage on the road to that place and he was ready to make the journey.

"I'll lay up, get stronger and smarter, then I'll be back," he said to me.

He told me to go ahead and make a deal. He had five thousand dollars delivered to me in a money order — I didn't ask where it came from — and I went back to the prosecutor, got both pending cases folded into one, and McGinley agreed to plead guilty. The only thing he ever asked me to try to get for him was an assignment to a prison close by so his mother and his three young children wouldn't have to be driven too far or too long to visit him.

When court was called into session, Judge Daniel Flynn came through the door of his chambers in an emerald green robe, which brought false smiles from many of the lawyers and court workers in the room. He was known to wear the green on two occasions each year—St. Patrick's Day and the Friday before the Notre Dame Fighting Irish took on the Southern Cal Trojans on the football field. He was also known among the lawyers who worked the Compton courthouse as "Danny Boy," as in, "Danny Boy sure is an insensitive Irish prick, isn't he?"

The clerk called the case and I stepped up and announced. McGinley was brought in through a side door and stood next to me in an orange jumpsuit with his wrists locked to a waist chain. He had no one out in the gallery to watch him go down. He was alone except for me.

"Top o' the morning to you, Mr. McGinley," Flynn said in an Irish brogue. "You know what today is?"

I lowered my eyes to the floor. McGinley mumbled his response.

"The day I get my sentence."

"That, too. But I am talking about St. Patrick's Day, Mr. McGinley. A day to revel in Irish heritage."

McGinley turned slightly and looked at me. He was street smart but not life smart. He didn't understand what was happening, whether this was part of the sentencing or just some form of white man disrespect. I wanted to tell him that the judge was being insensitive and probably racist. Instead I leaned over and whispered in his ear, "Just be cool. He's an asshole."

"Do you know the origin of your name, Mr. McGinley?" the judge asked.

"No, sir."

"Do you care?"

"Not really, sir. It's a name from a slaveholder, I 'spect. Why would I care who that motherfucka be?"

"Excuse me, Your Honor," I said quickly.

I leaned over to McGinley again.

"Darius, cool it," I whispered. "And watch your language."

"He's dissing me," he said back, a little louder than a whisper.

"And he hasn't sentenced you yet. You want to blow the deal?"

McGinley stepped back from me and looked up at the judge.

"Sorry about my language, Y'Honor. I come from the street."

"I can tell that," Flynn said. "Well, it is a shame you feel that way about your history. But if you don't care about your name, then I don't either. Let's get on with the sentencing and get you off to prison, shall we?"

He said the last part cheerfully, as if he were taking great delight in sending McGinley off to Disneyland, the happiest place on earth.

The sentencing went by quickly after that. There was nothing in the pre-sentencing investigation report besides what everybody already knew. Darius McGinley had had only one profession since age eleven, drug dealer. He'd had only one true family, a gang. He'd never gotten a driver's license, though he drove a BMW. He'd never gotten married, though he'd fathered three babies. It was the same old story and same old cycle trotted out a dozen times a day in courtrooms across the county. McGinley lived in a society that intersected mainstream America only in the courtrooms. He was just fodder for the machine. The machine needed to eat and McGinley was on the plate. Flynn sentenced him to the agreed-upon three to five years in prison and read all of the standard legal language that came with a plea agreement. For laughs — though only his own courtroom staff complied — he read the boilerplate using his brogue again. And then it was over.

I know McGinley dealt death and destruction in the form of rock cocaine and probably committed untold violence and other offenses he was never charged with, but I still felt bad for him. I felt like he was another one who'd never had a shot at anything but thug life in the first place. He'd never known his father and had dropped out of school in the sixth grade to learn the rock trade. He could accurately count money in a rock house but he had never had a checking account. He had never been to a county beach, let alone outside of Los Angeles. And now his first trip out would be on a bus with bars over the windows.

Before he was led back into the holding cell for processing and transfer to prison I shook his hand, his movement restricted by the waist chain, and wished him good luck. It is something I rarely do with my clients.

"No sweat," he said to me. "I'll be back."

And I didn't doubt it. In a way, Darius McGinley was just as much a franchise client as Louis Roulet. Roulet was most likely a one-shot deal. But over the years, I had a feeling McGinley would be one of what I call my "annuity clients." He would be the gift that would keep on giving — as long as he defied the odds and kept on living.

I put the McGinley file in my briefcase and headed back through the gate while the next case was called. Outside the courtroom Raul Levin was waiting for me in the crowded hallway. We had a scheduled meeting to go over his findings in the Roulet case. He'd had to come to Compton because I had a busy schedule.

"Top o' the morning," Levin said in an exaggerated Irish accent.

"Yeah, you saw that?"

"I stuck my head in. The guy's a bit of a racist, isn't he?"

"And he can get away with it because ever since they unified the courts into one countywide district, his name goes on the ballot everywhere. Even if the people of Compton rose up like a wave to vote him off, the Westsiders could still cancel them out. It's fucked up."

"How'd he get on the bench in the first place?"

"Hey, you get a law degree and make the right contributions to the right people and you could be a judge, too. He was appointed by the governor. The hard part is winning that first retention election. He did. You've never heard the 'In like Flynn' story?"

"Nope."

"You'll love it. About six years ago Flynn gets his appointment from the governor. This is before unification. Back then judges were elected by the voters of the district where they presided. The supervising judge for L.A. County checks out his credentials and pretty quickly realizes that he's got a guy with lots of political connections but no talent or courthouse experience to go with it. Flynn was basically an office lawyer. Probably couldn't find a courthouse, let alone try a case, if you paid him. So the presiding judge dumps him down here in Compton criminal because the rule is you have to run for retention the year after being appointed to the bench. He figures Flynn will fuck up, anger the folks and get voted out. One year and out."

"Headache over."

"Exactly. Only it didn't work that way. In the first hour on the first day of filing for the ballot that year, Fredrica Brown walks into the clerk's office and puts in her papers to run against Flynn. You know Downtown Freddie Brown?"

"Not personally. I know of her."

"So does everybody else around here. Besides being a pretty good defense lawyer, she's black, she's a woman and she's popular in the community. She would have crushed Flynn five to one or better."

"Then how the hell did Flynn keep the seat?"

"That's what I'm getting to. With Freddie on the ballot, nobody else filed to run. Why bother, she was a shoo-in — though it was kind of curious why she'd want to be a judge and take the pay cut. Back then she had to have been well into mid six figures with her practice."

"So what happened?"

"What happened was, a couple months later on the last hour before filing closed, Freddie walks back into the clerk's office and withdraws from the ballot."

Levin nodded.

"So Flynn ends up running unopposed and keeps the seat," he said.

"You got it. Then unification comes in and they'll never be able to get him out of there."

Levin looked outraged.

"That's bullshit. They had some kind of deal and that's gotta be a violation of election laws."

"Only if you could prove there was a deal. Freddie has always maintained that she wasn't paid off or part of some plan Flynn cooked up to stay on the bench. She says she just changed her mind and pulled out because she realized she couldn't sustain her lifestyle on a judge's pay. But I'll tell you one thing, Freddie sure seems to do well whenever she has a case in front of Flynn."

"And they call it a justice system."

"Yeah, they do."

"So what do you think about Blake?"

It had to be brought up. It was all anybody else was talking about. Robert Blake, the movie and television actor, had been acquitted of murdering his wife the day before in Van Nuys Superior Court. The DA and the LAPD had lost another big media case and you couldn't go anywhere without it being the number one topic of discussion. The media and most people who lived and worked outside the machine didn't get it. The question wasn't whether Blake did it, but whether there was enough evidence presented in trial to convict him of doing it. They were two distinctly separate things but the public discourse that had followed the verdict had entwined them.

"What do I think?" I said. "I think I admire the jury for staying focused on the evidence. If it wasn't there, it wasn't there. I hate it when the DA thinks they can ride in a verdict on common sense — 'If it wasn't him, who else could it have been?' Give me a break with that. You want to convict a man and put him in a cage for life, then put up the fucking evidence. Don't hope a jury is going to bail your ass out on it."

"Spoken like a true defense attorney."

"Hey, you make your living off defense attorneys, pal. You should memorize that rap. So forget Blake. I'm jealous and I'm already tired of hearing about it. You said on the phone that you had good news for me."

"I do. Where do you want to go to talk and look at what I've got?"

I looked at my watch. I had a calendar call on a case in the Criminal Courts Building downtown. I had until eleven to be there and I couldn't miss it because I had missed it the day before. After that I was supposed to go up to Van Nuys to meet for the first time with Ted Minton, the prosecutor who had taken the Roulet case over from Maggie McPherson.

"I don't have time to go anywhere," I said. "We can go sit in my car and grab a coffee. You got your stuff with you?"

In answer Levin raised his briefcase and rapped his knuckles on its side.

"But what about your driver?"

"Don't worry about him."

"Then let's do it."

11

After we were in the Lincoln I told Earl to drive around and see if he could find a Starbucks. I needed coffee.

"Ain' no Starbuck 'round here," Earl responded.

I knew Earl was from the area but I didn't think it was possible to be more than a mile from a Starbucks at any given point in the county, maybe even the world. But I didn't argue the point. I just wanted coffee.

"Okay, well, drive around and find a place that has coffee. Just don't go too far from the courthouse. We need to get back to drop Raul off after."

"You got it."

"And Earl? Put on your earphones while we talk about a case back here for a while, okay?"

Earl fired up his iPod and plugged in the earbuds. He headed the Lincoln down Acacia in search of java. Soon we could hear the tinny sound of hip-hop coming from the front seat and Levin opened his briefcase on the fold-down table built into the back of the driver's seat.

"Okay, what do you have for me?" I said. "I'm going to see the prosecutor today and I want to have more aces in my hand than he does. We also have the arraignment Monday."

"I think I've got a few aces here," Levin replied.

He sorted through things in his briefcase and then started his presentation.

"Okay," he said, "let's begin with your client and then we'll check in on Reggie Campo. Your guy is pretty squeaky. Other than parking and speeding tickets — which he seems to have a problem avoiding and then a bigger problem paying — I couldn't find squat on him. He's pretty much your standard citizen."

"What's with the tickets?"

"Twice in the last four years he's let parking tickets — a lot of them — and a couple speeding tickets accumulate unpaid. Both times it went to warrant and your colleague C. C. Dobbs stepped in to pay them off and smooth things over."

"I'm glad C.C.'s good for something. By 'paying them off,' I assume you mean the tickets, not the judges."

"Let's hope so. Other than that, only one blip on the radar with Roulet."

"What?"

"At the first meeting when you were giving him the drill about what to expect and so on and so forth, it comes out that he'd had a year at UCLA law and knew the system. Well, I checked on that. See, half of what I do is try to find out who is lying or who is the biggest liar of the bunch. So I check damn near everything. And most of the time it's easy to do because everything's on computer."

"Right, I get it. So what about the law school, was that a lie?"

"Looks like it. I checked the registrar's office and he's never been enrolled in the law school at UCLA."

I thought about this. It was Dobbs who had brought up UCLA law and Roulet had just nodded. It was a strange lie for either one of them to have told because it didn't really get them anything. It made me think about the psychology behind it. Was it something to do with me? Did they want me to think of Roulet as being on the same level as me?

"So if he lied about something like that...," I said, thinking out loud.

"Right," Levin said. "I wanted you to know about it. But I gotta say, that's it on the negative side for Mr. Roulet so far. He might've lied about law school but it looks like he didn't lie about his story — at least the parts I could check out."

"Tell me."

"Well, his track that night checks out. I got wits in here who put him at Nat's North, Morgan's and then the Lamplighter, bing, bing, bing. He did just what he told us he did. Right down to the number of martinis. Four total and at least one of them he left on the bar unfinished."

"They remember him that well? They remember that he didn't even finish his drink?"

I am always suspicious of perfect memory because there is no such thing. And it is my job and my skill to find the faults in the memory of witnesses. Whenever someone remembers too much, I get nervous — especially if the witness is for the defense.

"No, I'm not just relying on a bartender's memory. I've got something here that you are going to love, Mick. And you better love me for it because it cost me a grand."

From the bottom of his briefcase he pulled out a padded case that contained a small DVD player. I had seen people using them on planes before and had been thinking about getting one for the car. The driver could use it while waiting on me in court. And I could probably use it from time to time on cases like this one.

Levin started loading in a DVD. But before he could play it the car pulled to a stop and I looked up. We were in front of a place called The Central Bean.

"Let's get some coffee and then see what you've got there," I said.

I asked Earl if he wanted anything and he declined the offer. Levin and I got out and went in. There was a short line for coffee. Levin spent the waiting time telling me about the DVD we were about to watch in the car.

"I'm in Morgan's and want to talk to this bartender named Janice but she says I have to clear it first with the manager. So I go back to see him in the office and he's asking me what exactly I want to ask Janice about. There's something off about this guy. I'm wondering why he wants to know so much, you know? Then it comes clear when he makes an offer. He tells me that last year they had a problem behind the bar. Pilferage from the cash register. They have as many as a dozen bartenders working back there in a given week and he couldn't figure out who had sticky fingers."

"He put in a camera."

"You got it. A hidden camera. He caught the thief and fired his ass. But it worked so good he kept the camera in place. The system records on high-density tape from eight till two every night. It's on a timer. He gets four nights on a tape. If there is ever a problem or a shortage he can go back and check it. Because they do a weekly profit-and-loss check, he rotates two tapes so he always has a week's worth of film to look at."

"He had the night in question on tape?"

"Yes, he did."

"And he wanted a thousand dollars for it."

"Right again."

"The cops don't know about it?"

"They haven't even come to the bar yet. They're just going with Reggie's story so far."

I nodded. This wasn't all that unusual. There were too many cases for the cops to investigate thoroughly and completely. They were already loaded for bear, anyway. They had an eyewitness victim, a suspect caught in her apartment, they had the victim's blood on the suspect and even the weapon. To them, there was no reason to go further.

"But we're interested in the bar, not the cash register," I said.

"I know that. And the cash register is against the wall behind the bar. The camera is up above it in a smoke detector on the ceiling. And the back wall is a mirror. I looked at what he had and pretty quickly realized that you can see the whole bar in the mirror. It's just reversed. I had the tape transferred to a disc because we can manipulate the image better. Blow it up and zero in, that sort of thing."

It was our turn in line. I ordered a large coffee with cream and sugar and Levin ordered a bottle of water. We took our refreshments back to the car. I told Earl not to drive until after we'd viewed the DVD. I can read while riding in a car but I thought looking at the small screen of Levin's player while bumping along south county streets might give me a dose of motion sickness.

Levin started the DVD and gave a running commentary to go with the visuals.

On the small screen was a downward view of the rectangular-shaped bar at Morgan's. There were two bartenders on patrol, both women in black jeans and white shirts tied off to show flat stomachs, pierced navels and tattoos creeping up out of their rear belt lines. As Levin had explained, the camera was angled toward the back of the bar area and cash register but the mirror that covered the wall behind the register displayed the line of customers sitting at the bar. I saw Louis Roulet sit down by himself in the dead center of the frame. There was a frame counter in the bottom left corner and a time and date code in the right corner. It said that it was 8:11 P.M. on March 6.

"There's Louis showing up," Levin said. "And over here is Reggie Campo."

He manipulated buttons on the player and froze the image. He then shifted it, bringing the right margin into the center. On the short side of the bar to the right a woman and a man sat next to each other. Levin zoomed in on them.

"Are you sure?" I asked.

I had only seen pictures of the woman with her face badly bruised and swollen.

"Yeah, it's her. And that's our Mr. X."

"Okay."

"Now watch."

He started the film moving again and widened the picture back to full frame. He then started moving it in fast-forward mode.

"Louis drinks his martini, he talks with the bartenders and nothing much happens for almost an hour," Levin said.

He checked a notebook page that had notes attributed to specific frame numbers. He slowed the image to normal speed at the right moment and shifted the frame again so that Reggie Campo and Mr. X were in the center of the screen. I noticed that we had advanced to 8:43 on the time code.

On the screen Mr. X took a pack of cigarettes and a lighter off the bar and slid off his stool. He then walked out of camera range to the right.

"He's heading to the front door," Levin said. "They have a smoking porch in the front."

Reggie Campo appeared to watch Mr. X go and then she slid off her stool and started walking along the front of the bar, just behind the patrons on stools. As she passed by Roulet she appeared to drag the fingers of her left hand across his shoulders, almost in a tickling gesture. This made Roulet turn and watch her as she kept going.

"She just gave him a little flirt there," Levin said. "She's heading to the bathroom."

"That's not how Roulet said it went down," I said. "He claimed she came on to him, gave him her—"

"Just hold your horses," Levin said. "She's got to come back from the can, you know."

I waited and watched Roulet at the bar. I checked my watch. I was doing okay for the time being but I couldn't miss the calendar call at the CCB. I had already pushed the judge's patience to the max by not showing up the day before.

"Here she comes," Levin said.

Leaning closer to the screen I watched as Reggie Campo came back along the bar line. This time when she got to Roulet she squeezed up to the bar between him and a man on the next stool to the right. She had to move into the space sideways and her breasts were clearly pushed against Roulet's right arm. It was a come-on if I had ever seen one. She said something and Roulet bent over closer to her lips to hear. After a few moments he nodded and then I saw her put what looked like a crumpled cocktail napkin into his hand. They had one more verbal exchange and then Reggie Campo kissed Louis Roulet on the cheek and pulled backwards away from the bar. She headed back to her stool.

"You're beautiful, Mish," I said, using the name I gave him after he told me of his mishmash of Jewish and Mexican descent.

"And you say the cops don't have this?" I added.

"They didn't know about it last week when I got it and I still have the tape. So, no, they don't have it and probably don't know about it yet."

Under the rules of discovery, I would need to turn it over to the prosecution after Roulet was formally arraigned. But there was still some play in that. I didn't technically have to turn over anything until I was sure I planned to use it in trial. That gave me a lot of leeway and time.

I knew that what was on the DVD was important and no doubt would be used in trial. All by itself it could be cause for reasonable doubt. It seemed to show a familiarity between victim and alleged attacker that was not included in the state's case. More important, it also caught the victim in a position in which her behavior could be interpreted as being at least partially responsible for drawing the action that followed. This was not to suggest that what followed was acceptable or not criminal, but juries are always interested in the causal relationships of crime and the individuals involved. What the video did was move a crime that might have been viewed through a black-and-white prism into the gray area. As a defense attorney I lived in the gray areas.

The flip side of that was that the DVD was so good it might be too good. It directly contradicted the victim's statement to police about not knowing the man who attacked her. It impeached her, showed her in a lie. It only took one lie to knock a case down. The tape was what I called "walking proof." It would end the case before it even got to trial. My client would simply walk away.

And with him would go the big franchise payday.

Levin was fast-forwarding the image again.

"Now watch this," he said. "She and Mr. X split at nine. But watch when he gets up."

Levin had shifted the frame to focus on Campo and the unknown man. When the time code hit 8:59 he put the playback in slow motion.

"Okay, they're getting ready to leave," he said. "Watch the guy's hands."

I watched. The man took a final draw on his drink, tilting his head far back and emptying the glass. He then slipped off his stool, helped Campo off hers and they walked out of the camera frame to the right.

"What?" I said. "What did I miss?"

Levin moved the image backwards until he got to the moment the unknown man was finishing his drink. He then froze the image and pointed to the screen. The man had his left hand down flat on the bar for balance as he reared back to drink.

"He drinks with his right hand," he said. "And on his left you can see a watch on his wrist. So it looks like the guy is right-handed, right?"

"Yeah, so? What does that get us? The injuries to the victim came from blows from the left."

"Think about what I've told you."

I did. And after a few moments I got it.

"The mirror. Everything's backwards. He's left-handed."

Levin nodded and made a punching motion with his left fist.

"This could be the whole case right here," I said, not sure that was a good thing.

"Happy Saint Paddy's Day, lad," Levin said in his brogue again, not realizing I might be staring at the end of the gravy train.

I took a long drink of hot coffee and tried to think about a strategy for the video. I didn't see any way to hold it for trial. The cops would eventually get around to the follow-up investigations and they would find out about it. If I held on to it, it could blow up in my face.

"I don't know how I'm going to use it yet," I said. "But I think it's safe to say Mr. Roulet and his mother and Cecil Dobbs are going to be very happy with you."

"Tell them they can always express their thanks financially."

"All right, anything else on the tape?"

Levin started to fast-forward the playback.

"Not really. Roulet reads the napkin and memorizes the address. He then hangs around another twenty minutes and splits, leaving a fresh drink on the bar."

He slowed the image down at the point Roulet was leaving. Roulet took one sip out of his fresh martini and put it down on the bar. He picked up the napkin Reggie Campo had given him, crumpled it in his hand and then dropped it to the floor as he got up. He left the bar, leaving the drink behind.

Levin ejected the DVD and returned it to its plastic sleeve. He then turned off the player and started to put it away.

"That's it on the visuals that I can show you here."

I reached forward and tapped Earl on the shoulder. He had his sound buds in. He pulled out one of the ear plugs and looked back at me.

"Let's head back to the courthouse," I said. "Keep your plugs in."

Earl did as instructed.

"What else?" I said to Levin.

"There's Reggie Campo," he said. "She's not Snow White."

"What did you find out?"

"It's not necessarily what I found out. It's what I think. You saw how she was on the tape. One guy leaves and she's dropping love notes on another guy alone at the bar. Plus, I did some checking. She's an actress but she's not currently working as an actress. Except for private auditions, you could say."

He handed me a professional photo collage that showed Reggie Campo in different poses and characters. It was the kind of photo sheet sent to casting directors all over the city. The largest photo on the sheet was a head shot. It was the first time I had seen her face up close without the ugly bruises and swelling. Reggie Campo was a very attractive woman and something about her face was familiar to me but I could not readily place it. I wondered if I had seen her in a television show or a commercial. I flipped the head shot over and read her credits. They were for shows I never watched and commercials I didn't remember.

"In the police reports she lists her current employer as Topsail Telemarketing. They're over in the Marina. They take the calls for a lot of the crap they sell on late-night TV. Workout machines and stuff like that. Anyway, it's day work. You work when you want. The only thing is, Reggie hasn't worked a day there for five months."

"So what are you telling me, she's been tricking?"

"I've been watching her the last three nights and —"

"You what?"

I turned and looked at him. If a private eye working for a criminal defendant was caught tailing the victim of a violent crime, there could be hell to pay and I would be the one to pay it. All the prosecution would have to do is go see a judge and claim harassment and intimidation and I'd be held in contempt faster than the Santa Ana wind through the Sepulveda Pass. As a crime victim Reggie Campo was sacrosanct until she was on the stand. Only then was she mine.

"Don't worry, don't worry," Levin said. "It was a very loose tail. Very loose. And I'm glad I did it. The bruises and the swelling and all of that have either gone away or she's using a lot of makeup, because this lady has been getting a lot of visitors. All men, all alone, all different times of the night. It looks like she tries to fit at least two into her dance card each night."

"Is she picking them up in the bars?"

"No, she's been staying in. These guys must be regulars or something because they know their way to her door. I got some plate numbers. If necessary I can visit them and try to get some answers. I also shot some infrared video but I haven't transferred it to disc yet."

"No, let's hold off on visiting any of these guys for now. Word could get back to her. We have to be very careful around her. I don't care if she's tricking or not."

I drank some more coffee and tried to decide how to move with this.

"You ran a check on her, right? No criminal record?"

"Right, she's clean. My guess is that she's new to the game. You know, these women who want to be actresses, it's a tough gig. It wears you down. She probably started by taking a little help from these guys here and there, then it became a business. She went from amateur to pro."

"And none of this is in the reports you got before?"

"Nope. Like I told you, there hasn't been a lot of follow-up by the cops. At least so far."

"If she graduated from amateur to pro, she could've graduated to setting a guy like Roulet up. He drives a nice car, wears nice clothes…have you seen his watch?"

"Yeah, a Rolex. If it's real, then he's wearing ten grand right there on his wrist. She could have seen that from across the bar. Maybe that's why she picked him out of all the rest."

We were back by the courthouse. I had to start heading toward downtown. I asked Levin where he was parked and he directed Earl to the lot.

"This is all good," I said. "But it means Louis lied about more than UCLA."

"Yeah," Levin agreed. "He knew he was going into a pay-for-play deal with her. He should have told you about it."

"Yeah, and now I'm going to talk to *him* about it."

We pulled up next to the curb outside a pay lot on Acacia. Levin took a file out of his briefcase. It had a rubber band around it that held a piece of paper to the outside cover. He held it out to me and I saw the document was an invoice for almost six thousand dollars for eight days of investigative services and expenses. Based on what I had heard during the last half hour, the price was a bargain.

"That file has everything we just talked about, plus a copy of the video from Morgan's on disc," Levin said.

I hesitantly took the file. By taking it I was moving it into the realm of discovery. Not accepting it and keeping everything with Levin would have given me a buffer, wiggle room if I got into a discovery scrap with the prosecutor.

I tapped the invoice with my finger.

"I'll call this in to Lorna and we'll send out a check," I said.

"How is Lorna? I miss seeing her."

When we were married, Lorna used to ride with me a lot and go into court with me to watch. Sometimes when I was short a driver she would take the wheel. Levin saw her more often back then.

"She's doing great. She's still Lorna."

Levin cracked his door open but didn't get out.

"You want me to stay on Reggie?"

That was the question. If I approved I would lose all deniability if something went wrong. Because now I would know what he was doing. I hesitated but then I nodded.

"Very loose. And don't farm it out. I only trust you on it."

"Don't worry. I'll handle it myself. What else?"

"The left-handed man. We have to figure out who Mr. X is and whether he was part of this thing or just another customer."

Levin nodded and pumped his left-handed fist again.

"I'm on it."

He put on his sunglasses, opened the door and slid out. He reached back in for his briefcase and his unopened bottle of water, then said good-bye and closed the door. I watched him start walking through the lot in search of his car. I should have been ecstatic about all I had just learned. It tilted everything steeply toward my client. But I still felt uneasy about something I couldn't quite put my finger on.

Earl had turned his music off and was awaiting direction.

"Take me downtown, Earl," I said.

"You got it," he replied. "The CCB?"

"Yeah and, hey, who was that you were listening to on the 'Pod? I could sort of hear it."

"That was Snoop. Gotta play him up loud."

I nodded. L.A.'s own. And a former defendant who faced down the machine on a murder charge and walked away. There was no better story of inspiration on the street.

"Earl?" I said. "Take the seven-ten. We're running late."

12

Sam Scales was a Hollywood con man. He specialized in Internet schemes designed to gather credit card numbers and verification data that he would then turn and sell in the financial underworld. The first time we had worked together he had been arrested for selling six hundred card numbers and their attendant verification information — expiration dates and the addresses, social security numbers and passwords of the rightful owners of the cards — to an undercover sheriff's deputy.

Scales had gotten the numbers and information by sending out an e-mail to five thousand people who were on the customer list of a Delaware-based company that sold a weight-loss product called TrimSlim6 over the Internet. The list had been stolen from the company's computer by a hacker who did freelance work for Scales. Using a rent-by-the-hour computer in a Kinko's and a temporary e-mail address, Scales then sent out a mass mailing to all those on the list. He identified himself as counsel for the federal Food and Drug Administration and told the recipients that their credit cards would be refunded the full amount of their purchases of TrimSlim6 following an FDA recall of the product. He said FDA testing of the product proved it to be ineffective in promoting weight loss. He said the makers of the product had agreed to refund all purchases in an effort to avoid fraud charges. He concluded the e-mail with instructions for confirming the refund. These included providing the credit card number, expiration date and all other pertinent verification data.

Of the five thousand recipients of the message, there were six hundred who bit. Scales then made an Internet contact in the underworld and set up a hand-to-hand sale, six hundred credit card numbers and vitals for ten thousand in cash. It meant that within days the numbers would be stamped on plastic blanks and then put to use. It was a fraud that would reach into the millions of dollars in losses.

But it was stunted in a West Hollywood coffee shop where Scales handed over a printout to his buyer and was given a thick envelope containing cash in return. When he walked out carrying the envelope and an iced decaf latte he was met by sheriff's deputies. He had sold his numbers to an undercover.

Scales hired me to get him a deal. He was thirty-three years old at the time and had a clean record, even though there were indications and evidence that he had never held a lawful job. By focusing the prosecutor assigned to the case on the theft of card numbers rather than the potential losses of the fraud, I was able to get Scales a disposition to his liking. He pleaded guilty to one felony count of identity theft and received a one-year suspended sentence, sixty days of CalTrans work and four years of probation.

That was the first time. That was three years ago. Sam Scales did not take the opportunity afforded him by the no-jail sentence. He was now back in custody and I was defending him in a fraud case so reprehensible that it was clear from the start that it was going to be beyond my ability to keep him out of prison.

On December 28 of the previous year Scales used a front company to register a domain name of SunamiHelp.com on the World Wide Web. On the home page of the website he put photographs of the destruction and death left two days earlier when a tsunami in the Indian Ocean devastated parts of Indonesia, Sri Lanka, India and Thailand. The site asked viewers to please help by making a donation to SunamiHelp which would then distribute it among the numerous agencies responding to the disaster. The site also carried the photograph of a handsome white man identified as Reverend Charles, who was engaged in the work of bringing Christianity to Indonesia. A personal note from Reverend Charles was posted on the site and it asked viewers to give from the heart.

Scales was smart but not that smart. He didn't want to steal the donations made to the site. He only wanted to steal the credit card information used to make the donations. The investigation that followed his arrest showed that all contributions made through the site actually were forwarded to the American Red Cross and did go to efforts to help victims of the devastating tsunami.

But the numbers and information from the credit cards used to make those donations were also forwarded to the financial underworld. Scales was arrested when a detective with the LAPD's fraud-by-trick unit named Roy Wunderlich found the website. Knowing that disasters always drew out the con artists in droves, Wunderlich had started typing in possible website names in which the word *tsunami* was misspelled. There were several legitimate tsunami donation sites on the web and he typed in variations of these, always misspelling the word. His thinking was that the con artists would misspell the word when they set up fraud sites in an effort to draw potential victims who were likely to be of a lower education level. SunamiHelp.com was among several questionable sites the detective found. Most of these he forwarded to an FBI task force looking at the problem on a nationwide scale. But when he checked the domain registration of SunamiHelp.com, he found a Los Angeles post office box. That gave Wunderlich jurisdiction. He was in business. He kept SunamiHelp.com for himself.

The PO box turned out to be a dead address but Wunderlich was undeterred. He floated a balloon, meaning he made a controlled purchase, or in this case a controlled donation.

The credit card number the detective provided while making a twenty-dollar donation would be monitored twenty-four hours a day by the Visa fraud unit and he would be informed instantly of any purchase made on the account. Within three days of the donation the credit card was used to purchase an eleven-dollar lunch at the Gumbo Pot restaurant in the Farmers Market at Fairfax and Third. Wunderlich knew that it had simply been a test purchase. Something small and easily coverable with cash if the user of the counterfeit credit card encountered a problem at the point of purchase.

The restaurant purchase was allowed to go through and Wunderlich and four other detectives from the trick unit were dispatched to the Farmers Market, a sprawling blend of old and new shops and restaurants that was always crowded and therefore a perfect place for credit card con artists to operate. The investigators would spread out in the complex and wait while Wunderlich continued to monitor the card's use by phone.

Two hours after the first purchase the control number was used again to purchase a six-hundred-dollar leather jacket at the Nordstrom in the market. The credit card approval was delayed but not stopped. The detectives moved in and arrested a young woman as she was completing the purchase of the jacket. The case then became what is known as a "snitch chain," the police following one suspect to the next as they snitched each other off and the arrests moved up the ladder.

Eventually they came to the man sitting at the top of that ladder, Sam Scales. When the story broke in the press Wunderlich referred to him as the Tsunami Svengali because so many victims of the scam turned out to be women who had wanted to help the handsome minister pictured on the website. The nickname angered Scales, and in my discussions with him he took to referring to the detective who had brought him down as Wunder Boy.

I got to Department 124 on the thirteenth floor of the Criminal Courts

Building by 10:45 but the courtroom was empty except for Marianne, the judge's clerk. I went through the bar and approached her station.

"You guys still doing the calendar?" I asked.

"Just waiting on you. I'll call everybody and tell the judge."

"She mad at me?"

Marianne shrugged. She wouldn't answer for the judge. Especially to a defense attorney. But in a way, she was telling me that the judge wasn't happy.

"Is Scales still back there?"

"Should be. I don't know where Joe went."

I turned and went over to the defense table and sat down and waited. Eventually, the door to the lockup opened and Joe Frey, the bailiff assigned to 124, stepped out.

"You still got my guy back there?"

"Just barely. We thought you were a no-show again. You want to go back?"

He held the steel door open for me and I stepped into a small room with a stairwell going up to the courthouse jail on the fourteenth floor and two doors leading to the smaller holding rooms for 124. One of the doors had a glass panel. It was for attorney-client meetings and I could see Sam Scales sitting by himself at a table behind the glass. He was wearing an orange jumpsuit and had steel cuffs on his wrists. He was being held without bail because his latest arrest violated his probation on the TrimSlim6 conviction. The sweet deal I had gotten him on that was about to go down the tubes.

"Finally," Scales said as I walked in.

"Like you're going anywhere. You ready to do this?"

"If I have no choice."

I sat down across from him.

"Sam, you always have a choice. But let me explain it again. They've got you cold on this, okay? You were caught ripping off people who wanted to help the people caught in one of the worst natural disasters in recorded history. They've got three co-conspirators who took deals to testify against you. They have the list of card numbers found in your possession. What I am saying is that at the end of the day, you are going to get about as much sympathy from the judge and a jury — if it should come to that — as they would give a child raper. Maybe even less."

"I know all of that but I am a useful asset to society. I could educate people. Put me in the schools. Put me in the country clubs. Put me on probation and I'll tell people what to watch out for out there."

"*You* are who they have to watch out for. You blew your chance with the last one and the prosecution said this is the final offer on this one. You don't take it and they're going to go to the wall on this. The one thing I can guarantee you is that there will be no mercy."

So many of my clients are like Sam Scales. They hopelessly believe there is a light behind the door. And I'm the one who has to tell them the door is locked and that the bulb burned out long ago anyway.

"Then I guess I have to do it," Scales said, looking at me with eyes that blamed me for not finding a way out for him.

"It's your choice. You want a trial, we'll go to trial. Your exposure will be ten years plus the one you've got left on the probation. You make 'em real mad and they can also ship you over to the FBI so the feds can take a swing at you on interstate wire fraud if they want."

"Let me ask you something. If we go to trial, could we win?"

I almost laughed but I still had some sympathy left for him.

"No, Sam, we can't win. Haven't you been listening to what I've been telling you for two months? They got you. You can't win. But I'm here to do what you want. Like I said, if you want a trial we'll go to trial. But I gotta tell you that if we go, you'll have to get your mother to pay me again. I'm only good through today."

"How much did she pay you already?"

"Eight thousand."

"Eight grand! That's her fucking retirement account money!"

"I'm surprised she has anything left in the account with you for a son."

He looked at me sharply.

"I'm sorry, Sam. I shouldn't have said that. From what she told me, you're a good son."

"Jesus Christ, I should have gone to fucking law school. You're a con no different from me. You know that, Haller? Only that paper they give you makes you street legal, that's all."

They always blame the lawyer for making a living. As if it's a crime to want to be paid for doing a day's work. What Scales had just said to me would have brought a near violent reaction back when I was maybe a year or two out of law school. But I'd heard the same insult too many times by now to do anything but roll with it.

"What can I say, Sam? We've already had this conversation."

He nodded and didn't say anything. I took it to mean he would take the DA's offer. Four years in the state penal system and a ten-thousand-dollar fine, followed by five years' parole. He'd be out in two and a half but the parole would be a killer for a natural-born con man to make it through unscathed. After a few minutes I got up and left the room. I knocked on the outer door and Deputy Frey let me back into the courtroom.

"He's good to go," I said.

I took my seat at the defense table and soon Frey brought Scales out and sat him next to me. He still had the cuffs on. He said nothing to me. In another few minutes Glenn Bernasconi, the prosecutor who worked 124, came down from his office on the fifteenth floor and I told him we were ready to accept the case disposition.

At 11 A.M. Judge Judith Champagne came out of chambers and onto the bench and Frey called the courtroom to order. The judge was a diminutive, attractive blonde and ex-prosecutor who had been on the bench at least as long as I'd had my ticket. She was old school all the way, fair but tough, running her courtroom as a fiefdom. Sometimes she even brought her dog, a German shepherd named Justice, to work with her. If the judge had had any kind of discretion in the sentence when Sam Scales faced her, he would have gone down hard. That was what I did for Sam Scales, whether he knew it or not. With this deal I had saved him from that.

"Good morning," the judge said. "I am glad you could make it today, Mr. Haller."

"I apologize, Your Honor. I got held up in Judge Flynn's court in Compton."

That was all I had to say. The judge knew about Flynn. Everybody did.

"And on St. Patrick's Day, no less," she said.

"Yes, Your Honor."

"I understand we have a disposition in the Tsunami Svengali matter."

She immediately looked over at her court reporter.

"Michelle, strike that."

She looked back at the lawyers.

"I understand we have a disposition in the Scales case. Is that correct?"

"That is correct," I said. "We're ready to go on that."

"Good."

Bernasconi half read, half repeated from memory the legalese needed to take a plea from the defendant. Scales waived his rights and pleaded guilty to the charges. He said nothing other than the word. The judge accepted the disposition agreement and sentenced him accordingly.

"You're a lucky man, Mr. Scales," she said when it was over. "I believe Mr. Bernasconi was quite generous with you. I would not have been."

"I don't feel so lucky, Judge," Scales said.

Deputy Frey tapped him on the shoulder from behind. Scales stood up and turned to me.

"I guess this is it," he said.

"Good luck, Sam," I said.

He was led off through the steel door and I watched it close behind them. I had not shaken his hand.

13

≈≈≈

The Van Nuys Civic Center is a long concrete plaza enclosed by government buildings. Anchoring one end is the Van Nuys Division of the LAPD. Along one side are two courthouses sitting opposite a public library and a city administration building. At the end of the concrete and glass channel is a federal administration building and post office. I waited for Louis Roulet in the plaza on one of the concrete benches near the library. The plaza was largely deserted despite the great weather. Not like the day before, when the place was overrun with cameras and the media and the gadflies, all crowding around Robert Blake and his lawyers as they tried to spin a not-guilty verdict into innocence.

It was a nice, quiet afternoon and I usually liked being outside. Most of my work is done in windowless courtrooms or the backseat of my Town Car, so I take it outside whenever I can. But I wasn't feeling the breeze or noticing the fresh air this time. I was annoyed because Louis Roulet was late and because what Sam Scales had said to me about being a street-legal con was festering like cancer in my mind. When finally I saw Roulet crossing the plaza toward me I got up to meet him.

"Where've you been?" I said abruptly.

"I told you I'd get here as soon as I could. I was in the middle of a showing when you called."

"Let's walk."

I headed toward the federal building because it would give us the longest stretch before we would have to turn around to cross back. I had my meeting with Minton, the new prosecutor assigned to his case, in twenty-five minutes in the older of the two courthouses. I realized that we didn't look like a lawyer and his client discussing a case. Maybe a lawyer and his realtor discussing a land grab. I was in my Hugo Boss and Roulet was in a tan suit over a green turtleneck. He had on loafers with small silver buckles.

"There won't be any showings up in Pelican Bay," I said to him.

"What's that supposed to mean? Where's that?"

"It's a pretty name for a super max prison where they send violent sex offenders. You're going to fit in there pretty good in your turtleneck and loafers."

"Look, what's the matter? What's this about?"

"It's about a lawyer who can't have a client who lies to him. In twenty minutes I'm about to go up to see the guy who wants to send you to Pelican

Bay. I need everything I can get my hands on to try to keep you out of there and it doesn't help when I find out you're lying to me."

Roulet stopped and turned to me. He raised his hands out, palms open.

"I haven't lied to you! I did not do this thing. I don't know what that woman wants but I —"

"Let me ask you something, Louis. You and Dobbs said you took a year of law at UCLA, right? Did they teach you anything at all about the lawyer-client bond of trust?"

"I don't know. I don't remember. I wasn't there long enough."

I took a step toward him, invading his space.

"You see? You are a fucking liar. You didn't go to UCLA law school for a year. You didn't even go for a goddamn day."

He brought his hands down and slapped them against his sides.

"Is that what this is all about, Mickey?"

"Yeah, that's right and from now on, don't call me Mickey. My friends call me that. Not my lying clients."

"What does whether or not I went to law school ten years ago have to do with this case? I don't —"

"Because if you lied to me about that, then you'd lie to me about anything, and I can't have that and be able to defend you."

I said it too loud. I saw a couple of women on a nearby bench watching us. They had juror badges on their blouses.

"Come on. This way."

I started walking back the other way, heading toward the police station.

"Look," Roulet said in a weak voice. "I lied because of my mother, okay?"

"No, not okay. Explain it to me."

"Look, my mother and Cecil think I went to law school for a year. I want them to continue to believe that. He brought it up with you and so I just sort of agreed. But it was ten years ago! What is the harm?"

"The harm is in lying to me," I said. "You can lie to your mother, to Dobbs, to your priest and to the police. But when I ask you something directly, do not lie to me. I need to operate from the standpoint of having facts from you. Incontrovertible facts. So when I ask you a question, tell me the truth. All the rest of the time you can say what you want and whatever makes you feel good."

"Okay, okay."

"If you weren't in law school, where were you?"

Roulet shook his head.

"Nowhere. I just didn't do anything for a year. Most of the time I stayed in my apartment near campus and read and thought about what I really wanted to do with my life. The only thing I knew for sure was that I didn't want to be a lawyer. No offense intended."

"None taken. So you sat there for a year and came up with selling real estate to rich people."

"No, that came later."

He laughed in a self-deprecating way.

"I actually decided to become a writer—I had majored in English lit—and I tried to write a novel. It didn't take me long to figure out that I couldn't do it. I eventually went to work for Mother. She wanted me to."

I calmed down. Most of my anger had been a show, anyway. I was trying to soften him up for the more important questioning. I thought he was now ready for it.

"Well, now that you are coming clean and confessing everything, Louis, tell me about Reggie Campo."

"What about her?"

"You were going to pay her for sex, weren't you?"

"What makes you say—"

I shut him up when I stopped again and grabbed him by one of his expensive lapels. He was taller than me and bigger, but I had the power in this conversation. I was pushing him.

"Answer the fucking question."

"All right, yes, I was going to pay. But how did you know that?"

"Because I'm a good goddamn lawyer. Why didn't you tell me this on that first day? Don't you see how that changes the case?"

"My mother. I didn't want my mother to know I...you know."

"Louis, let's sit down."

I walked him over to one of the long benches by the police station. There was a lot of space and no one could overhear us. I sat in the middle of the bench and he sat to my right.

"Your mother wasn't even in the room when we were talking about the case. I don't even think she was in there when we talked about law school."

"But Cecil was and he tells her everything."

I nodded and made a mental note to cut Cecil Dobbs completely out of the loop on case matters from now on.

"Okay, I think I understand. But how long were you going to let it go without telling me? Don't you see how this changes everything?"

"I'm not a lawyer."

"Louis, let me tell you a little bit about how this works. You know what I am? I'm a neutralizer. My job is to neutralize the state's case. Take each piece of evidence or proof and find a way to eliminate it from contention. Think of it like one of those street entertainers you see on the Venice boardwalk. You ever gone down there and seen the guy spinning all those plates on those little sticks?"

"I think so. I haven't been down there in a long time."

"Doesn't matter. The guy has these thin little sticks and he puts a plate on each one and starts spinning the plate so it will stay balanced and upright. He gets a lot of them going at once and he moves from plate to plate and stick to stick making sure everything is spinning and balanced and staying up. You with me?"

"Yes. I understand."

"Well, that's the state's case, Louis. A bunch of spinning plates. And every one of those plates is an individual piece of evidence against you. My job is to take each plate, stop it from spinning and knock it to the ground so hard that it shatters and can't be used anymore. If the blue plate contains the victim's blood on your hands, then I need to find a way to knock it down. If the yellow plate has a knife with your bloody fingerprints on it, then once again I need to knock that sucker down. Neutralize it. You follow?"

"Yes, I follow. I—"

"Now, in the middle of this field of plates is a big one. It's a fucking platter, Louis, and if that baby falls over it's going to take everything down with it. Every plate. The whole case goes down. Do you know what that platter is, Louis?"

He shook his head no.

"That big platter is the victim, the chief witness against you. If we can knock that platter over, then the whole act is over and the crowd moves on."

I waited a moment to see if he would react. He said nothing.

"Louis, for almost two weeks you have concealed from me the method by which I could knock the big platter down. It asks the question why. Why would a guy with money at his disposal, a Rolex watch on his wrist, a Porsche out in the parking lot and a Holmby Hills address need to use a knife to get sex from a woman who sells it anyway? When you boil it all down to that question, the case starts to collapse, Louis, because the answer is simple. He wouldn't. Common sense says he wouldn't. And when you come to that conclusion, all the plates stop spinning. You see the setup, you see the trap, and now it's the defendant who starts to look like the victim."

I looked at him. He nodded.

"I'm sorry," he said.

"You should be," I said. "The case would have started coming apart almost two weeks ago and we probably wouldn't be sitting here right now if you had been up-front with me from the start."

In that moment I realized where my anger was truly coming from and it wasn't because Roulet had been late or had lied or because of Sam Scales calling me a street-legal con. It was because I saw the franchise slipping away. There would be no trial in this case, no six-figure fee. I'd be lucky just to keep the retainer I'd gotten at the start. The case was going to end today when I walked into the DA's office and told Ted Minton what I knew and what I had.

"I'm sorry," Roulet said again in a whiny voice. "I didn't mean to mess things up."

I was looking down at the ground between my feet now. Without looking at him I reached over and put my hand on his shoulder.

"I'm sorry I yelled at you before, Louis."

"What do we do now?"

"I have a few more questions to ask you about that night, and then I'm going to go up into that building over there and meet the prosecutor and knock down all his plates. I think that by the time I come out of there this may all be over and you'll be free to go back to showing your mansions to rich people."

"Just like that?"

"Well, formally he may want to go into court and ask a judge to dismiss the case."

Roulet opened his mouth in shock.

"Mr. Haller, I can't begin to tell you how—"

"You can call me Mickey. Sorry about that before."

"No problem. Thank you. What questions do you want to ask?"

I thought for a moment. I really didn't need anything else to go into the meeting with Minton. I was locked and loaded. I had walking proof.

"What did the note say?" I asked.

"What note?"

"The one she gave you at the bar in Morgan's."

"Oh, it said her address and then underneath she wrote 'four hundred dollars' and then under that she wrote 'Come after ten.'"

"Too bad we don't have that. But I think we have enough."

I nodded and looked at my watch. I still had fifteen minutes until the meeting but I was finished with Roulet.

"You can go now, Louis. I'll call you when it's all over."

"You sure? I could wait out here if you want."

"I don't know how long it will take. I'm going to have to lay it all out for him. He'll probably have to take it to his boss. It could be a while."

"All right, well, I guess I'll go then. But you'll call me, right?"

"Yes, I will. We'll probably go in to see the judge Monday or Tuesday, then it will all be over."

He put his hand out and I shook it.

"Thanks, Mick. You're the best. I knew I had the best lawyer when I got you."

I watched him walk back across the plaza and go between the two courthouses toward the public parking garage.

"Yeah, I'm the best," I said to myself.

I felt the presence of someone and turned to see a man sit down on the bench next to me. He turned and looked at me and we recognized each other at the same time. It was Howard Kurlen, a homicide detective from the Van Nuys Division. We had bumped up against each other on a few cases over the years.

"Well, well, well," Kurlen said. "The pride of the California bar. You're not talking to yourself, are you?"

"Maybe."

"That could be bad for a lawyer if that got around."

"I'm not worried. How are you doing, Detective?"

Kurlen was unwrapping a sandwich he had taken out of a brown bag.

"Busy day. Late lunch."

He produced a peanut butter sandwich from the wrap. There was a layer of something else besides peanut butter in it but it wasn't jelly. I couldn't identify it. I looked at my watch. I still had a few minutes before I needed to get in line for the metal detectors at the courthouse entrance but I wasn't sure I wanted to spend them with Kurlen and his horrible-looking sandwich. I thought about bringing up the Blake verdict, sticking it to the LAPD a little bit, but Kurlen stuck one in me first.

"How's my man Jesus doin'?" the detective asked.

Kurlen had been lead detective on the Jesus Menendez case. He had wrapped him up so tightly that Menendez had no choice but to plead and hope for the best. He still got life.

"I don't know," I answered. "I don't talk to Jesus anymore."

"Yeah, I guess once they plead out and go upstate they're not much use to you. No appeal work, no nothing."

I nodded. Every cop had a jaundiced eye when it came to defense lawyers. It was as if they believed their own actions and investigations were beyond questioning or reproach. They didn't believe in a justice system based on checks and balances.

"Just like you, I guess," I said. "On to the next one. I hope your busy day means you're working on getting me a new client."

"I don't look at it that way. But I was wondering, do you sleep well at night?"

"You know what I was wondering? What the hell is in that sandwich?"

He held what was left of the sandwich up on display.

"Peanut butter and sardines. Lots of good protein to get me through another day of chasing scumbags. Talking to them, too. You didn't answer my question."

"I sleep fine, Detective. You know why? Because I play an important part in the system. A needed part—just like your part. When somebody is accused of a crime, they have the opportunity to test the system. If they want to do that, they come to me. That's all any of this is about. When you understand that, you have no trouble sleeping."

"Good story. When you close your eyes I hope you believe it."

"How about you, Detective? You ever put your head on the pillow and wonder whether you've put innocent people away?"

"Nope," he said quickly, his mouth full of sandwich. "Never happened, never will."

"Must be nice to be so sure."

"A guy told me once that when you get to the end of your road, you have to look at the community woodpile and decide if you added to it while you were here or whether you just took from it. Well, I add to the woodpile, Haller. I sleep good at night. But I wonder about you and your kind. You lawyers are all takers from the woodpile."

"Thanks for the sermon. I'll keep it in mind next time I'm chopping wood."

"You don't like that, then I've got a joke for you. What's the difference between a catfish and a defense attorney?"

"Hmmm, I don't know, Detective."

"One's a bottom-feeding scum sucker and one's a fish."

He laughed uproariously. I stood up. It was time to go.

"I hope you brush your teeth after you eat something like that," I said. "I'd hate to be your partner if you don't."

I walked away, thinking about what he had said about the woodpile and what Sam Scales had said about my being a street-legal con. I was getting it from all sides today.

"Thanks for the tip," Kurlen called after me.

14

Ted Minton had arranged for us to discuss the Roulet case in private by scheduling our conference at a time he knew the deputy district attorney he shared space with had a hearing in court. Minton met me in the waiting area and walked me back. He did not look to me to be older than thirty but he had a self-assured presence. I probably had ten years and a hundred trials on him, yet he showed no sign of deference or respect. He acted as though the meeting was a nuisance he had to put up with. That was fine. That was the usual. And it put more fuel in my tank.

When we got to his small, windowless office, he offered me his office partner's seat and closed the door. We sat down and looked at each other. I let him go first.

"Okay," he said. "First off, I wanted to meet you. I'm sort of new up here in the Valley and haven't met a lot of the members of the defense bar. I know you're one of those guys that covers the whole county but we haven't run across each other before."

"Maybe that's because you haven't worked many felony trials before."

He smiled and nodded like I had scored a point of some kind.

"That might be true," he said. "Anyway, I gotta tell you, when I was in law school at SC I read a book about your father and his cases. I think it was called *Haller for the Defense*. Something like that. Interesting guy and interesting times."

I nodded back.

"He was gone before I really knew him, but there were a few books about him and I read them all more than a few times. It's probably why I ended up doing this."

"That must have been hard, getting to know your father through books."

I shrugged. I didn't think that Minton and I needed to know each other that well, particularly in light of what I was about to do to him.

"I guess it happens," he said.

"Yeah."

He clapped his hands together once, a let's-get-down-to-business gesture.

"Okay, so we're here to talk about Louis Roulet, aren't we?"

"It's pronounced Roo-*lay*."

"Roooo-*lay*. Got it. So, let's see, I have some things for you here."

He swiveled his seat to turn back to his desk. He picked up a thin file and turned back to hand it to me.

"I want to play fair. That's the up-to-the-minute discovery for you. I know I don't have to give it to you until after the arraignment but, hell, let's be cordial."

My experience is that when prosecutors tell you they are playing fair or better than fair, then you better watch your back. I fanned through the discovery file but didn't really read anything. The file Levin had gathered for me was at least four times as thick. I wasn't thrilled because Minton had so little. I was suspicious that he was holding back on me. Most prosecutors made you work for the discovery by having to demand it repeatedly, to the point of going to court to complain to the judge about it. But Minton had just casually handed at least some of it over. Either he had more to learn than I imagined about felony prosecutions or there was some sort of play here.

"This is everything?" I asked.

"Everything I've gotten."

That was always the way. If the prosecutor didn't have it, then he could stall its release to the defense. I knew for a fact — as in having been married to a prosecutor — that it was not out of the ordinary for a prosecutor to tell the police investigators on a case to take their time getting all the paperwork in. They could then turn around and tell the defense lawyer they wanted to play fair and hand over practically nothing. The rules of discovery were often referred to by defense pros as the rules of dishonesty. This of course went both ways. Discovery was supposed to be a two-way street.

"And you're going to trial with this?"

I waved the file as if to say its thin contents were as thin as the case.

"I'm not worried about it. But if you want to talk about a disposition, I'll listen."

"No, no disposition on this. We're going balls out. We're going to waive the prelim and go right to trial. No delays."

"He won't waive speedy?"

"Nope. You've got sixty days from Monday to put up or shut up."

Minton pursed his lips as though what I had just told him were only a minor inconvenience and surprise. It was a good cover-up. I knew I had landed a solid punch.

"Well, then, I guess we ought to talk about unilateral discovery. What do you have for me?"

He had dropped the pleasant tone.

"I'm still putting it together," I said. "But I'll have it at the arraignment Monday. But most of what I've got is probably already in this file you gave me, don't you think?"

"Most likely."

"You have that the supposed victim is a prostitute who had solicited my client in here, right? And that she has continued that line of work since the alleged incident, right?"

Minton's mouth opened maybe a half inch and then closed, but it was a good tell. I had hit him with another solid shot. But then he recovered quickly.

"As a matter of fact," he said, "I am aware of her occupation. But what surprises me is that you know this already. I hope you aren't sniffing around my victim, Mr. Haller?"

"Call me Mickey. And what I am doing is the least of your problems. You better take a good look at this case, Ted. I know you're new to felony trials and you don't want to come out of the box with a loser like this. Especially after the Blake fiasco. But this one's a dog and it's going to bite you on the ass."

"Really? How so?"

I looked past his shoulder at the computer on his desk.

"Does that thing play DVDs?"

Minton looked back at the computer. It looked ancient.

"It should. What have you got?"

I realized that showing him the surveillance video from the bar at Morgan's would be giving an early reveal of the biggest ace that I held, but I was confident that once he saw it, there would be no arraignment Monday and no case. My job was to neutralize the case and get my client out from under the government's weight. This was the way to do it.

"I don't have all my discovery together but I do have this," I said.

I handed Minton the DVD I had gotten earlier from Levin. The prosecutor put it into his computer.

"This is from the bar at Morgan's," I told him as he tried to get it playing.

"Your guys never went there but my guy did. This is the Sunday night of the supposed attack."

"And this could have been doctored."

"It could have been but it wasn't. You can have it checked. My investigator has the original and I will tell him to make it available after the arraignment."

After a short struggle Minton got the DVD to play. He watched silently as I pointed out the time code and all the same details Levin had pointed out to me, including Mr. X and his left-handedness. Minton fast-forwarded as I instructed and then slowed it to watch the moment when Reggie Campo approached my client at the bar. He had a frown of concentration on his face. When it was over he ejected the disc and held it up.

"Can I keep this until I get the original?"

"Be my guest."

Minton put the disc back in its case and placed it on top of a stack of files on his desk.

"Okay, what else?" he asked.

Now my mouth let some light in.

"What do you mean, what else? Isn't that enough?"

"Enough for what?"

"Look, Ted, why don't we cut the bullshit?"

"Please do."

"What are we talking about here? That disc blows this case out of the water. Let's forget about arraignment and trial and talk about going into court next week with a joint motion to dismiss. I want this shit-canned with prejudice, Ted. No coming back at my guy if somebody in here decides to change their mind."

Minton smiled and shook his head.

"Can't do that, Mickey. This woman was injured quite badly. She was victimized by an animal and I'm not going to dismiss anything against—"

"Quite badly? She's been turning tricks again all week. You—"

"How do you know that?"

I shook my head.

"Man, I am trying to help you here, save you some embarrassment, and all you're worried about is whether I've crossed some line with the victim. Well, I've got news for you. She ain't the victim. Don't you see what you have here? If this thing gets to a jury and they see that disc, all the plates fall, Ted. Your case is over and you have to come back in here and explain to your boss Smithson why you didn't see it coming. I don't know Smithson all that well, but I do know one thing about him. He doesn't like to lose. And after what happened yesterday, I would say that he feels a little more urgent about that."

"Prostitutes can be victims, too. Even amateurs."

I shook my head. I decided to show my whole hand.

"She set him up," I said. "She knew he had money and she laid a trap. She wants to sue him and cash in. She either hit herself or she had her boyfriend from the bar, the left-handed man, do it. No jury in the world is going to buy what you're selling. Blood on the hand or fingerprints on the knife — it was all staged after he was knocked out."

Minton nodded as if he followed the logic but then came out with something from left field.

"I'm concerned that you may be trying to intimidate my victim by following her and harassing her."

"What?"

"You know the rules of engagement. Leave the victim alone or we'll next talk about it with a judge."

I shook my head and spread my hands wide.

"Are you listening to anything I'm saying here?"

"Yes, I have listened to it all and it doesn't change the course I am taking. I do have an offer for you, though, and it will be good only until Monday's arraignment. After that, all bets are off. Your client takes his chances with a judge and jury. And I'm not intimidated by you or the sixty days. I will be ready and waiting."

I felt like I was underwater and everything that I said was trapped in bubbles that were drifting up and away. No one could hear me correctly. Then I realized that there was something I was missing. Something important. It didn't matter how green Minton was, he wasn't stupid and I had just mistakenly thought he was acting stupid. The L.A. County DA's office got some of the best of the best out of law school. He had already mentioned Southern Cal and I knew that was a law school that turned out top-notch lawyers. It was only a matter of experience. Minton might be short on experience but it didn't mean he was short on legal intelligence. I realized that I should be looking at myself, not Minton, for understanding.

"What am I missing here?" I asked.

"I don't know," Minton said. "You're the one with the high-powered defense. What could you be missing?"

I stared at him for a moment and then knew. There was a glitch in the discovery. There was something in his thin file that was not in the thick one Levin had put together. Something that would get the prosecution past the fact that Reggie Campo was selling it. Minton had so much as told me already. *Prostitutes can be victims, too.*

I wanted to stop everything and look through the state's discovery file to compare it with everything about the case that I knew. But I could not do it now in front of him.

"Okay," I said. "What's your offer? He won't take it but I'll present it."

"Well, he's got to do prison time. That's a given. We're willing to drop it all down to an ADW and attempted sexual battery. We'll go to the middle of the guidelines, which would put him at about seven years."

I nodded. Assault with a deadly weapon and attempted sexual battery. A seven-year sentence would likely mean four years actual. It wasn't a bad offer but only from the standpoint of Roulet having committed the crime. If he was innocent, then no offer was acceptable.

I shrugged.

"I'll take it to him," I said.

"Remember, only until the arraignment. So if he wants it you better call me Monday morning first thing."

"Right."

I closed my briefcase and stood up to go. I was thinking about how Roulet was probably waiting for a phone call from me, telling him the nightmare was over. Instead, I would be calling about a seven-year deal.

Minton and I shook hands and I said I would call him, then I headed out. In the hallway leading to the reception area I ran into Maggie McPherson.

"Hayley had a great time Saturday," she said about our daughter. "She's still talking about it. She said you were going to see her this weekend, too."

"Yeah, if that's okay."

"Are you all right? You look like you're in a daze."

"It's turning into a long week. I'm glad I have an empty calendar tomorrow. Which works better for Hayley, Saturday or Sunday?"

"Either's fine. Were you just meeting Ted on the Roulet thing?"

"Yeah. I got his offer."

I raised my briefcase to show I was taking the prosecution's plea offer with me.

"Now I have to go try to sell it," I added. "That's going to be tough. Guy says he didn't do it."

"I thought they all said that."

"Not like this guy."

"Well, good luck."

"Thanks."

We headed opposite ways in the hallway and then I remembered something and called back to her.

"Hey, Happy St. Patrick's."

"Oh."

She turned and came back toward me.

"Stacey's staying a couple hours late with Hayley and a bunch of us are going over to Four Green Fields after work. You feel like a pint of green beer?"

Four Green Fields was an Irish pub not far from the civic center. It was frequented by lawyers from both sides of the bar. Animosities grew slack under the taste of room-temperature Guinness.

"I don't know," I said. "I think I have to head over the hill to see my client but you never know, I might come back."

"Well, I only have till eight and then I have to go relieve Stacey."

"Okay."

We parted again and I left the courthouse. The bench where I had sat with Roulet and then Kurlen was empty. I sat down, opened my case and pulled out the discovery file Minton had given me. I flipped through reports I already had gotten copies of through Levin. There seemed to be nothing new until I came to a comparative fingerprint analysis report that confirmed what we had thought all along; the bloody fingerprints on the knife belonged to my client, Louis Roulet.

It still wasn't enough to justify Minton's demeanor. I kept looking and then I found it in the weapon analysis report. The report I had gotten from Levin was completely different, as if from another case and another weapon. As I quickly read it I felt perspiration popping in my hair. I had been set up. I had been embarrassed in the meeting with Minton and worse yet had tipped him early to my hole card. He had the video from Morgan's and had all the time he would need to prepare for it in court.

Finally, I slapped the folder closed and pulled out my cell phone. Levin answered after two rings.

"How'd it go?" he asked. "Bonuses for everybody?"

"Not quite. Do you know where Roulet's office is?"

"Yeah, on Canon in Beverly Hills. I've got the exact address in the file."

"Meet me there."

"Now?"

"I'll be there in thirty minutes."

I punched the button, ending the call without further discussion, and then called Earl on speed dial. He must have had his iPod plugs in his ears because he didn't answer until the seventh ring.

"Come get me," I said. "We're going over the hill."

I closed the phone and got off the bench. Walking toward the opening between the two courthouses and the place where Earl would pick me up, I felt angry. At Roulet, at Levin, and most of all at myself. But I also was aware of the positive side of this. The one thing that was certain now was that the franchise — and the big payday that came with it — was back in play. The case was going to go the distance to trial unless Roulet took the state's offer. And I thought the chances of that were about the same as the chances for snow in L.A. It could happen but I wouldn't believe it until I saw it.

15

When the rich in Beverly Hills want to drop small fortunes on clothes and jewelry, they go to Rodeo Drive. When they want to drop larger fortunes on houses and condominiums, they walk a few blocks over to Canon Drive, where the high-line real estate companies roost, photographs of their multimillion-dollar offerings presented in showroom windows on ornate gold easels like Picassos and Van Goghs. This is where I found Windsor Residential Estates and Louis Roulet on Thursday afternoon.

By the time I got there, Raul Levin was already waiting — and I mean waiting. He had been kept in the showroom with a fresh bottle of water while Louis worked the phone in his private office. The receptionist, an overly tanned blonde with a haircut that hung down one side of her face like a scythe, told me it would be just a few minutes more and then we both could go in. I nodded and stepped away from her desk.

"You want to tell me what's going on?" Levin asked.

"Yeah, when we get in there with him."

The showroom was lined on both sides with steel wires that ran from ceiling to floor and on which were attached 8 × 10 frames containing the photos and pedigrees of the estates offered for sale. Acting like I was studying the rows of houses I couldn't hope to afford in a hundred years, I moved toward the back hallway that led to the offices. When I got there I noticed an open door and heard Louis Roulet's voice. It sounded like he was setting up a showing of a Mulholland Drive mansion for a client he told the realtor on the other end of the phone wanted his name kept confidential. I looked back at Levin, who was still near the front of the showroom.

"This is bullshit," I said and signaled him back.

I walked down the hallway and into Roulet's plush office. There was the requisite desk stacked with paperwork and thick multiple-listing catalogs. But Roulet wasn't there. He was in a sitting area to the right of the desk, slouched on a sofa with a cigarette in one hand and the phone in the other. He looked shocked to see me and I thought maybe the receptionist hadn't even told him he had visitors.

Levin came into the office behind me, followed by the receptionist, the hair scythe swinging back and forth as she hurried to catch up. I was worried that the blade might cut off her nose.

"Mr. Roulet, I'm sorry, these men just came back here."

"Lisa, I have to go," Roulet said into the phone. "I'll call you back."

He put the phone down in its cradle on the glass coffee table.

"It's okay, Robin," he said. "You can go now."

He made a dismissive gesture with the back of his hand. Robin looked at me like I was wheat she wanted to cut down with that blond blade and then left the room. I closed the door and looked back at Roulet.

"What happened?" he said. "Is it over?"

"Not by a long shot," I said.

I was carrying the state's discovery file. The weapon report was front and center. I stepped over and dropped it onto the coffee table.

"I only succeeded in embarrassing myself in the DA's office. The case against you still stands and we'll probably be going to trial."

Roulet's face dropped.

"I don't understand," he said. "You said you were going to tear that guy a new asshole."

"Turns out the only asshole in there was me. Because once again you didn't level with me."

Then, turning to look at Levin, I said, "And because you got us set up."

Roulet opened the file. On the top page was a color photograph of a knife with blood on its black handle and the tip of its blade. It was not the same knife that was photocopied in the records Levin got from his police sources and that he had showed us in the meeting in Dobbs's office the first day of the case.

"What the hell is that?" said Levin, looking down at the photo.

"That is a knife. The real one, the one Roulet had with him when he went to Reggie Campo's apartment. The one with her blood and his *initials* on it."

Levin sat down on the couch on the opposite side from Roulet. I stayed standing and they both looked up at me. I started with Levin.

"I went in to see the DA to kick his ass today and he ended up kicking mine with that. Who was your source, Raul? Because he gave you a marked deck."

"Wait a minute, wait a minute. That's not—"

"No, you wait a minute. The report you had on the knife being untraceable was bogus. It was put in there to fuck us up. To trick us and it worked perfectly, because I waltzed in there thinking I couldn't lose today and just gave him the Morgan's bar video. Just trotted it out like it was the hammer. Only it wasn't, goddamn it."

"It was the runner," Levin said.

"What?"

"The runner. The guy who runs the reports between the police station and the DA's office. I tell him which cases I'm interested in and he makes extra copies for me."

"Well, they're onto his ass and they worked it perfectly. You better call him and tell him if he needs a good criminal defense attorney I'm not available."

I realized I was pacing in front of them on the couch but I didn't stop.

"And you," I said to Roulet. "I now get the real weapon report and find out not only is the knife a custom-made job but it is traceable right back to you because it has your fucking initials on it! You lied to me again!"

"I didn't lie," Roulet yelled back. "I tried to tell you. I said it wasn't my knife. I said it twice but nobody listened to me."

"Then you should have clarified what you meant. Just saying it wasn't your knife was like saying you didn't do it. You should have said, 'Hey, Mick, there might be a problem with the knife because I did have a knife but this picture isn't it.' What did you think, that it was just going to go away?"

"Please, can you keep it down," Roulet protested. "There might be customers out there."

"I don't care! Fuck your customers. You're not going to need customers anymore where you're going. Don't you see that this knife trumps everything we've got? You took a murder weapon to a meeting with a prostitute. The knife was no plant. It was yours. And that means we no longer have the setup. How can we claim she set you up when the prosecutor can prove you had that knife with you when you walked through the door?"

He didn't answer but I didn't give him a lot of time to.

"You fucking did this thing and they've got you," I said, pointing at him. "No wonder they didn't bother with any follow-up investigation at the bar. No follow-up needed when they've got *your* knife and *your* fingerprints in blood on it."

"I didn't do it! It's a setup. I'm TELLING YOU! It was—"

"Who's yelling now? Look, I don't care what you're telling me. I can't deal with a client who doesn't level, who doesn't see the percentage in telling his own attorney what is going on. So the DA has made an offer to you and I think you better take it."

Roulet sat up straight and grabbed the pack of cigarettes off the table. He took one out and lit it off the one he already had going.

"I'm not pleading guilty to something I didn't do," he said, his voice suddenly calm after a deep drag off the fresh smoke.

"Seven years. You'll be out in four. You have till court time Monday and then it disappears. Think about it, then tell me you want to take it."

"I won't take it. I didn't do this thing and if you won't take it to trial, then I will find somebody who will."

Levin was holding the discovery file. I reached down and rudely grabbed it out of his hands so I could read directly from the weapon report.

"You didn't do it?" I said to Roulet. "Okay, if you didn't do it, then would you mind telling me why you went to see this prostitute with a custom-made Black Ninja knife with a five-inch blade, complete with your initials engraved not once, but twice on both sides of the blade?"

Finished reading from the report, I threw it back to Levin. It went through his hands and slapped against his chest.

"Because I always carry it!"

The force of Roulet's response quieted the room. I paced back and forth once, staring at him.

"You always carry it," I said, not a question.

"That's right. I'm a realtor. I drive expensive cars. I wear expensive jewelry. And I often meet strangers alone in empty houses."

Again he gave me pause. As hyped up as I was, I still knew a glimmer when I saw one. Levin leaned forward and looked at Roulet and then at me. He saw it, too.

"What are you talking about?" I said. "You sell homes to rich people."

"How do you know they are rich when they call you up and say they want to see a place?"

I stretched my hands out in confusion.

"You must have some sort of system for checking them out, right?"

"Sure, we can run a credit report and we can ask for references. But it still comes down to what they give us and these kind of people don't like to wait. When they want to see a piece of property, they want to see it. There are a lot of realtors out there. If we don't act quickly, there will be some-body else who will."

I nodded. The glimmer was getting brighter. There might be something here I could work with.

"There have been murders, you know," Roulet said. "Over the years. Every realtor knows the danger exists when you go to some of these places alone. For a while there was somebody out there called the Real Estate Rapist. He attacked and robbed women in empty houses. My mother..."

He didn't finish. I waited. Nothing.

"What about your mother?"

Roulet hesitated before answering.

"She was showing a place in Bel-Air once. She was alone and she thought it was safe because it was Bel-Air. The man raped her. He left her tied up. When she didn't come back to the office, I went to the house. I found her."

Roulet's eyes were staring at the memory.

"How long ago was this?" I asked.

"About four years. She stopped selling after it happened. Just stayed in her office and never showed another property again. I did the selling. And that's when and why I got the knife. I've had it for four years and carry it everywhere but on planes. It was in my pocket when I went to that apart-ment. I didn't think anything about it."

I dropped into the chair across the table from the couch. My mind was working. I was seeing how it could work. It was still a defense that relied on

coincidence. Roulet was set up by Campo and the setup was aided coinciden-
tally when she found the knife on him after knocking him out. It could work.

"Did your mother file a police report?" Levin asked. "Was there an investigation?"

Roulet shook his head as he stubbed out his cigarette in the ashtray.

"No, she was too embarrassed. She was afraid it would get into the
paper."

"Who else knows about it?" I asked.

"Uh, me...and Cecil I'm sure knows. Probably nobody else. You can't
use this. She would—"

"I won't use it without her permission," I said. "But it could be important. I'll have to talk to her about it."

"No, I don't want you—"

"Your life and livelihood are on the line here, Louis. You get sent to
prison and you're not going to make it. Don't worry about your mother. A
mother will do what she has to do to protect her young."

Roulet looked down and shook his head.

"I don't know...," he said.

I exhaled, trying to lose all my tension with the breath. Disaster may
have been averted.

"I know one thing," I said. "I'm going to go back to the DA and say pass
on the deal. We'll go to trial and take our chances."

16

The hits kept coming. The other shoe didn't drop on the prosecution's case
until after I'd dropped Earl off at the commuter lot where he parked his
own car every morning and I drove the Lincoln back to Van Nuys and Four
Green Fields. It was a shotgun pub on Victory Boulevard—maybe that was
why lawyers liked the place—with the bar running down the left side and
a row of scarred wooden booths down the right. It was crowded as only an
Irish bar can be the night of St. Patrick's Day. My guess was that the crowd
was swollen even bigger than in previous years because of the fact that the
drinker's holiday fell on a Thursday and many revelers were kicking off a
long weekend. I had made sure my own calendar was clear on Friday. I
always clear the day after St. Pat's.

As I started to fight my way through the mass in search of Maggie
McPherson, the required "Danny Boy" started blaring from a jukebox
somewhere in the back. But it was a punk rock version from the early eight-

ies and its driving beat obliterated any chance I had of hearing anything when I saw familiar faces and said hello or asked if they had seen my ex-wife. The small snippets of conversation I overheard as I pushed through seemed to all be about Robert Blake and the stunning verdict handed down the day before.

I ran into Robert Gillen in the crowd. The cameraman reached into his pocket and pulled out four crisp hundred-dollar bills and handed them to me. The bills were probably four of the original ten I had paid him two weeks earlier in the Van Nuys courthouse as I tried to impress Cecil Dobbs with my media manipulation skills. I had already expensed the thousand to Roulet. The four hundred was profit.

"I thought I'd run into you here," he yelled in my ear.

"Thanks, Sticks," I replied. "It'll go toward my bar tab."

He laughed. I looked past him into the crowd for my ex-wife.

"Anytime, my man," he said.

He slapped me on the shoulder as I squeezed by him and pushed on. I finally found Maggie in the last booth in the back. It was full of six women, all prosecutors or secretaries from the Van Nuys office. Most I knew at least in passing but the scene was awkward because I had to stand and yell over the music and the crowd. Plus the fact that they were prosecutors and viewed me as being in league with the devil. They had two pitchers of Guinness on the table and one was full. But my chances of getting through the crowd to the bar to get a glass were negligible. Maggie noticed my plight and offered to share her glass with me.

"It's all right," she yelled. "We've swapped spit before."

I smiled and knew the two pitchers on the table had not been the first two. I took a long drink and it tasted good. Guinness always gave me a solid center.

Maggie was in the middle on the left side of the booth and between two young prosecutors whom I knew she had taken under her wing. In the Van Nuys office, many of the younger females gravitated toward my ex-wife because the man in charge, Smithson, surrounded himself with attorneys like Minton.

Still standing at the side of the booth, I raised the glass in toast to her but she couldn't respond because I had her glass. She reached over and raised the pitcher.

"Cheers!"

She didn't go so far as to drink from the pitcher. She put it down and whispered to the woman on the outside of the booth. She got up to let Maggie out. My ex-wife stood up and kissed me on the cheek and said, "It's always easier for a lady to get a glass in these sorts of situations."

"Especially beautiful ladies," I said.

She gave me one of her looks and turned toward the crowd that was five deep between us and the bar. She whistled shrilly and it caught the attention of one of the pure-bred Irish guys who worked the tap handles and could etch a harp or an angel or a naked lady in the foam at the top of the glass.

"I need a pint glass," she yelled.

The bartender had to read her lips. And like a teenager being passed over the heads of the crowd at a Pearl Jam concert, a clean glass made its way back to us hand to hand. She filled it from the freshest pitcher on the booth's table and then we clicked glasses.

"So," she said. "Are you feeling a little better than when I saw you today?"

I nodded.

"A little."

"Did Minton sandbag you?"

I nodded again.

"Him *and* the cops did, yeah."

"With that guy Corliss? I told them he was full of shit. They all are."

I didn't respond and tried to act like what she had just said was not news to me and that Corliss was a name I already knew. I took a long and slow drink from my glass.

"I guess I shouldn't have said that," she said. "But my opinion doesn't matter. If Minton is dumb enough to use him, then you'll take the guy's head off, I'm sure."

I guessed that she was talking about a witness. But I had seen nothing in my review of the discovery file that mentioned a witness named Corliss. The fact that it was a witness she didn't trust led me further to believe that Corliss was a snitch. Most likely a jailhouse snitch.

"How come you know about him?" I finally asked. "Minton talked to you about him?"

"No, I'm the one who sent him to Minton. Doesn't matter what I think of what he said, it was my duty to send him to the right prosecutor and it was up to Minton to evaluate him."

"I mean, why did he come to you?"

She frowned at me because the answer was so obvious.

"Because I handled the first appearance. He was there in the pen. He thought the case was still mine."

Now I understood. Corliss was a C. Roulet was taken out of alphabetical order and called first. Corliss must have been in the group of inmates taken into the courtroom with him. He had seen Maggie and me argue over Roulet's bail. He therefore thought Maggie still had the case. He must have made a snitch call to her.

"When did he call you?" I asked.

"I am telling you too much, Haller. I'm not—"

"Just tell me when he called you. That hearing was on a Monday, so was it later that day?"

The case did not make any notice in the newspapers or on TV. So I was

curious as to where Corliss would have gotten the information he was trying to trade to prosecutors. I had to assume it didn't come from Roulet. I
was pretty sure I had scared him silent. Without a media information
point, Corliss would have been left with the information gleaned in court
when the charges were read and Maggie and I argued bail.

It was enough, I realized. Maggie had been specific in detailing Regina
Campo's injuries as she was trying to impress the judge to hold Roulet
without bail. If Corliss had been in court, he'd have been privy to all the
details he would need to make up a jailhouse confession from my client.
Add that to his proximity to Roulet and a jailhouse snitch is born.

"Yes, he called me late Monday," Maggie finally answered.

"So why did you think he was full of shit? He's done it before, hasn't he?
The guy's a professional snitch, right?"

I was fishing and she knew it. She shook her head.

"I am sure you will find out all you need to know during discovery. Can
we just have a friendly pint of Guinness here? I have to leave in about an
hour."

I nodded but wanted to know more.

"Tell you what," I said. "You've probably had enough Guinness for one
St. Patrick's Day. How about we get out of here and get something to eat?"

"Why, so you can keep asking me about your case?"

"No, so we can talk about our daughter."

Her eyes narrowed.

"Is something wrong?" she asked.

"Not that I know of. But I want to talk to you about her."

"Where are you taking me to dinner?"

I mentioned an expensive Italian restaurant on Ventura in Sherman
Oaks and her eyes got warm. It had been a place we had gone to celebrate
anniversaries and getting pregnant. Our apartment, which she still had,
was a few blocks away on Dickens.

"Think we can eat there in an hour?" she asked.

"If we leave right now and order without looking."

"You're on. Let me just say some quick good-byes."

"I'll drive."

And it was a good thing I drove because she was unsteady on her feet. We
had to walk hip to hip to the Lincoln and then I helped her get in.

I took Van Nuys south to Ventura. After a few moments Maggie reached
beneath her legs and pulled out a CD case she had been uncomfortably sitting on. It was Earl's. One of the CDs he listened to on the car stereo when
I was in court. It saved juice on his iPod. The CD was by a dirty south per-
former named Ludacris.

"No wonder I was so uncomfortable," she said. "Is this what you're listening to while driving between courthouses?"

"Actually, no. That's Earl's. He's been doing the driving lately. Ludacris isn't really to my liking. I'm more of an old school guy. Tupac and Dre and people like that."

She laughed because she thought I was kidding. A few minutes later we drove down the narrow alley that led to the door of the restaurant. A valet took the car and we went in. The hostess recognized us and acted like it had only been a couple weeks since the last time we had been in. The truth was, we had probably both been in there recently, but each with other partners.

I asked for a bottle of Singe Shiraz and we ordered pasta dishes without looking at a menu. We skipped salads and appetizers and told the waiter not to delay bringing the food out. After he left I checked my watch and saw we still had forty-five minutes. Plenty of time.

The Guinness was catching up with Maggie. She smiled in a fractured sort of way that told me she was drunk. Beautifully drunk. She never got mean under a buzz. She always got sweeter. It was probably how we'd ended up having a child together.

"You should probably lay off the wine," I told her. "Or you'll have a headache tomorrow."

"Don't worry about me. I'll lay what I want and lay off what I want."

She smiled at me and I smiled back.

"So how you been, Haller? I mean really."

"Fine. You? And I mean really."

"Never better. Are you past Lorna now?"

"Yeah, we're even friends."

"And what are we?"

"I don't know. Sometimes adversaries, I guess."

She shook her head.

"We can't be adversaries if we can't stay on the same case together. Besides, I'm always looking out for you. Like with that dirtbag, Corliss."

"Thanks for trying, but he still did the damage."

"I just have no respect for a prosecutor who would use a jailhouse snitch. Doesn't matter that your client is an even bigger dirtbag."

"He wouldn't tell me exactly what Corliss said my guy said."

"What are you talking about?"

"He just said he had a snitch. He wouldn't reveal what he said."

"That's not fair."

"That's what I said. It's a discovery issue but we don't get a judge assigned until after the arraignment Monday. So there's nobody I can really complain to yet. Minton knows that. It's like you warned me. He doesn't play fair."

Her cheeks flushed. I had pushed the right buttons and she was angry. For Maggie, winning fair was the only way to win. That was why she was a good prosecutor.

We were sitting at the end of the banquette that ran along the back wall of the restaurant. We were on both sides of a corner. Maggie leaned toward me but went too far and we banged heads. She laughed but then tried again. She spoke in a low voice.

"He said that he asked your guy what he was in for and your guy said, 'For giving a bitch exactly what she deserved.' He said your client told him he punched her out as soon as she opened her door."

She leaned back and I could tell she had moved too quickly, bringing on a swoon of vertigo.

"You okay?"

"Yes, but can we change the subject? I don't want to talk about work anymore. There are too many assholes and it's too frustrating."

"Sure."

Just then the waiter brought our wine and our dinners at the same time. The wine was good and the food was like home comfort. We started out eating quietly. Then Maggie hit me with a pitch right out of the blue.

"You didn't know anything about Corliss, did you? Not till I opened my big mouth."

"I knew Minton was hiding something. I thought it was a jailhouse—"

"Bullshit. You got me drunk so you could find out what I knew."

"Uh, I think you were already drunk when I hooked up with you tonight."

She was poised with her fork up over her plate, a long string of linguine with pesto sauce hanging off it. She then pointed the fork at me.

"Good point. So what about our daughter?"

I wasn't expecting her to remember that. I shrugged.

"I think what you said last week is right. She needs her father more in her life."

"And?"

"And I want to play a bigger part. I like watching her. Like when I took her to that movie on Saturday. I was sort of sitting sideways so I could watch her watching the movie. Watch her eyes, you know?"

"Welcome to the club."

"So I don't know. I was thinking maybe we should set up a schedule, you know? Like make it a regular thing. She could even stay overnight some-times—I mean, if she wanted."

"Are you sure about all of that? This is new from you."

"It's new because I didn't know about it before. When she was smaller and I couldn't really communicate with her, I didn't really know what to do with her. I felt awkward. Now I don't. I like talking to her. Being with her. I learn more from her than she does from me, that's for sure."

I suddenly felt her hand on my leg under the table.

"This is great," she said. "I am so happy to hear you say that. But let's move slow. You haven't been around her much for four years and I am not going to let her build up her hopes only to have you pull a disappearing act."

"I understand. We can take it any way you want. I'm just telling you I am going to be there. I promise."

She smiled, wanting to believe. And I made the same promise I just made to her to myself.

"Well, great," she said. "I'm really glad you want to do this. Let's get a calendar and work out some dates and see how it goes."

She took her hand away and we continued eating in silence until we both had almost finished. Then Maggie surprised me once again.

"I don't think I can drive my car tonight," she said.

I nodded.

"I was thinking the same thing."

"You seem all right. You only had half a pint at —"

"No, I mean I was thinking the same thing about you. But don't worry, I'll drive you home."

"Thank you."

Then she reached across the table and put her hand on my wrist.

"And will you take me back to get my car in the morning?"

She smiled sweetly at me. I looked at her, trying to read this woman who had told me to hit the road four years before. The woman I had never been able to get by or get over, whose rejection sent me reeling into a relationship I knew from the beginning couldn't go the distance.

"Sure," I said. "I'll take you."

17

Friday, March 18

In the morning I awoke to find my eight-year-old daughter sleeping between me and my ex-wife. Light was leaking in from a cathedral window high up on the wall. When I had lived here that window had always bothered me because it let in too much light too early in the mornings. Looking up at the pattern it threw on the inclined ceiling, I reviewed what had happened the night before and remembered that I had ended up drinking all but one glass of the bottle of wine at the restaurant. I remembered taking Maggie home to the apartment and coming in to find our daughter had already fallen asleep for the night — in her own bed.

After the babysitter had been released, Maggie opened another bottle of wine. When we finished it she took me by the hand and led me to the bedroom we had shared for four years, but not in four years. What bothered me now was that my memory had absorbed all the wine and I could not remember whether it had been a triumphant return to the bedroom or a failure. I also could not remember what words had been spoken, what promises had possibly been made.

"This is not fair to her."

I turned my head on the pillow. Maggie was awake. She was looking at our sleeping daughter's angelic face.

"What isn't fair?"

"Her waking up and finding you here. She might get her hopes up or just get the wrong idea."

"How'd she get in here?"

"I carried her in. She had a nightmare."

"How often does she have nightmares?"

"Usually, when she sleeps alone. In her room."

"So she sleeps in here all the time?"

Something about my tone bothered her.

"Don't start. You have no idea what it's like to raise a child by yourself."

"I know. I'm not saying anything. So what do you want me to do, leave before she wakes up? I could get dressed and act like I just came by to get you and drive you back to your car."

"I don't know. Get dressed for now. Try not to wake her up."

I slipped out of the bed, grabbed my clothes and went down the hall to the guest bathroom. I was confused by how much Maggie's demeanor toward me had changed overnight. Alcohol, I decided. Or maybe something I did or said after we'd gotten back to the apartment. I quickly got dressed and went back up the hallway to the bedroom and peeked in.

Hayley was still asleep. With her arms spread across two pillows she looked like an angel with wings. Maggie was pulling a long-sleeve T-shirt over an old pair of sweats she'd had since back when we were married. I walked in and stepped over to her.

"I'm going to go and come back," I whispered.

"What?" she said with annoyance. "I thought we were going to get the car."

"But I thought you didn't want her to wake up and see me. So let me go and I'll have some coffee or something and be back in an hour. We can all go together and get your car and then I'll take Hayley to school. I'll even pick her up later if you want. My calendar's clear today."

"Just like that? You're going to start driving her to school?"

"She's my daughter. Don't you remember anything I told you last night?"

She shifted the line of her jaw and I knew from experience that this was when the heavy artillery came out. I was missing something. Maggie had shifted gears.

"Well, yes, but I thought you were just saying that," she said.

"What do you mean?"

"I just thought you were trying to get into my head on your case or just plain get me into bed. I don't know."

I laughed and shook my head. Any fantasies about us that I'd had the night before were vanishing quickly.

"I wasn't the one who led the other up the steps to the bedroom," I said.

"Oh, so it was really about the case. You wanted what I knew about your case."

I just stared at her for a long moment.

"I can't win with you, can I?"

"Not when you're underhanded, when you act like a criminal defense attorney."

She was always the better of the two of us when it came to verbal knife throwing. The truth was, I was thankful we had a built-in conflict of interest and I would never have to face her in trial. Over the years some people — mostly defense pros who suffered at her hands — had gone so far as to say that was the reason I had married her. To avoid her professionally.

"Tell you what," I said. "I'll be back in an hour. If you want a ride to the car that you were too drunk to drive last night, be ready and have her ready."

"It's okay. We'll take a cab."

"I will drive you."

"No, we'll take a cab. And keep your voice down."

I looked over at my daughter, still asleep despite her parents' verbal sparring.

"What about her? Do you want me to take her tomorrow or Sunday?"

"I don't know. Call me tomorrow."

"Fine. Good-bye."

I left her there in the bedroom. Outside the apartment building I walked a block and a half down Dickens before finding the Lincoln parked awkwardly against the curb. There was a ticket on the windshield citing me for parking next to a fire hydrant. I got in the car and threw it into the backseat. I'd deal with it the next time I was riding back there. I wouldn't be like Louis Roulet, letting my tickets go to warrant. There was a county full of cops out there who would love to book me on a warrant.

Fighting always made me hungry and I realized I was starved. I worked my way back to Ventura and headed toward Studio City. It was early, especially for the morning after St. Patrick's Day, and I got to the DuPar's by Laurel Canyon Boulevard before it was crowded. I got a booth in the back and ordered a short stack of pancakes and coffee. I tried to forget about Maggie McFierce by opening up my briefcase and pulling out a legal pad and the Roulet files.

Before diving into the files I made a call to Raul Levin, waking him up at his home in Glendale.

"I've got something for you to do," I said.

"Can't this wait till Monday? I just got home a couple hours ago. I was going to start the weekend today."

"No, it can't wait and you owe me one after yesterday. Besides, you're not even Irish. I need you to background somebody."

"All right, wait a minute."

I heard him put down the phone while he probably grabbed pen and paper to take notes.

"Okay, go ahead."

"There's a guy named Corliss who was arraigned right after Roulet back on the seventh. He was in the first group out and they were in the holding pen at the same time. He's now trying to snitch Roulet off and I want to know everything there is to know about the guy so I can put his dick in the dirt."

"Got a first name?"

"Nope."

"Do you know what he's in there for?"

"No, and I don't even know if he is still in there."

"Thanks for the help. What's he saying Roulet told him?"

"That he beat up some bitch who had it coming. Words to that effect."

"Okay, what else you got?"

"That's it other than I got a tip that he's a repeat snitch. Find out who he's crapped on in the past and there might be something there I can use. Go back as far as you can go with this guy. The DA's people usually don't. They're afraid of what they might find. They'd rather be ignorant."

"Okay, I'll get on it."

"Let me know when you know."

I closed the phone just as my pancakes arrived. I doused them liberally with maple syrup and started eating while looking through the file containing the state's discovery.

The weapon report remained the only surprise. Everything else in the file, except the color photos, I had already seen in Levin's file.

I moved on to that. As expected with a contract investigator, Levin had larded the file with everything found in the net he had cast. He even had copies of the parking tickets and speeding citations Roulet had accumulated and failed to pay in recent years. It annoyed me at first because there was so much to weed through to get to what was going to be germane to Roulet's defense.

I was nearly through it all when the waitress swung by my booth with a coffee pot, looking to refill my mug. She recoiled when she saw the battered face of Reggie Campo in one of the color photos I had put to the side of the files.

"Sorry about that," I said.

I covered the photo with one of the files and signaled her back. The waitress came back hesitantly and poured the coffee.

"It's work," I said in feeble explanation. "I didn't mean to do that to you."

"All I can say is I hope you get the bastard that did that to her."

I nodded. She thought I was a cop. Probably because I hadn't shaved in twenty-four hours.

"I'm working on it," I said.

She went away and I went back to the file. As I slid the photo of Reggie Campo out from underneath it I saw the undamaged side of her face first. The left side. Something struck me and I held the file in position so that I was only looking at the good half of her face. The wave of familiarity came over me again. But again I could not place its origin. I knew this woman looked like another woman I knew or was at least familiar with. But who?

I also knew it was going to bother me until I figured it out. I thought about it for a long time, sipping my coffee and drumming my fingers on the table, and then decided to try something. I took the face shot of Campo and folded it lengthwise down the middle so that one side of the crease showed the damaged right side of her face and the other showed the unblemished left side. I then slipped the folded photo into the inside pocket of my jacket and got up from the booth.

There was no one in the restroom. I quickly went to the sink and took out the folded photo. I leaned over the sink and held the crease of the photo against the mirror with the undamaged side of Reggie Campo's face on display. The mirror reflected the image, creating a full and undamaged face. I stared at it for a long time and then finally realized why the face was familiar.

"Martha Renteria," I said.

The door to the restroom suddenly burst open and two teenagers stormed in, their hands already tugging on their zippers. I quickly pulled the photo back from the mirror and shoved it inside my jacket. I turned and walked toward the door. I heard them burst into laughter as I left. I couldn't imagine what it was they thought I was doing.

Back at the booth I gathered my files and photos and put them all back into my briefcase. I left a more than adequate amount of cash on the table for tab and tip and left the restaurant in a hurry. I felt like I was having a strange food reaction. My face felt flushed and I was hot under the collar. I thought I could hear my heart pounding beneath my shirt.

Fifteen minutes later I was parked in front of my storage warehouse on Oxnard Avenue in North Hollywood. I have a fifteen-hundred-square-foot space behind a double-wide garage door. The place is owned by a man whose son I defended on a possession case, getting him out of jail and into pretrial intervention. In lieu of a fee, the father gave me the warehouse rent-free for a year. But his son the drug addict kept getting into trouble and I kept getting free years of warehouse rent.

I keep the boxes of files from dead cases in the warehouse as well as two other Lincoln Town Cars. Last year when I was flush I bought four Lincolns at once so I could get a fleet rate. The plan was to use each one until it hit sixty thousand on the odometer and then dump it on a limousine service to be used to ferry travelers to and from the airport. The plan was working out so far. I was on the second Lincoln and it would soon be time for the third.

Once I got one of the garage doors up I went to the archival area, where the file boxes were arranged by year on industrial shelving. I found the section of shelves for boxes from two years earlier and ran my finger down the list of client names written on the side of each box until I found the name Jesus Menendez.

I pulled the box off the shelf and squatted down and opened it on the floor. The Menendez case had been short-lived. He took a plea early, before the DA pulled it back off the table. So there were only four files and these mostly contained copies of the documents relating to the police investigation. I paged through the files looking for photographs and finally saw what I was looking for in the third file.

Martha Renteria was the woman Jesus Menendez had pleaded guilty to murdering. She was a twenty-four-year-old dancer who had a dark beauty and a smile of big white teeth. She had been found stabbed to death in her Panorama City apartment. She had been beaten before she was stabbed and her facial injuries were to the left side of her face, the opposite of Reggie Campo. I found the close-up shot of her face contained in the autopsy report. Once more I folded the photo lengthwise, one side of her face damaged, one side untouched.

On the floor I took the two folded photographs, one of Reggie and one of Martha, and fitted them together along the fold lines. Putting aside the fact that one woman was dead and one wasn't, the half faces damn near formed a perfect match. The two women looked so much alike they could have passed for sisters.

18

Jesus Menendez was serving a life sentence in San Quentin because he had wiped his penis on a bathroom towel. No matter how you looked at it, that is what it really came down to. That towel had been his biggest mistake.

Sitting spread-legged on the concrete floor of my warehouse, the contents of Menendez files fanned out around me, I was reacquainting myself with the facts of the case I had worked two years before. Menendez was convicted of killing Martha Renteria after following her home to Panorama City from a strip club in East Hollywood called The Cobra Room. He raped her and then stabbed her more than fifty times, causing so much blood to leave her body that it seeped through the bed and formed a puddle on the wood floor below it. In another day it seeped through cracks in the floor and formed a drip from the ceiling in the apartment below. That is when the police were called.

The case against Menendez was formidable but circumstantial. He had also hurt himself by admitting to police — before I was on the case — that he had been in her apartment on the night of the murder. But it was the DNA on the fluffy pink towel in the victim's bathroom that ultimately did him in. It couldn't be neutralized. It was a spinning plate that couldn't be knocked down. Defense pros call a piece of evidence like this the iceberg because it is the evidence that sinks the ship.

I had taken on the Menendez murder case as what I would call a "lost leader." Menendez had no money to pay for the kind of time and effort it would take to mount a thorough defense but the case had garnered substantial publicity and I was willing to trade my time and work for the free advertising. Menendez had come to me because just a few months before his arrest I had successfully defended his older brother Fernando in a heroin case. At least in my opinion I had been successful. I had gotten a possession and sales charge knocked down to a simple possession. He got probation instead of prison.

Those good efforts resulted in Fernando calling me on the night Jesus was arrested for the murder of Martha Renteria. Jesus had gone to the Van Nuys Division to voluntarily talk to detectives. A drawing of his face had been shown on every television channel in the city and was getting heavy rotation in particular on the Spanish channels. He had told his family that he would go to the detectives to straighten things out and be back. But he never came back, so his brother called me. I told the brother that the lesson to be learned was never to go to the detectives to straighten things out until after you've consulted an attorney.

I had already seen numerous television news reports on the murder of the exotic dancer, as Renteria had been labeled, when Menendez's brother called me. The reports had included the police artist's drawing of the Latin male believed to have followed her from the club. I knew that the pre-arrest media interest meant the case would likely be carried forward in the public consciousness by the television news and I might be able to get a good ride out of it. I agreed to take the case on the come line. For free. Pro bono. For the good of the system. Besides, murder cases are few and far between. I take them when I can get them. Menendez was the twelfth accused murderer I had defended. The first eleven were still in prison but none of them were on death row. I considered that a good record.

By the time I got to Menendez in a holding cell at Van Nuys Division, he had already given a statement that implicated him to the police. He had told detectives Howard Kurlen and Don Crafton that he had not followed Renteria home, as suggested by the news reports, but had been an invited guest to her apartment. He explained that earlier in the day he had won eleven hundred dollars on the California lotto and had been willing to trade some of it to Renteria for some of her attention. He said that at her apartment they had engaged in consensual sex—although he did not use those words—and that when he left she was alive and five hundred dollars in cash richer.

The holes Kurlen and Crafton punched in Menendez's story were many. First of all, there had been no state lotto on the day of or day before the murder and the neighborhood mini-market where he said he had cashed his winning ticket had no record of paying out an eleven-hundred-dollar win to Menendez or anyone else. Additionally, no more than eighty dollars in cash was found in the victim's apartment. And lastly, the autopsy report indicated that bruising and other damage to the interior of the victim's vagina precluded what could be considered consensual sexual relations. The medical examiner concluded that she had been brutally raped.

No fingerprints other than the victim's were found in the apartment. The place had been wiped clean. No semen was found in the victim's body, indicating her rapist had used a condom or had not ejaculated during the assault. But in the bathroom off the bedroom where the attack and murder had taken place, a crime scene investigator using a black light found a small amount of semen on a pink towel hanging on a rack near the toilet. The theory that came into play was that after the rape and murder the killer had stepped into the bathroom, removed the condom and flushed it down the toilet. He had then wiped his penis with the nearby towel and then hung the towel back on the rack. When cleaning up after the crime and wiping surfaces he might have touched, he forgot about that towel.

The investigators kept the discovery of the DNA deposit and their attendant theory secret. It never made it into the media. It would become Kurlen and Crafton's hole card.

Based on Menendez's lies and the admission that he had been in the victim's apartment, he was arrested on suspicion of murder and held without bail. Detectives got a search warrant, and oral swabs were collected from Menendez and sent to the lab for DNA typing and comparison to the DNA recovered from the bathroom towel.

That was about when I entered the case. As they say in my profession, by then the *Titanic* had already left the dock. The iceberg was out there waiting. Menendez had badly hurt himself by talking—and lying—to the detectives. Still, unaware of the DNA comparison that was under way, I saw a glimmer of light for Jesus Menendez. There was a case to be made for neutralizing his interview with detectives—which, by the way, became a full-blown confession by the time it got reported by the media. Menendez was Mexican born and had come to this country at age eight. His family spoke only Spanish at home and he had attended a school for Spanish speakers until dropping out at age fourteen. He spoke only rudimentary English, and his cognition level of the language seemed to me to be even lower than his speaking level. Kurlen and Crafton made no effort to bring in a translator and, according to the taped interview, not once asked if Menendez even wanted one.

This was the crack I would work my way into. The interview was the foundation of the case against Menendez. It was the spinning platter. If I could knock it down most of the other plates would come down with it. My plan was to attack the interview as a violation of Menendez's rights because he could not have understood the Miranda warning he had been read by Kurlen or the document listing these rights in English that he had signed at the detective's request.

This is where the case stood until two weeks after Menendez's arrest when the lab results came back matching his DNA to that found on the towel in the victim's bathroom. After that the prosecution didn't need the interview or his admissions. The DNA put Menendez directly on the scene of a brutal rape and murder. I could try an O.J. defense — attack the credibility of the DNA match. But prosecutors and lab techs had learned so much from that debacle and in the years since that I knew I was unlikely of prevailing with a jury. The DNA was the iceberg and the momentum of the ship made it impossible to steer around it in time.

The district attorney himself revealed the DNA findings at a press conference and announced that his office would seek the death penalty for Menendez. He added that detectives had also located three eyewitnesses who had seen Menendez throw a knife into the Los Angeles River. The DA said the river was searched for the weapon but it was not recovered. Regardless, he characterized the witness accounts as solid — they were Menendez's three roommates.

Based on the prosecution's case coming together and the threat of the death penalty, I decided the O.J. defense would be too risky. Using Fernando Menendez as my translator, I went to the Van Nuys jail and told Jesus that his only hope was for a deal the DA had floated by me. If Menendez would plead guilty to murder I could get him a life sentence with the possibility of parole. I told him he'd be out in fifteen years. I told him it was the only way.

It was a tearful discussion. Both brothers cried and beseeched me to find another way. Jesus insisted that he did not kill Martha Renteria. He said he had lied to the detectives to protect Fernando, who had given him the money after a good month selling tar heroin. Jesus thought that revealing his brother's generosity would lead to another investigation of Fernando and his possible arrest.

The brothers urged me to investigate the case. Jesus told me Renteria had had other suitors that night in The Cobra Room. The reason he had paid her so much money was because she had played him off another bidder for her services.

Lastly, Jesus told me it was true that he had thrown a knife into the river but it was because he was afraid. It wasn't the murder weapon. It was just a knife he used on day jobs he picked up in Pacoima. It looked like the knife they were describing on the Spanish channel and he got rid of it before going to the police to straighten things out.

I listened and then told them that none of their explanations mattered. The only thing that mattered was the DNA. Jesus had a choice. He could take the fifteen years or go to trial and risk getting the death penalty or life *without* the possibility of parole. I reminded Jesus that he was a young man. He could be out by age forty. He could still have a life.

By the time I left the jailhouse meeting, I had Jesus Menendez's consent to make the deal. I only saw him one more time after that. At his plea-and-sentencing hearing when I stood next to him in front of the judge and coached him through the guilty plea. He was shipped off to Pelican Bay initially and then down to San Quentin after that. I had heard through the courthouse grapevine that his brother had gotten himself popped again — this time for using heroin. But he didn't call me. He went with a different lawyer and I didn't have to wonder why.

On the warehouse floor I opened the report on the autopsy of Martha Renteria. I was looking for two specific things that had probably not been looked at very closely by anyone else before. The case was closed. It was a dead file. Nobody cared anymore.

The first was the part of the report that dealt with the fifty-three stab wounds Renteria suffered during the attack on her bed. Under the heading "Wound Profile" the unknown weapon was described as a blade no longer than five inches and no wider than an inch. Its thickness was placed at one-eighth of an inch. Also noted in the report was the occurrence of jagged skin tears at the top of the victim's wounds, indicating that the top of the blade had an uneven line, to wit, it was designed as a weapon that would inflict damage going in as well as coming out. The shortness of the blade suggested that the weapon might be a folding knife.

There was a crude drawing in the report that depicted the outline of the blade without a handle. It looked familiar to me. I pulled my briefcase across the floor from where I had put it down and opened it up. From the state's discovery file I pulled the photo of the open folding knife with Louis Roulet's initials etched on the blade. I compared the blade to the outline drawn on the page in the autopsy report. It wasn't an exact match but it was damn close.

I then pulled out the recovered weapon analysis report and read the same paragraph I had read during the meeting in Roulet's office the day before. The knife was described as a custom-made Black Ninja folding knife with a blade measuring five inches long, one inch wide and one-eighth of an inch thick — the same measurements belonging to the unknown knife used to kill Martha Renteria. The knife Jesus Menendez supposedly threw into the L.A. River.

I knew that a five-inch blade wasn't unique. Nothing was conclusive but my instincts told me I was moving toward something. I tried not to let the burn that was building in my chest and throat distract me. I tried to stay on point. I moved on. I needed to check for a specific wound but I didn't want to look at the photos contained in the back of the report, the photos that coldly documented the horribly violated body of Martha Renteria. Instead I went to the page that had two side-by-side generic body profiles, one for the front and one for the back. On these the medical examiner had marked the wounds and numbered them. Only the front profile had been used. Dots and numbers 1 through 53. It looked like a macabre connect-the-dots puzzle and I didn't doubt that Kurlen or some detective looking for anything in the days before Menendez walked in had connected them, hoping the killer had left his initials or some other bizarre clue behind.

I studied the front profile's neck and saw two dots on either side of the neck. They were numbered 1 and 2. I turned the page and looked at the list of individual wound descriptions.

The description for wound number 1 read: *Superficial puncture on the lower right neck with ante-mortem histamine levels, indicative of coercive wound.*

The description for wound number 2 read: *Superficial puncture on the lower left neck with ante-mortem histamine levels, indicative of coercive wound. This puncture measures 1 cm larger than wound No. 1.*

The descriptions meant the wounds had been inflicted while Martha Renteria was still alive. And that was likely why they had been the first wounds listed and described. The examiner had suggested it was likely that the wounds resulted from a knife being held to the victim's neck in a coercive manner. It was the killer's method of controlling her.

I turned back to the state's discovery file for the Campo case. I pulled the photographs of Reggie Campo and the report on her physical examination at Holy Cross Medical Center. Campo had a small puncture wound on the lower left side of her neck and no wounds on her right side. I next scanned through her statement to the police until I found the part in which she described how she got the wound. She said that her attacker pulled her up off the floor of the living room and told her to lead him toward the bedroom. He controlled her from behind by gripping the bra strap across her back with his right hand and holding the knife point against the left side of her neck with his left hand. When she felt him momentarily rest his wrist on her shoulder she made her move, suddenly pivoting and pushing backwards, knocking her attacker into a large floor vase, and then breaking away.

I thought I understood now why Reggie Campo had only one wound on her neck, compared with the two Martha Renteria ended up with. If Campo's attacker had gotten her to the bedroom and put her down on the bed, he would have been facing her when he climbed on top of her. If he kept his knife in the same hand — the left — the blade would shift to the other side of her neck. When they found her dead in the bed, she'd have coercive punctures on both sides of her neck.

I put the files aside and sat cross-legged on the floor without moving for a long time. My thoughts were whispers in the darkness inside. In my mind

I held the image of Jesus Menendez's tear-streaked face when he had told me that he was innocent—when he'd begged me to believe him—and I had told him that he must plead guilty. It had been more than legal advice I was dispensing. He had no money, no defense and no chance—in that order—and I told him he had no choice. And though ultimately it was his decision and from his mouth that the word *guilty* was uttered in front of the judge, it felt to me now as though it had been me, his own attorney, holding the knife of the system against his neck and forcing him to say it.

19

I got out of the huge new rent-a-car facility at San Francisco International by one o'clock and headed north to the city. The Lincoln they gave me smelled like it had last been used by a smoker, maybe the renter or maybe just the guy who cleaned it up for me.

I don't know how to get anywhere in San Francisco. I just know how to drive through it. Three or four times a year I need to go to the prison by the bay, San Quentin, to talk to clients or witnesses. I could tell you how to get there, no sweat. But ask me how to get to Coit Tower or Fisherman's Wharf and we have a problem.

By the time I got through the city and over the Golden Gate it was almost two. I was in good shape. I knew from past experience that attorney visiting hours ended at four.

San Quentin is over a century old and looks as though the soul of every prisoner who lived or died there is etched on its dark walls. It was as foreboding a prison as I had ever visited, and at one time or another I had been to every one in California.

They searched my briefcase and made me go through a metal detector. After that they still passed a wand over me to make extra sure. Even then I wasn't allowed direct contact with Menendez because I had not formally scheduled the interview the required five days in advance. So I was put in a no-contact room—a Plexiglas wall between us with dime-size holes to speak through. I showed the guard the six-pack of photos I wanted to give Menendez and he told me I would have to show him the pictures through the Plexiglas. I sat down, put the photos away and didn't have to wait long until they brought Menendez in on the other side of the glass.

Two years ago, when he was shipped off to prison, Jesus Menendez had been a young man. Now he looked like he was already the forty years old I told him he could beat if he pleaded guilty. He looked at me with eyes as dead as the gravel stones out in the parking lot. He saw me and sat down reluctantly. He didn't have much use for me anymore.

We didn't bother with hellos and I got right into it.

"Look, Jesus, I don't have to ask you how you've been. I know. But something's come up and it could affect your case. I need to ask you a few questions. You understand me?"

"Why questions now, man? You had no questions before."

I nodded.

"You're right. I should've asked you more questions back then and I didn't. I didn't know then what I know now. Or at least what I think I know now. I am trying to make things right."

"What do you want?"

"I want you to tell me about that night at The Cobra Room."

He shrugged.

"The girl was there and I talked. She tol' me to follow her home."

He shrugged again.

"I went to her place, man, but I didn't kill her like that."

"Go back to the club. You told me that you had to impress the girl, that you had to show her the money and you spent more than you wanted to. You remember?"

"Is right."

"You said there was another guy trying to get with her. You remember that?"

"Si, he was there talking. She went to him but she came back to me."

"You had to pay her more, right?"

"Like that."

"Okay, do you remember that guy? If you saw a picture of him, would you remember him?"

"The guy who talked big? I think I 'member."

"Okay."

I opened my briefcase and took out the spread of mug shots. There were six photos and they included the booking photo of Louis Ross Roulet and five other men whose mug shots I had culled out of my archive boxes. I stood up and one by one started holding them up on the glass. I thought that by spreading my fingers I would be able to hold all six against the glass. Menendez stood up to look closely at the photos.

Almost immediately a voice boomed from an overhead speaker.

"Step back from the glass. Both of you step back from the glass and remain seated or the interview will be terminated."

I shook my head and cursed. I gathered the photos together and sat down. Menendez sat back down as well.

"Guard!" I said loudly.

I looked at Menendez and waited. The guard didn't enter the room.

"Guard!" I called again, louder.

Finally, the door opened and the guard stepped into my side of the interview room.

"You done?"

"No. I need him to look at these photos."

I held up the stack.

"Show him through the glass. He's not allowed to receive anything from you."

"But I'm going to take them right back."

"Doesn't matter. You can't give him anything."

"But if you don't let him come to the glass, how is he going to see them?"

"It's not my problem."

I waved in surrender.

"All right, okay. Then can you stay here for a minute?"

"What for?"

"I want you to watch this. I'm going to show him the photos and if he makes an ID, I want you to witness it."

"Don't drag me into your bullshit."

He walked to the door and left.

"Goddamn it," I said.

I looked at Menendez.

"All right, Jesus, I'm going to show you, anyway. See if you recognize any of them from where you are sitting."

One by one I held the photos up about a foot from the glass. Menendez leaned forward. As I showed each of the first five he looked, thought about it and then shook his head no. But on the sixth photo I saw his eyes flare. It seemed as though there was some life in them after all.

"That one," he said. "Is him."

I turned the photo toward me to be sure. It was Roulet.

"I 'member," Menendez said. "He's the one."

"And you're sure?"

Menendez nodded.

"What makes you so sure?"

"Because I know. In here I think on that night all of my time."

I nodded.

"Who is the man?" he asked.

"I can't tell you right now. Just know that I am trying to get you out of here."

"What do I do?"

"What you have been doing. Sit tight, be careful and stay safe."

"Safe?"

"I know. But as soon as I have something, you will know about it. I'm trying to get you out of here, Jesus, but it might take a little while."

"You were the one who tol' me to come here."

"At the time I didn't think there was a choice."

"How come you never ask me, did you murder this girl? You my lawyer, man. You din't care. You din't listen."

I stood up and loudly called for the guard. Then I answered his question.

"To legally defend you I didn't need to know the answer to that question. If I asked my clients if they were guilty of the crimes they were charged with, very few would tell me the truth. And if they did, I might not be able to defend them to the best of my ability."

The guard opened the door and looked in at me.

"I'm ready to go," I said.

I checked my watch and figured that if I was lucky in traffic I might be able to catch the five o'clock shuttle back to Burbank. The six o'clock at the latest. I dropped the photos into my briefcase and closed it. I looked back at Menendez, who was still in his chair on the other side of the glass.

"Can I just put my hand on the glass?" I asked the guard.

"Hurry up."

I leaned across the counter and put my hand on the glass, fingers spread. I waited for Menendez to do the same, creating a jailhouse handshake.

Menendez stood, leaned forward and spit on the glass where my hand was.

"You never shake my hand," he said. "I don't shake yours."

I nodded. I thought I understood just where he was coming from.

The guard smirked and told me to step through the door. In ten minutes I was out of the prison and crunching across the gravel to my rental car.

I had come four hundred miles for five minutes but those minutes were devastating. I think the lowest point of my life and professional career came an hour later when I was on the rent-a-car train being delivered back to the United terminal. No longer concentrating on the driving and making it back in time, I had only the case to think about. Cases, actually.

I leaned down, elbows on my knees and my face in my hands. My greatest fear had been realized, realized for two years but I hadn't known it. Not until now. I had been presented with innocence but I had not seen it or grasped it. Instead, I had thrown it into the maw of the machine like everything else. Now it was a cold, gray innocence, as dead as gravel and hidden in a fortress of stone and steel. And I had to live with it.

There was no solace to be found in the alternative, the knowledge that had we rolled the dice and gone to trial, Jesus would likely be on death row right now. There could be no comfort in knowing that fate was avoided, because I knew as sure as I knew anything else in the world that Jesus Menendez had been innocent. Something as rare as a true miracle — an innocent man — had come to me and I hadn't recognized it. I had turned away.

"Bad day?"

I looked up. There was a man across from me and a little bit further down the train car. We were the only ones on this link. He looked to be a decade older and had receding hair that made him look wise. Maybe he was even a lawyer, but I wasn't interested.

"I'm fine," I said. "Just tired."

And I held up a hand, palm out, a signal that I did not want conversation. I usually travel with a set of earbuds like Earl uses. I put them in and run the wire into a jacket pocket. It connects with nothing but it keeps people from talking to me. I had been in too much of a hurry this morning to think about them. Too much of a hurry to reach this point of desolation.

The man across the train got the message and said nothing else. I went back to my dark thoughts about Jesus Menendez. The bottom line was that I believed that I had one client who was guilty of the murder another client was serving a life sentence for. I could not help one without hurting the other. I needed an answer. I needed a plan. I needed proof. But for the moment on the train, I could only think of Jesus Menendez's dead eyes, because I knew I was the one who had killed the light in them.

As soon as I got off the shuttle at Burbank I turned on my cell. I had not come up with a plan but I had come up with my next step and that started with a call to Raul Levin. The phone buzzed in my hand, which meant I had messages. I decided I would get them after I set Levin in motion.

He answered my call and the first thing he asked was whether I had gotten his message.

"I just got off a plane," I said. "I missed it."

"A plane? Where were you?"

"Up north. What was the message?"

"Just an update on Corliss. If you weren't calling about that, what were you calling about?"

"What are you doing tonight?"

"Just hanging out. I don't like going out on Fridays and Saturdays. It's amateur hour. Too many drunks on the road."

"Well, I want to meet. I've got to talk to somebody. Bad things are happening."

Levin apparently sensed something in my voice because he immediately changed his stay-at-home-on-Friday-night policy and we agreed to meet at the Smoke House over by the Warner Studios. It was not far from where I was and not far from his home.

At the airport valet window I gave my ticket to a man in a red jacket and checked messages while waiting for the Lincoln.

Three messages had come in, all during the hour flight down from San Francisco. The first was from Maggie McPherson.

"Michael, I just wanted to call and say I'm sorry about how I was this morning. To tell you the truth, I was mad at myself for some of the things I said last night and the choices I made. I took it out on you and I should not have done that. Um, if you want to take Hayley out tomorrow or Sunday she would love it and, who knows, maybe I could come, too. Either way, just let me know."

She didn't call me Michael too often, even when we were married. She was one of those women who could use your last name and turn it into an endearment. That is, if she wanted to. She had always called me Haller. From the day we met in line to go through a metal detector at the CCB. She was headed to orientation at the DA's office and I was headed to misdemeanor arraignment court to handle a DUI.

I saved the message to listen to again sometime and went on to the next. I was expecting it to be from Levin but the automated voice reported the call came from a number with a 310 area code. The next voice I heard was Louis Roulet's.

"It's me, Louis. I was just checking in. I was just wondering after yesterday where things stood. I also have something I want to tell you."

I hit the erase button and moved on to the third and last message. This was Levin's.

"Hey, Bossman, give me a call. I have some stuff on Corliss. Anyway, the name is Dwayne Jeffery Corliss. That's Dwayne with a *D-W*. He's a hype and he's done the snitch thing a couple other times here in L.A. What's new, right? Anyway, he was actually arrested for stealing a bike he probably planned to trade for a little Mexican tar. He has parlayed snitching off Roulet into a ninety-day lockdown program at County-USC. So we won't be able to get to him and talk to him unless you got a judge that will set it up. Pretty shrewd move by the prosecutor. Anyway, I'm still running him down. Something came up on the Internet in Phoenix that looks pretty good for us if it was the same guy. Something that blew up in his face. I should be able to confirm it by Monday. So that's it for now. Give me a call over the weekend. I'm just hanging out."

I erased the message and closed the phone.

"Say no more," I said to myself.

Once I heard that Corliss was a hype, I needed to know nothing else. I understood why Maggie had not trusted the guy. Hypes — needle addicts — were the most desperate and unreliable people you could come across in the machine. Given the opportunity, they would snitch off their own mothers to get the next injection, or into the next methadone program. Every one of them was a liar and every one of them could easily be shown as such in court.

I was, however, puzzled by what the prosecutor was up to. The name Dwayne Corliss was not in the discovery material Minton had given me. Yet the prosecutor was making the moves he would make with a witness. He had stuck Corliss into a ninety-day program for safekeeping. The Roulet trial would come and go in that time. Was he hiding Corliss? Or was he simply putting the snitch on a shelf in the closet so he would know exactly where he was and where he'd been in case the time came in trial that his testimony would be needed? He was obviously operating under the belief that I didn't know about Corliss. And if it hadn't been for a slip by Maggie McPherson, I wouldn't. It was still a dangerous move, nevertheless. Judges do not look kindly on prosecutors who so openly flout the rules of discovery.

It led me to thinking of a possible strategy for the defense. If Minton was foolish enough to try to spring Corliss in trial, I might not even object under the rules of discovery. I might let him put the heroin addict on the stand so I would get the chance to shred him in front of the jury like a credit card receipt. It would all depend on what Levin could come up with. I planned to tell him to continue to dig into Dwayne Jeffery Corliss. To hold nothing back.

I also thought about Corliss being in a lockdown program at County-USC. Levin was wrong and so was Minton if he was thinking I couldn't reach his witness in lockdown. By coincidence, my client Gloria Dayton had been placed in a lockdown program at County-USC after she snitched off her drug-dealing client. While there were a number of such programs at County, it was likely that she shared group therapy sessions or even mealtime with Corliss. I might not be able to get directly to Corliss but as Dayton's attorney I could get to her, and she in turn could get a message to Corliss.

The Lincoln pulled up and I gave the man in the red jacket a couple dollars. I exited the airport and drove south on Hollywood Way toward the center of Burbank, where all the studios were. I got to the Smoke House ahead of Levin and ordered a martini at the bar. On the overhead TV was an update on the start of the college basketball tournament. Florida had defeated Ohio in the first round. The headline on the bottom of the screen said "March Madness" and I toasted my glass to it. I knew what real March Madness was beginning to feel like.

Levin came in and ordered a beer before we sat down to dinner. It was still green, left over from the night before. Must have been a slow night. Maybe everybody had gone to Four Green Fields.

"Nothing like hair of the dog that bit ya, as long as it's green hair," he said in that brogue that was getting old.

He sipped the level of the glass down so he could walk with it and we stepped out to the hostess station so we could go to a table. She led us to a red padded booth that was shaped like a U. We sat across from each other and I put my briefcase down next to me. When the waitress came for a cocktail order we ordered the whole shooting match: salads, steaks and potatoes. I also asked for an order of the restaurant's signature garlic cheese bread.

"Good thing you don't like going out on weekends," I said to Levin after she was gone. "You eat the cheese bread and your breath will probably kill anybody you come in contact with after this."

"I'll have to take my chances."

We were quiet for a long moment after that. I could feel the vodka working its way into my guilt. I would be sure to order another when the salads came.

"So?" Levin finally said. "You called the meeting."

I nodded.

"I want to tell you a story. Not all of the details are set or known. But I'll tell it to you in the way I think it goes and then you tell me what you think and what I should do. Okay?"

"I like stories. Go ahead."

"I don't think you'll like this one. It starts two years ago with —"

I stopped and waited while the waitress put down our salads and the cheese bread. I asked for another vodka martini even though I was only halfway through the one I had. I wanted to make sure there was no gap.

"So," I said after she was gone. "This whole thing starts two years ago with Jesus Menendez. You remember him, right?"

"Yeah, we mentioned him the other day. The DNA. He's the client you always say is in prison because he wiped his prick on a fluffy pink towel."

He smiled because it was true that I had often reduced Menendez's case to such an absurdly vulgar basis. I had often used it to get a laugh when trading war stories at Four Green Fields with other lawyers. That was before I knew what I now knew.

I did not return the smile.

"Yeah, well, it turns out Jesus didn't do it."

"What do you mean? Somebody else wiped his prick on the towel?"

This time Levin laughed out loud.

"No, you don't get it. I'm telling you Jesus Menendez was innocent."

Levin's face grew serious. He nodded, putting something together.

"He's in San Quentin. You were up at the Q today."

I nodded.

"Let me back up and tell the story," I said. "You didn't do much work for me on Menendez because there was nothing to be done. They had the DNA, his own incriminating statement and three witnesses who saw him throw a knife into the river. They never found the knife but they had the witnesses—his own roommates. It was a hopeless case. Truth is, I took it on the come line for publicity value. So basically all I did was walk him to a plea. He didn't like it, said he didn't do it, but there was no choice. The DA was going for the death penalty. He'd have gotten that or life without. I got him life with and I made the little fucker take it. I made him."

I looked down at my untouched salad. I realized I didn't feel like eating. I just felt like drinking and pickling the cork in my brain that contained all the guilt cells.

Levin waited me out. He wasn't eating, either.

"In case you don't remember, the case was about the murder of a woman named Martha Renteria. She was a dancer at The Cobra Room on East Sunset. You didn't end up going there on this, did you?"

Levin shook his head.

"They don't have a stage," I said. "They have like a pit in the center and for each number, these guys dressed like Aladdin come out carrying this big cobra basket between two bamboo poles. They put it down and the music starts. Then the top comes off the basket and the girl comes up dancing. Then her top comes off, too. Kind of a new take on the dancer coming out of the cake."

"It's Hollywood, baby," Levin said. "You gotta have a show."

"Well, Jesus Menendez liked the show. He had eleven hundred dollars his brother the drug dealer gave him and he took a fancy to Martha Renteria. Maybe because she was the only dancer who was shorter than him. Maybe because she spoke Spanish to him. After her set they sat and talked and then she circulated a little bit and came back and pretty soon he knew he was in competition with another guy in the club. He trumped the other guy by offering her five hundred if she'd take him home."

"But he didn't kill her when he got there?"

"Uh-uh. He followed her car in his. Got there, had sex, flushed the condom, wiped his prick on the towel and then he went home. The story starts after he left."

"The real killer."

"The real killer knocks on the door, maybe fakes like it's Jesus and that he's forgotten something. She opens the door. Or maybe it was an appointment. She was expecting the knock and she opens the door."

"The guy from the club? The one Menendez was bidding against?"

I nodded.

"Exactly. He comes in, punches her a few times to soften her up and then takes out his folding knife and holds it against her neck while he walks her to the bedroom. Sound familiar? Only she isn't lucky like Reggie Campo would be in a couple years. He puts her on the bed, puts on a condom and climbs on top. Now the knife is on the other side of her neck and he keeps it there while he rapes her. And when he's done, he kills her. He stabs her with that knife again and again. It's a case of overkill if there ever was one. He's working out something in his sick fucking mind while he's doing it."

My second martini came and I took it right from the waitress's hand and gulped half of it down. She asked if we were finished with our salads and we both waved them away untouched.

"Your steaks will be right out," she said. "Or do you want me to just dump them in the garbage and save you the time?"

I looked up at her. She was smiling but I was so caught up in the story I was telling that I had missed what it was she had said.

"Never mind," she said. "They'll be right out."

I got right back to the story. Levin said nothing.

"After she's dead the killer cleans up. He takes his time, because what's the hurry, she's not going anywhere or calling anybody. He wipes the place down to take care of any fingerprints he might have left. And in the process he wipes away Menendez's prints. This will look bad for Menendez when he later goes to the police to explain that he is the guy in the sketches but he didn't kill Martha. They'll look at him and say, 'Then why'd you wear gloves when you were there?'"

Levin shook his head.

"Oh man, if this is true..."

"Don't worry, it's true. Menendez gets a lawyer who once did a good job for his brother but this lawyer wouldn't know an innocent man if he kicked him in the nuts. This lawyer is all about the deal. He never even asks the kid if he did it. He just assumes he did it because they got his fucking DNA on the towel and the witnesses who saw him toss the knife. The lawyer goes to work and gets the best possible deal he could get. He actually feels pretty good about it because he's going to keep Menendez off death row and get him a shot at parole someday. So he goes to Menendez and brings down the hammer. He makes him take the deal and stand up there in court and say 'Guilty.' Jesus then goes off to prison and everybody's happy. The state's happy because it saves money on a trial and Martha Renteria's family is happy because they don't have to face a trial with all those autopsy photos and stories about their daughter dancing naked and taking men home for money. And the lawyer's happy because he got on TV with the case at least six times, plus he kept another client off death row."

I gulped down the rest of the martini and looked around for our waitress. I wanted another.

"Jesus Menendez goes off to prison a young man. I just saw him and he's twenty-six going on forty. He's a small guy. You know what happens to the little ones up there."

I was looking straight down at the empty space on the table in front of me when an egg-shaped platter with a sizzling steak and steaming potato was put down. I looked up at the waitress and told her to bring me another martini. I didn't say please.

"You better take it easy," Levin said after she was gone. "There probably isn't a cop in this county who wouldn't love to pull you over on a deuce, take you back to lockup and put the flashlight up your ass."

"I know, I know. It will be my last. And if it's too much I won't drive. They always have a cab out front of this place."

Deciding that food might help I cut into my steak and ate a piece. I then took a piece of cheese bread out of the napkin it was folded into a basket with, but it was no longer warm. I dropped it on my plate and put my fork down.

"Look, I know you're beating yourself up over this but you are forgetting something," Levin said.

"Yeah? What's that?"

"His exposure. He was facing the needle, man, and the case was a dog. I didn't work it for you because there was nothing to work. They had him and you saved him from the needle. That's your job and you did it well. So now you think you know what really went down. You can't beat yourself up for what you didn't know then."

I held my hand up in a *stop there* gesture.

"The guy was innocent. I should've seen it. I should've done something about it. Instead, I just did my usual thing and went through the motions with my eyes closed."

"Bullshit."

"No, no bullshit."

"Okay, go back to the story. Who was the second guy who came to her door?"

I opened my briefcase next to me and reached into it.

"I went up to San Quentin today and showed Menendez a six-pack. All mug shots of my clients. Mostly former clients. Menendez picked one out in less than ten seconds."

I tossed the mug shot of Louis Roulet across the table. It landed facedown. Levin picked it up and looked at it for a few moments, then put it back facedown on the table.

"Let me show you something else," I said.

My hand went back into the briefcase and pulled out the two folded photographs of Martha Renteria and Reggie Campo. I looked around to make sure the waitress wasn't about to deliver my martini and then handed them across the table.

"It's like a puzzle," I said. "Put them together and see what you get."

Levin put the one face together from the two and nodded as he understood the significance. The killer—Roulet—zeroed in on women that fit a model or profile he desired. I next showed him the weapon sketch drawn by the medical examiner on the Renteria autopsy and read him the description of the two coercive wounds found on her neck.

"You know that video you got from the bar?" I asked. "What it shows is a killer at work. Just like you, he saw that Mr. X was left-handed. When he attacked Reggie Campo he punched with his left and then held the knife with his left. This guy knows what he is doing. He saw an opportunity and took it. Reggie Campo is the luckiest woman alive."

"You think there are others? Other murders, I mean."

"Maybe. That's what I want you to look into. Check out all the knife murders of women in the last few years. Then get the victim's pictures and see if they match the physical profile. And don't look at unsolved cases only. Martha Renteria was supposedly among the closed cases."

Levin leaned forward.

"Look, man, I'm not going to throw a net over this like the police can. You have to bring the cops in on this. Or go to the FBI. They got their serial killer specialists."

I shook my head.

"Can't. He's my client."

"Menendez is your client, too, and you have to get him out."

"I'm working on that. And that's why I need you to do this for me, Mish."

We both knew that I called him Mish whenever I needed something that crossed the lines of our professional relationship into the friendship that was underneath it.

"What about a hitman?" Levin said. "That would solve our problems."

I nodded, knowing he was being facetious.

"Yeah, that would work," I said. "It would make the world a better place, too. But it probably wouldn't spring Menendez."

Levin leaned forward again. Now he was serious.

"I'll do what I can, Mick, but I don't think this is the right way to go. You can declare conflict of interest and dump Roulet. Then work on jumping Menendez out of the Q."

"Jump him out with what?"

"The ID he made on the six-pack. That was solid. He didn't know Roulet from a hole in the ground and he goes and picks him out of the pack."

"Who is going to believe that? I'm his lawyer! Nobody from the cops to the clemency board is going to believe I didn't set that up. This is all theory, Raul. You know it and I know it to be true but we can't prove a damn thing."

"What about the wounds? They could match the knife they got from the Campo case to Martha Renteria's wounds."

I shook my head.

"She was cremated. All they have is the descriptions and photos from the autopsy and it wouldn't be conclusive. It's not enough. Besides, I can't be seen as the guy pushing this on my own client. If I turn against a client, then I turn against all my clients. It can't look that way or I'll lose them all. I have to figure something else out."

"I think you're wrong. I think—"

"For now I go along as if I don't know any of this, you understand? But you look into it. All of it. Keep it separate from Roulet so I don't have a discovery issue. File it all under Jesus Menendez and bill the time to me on that case. You understand?"

Before Levin could answer, the waitress brought my third martini. I waved it away.

"I don't want it. Just the check."

"Well, I can't pour it back into the bottle," she said.

"Don't worry, I'll pay for it. I just don't want to drink it. Give it to the guy who makes the cheese bread and just bring me the check."

She turned and walked away, probably annoyed that I hadn't offered the drink to her. I looked back at Levin. He looked like he was pained by everything that had been revealed to him. I knew just how he felt.

"Some franchise I got, huh?"

"Yeah. How are you going to be able to act straight with this guy when you have to deal with him and meantime you're digging out this other shit on the side?"

"With Roulet? I plan to see him as little as possible. Only when it's necessary. He left me a message today, has something to tell me. But I'm not calling back."

"Why did he pick you? I mean, why would he pick the one lawyer who might put this thing together?"

I shook my head.

"I don't know. I thought about it the whole plane ride down. I think maybe he was worried I might hear about the case and put it together anyway. But if he was my client, then he knew I'd be ethically bound to protect him. At least at first. Plus there's the money."

"What money?"

"The money from Mother. The franchise. He knows how big a payday this is for me. My biggest ever. Maybe he thought I'd look the other way to keep the money coming in."

Levin nodded.

"Maybe I should, huh?" I said.

It was a vodka-spurred attempt at humor, but Levin didn't smile and then I remembered Jesus Menendez's face behind the prison Plexiglas and I couldn't even bring myself to smile.

"Listen, there's one other thing I need you to do," I said. "I want you to look at him, too. Roulet. Find out all you can without getting too close. And check out that story about the mother, about her getting raped in a house she was selling in Bel-Air."

Levin nodded.

"I'm on it."

"And don't farm it out."

This was a running joke between us. Like me, Levin was a one-man shop. He had no one to farm it out to.

"I won't. I'll handle it myself."

It was his usual response but this time it lacked the false sincerity and humor he usually gave it. He'd answered by habit.

The waitress moved by the table and put our check down without a thank you. I dropped a credit card on it without even looking at the damage. I just wanted to leave.

"You want her to wrap up your steak?" I asked.

"That's okay," Levin said. "I've kind of lost my appetite for right now."

"What about that attack dog you've got at home?"

"That's an idea. I forgot about Bruno."

He looked around for the waitress to ask for a box.

"Take mine, too," I said. "I don't have a dog."

21

Despite the vodka glaze, I made it through the slalom that was Laurel Canyon without cracking up the Lincoln or getting pulled over by a cop. My house is on Fareholm Drive, which terraces up off the southern mouth of the canyon. All the houses are built to the street line and the only problem I had coming home was when I found that some moron had parked his SUV in front of my garage and I couldn't get in. Parking on the narrow street is always difficult and the opening in front of my garage door was usually just too inviting, especially on a weekend night, when invariably someone on the street was throwing a party.

I motored by the house and found a space big enough for the Lincoln about a block and a half away. The further I had gotten from my house, the angrier I had gotten with the SUV. The fantasy grew from spitting on the windshield to breaking off the side mirror, flattening the tires and kicking in the side panels. But instead I wrote a sedate little note on a page of yellow legal paper: *This is not a parking space! Next time you will be towed*. After all, you never know who's driving an SUV in L.A., and if you threaten someone for parking in front of your garage, then they know where you live.

I walked back and was placing the note under the violator's windshield wiper when I noticed the SUV was a Range Rover. I put my hand on the hood and it was cool to the touch. I looked up above the garage to the windows of my house that I could see, but they were dark. I slapped the folded note under the windshield wiper and started up the stairs to the front deck and door. I half expected Louis Roulet to be sitting in one of the tall director chairs, taking in the twinkling view of the city, but he was not there.

Instead, I walked to the corner of the porch and looked out on the city. It was this view that had made me buy the place. Everything about the house once you went through the door was ordinary and outdated. But the front porch and the view right above Hollywood Boulevard could launch a million dreams. I had used money from the last franchise case for a down payment. But once I was in and there wasn't another franchise, I took the equity out in a second mortgage. The truth was I struggled every month just to pay the nut. I needed to get out from under it but that view off the front deck paralyzed me. I'd probably be staring out at the city when they came to take the key and foreclose on the place.

I know the question my house prompts. Even with my struggles to stay afloat with it, how fair is it that when a prosecutor and defense attorney divorce, the defense attorney gets the house on the hill with a million-dollar view while the prosecutor with the daughter gets the two-bedroom apartment in the Valley. The answer is that Maggie McPherson could buy a house of her choosing and I would help her to my maximum ability. But she had refused to move while she waited to be tapped for a promotion to the downtown office. Buying a house in Sherman Oaks or anywhere else would send the wrong message, one of sedentary contentment. She was not content to be Maggie McFierce of the Van Nuys Division. She was not content to be passed over by John Smithson or any of his young guns. She was ambitious and wanted to get downtown, where supposedly the best and brightest prosecuted the most important crimes. She refused to accept the simple truism that the better you were, the bigger threat you were to those at the top, especially if they are elected. I knew that Maggie would never be invited downtown. She was too damn good.

Every now and then this realization would seep through and she would lash out in unexpected ways. She would make a cutting remark at a press conference or she would refuse to cooperate with a downtown investigation. Or she would drunkenly reveal to a criminal defense attorney and ex-husband something about a case he shouldn't be told.

The phone started to ring from inside the house. I moved to the front door and fumbled with my keys to unlock it and get inside in time. My phone numbers and who has them could form a pyramid chart. The number in the yellow pages everybody has or could have. Next up the pyramid is my cell phone, which has been disseminated to key colleagues, investigators, bondsmen, clients and other cogs in the machine. My home phone—the land line—was the top of the pyramid. Very few had the number. No clients and no other lawyers except for one.

I got in and grabbed the phone off the kitchen wall before it went to message. The caller was that one other lawyer with the number. Maggie McPherson.

"Did you get my messages?"

"I got the one on my cell. What's wrong?"

"Nothing's wrong. I left one on this number a lot earlier."

"Oh, I've been gone all day. I just got in."

"Where have you been?"

"Well, I've been up to San Francisco and back and I just got in from having dinner with Raul Levin. Is all of that all right with you?"

"I'm just curious. What was in San Francisco?"

"A client."

"So what you really mean is you were up to San Quentin and back."

"You were always too smart for me, Maggie. I can never fool you. Is there a reason for this call?"

"I just wanted to see if you got my apology and I also wanted to find out if you were going to do something with Hayley tomorrow."

"Yes and yes. But Maggie, no apology is necessary and you should know that. I am sorry for the way I acted before I left. And if my daughter wants to be with me tomorrow, then I want to be with her. Tell her we can go down to the pier or to a movie if she wants. Whatever she wants."

"Well, she actually wants to go to the mall."

She said it as if she were stepping on glass.

"The mall? The mall is fine. I'll take her. What's wrong with the mall? Is there something in particular she wants?"

I suddenly noticed a foreign odor in the house. The smell of smoke. While standing in the middle of the kitchen I checked the oven and the stove. They were off. I was tethered to the kitchen because the phone wasn't cordless. I stretched it to the door and flicked on the light to the dining room. It was empty and its light was cast into the next room, the living room through which I had passed when I had entered. It looked empty as well.

"They have a place there where you make your own teddy bear and you pick the style and its voice box and you put a little heart in with the stuffing. It's all very cute."

I now wanted to get off the line and explore further into my house.

"Fine. I'll take her. What time is good?"

"I was thinking about noon. Maybe we could have lunch first."

"We?"

"Would that bother you?"

"No, Maggie, not at all. How about I come by at noon?"

"Great."

"See you then."

I hung the phone up before she could say good-bye. I owned a gun but it was a collector piece that hadn't been fired in my lifetime and was stored in a box in my bedroom closet at the rear of the house. So I quietly opened a kitchen drawer and took out a short but sharp steak knife. I then walked through the living room toward the hallway that led to the rear of the house. There were three doorways in the hall. They led to my bedroom, a bathroom and another bedroom I had turned into a home office, the only real office I had.

The desk light was on in the office. It was not visible from the angle I had in the hallway but I could tell it was on. I had not been home in two days but I did not remember leaving it on. I approached the open door to the room slowly, aware that this is what I may have been meant to do. Focus on the light in one room while the intruder is waiting in the darkness of the bedroom or bathroom.

"Come on back, Mick. It's just me."

I knew the voice but it didn't make me feel at ease. Louis Roulet was waiting in the room. I stepped to the threshold and stopped. He was sitting in the black leather desk seat. He swiveled it around so that he was facing me and crossed his legs. His pants rode up on his left leg and I could see the tracking bracelet that Fernando Valenzuela had made him wear. I knew that if Roulet had come to kill me, at least he would leave a trail. It wasn't all that comforting, though. I leaned against the door frame so that I could hold the knife behind my hip without being too obvious about it.

"So this is where you do your great legal work?" Roulet asked.

"Some of it. What are you doing here, Louis?"

"I came to see you. You didn't return my call and so I wanted to make sure we were still a team, you know?"

"I was out of town. I just got back."

"What about dinner with Raul? Isn't that what you said to your caller?"

"He's a friend. I had dinner on my way in from Burbank Airport. How did you find out where I live, Louis?"

He cleared his throat and smiled.

"I work in real estate, Mick. I can find out where anybody lives. In fact, I used to be a source for the *National Enquirer*. Did you know that? I could tell them where any celebrity lived, no matter what fronts and corporations they hid their purchases behind. But I gave it up after a while. The money was good but it was so...tawdry. You know what I mean, Mick? Anyway, I stopped. But I can still find out where anyone lives. I can also find out whether they've maxed the mortgage value out and even if they're making their payments on time."

He looked at me with a knowing smile. He was telling me he knew the house was a financial shell, that I had nothing in the place and usually ran a month behind on the two mortgages. Fernando Valenzuela probably wouldn't even accept the place as collateral on a five-thousand-dollar bond.

"How'd you get in?" I asked.

"Well, that's the funny thing about this. It turns out I had a key. Back when this place was for sale — what was that, about eighteen months ago? Anyway, I wanted to see it because I thought I had a client who might be interested because of the view. So I came and got the key out of the realtor's combo box. I came in and looked around and knew immediately it wasn't right for my client—he wanted something nicer—so I left. And I forgot to put the key back. I have a bad habit of doing that. Isn't that strange that all this time later my lawyer would be living in this house? And by the way, I see you haven't done a thing with it. You have the view, of course, but you really need to do some updating."

I knew then that he had been keeping tabs on me since the Menendez case. And that he probably knew I had just been up to San Quentin visiting him. I thought about the man on the car-rental train. *Bad day?* I had later seen him on the shuttle to Burbank. Had he been following me? Was he working for Roulet? Was he the investigator Cecil Dobbs had tried to push onto the case? I didn't know all the answers but I knew that the only reason Roulet would be in my house waiting for me was because he knew what I knew.

"What do you really want, Louis? Are you trying to scare me?"

"No, no, I'm the one who should be scared. I assume you have a weapon of some sort behind your back there. What is it, a gun?"

I gripped the knife tighter but did not display it.

"What is it you want?" I repeated.

"I want to make you an offer. Not on the house. On your services."

"You already have my services."

He swiveled back and forth in the chair before responding. My eyes scanned the desk, checking if anything was missing. I noticed he had used a little pottery dish my daughter had made for me as an ashtray. It was supposed to be for paperclips.

"I was thinking about our fee arrangement and the difficulties the case presents," he said. "Frankly, Mick, I think you are underpaid. So I want to set up a new fee schedule. You will be paid the amount already agreed upon and you will be paid in full before the trial begins. But I am now going to add a performance bonus. When I am found by a jury of my peers to be not guilty of this ugly crime, your fee automatically doubles. I will write the check in your Lincoln as we drive away from the courthouse."

"That's nice, Louis, but the California bar refuses to allow defense attorneys to accept bonuses based on results. I couldn't accept it. It's more than generous but I can't."

"But the California bar isn't here, Mick. And we don't have to treat it as a performance bonus. It's just part of the fee schedule. Because, after all, you will be successful in defending me, won't you?"

He looked intently at me and I read the threat.

"There are no guarantees in the courtroom. Things can always go badly. But I still think it looks good."

Roulet's face slowly broke into a smile.

"What can I do to make it look even better?"

I thought about Reggie Campo. Still alive and ready to go to trial. She had no idea whom she would be testifying against.

"Nothing," I answered. "Just sit tight and wait it out. Don't get any ideas. Don't do anything. The case is coming together and we'll be all right."

He didn't respond. I wanted to get him away from thoughts about the threat Reggie Campo presented.

"There is one thing that has come up, though," I said.

"Really? What's that?"

"I don't have the details. What I know I only know from a source who can't tell me any more. But it looks like the DA has a snitch from the jail. You didn't talk to anybody about the case when you were in there, did you? Remember, I told you not to talk to anybody."

"And I didn't. Whoever they have, he is a liar."

"Most of them are. I just wanted to be sure. I'll deal with it if it comes up."

"Good."

"One other thing. Have you talked to your mother about testifying about the attack in the empty house? We need it to set up the defense of you carrying the knife."

Roulet pursed his lips but didn't answer.

"I need you to work on her," I said. "It could be very important to establish that solidly with the jury. Besides that, it could swing sympathy toward you."

Roulet nodded. He saw the light.

"Can you please ask her?" I asked.

"I will. But she'll be tough. She never reported it. She never told anyone but Cecil."

"We need her to testify and then we can get Cecil to testify and back her up. It's not as good as a police report but it will work. We need her, Louis. I think if she testifies, she can convince them. Juries like old ladies."

"Okay."

"Did she ever tell you what the guy looked like or how old he was, anything like that?"

He shook his head.

"She couldn't tell. He wore a ski mask and goggles. He jumped on her as soon as she came in the door. He had been hiding behind it. It was very quick and very brutal."

His voice quavered as he described it. I became puzzled.

"I thought you said the attacker was a prospective buyer she was supposed to meet there," I said. "He was already in the house?"

He brought his eyes up to mine.

"Yes. Somehow he had already gotten in and was waiting for her. It was terrible."

I nodded. I didn't want to go further with him at the moment. I wanted him out of my house.

"Listen, thank you for your offer, Louis. Now if you would excuse me, I want to go to bed. It's been a long day."

I gestured with my free hand toward the hallway leading to the front of the house. Roulet got up from the desk chair and came toward me. I backed into the hallway and then into the open door of my bedroom. I kept the knife behind me and ready. But Roulet passed by without incident.

"And tomorrow you have your daughter to entertain," he said.

That froze me. He had listened to the call from Maggie. I didn't say anything. He did.

"I didn't know you had a daughter, Mick. That must be nice."

He glanced back at me, smiling as he moved down the hall.

"She's beautiful," he said.

My inertia turned to momentum. I stepped into the hall and started following him, anger building with each step. I gripped the knife tightly.

"How do you know what she looks like?" I demanded.

He stopped and I stopped. He looked down at the knife in my hand and then at my face. He spoke calmly.

"The picture of her on your desk."

I had forgotten about the photo. A small framed shot of her in a teacup at Disneyland.

"Oh," I said.

He smiled, knowing what I had been thinking.

"Good night, Mick. Enjoy your daughter tomorrow. You probably don't get to see her enough."

He turned and crossed the living room and opened the front door. He looked back at me before stepping out.

"What you need is a good lawyer," he said. "One that will get you custody."

"No. She's better off with her mother."

"Good night, Mick. Thanks for the conversation."

"Good night, Louis."

I stepped forward to close the door.

"Nice view," he said from out on the front porch.

"Yeah," I said as I closed and locked the door.

I stood there with my hand on the knob, waiting to hear his steps going down the stairs to the street. But a few moments later he knocked on the door. I closed my eyes, held the knife at the ready and opened it. Roulet raised his hand out. I took a step back.

"Your key," he said. "I figured you should have it."

I took the key off his outstretched palm.

"Thanks."

"Don't mention it."

I closed the door and locked it once again.

22

Tuesday, April 12

The day started better than any defense attorney could ask for. I had no courtroom to be in, no client to meet. I slept late, spent the morning reading the newspaper cover to cover and had a box ticket to the home opener of the Los Angeles Dodgers baseball season. It was a day game and a time-honored tradition among those on the defense side of the aisle to attend. My ticket had come from Raul Levin, who was taking five of the defense pros he did work for to the game as a gesture of thanks for their business. I was sure the others would grumble and complain at the game about how I was monopolizing Levin as I prepared for the Roulet trial. But I wasn't going to let it bother me.

We were in the outwardly slow time before trial, when the machine moves with a steady, quiet momentum. Louis Roulet's trial was set to begin in a month. As it was growing nearer I was taking on fewer and fewer clients. I needed the time to prepare and strategize. Though the trial was weeks away it would likely be won or lost with the information gathered now. I needed to keep my schedule clear for this. I took cases from repeat customers only — and only if the money was right and it came up front.

A trial was a slingshot. The key was in the preparation. Pretrial is when the sling is loaded with the proper stone and slowly the elastic is pulled back and stretched to its limit. Finally, at trial you let it go and the projectile shoots forward, unerringly at the target. The target is acquittal. Not guilty. You only hit that target if you have properly chosen the stone and pulled back carefully on the sling, stretching it as far as possible.

Levin was doing most of the stretching. He had continued to dig into the lives of the players in both the Roulet and Menendez cases. We had hatched a strategy and plan we were calling a "double slingshot" because it had two intended targets. I had no doubt that when the trial began in May, we would be stretched back to the limit and ready to let go.

The prosecution did its part to help us load the slingshot, as well. In the weeks since Roulet's arraignment the state's discovery file grew thicker as scientific reports filtered in, further police investigations were carried out and new developments occurred.

Among the new developments of note was the identification of Mr. X, the left-handed man who had been with Reggie Campo at Morgan's the night of the attack. LAPD detectives, using the video I had alerted the prosecution to, were able to identify him by showing a frame taken off the video to known prostitutes and escorts when they were arrested by the Administrative Vice section. Mr. X was identified as Charles Talbot. He was known to many of the sex providers as a regular. Some said that he owned or worked at a convenience store on Reseda Boulevard.

The investigative reports forwarded to me through discovery requests revealed that detectives interviewed Talbot and learned that on the night of March 6 he left Reggie Campo's apartment shortly before ten and went to the previously mentioned twenty-four-hour convenience store. Talbot owned the business. He went to the store so that he could check on things and open a cigarette storage cabinet that only he carried the key for. Tape from surveillance cameras in the store confirmed that he was there from 10:09 to 10:51 P.M. restocking the cigarette bins beneath the front counter. The investigator's summary dismissed Talbot as having no bearing or part in the events that occurred after he left Campo's apartment. He was just one of her customers.

Nowhere in the state's discovery was there mention of Dwayne Jeffery Corliss, the jailhouse snitch who had contacted the prosecution with a tale to tell about Louis Roulet. Minton had either decided not to use him as a witness or was keeping him under wraps for emergency use only. I tended to think it was the latter. Minton had sequestered him in the lockdown program. He wouldn't have gone to the trouble unless he wanted to keep Corliss offstage but ready. This was fine with me. What Minton didn't know was that Corliss was the stone I was going to put into the slingshot.

And while the state's discovery contained little information on the victim of the crime, Raul Levin was vigorously pursuing Reggie Campo. He located a website called PinkMink.com on which she advertised her services. What was important about the discovery was not necessarily that it further established that she was engaged in prostitution but that the ad copy stated that she was "very open-minded and liked to get wild" and was "available for S&M role play — you spank me or I'll spank you." It was good ammunition to have. It was the kind of stuff that could help color a victim or witness in a jury's eyes. And she was both.

Levin also was digging deeper into the life and times of Louis Roulet and had learned that he had been a poor student who'd attended five different private schools in and around Beverly Hills as a youth. He did go on to attend and graduate from UCLA with a degree in English literature but Levin located fellow classmates who had said Roulet paid his way through by purchasing from other students completed class assignments, test answers and even a ninety-page senior thesis on the life and work of John Fante.

A far darker profile emerged of Roulet as an adult. Levin found numerous female acquaintances who said Roulet had mistreated them, either physically or mentally, or both. Two women who had known Roulet while they were students at UCLA told Levin that they suspected that Roulet had spiked their drinks at a fraternity party with a date-rape drug and then took sexual advantage of them. Neither reported their suspicions to authorities but one woman had her blood tested the day after the party. She said traces of ketamine hydrochloride, a veterinary sedative, were found. Luckily for the defense, neither woman had so far been located by investigators for the prosecution.

Levin took a look at the so-called Real Estate Rapist cases of five years before as well. Four women — all realtors — reported being overpowered and raped by a man who was waiting inside when they entered homes they believed had been vacated by their owners for a showing. The attacks went unsolved but stopped eleven months after the first one was reported. Levin spoke to an LAPD sex crimes expert who worked the cases. He said that his gut instinct had always been that the rapist wasn't an outsider. The assailant seemed to know how to get into the houses and how to draw the female sales agents to them alone. The investigator was convinced the rapist was in the real estate community, but with no arrest ever made, he never proved his theory.

Added to this branch of his investigation, Levin could find little to confirm that Mary Alice Windsor had been one of the unreported victims of the rapist. She had granted us an interview and agreed to testify about her secret tragedy but only if her testimony was vitally needed. The date of the attack she provided fell within the dates of the documented assaults attributed to the Real Estate Rapist, and Windsor provided an appointment book and other documentation showing she was indeed the realtor on record in regard to the sale of the Bel-Air home where she said she was attacked. But ultimately we only had her word for it. There were no medical or hospital records indicative of treatment for a sexual assault. And no police record.

Still, when Mary Windsor recounted her story, it matched Roulet's telling of it in almost all details. Afterward, it had struck both Levin and me as odd that Louis had known so much about the attack. If his mother had decided to keep it secret and unreported, then why would she share so many details of her harrowing ordeal with her son? That question led Levin to postulate a theory that was as repulsive as it was intriguing.

"I think he knows all the details because he was there," Levin had said after the interview and we were by ourselves.

"You mean he watched it without doing anything to stop it?"

"No, I mean I think he was the man in the ski mask and goggles."

I was silent. I think on a subliminal level I may have been thinking the same thing but the idea was too creepy to have broken through to the surface.

"Oh, man...," I said.

Levin, thinking I was disagreeing, pressed his case forward.

"This is a very strong woman," he said. "She built that company from nothing and real estate in this town is cutthroat. She's a tough lady and I can't see her not reporting this, not wanting the guy who did it to be caught. I view people two ways. They're either eye-for-an-eye people or they are turn-the-cheek people. She's definitely an eye-for-an-eye person and I can't see her keeping it quiet unless she was protecting that guy. Unless that guy was our guy. I'm telling you, man, Roulet is evil. I don't know where it comes from or how he got it, but the more I look at him, the more I see the devil."

All of this backgrounding was completely sub rosa. It obviously was not the kind of background that would in any way be brought forward as a means of defense. It had to be hidden from discovery, so little of what Levin or I found was put down on paper. But it was still information that I had to know as I made my decisions and set up the trial and the play within it.

At 11:05 my home phone rang as I was standing in front of a mirror and fitting a Dodgers cap onto my head. I checked the caller ID before answering and saw that it was Lorna Taylor.

"Why is your cell phone off?" she asked.

"Because I'm off. I told you, no calls today. I'm going to the ballgame with Mish and I'm supposed to get going to meet him early."

"Who's Mish?"

"I mean Raul. Why are you bothering me?"

I said it good-naturedly.

"Because I think you are going to want to be bothered with this. The mail came in a little early today and with it you got a notice from the Second."

The Second District Court of Appeal reviewed all cases emanating from L.A. County. They were the first appellate hurdle on the way to the Supreme Court. But I didn't think Lorna would be calling me to tell me I had lost an appeal.

"Which case?"

At any given time I usually have four or five cases on appeal to the Second.

"One of your Road Saints. Harold Casey. You won!"

I was shocked. Not at winning, but at the timing. I had tried to move quickly with the appeal. I had written the brief before the verdict had come in and paid extra for expedited daily transcripts from the trial. I filed the notice of appeal the day after the verdict and asked for an expedited review. Even still, I wasn't expecting to hear anything on Casey for another two months.

I asked Lorna to read the opinion and a smile widened on my face. The summary was literally a rewrite of my brief. The three-judge panel had agreed with me right down the line on my contention that the low flyover of the sheriff's surveillance helicopter above Casey's ranch constituted an invasion of privacy. The court overturned Casey's conviction, saying that the search that led to the discovery of the hydroponic pot farm was illegal.

The state would now have to decide whether to retry Casey and, realistically, a retrial was out of the question. The state would have no evidence, since the appeals court ruled everything garnered during the search of the ranch was inadmissible. The Second's ruling was clearly a victory for the defense, and they don't come that often.

"Man, what a day for the underdog!"

"Where is he, anyway?" Lorna asked.

"He may still be at the reception center but they were moving him to Corcoran. Here's what you do. Make about ten copies of the ruling and put them in an envelope and send it to Casey at Corcoran. You should have the address."

"Well, won't they be letting him go?"

"Not yet. His parole was violated after his arrest and the appeal doesn't affect that. He won't get out until he goes to the parole board and argues fruit of the poisonous tree, that he got violated because of an illegal search. It will probably take about six weeks for all that to work itself out."

"Six weeks? That's unbelievable."

"Don't do the crime if you can't do the time."

I sang it like Sammy Davis did on that old television show.

"Please don't sing to me, Mick."

"Sorry."

"Why are we sending ten copies to him? Isn't one enough?"

"Because he'll keep one for himself and spread the other nine around the prison and then your phone will start ringing. An attorney who can win on appeal is like gold in prison. They'll come calling and you're going to have to weed 'em out and find the ones who have family and can pay."

"You always have an angle, don't you?"

"I try to. Anything else happening?"

"Just the usual. The calls you told me you didn't want to hear about. Did you get in to see Glory Days yesterday at County?"

"It's Gloria Dayton and, yes, I got in to see her. She looks like she's over the hump. She's still got more than a month to go."

The truth was, Gloria Dayton looked better than over the hump. I hadn't seen her so sharp and bright-eyed in years. I'd had a purpose for going down to County-USC Medical Center to talk to her, but seeing her on the downhill side of recovery was a nice bonus.

As expected, Lorna was the doomsayer.

"And how long will it last this time before she calls your number again and says, 'I'm in jail. I need Mickey'?"

She said the last part with a whiny, nasal impression of Gloria Dayton. It was quite accurate but it annoyed me anyway. Then she topped it with a little song to the tune of the Disney classic.

"M-I-C..., see you real soon. K-E-Y..., why, because you never charge me! M-O-U-T-H. Mickey Mouth...Mickey Mouth, the lawyer every—"

"Please don't sing to me, Lorna."

She laughed into the phone.

"I'm just making a point."

I was smiling but trying to keep it out of my voice.

"Fine. I get it. I have to get going now."

"Well, have a great time...Mickey Mouth."

"You could sing that song all day and the Dodgers could lose twenty-zip to the Giants and I'd still have a great time. After hearing the news from you, what could go wrong?"

After ending the call I went into my home office and got a cell number for Teddy Vogel, the outside leader of the Saints. I gave him the good news and suggested that he could probably pass it on to Hard Case faster than I could. There are Road Saints in every prison. They have a communication system the CIA and FBI might be able to learn something from. Vogel said he'd handle it. Then he said the ten grand he gave me the month before on the side of the road near Vasquez Rocks was a worthy investment.

"I appreciate that, Ted," I said. "Keep me in mind next time you need an attorney."

"Will do, Counselor."

He clicked off and I clicked off. I then grabbed my first baseman's glove out of the hallway closet and headed out the front door.

Having given Earl the day off with pay, I drove myself toward downtown and Dodger Stadium. Traffic was light until I got close. The home opener is always a sell-out, even though it is a day game on a weekday. The start of baseball season is a rite of spring that draws downtown workers by the thousands. It's the only sporting event in laid-back L.A. where you see men all in stiff white shirts and ties. They're all playing hooky. There is nothing like the start of a season, before all the one-run losses, pitching break-downs and missed opportunities. Before reality sets in.

I was the first one to the seats. We were three rows from the field in seats added to the stadium during the off-season. Levin must have busted a nut buying the tickets from one of the local brokers. At least it was probably deductible as a business entertainment expense.

The plan was for Levin to get there early as well. He had called the night before and said he wanted some private time with me. Besides watching batting practice and checking out all the improvements the new owner had made to the stadium, we would discuss my visit with Gloria Dayton and Raul would give me the latest update on his various investigations relating to Louis Roulet.

But Levin never made it for BP. The other four lawyers showed up—three of them in ties, having come from court—and we missed our chance to talk privately.

I knew the other four from some of the boat cases we had tried together. In fact, the tradition of defense pros taking in Dodgers games together started with the boat cases. Under a wide-ranging mandate to stop drug flow to the United States, the U.S. Coast Guard had taken to stopping suspect vessels anywhere on the oceans. When they struck gold—or, that is, cocaine—they seized the vessels and crews. Many of the prosecutions were funneled to the U.S. District Court in Los Angeles. This resulted in prosecutions of sometimes twelve or more defendants at a time. Every defendant got his own lawyer, most of them appointed by the court and paid by Uncle Sugar. The cases were lucrative and steady and we had fun. Somebody had the idea of having case meetings at Dodger Stadium. One time we all pitched in and bought a private suite for a Cubs game. We actually did talk about the case for a few minutes during the seventh-inning stretch.

The pre-game ceremonies started and there was no sign of Levin. Hundreds of doves were released from baskets on the field and they formed up, circled the stadium to loud cheering and then flew up and away. Shortly after, a B-2 stealth bomber buzzed the stadium to even louder applause. That was L.A. Something for everyone and a little irony to boot.

The game started and still no Levin. I turned my cell phone on and tried to call him, even though it was hard to hear. The crowd was loud and boisterous, hopeful of a season that would not end in disappointment again. The call went to a message.

"Mish, where you at, man? We're at the game and the seats are fantastic, but we got one empty one. We're waiting on you."

I closed the phone, looked at the others and shrugged.

"I don't know," I said. "He didn't answer his cell."

I left my phone on and put it back on my belt.

Before the first inning was over I was regretting what I had said to Lorna about not caring if the Giants drilled us 20–zip. They built a 5–0 lead before the Dodgers even got their first bats of the season and the crowd grew frustrated early. I heard people complaining about the prices, the renovation and the overcommercialization of the stadium. One of the lawyers, Roger Mills, surveyed the surfaces of the stadium and remarked that the place was more crowded with corporate logos than a NASCAR race car.

The Dodgers were able to bite into the lead, but in the fourth inning the wheels came off and the Giants chased Jeff Weaver with a three-run shot over the centerfield wall. I used the downtime during the pitching change to brag about how fast I had heard from the Second on the Casey case. The other lawyers were impressed, though one of them, Dan Daly, suggested that I had only received the quick appellate review because the three judges were on my Christmas list. I remarked to Daly that he had apparently missed the bar memo regarding juries' distrust of lawyers with ponytails. His went halfway down his back.

It was also during this lull in the game that I heard my phone ringing. I grabbed it off my hip and flipped it open without looking at the screen.

"Raul?"

"No, sir, this is Detective Lankford with the Glendale Police Department. Is this Michael Haller?"

"Yes," I said.

"Do you have a moment?"

"I have a moment but I am not sure how well I'll be able to hear you. I'm at the Dodgers game. Can this wait until I can call you back?"

"No, sir, it can't. Do you know a man named Raul Aaron Levin? He's a—"

"Yes, I know him. What's wrong?"

"I'm afraid Mr. Levin is dead, sir. He's been the victim of a homicide in his home."

My head dropped so low and so forward that I banged it into the back of the man seated in front of me. I then pulled back and held one hand to one ear and pressed the phone against the other. I blanked out everything around me.

"What happened?"

"We don't know," Lankford said. "That's why we are here. It looks like he was working for you recently. Is there any chance you could come here to possibly answer some questions and assist us?"

I blew out my breath and tried to keep my voice calm and modulated.

"I'm on my way," I said.

23

Raul Levin's body was in the back room of his bungalow a few blocks off of Brand Boulevard. The room had likely been designed as a sunroom or maybe a TV room but Raul had turned it into his home office. Like me he'd had no need for a commercial space. His was not a walk-in business. He wasn't even in the yellow pages. He worked for attorneys and got jobs by word of mouth. The five lawyers that were to join him at the baseball game were testimony to his skill and success.

The uniformed cops who had been told to expect me made me wait in the front living room until the detectives could come from the back and talk to me. A uniformed officer stood by in the hallway in case I decided to make a mad dash for the back room or the front door. He was in position to handle it either way. I sat there waiting and thinking about my friend.

I had decided on the drive from the stadium that I knew who had killed Raul Levin. I didn't need to be led to the back room to see or hear the evidence to know who the killer was. Deep down I knew that Raul had gotten too close to Louis Roulet. And I was the one who had sent him. The only question left for me was what was I going to do about it.

After twenty minutes two detectives came from the back of the house and into the living room. I stood up and we talked while standing. The man identified himself as Lankford, the detective who had called me. He was older, the veteran. His partner was a woman named Sobel. She didn't look like she had been investigating homicides for very long.

We didn't shake hands. They were wearing rubber gloves. They also had paper booties over their shoes. Lankford was chewing gum.

"Okay, this is what we've got," he said gruffly. "Levin was in his office, sitting in his desk chair. The chair was turned from the desk, so he was facing the intruder. He was shot one time in the chest. Something small, looks like a twenty-two to me but we'll wait on the coroner for that."

Lankford tapped his chest dead center. I could hear the hard sound of a bullet-proof vest beneath his shirt.

I corrected him. He had pronounced the name here and on the phone earlier as Levine. I said the name rhymed with heaven.

"Levin, then," he said, getting it right. "Anyway, after the shot, he tried to get up or just fell forward to the floor. He expired facedown on the floor. The intruder ransacked the office and we are currently at a loss to determine what he was looking for or what he might have taken."

"Who found him?" I asked.

"A neighbor who found his dog running loose. The intruder must have let the dog out before or after the killing. The neighbor found it wandering around, recognized it and brought it back. She found the front door open, came in and found the body. It didn't look like much of a watchdog, you ask me. It's one of those little hair balls."

"A shih tzu," I said.

I had seen the dog before and heard Levin talk about it, but I couldn't remember its name. It was something like Rex or Bronco—a name that belied the dog's small stature.

Sobel referred to a notebook she was holding before continuing the questioning.

"We haven't found anything that can lead us to next of kin," she said. "Do you know if he had any family?"

"I think his mother lives back east. He was born in Detroit. Maybe she's there. I don't think they had much of a relationship."

She nodded.

"We have found his time and hours calendar. He's got your name on almost every day for the last month. Was he working on a specific case for you?"

I nodded.

"A couple different cases. One mostly."

"Do you care to tell us about it?" she asked.

"I have a case about to go to trial. Next month. It's an attempted rape and murder. He was running down the evidence and helping me to get ready."

"You mean helping you try to backdoor the investigation, huh?" Lankford said.

I realized then that Lankford's politeness on the phone was merely sweet talk to get me to come to the house. He would be different now. He even seemed to be chewing his gum more aggressively than when he had first entered the room.

"Whatever you want to call it, Detective. Everybody is entitled to a defense."

"Yeah, sure, and they're all innocent, only it's their parents' fault for taking them off the tit too soon," Lankford said. "Whatever. This guy Levin was a cop before, right?"

He was back to mispronouncing the name.

"Yes, he was LAPD. He was a detective on a Crimes Against Persons squad but he retired after twelve years on the force. I think it was twelve years. You'll have to check. And it's Levin."

"Right, as in heaven. I guess he couldn't hack working for the good guys, huh?"

"Depends on how you look at it, I guess."

"Can we get back to your case?" Sobel asked. "What is the name of the defendant?"

"Louis Ross Roulet. The trial's in Van Nuys Superior before Judge Fullbright."

"Is he in custody?"

"No, he's out on a bond."

"Any animosity between Roulet and Mr. Levin?"

"Not that I know of."

I had decided. I was going to deal with Roulet in the way I knew how. I was sticking with the plan I had concocted — with the help of Raul Levin. Drop a depth charge into the case and make sure to get clear. I felt I owed it to my friend Mish. He would have wanted it this way. I wouldn't farm it out. I would handle it personally.

"Could this have been a gay thing?" Lankford asked.

"What? Why do you say that?"

"Prissy dog and then all around the house, he's only got pictures of guys and the dog. Everywhere. On the walls, next to the bed, on the piano."

"Look closely, Detective. It is probably one guy. His partner died a few years ago. I don't think he's been with anybody since then."

"Died of AIDS, I bet."

I didn't confirm that for him. I just waited. On the one hand, I was annoyed with Lankford's manner. On the other hand, I figured that his torch-the-ground method of investigation would preclude him from being able to tag Roulet with this. That was fine with me. I only needed to stall him for five or six weeks and then I wouldn't care if they put it together or not. I'd be finished with my own play by then.

"Did this guy go out patrolling the gay joints?" Lankford asked.

I shrugged.

"I have no idea. But if it was a gay murder, why was his office ransacked and not the rest of the house?"

Lankford nodded. He seemed to be momentarily taken aback by the logic of my question. But then he hit me with a surprise punch.

"So where were you this morning, Counselor?"

"What?"

"It's just routine. The scene indicates the victim knew his killer. He let the shooter right into the back room. As I said before, he was probably sitting in his desk chair when he took the bullet. Looks to me like he was quite comfortable with his killer. We are going to have to clear all acquaintances, professional and social."

"Are you saying I'm a suspect in this?"

"No, I'm just trying to clear things up and tighten the focus."

"I was home all morning. I was getting ready to meet Raul at Dodger Stadium. I left for the stadium about twelve and that's where I was when you called."

"What about before that?"

"Like I said, I was home. I was alone. But I got a phone call about eleven that will put me in my house and I'm at least a half hour from here. If he was killed after eleven, then I'm clear."

Lankford didn't rise to the bait. He didn't give me the time of death. Maybe it was unknown at the moment.

"When was the last time you spoke to him?" he asked instead.

"Last night by telephone."

"Who called who and why?"

"He called me and asked if I could get to the game early. I said I could."

"How come?"

"He likes to — he liked to watch batting practice. He said we could jaw over the Roulet case a little bit. Nothing specific but he hadn't updated me in about a week."

"Thank you for your cooperation," Lankford said, sarcasm heavy in his voice.

"You realize that I just did what I tell every client and anybody who will listen not to do? I talked to you without a lawyer present, gave you my alibi. I must be out of my mind."

"I said thank you."

Sobel spoke up.

"Is there anything else you can tell us, Mr. Haller? About Mr. Levin or his work."

"Yeah, there is one other thing. Something you should probably check out. But I want to remain confidential on it."

I looked past them at the uniformed officer still standing in the hallway. Sobel followed my eyes and understood I wanted privacy.

"Officer, you can wait out front, please," she said.

The officer left, looking annoyed, probably because he had been dismissed by a woman.

"Okay," Lankford said. "What have you got?"

"I'll have to look up the exact dates but a few weeks ago, back in March, Raul did some work for me on another case that involved one of my clients snitching off a drug dealer. He made some calls, helped ID the guy. I heard afterward that the guy was a Colombian and he was pretty well connected. He could have had friends who..."

I left it for them to fill in the blanks.

"I don't know," Lankford said. "This was pretty clean. Doesn't look like a revenge deal. They didn't cut his throat or take his tongue. One shot, plus they ransacked the office. What would the dealer's people be looking for?"

I shook my head.

"Maybe my client's name. The deal I made kept it out of circulation."

Lankford nodded thoughtfully.

"What is the client's name?"

"I can't tell you. Attorney-client privilege."

"Okay, here we go with that bullshit. How are we going to investigate this if we don't even know your client's name? Don't you care about your friend in there on the floor with a piece of lead in his heart?"

"Yes, I care. I'm obviously the only one here who does care. But I am also bound by the rules and ethics of law."

"Your client could be in danger."

"My client is safe. My client is in lockdown."

"It's a woman, isn't it?" Sobel said. "You keep saying 'client' instead of he or she."

"I'm not talking to you about my client. If you want the name of the dealer, it's Hector Arrande Moya. He's in federal custody. I believe the originating charge came out of a DEA case in San Diego. That's all I can tell you."

Sobel wrote it all down. I believed I had now given them sufficient reason to look beyond Roulet and the gay angle.

"Mr. Haller, have you ever been in Mr. Levin's office before?" Sobel asked.

"A few times. Not in a couple months, at least."

"Do you mind walking back with us anyway? Maybe you'll see something out of place or notice something that's missing."

"Is he still back there?"

"The victim? Yes, he's still as he was found."

I nodded. I wasn't sure I wanted to see Raul Levin's body in the center of a murder scene. I then decided all at once that I must see him and I must not forget the vision. I would need it to fuel my resolve and my plan.

"Okay, I'll go back."

"Then put these on and don't touch anything while you're back there," Lankford said. "We're still processing the scene."

From his pocket he produced a folded pair of paper booties. I sat down on Raul's couch and put them on. Then I followed them down the hallway to the death room.

Raul Levin's body was in situ — as they had found it. He was chest-down on the floor, his face turned to his right, his mouth and eyes open. His body was in an awkward posture, one hip higher than the other and his arms and hands beneath him. It seemed clear that he had fallen from the desk chair that was behind him.

I immediately regretted my decision to come into the room. I suddenly knew that the final look on Raul's face would crowd out all other visual memories I had of him. I would be forced to try to forget him, so I would not have to look at those eyes in my mind again.

It was the same with my father. My only visual memory was of a man in a bed. He was a hundred pounds tops and was being ravaged from the inside out by cancer. All the other visuals I carried of him were false. They came from pictures in books I had read.

There were a number of people working in the room. Crime scene investigators and people from the medical examiner's office. My face must have shown the horror I was feeling.

"You know why we can't cover him up?" Lankford asked me. "Because of people like you. Because of O.J. It's what they call *evidence transference*. Something you lawyers like to jump all over on. So no sheets over the body anymore. Not till we move it out of here."

I didn't say anything. I just nodded. He was right.

"Can you step over here to the desk and tell us if you see anything unusual?" Sobel asked, apparently having some sympathy for me.

I was thankful to do it because I could keep my back to the body. I walked over to the desk, which was a conjoining of three worktables forming a turn in the corner of the room. It was furniture I recognized had come from the IKEA store in nearby Burbank. It was nothing fancy. It was simple and useful. The center table in the corner had a computer on top and a pull-out tray for a keyboard. The tables to either side looked like twin work spaces and possibly were used by Levin to keep separate investigations from mingling.

My eyes lingered on the computer as I wondered what Levin may have put on electronic files about Roulet. Sobel noticed.

"We don't have a computer expert," she said. "Too small a department.

We've got a guy coming from the sheriff's office but it looks to me like the whole drive was pulled out."

She pointed with her pen under the table to where the PC unit was sitting upright but with one side of its plastic cowling having been removed and placed to the rear.

"Probably won't be anything there for us," she said. "What about the desks?"

My eyes moved over the table to the left of the computer first. Papers and files were spread across it in a haphazard way. I looked at some of the tabs and recognized the names.

"Some of these are my clients but they're old cases. Not active."

"They probably came from the file cabinets in the closet," Sobel said. "The killer could have dumped them here to confuse us. To hide what he was really looking for or taking. What about over here?"

We stepped over to the table to the right of the computer. This one was not in as much disarray. There was a calendar blotter on which it was clear Levin kept a running account of his hours and which attorney he was working for at the time. I scanned the blocks and saw my name numerous times going back five weeks. It was as they had told me, he had practically been working full-time for me.

"I don't know," I said. "I don't know what to look for. I don't see anything that could help."

"Well, most attorneys aren't that helpful," Lankford said from behind me.

I didn't bother to turn around to defend myself. He was by the body and I didn't want to see what he was doing. I reached out to turn the Rolodex that was on the table just so I could look through the names on the cards.

"Don't touch that!" Sobel said instantly.

I jerked my hand back.

"Sorry. I was just going to look through the names. I don't..."

I didn't finish. I was at sea here. I wanted to leave and get something to drink. I felt like the Dodger dog that had tasted so good back at the stadium was about to come up.

"Hey, check it out," Lankford said.

I turned with Sobel and saw that the medical examiner's people were slowly turning Levin's body over. Blood had stained the front of the Dodgers shirt he was wearing. But Lankford was pointing to the dead man's hands, which had not been visible beneath the body before. The two middle fingers of his left hand were folded down against the palm while the two outside fingers were fully extended.

"Was this guy a Texas Longhorns fan or what?" Lankford asked.

Nobody laughed.

"What do you think?" Sobel said to me.

I stared down at my friend's last gesture and just shook my head.

"Oh, I got it," Lankford said. "It's like a signal. A code. He's telling us that the devil did it."

I thought of Raul calling Roulet the devil, of having the proof that he was evil. And I knew what my friend's last message to me meant. As he died on the floor of his office, he tried to tell me. Tried to warn me.

24

I went to Four Green Fields and ordered a Guinness but quickly escalated to vodka over ice. I didn't think there was any sense in delaying things. The Dodgers game was finishing up on the TV over the bar. The boys in blue were rallying, down now by just two with the bases loaded in the ninth. The bartender had his eyes glued to the screen but I didn't care anymore about the start of new seasons. I didn't care about ninth-inning rallies.

After the second vodka assault, I brought the cell phone up onto the bar and started making calls. First I called the four other lawyers from the game. We had all left when I had gotten the word but they went home only knowing that Levin was dead, none of the details. Then I called Lorna and she cried on the phone. I talked her through it for a little while and then she asked the question I was hoping to avoid.

"Is this because of your case? Because of Roulet?"

"I don't know," I lied. "I told the cops about it but they seemed more interested in him being gay than anything else."

"He was gay?"

I knew it would work as a deflection.

"He didn't advertise it."

"And you knew and didn't tell me?"

"There was nothing to tell. It was his life. If he wanted to tell people, he would have told people, I guess."

"The detectives said that's what happened?"

"What?"

"You know, that his being gay is how he got murdered."

"I don't know. They kept asking about it. I don't know what they think. They'll look at everything and hopefully it will lead to something."

There was silence. I looked up at the TV just as the winning run crossed the plate for the Dodgers and the stadium erupted in bedlam and joy. The bartender whooped and used a remote to turn up the broadcast. I looked away and put a hand over my free ear.

"Makes you think, doesn't it?" Lorna said.

"About what?"

"About what we do. Mickey, when they catch the bastard who did this, he might call me to hire you."

I got the bartender's attention by shaking the ice in my empty glass. I wanted a refill. What I didn't want was to tell Lorna that I believed I was already working for the bastard who had killed Raul.

"Lorna, take it easy. You're getting—"

"It could happen!"

"Look, Raul was my colleague and he was also my friend. But I'm not going to change what I do or what I believe in because—"

"Maybe you should. Maybe we all should. That's all I'm saying."

She started crying again. The bartender brought my fresh drink and I took a third of it down in one gulp.

"Lorna, do you want me to come over there?"

"No, I don't want anything. I don't know what I want. This is just so awful."

"Can I tell you something?"

"What? Of course you can."

"You remember Jesus Menendez? My client?"

"Yes, but what's he have—"

"He was innocent. And Raul was working on it. We were working on it. We're going to get him out."

"Why are you telling me this?"

"I'm telling you because we can't take what happened to Raul and just stop in our tracks. What we do is important. It's necessary."

The words sounded hollow as I said them. She didn't respond. I had probably confused her because I had confused myself.

"Okay?" I asked.

"Okay."

"Good. I have to make some more calls, Lorna."

"Will you tell me when you find out about the services?"

"I will."

After closing my phone I decided to take a break before making another call. I thought about Lorna's last question and realized I might be the one organizing the services she asked about. Unless an old woman in Detroit who had disowned Raul Levin twenty-five years ago stepped up to the plate.

I pushed my glass to the edge of the bar gutter and said to the bartender, "Gimme a Guinness and give yourself one, too."

I decided it was time to slow down and one way was to drink Guinness, since it took so long to fill a glass out of the tap. When the bartender finally brought it to me I saw that he had etched a harp in the foam with the tap nozzle. An angel's harp. I hoisted the glass before drinking from it.

"God bless the dead," I said.

"God bless the dead," the bartender said.

I drank heavily from the glass and the thick ale was like mortar I was sending down to hold the bricks together inside. All at once I felt like crying. But then my phone rang. I grabbed it up without looking at the screen and said hello. The alcohol had bent my voice into an unrecognizable shape.

"Is this Mick?" a voice asked.

"Yeah, who's this?"

"It's Louis. I just heard the news about Raul. I'm so sorry, man."

I pulled the phone away from my ear as if it were a snake about to bite me. I pulled my arm back, ready to throw it at the mirror behind the bar, where I saw my own reflection. Then I stopped and brought it back.

"Yeah, motherfucker, how did you—"

I broke off and started laughing as I realized what I had just called him and what Raul Levin's theory about Roulet had been.

"Excuse me," Roulet said. "Are you drinking?"

"You're damn right I'm drinking," I said. "How the fuck do you already know what happened to Mish?"

"If by Mish you mean Mr. Levin, I just got a call from the Glendale police. A detective said she wanted to speak to me about him."

That answer squeezed at least two of the vodkas right out of my liver. I straightened up on my stool.

"Sobel? Is that who called?"

"Yeah, I think so. She said she got my name from you. She said it would be routine questions. She's coming here."

"Where?"

"The office."

I thought about it for a moment but didn't think Sobel was in any kind of danger, even if she came without Lankford. Roulet wouldn't try anything with a cop, especially in his own office. My greater concern was that somehow Sobel and Lankford were already onto Roulet and I would be robbed of my chance to personally avenge Raul Levin and Jesus Menendez. Had Roulet left a fingerprint behind? Had a neighbor seen him go into Levin's house?

"That's all she said?"

"Yes. She said they were talking to all of his recent clients and I was the most recent."

"Don't talk to them."

"You sure?"

"Not without your lawyer present."

"Won't they get suspicious if I don't talk to them, like give them an alibi or something?"

"It doesn't matter. They don't talk to you unless I give my permission. And I'm not giving it."

I gripped my free hand into a fist. I couldn't stand the idea of giving legal advice to the man I was sure had killed my friend that very morning.

"Okay," Roulet said. "I'll send her on her way."

"Where were you this morning?"

"Me? I was here at the office. Why?"

"Did anybody see you?"

"Well, Robin came in at ten. Not before that."

I pictured the woman with the hair cut like a scythe. I didn't know what to tell Roulet because I didn't know what the time of death was. I didn't want to mention anything about the tracking bracelet he supposedly had on his ankle.

"Call me after Detective Sobel leaves. And remember, no matter what she or her partner says to you, do not talk to them. They can lie to you as much as they want. And they all do. Consider anything they tell you to be a lie. They're just trying to trick you into talking to them. If they tell you I said it was okay to talk, that is a lie. Pick up the phone and call me, I will tell them to get lost."

"All right, Mick. That's how I'll play it. Thanks."

He ended the call. I closed my phone and dropped it on the bar like it was something dirty and discarded.

"Yeah, don't mention it," I said.

I drained a good quarter of my pint, then picked up the phone again. Using speed dial I called Fernando Valenzuela's cell number. He was at home, having just gotten in from the Dodgers game. That meant that he had left early to beat the traffic. Typical L.A. fan.

"Do you still have a tracking bracelet on Roulet?"

"Yeah, he's got it."

"How's it work? Can you track where he's been or only where he's at?"

"It's global positioning. It sends up a signal. You can track it backwards to tell where somebody's been."

"You got it there or is it at the office?"

"It's on my laptop, man. What's up?"

"I want to see where he's been today."

"Well, let me boot it up. Hold on."

I held on, finished my Guinness and had the bartender start filling another before Valenzuela had his laptop fired up.

"Where're you at, Mick?"

"Four Green Fields."

"Anything wrong?"

"Yeah, something's wrong. Do you have it up or what?"

"Yeah, I'm looking at it right here. How far back do you want to check?"

"Start at this morning."

"Okay. He, uh...he hasn't done much today. I track it from his home to his office at eight. Looks like he took a little trip nearby—a couple blocks, probably for lunch—and then back to the office. He's still there."

I thought about this for a few moments. The bartender delivered my next pint.

"Val, how do you get that thing off your ankle?"

"You mean if you were him? You don't. You can't. It bolts on and the little wrench you use is unique. It's like a key. I got the only one."

"You're sure about that?"

"I'm sure. I got it right here on my key chain, man."

"No copies — like from the manufacturer?"

"Not supposed to be. Besides, it doesn't matter. If the ring is broken — like even if he did open it — I get an alarm on the system. It also has what's called a 'mass detector.' Once I put that baby around his ankle, I get an alarm on the computer the moment it reads that there is nothing there. That didn't happen, Mick. So you are talking about a saw being the only way. Cut off the leg, leave the bracelet on the ankle. That's the only way."

I drank the top off my new beer. The bartender hadn't bothered with any artwork this time.

"What about the battery? What if the battery's dead, you lose the signal?"

"No, Mick. I got that covered, too. He's got a charger and a receptacle on the bracelet. Every few days he's got to plug it in for a couple hours to juice it. You know, while he's at his desk or something or taking a nap. If the battery goes below twenty percent I get an alarm on my computer and I call him and say plug it in. If he doesn't do it then, I get another alarm at fifteen percent, and then at ten percent *he* starts beeping and he's got no way to take it off or turn it off. Doesn't make for a good getaway. And that last ten percent still gives me five hours of tracking. I can find him in five hours, no sweat."

"Okay, okay."

I was convinced by the science.

"What's going on?"

I told him about Levin and told him that the police would likely have to check out Roulet, and the ankle bracelet and tracking system would likely be our client's alibi. Valenzuela was stunned by the news. He might not have been as close to Levin as I had been, but he had known him just as long.

"What do you think happened, Mick?" he asked me.

I knew that he was asking if I thought Roulet was the killer or somehow behind the killing. Valenzuela was not privy to all that I knew or that Levin had found out.

"I don't know what to think," I said. "But you should watch yourself with this guy."

"And you watch yourself."

"I will."

I closed the phone, wondering if there was something Valenzuela didn't know. If Roulet had somehow found a way to take the ankle bracelet off or to subvert the tracking system. I was convinced by the science of it but not the human side of it. There are always human flaws.

The bartender sauntered over to my spot at the bar.

"Hey, buddy, did you lose your car keys?" he said.

I looked around to make sure he was talking to me and then shook my head.

"No," I said.

"Are you sure? Somebody found keys in the parking lot. You better check."

I reached into the pocket of my suit jacket, then brought my hand out and extended it, palm up. My key ring was displayed on my hand.

"See, I tol—"

In a quick and unexpected move, the bartender grabbed the keys off my hand and smiled.

"Falling for that should be a sobriety test in and of itself," he said. "Anyway, pal, you're not driving—not for a while. When you're ready to go, I'll call you a taxi."

He stepped back from the bar in case I had a violent objection to the ruse. But I just nodded.

"You got me," I said.

He tossed my keys onto the back counter, where the bottles were lined up. I looked at my watch. It wasn't even five o'clock. Embarrassment burned through the alcohol padding. I had taken the easy way out. The coward's way, getting drunk in the face of a terrible occurrence.

"You can take it," I said, pointing to my glass of Guinness.

I picked up the phone and punched in a speed-dial number. Maggie McPherson answered right away. The courts usually closed by four-thirty. The prosecutors were usually at their desks in that last hour or two before the end of the day.

"Hey, is it quitting time yet?"

"Haller?"

"Yeah."

"What's going on? Are you drinking? Your voice is different."

"I think I might need you to drive *me* home this time."

"Where are you?"

"For Greedy Fucks."

"What?"

"Four Green Fields. I've been here awhile."

"Michael, what is—"

"Raul Levin is dead."

"Oh my God, what—"

"Murdered. So this time can you drive *me* home? I've had too much."

"Let me call Stacey and get her to stay late with Hayley, then I'll be on my way. Do not try to leave there, okay? Just don't leave."

"Don't worry, the bartender isn't gonna let me."

25

After closing my phone I told the bartender I had changed my mind and I'd have one more pint while waiting for my ride. I took out my wallet and put a credit card on the bar. He ran my tab first, then got me the Guinness. He took so long filling the glass, spooning foam over the side to give me a full pour, that I had barely tasted it by the time Maggie got there.

"That was too quick," I said. "You want a drink?"

"No, it's too early. Let's just get you home."

"Okay."

I got off the stool, remembered to collect my credit card and phone, and left the bar with my arm around her shoulders and feeling like I had poured more Guinness and vodka down the drain than my own throat.

"I'm right out front," Maggie said. "Four Greedy Fucks, how did you come up with that? Do four people own this place?"

"No, *for*, as in *for the people*. As in Haller *for the defense*. Not the number four. Greedy fucks as in lawyers."

"Thank you."

"Not you. You're not a lawyer. You're a prosecutor."

"How much did you drink, Haller?"

"Somewhere between too much and a lot."

"Don't puke in my car."

"I promise."

We got to the car, one of the cheap Jaguar models. It was the first car she had ever bought without me holding her hand and being involved in running down the choices. She'd gotten the Jag because it made her feel classy, but anybody who knew cars knew it was just a dressed-up Ford. I didn't spoil it for her. Whatever made her happy made me happy — except the time she thought divorcing me would make her life happier. That didn't do much for me.

She helped me in and then we were off.

"Don't pass out, either," she said as she pulled out of the parking lot. "I don't know the way."

"Just take Laurel Canyon over the hill. After that, it's just a left turn at the bottom."

Even though it was supposed to be a reverse commute, it took almost forty-five minutes in end-of-the-day traffic to get to Fareholm Drive. Along the way I told her about Raul Levin and what had happened. She didn't react like Lorna had because she had never known Levin. Though I had known him and used him as an investigator for years, he didn't become a friend until after we had divorced. In fact, it was Raul who had driven me home on more than one night from Four Green Fields as I was getting through the end of my marriage.

My garage opener was in the Lincoln back at the bar so I told her to just park in the opening in front of the garage. I also realized my front door key was on the ring that had the Lincoln's key and that had been confiscated by the bartender. We had to go down the side of the house to the back deck and get the spare key—the one Roulet had given me—from beneath an ashtray on the picnic table. We went in the back door, which led directly into my office. This was good because even in my inebriated state I was pleased that we avoided climbing the stairs to the front door. Not only would it have worn me out but she would have seen the view and been reminded of the inequities between life as a prosecutor and life as a greedy fuck.

"Ah, that's nice," she said. "Our little teacup."

I followed her eyes and saw she was looking at the photo of our daughter I kept on the desk. I thrilled at the idea I had inadvertently scored a point of some kind with her.

"Yeah," I said, fumbling any chance of capitalizing.

"Which way to the bedroom?" she asked.

"Well, aren't you being forward. To the right."

"Sorry, Haller, I'm not staying long. I only got a couple extra hours out of Stacey, and with that traffic, I've got to turn around and head back over the hill soon."

She walked me into the bedroom and we sat down next to each other on the bed.

"Thank you for doing this," I said.

"One good turn deserves another, I guess," she said.

"I thought I got my good turn that night I took you home."

She put her hand on my cheek and turned my face toward hers. She kissed me. I took this as confirmation that we actually had made love that night. I felt incredibly left out at not remembering.

"Guinness," she said, tasting her lips as she pulled away.

"And some vodka."

"Good combination. You'll be hurting in the morning."

"It's so early I'll be hurting tonight. Tell you what, why don't we go get dinner at Dan Tana's? Craig's on the door now and—"

"No, Mick. I have to go home to Hayley and you have to go to sleep."

I made a gesture of surrender.

"Okay, okay."

"Call me in the morning. I want to talk to you when you're sober."

"Okay."

"You want to get undressed and get under the covers?"

"No, I'm all right. I'll just..."

I leaned back on the bed and kicked my shoes off. I then rolled over to the edge and opened a drawer in the night table. I took out a bottle of Tylenol and a CD that had been given to me by a client named Demetrius Folks. He was a banger from Norwalk known on the street as Lil' Demon. He had told me once that he'd had a vision one night and that he knew he was destined to die young and violently. He gave me the CD and told me to play it when he was dead. And I did. Demetrius's prophecy came true. He was killed in a drive-by shooting about six months after he had given me the disc. In Magic Marker he had written *Wreckrium for Lil' Demon* on it. It was a collection of ballads he had burned off of Tupac CDs.

I loaded the CD into the Bose player on the night table and soon the rhythmic beat of "God Bless the Dead" started to play. The song was a salute to fallen comrades.

"You listen to this stuff?" Maggie asked, her eyes squinting at me in disbelief.

I shrugged as best I could while leaning on an elbow.

"Sometimes. It helps me understand a lot of my clients better."

"These are the people who should be in jail."

"Maybe some of them. But a lot of them have something to say. Some are true poets and this guy was the best of them."

"Was? Who is it, the one that got shot outside the car museum on Wilshire?"

"No, you're talking about Biggie Smalls. This is the late great Tupac Shakur."

"I can't believe you listen to this stuff."

"I told you. It helps me."

"Do me a favor. Do not listen to this around Hayley."

"Don't worry about it, I won't."

"I've gotta go."

"Just stay a little bit."

She complied but she sat stiffly on the edge of the bed. I could tell she was trying to pick up the lyrics. You needed an ear for it and it took some time. The next song was "Life Goes On," and I watched her neck and shoulders tighten as she caught some of the words.

"Can I please go now?" she asked.

"Maggie, just stay a few minutes."

I reached over and turned it down a little.

"Hey, I'll turn it off if you'll sing to me like you used to."

"Not tonight, Haller."

"Nobody knows the Maggie McFierce I know."

She smiled a little and I was quiet for a moment while I remembered those times.

"Maggie, why do you stay with me?"

"I told you, I can't stay."

"No, I don't mean tonight. I'm talking about how you stick with me, how you don't run me down with Hayley and how you're there when I need you. Like tonight. I don't know many people who have ex-wives who still like them."

She thought a little bit before answering.

"I don't know. I guess because I see a good man and a good father in there waiting to break out one day."

I nodded and hoped she was right.

"Tell me something. What would you do if you couldn't be a prosecutor?"

"Are you serious?"

"Yeah, what would you do?"

"I've never really thought about it. Right now I get to do what I've always wanted to do. I'm lucky. Why would I want to change?"

I opened the Tylenol bottle and popped two without a chaser. The next song was "So Many Tears," another ballad for all of those lost. It seemed appropriate.

"I think I'd be a teacher," she finally said. "Grade school. Little girls like Hayley."

I smiled.

"Mrs. McFierce, Mrs. McFierce, my dog ate my homework."

She slugged me on the arm.

"Actually, that's nice," I said. "You'd be a good teacher…except when you're sending kids off to detention without bail."

"Funny. What about you?"

I shook my head.

"I wouldn't be a good teacher."

"I mean what would you do if you weren't a lawyer."

"I don't know. But I've got three Town Cars. I guess I could start a limo service, take people to the airport."

Now she smiled at me.

"I'd hire you."

"Good. There's one customer. Give me a dollar and I'll tape it to the wall."

But the banter wasn't working. I leaned back, put my palms against my eyes and tried to push away the day, to push out the memory of Raul Levin on the floor of his house, eyes staring at a permanent black sky.

"You know what I used to be afraid of?" I asked.

"What?"

"That I wouldn't recognize innocence. That it would be there right in front of me and I wouldn't see it. I'm not talking about guilty or not guilty. I mean innocence. Just innocence."

She didn't say anything.

"But you know what I should have been afraid of?"

"What, Haller?"

"Evil. Pure evil."

"What do you mean?"

"I mean, most of the people I defend aren't evil, Mags. They're guilty, yeah, but they aren't evil. You know what I mean? There's a difference. You listen to them and you listen to these songs and you know why they make the choices they make. People are just trying to get by, just to live with what they're given, and some of them aren't given a damn thing in the first place. But evil is something else. It's different. It's like...I don't know. It's out there and when it shows up...I don't know. I can't explain it."

"You're drunk, that's why."

"All I know is I should have been afraid of one thing but I was afraid of the complete opposite."

She reached over and rubbed my shoulder. The last song was "to live & die in l.a.," and it was my favorite on the homespun CD. I started to softly hum and then I sang along with the refrain when it came up on the track.

> to live & die in l.a.
> it's the place to be
> you got to be there to know it
> ev'ybody wanna see

Pretty soon I stopped singing and pulled my hands down from my face. I fell asleep with my clothes on. I never heard the woman I had loved more than anyone else in my life leave the house. She would tell me later that the last thing I had mumbled before passing out was, "I can't do this anymore."

I wasn't talking about my singing.

26

Wednesday, April 13

I slept almost ten hours but I still woke up in darkness. It said 5:18 on the Bose. I tried to go back to the dream but the door was closed. By 5:30 I rolled out of bed, struggled for equilibrium, and hit the shower. I stayed under the spray until the hot-water tank ran cold. Then I got out and got dressed for another day of fighting the machine.

It was still too early to call Lorna to check on the day's schedule but I keep a calendar on my desk that is usually up-to-date. I went into the home office to check it and the first thing I noticed was a dollar bill taped to the wall over the desk.

My adrenaline jogged up a couple notches as my mind raced and I thought an intruder had left the money on the wall as some sort of threat or message. Then I remembered.

"Maggie," I said out loud.

I smiled and decided to leave the dollar bill taped to the wall.

I got the calendar out of the briefcase and checked my schedule. It looked like I had the morning free until an 11 A.M. hearing in San Fernando Superior. The case was a repeat client charged with possession of drug paraphernalia. It was a bullshit charge, hardly worth the time and money, but Melissa Menkoff was already on probation for a variety of drug offenses. If she took a fall for something as minor as drug paraphernalia, her probated sentence would kick in and she would end up behind a steel door for six to nine months.

That was all I had on the calendar. After San Fernando my day was clear and I silently congratulated myself for the foresight I must have used in keeping the day after opening day clear. Of course, I didn't know when I set up the schedule that the death of Raul Levin would send me into Four Green Fields so early, but it was good planning just the same.

The hearing on the Menkoff matter involved my motion to suppress the crack pipe found during a search of her vehicle after a reckless driving stop in Northridge. The pipe had been found in the closed center console of her car. She had told me that she had not given permission to the police to search the car but they did anyway. My argument was that there was no consent to search and no probable cause to search. If Menkoff had been pulled over by police for driving erratically, then there was no reason to search the closed compartments of her car.

It was a loser and I knew it, but Menkoff's father paid me well to do the best I could for his troubled daughter. And that was exactly what I was going to do at eleven o'clock in San Fernando Court.

For breakfast I had two Tylenols and chased them with fried eggs, toast and coffee. I doused the eggs liberally with pepper and salsa. It all hit the right spots and gave me the fuel to carry on the battle. I turned the pages of the *Times* as I ate, looking for a story on the murder of Raul Levin. Inexplicably, there was no story. I didn't understand this at first. Why would Glendale keep the wraps on this? Then I remembered that the *Times* put out several regional editions of the paper each morning. I lived on the Westside, and Glendale was considered part of the San Fernando Valley. News of a murder in the Valley may have been deemed by *Times* editors as unimportant to Westside readers, who had their own region's murders to worry about. I got no story on Levin.

I decided I would have to buy a second copy of the *Times* off a newsstand on the way to San Fernando Court and check again. Thoughts about which newsstand I would direct Earl Briggs to reminded me that I had no car. The Lincoln was in the parking lot at Four Green Fields—unless it had been stolen during the night—and I couldn't get my keys until the pub opened at eleven for lunch. I had a problem. I had seen Earl's car in the commuter lot where I picked him up each morning. It was a pimped-out Toyota with a low-rider profile and spinning chrome rims. My guess was that it had the permanent stink of weed in it, too. I didn't want to ride in it. In the north county it was an invitation to a police stop. In the south county it was an invitation to get shot at. I also didn't want Earl to pick me up at the house. I never let my drivers know where I live.

The plan I came up with was to take a cab to my warehouse in North Hollywood and use one of the new Town Cars. The Lincoln at Four Green Fields had over fifty thousand miles on it, anyway. Maybe breaking out the new wheels would help me get past the depression sure to set in because of Raul Levin.

After I had cleaned the frying pan and the dish in the sink I decided it was late enough to risk waking Lorna with a call to confirm my day's schedule. I went back into the home office and when I picked up the house phone to make the call I heard the broken dial tone that told me I had at least one message waiting.

I called the retrieval number and was told by an electronic voice that I had missed a call at 11:07 A.M. the day before. When the voice recited the number that the missed call had come from, I froze. The number was Raul Levin's cell phone. I had missed his last call.

"Hey, it's me. You probably left for the game already and I guess you got your cell turned off. If you don't get this I'll just catch you there. But I've got another ace for you. I guess you—"

He broke off for a moment at the background sound of a dog barking.

"—could say I've got Jesus's ticket out of the Q. I've gotta go, lad."

That was it. He hung up without a good-bye and had used that stupid brogue at the end. The brogue had always annoyed me. Now it sounded endearing. I missed it already.

I pushed the button to replay the message and listened again and then did it three more times before finally saving the message and hanging up. I then sat there in my desk chair and tried to apply the message to what I knew. The first puzzle involved the time of the call. I did not leave for the game until at least 11:30, yet I had somehow missed the call from Levin that had come in more than twenty minutes earlier.

This made no sense until I remembered the call from Lorna. At 11:07 I had been on the phone with Lorna. My home phone was used so infrequently and so few people had the number that I did not bother to have call waiting installed on the line. This meant that Levin's last call would have been kicked over to the voicemail system and I would have never known about it as I spoke to Lorna.

That explained the circumstances of the call but not its contents.

Levin had obviously found something. He was no lawyer but he certainly knew evidence and how to evaluate it. He had found something that could help me get Menendez out of prison. He had found Jesus's ticket out.

The last thing left to consider was the interruption of the dog barking and that was easy. I had been to Levin's home before and I knew the dog was a high-strung yapper. Every time I had come to the house, I had heard the dog start barking before I had even knocked on the door. The barking in the background on the phone message and Levin hurriedly ending the call told me someone was coming to his door. He had a visitor and it may very well have been his killer.

I thought about things for a few moments and decided that the timing of the call was something I could not in good conscience keep from the police. The contents of the message would raise new questions that I might have difficulty answering, but that was outweighed by the value of the call's timing. I went into the bedroom and dug through the pockets of the blue jeans I had worn the day before to the game. In one of the back pockets I found the ticket stub from the game and the business cards Lankford and Sobel had given me at the end of my visit to Levin's house.

I chose Sobel's card and noticed it only said *Detective Sobel* on it. No first name. I wondered why that was as I made the call. Maybe she was like me, with two different business cards in alternate pockets. One with her complete name in one, one with the more formal name in the other.

She answered the call right away and I decided to see what I could get from her before I gave her what I had.

"Anything new on the investigation?" I asked.

"Not a lot. Not a lot that I can share with you. We are sort of organizing the evidence we have. We got some ballistics back and —"

"They already did an autopsy?" I said. "That was quick."

"No, the autopsy won't be until tomorrow."

"Then how'd you get ballistics already?"

She didn't answer but then I figured it out.

"You found a casing. He was shot with an automatic that ejected the shell."

"You're good, Mr. Haller. Yes, we found a cartridge."

"I've done a lot of trials. And call me Mickey. It's funny, the killer ransacked the place but didn't pick up the shell."

"Maybe that's because it rolled across the floor and fell into a heating vent. The killer would have needed a screwdriver and a lot of time."

I nodded. It was a lucky break. I couldn't count the number of times clients had gone down because the cops had caught a lucky break. Then again, there were a lot of clients who walked because they caught the break. It all evened out in the end.

"So, was your partner right about it being a twenty-two?"

She paused before answering, deciding whether to cross some threshold of revealing case information to me, an involved party in the case but the enemy—a defense lawyer—nonetheless.

"He was right. And thanks to the markings on the cartridge, we even know the exact gun we are looking for."

I knew from questioning ballistics experts and firearms examiners in trials over the years that marks left on bullet casings during the firing process could identify the weapon even without the weapon in hand. With an automatic, the firing pin, breech block, ejector and extractor all leave signature marks on the bullet casing in the split second the weapon is fired. Analyzing the four markings in unison can lead to a specific make and model of the weapon being identified.

"It turns out that Mr. Levin owned a twenty-two himself," Sobel said. "But we found it in a closet safe in the house and it's not a Woodsman. The one thing we have not found is his cell phone. We know he had one but we—"

"He was talking to me on it right before he was killed."

There was a moment of silence.

"You told us yesterday that the last time you spoke to him was Friday night."

"That's right. But that's why I am calling. Raul called me yesterday morning at eleven-oh-seven and left me a message. I didn't get it until today because after I left you people yesterday I just went out and got drunk. Then I went to sleep and didn't realize I had a message from him till right now. He called about one of the cases he was working on for me sort of on the side. It's an appellate thing and the client's in prison. A no-rush thing. Anyway, the content of the message isn't important but the call helps with the timing. And get this, while he's leaving the message, you hear the dog start to bark. It did that whenever somebody came to the door. I know because I'd been there before and the dog always barked."

Again she hit me with some silence before responding.

"I don't understand something, Mr. Haller."

"What's that?"

"You told us yesterday you were at home until around noon before you left for the game. And now you say that Mr. Levin left a message for you at eleven-oh-seven. Why didn't you answer the phone?"

"Because I was on it and I don't have call waiting. You can check my records, you'll see I got a call from my office manager, Lorna Taylor. I was talking to her when Raul called. Without call waiting I didn't know. And of course he thought I had already left for the game so he just left a message."

"Okay, I understand. We'll probably want your permission in writing to look at those records."

"No problem."

"Where are you now?"

"I'm at home."

I gave her the address and she said that she and her partner were coming. "Make it soon. I have to leave for court in about an hour."

"We're coming right now."

I closed the phone feeling uneasy. I had defended a dozen murderers over the years and that had brought me into contact with a number of homicide investigators. But I had never been questioned myself about a murder before. Lankford and now Sobel seemed to be suspicious of every answer I could give. It made me wonder what they knew that I didn't.

I straightened up things on the desk and closed my briefcase. I didn't want them seeing anything I didn't want them to see. I then walked through my house and checked every room. My last stop was the bedroom. I made the bed and put the CD case for *Wreckrium for Lil' Demon* back in the night table drawer. And then it hit me. I sat on the bed as I remembered something Sobel had said. She had made a slip and at first it had gone right by me. She had said that they had found Raul Levin's .22 caliber gun but it was not the murder weapon. She said it was not a Woodsman.

She had inadvertently revealed to me the make and model of the murder weapon. I knew the Woodsman was an automatic pistol manufactured by Colt. I knew this because I owned a Colt Woodsman Sport Model. It had been bequeathed to me many years ago by my father. Upon his death. Once old enough to handle it, I had never even taken it out of its wooden box.

I got up from the bed and went to the walk-in closet. I moved as if in a heavy fog. My steps were tentative and I put my hand out to the wall and then the door casement as if needing my bearings. The polished wooden box was on the shelf where it was supposed to be. I reached up with both hands to bring it down and then walked it out to the bedroom.

I put the box down on the bed and flipped open the brass latch. I raised the lid and pulled away the oilcloth covering.

The gun was gone.

PART TWO
—A World Without Truth

27

Monday, May 23

The check from Roulet cleared. On the first day of trial I had more money in my bank account than I'd ever had in my life. If I wanted, I could drop the bus benches and go with billboards. I could also take the back cover of the yellow pages instead of the half page I had inside. I could afford it. I finally had a franchise case and it had paid off. In terms of money, that is. The loss of Raul Levin would forever make this franchise a losing proposition.

We had been through three days of jury selection and were now ready to put on the show. The trial was scheduled for another three days at the most — two for the prosecution and one for the defense. I had told the judge that I would need a day to put my case before the jury, but the truth was, most of my work would be done during the prosecution's presentation.

There's always an electric feel to the start of a trial. A nervousness that attacks deep in the gut. So much is on the line. Reputation, personal freedom, the integrity of the system itself. Something about having those twelve strangers sit in judgment of your life and work always jumps things up inside. And I am referring to me, the defense attorney — the judgment of the defendant is a whole other thing. I've never gotten used to it, and the truth is, I never want to. I can only liken it to the anxiety and tension of standing at the front of a church on your wedding day. I'd had that experience twice and I was reminded of it every time a judge called a trial to order.

Though my experience in trial work severely outweighed my opponent's, there was no mistake about where I stood. I was one man standing before the giant maw of the system. Without a doubt I was the underdog. Yes, it was true that I faced a prosecutor in his first major felony trial. But that advantage was evened and then some by the power and might of the state. At the prosecutor's command were the forces of the entire justice system. And against this all I had was myself. And a guilty client.

I sat next to Louis Roulet at the defense table. We were alone. I had no second and no investigator behind me — out of some strange loyalty to Raul Levin I had not hired a replacement. I didn't really need one, either. Levin had given me everything I needed. The trial and how it played out would serve as a last testament to his skills as an investigator.

In the first row of the gallery sat C. C. Dobbs and Mary Alice Windsor. In accordance with a pretrial ruling, the judge was allowing Roulet's mother to be in the courtroom during opening statements only. Because she was listed as a defense witness, she would not be allowed to listen to any of the testimony that followed. She would remain in the hallway outside, with her loyal lapdog Dobbs at her side, until I called her to the stand.

Also in the first row but not seated next to them was my own support section: my ex-wife Lorna Taylor. She had gotten dressed up in a navy suit and white blouse. She looked beautiful and could have blended in easily with the phalanx of female attorneys who descended on the courthouse every day. But she was there for me and I loved her for it.

The rest of the rows in the gallery were sporadically crowded. There were a few print reporters there to grab quotes from the opening statements and a few attorneys and citizen onlookers. No TV had shown up. The trial had not yet drawn more than cursory attention from the public, and this was good. This meant our strategy of publicity containment had worked well.

Roulet and I were silent as we waited for the judge to take the bench and order the jury into the box so that we could begin. I was attempting to calm myself by rehearsing what I wanted to say to the jurors. Roulet was staring straight ahead at the State of California seal affixed to the front of the judge's bench.

The courtroom clerk took a phone call, said a few words and then hung up.

"Two minutes, people," he said loudly. "Two minutes."

When a judge called ahead to the courtroom, that meant people should be in their positions and ready to go. We were. I glanced over at Ted Minton at the prosecution's table and saw he was doing the same thing that I was doing. Calming himself by rehearsing. I leaned forward and studied the notes on the legal pad in front of me. Then Roulet unexpectedly leaned forward and almost right into me. He spoke in a whisper, even though it wasn't necessary yet.

"This is it, Mick."

"I know."

Since the death of Raul Levin, my relationship with Roulet had been one of cold endurance. I put up with him because I had to. But I saw him as little as possible in the days and weeks before the trial, and spoke to him as little as possible once it started. I knew the one weakness in my plan was my own weakness. I feared that any interaction with Roulet could lead me into acting out my anger and desire to personally, physically avenge my friend. The three days of jury selection had been torture. Day after day I had to sit right next to him and listen to his condescending comments about prospective jurors. The only way I got through it was to pretend he wasn't there.

"You ready?" he asked me.

"Trying to be," I said. "Are you?"

"I'm ready. But I wanted to tell you something before we began."

I looked at him. He was too close to me. It would have been invasive even if I loved him and not hated him. I leaned back.

"What?"

He followed me, leaning back next to me.

"You're my lawyer, right?"

I leaned forward, trying to get away.

"Louis, what is this? We've been together on this more than two months and now we're sitting here with a jury picked and ready for trial. You have paid me more than a hundred and fifty grand and you have to ask if I'm your lawyer? Of course I'm your lawyer. What is it? What is wrong?"

"Nothing's wrong."

He leaned forward and continued.

"I mean, like, if you're my lawyer, I can tell you stuff and you have to hold it as a secret, even if it's a crime I tell you about. More than one crime. It's covered by the attorney-client relationship, right?"

I felt the low rumbling of upset in my stomach.

"Yes, Louis, that's right—unless you are going to tell me about a crime about to be committed. In that case I can be relieved of the code of ethics and can inform the police so they can stop the crime. In fact, it would be my duty to inform them. A lawyer is an officer of the court. So what is it that you want to tell me? You just heard we got the two-minute warning. We're about to start here."

"I've killed people, Mick."

I looked at him for a moment.

"What?"

"You heard me."

He was right. I had heard him. And I shouldn't have acted surprised. I already knew he had killed people. Raul Levin was among them and he had even used my gun—though I hadn't figured out how he had defeated the GPS bracelet on his ankle. I was just surprised he had decided to tell me in such a matter-of-fact manner two minutes before his trial was called to order.

"Why are you telling me this?" I asked. "I'm about to try to defend you in this thing and you—"

"Because I know you already know. And because I know what your plan is."

"My plan? What plan?"

He smiled slyly at me.

"Come on, Mick. It's simple. You defend me on this case. You do your best, you get paid the big bucks, you win and I walk away. But then, once it's all over and you've got your money in the bank, you turn against me because I'm not your client anymore. You throw me to the cops so you can get Jesus Menendez out and redeem yourself."

I didn't respond.

"Well, I can't let that happen," he said quietly. "Now, I am yours forever, Mick. I am telling you I've killed people, and guess what? Martha Renteria was one of them. I gave her just what she deserved, and if you go to the cops or use what I've told you against me, then you won't be practicing law for very long. Yes, you might succeed in raising Jesus from the dead. But I'll never be prosecuted because of your misconduct. I believe it is called 'fruit of the poisonous tree,' and you are the tree, Mick."

I still couldn't respond. I just nodded again. Roulet had certainly thought it through. I wondered how much help he had gotten from Cecil Dobbs. He had obviously had somebody coach him on the law.

I leaned toward him and whispered.

"Follow me."

I got up and walked quickly through the gate and toward the rear door of the courtroom. From behind I heard the clerk's voice.

"Mr. Haller? We're about to start. The judge —"

"One minute," I called out without turning around.

I held one finger up as well. I then pushed through the doors into the dimly lit vestibule designed as a buffer to keep hallway sounds from the courtroom. A set of double doors on the other side led to the hallway. I moved to the side and waited for Roulet to step into the small space.

As soon as he came through the door I grabbed him and spun him into the wall. I held him pressed against it with both of my hands on his chest.

"What the fuck do you think you are doing?"

"Take it easy, Mick. I just thought we should know where we both —"

"You son of a bitch. You killed Raul and all he was doing was working for you! He was trying to help you!"

I wanted to bring my hands up to his neck and choke him out on the spot.

"You're right about one thing. I am a son of a bitch. But you are wrong about everything else, Mick. Levin wasn't trying to help me. He was trying to bury me and he was getting too close. He got what he deserved for that."

I thought about Levin's last message on my phone at home. *I've got Jesus's ticket out of the Q.* Whatever it was that he had found, it had gotten him killed. And it had gotten him killed before he could deliver the information to me.

"How did you do it? You're confessing everything to me here, then I want to know how you did it. How'd you beat the GPS? Your bracelet showed you weren't even near Glendale."

He smiled at me, like a boy with a toy he wasn't going to share.

"Let's just say that is proprietary information and leave it at that. You never know, I may have to pull the old Houdini act again."

In his words I heard the threat and in his smile I saw the evil that Raul Levin had seen.

"Don't get any ideas, Mick," he said. "As you probably know, I do have an insurance policy."

I pressed harder against him and leaned in closer.

"Listen, you piece of shit. I want the gun back. You think you have this thing wired? You don't have shit. *I've* got it wired. And you won't make it through the week if I don't get that gun back. You got that?"

Roulet slowly reached up, grabbed my wrists and pulled my hands off his chest. He started straightening his shirt and tie.

"Might I suggest an agreement," he said calmly. "At the end of this trial I walk out of the courtroom a free man. I continue to maintain my freedom, and in exchange for this, the gun never falls into, shall we say, the wrong hands."

Meaning Lankford and Sobel.

"Because I'd really hate to see that happen, Mick. A lot of people depend on you. A lot of clients. And you, of course, wouldn't want to go where they are going."

I stepped back from him, using all my will not to raise my fists and attack. I settled for a voice that quietly seethed with all of my anger and hate.

"I promise you," I said, "if you fuck with me you will never be free of me. Are we clear on that?"

Roulet started to smile. But before he could respond the door from the courtroom opened and Deputy Meehan, the bailiff, looked in.

"The judge is on the bench," he said sternly. "She wants you in here. Now."

I looked back at Roulet.

"I said, are we clear?"

"Yes, Mick," he said good-naturedly. "We're crystal clear."

I stepped away from him and entered the courtroom, striding up the aisle to the gate. Judge Constance Fullbright was staring me down every step of the way.

"So nice of you to consider joining us this morning, Mr. Haller."

Where had I heard that before?

"I am sorry, Your Honor," I said as I came through the gate. "I had an emergency situation with my client. We had to conference."

"Client conferences can be handled right at the defense table," she responded.

"Yes, Your Honor."

"I don't think we are starting off correctly here, Mr. Haller. When my clerk announces that we will be in session in two minutes, then I expect everyone — including defense attorneys and their clients — to be in place and ready to go."

"I apologize, Your Honor."

"That's not good enough, Mr. Haller. Before the end of court today I want you to pay a visit to my clerk with your checkbook. I am fining you five hundred dollars for contempt of court. You are not in charge of this courtroom, sir. I am."

"Your Honor —"

"Now, can we please have the jury," she ordered, cutting off my protest.

The bailiff opened the jury room door and the twelve jurors and two alternates started filing into the jury box. I leaned over to Roulet, who had just sat down, and whispered.

"You owe me five hundred dollars."

28

Ted Minton's opening statement was a by-the-numbers model of prosecutorial overkill. Rather than tell the jurors what evidence he would present and what it would prove, the prosecutor tried to tell them what it all meant. He was going for a big picture and this was almost always a mistake. The big picture involves inferences and suggestions. It extrapolates givens to the level of suspicions. Any experienced prosecutor with a dozen or more felony trials under his belt will tell you to keep it small. You want them to convict, not necessarily to understand.

"What this case is about is a predator," he told them. "Louis Ross Roulet is a man who on the night of March sixth was stalking prey. And if it were not for the sheer determination of a woman to survive, we would be here prosecuting a murder case."

I noticed early on that Minton had picked up a scorekeeper. This is what I call a juror who incessantly takes notes during trial. An opening statement is not an offer of evidence and Judge Fullbright had so admonished the jury, but the woman in the first seat in the front row had been writing since the start of Minton's statement. This was good. I like scorekeepers because they document just what the lawyers say will be presented and proved at trial and at the end they go back to check. They keep score.

I looked at the jury chart I had filled in the week before and saw that the scorekeeper was Linda Truluck, a homemaker from Reseda. She was one of only three women on the jury. Minton had tried hard to keep the female content to a minimum because, I believe, he feared that once it was established in trial that Regina Campo had been offering sexual services for money, he might lose the females' sympathy and ultimately their votes on a verdict. I believed he was probably correct in that assumption and I worked just as diligently to get women on the panel. We both ended up using all of our twenty challenges and it was probably the main reason it took three days to seat a jury. In the end I got three women on the panel and only needed one to head off a conviction.

"Now, you are going to hear testimony from the victim herself about her lifestyle being one that we would not condone," Minton told the jurors. "The bottom line is she was selling sex to the men she invited to her home. But I want you to remember that what the victim in this case did for a living is not what this trial is about. Anyone can be a victim of a violent crime. Anyone. No matter what someone does for a living, the law does not allow for them to be beaten, to be threatened at knifepoint or to be put in fear of their lives. It doesn't matter what they do to make money. They enjoy the same protections that we all do."

It was pretty clear to me that Minton didn't even want to use the word *prostitution* or *prostitute* for fear it would hurt his case. I wrote the word down on the legal pad I would take with me to the lectern when I made my statement. I planned to make up for the prosecutor's omissions.

Minton gave an overview of the evidence. He spoke about the knife with the defendant's initials on the blade. He talked about the blood found on his left hand. And he warned the jurors not to be fooled by the defense's efforts to confuse or muddle the evidence.

"This is a very clear-cut and straightforward case," he said as he was winding up. "You have a man who attacked a woman in her home. His plan was to rape and then kill her. It is only by the grace of God that she will be here to tell you the story."

With that he thanked them for their attention and took his seat at the prosecution table. Judge Fullbright looked at her watch and then looked at me. It was 11:40 and she was probably weighing whether to go to a break or let me proceed with my opener. One of the judge's chief jobs during trial is jury management. The judge's duty is to make sure the jury is comfortable and engaged. Lots of breaks, short and long, is often the answer.

I had known Connie Fullbright for at least twelve years, since long before she was a judge. She had been both a prosecutor and defense lawyer. She knew both sides. Aside from being overly quick with contempt citations, she was a good and fair judge — until it came to sentencing. You went into Fullbright's court knowing you were on an even level with the prosecution. But if the jury convicted your client, be prepared for the worst. Fullbright was one of the toughest sentencing judges in the county. It was as if she were punishing you and your client for wasting her time with a trial. If there was any room within the sentencing guidelines, she always went to the max, whether it was prison or probation. It had gotten her a telling sobriquet among the defense pros who worked the Van Nuys courthouse. They called her Judge Fullbite.

"Mr. Haller," she said, "are you planning to reserve your statement?"

"No, Your Honor, but I believe I am going to be pretty quick."

"Very good," she said. "Then we'll hear from you and then we'll take lunch."

The truth was I didn't know how long I would be. Minton had been about forty minutes and I knew I would take close to that. But I had told the judge I'd be quick simply because I didn't like the idea of the jury going to lunch with only the prosecutor's side of the story to think about as they chewed their hamburgers and tuna salads.

I got up and went to the lectern located between the prosecution and defense tables. The courtroom was one of the recently rehabbed spaces in the old courthouse. It had twin jury boxes on either side of the bench. Everything was done in a blond wood, including the rear wall behind the bench. The door to the judge's chambers was almost hidden in the wall, its lines camouflaged in the lines and grain of the wood. The doorknob was the only giveaway.

Fullbright ran her trials like a federal judge. Attorneys were not allowed to approach witnesses without permission and never allowed to approach the jury box. They were required to speak from the lectern only.

Standing now at the lectern, the jury was in the box to my right and closer to the prosecution table than to the defense's. This was fine with me. I didn't want them to get too close a look at Roulet. I wanted him to be a bit of a mystery to them.

"Ladies and gentlemen of the jury," I began, "my name is Michael Haller and I am representing Mr. Roulet during this trial. I am happy to tell you that this trial will most likely be a quick one. Just a few more days of your time will be taken. In the long run you will probably see that it took us longer to pick all of you than it will take to present both sides of the case. The prosecutor, Mr. Minton, seemed to spend his time this morning telling you about what he thinks all the evidence means and who Mr. Roulet really is. I would advise you to simply sit back, listen to the evidence and let your common sense tell you what it all means and who Mr. Roulet is."

I kept my eyes moving from juror to juror. I rarely looked down at the pad I had placed on the lectern. I wanted them to think I was shooting the breeze with them, talking off the top of my head.

"Usually, what I like to do is reserve my opening statement. In a criminal trial the defense always has the option of giving an opener at the start of the trial, just as Mr. Minton did, or right before presenting the defense's case. Normally, I would take the second option. I would wait and make my statement before trotting out all the defense's witnesses and evidence. But this case is different. It's different because the prosecution's case is also going to be the defense's case. You'll certainly hear from some defense witnesses, but the heart and soul of this case is going to be the prosecution's evidence and witnesses and how you decide to interpret them. I guarantee you that a version of the events and evidence far different from what Mr. Minton just outlined is going to emerge in this courtroom. And when it comes time to present the defense's case, it probably won't even be necessary."

I checked the scorekeeper and saw her pencil moving across the page of her notebook.

"I think that what you are going to find here this week is that this whole case will come down to the actions and motivations of one person. A prostitute who saw a man with outward signs of wealth and chose to target him. The evidence will show this clearly and it will be shown by the prosecution's own witnesses."

Minton stood up and objected, saying I was going out of bounds in trying to impeach the state's main witness with unsubstantiated accusations. There was no legal basis for the objection. It was just an amateurish attempt to send a message to the jury. The judge responded by inviting us to a sidebar.

We walked to the side of the bench and the judge flipped on a sound neutralizer which sent white noise from a speaker on the bench toward the jury and prevented them from hearing what was whispered in the sidebar. The judge was quick with Minton, like an assassin.

"Mr. Minton, I know you are new to felony trial work, so I see I will have to school you as we go. But don't you ever object during an opening statement in my courtroom. This isn't evidence he's presenting. I don't care if he says your own mother is the defendant's alibi witness, you don't object in front of my jury."

"Your Hon—"

"That's it. Go back."

She rolled her seat back to the center of the bench and flicked off the white noise. Minton and I returned to our positions without further word.

"Objection overruled," the judge said. "Continue, Mr. Haller, and let me remind you that you said you would be quick."

"Thank you, Your Honor. That is still my plan."

I referred to my notes and then looked back at the jury. Knowing that Minton would have been intimidated to silence by the judge, I decided to raise the rhetoric up a notch, go off notes and get directly to the windup.

"Ladies and gentlemen, in essence, what you will be deciding here is who the real predator was in this case. Mr. Roulet, a successful businessman with a spotless record, or an admitted prostitute with a successful business in taking money from men in exchange for sex. You will hear testimony that the alleged victim in this case was engaged in an act of prostitution with another man just moments before this supposed attack occurred. And you will hear testimony that within days of this supposedly life-threatening assault, she was back in business once again, trading sex for money."

I glanced at Minton and saw he was doing a slow burn. He had his eyes downcast on the table in front of him and he was slowly shaking his head. I looked up at the judge.

"Your Honor, could you instruct the prosecutor to refrain from demonstrating in front of the jury? I did not object or in any way try to distract the jury during his opening statement."

"Mr. Minton," the judge intoned, "please sit still and extend the courtesy to the defense that was extended to you."

"Yes, Your Honor," Minton said meekly.

The jury had now seen the prosecutor slapped down twice and we weren't even past openers. I took this as a good sign and it fed my momentum. I looked back at the jury and noticed that the scorekeeper was still writing.

"Finally, you will receive testimony from many of the state's own witnesses that will provide a perfectly acceptable explanation for much of the physical evidence in this case. I am talking about the blood and about the knife Mr. Minton mentioned. Taken individually or as a whole, the prosecution's own case will provide you with more than reasonable doubt about the guilt of my client. You can mark it down in your notebooks. I guarantee you will find that you have only one choice at the end of this case. And that is to find Mr. Roulet not guilty of these charges. Thank you."

As I walked back to my seat I winked at Lorna Taylor. She nodded at me as if to say I had done well. My attention was then drawn to the two figures sitting two rows behind her. Lankford and Sobel. They had slipped in after I had first surveyed the gallery.

I took my seat and ignored the thumbs-up gesture given me by my client. My mind was on the two Glendale detectives, wondering what they were doing in the courtroom. Watching me? Waiting for me?

The judge dismissed the jury for lunch and everyone stood while the scorekeeper and her colleagues filed out. After they were gone Minton asked the judge for another sidebar. He wanted to try to explain his objection and repair the damage but not in open court. The judge said no.

"I'm hungry, Mr. Minton, and we're past that now. Go to lunch."

She left the bench, and the courtroom that had been so silent except for the voices of lawyers then erupted in chatter from the gallery and the court workers. I put my pad in my briefcase.

"That was really good," Roulet said. "I think we're already ahead of the game."

I looked at him with dead eyes.

"It's no game."

"I know that. It's just an expression. Listen, I am having lunch with Cecil and my mother. We would like you to join us."

I shook my head.

"I have to defend you, Louis, but I don't have to eat with you."

I took my checkbook out of my briefcase and left him there. I walked around the table to the clerk's station so that I could write out a check for five hundred dollars. The money didn't hurt as much as I knew the bar review that follows any contempt citation would.

When I was finished I turned back to find Lorna waiting for me at the gate with a smile. We planned to go to lunch and then she would go back to manning the phone in her condo. In three days I would be back in business and needed clients. I was depending on her to start filling in my calendar.

"Looks like I better buy you lunch today," she said.

I threw my checkbook into the briefcase and closed it. I joined her at the gate.

"That would be nice," I said.

I pushed through the gate and checked the bench where I had seen Lankford and Sobel sitting a few moments before.

They were gone.

29

The prosecution began presenting its case to the jury in the afternoon session and very quickly Ted Minton's strategy became clear to me. The first four witnesses were a 911 dispatch operator, the patrol officers who responded to Regina Campo's call for help and the paramedic who treated her before she was transported to the hospital. In anticipation of the defense strategy, it was clear that Minton wanted to firmly establish that Campo had been brutally assaulted and was indeed the victim in this crime. It wasn't a bad strategy. In most cases it would get the job done.

The dispatch operator was essentially used as the warm body needed to introduce a recording of Campo's 911 call for help. Printed transcripts of the call were handed out to jurors so they could read along with a scratchy audio playback. I objected on the grounds that it was prejudicial to play the audio recording when the transcript would suffice but the judge quickly overruled me before Minton even had to counter. The recording was played and there was no doubt that Minton had started out of the gate strong as the jurors sat raptly listening to Campo scream and beg for help. She sounded genuinely distraught and scared. It was exactly what Minton wanted the jurors to hear and they certainly got it. I didn't dare question the dispatcher on cross-examination because I knew it might give Minton the opportunity to play the recording again on redirect.

The two patrol officers who followed offered different testimony because they did separate things upon arriving at the Tarzana apartment complex in response to the 911 call. One primarily stayed with the victim while the other went up to the apartment and handcuffed the man Campo's neighbors were sitting on — Louis Ross Roulet.

Officer Vivian Maxwell described Campo as disheveled, hurt and frightened. She said Campo kept asking if she was safe and if the intruder had been caught. Even after she was assured on both questions, Campo remained scared and upset, at one point telling the officer to unholster her weapon and have it ready in case the attacker broke free. When Minton was through with this witness, I stood up to conduct my first cross-examination of the trial.

"Officer Maxwell," I asked, "did you at any time ask Ms. Campo what had happened to her?"

"Yes, I did."

"What exactly did you ask her?"

"I asked what had happened and who did this to her. You know, who had hurt her."

"What did she tell you?"

"She said a man had come to her door and knocked and when she opened it he punched her. She said he hit her several times and then took out a knife."

"She said he took the knife out after he punched her?"

"That's how she said it. She was upset and hurt at the time."

"I understand. Did she tell you who the man was?"

"No, she said she didn't know the man."

"You specifically asked if she knew the man?"

"Yes. She said no."

"So she just opened her door at ten o'clock at night to a stranger."

"She didn't say it that way."

"But you said she told you she didn't know him, right?"

"That is correct. That is how she said it. She said, 'I don't know who he is.'"

"And did you put this in your report?"

"Yes, I did."

I introduced the patrol officer's report as a defense exhibit and had Maxwell read parts of it to the jury. These parts involved Campo saying that the attack was unprovoked and at the hands of a stranger.

"'The victim does not know the man who assaulted her and did not know why she was attacked,'" she read from her own report.

Maxwell's partner, John Santos, testified next, telling jurors that Campo directed him to her apartment, where he found a man on the floor near the entrance. The man was semiconscious and was being held on the ground by two of Campo's neighbors, Edward Turner and Ronald Atkins. One man was straddling the man's chest and the other was sitting on his legs.

Santos identified the man being held on the floor as the defendant, Louis Ross Roulet. Santos described him as having blood on his clothes and his left hand. He said Roulet appeared to be suffering from a concussion or some sort of head injury and initially was not responsive to commands. Santos turned him over and handcuffed his hands behind his back. The officer then put a plastic evidence bag he carried in a compartment on his belt over Roulet's bloody hand.

Santos testified that one of the men who had been holding Roulet handed over a folding knife that was open and had blood on its handle and blade. Santos told jurors he bagged this item as well and turned it over to Detective Martin Booker as soon as he arrived on the scene.

On cross-examination I asked Santos only two questions.

"Officer, was there blood on the defendant's right hand?"

"No, there was no blood on his right hand or I would have bagged that one, too."

"I see. So you have blood on the left hand only and a knife with blood on the handle. Would it then appear to you that if the defendant had held that knife, then he would have to have held it in his left hand?"

Minton objected, saying that Santos was a patrol officer and that the question was beyond the scope of his expertise. I argued that the question required only a commonsense answer, not an expert. The judge overruled the objection and the court clerk read the question back to the witness.

"It would seem that way to me," Santos answered.

Arthur Metz was the paramedic who testified next. He told jurors about Campo's demeanor and the extent of her injuries when he treated her less than thirty minutes after the attack. He said that it appeared to him that she had suffered at least three significant impacts to the face. He also described a small puncture wound to her neck. He described all the injuries as superficial but painful. A large blowup of the same photograph of Campo's face I had seen on the first day I was on the case was displayed on an easel in front of the jury. I objected to this, arguing that the photo was prejudicial because it had been blown up to larger-than-life size, but I was overruled by Judge Fullbright.

Then, when it was my turn to cross-examine Metz, I used the photo I had just objected to.

"When you tell us that it appeared that she suffered at least three impacts to the face, what do you mean by 'impact'?" I asked.

"She was struck with something. Either a fist or a blunt object."

"So basically someone hit her three times. Could you please use this laser pointer and show the jury on the photograph where these impacts occurred."

From my shirt pocket I unclipped a laser pointer and held it up for the judge to see. She granted me permission to carry it to Metz. I turned it on and handed it to him. He then put the red eye of the laser beam on the photo of Campo's battered face and drew circles in the three areas where he believed she had been struck. He circled her right eye, her right cheek and an area encompassing the right side of her mouth and nose.

"Thank you," I said, taking the laser back from him and returning to the lectern. "So if she was hit three times on the right side of her face, the impacts would have come from the left side of her attacker, correct?"

Minton objected, once more saying the question was beyond the scope of the witness's expertise. Once more I argued common sense and once more the judge overruled the prosecutor.

"If the attacker was facing her, he would have punched her from the left, unless it was a backhand," Metz said. "Then it could have been a right."

He nodded and seemed pleased with himself. He obviously thought he was helping the prosecution but his effort was so disingenuous that he was actually probably helping the defense.

"You are suggesting that Ms. Campo's attacker hit her three times with a backhand and caused this degree of injury?"

I pointed to the photo on the exhibit easel. Metz shrugged, realizing he had probably not been so helpful to the prosecution.

"Anything is possible," he said.

"Anything is possible," I repeated. "Well, is there any other possibility you can think of that would explain these injuries as coming from anything other than direct left-handed punches?"

Metz shrugged again. He was not an impressive witness, especially following two cops and a dispatcher who had been very precise in their testimony.

"What if Ms. Campo were to have hit her face with her own fist? Wouldn't she have used her right—"

Minton jumped up immediately and objected.

"Your Honor, this is outrageous! To suggest that this victim did this to herself is not only an affront to this court but to all victims of violent crime everywhere. Mr. Haller has sunk to—"

"The witness said anything is possible," I argued, trying to knock Minton off the soapbox. "I am trying to explore what—"

"Sustained," Fullbright said, ending it. "Mr. Haller, don't go there unless you are making more than an exploratory swing through the possibilities."

"Yes, Your Honor," I said. "No further questions."

I sat down and glanced at the jurors and knew from their faces that I had made a mistake. I had turned a positive cross into a negative. The point I had made about a left-handed attacker was obscured by the point I had lost with the suggestion that the injuries to the victim's face were self-inflicted. The three women on the panel looked particularly annoyed with me.

Still, I tried to focus on a positive aspect. It was good to know the jury's feelings on this now, before Campo was in the witness box and I asked the same thing.

Roulet leaned toward me and whispered, "What the fuck was that?"

Without responding I turned my back to him and took a scan around the courtroom. It was almost empty. Lankford and Sobel had not returned to the courtroom and the reporters were gone as well. That left only a few other onlookers. They appeared to be a disparate collection of retirees, law students and lawyers resting their feet until their own hearings began in other courtrooms. But I was counting on one of these onlookers being a plant from the DA's office. Ted Minton might be flying solo but my guess was that his boss would have a means of keeping tabs on him and the case. I knew I was playing as much to the plant as I was to the jury. By the trial's end I needed to send a note of panic down to the second floor that would then echo back to Minton. I needed to push the young prosecutor toward taking a desperate measure.

The afternoon dragged on. Minton still had a lot to learn about pacing and jury management, knowledge that comes only with courtroom experience. I kept my eyes on the jury box—where the real judges sat—and saw the jurors were growing bored as witness after witness offered testimony that filled in small details in the prosecutor's linear presentation of the events of March 6. I asked few questions on cross and tried to keep a look on my face that mirrored those I saw in the jury box.

Minton obviously wanted to save his most powerful stuff for day two. He would have the lead investigator, Detective Martin Booker, to bring all the details together, and then the victim, Regina Campo, to bring it all home to the jury. It was a tried-and-true formula — ending with muscle and emotion — and it worked ninety percent of the time, but it was making the first day move like a glacier.

Things finally started to pop with the last witness of the day. Minton brought in Charles Talbot, the man who had picked up Regina Campo at Morgan's and gone with her to her apartment on the night of the sixth. What Talbot had to offer to the prosecution's case was negligible. He was basically hauled in to testify that Campo had been in good health and uninjured when he left her. That was it. But what caused his arrival to rescue the trial from the pit of boredom was that Talbot was an honest-to-God alternate lifestyle man and jurors always loved visiting the other side of the tracks.

Talbot was fifty-five years old with dyed blond hair that wasn't fooling anyone. He had blurred Navy tattoos on both forearms. He was twenty years divorced and owned a twenty-four-hour convenience store called Kwik Kwik. The business gave him a comfortable living and lifestyle with an apartment in the Warner Center, a late-model Corvette and a nightlife that included a wide sampling of the city's professional sex providers.

Minton established all of this in the early stages of his direct examination. You could almost feel the air go still in the courtroom as the jurors plugged into Talbot. The prosecutor then brought him quickly to the night of March 6, and Talbot described hooking up with Reggie Campo at Morgan's on Ventura Boulevard.

"Did you know Ms. Campo before you met her in the bar that night?"

"No, I did not."

"How did it come about that you met her there?"

"I just called her up and said I wanted to get together with her and she suggested we meet at Morgan's. I knew the place, so I said sure."

"And how did you call her up?"

"With the telephone."

Several jurors laughed.

"I'm sorry. I understand that you used a telephone to call her. I meant how did you know *how* to contact her?"

"I saw her ad on the website and I liked what I saw and so I went ahead and called her up and we made a date. It's as simple as that. Her number is on her website ad."

"And you met at Morgan's."

"Yes, that's where she meets her dates, she told me. So I went there and we had a couple drinks and we talked and we liked each other and that was that. I followed her back to her place."

"When you went to her apartment did you engage in sexual relations?"

"Sure did. That's what I was there for."

"And you paid her?"

"Four hundred bucks. It was worth it."

I saw a male juror's face turning red and I knew I had pegged him perfectly during selection the week before. I had wanted him because he had brought a Bible with him to read while other prospective jurors were being questioned. Minton had missed it, focusing only on the candidates as they were being questioned. But I had seen the Bible and asked few questions of the man when it was his turn. Minton accepted him on the jury and so did I. I figured he would be easy to turn against the victim because of her occupation. His reddening face confirmed it.

"What time did you leave her apartment?" Minton asked.

"About five minutes before ten," Talbot answered.

"Did she tell you she was expecting another date at the apartment?"

"No, she didn't say anything about that. In fact, she was sort of acting like she was done for the night."

I stood up and objected.

"I don't think Mr. Talbot is qualified here to interpret what Ms. Campo was thinking or planning by her actions."

"Sustained," the judge said before Minton could offer an argument.

The prosecutor moved right along.

"Mr. Talbot, could you please describe the physical state Ms. Campo was in when you left her shortly before ten o'clock on the night of March sixth?"

"Completely satisfied."

There was a loud blast of laughter in the courtroom and Talbot beamed proudly. I checked the Bible man and it looked like his jaw was tightly clenched.

"Mr. Talbot," Minton said. "I mean her physical state. Was she hurt or bleeding when you left her?"

"No, she was fine. She was okay. When I left her she was fit as a fiddle and I know because I had just played her."

He smiled, proud of his use of language. This time there was no laughter and the judge had finally had enough of his use of the double entendre. She admonished him to keep his more off-color remarks to himself.

"Sorry, Judge," he said.

"Mr. Talbot," Minton said. "Ms. Campo was not injured in any way when you left her?"

"Nope. No way."

"She wasn't bleeding?"

"No."

"And you didn't strike her or physically abuse her in any way?"

"No again. What we did was consensual and pleasurable. No pain."

"Thank you, Mr. Talbot."

I looked at my notes for a few moments before standing up. I wanted a break of time to clearly mark the line between direct and cross-examination.

"Mr. Haller?" the judge prompted. "Do you wish to cross-examine the witness?"

I stood up and moved to the lectern.

"Yes, Your Honor, I do."

I put my pad down and looked directly at Talbot. He was smiling pleasantly at me but I knew he wouldn't like me for very long.

"Mr. Talbot, are you right- or left-handed?"

"I'm left-handed."

"Left-handed," I echoed. "And isn't it true that on the night of the sixth, before leaving Regina Campo's apartment, she asked you to strike her with your fist repeatedly in the face?"

Minton stood up.

"Your Honor, there is no basis for this sort of questioning. Mr. Haller is simply trying to muddy the waters by taking outrageous statements and turning them into questions."

The judge looked at me and waited for a response.

"Judge, it is part of the defense theory as outlined in my opening statement."

"I am going to allow it. Just be quick about it, Mr. Haller."

The question was read to Talbot and he smirked and shook his head.

"That is not true. I've never hurt a woman in my life."

"You struck her with your fist three times, didn't you, Mr. Talbot?"

"No, I did not. That is a lie."

"You said you have never hurt a woman in your life."

"That's right. Never."

"Do you know a prostitute named Shaquilla Barton?"

Talbot had to think before answering.

"Doesn't ring a bell."

"On the website where she advertises her services she uses the name Shaquilla Shackles. Does that ring a bell now, Mr. Talbot?"

"Okay, yeah, I think so."

"Have you ever engaged in acts of prostitution with her?"

"One time, yes."

"When was that?"

"Would've been at least a year ago. Maybe longer."

"And did you hurt her on that occasion?"

"No."

"And if she were to come to this courtroom and say that you did hurt her by punching her with your left hand, would she be lying?"

"She damn sure would be. I tried her out and didn't like that rough stuff. I'm strictly a missionary man. I didn't touch her."

"You didn't touch her?"

"I mean I didn't punch her or hurt her in any way."

"Thank you, Mr. Talbot."

I sat down. Minton did not bother with a redirect. Talbot was excused and Minton told the judge that he had only two witnesses remaining to present in the case but that their testimony would be lengthy. Judge Fullbright checked the time and recessed court for the day.

Two witnesses left. I knew that had to be Detective Booker and Reggie Campo. It looked like Minton was going to go without the testimony of the jailhouse snitch he had stashed in the PTI program at County-USC. Dwayne Corliss's name had never appeared on any witness list or any other discovery document associated with the prosecution of the case. I thought maybe Minton had found out what Raul Levin had found out about Corliss before Raul was murdered. Either way, it seemed apparent that Corliss had been dropped by the prosecution. And that was what I needed to change.

As I gathered my papers and documents in my briefcase, I also gathered the resolve to talk to Roulet. I glanced over at him. He was sitting there waiting to be dismissed by me.

"So what do you think?" I asked.

"I think you did very well. More than a few moments of reasonable doubt."

I snapped the latches on the briefcase closed.

"Today I was just planting seeds. Tomorrow they'll sprout and on Wednesday they'll bloom. You haven't seen anything yet."

I stood up and lifted the briefcase off the table. It was heavy with all the case documents and my computer.

"See you tomorrow."

I walked out through the gate. Cecil Dobbs and Mary Windsor were waiting for Roulet in the hallway near the courtroom door. As I came out they turned to speak to me but I walked on by.

"See you tomorrow," I said.

"Wait a minute, wait a minute," Dobbs called to my back.

I turned around.

"We're stuck out here," he said as he and Windsor walked to me. "How is it going in there?"

I shrugged.

"Right now it's the prosecution's case," I answered. "All I'm doing is bobbing and weaving, trying to protect. I think tomorrow will be our round. And Wednesday we go for the knockout. I've got to go prepare."

As I headed to the elevator, I saw that a number of the jurors from the case had beaten me to it and were waiting to go down. The scorekeeper was among them. I went into the restroom next to the bank of elevators so I didn't have to ride down with them. I put my briefcase on the counter between the sinks and washed my face and hands. As I stared at myself in the mirror I looked for signs of stress from the case and everything associated with it. I looked reasonably sane and calm for a defense pro who was playing both his client and the prosecution at the same time.

The cold water felt good and I felt refreshed as I came out of the restroom, hoping the jurors had cleared out.

The jurors were gone. But standing in the hallway by the elevator were Lankford and Sobel. Lankford was holding a folded sheaf of documents in one hand.

"There you are," he said. "We've been looking for you."

30

The document Lankford handed me was a search warrant granting the police the authority to search my home, office and car for a .22 caliber Colt Woodsman Sport Model pistol with the serial number 656300081-52. The authorization said the pistol was believed to have been the murder weapon in the April 12 homicide of Raul A. Levin. Lankford had handed the warrant to me with a proud smirk on his face. I did my best to act like it was business as usual, the kind of thing I handled every other day and twice on Fridays. But the truth was, my knees almost buckled.

"How'd you get this?" I said.

It was a nonsensical response to a nonsensical moment.

"Signed, sealed and delivered," Lankford said. "So where do you want to start? You have your car here, right? That Lincoln you're chauffeured around in like a high-class hooker."

I checked the judge's signature on the last page and saw it was a Glendale muni-court judge I had never heard of. They had gone to a local who probably knew he'd need the police endorsement come election time. I started to recover from the shock. Maybe the search was a front.

"This is bullshit," I said. "You don't have the PC for this. I could have this thing quashed in ten minutes."

"It looked pretty good to Judge Fullbright," Lankford said.

"Fullbright? What does she have to do with this?"

"Well, we knew you were in trial, so we figured we ought to ask her if it was okay to drop the warrant on you. Don't want to get a lady like that mad, you know. She said after court was over was fine by her—and she didn't say shit about the PC or anything else."

They must have gone to Fullbright on the lunch break, right after I had seen them in the courtroom. My guess was, it had been Sobel's idea to check with the judge first. A guy like Lankford would have enjoyed pulling me right out of court and disrupting the trial.

I had to think quickly. I looked at Sobel, the more sympathetic of the two.

"I'm in the middle of a three-day trial," I said. "Any way we can put this on hold until Thursday?"

"No fucking way," Lankford answered before his partner could. "We're not letting you out of our sight until we execute the search. We're not going to give you the time to dump the gun. Now where's your car, Lincoln lawyer?"

I checked the authorization of the warrant. It had to be very specific and I was in luck. It called for the search of a Lincoln with the California license plate NT GLTY. I realized that someone must have written the plate down on the day I was called to Raul Levin's house from the Dodgers game. Because that was the old Lincoln — the one I was driving that day.

"It's at home. Since I'm in trial I don't use the driver. I got a ride in with my client this morning and I was just going to ride back with him. He's probably waiting down there."

I lied. The Lincoln I had been driving was in the courthouse parking garage. But I couldn't let the cops search it because there was a gun in a compartment in the backseat armrest. It wasn't the gun they were looking for but it was a replacement. After Raul Levin was murdered and I'd found my pistol box empty, I asked Earl Briggs to get me a gun for protection. I knew that with Earl there would be no ten-day waiting period. But I didn't know the gun's history or registration and I didn't want to find out through the Glendale Police Department.

But I was in luck because the Lincoln with the gun inside wasn't the one described in the warrant. That one was in my garage at home, waiting on the buyer from the limo service to come by and take a look at. And that would be the Lincoln that would be searched.

Lankford grabbed the warrant out of my hand and shoved it into an inside coat pocket.

"Don't worry about your ride," Lankford said. "We're your ride. Let's go."

On the way down and out of the courthouse, we didn't run into Roulet or his entourage. And soon I was riding in the back of a Grand Marquis, thinking that I had made the right choice when I had gone with the Lincoln. There was more room in the Lincoln and the ride was smoother.

Lankford did the driving and I sat behind him. The windows were up and I could hear him chewing gum.

"Let me see the warrant again," I said.

Lankford made no move.

"I'm not letting you inside my house until I've had a chance to completely study the warrant. I could do it on the way and save you some time. Or..."

Lankford reached inside his jacket and pulled out the warrant. He handed it over his shoulder to me. I knew why he was hesitant. Cops usually had to lay out their whole investigation in the warrant application in order to convince a judge of probable cause. They didn't like the target reading it, because it gave away the store.

I glanced out the window as we were passing the car lots on Van Nuys Boulevard. I saw a new model Town Car on a pedestal in front of the Lincoln dealership. I looked back down at the warrant, opened it to the summary section and read.

Lankford and Sobel had started out doing some good work. I had to give them that. One of them had taken a shot — I was guessing Sobel — and put my name into the state's Automated Firearm System and hit the lotto. The AFS computer said I was the registered owner of a pistol of the same make and model as the murder weapon.

It was a smooth move but it still wasn't enough to make probable cause. Colt made the Woodsman for more than sixty years. That meant there were probably a million of them out there and a million suspects who owned them.

They had the smoke. They then rubbed other sticks together to make the required fire. The application summary stated that I had hidden from the investigators the fact that I owned the gun in question. It said I had also fabricated an alibi when initially interviewed about Levin's death, then attempted to throw detectives off the track by giving them a phony lead on the drug dealer Hector Arrande Moya.

Though motivation was not necessarily a subject needed to obtain a search warrant, the PC summary alluded to it anyway, stating that the victim — Raul Levin — had been extorting investigative assignments from me and that I had refused to pay him upon completion of those assignments.

The outrage of such an assertion aside, the alibi fabrication was the key point of probable cause. The statement said that I had told the detectives I was home at the time of the murder, but a message on my home phone was left just before the suspected time of death and this indicated that I was not home, thereby collapsing my alibi and proving me a liar at the same time.

I slowly read the PC statement twice more but my anger did not subside. I tossed the warrant onto the seat next to me.

"In some ways it's really too bad I am not the killer," I said.

"Yeah, why is that?" Lankford said.

"Because this warrant is a piece of shit and you both know it. It won't stand up to challenge. I told you that message came in when I was already on the phone and that can be checked and proven, only you were too lazy or you didn't want to check it because it would have made it a little difficult to get your warrant. Even with your pocket judge in Glendale. You lied by omission and commission. It's a bad-faith warrant."

Because I was sitting behind Lankford I had a better angle on Sobel. I watched her for signs of doubt as I spoke.

"And the suggestion that Raul was extorting business from me and that I wouldn't pay is a complete joke. Extorted me with what? And what didn't I pay him for? I paid him every time I got a bill. Man, I tell you, if this is how you work all your cases, I gotta open up an office in Glendale. I'm going to shove this warrant right up your police chief's ass."

"You lied about the gun," Lankford said. "And you owed Levin money. It's right there in his accounts book. Four grand."

"I didn't lie about anything. You never asked if I owned a gun."

"Lied by omission. Right back at ya."

"Bullshit."

"Four grand."

"Oh yeah, the four grand — I killed him because I didn't want to pay him four grand," I said with all the sarcasm I could muster. "You got me there, Detective. Motivation. But I guess it never occurred to you to see if he had even billed me for the four grand yet, or to see if I hadn't just paid an invoice from him for six thousand dollars a week before he was murdered."

Lankford was undaunted. But I saw the doubt start to creep into Sobel's face.

"Doesn't matter how much or when you paid him," Lankford said. "A blackmailer is never satisfied. You never stop paying until you reach the point of no return. That's what this is about. The point of no return."

I shook my head.

"And what exactly was it that he had on me that made me give him jobs and pay him until I reached the point of no return?"

Lankford and Sobel exchanged a look and Lankford nodded. Sobel reached down to a briefcase on the floor and took out a file. She handed it over the seat to me.

"Take a look," Lankford said. "You missed it when you were ransacking his place. He'd hidden it in a dresser drawer."

I opened the file and saw that it contained several 8 × 10 color photos. They were taken from afar and I was in each one of them. The photographer had trailed my Lincoln over several days and several miles. Each image a frozen moment in time, the photos showed me with various individuals whom I easily recognized as clients. They were prostitutes, street dealers and Road Saints. The photos could be interpreted as suspicious because they showed one split second of time. A male prostitute in mini-shorts alighting from the backseat of the Lincoln. Teddy Vogel handing me a thick roll of cash through the back window. I closed the file and tossed it back over the seat.

"You're kidding me, right? You're saying Raul came to me with that? He extorted me with that? Those are my clients. Is this a joke or am I just missing something?"

"The California bar might not think it's a joke," Lankford said. "We hear you're on thin ice with the bar. Levin knew it. He worked it."

I shook my head.

"Incredible," I said.

I knew I had to stop talking. I was doing everything wrong with these people. I knew I should just shut up and ride it out. But I felt an almost over-powering need to convince them. I began to understand why so many cases were made in the interview rooms of police stations. People just can't shut up.

I tried to place the photographs that were in the file. Vogel giving me the roll of cash was in the parking lot outside the Saints' strip club on Sepulveda. That happened after Harold Casey's trial and Vogel was paying me for filing the appeal. The prostitute was named Terry Jones and I handled a soliciting charge for him the first week of April. I'd had to find him on the Santa Monica Boulevard stroll the night before a hearing to make sure he was going to show up.

It became clear that the photos had all been taken between the morning I had caught the Roulet case and the day Raul Levin was murdered. They were then planted at the crime scene by the killer—all part of Roulet's plan to set me up so that he could control me. The police would have everything they needed to put the Levin murder on me—except the murder weapon. As long as Roulet had the gun, he had me.

I had to admire the plan and the ingenuity at the same time that it made me feel the dread of desperation. I tried to put the window down but the button wouldn't work. I asked Sobel to open a window and she did. Fresh air started blowing into the car.

After a while Lankford looked at me in the rearview and tried to jump-start the conversation.

"We ran the history on that Woodsman," he said. "You know who owned it once, don't you?"

"Mickey Cohen," I answered matter-of-factly, staring out the window at the steep hillsides of Laurel Canyon.

"How'd you end up with Mickey Cohen's gun?"

I answered without turning from the window.

"My father was a lawyer. Mickey Cohen was his client."

Lankford whistled. Cohen was one of the most famous gangsters to ever call Los Angeles home. He was from back in the day when the gangsters competed with movie stars for the gossip headlines.

"And what? He just gave your old man a gun?"

"Cohen was charged in a shooting and my father defended him. He claimed self-defense. There was a trial and my father got a not-guilty verdict. When the weapon was returned Mickey gave it to my father. Sort of a keepsake, you could say."

"Your old man ever wonder how many people the Mick whacked with it?"

"I don't know. I didn't really know my father."

"What about Cohen? You ever meet him?"

"My father represented him before I was even born. The gun came to me in his will. I don't know why he picked me to have it. I was only five years old when he died."

"And you grew up to be a lawyer like dear old dad, and being a good lawyer you registered it."

"I thought if it was ever stolen or something I would want to be able to get it back. Turn here on Fareholm."

Lankford did as I instructed and we started climbing up the hill to my home. I then gave them the bad news.

"Thanks for the ride," I said. "You guys can search my house and my office and my car for as long as you want, but I have to tell you, you are wasting your time. Not only am I the wrong guy for this, but you aren't going to find that gun."

I saw Lankford's head jog up and he was looking at me in the rearview again.

"And why is that, Counselor? You already dumped it?"

"Because the gun was stolen out of my house and I don't know where it is."

Lankford started laughing. I saw the joy in his eyes.

"Uh-huh, stolen. How convenient. When did this happen?"

"Hard to tell. I hadn't checked on the gun in years."

"You make a police report on it or file an insurance claim?"

"No."

"So somebody comes in and steals your Mickey Cohen gun and you don't report it. Even after you just told us you registered it in case this very thing happened. You being a lawyer and all, doesn't that sound a little screwy to you?"

"It does, except I knew who stole it. It was a client. He told me he took it and if I were to report it, I would be violating a client trust because my police report would lead to his arrest. Kind of a catch-twenty-two, Detective."

Sobel turned and looked back at me. I think maybe she thought I was making it up on the spot, which I was.

"That sounds like legal jargon and bullshit, Haller," Lankford said.

"But it's the truth. We're here. Just park in front of the garage."

Lankford pulled the car into the space in front of my garage and killed the engine. He turned to look back at me before getting out.

"Which client stole the gun?"

"I told you, I can't tell you."

"Well, Roulet's your only client right now, isn't he?"

"I have a lot of clients. But I told you, I can't tell you."

"Think maybe we should run the charts from his ankle bracelet and see if he's been to your place lately?"

"Do whatever you want. He actually has been here. We had a meeting here once. In my office."

"Maybe that's when he took it."

"I'm not telling you he took it, Detective."

"Yeah, well, that bracelet gives Roulet a pass on the Levin thing, anyway. We checked the GPS. So I guess that leaves you, Counselor."

"And that leaves you wasting your time."

I suddenly realized something about Roulet's ankle bracelet but tried not to show it. Maybe a line on the trapdoor to his Houdini act. It was something I would need to check into later.

"Are we just going to sit here?"

Lankford turned and got out. He then opened my door because the inside handle had been disabled for transporting suspects and custodies. I looked at the two detectives.

"You want me to show you the gun box? Maybe when you see it is empty, you can just leave and save us all the time."

"Not quite, Counselor," Lankford said. "We're going through this whole place. I'll take the car and Detective Sobel will start in the house."

I shook my head.

"Not quite, Detective. It doesn't work that way. I don't trust you. Your warrant is bent, so as far as I'm concerned, you're bent. You stay together so I can watch you both or we wait until I can get a second observer up here. My case manager could be here in ten minutes. I could bring her up here to watch and you could also ask her about calling me on the morning Raul Levin got killed."

Lankford's face grew dark with insult and anger that he looked like he was having trouble controlling. I decided to push it. I took out my cell phone and opened it.

"I'm going to call your judge right now and see if he —"

"Fine," Lankford said. "We'll start with the car. Together. We'll work our way inside the house."

I closed the phone and put it back in my pocket.

"Fine."

I walked over to a keypad on the wall outside the garage. I tapped in the combination and the garage door started to rise, revealing the blue-black Lincoln awaiting inspection. Its license plate read NT GLTY. Lankford looked at it and shook his head.

"Yeah, right."

He stepped into the garage, his face still tight with anger. I decided to ease things a little bit.

"Hey, Detective," I said. "What's the difference between a catfish and a defense attorney?"

He didn't respond. He stared angrily at the license plate on my Lincoln.

"One's a bottom-feeding shit sucker," I said. "And the other one's a fish."

For a moment his face remained frozen. Then a smile creased it and he broke into a long and hard laugh. Sobel stepped into the garage, having not heard the joke.

"What?" she said.

"I'll tell you later," Lankford said.

31

~~~

It took them a half hour to search the Lincoln and then move into the house, where they started with the office. I watched the whole time and only spoke when offering explanation about something that gave them pause in their search. They didn't talk much to each other and it was becoming increasingly clear that there was a rift between the two partners over the direction Lankford had taken the investigation.

At one point Lankford got a call on his cell phone and he went out the front door onto the porch to talk privately. I had the shades up and if I stood in the hallway I could look one way and see him out there and the other way and see Sobel in my office.

"You're not too happy about this, are you?" I said to Sobel when I was sure her partner couldn't hear.

"It doesn't matter how I am. We're following the case and that's it."

"Is your partner always like that, or only with lawyers?"

"He spent fifty thousand dollars on a lawyer last year, trying to get custody of his kids. He didn't. Before that we lost a big case — a murder — on a legal technicality."

I nodded.

"And he blamed the lawyer. But who broke the rules?"

She didn't respond and that as much as confirmed it had been Lankford who had made the technical misstep.

"I get the picture," I said.

I checked on Lankford on the porch again. He was gesturing impatiently like he was trying to explain something to a moron. Must have been his custody lawyer. I decided to change the subject with Sobel.

"Do you think you are being manipulated at all on this case?"

"What are you talking about?"

"The photos stashed in the bureau, the bullet casing in the floor vent. Pretty convenient, don't you think?"

"What are you saying?"

"I'm not saying anything. I'm asking questions your partner doesn't seem interested in."

I checked on Lankford. He was tapping in numbers on his cell, making a new call. I turned and stepped into the open doorway of the office. Sobel was looking behind the files in a drawer. Finding no gun, she closed the drawer and stepped over to the desk. I spoke in a low voice.

"What about Raul's message to me?" I said. "About finding Jesus Menendez's ticket out, what do you think he meant?"

"We haven't figured that out yet."

"Too bad. I think it's important."

"Everything's important until it isn't."

I nodded, not sure what she meant by that.

"You know, the case I'm trying is pretty interesting. You ought to come back by and watch. You might learn something."

She looked from the desk to me. Our eyes held for a moment. Then she squinted with suspicion, like she was trying to judge whether a supposed murder suspect was actually coming on to her.

"Are you serious?"

"Yeah, why not?"

"Well, for one thing, you might have trouble getting to court if you're in lockup."

"Hey, no gun, no case. That's why you're here, right?"

She didn't answer.

"Besides, this is your partner's thing. You're not riding with him on this. I can tell."

"Typical lawyer. You think you know all the angles."

"No, not me. I'm finding out I don't know any of them."

She changed the subject.

"Is this your daughter?"

She pointed to the framed photograph on the desk.

"Yeah. Hayley."

"Nice alliteration. Hayley Haller. Named after the comet?"

"Sort of. Spelled differently. My ex-wife came up with it."

Lankford came in then, talking to Sobel loudly about the call he had gotten. It had been from a supervisor telling them that they were back in play and would handle the next Glendale homicide whether the Levin case was still active or not. He didn't say anything about the call he had made.

Sobel told him she had finished searching the office. No gun.

"I'm telling you, it's not here," I said. "You are wasting your time. And mine. I have court tomorrow and need to prepare for witnesses."

"Let's do the bedroom next," Lankford said, ignoring my protest.

I backed up into the hallway to give them space to come out of one room and go into the next. They walked down the sides of the bed to where twin night tables waited. Lankford opened the top drawer of his table and lifted out a CD.

"*Wreckrium for Lil' Demon*," he read. "You have to be fucking kidding me."

I didn't respond. Sobel quickly opened the two drawers of her table and found them empty except for a strip of condoms. I looked the other way.

"I'll take the closet," Lankford said after he had finished with his night table—leaving the drawers open in typical police search fashion. He walked into the closet and soon spoke from inside it.

"Here we go."

He stepped back out of the closet holding the wooden gun box.

"Bingo," I said. "You found an empty gun box. You must be a detective."

Lankford shook the box in his hands before putting it down on the bed. Either he was trying to play with me or the box had a solid heft to it. I felt a little charge go down the back of my neck as I realized that Roulet could have just as easily snuck back into my house to return the gun. It would have been the perfect hiding place for it. The last place I might think to check again once I had determined that the gun was gone. I remembered the odd smile on Roulet's face when I had told him I wanted my gun back. Was he smiling because I already had the gun back?

Lankford flipped the box's latch and lifted the top. He pulled back the oilcloth covering. The cork cutout which once held Mickey Cohen's gun was still empty. I breathed out so heavily it almost came out as a sigh.

"What did I tell you?" I said quickly, trying to cover up.

"Yeah, what did you tell us," Lankford said. "Heidi, you got a bag? We're going to take the box."

I looked at Sobel. She didn't look like a Heidi to me. I wondered if it was some sort of a squad room nickname. Or maybe it was the reason she didn't put her first name on her business card. It didn't sound homicide tough.

"In the car," she said.

"Go get it," Lankford said.

"You are going to take an empty gun box?" I asked. "What good does it do you?"

"All part of the chain of evidence, Counselor. You should know that. Besides, it will come in handy, since I have a feeling we'll never find the gun."

I shook my head.

"Maybe handy in your dreams. The box is evidence of nothing."

"It's evidence that you had Mickey Cohen's gun. Says it right on this little brass plaque your daddy or somebody had made."

"So fucking what?"

"Well, I just made a call while I was out on your front porch, Haller. See, we had somebody checking on Mickey Cohen's self-defense case. Turns out that over there in LAPD's evidence archive they still have all the ballistic evidence from that case. That's a lucky break for us, the case being, what, fifty years old?"

I understood immediately. They would take the bullet slugs and casings from the Cohen case and compare them with the same evidence recovered in the Levin case. They would match the Levin murder to Mickey Cohen's gun which they would then tie to me with the gun box and the state's AFS computer. I doubted Roulet could have realized how the police would be able to make a case without even having the gun when he thought out his scheme to control me.

I stood there silently. Sobel left the room without a glance at me and Lankford looked up from the box at me with a killer smile.

"What's the matter, Counselor?" he asked. "Evidence got your tongue?"

I finally was able to speak.

"How long will ballistics take?" I managed to ask.

"Hey, for you, we're going to put a rush on it. So get out there and enjoy yourself while you can. But don't leave town."

He laughed, almost giddy with himself.

"Man, I thought they only said that in movies. But there, I just said it! I wish my partner had been here."

Sobel came back in with a large brown bag and a roll of red evidence tape. I watched her put the gun box into the bag and then seal it with the tape. I wondered how much time I had and if the wheels had just come off of everything I had put into motion. I started to feel as empty as the wooden box Sobel had just sealed inside the brown paper bag.

32

Fernando Valenzuela lived out in Valencia. From my home it was easily an hour's drive north in the last remnants of rush-hour traffic. Valenzuela had moved out of Van Nuys a few years earlier because his three daughters were nearing high school age and he feared for their safety and education. He moved into a neighborhood filled with people who had also fled from the city and his commute went from five minutes to forty-five. But he was happy. His house was nicer and his children safer. He lived in a Spanish-style house with a red tile roof in a planned community full of Spanish-style houses with red tile roofs. It was more than a bail bondsman could ever dream of having, but it came with a stiff monthly price tag.

It was almost nine by the time I got there. I pulled up to the garage, which had been left open. One space was taken by a minivan and the other by a pickup. On the floor between the pickup and a fully equipped tool bench was a large cardboard box that said SONY on it. It was long and thin. I looked closer and saw it was a box for a fifty-inch plasma TV. I got out and went to the front door and knocked. Valenzuela answered after a long wait.

"Mick, what are you doing up here?"

"Do you know your garage door is open?"

"Holy shit! I just had a plasma delivered."

He pushed by me and ran across the yard to look into the garage. I closed his front door and followed him to the garage. When I got there he was standing next to his TV, smiling.

"Oh, man, you know that would've never happened in Van Nuys," he said. "That sucker woulda been long gone. Come on, we'll go in through here."

He headed toward a door that would take us from the garage into the house. He hit a switch that made the garage door start to roll down.

"Hey, Val, wait a minute," I said. "Let's just talk out here. It's more private."

"But Maria probably wants to say hello."

"Maybe next time."

He came back over to me, concern in his eyes.

"What's up, Boss?"

"What's up is I spent some time today with the cops working on Raul's murder. They said they cleared Roulet on it because of the ankle bracelet."

Valenzuela nodded vigorously.

"Yeah, yeah, they came to see me a few days after it happened. I showed them the system and how it works and I pulled up Roulet's track for that day. They saw he was at work. And I also showed them the other bracelet I got and explained how it couldn't be tampered with. It's got a mass detector. Bottom line is you can't take it off. It would know and then I would know."

I leaned back against the pickup and folded my arms.

"So did those two cops ask where *you* were on that Saturday?"

It hit Valenzuela like a punch.

"What did you say, Mick?"

My eyes lowered to the plasma TV box and then back up to his.

"Somehow, some way, he killed Raul, Val. Now my ass is on the line and I want to know how he did it."

"Mick, listen to me, he's clear. I'm telling you, that bracelet didn't come off his ankle. The machine doesn't lie."

"Yeah, I know, the machine doesn't lie..."

After a moment he got it.

"What are you saying, Mick?"

He stepped in front of me, his body posture stiffening aggressively. I stopped leaning on the truck and dropped my hands to my sides.

"I'm asking, Val. Where were you on that Tuesday morning?"

"You son of a bitch, how could you ask me that?"

He had moved into a fight stance. I was momentarily taken off guard as I thought about him calling me what I had called Roulet earlier in the day.

Valenzuela suddenly lunged at me and shoved me hard against his truck. I shoved him back harder and he went backwards into the TV box. It tipped over and hit the floor with a loud, heavy *whump* and then he came down on it in a seated position. There was a sharp snap sound from inside the box.

"Oh, fuck!" he cried. "Oh, fuck! You broke the screen!"

"You pushed me, Val. I pushed back."

"Oh, fuck!"

He scrambled to the side of the box and tried to lift it back up but it was too heavy and unwieldy. I walked over to the other side and helped him right it. As the box came upright we heard small bits of material inside it slide down. It sounded like glass.

"Motherfuck!" Valenzuela yelled.

The door leading into the house opened and his wife, Maria, looked out.

"Hi, Mickey. Val, what is all the noise?"

"Just go inside," her husband ordered.

"Well, what is—"

"Shut the fuck up and go inside!"

She paused for a moment, staring at us, then closed the door. I heard her lock it. It looked like Valenzuela was sleeping with the broken TV tonight. I looked back at him. His mouth was spread in shock.

"That was eight thousand dollars," he whispered.

"They make TVs that cost eight thousand dollars?"

I was shocked. What was the world coming to?

"That was with a discount."

"Val, where'd you get the money for an eight-thousand-dollar TV?"

He looked at me and the fire came back.

"Where the fuck do you think? Business, man. Thanks to Roulet I'm having a hell of a year. But goddamn, Mick, I didn't cut him loose from the bracelet so he could go out and kill Raul. I knew Raul just as long as you did. I did not do that. I did not put the bracelet on and wear it while he went to kill Raul. And I did not go and kill Raul for him for a fucking TV. If you can't believe that, then just get the hell out of here and out of my life!"

He said it all with the desperate intensity of a wounded animal. A flash thought of Jesus Menendez came to my mind. I had failed to see the innocence in his pleas. I didn't want that to ever happen again.

"Okay, Val," I said.

I walked over to the house door and pushed the button that raised the garage door. When I turned back I saw he had taken a box cutter from the tool bench and was cutting the tape on the top of the TV box. It looked like he was trying to confirm what we already knew about the plasma. I walked past him and out of the garage.

"I'll split it with you, Val," I said. "I'll have Lorna send you a check in the morning."

"Don't bother. I'll tell them it was delivered this way."

I got to my car door and looked back at him.

"Then give me a call when they arrest you for fraud. After you bail yourself out."

I got in the Lincoln and backed out of the driveway. When I glanced back into the garage, I saw Valenzuela had stopped cutting open the box and was just standing there looking at me.

Traffic going back into the city was light and I made good time. I was just coming in through the front door when the house phone started to ring. I grabbed it in the kitchen, thinking maybe it was Valenzuela calling to tell me he was taking his business to another defense pro. At the moment I didn't care.

Instead, it was Maggie McPherson.

"Everything all right?" I asked. She usually didn't call so late.

"Fine."

"Where's Hayley?"

"Asleep. I didn't want to call until she went down."

"What's up?"

"There was a strange rumor about you floating around the office today."

"You mean the one about me being Raul Levin's murderer?"

"Haller, is this serious?"

The kitchen was too small for a table and chairs. I couldn't go far with the phone cord tether so I hoisted myself up onto the counter. Through the window over the sink I could see the lights of downtown twinkling in the distance and a glow on the horizon that I knew came from Dodger Stadium.

"I would say, yes, the situation is serious. I am being set up to take the fall for Raul's murder."

"Oh my God, Michael, how is this possible?"

"A lot of different ingredients — evil client, cop with a grudge, stupid lawyer, add sugar and spice and everything nice."

"Is it Roulet? Is he the one?"

"I can't talk about my clients with you, Mags."

"Well, what are you planning to do?"

"Don't worry, I've got it covered. I'll be okay."

"What about Hayley?"

I knew what she was saying. She was warning me to keep it away from Hayley. Don't let her go to school and hear kids talking about her father the murder suspect with a face and name splashed across the news.

"Hayley will be fine. She'll never know. Nobody will ever know if I play this thing right."

She didn't say anything and there was nothing else I could do to reassure her. I changed the subject. I tried to sound confident, even cheerful.

"How did your boy Minton look after court today?"

She didn't answer at first, probably reluctant to change the subject.

"I don't know. He looked fine. But Smithson sent an observer up because it's his first solo."

I nodded. I was counting on Smithson, who ran the DA's Van Nuys branch, having sent somebody to keep a watch on Minton.

"Any feedback?"

"No, not yet. Nothing that I heard. Look, Haller, I am really worried about this. The rumor was that you were served a search warrant in the courthouse. Is that true?"

"Yeah, but don't worry about it. I'm telling you, I have things under control. It will all come out okay. I promise."

I knew I had not quelled her fears. She was thinking about our daughter and the possible scandal. She was probably also thinking a little bit about herself and what having an ex-husband disbarred or accused of murder would do to her chances of advancement.

"Besides, if it all goes to shit, you're still going to be my first customer, right?"

"What are you talking about?"

"The Lincoln Lawyer Limousine Service. You're in, right?"

"Haller, it doesn't sound like this is a time to be making jokes."

"It's no joke, Maggie. I've been thinking about quitting. Even before all of this bullshit came up. It's like I told you that night, I can't do this anymore."

There was a long silence before she responded.

"Whatever you want to do is going to be fine by me and Hayley."

I nodded.

"You don't know how much I appreciate that."

She sighed into the phone.

"I don't know how you do it, Haller."

"Do what?"

"You're a sleazy defense lawyer with two ex-wives and an eight-year-old daughter. And we all still love you."

Now I was silent. Despite everything I smiled.

"Thank you, Maggie McFierce," I finally said. "Good night."

And I hung up the phone.

33

≈≈≈

Tuesday, May 24

The second day of trial began with a forthwith to the judge's chambers for Minton and me. Judge Fullbright wanted only to speak to me but the rules of trial made it improper for her to meet privately with me about any matter and exclude the prosecution. Her chambers were spacious, with a desk and separate seating area surrounded by three walls of shelves containing law books. She told us to sit in the seats in front of her desk.

"Mr. Minton," she began, "I can't tell you not to listen but I'm going to have a conversation with Mr. Haller that I don't expect you to join or interrupt. It doesn't concern you or, as far as I know, the Roulet case."

Minton, taken by surprise, didn't quite know how to react other than to drop his jaw a couple inches and let light into his mouth. The judge turned in her desk chair toward me and clasped her hands together on the desk.

"Mr. Haller, is there anything you need to bring up with me? Keeping in mind that you are sitting next to a prosecutor."

"No, Judge, everything's fine. Sorry if you were bothered yesterday."

I did my best to put a rueful smile on my face, as if to show the search warrant had been nothing more than an embarrassing inconvenience.

"It is hardly a bother, Mr. Haller. We've invested a lot of time on this case. The jury, the prosecution, all of us. I am hoping that it is not going to be for naught. I don't want to do this again. My calendar is already overflowing."

"Excuse me, Judge Fullbright," Minton said. "Could I just ask what —"

"No, you may not," she said, cutting him off. "What we are talking about does not concern the trial other than the timing of it. If Mr. Haller is assuring me that we don't have a problem, then I will take him at his word. You need no further explanation than that."

She looked pointedly at me.

"Do I have your word on this, Mr. Haller?"

I hesitated before nodding. What she was telling me was that there would be hell to pay if I broke my word and the Glendale investigation caused a disruption or mistrial in the Roulet case.

"You've got my word," I said.

She immediately stood up and turned toward the hat rack in the corner. Her black robe hung there on a hanger.

"Okay, then, gentlemen, let's get to it. We've got a jury waiting."

Minton and I left the chambers and entered the courtroom through the clerk's station. Roulet was seated in the defendant's chair and waiting.

"What the hell was that all about?" Minton whispered to me.

He was playing dumb. He had to have heard the same rumors my ex-wife had picked up in the halls of the DA's office.

"Nothing, Ted. Just some bullshit involving another case of mine. You going to wrap it up today?"

"Depends on you. The longer you take, the longer I take cleaning up the bullshit you sling."

"Bullshit, huh? You're bleeding to death and don't even know it."

He smiled confidently at me.

"I don't think so."

"Call it death by a thousand razor blades, Ted. One doesn't do it. They all do it. Welcome to felony practice."

I separated from him and went to the defense table. As soon as I sat down, Roulet was in my ear.

"What was that about with the judge?" he whispered.

"Nothing. She was just warning me about how I handle the victim on cross."

"Who, the woman? She actually called her a victim?"

"Louis, first of all, keep your voice down. And second, she *is* the victim in this thing. You may have that rare ability to convince yourself of almost anything, but we still—no, make that I—still need to convince the jury."

He took the rebuke like I was blowing bubbles in his face and moved on.

"Well, what did she say?"

"She said she isn't going to allow me a lot of freedom in cross-examination. She reminded me that Regina Campo is a victim."

"I'm counting on you to rip her to shreds, to borrow a quote from you on the day we met."

"Yeah, well, things are a lot different than on the day we met, aren't they? And your little scheme with my gun is about to blow up in my face. And I'm telling you right now, I'm not going down for it. If I have to drive people to the airport the rest of my life, I will do that and do it gladly if it's my only way out from this. You understand, Louis?"

"I understand, Mick," he said glibly. "I'm sure you'll figure something out. You're a smart man."

I turned and looked at him. Luckily, I didn't have to say anything further. The bailiff called the court to order and Judge Fullbright took the bench.

Minton's first witness of the day was LAPD Detective Martin Booker. He was a solid witness for the prosecution. A rock. His answers were clear and concise and given without hesitation. Booker introduced the key piece of evidence, the knife with my client's initials on it, and under Minton's questioning he took the jury through his entire investigation of the attack on Regina Campo.

He testified that on the night of March 6 he had been working night duty out of Valley Bureau in Van Nuys. He was called to Regina Campo's apartment by the West Valley Division watch commander, who believed, after being briefed by his patrol officers, that the attack on Campo merited immediate attention from an investigator. Booker explained that the six detective bureaus in the Valley were only staffed during daytime hours. He said the night-duty detective was a quick-response position and often assigned cases of a pressing nature.

"What made this case of pressing nature, Detective?" Minton asked.

"The injuries to the victim, the arrest of a suspect and the belief that a greater crime had probably been averted," Booker answered.

"That greater crime being what?"

"Murder. It sounded like the guy was planning to kill her."

I could have objected but I planned to exploit the exchange on cross-examination, so I let it go.

Minton walked Booker through the investigative steps he took at the crime scene and later while interviewing Campo as she was being treated at a hospital.

"Before you got to the hospital you had been briefed by Officers Maxwell and Santos on what the victim had reported had happened, correct?"

"Yes, they gave me an overview."

"Did they tell you that the victim was engaged in selling sex to men for a living?"

"No, they didn't."

"When did you find that out?"

"Well, I was getting a pretty good sense of it when I was in her apartment and I saw some of the property she had there."

"What property?"

"Things I would describe as sex aids, and in one of the bedrooms, there was a closet that only had negligees and clothing of a sexually provocative nature in it. There was also a television in that room and a collection of pornographic tapes in the drawers beneath it. I had been told that she did not have a roommate but it looked to me like both bedrooms were in active use. I started to think that one room was hers, like it was the one she slept in when she was alone, and the other was for her professional activities."

"A trick pad?"

"You could call it that."

"Did it change your opinion of her as a victim of this attack?"

"No, it didn't."

"And why not?"

"Because anybody can be a victim. Prostitute or pope, doesn't matter. A victim is a victim."

Spoken just as rehearsed, I thought. Minton made a check mark on his pad and moved on.

"Now, when you got to the hospital, did you ask the victim about your theory in regard to her bedrooms and what she did for a living?"

"Yes, I did."

"What did she tell you?"

"She flat out said she was a working girl. She didn't try to hide it."

"Did anything she said to you differ from the accounts of the attack you had already gathered at the crime scene?"

"No, not at all. She told me she opened the door to the defendant and he immediately punched her in the face and drove her backwards into the apartment. He assaulted her further and produced a knife. He told her he was going to rape her and then kill her."

Minton continued to probe the investigation in more detail and to the point of boring the jury. When I was not writing down questions to ask Booker during cross, I watched the jurors and saw their attention lag under the weight of so much information.

Finally, after ninety minutes of direct examination it was my turn with the police detective. My goal was to get in and get out. While Minton performed the whole case autopsy, I only wanted to go in and scrape cartilage out of the knees.

"Detective Booker, did Regina Campo explain why she lied to the police?"

"She didn't lie to me."

"Maybe not to you but she told the first officers on the scene, Maxwell and Santos, that she did not know why the suspect had come to her apartment, didn't she?"

"I wasn't present when they spoke to her so I can't testify to that. I do know that she was scared, that she had just been beaten and threatened with rape and death at the time of the first interview."

"So you are saying that under those circumstances it is acceptable to lie to the police."

"No, I did not say that."

I checked my notes and moved on. I wasn't going for a linear continuum of questions. I was potshotting, trying to keep him off balance.

"Did you catalog the clothing you found in the bedroom you said Ms. Campo used for her prostitution business?"

"No, I did not. It was just an observation I made. It was not important to the case."

"Would any of the outfits you saw in the closet have been appropriate to sadomasochistic sexual activities?"

"I wouldn't know that. I am not an expert in that field."

"How about the pornographic videos? Did you write down the titles?"

"No, I did not. Again, I did not believe that it was pertinent to the investigation of who had brutally assaulted this woman."

"Do you recall if the subject matter of any of the videos involved sadomasochism or bondage or anything of that nature?"

"No, I do not."

"Now, did you instruct Ms. Campo to get rid of those tapes and the clothing from the closet before members of Mr. Roulet's defense team could view the apartment?"

"I certainly did not."

I checked that one off my list and moved on.

"Have you ever spoken to Mr. Roulet about what happened in Ms. Campo's apartment that night?"

"No, he lawyered up before I got to him."

"Do you mean he exercised his constitutional right to remain silent?"

"Yes, that's exactly what he did."

"So, as far as you know, he never spoke to the police about what happened."

"That is correct."

"In your opinion, was Ms. Campo struck with great force?"

"I would say so, yes. Her face was very badly cut and swollen."

"Then please tell the jury about the impact injuries you found on Mr. Roulet's hands."

"He had wrapped a cloth around his fist to protect it. There were no injuries on his hands that I could see."

"Did you document this lack of injury?"

Booker looked puzzled by the question.

"No," he said.

"So you had Ms. Campo's injuries documented by photographs but you didn't see the need to document Mr. Roulet's lack of injuries, correct?"

"It didn't seem to me to be necessary to photograph something that wasn't there."

"How do you know he wrapped his fist in a cloth to protect it?"

"Ms. Campo told me she saw that his hand was wrapped right before he punched her at the door."

"Did you find this cloth he supposedly wrapped his hand in?"

"Yes, it was in the apartment. It was a napkin, like from a restaurant. It had her blood on it."

"Did it have Mr. Roulet's blood on it?"

"No."

"Was there anything that identified it as belonging to the defendant?"

"No."

"So we have Ms. Campo's word for it, right?"

"That's right."

I let some time pass while I scribbled a note on my pad. I then continued to question the detective.

"Detective, when did you learn that Louis Roulet denied assaulting or threatening Ms. Campo and that he would be vigorously defending himself against the charges?"

"That would have been when he hired you, I guess."

There was a murmur of laughter in the courtroom.

"Did you pursue other explanations for Ms. Campo's injuries?"

"No, she told me what happened. I believed her. He beat her and was going to—"

"Thank you, Detective Booker. Just try to answer the question I ask."

"I was."

"If you looked for no other explanation because you believed the word of Ms. Campo, is it safe to say that this whole case relies upon her word and what she said occurred in her apartment on the night of March sixth?"

Booker deliberated a moment. He knew I was leading him into a trap of his own words. As the saying goes, there is no trap so deadly as the one you set for yourself.

"It's not just her word," he said after thinking he saw a way out. "There is physical evidence. The knife. Her injuries. More than just her word on this."

He nodded affirmatively.

"But doesn't the state's explanation for her injuries and the other evidence begin with her telling of what happened?"

"You could say that, yes," he said reluctantly.

"She is the tree on which all of these fruits grow, is she not?"

"I probably wouldn't use those words."

"Then what words would you use, Detective?"

I had him now. Booker was literally squirming in his seat. Minton stood up and objected, saying I was badgering the witness. It must have been something he had seen on TV or in a movie. He was told to sit down by the judge.

"You can answer the question, Detective," the judge said.

"What was the question?" Booker asked, trying to buy some time.

"You disagreed with me when I characterized Ms. Campo as the tree from which all the evidence in the case grows," I said. "If I am wrong, how would you describe her position in this case?"

Booker raised his hands in a quick gesture of surrender.

"She's the victim! Of course she's important because she told us what happened. We have to rely on her to set the course of the investigation."

"You rely on her for quite a bit in this case, don't you? Victim and chief witness against the defendant, correct?"

"That's right."

"Who else saw the defendant attack Ms. Campo?"

"Nobody else."

I nodded, to underline the answer for the jury. I looked over and exchanged eye contact with those in the front row.

"Okay, Detective," I said. "I want to ask you about Charles Talbot now. How did you find out about this man?"

"Uh, the prosecutor, Mr. Minton, told me to find him."

"And do you know how Mr. Minton came to know about his existence?"

"I believe you were the one who informed him. You had a videotape from a bar that showed him with the victim a couple hours before the attack."

I knew this could be the point to introduce the video but I wanted to wait on that. I wanted the victim on the stand when I showed the tape to the jury.

"And up until that point you didn't think it was important to find this man?"

"No, I just didn't know about him."

"So when you finally did know about Talbot and you located him, did you have his left hand examined to determine if he had any injuries that could have been sustained while punching someone repeatedly in the face?"

"No, I didn't."

"Is that because you were confident in your choice of Mr. Roulet as the person who punched Regina Campo?"

"It wasn't a choice. It was where the investigation led. I didn't locate Charles Talbot until more than two weeks after the crime occurred."

"So what you are saying is that if he'd had injuries, they would have been healed by then, correct?"

"I'm no expert on it but that was my thinking, yes."

"So you never looked at his hand, did you?"

"Not specifically, no."

"Did you question any coworkers of Mr. Talbot about whether they saw bruising or other injuries on his hand around the time of the crime?"

"No, I did not."

"So you never really looked beyond Mr. Roulet, did you?"

"That is wrong. I come into every case with an open mind. But Roulet was there and in custody from the start. The victim identified him as her attacker. He was obviously a focus."

"Was he *a* focus or *the* focus, Detective Booker?"

"He was both. At first he was *a* focus and later—after we found his initials on the weapon that had been held to Reggie Campo's throat—he became *the* focus, you could say."

"How do you know that knife was held to Ms. Campo's throat?"

"Because she told us and she had the puncture wound to show for it."

"Are you saying there was some sort of forensic analysis that matched the knife to the wound on her neck?"

"No, that was impossible."

"So again we have Ms. Campo's word that the knife was held to her throat by Mr. Roulet."

"I had no reason to doubt her then. I have none now."

"Now without any explanation for it, I guess you would consider the knife with the defendant's initials on it to be a highly important piece of evidence of guilt, wouldn't you?"

"Yes. Even with explanation, I would say. He brought that knife in there with one purpose in mind."

"You are a mind reader, are you, Detective?"

"No, I'm a detective. And I am just saying what I think."

"Accent on *think*."

"It's what I know from the evidence in the case."

"I'm glad you are so confident, sir. I have no further questions at this time. I reserve the right to recall Detective Booker as a witness for the defense."

I had no intention of calling Booker back to the stand but I thought the threat might sound good to the jury.

I returned to my seat while Minton tried to bandage up Booker on redirect. The damage was in perceptions and there wasn't a lot that he could do with that. Booker had only been a setup man for the defense. The real damage would come later.

After Booker stepped down, the judge called for the mid-morning break. She told the jurors to be back in fifteen minutes but I knew the break would last longer. Judge Fullbright was a smoker and had already faced highly publicized administrative charges for sneaking smokes in her chambers. That meant that for her to take care of her habit and avoid further scandal, she had to take the elevator down and leave the building and stand in the entry port where the jail buses come in. I figured I had at least a half hour.

I went out into the hallway to talk to Mary Alice Windsor and work my cell phone. It looked like I would be putting on witnesses in the afternoon session.

I was first approached by Roulet, who wanted to talk about my cross-examination of Booker.

"It looked to me like it went really well for us," he said.

"Us?"

"You know what I mean."

"You can't tell whether it's gone well until you get the verdict. Now leave me alone, Louis. I have to make some calls. And where is your mother? I am probably going to need her this afternoon. Is she going to be here?"

"She had an appointment this morning but she'll be here. Just call Cecil and he'll bring her in."

After he walked away Detective Booker took his place, walking up to me and pointing a finger in my face.

"It's not going to fly, Haller," he said.

"What's not going to fly?" I asked.

"Your whole bullshit defense. You're going to crash and burn."

"We'll see."

"Yeah, we'll see. You know, you have some balls trying to trash Talbot with this. Some balls. You must need a wheelbarrow to carry them around in."

"I'm just doing my job, Detective."

"And some job it is. Lying for a living. Tricking people from looking at the truth. Living in a world without truth. Let me ask you something. You know the difference between a catfish and a lawyer?"

"No, what's the difference?"

"One's a bottom-feeding, shit-eating scum sucker. The other's a fish."

"That's a good one, Detective."

He left me then and I stood there smiling. Not because of the joke or the understanding that Lankford had probably been the one to elevate the insult from defense attorneys to all of lawyerdom when he had retold the joke to Booker. I smiled because the joke was confirmation that Lankford and Booker were in communication. They were talking and it meant that things were moving and in play. My plan was still holding together. I still had a chance.

34

Every trial has a main event. A witness or a piece of evidence that becomes the fulcrum upon which everything swings one way or the other. In this case the main event was billed as Regina Campo, victim and accuser, and the case would seem to rest upon her performance and testimony. But a good defense attorney always has an understudy and I had mine, a witness secretly waiting in the wings upon whom I hoped to shift the weight of the trial.

Nevertheless, when Minton called Regina Campo to the stand after the break, it was safe to say all eyes were on her as she was led in and walked to the witness box. It was the first time anyone in the jury had seen her in person. It was also the first time I had ever seen her. I was surprised, but not in a good way. She was diminutive and her hesitant walk and slight posture belied the picture of the scheming mercenary I had been building in the jury's collective consciousness.

Minton was definitely learning as he was going. With Campo he seemed to have arrived at the conclusion that less was more. He economically led her through the testimony. He first started with personal background before moving on to the events of March 6.

Regina Campo's story was sadly unoriginal and that was what Minton was counting on. She told the story of a young, attractive woman coming to Hollywood from Indiana a decade before with hopes of celluloid glory. There were starts and stops to a career, an appearance on a television show here and there. She was a fresh face and there were always men willing to put her in small meaningless parts. But when she was no longer a fresh face, she found work in a series of straight-to-cable films which often required her to appear nude. She supplemented her income with nude modeling jobs and slipped easily into a world of trading sex for favors. Eventually, she skipped the façade altogether and started trading sex for money. It finally brought her to the night she encountered Louis Roulet.

Regina Campo's courtroom version of what happened that night did not differ from the accounts offered by all previous witnesses in the trial. But where it was dramatically different was in the delivery. Campo, with her face framed by dark, curly hair, seemed like a little girl lost. She appeared scared and tearful during the latter half of her testimony. Her lower lip and finger shook with fear as she pointed to the man she identified as her attacker. Roulet stared right back, a blank expression on his face.

"It was him," she said in a strong voice. "He's an animal who should be put away!"

I let that go without objection. I would get my chance with her soon enough. Minton continued the questioning, taking Campo through her escape, and then asked why she had not told the responding officers the truth about knowing who the man who attacked her was and why he was there.

"I was scared," she said. "I wasn't sure they would believe me if I told them why he was there. I wanted to make sure they arrested him because I was very afraid of him."

"Do you regret that decision now?"

"Yes, I do because I know it might help him get free to do this again to somebody."

I did object to that answer as prejudicial and the judge sustained it. Minton threw a few more questions at his witness but seemed to know he was
past the apex of the testimony and that he should stop before he obscured
the trembling finger of identification.

Campo had testified on direct examination for slightly less than an hour.
It was almost 11:30 but the judge did not break for lunch as I had expected.
She told the jurors she wanted to get as much testimony in as possible during the day and that they would go to a late, abbreviated lunch. This made
me wonder if she knew something I didn't. Had the Glendale detectives
called her during the mid-morning break to warn of my impending arrest?

"Mr. Haller, your witness," she said to prompt me and keep things going.

I went to the lectern with my legal pad and looked at my notes. If I was
engaged in a defense of a thousand razors, I had to use at least half of them
on this witness. I was ready.

"Ms. Campo, have you engaged the services of an attorney to sue Mr.
Roulet over the alleged events of March sixth?"

She looked as though she had expected the question, but not as the first
one out of the shoot.

"No, I haven't."

"Have you talked to an attorney about this case?"

"I haven't hired anybody to sue him. Right now, all I am interested in is
seeing that justice is —"

"Ms. Campo," I interrupted. "I didn't ask whether you hired an attorney
or what your interests are. I asked if you had *talked* to an attorney—any
attorney—about this case and a possible lawsuit against Mr. Roulet."

She was looking closely at me, trying to read me. I had said it with the
authority of someone who knew something, who had the goods to back up
the charge. Minton had probably schooled her on the most important
aspect of testifying: don't get trapped in a lie.

"Talked to an attorney, yes. But it was nothing more than talk. I didn't
hire him."

"Is that because the prosecutor told you not to hire anybody until the
criminal case was over?"

"No, he didn't say anything about that."

"Why did you talk to an attorney about this case?"

She had dropped into a routine of hesitating before every answer. This
was fine with me. The perception of most people is that it takes time to tell
a lie. Honest responses come easily.

"I talked to him because I wanted to know my rights and to make sure I
was protected."

"Did you ask him if you could sue Mr. Roulet for damages?"

"I thought what you say to your attorney is private."

"If you wish, you can tell the jurors what you spoke to the attorney
about."

There was the first deep slash with the razor. She was in an untenable position. No matter how she answered she would not look good.

"I think I want to keep it private," she finally said.

"Okay, let's go back to March sixth, but I want to go a little further back than Mr. Minton did. Let's go back to the bar at Morgan's when you first spoke to the defendant, Mr. Roulet."

"Okay."

"What were you doing at Morgan's that night?"

"I was meeting someone."

"Charles Talbot?"

"Yes."

"Now, you were meeting him there to sort of size up whether you wanted to lead him back to your place to engage in sex for hire, correct?"

She hesitated but then nodded.

"Please answer verbally," the judge told her.

"Yes."

"Would you say that practice is a safety precaution?"

"Yes."

"A form of safe sex, right?"

"I guess so."

"Because in your profession you deal intimately with strangers, so you must protect yourself, correct?"

"Yes, correct."

"People in your profession call this the 'freak test,' don't they?"

"I've never called it that."

"But it is true that you meet your prospective clients in a public place like Morgan's to test them out and make sure they aren't freaks or dangerous before you take them to your apartment. Isn't that right?"

"You could say that. But the truth is, you can never be sure about somebody."

"That is true. So when you were at Morgan's you noticed Mr. Roulet sitting at the same bar as you and Mr. Talbot?"

"Yes, he was there."

"And had you ever seen him before?"

"Yes, I had seen him there and a few other places before."

"Had you ever spoken to him?"

"No, we never talked."

"Had you ever noticed that he wore a Rolex watch?"

"No."

"Had you ever seen him drive up or away from one of these places in a Porsche or a Range Rover?"

"No, I never saw him driving."

"But you had seen him before in Morgan's and other places like it."

"Yes."

"But never spoke to him."

"Correct."

"Then, what made you approach him?"

"I knew he was in the life, that's all."

"What do you mean by 'in the life'?"

"I mean that the other times I had seen him I could tell he was a player. I'd seen him leave with girls that do what I do."

"You saw him leave with other prostitutes?"

"Yes."

"Leave to where?"

"I don't know, leave the premises. Go to a hotel or the girl's apartment. I don't know that part."

"Well, how do you know they even left the premises? Maybe they went outside for a smoke."

"I saw them get into his car and drive away."

"Ms. Campo, you testified a minute ago that you never saw Mr. Roulet's cars. Now you are saying that you saw him get into his car with a woman who is a prostitute like yourself. Which is it?"

She realized her misstep and froze for a moment until an answer came to her.

"I saw him get into a car but I didn't know what kind it was."

"You don't notice things like that, do you?"

"Not usually."

"Do you know the difference between a Porsche and a Range Rover?"

"One's big and one's small, I guess."

"What kind of car did you see Mr. Roulet get into?"

"I don't remember."

I paused a moment and decided I had milked her contradiction for all it was worth. I looked down at my list of questions and moved on.

"These women that you saw leave with Mr. Roulet, were they ever seen again?"

"I don't understand."

"Did they disappear? Did you ever see them again?"

"No, I saw them again."

"Had they been beaten or injured?"

"Not that I know of but I didn't ask."

"But all of this added up to you believing that you were safe as far as approaching and soliciting him, correct?"

"I don't know about safe. I just knew he was probably there looking for a girl and the man I was with already told me he would be finished by ten because he had to go to his business."

"Well, can you tell the jury why it was that you did not have to sit with Mr. Roulet like you did with Mr. Talbot and subject him to a freak test?"

Her eyes drifted over to Minton. She was hoping for a rescue but none was coming.

"I just thought he was a known quantity, that's all."

"You thought he was safe."

"I guess so. I don't know. I needed the money and I made a mistake with him."

"Did you think he was rich and could solve your need for money?"

"No, nothing like that. I saw him as a potential customer who wasn't new to the game. Somebody who knew what he was doing."

"You testified that on prior occasions you had seen Mr. Roulet with other women who practice the same profession as yourself?"

"Yes."

"They're prostitutes."

"Yes."

"Do you know them?"

"We're acquaintances."

"And do you extend professional courtesy to these women in terms of alerting them to customers who might be dangerous or unwilling to pay?"

"Sometimes."

"And they extend the same professional courtesy to you, right?"

"Yes."

"How many of them warned you about Louis Roulet?"

"Well, nobody did, or I wouldn't have gone with him."

I nodded and looked at my notes for a long moment before continuing. I then led her in more detail through the events at Morgan's and then introduced the video surveillance tape from the bar's overhead camera. Minton objected to it being shown to the jury without proper foundation but he was overruled. A television on an industrial stand was wheeled in front of the jury and the video was played. I could tell by the rapt attention they paid to it that they were enamored with the idea of watching a prostitute at work as well as the aspect of seeing the two main players in the case in unguarded moments.

"What did the note say that you passed him?" I asked after the television was pushed to the side of the courtroom.

"I think it just said my name and address."

"You didn't quote him a price for the services you would perform?"

"I may have. I don't remember."

"What is the going rate that you charge?"

"Usually I get four hundred dollars."

"Usually? What would make you differentiate from that?"

"Depends on what the client wants."

I looked over at the jury box and saw that the Bible man's face was getting tight with discomfort.

"Do you ever engage in bondage and domination with your clients?"

"Sometimes. It's only role playing, though. Nobody ever gets hurt. It's just playacting."

"Are you saying that before the night of March sixth, you have never been hurt by a client?"

"Yes, that's what I am saying. That man hurt me and tried to kill—"

"Please just answer the question I ask, Ms. Campo. Thank you. Now, let's go back to Morgan's. Yes or no, at the moment you gave Mr. Roulet the napkin with your address and price on it, you were confident that he would not be a danger to you and that he was carrying sufficient cash funds to pay the four hundred dollars you demand for your services?"

"Yes."

"So, why didn't Mr. Roulet have any cash on him when the police searched him?"

"I don't know. I didn't take it."

"Do you know who did?"

"No."

I hesitated for a long moment, preferring to punctuate my shifts in questioning streams with an underscore of silence.

"Now, uh, you are still working as a prostitute, correct?" I asked.

Campo hesitated before saying yes.

"And are you happy working as a prostitute?" I asked.

Minton stood.

"Your Honor, what does this have to do with—"

"Sustained," the judge said.

"Okay," I said. "Then, isn't it true, Ms. Campo, that you have told several of your clients that your hope is to leave the business?"

"Yes, that's true," she answered without hesitation for the first time in many questions.

"Isn't it also true that you see the potential financial aspects of this case as a means of getting out of the business?"

"No, that's not true," she said forcefully and without hesitation. "That man attacked me. He was going to kill me! That's what this is about!"

I underlined something on my pad, another punctuation of silence.

"Was Charles Talbot a repeat customer?" I asked.

"No, I met him for the first time that night at Morgan's."

"And he passed your safety test."

"Yes."

"Was Charles Talbot the man who punched you in the face on March sixth?"

"No, he was not," she answered quickly.

"Did you offer to split the profits you would receive from a lawsuit against Mr. Roulet with Mr. Talbot?"

"No, I did not. That's a lie!"

I looked up at the judge.

"Your Honor, can I ask my client to stand up at this time?"

"Be my guest, Mr. Haller."

I signaled Roulet to stand at the defense table and he obliged. I looked back at Regina Campo.

"Now, Ms. Campo, are you sure that this is the man who struck you on the night of March sixth?"

"Yes, it's him."

"How much do you weigh, Ms. Campo?"

She leaned back from the microphone as if put out by what was an invasive question, even coming after so many questions pertaining to her sex life. I noticed Roulet start to sit back down and I signaled him to remain standing.

"I'm not sure," Campo said.

"On your ad on the website you list your weight at one hundred and five pounds," I said. "Is that correct?"

"I think so."

"So if the jury is to believe your story about March sixth, then they must believe that you were able to overpower and break free of Mr. Roulet."

I pointed to Roulet, who was easily six feet and outweighed her by at least seventy-five pounds.

"Well, that's what I did."

"And this was while he supposedly was holding a knife to your throat."

"I wanted to live. You can do some amazing things when your life is in danger."

She used her last defense. She started crying, as if my question had reawakened the horror of coming so close to death.

"You can sit down, Mr. Roulet. I have nothing else for Ms. Campo at this time, Your Honor."

I took my seat next to Roulet. I felt the cross had gone well. My razor work had opened up a lot of wounds. The state's case was bleeding. Roulet leaned over and whispered one word to me. "Brilliant!"

Minton went back in for a redirect but he was just a gnat flitting around an open wound. There was no going back on some of the answers his star witness had given, and there was no way to change some of the images I had planted in the jurors' minds.

In ten minutes he was through and I waived off a recross, feeling that Minton had accomplished little during his second effort and I could leave well enough alone. The judge asked the prosecutor if he had any further witnesses and Minton said he would like to think about it through lunch before deciding whether to rest the state's case.

Normally, I would have objected to this because I would want to know if I had to put a witness on the stand directly after lunch. But I let it go. I believed that Minton was feeling the pressure and was wavering. I wanted to push him toward a decision and thought maybe giving him the lunch hour would help.

The judge excused the jury to lunch, giving them only an hour instead of the usual ninety minutes. She was going to keep things moving. She said court would recess until 1:30 and then abruptly left the bench. She probably needed a cigarette, I guessed.

I asked Roulet if his mother could join us for lunch so that we could talk about her testimony, which I thought would come in the afternoon if not directly after lunch. He said he would arrange it and suggested we meet at a French restaurant on Ventura Boulevard. I told him we had less than an hour and that his mother should meet us at Four Green Fields. I didn't like the idea of bringing them into my sanctuary but I knew we could eat there quickly and be back to court on time. The food probably wasn't up to the standards of the French bistro on Ventura but I wasn't worried about that.

When I got up and turned from the defense table, I saw the rows of the gallery were empty. Everybody had hustled out to lunch. Only Minton was waiting by the rail for me.

"Can I talk to you for a minute?" he asked.

"Sure."

We waited until Roulet had gone through the gate and left the courtroom before either one of us spoke. I knew what was coming. It was customary for the prosecutor to throw out a low-ball disposition at the first sign of trouble. Minton knew he had trouble. The main-event witness was a draw at best.

"What's up?" I said.

"I was thinking about what you said about the thousand razors."

"And?"

"And, well, I want to make you an offer."

"You're new at this, kid. Don't you need somebody in charge to approve a plea agreement?"

"I have some authority."

"Okay, then give me what you are authorized to offer."

"I'll drop it all down to an aggravated assault with GBI."

"And?"

"I'll go down to four."

The offer was a substantial reduction but Roulet, if he took it, would still be sentenced to four years in prison. The main concession was that it knocked the case out of sex crime status. Roulet would not have to register with local authorities as a sex offender after he got out of prison.

I looked at him as if he had just insulted my mother's memory.

"I think that's a little strong, Ted, considering how your ace just held up on the stand. Did you see the juror who is always carrying the Bible? He looked like he was about to shit the Good Book when she was testifying."

Minton didn't respond. I could tell he hadn't even noticed a juror carrying a Bible.

"I don't know," I said. "It's my duty to bring your offer to my client and I will do that. But I'm also going to tell him he'd be a fool to take it."

"Okay, then, what do you want?"

"A case like this, there's only one verdict, Ted. I'm going to tell him he should ride it out. I think it's clear sailing from here. Have a good lunch."

I left him there at the gate, halfway expecting him to shout a new offer to my back as I went down the center aisle of the gallery. But Minton held his ground.

"That offer's good only until one-thirty, Haller," he called after me, an odd tone in his voice.

I raised a hand and waved without looking back. As I went through the courtroom door, I was sure that what I had heard was the sound of desperation creeping into his voice.

35

After we came back into court from Four Green Fields I purposely ignored Minton. I wanted to keep him guessing as long as possible. It was all part of the plan to push him in a direction I wanted him and the trial to go. When we were all seated at the tables and ready for the judge, I finally looked over at him, waited for the eye contact, and then just shook my head. No deal. He nodded, trying his best to give me a show of confidence in his case and confusion over my client's decision. One minute later the judge took the bench, brought out the jury, and Minton promptly folded his tent.

"Mr. Minton, do you have another witness?" the judge asked.

"Your Honor, at this time the state rests."

There was the slightest hesitation in Fullbright's response. She stared at Minton for just a second longer than she should have. I think it sent a message of surprise to the jury. She then looked over at me.

"Mr. Haller, are you ready to proceed?"

The routine procedure would be to ask the judge for a directed verdict of acquittal at the end of the state's case. But I didn't, fearing that this could be the rare occasion that the request was granted. I couldn't let the case end yet. I told the judge I was ready to proceed with a defense.

My first witness was Mary Alice Windsor. She was escorted into the courtroom by Cecil Dobbs, who then took a seat in the front row of the gallery. Windsor was wearing a powder blue suit with a chiffon blouse. She had a regal bearing as she crossed in front of the bench and took a seat in the witness box. Nobody would have guessed she had eaten shepherd's pie for lunch. I very quickly went through the routine identifiers and established her relationship by both blood and business to Louis Roulet. I then asked the judge for permission to show the witness the knife the prosecution had entered as evidence in the case.

Permission granted, I went to the court clerk to retrieve the weapon, which was still wrapped in a clear plastic evidence bag. It was folded so that the initials on the blade were visible. I took it to the witness box and put it down in front of the witness.

"Mrs. Windsor, do you recognize this knife?"

She picked up the evidence bag and attempted to smooth the plastic over the blade so she could look for and read the initials.

"Yes, I do," she finally said. "It's my son's knife."

"And how is it that you would recognize a knife owned by your son?"

"Because he showed it to me on more than one occasion. I knew he always carried it and sometimes it came in handy at the office when our brochures came in and we needed to cut the packing straps. It was very sharp."

"How long did he have the knife?"

"Four years."

"You seem pretty exact about that."

"I am."

"How can you be so sure?"

"Because he got it for protection four years ago. Almost exactly."

"Protection from what, Mrs. Windsor?"

"In our business we often show homes to complete strangers. Sometimes we are the only ones in the home with these strangers. There has been more than one incident of a realtor being robbed or hurt...or even murdered or raped."

"As far as you know, was Louis ever the victim of such a crime?"

"Not personally, no. But he knew someone who had gone into a home and that happened to them..."

"What happened?"

"She got raped and robbed by a man with a knife. Louis was the one who found her after it was over. The first thing he did was go out and get a knife for protection after that."

"Why a knife? Why not a gun?"

"He told me that at first he was going to get a gun but he wanted something he could always carry and not be noticeable with. So he got a knife and he got me one, too. That's how I know it was almost exactly four years ago that he got this."

She held the bag up containing the knife.

"Mine's exactly the same, only the initials are different. We both have been carrying them ever since."

"So would it seem to you that if your son was carrying that knife on the night of March sixth, then that would be perfectly normal behavior from him?"

Minton objected, saying I had not built the proper foundation for

Windsor to answer the question and the judge sustained it. Mary Windsor, being unschooled in criminal law, assumed that the judge was allowing her to answer.

"He carried it every day," she said. "March sixth would have been no dif—"

"Mrs. Windsor," the judge boomed. "I sustained the objection. That means you do not answer. The jury will disregard her answer."

"I'm sorry," Windsor said in a weak voice.

"Next question, Mr. Haller," the judge ordered.

"That's all I have, Your Honor. Thank you, Mrs. Windsor."

Mary Windsor started to get up but the judge admonished her again, telling her to stay seated. I returned to my seat as Minton got up from his. I scanned the gallery and saw no recognizable faces save that of C. C. Dobbs. He gave me an encouraging smile, which I ignored.

Mary Windsor's direct testimony had been perfect in terms of her adhering to the choreography we had worked up at lunch. She had succinctly delivered to the jury the explanation for the knife, yet she had also left in her testimony a minefield that Minton would have to cross. Her direct testimony had covered no more than I had provided Minton in a discovery summary. If he strayed from it he would quickly hear the deadly *click* under his foot.

"This incident that inspired your son to start carrying around a five-inch folding knife, when exactly was that?"

"It happened on June ninth in two thousand and one."

"You're sure?"

"Absolutely."

I turned in my seat so I could more fully see Minton's face. I was reading him. He thought he had something. Windsor's exact memory of a date was obvious indication of planted testimony. He was excited. I could tell.

"Was there a newspaper story about this supposed attack on a fellow realtor?"

"No, there wasn't."

"Was there a police investigation?"

"No, there wasn't."

"And yet you know the exact date. How is that, Mrs. Windsor? Were you given this date before testifying here?"

"No, I know the date because I will never forget the day I was attacked."

She waited a moment. I saw at least three of the jurors open their mouths silently. Minton did the same. I could almost hear the *click*.

"My son will never forget it, either," Windsor continued. "When he came looking for me and found me in that house, I was tied up, naked. There was blood. It was traumatic for him to see me that way. I think that was one of the reasons he took to carrying a knife. I think in some ways he wished he had gotten there earlier and been able to stop it."

"I see," Minton said, staring down at his notes.

He froze, unsure how to proceed. He didn't want to raise his foot for fear that the mine would detonate and blow it off.

"Mr. Minton, anything else?" the judge asked, a not so well disguised note of sarcasm in her voice.

"One moment, Your Honor," Minton said.

Minton gathered himself, reviewed his notes and tried to salvage something.

"Mrs. Windsor, did you or your son call the police after he found you?"

"No, we didn't. Louis wanted to but I did not. I thought that it would only further the trauma."

"So we have no official police documentation of this crime, correct?"

"That's correct."

I knew that Minton wanted to carry it further and ask if she had sought medical treatment after the attack. But sensing another trap, he didn't ask the question.

"So what you are saying here is that we only have your word that this attack even occurred? Your word and your son's, if he chooses to testify."

"It did occur. I live with it each and every day."

"But we only have you who says so."

She looked at the prosecutor with deadpan eyes.

"Is that a question?"

"Mrs. Windsor, you are here to help your son, correct?"

"If I can. I know him as a good man who would not have committed this despicable crime."

"You would be willing to do anything and everything in your power to save your son from conviction and possible prison, wouldn't you?"

"But I wouldn't lie about something like this. Oath or no oath, I wouldn't lie."

"But you want to save your son, don't you?"

"Yes."

"And saving him means lying for him, doesn't it?"

"No. It does not."

"Thank you, Mrs. Windsor."

Minton quickly returned to his seat. I had only one question on redirect.

"Mrs. Windsor, how old were you when this attack occurred?"

"I was fifty-four."

I sat back down. Minton had nothing further and Windsor was excused. I asked the judge to allow her to sit in the gallery for the remainder of the trial, now that her testimony was concluded. Without an objection from Minton the request was granted.

My next witness was an LAPD detective named David Lambkin, who was a national expert on sex crimes and had worked on the Real Estate Rapist investigation. In brief questioning I established the facts of the case and the five reported cases of rape that were investigated. I quickly got to the five key questions I needed to bolster Mary Windsor's testimony.

"Detective Lambkin, what was the age range of the known victims of the rapist?"

"These were all professional women who were pretty successful. They tended to be older than your average rape victim. I believe the youngest was twenty-nine and the oldest was fifty-nine."

"So a woman who was fifty-four years old would have fallen within the rapist's target profile, correct?"

"Yes."

"Can you tell the jury when the first reported attack occurred and when the last reported attack occurred?"

"Yes. The first was October one, two thousand, and the last one was July thirtieth of two thousand and one."

"So June ninth of two thousand and one was well within the span of this rapist's attacks on women in the real estate business, correct?"

"Yes, correct."

"In the course of your investigation of this case, did you come to a conclusion or belief that there were more than five rapes committed by this individual?"

Minton objected, saying the question called for speculation. The judge sustained the objection but it didn't matter. The question was what was important and the jury seeing the prosecutor keeping the answer from them was the payoff.

Minton surprised me on cross. He recovered enough from the misstep with Windsor to hit Lambkin with three solid questions with answers favorable to the prosecution.

"Detective Lambkin, did the task force investigating these rapes issue any kind of warning to women working in the real estate business?"

"Yes, we did. We sent out fliers on two occasions. The first went to all licensed real estate businesses in the area and the next mail-out went to all licensed real estate brokers individually, male and female."

"Did these mail-outs contain information about the rapist's description and methods?"

"Yes, they did."

"So if someone wished to concoct a story about being attacked by this rapist, the mail-outs would have provided all the information needed, correct?"

"That is a possibility, yes."

"Nothing further, Your Honor."

Minton proudly sat down and Lambkin was excused when I had nothing further. I asked the judge for a few minutes to confer with my client and then leaned in close to Roulet.

"Okay, this is it," I said. "You're all we have left. Unless there's something you haven't told me, you're clean and there isn't much Minton can come

back at you with. You should be safe up there unless you let him get to you.
Are you still cool with this?"

Roulet had said all along that he would testify and deny the charges. He
had reiterated his desire again at lunch. He demanded it. I always viewed
the risks of letting a client testify as evenly split. Anything he said could
come back to haunt him if the prosecution could bend it to the state's favor.
But I also knew that no matter what admonishments were given to a jury
about a defendant's right to remain silent, the jury always wanted to hear
the defendant say he didn't do it. You take that away from the jury and they
might hold a grudge.

"I want to do it," Roulet whispered. "I can handle the prosecutor."

I pushed my chair back and stood up.

"The defense calls Louis Ross Roulet, Your Honor."

36

Louis Roulet moved toward the witness box quickly, like a basketball
player pulled off the bench and sent to the scorer's table to check into the
game. He looked like a man anxious for the opportunity to defend himself. He knew this posture would not be lost on the jury.

After dispensing with the preliminaries, I got right down to the issues of
the case. Under my questioning Roulet freely admitted that he had gone to
Morgan's on the night of March 6 to seek female companionship. He said
he wasn't specifically looking to engage the services of a prostitute but was
not against the possibility.

"I had been with women I had to pay before," he said. "So I wouldn't
have been against it."

He testified that he had no conscious eye contact with Regina Campo
before she approached him at the bar. He said that she was the aggressor
but at the time that didn't bother him. He said the solicitation was open-
ended. She said she would be free after ten and he could come by if he was
not otherwise engaged.

Roulet described efforts made over the next hour at Morgan's and then
at the Lamplighter to find a woman he would not have to pay but said he
was unsuccessful. He then drove to the address Campo had given him and
knocked on the door.

"Who answered?"

"She did. She opened the door a crack and looked out at me."

"Regina Campo? The woman who testified this morning?"

"Yes, that's right."

"Could you see her whole face through the opening in the door?"

"No. She only opened up a crack and I couldn't see her. Only her left eye and a little bit of that side of her face."

"How did the door open? Was this crack through which you could see her on the right or left side?"

"As I was looking at the door the opening would have been on the right."

"So let's make sure we make this clear. The opening was on the right, correct?"

"Correct."

"So if she were standing behind the door and looking through the opening, she would be looking at you with her left eye."

"That is correct."

"Did you see her right eye?"

"No."

"So if she had a bruise or a cut or any damage on the right side of her face, could you have seen it?"

"No."

"Okay. So what happened next?"

"She saw it was me and she said come in. She opened the door wider but still sort of stood behind it."

"You couldn't see her?"

"Not completely. She was using the edge of the door as sort of a block."

"What happened next?"

"Well, it was kind of like an entry area, a vestibule, and she pointed through an archway to the living room. I went the way she pointed."

"Did this mean that she was then behind you?"

"Yes, when I turned toward the living room she was behind me."

"Did she close the door?"

"I think so. I heard it close."

"And then what?"

"Something hit me on the back of my head and I went down. I blacked out."

"Do you know how long you were out?"

"No. I think it was a while but none of the police or anybody ever told me."

"What do you remember when you regained consciousness?"

"I remember having a hard time breathing and when I opened my eyes, there was somebody sitting on me. I was on my back and he was sitting on me. I tried to move and that was when I realized somebody was sitting on my legs, too."

"What happened next?"

"They took turns telling me not to move and one of them told me they had my knife and if I tried to move or escape he would use it on me."

"Did there come a time that the police came and you were arrested?"

"Yes, a few minutes later the police were there. They handcuffed me and made me stand up. That was when I saw I had blood on my jacket."

"What about your hand?"

"I couldn't see it because it was handcuffed behind my back. But I heard one of the men who had been sitting on me tell the police officer that there was blood on my hand and then the officer put a bag over it. I felt that."

"How did the blood get on your hand and jacket?"

"All I know is that somebody put it on there because I didn't."

"Are you left-handed?"

"No, I am not."

"You didn't strike Ms. Campo with your left fist?"

"No, I did not."

"Did you threaten to rape her?"

"No, I did not."

"Did you tell her you were going to kill her if she didn't cooperate with you?"

"No, I did not."

I was hoping for some of the fire I had seen on that first day in C. C. Dobbs's office but Roulet was calm and controlled. I decided that before I finished with him on direct I needed to push things a little to get some of that anger back. I had told him at lunch I wanted to see it and wasn't sure what he was doing or where it had gone.

"Are you angry about being charged with attacking Ms. Campo?"

"Of course I am."

"Why?"

He opened his mouth but didn't speak. He seemed outraged that I would ask such a question. Finally, he responded.

"What do you mean, why? Have you ever been accused of something you didn't do and there's nothing you can do about it but wait? Just wait for weeks and months until you finally get a chance to go to court and say you've been set up. But then you have to wait even longer while the prosecutor puts on a bunch of liars and you have to listen to their lies and just wait your chance. Of course it makes you angry. I am innocent! I did not do this!"

It was perfect. To the point and playing to anybody who had ever been falsely accused of anything. There was more I could ask but I reminded myself of the rule: get in and get out. Less is always more. I sat down. If I decided there was anything I had missed I would clean it up on redirect.

I looked at the judge.

"Nothing further, Your Honor."

Minton was up and ready before I even got back to my seat. He moved to the lectern without breaking his steely glare away from Roulet. He was showing the jury what he thought of this man. His eyes were like lasers shooting across the room. He gripped the sides of the lectern so hard his knuckles were white. It was all a show for the jury.

"You deny touching Ms. Campo," he said.

"That's right," Roulet retorted.

"According to you she just punched herself or had a man she had never met before that night punch her lights out for her as part of this setup, is that correct?"

"I don't know who did it. All I know is that I didn't."

"But what you are saying is that this woman, Regina Campo, is lying. She came into this courtroom today and flat out lied to the judge and the jury and the whole wide world."

Minton punctuated the sentence by shaking his head with disgust.

"All I know is that I did not do the things she said I did. The only explanation is that one of us is lying. It's not me."

"That will be for the jury to decide, won't it?"

"Yes."

"And this knife you supposedly got for your own protection. Are you telling this jury that the victim in this case somehow knew you had a knife and used it as part of the setup?"

"I don't know what she knew. I had never shown the knife to her or in a bar where she would have been. So I don't see how she could have known about it. I think that when she went into my pocket for the money she found the knife. I always keep my knife and money in the same pocket."

"Oh, so now you have her stealing money out of your pocket as well. When does this end with you, Mr. Roulet?"

"I had four hundred dollars with me. When I was arrested it was gone. Someone took it."

Rather than try to pinpoint Roulet on the money, Minton was wise enough to know that no matter how he handled it, he would be facing a break-even proposition at best. If he tried to make a case that Roulet never had the money and that his plan was to attack and rape Campo rather than pay her, then he knew I would trot out Roulet's tax returns, which would throw serious doubt on the idea that he couldn't afford to pay a prostitute. It was an avenue of testimony commonly referred to by lawyers as a "cluster fuck" and he was staying away. He moved on to his finish.

In dramatic style Minton held up the evidence photo of Regina Campo's beaten and bruised face.

"So Regina Campo is a liar," he said.

"Yes."

"She had this done to her or maybe even did it herself."

"I don't know who did it."

"But not you."

"No, it wasn't me. I wouldn't do that to a woman. I wouldn't hurt a woman."

Roulet pointed to the photo Minton had continued to hold up.

"No woman deserves that," he said.

I leaned forward and waited. Roulet had just said the line I had told him to somehow find a way of putting into one of his answers during testi-mony. *No woman deserves that.* It was now up to Minton to take the bait. He was smart. He had to understand that Roulet had just opened a door.

"What do you mean by *deserves?* Do you think crimes of violence come down to a matter of whether a victim gets what they deserve?"

"No. I didn't mean it that way. I meant that no matter what she does for a living, she shouldn't have been beaten like that. Nobody deserves to have that happen to them."

Minton brought down the arm that held the photo. He looked at it him-self for a moment and then looked back up at Roulet.

"Mr. Roulet, I have nothing more to ask you."

37

I still felt that I was winning the razor fight. I had done everything possible to maneuver Minton into a position in which he had only one choice. It was now time to see if doing everything possible had been enough. After the young prosecutor sat down, I chose not to ask my client another ques-tion. He had held up well under Minton's attack and I felt the wind was in our sails. I stood up and looked back at the clock on the upper rear wall of the courtroom. It was only three-thirty. I then looked back at the judge.

"Your Honor, the defense rests."

She nodded and looked over my head at the clock. She told the jury to take the mid-afternoon break. Once the jurors were out of the courtroom, she looked at the prosecution table where Minton had his head down and was writing.

"Mr. Minton?"

The prosecutor looked up.

"We're still in session. Pay attention. Does the state have rebuttal?"

Minton stood.

"Your Honor, I would ask that we adjourn for the day so that the state has time to consider rebuttal witnesses."

"Mr. Minton, we still have at least ninety minutes to go today. I told you I wanted to be productive today. Where are your witnesses?"

"Frankly, Your Honor, I was not anticipating the defense resting after only three witnesses and I —"

"He gave fair warning of that in his opening statement."

"Yes, but still the case has moved faster than anticipated. We're a half day ahead. I would beg the court's indulgence. I would be hard-pressed to get the rebuttal witness I am considering even into court before six o'clock tonight."

I turned and looked at Roulet, who had returned to the seat next to mine. I nodded to him and winked with my left eye so the judge would not see the gesture. It looked like Minton had swallowed the bait. Now I just had to make sure the judge didn't make him spit it out. I stood up.

"Your Honor, the defense has no objection to the delay. Maybe we can use the time to prepare closing arguments and instructions to the jury."

The judge first looked at me with a puzzled frown. It was a rarity that the defense would not object to prosecutorial foot dragging. But then the seed I had planted began to bloom.

"You may have an idea there, Mr. Haller. If we adjourn early today I will expect that we will go to closing statements directly after rebuttal. No further delays except to consider jury instructions. Is that understood, Mr. Minton?"

"Yes, Your Honor, I will be ready."

"Mr. Haller?"

"It was my idea, Judge. I'll be ready."

"Very well, then. We have a plan. As soon as the jurors are back I will dismiss them for the day. They'll beat the traffic and tomorrow things will run so smoothly and quickly that I have no doubt they will be deliberating by the afternoon session."

She looked at Minton and then me, as if daring one of us to disagree with her. When we didn't, she got up and left the bench, probably in pursuit of a cigarette.

Twenty minutes later the jury was heading home and I was gathering my things at the defense table. Minton stepped over and said, "Can I talk to you?"

I looked at Roulet and told him to head out with his mother and Dobbs and that I would call him if I needed him for anything.

"But I want to talk to you, too," he said.

"About what?"

"About everything. How do you think I did up there?"

"You did good and everything is going good. I think we're in good shape."

I then nodded my head toward the prosecution table where Minton had returned and dropped my voice to a whisper.

"He knows it, too. He's about to make another offer."

"Should I stick around to hear what it is?"

I shook my head.

"No, it doesn't matter what it is. There's only one verdict, right?"

"That's right."

He patted my shoulder when he got up and I had to steady myself not to shrink away from the touch.

"Don't touch me, Louis," I said. "You want to do something for me, then give me my fucking gun back."

He didn't reply. He just smiled and moved toward the gate. After he was gone I turned to look at Minton. He now had the gleam of desperation in his eye. He needed a conviction — any conviction — on this case.

"What's up?"

"I have another offer."

"I'm listening."

"I'll drop it down further. Take it down to simple assault. Six months in county. The way they empty that place out at the end of every month, he probably won't do sixty days actual."

I nodded. He was talking about the federal mandate to stop overcrowding in the county jail system. It didn't matter what was handed down in a courtroom; out of necessity, sentences were often drastically cut. It was a good offer but I didn't show anything. I knew the offer had to have come from the second floor. Minton wouldn't have had the authority to go so low.

"He takes that and she'll rob him blind in civil," I said. "I doubt he'll go for it."

"That's a damn good offer," Minton said.

There was a hint of outrage in his voice. My guess was that the observer's report card on Minton was not good and he was under orders to close the case out with a guilty plea. Trash the trial and the judge's and jury's time, just get that plea. The Van Nuys office didn't like losing cases and we were only two months removed from the Robert Blake fiasco. It pleaded them out when the going got rough. Minton could go as low as he needed to go, just as long as he got something. Roulet had to go down — even if it was only for sixty days actual.

"Maybe from your side of things it's a damn good offer. But it still means I have to convince a client to plead to something he says he didn't do. Then on top of that, the dispo still opens the door to civil liability. So while he's sitting up there in county trying to protect his asshole for sixty days, Reggie Campo and her lawyer are down here taking him to the cleaners. You see? It's not so good when you look at it from his angle. If it was left to me, I'd ride the trial out. I think we're winning. I know we've got the Bible guy, so we've got a hanger at minimum. But who knows, maybe we've got all twelve."

Minton slapped his hand down on his table.

"What the fuck are you talking about? You know he did this thing, Haller. And six months — let alone sixty days — for what he did to that woman is a joke. It's a fucking travesty that I'll lose sleep over, but they've been watching and think you've got the jury, so I have to do it."

I closed my briefcase with an authoritative snap and stood up.

"Then I hope you got something good for rebuttal, Ted. Because you're going to get your wish for a jury verdict. And I have to tell you, man, you're looking more and more like a guy who came naked to a razor fight. Better get your hands off your nuts and fight back."

I headed through the gate. Halfway to the doors at the back of the courtroom I stopped and looked back at him.

"Hey, you know something? If you lose sleep over this or any other case, then you gotta quit the job and go do something else. Because you're not going to make it, Ted."

Minton sat at his table, staring straight ahead at the empty bench. He didn't acknowledge what I had said. I left him there thinking about it. I thought I had played it right. I'd find out in the morning.

I went back over to Four Green Fields to work on my closing. I wouldn't need the two hours the judge had given us. I ordered a Guinness at the bar and took it over to one of the tables to sit by myself. Table service didn't start again until six. I sketched out some basic notes but I instinctively knew I would largely be reacting to the state's presentation. In pretrial motions, Minton had already asked and received permission from Judge Fullbright to use a PowerPoint presentation to illustrate the case to the jury. It had become all the rage with young prosecutors to put up the screen and flash computer graphics on it, as if the jurors couldn't be trusted to think and make connections on their own. It now had to be fed to them like TV.

My clients rarely had the money to pay my fees, let alone for PowerPoint presentations. Roulet was an exception. Through his mother he could afford to hire Francis Ford Coppola to put together a PowerPoint for him if he wanted it. But I never even brought it up. I was strictly old school. I liked going into the ring on my own. Minton could throw whatever he wanted up on the big blue screen. When it was my turn I wanted the jury looking only at me. If I couldn't convince them, nothing from a computer could, either.

At 5:30 I called Maggie McPherson at her office.

"It's quitting time," I said.

"Maybe for big-shot defense pros. Us public servants have to work till after dark."

"Why don't you take a break and come meet me for a Guinness and some shepherd's pie, then you can go back to work and finish up."

"No, Haller. I can't do that. Besides, I know what you want."

I laughed. There was never a time that she didn't think she knew what I wanted. Most of the time she was right but not this time.

"Yeah? What do I want?"

"You're going to try to corrupt me again and find out what Minton is up to."

"Not a chance, Mags. Minton is an open book. Smithson's observer is giving him bad marks. So Smithson's told him to fold the tent, get something and get out. But Minton's been working on his little PowerPoint closing and wants to gamble, take it all the way to the house. Besides that, he's got genuine outrage in his blood, so he doesn't like the idea of folding up."

"Neither do I. Smithson's always afraid of losing—especially since Blake. He always wants to sell short. You can't be that way."

"I always said they lost the Blake case the minute they passed you over. You tell 'em, Maggie."

"If I ever get the chance."

"Someday."

She didn't like dwelling on her own stalled career. She moved on.

"So you sound chipper," she said. "Yesterday you were a murder suspect. Today you've got the DA by the short hairs. What changed?"

"Nothing. It's just the calm before the storm, I guess. Hey, let me ask you something. Have you ever put a rush on ballistics?"

"What kind of ballistics?"

"Matching casing to casing and slug to slug."

"Depends on who is doing it—which department, I mean. But if they put a real rush on it, they could have something in twenty-four hours."

I felt the dull thud of dread drop into my stomach. I knew I could be on borrowed time.

"Most of the time, though, that doesn't happen," she continued. "Two or three days is what it will usually take on a rush. And if you want the whole package—casing and slug comparisons—it could take longer because the slug could be damaged and tough to read. They have to work with it."

I nodded. I didn't think any of that could help me. I knew they had recovered a bullet casing at the crime scene. If Lankford and Sobel got a match on that to the casing of a bullet fired fifty years ago from Mickey Cohen's gun, they would come for me and worry about the slug comparison later.

"You still there?" Maggie asked.

"Yeah. I was just thinking of something."

"You don't sound so chipper anymore. You want to talk about this, Michael?"

"No, not right now. But if I end up needing a good lawyer, you know who I'll call."

"That'll be the day."

"You might be surprised."

I let some more silence into the conversation. Just having her on the other end of the line was a calming comfort. I liked it.

"Haller, I should get back to my job now."

"Okay, Maggie, put those bad guys away."

"I will."

"Good night."

I closed the phone and thought about things for a few moments, then opened it up again and called the Sheraton Universal to see if they had a room available. I had decided that as a precaution I would not go home this night. There might be two detectives from Glendale waiting for me.

38

Wednesday, May 25

After a sleepless night in a bad hotel bed I got to the courthouse early on Wednesday morning and found no welcoming party, no Glendale detectives waiting with smiles and a warrant for my arrest. A flash of relief went through me as I made my way through the metal detector. I was wearing the same suit I had worn the day before but was hoping no one would notice. I did have a fresh shirt and tie on. I keep spares in the trunk of the Lincoln for summer days when I'm working up in the desert and the car's air conditioner can get overwhelmed.

When I got to Judge Fullbright's courtroom I was surprised to find I was not the first of the trial's players to arrive. Minton was in the gallery, setting up the screen for his PowerPoint presentation. Because the courtroom had been designed before the era of computer-enhanced presentations, there was no place to put a twelve-foot screen in comfortable view of the jury, the judge, and the lawyers. A good chunk of the gallery space would be taken up by the screen, and any spectator who sat behind it wouldn't get to see the show.

"Bright and early," I said to Minton.

He looked over from his work and seemed a bit surprised to see me in early as well.

"Have to work out the logistics of this thing. It's kind of a pain."

"You could always do it the old-fashioned way and just look at the jury and talk directly to them."

"No, thanks. I like this better. Did you talk to your client about the offer?"

"Yeah, no sale. Looks like we ride this one to the end."

I put my briefcase down on the defense table and wondered if the fact that Minton was setting up for his closing argument meant he had decided against mounting any kind of rebuttal. A sharp jab of panic went through me. I looked over at the state's table and saw nothing that gave me a clue to what Minton was planning. I knew I could flat out ask him but I did not want to give away my appearance of disinterested confidence.

Instead, I sauntered over to the bailiff's desk to talk to Bill Meehan, the deputy who ran Fullbright's court. I saw on his desk a spread of paperwork. He would have the courtroom calendar as well as the list of custodies bused to the courthouse that morning.

"Bill, I'm going to grab a cup of coffee. You want something?"

"No, man, but thanks. I'm set on caffeine. For a while, at least."

I smiled and nodded.

"Hey, is that the custody list? Can I take a look and see if any of my clients are on it?"

"Sure."

Meehan handed me several pages that were stapled together. It was a listing by name of every inmate that was now housed in the courthouse's jails. Following the name was the courtroom each prisoner was headed to. Acting as nonchalant as I could I scanned the list and quickly found the name Dwayne Jeffery Corliss on it. Minton's snitch was in the building and was headed to Fullbright's court. I almost let out a sigh of relief but kept it all inside. It looked like Minton was going to play things the way I had hoped and planned.

"Something wrong?" Meehan asked.

I looked at him and handed back the list.

"No, why?"

"I don't know. You look like something happened, is all."

"Nothing's happened yet but it will."

I left the courtroom and went down to the cafeteria on the second floor. When I was in line paying for my coffee I saw Maggie McPherson walk in and go directly to the coffee urns. After I paid I walked up behind her as she was mixing powder from a pink packet into her coffee.

"Sweet'N Low," I said. "My ex-wife used to tell me that's how she liked it."

She turned and saw me.

"Stop, Haller."

But she smiled.

"Stop, Haller, or I'll holler," I said. "She used to have to say that, too. A lot."

"What are you doing? Shouldn't you be up on six getting ready to pull the plug on Minton's PowerPoint?"

"I'm not worried. In fact, you ought to come up and check it out. Old school versus new school, a battle for the ages."

"Hardly. By the way, isn't that the same suit you were wearing yesterday?"

"Yeah, it's my lucky suit. But how do you know what I was wearing yesterday?"

"Oh, I popped my head in Fullbite's court for a couple minutes yesterday. You were too busy questioning your client to notice."

I was secretly pleased that she would even notice my suits. I knew it meant something.

"So, then, why don't you pop your head in again this morning?"

"Today I can't. I'm too busy."

"What've you got?"

"I'm taking over a murder one for Andy Seville. He's quitting to go private and yesterday they divided up his cases. I got the good one."

"Nice. Does the defendant need a lawyer?"

"No way, Haller. I'm not losing another one to you."

"Just kidding. I've got my hands full."

She snapped a top onto her cup and picked it up off the counter, using a layer of napkins as insulation against its heat.

"Same here. So I'd wish you good luck today but I can't."

"Yeah, I know. Gotta keep the company line. Just cheer up Minton when he comes down with his hat in his hand."

"I'll try."

She left the cafeteria and I walked over to an empty table. I still had fifteen minutes before the trial was supposed to start up again. I pulled out my cell and called my second ex-wife.

"Lorna, it's me. We're in play with Corliss. Are you set?"

"I'm ready."

"Okay, I'm just checking. I'll call you."

"Good luck today, Mickey."

"Thanks. I'll need it. You be ready for the next call."

I closed the phone and was about to get up when I saw LAPD Detective Howard Kurlen cutting through the tables toward me. The man who put Jesus Menendez in prison didn't look like he was stopping in for a peanut butter and sardine sandwich. He was carrying a folded document. He got to my table and dropped it in front of my coffee cup.

"What is this shit?" he demanded.

I started unfolding the document, even though I knew what it was.

"Looks like a subpoena, Detective. I would've thought you'd know what it is."

"You know what I mean, Haller. What's the game? I've got nothing to do with that case up there and I don't want to be a part of your bullshit."

"It's no game and it's no bullshit. You've been subpoenaed as a rebuttal witness."

"To rebut what? I told you and you already know, I didn't have a goddamn thing to do with that case. It's Marty Booker's and I just talked to him and he said it's gotta be a mistake."

I nodded like I wanted to be accommodating.

"I'll tell you what, go on up to the courtroom and take a seat. If it's a mistake I'll get it straightened out as soon as I can. I doubt you'll be here another hour. I'll get you out of there and back chasing the bad guys."

"How about this? I leave now and you straighten it out whenever the fuck you want."

"I can't do that, Detective. That is a valid and lawful subpoena and you must appear in that courtroom unless otherwise discharged. I told you, I will do that as soon as I can. The state's got one witness and then it's my turn and I'll take care of it."

"This is such bullshit."

He turned from me and stalked back through the cafeteria toward the doorway. Luckily, he had left the subpoena with me, because it was phony. I had never registered it with the court clerk and the scribbled signature at the bottom was mine.

Bullshit or not, I didn't think Kurlen was leaving the courthouse. He was a man who understood duty and the law. He lived by it. It was what I was counting on. He would be in the courtroom until discharged. Or until he understood why I had called him there.

39

At 9:30 the judge put the jury in the box and immediately proceeded with the day's business. I glanced back at the gallery and caught sight of Kurlen in the back row. He had a pensive, if not angry, cast to his face. He was close to the door and I didn't know how long he would last. I was figuring I would need that whole hour I had told him about.

I glanced further around the room and saw that Lankford and Sobel were sitting on a bench next to the bailiff's desk that was designated for law enforcement personnel. Their faces revealed nothing but they still put the pause in me. I wondered if I would even get the hour I needed.

"Mr. Minton," the judge intoned, "does the state have any rebuttal?"

I turned back to the court. Minton stood up, adjusted his jacket and then seemed to hesitate and brace himself before responding.

"Yes, Your Honor, the state calls Dwayne Jeffery Corliss as a rebuttal witness."

I stood up and noticed to my right that Meehan, the bailiff, had stood up as well. He was going to go into the courtroom lockup to retrieve Corliss.

"Your Honor?" I said. "Who is Dwayne Jeffery Corliss and why wasn't I told about him before now?"

"Deputy Meehan, hold on a minute," Fullbright said.

Meehan stood frozen with the key to the lockup door poised in his hand. The judge then apologized to the jury but told them they had to go back into the deliberation room until recalled. After they filed through the door behind the box, the judge turned her focus onto Minton.

"Mr. Minton, do you want to tell us about your witness?"

"Dwayne Corliss is a cooperating witness who spoke with Mr. Roulet when he was in custody following his arrest."

"Bullshit!" Roulet barked. "I didn't talk to—"

"Be quiet, Mr. Roulet," the judge boomed. "Mr. Haller, instruct your client on the danger of outbursts in my courtroom."

"Thank you, Your Honor."

I was still standing. I leaned down to whisper in Roulet's ear.

"That was perfect," I said. "Now be cool and I'll take it from here."

He nodded and leaned back. He angrily folded his arms across his chest. I straightened up.

"I'm sorry, Your Honor, but I do share my client's outrage over this last-ditch effort by the state. This is the first we have heard of Mr. Corliss. I would like to know when he came forward with this supposed conversation."

Minton had remained standing. I thought it was the first time in the trial that we had stood side by side and argued to the judge.

"Mr. Corliss first contacted the office through a prosecutor who handled the first appearance of the defendant," Minton said. "However, that information was not passed on to me until yesterday when in a staff meeting I was asked why I had never acted on the information."

This was a lie but not one I wanted to expose. To do so would reveal Maggie McPherson's slip on St. Patrick's Day and it might also derail my plan. I had to be careful. I needed to argue vigorously against Corliss taking the stand but I also needed to lose the argument.

I put my best look of outrage on my face.

"This is incredible, Your Honor. Just because the DA's office has a communication problem, my client has to suffer the consequences of not being informed that the state had a witness against him? This man should clearly not be allowed to testify. It's too late to bring him in now."

"Your Honor," Minton said, jumping in quickly. "I have had no time to interview or depose Mr. Corliss myself. Because I was preparing my closing I simply made arrangements for him to be brought here today. His testimony is key to the state's case because it serves as rebuttal to Mr. Roulet's self-serving statements. To not allow his testimony is a serious disservice to the state."

I shook my head and smiled in frustration. With his last line Minton was threatening the judge with the loss of the DA's backing should she ever face an election with an opposing candidate.

"Mr. Haller?" the judge asked. "Anything before I rule?"

"I just want my objection on the record."

"So noted. If I were to give you time to investigate and interview Mr. Corliss, how much would you need?"

"A week."

Now Minton put on the fake smile and shook his head.

"That's ridiculous, Your Honor."

"Do you want to go back and talk to him?" the judge asked me. "I'll allow it."

"No, Your Honor. As far as I'm concerned all jailhouse snitches are liars. It would do me no good to interview him because anything that comes out of his mouth would be a lie. Anything. Besides, it's not what he has to say. It's what others have to say about him. That's what I would need time for."

"Then I am going to rule that he can testify."

"Your Honor," I said. "If you are going to allow him into this courtroom, could I ask one indulgence for the defense?"

"What is that, Mr. Haller?"

"I would like to step into the hallway and make a quick phone call to an investigator. It will take me less than a minute."

The judge thought for a moment and then nodded.

"Go ahead. I will bring the jury in while you do it."

"Thank you."

I hurried through the gate and down the middle aisle. My eyes caught those of Howard Kurlen and he gave me one of his best smirks.

In the hallway I speed-dialed Lorna Taylor's cell phone and she answered right away.

"Okay, how far away are you?"

"About fifteen minutes."

"Did you remember the printout and the tape?"

"Got it all right here."

I looked at my watch. It was a quarter to ten.   ·

"Okay, well, we're in play here. Don't delay getting here but then I want you to wait out in the hall outside the courtroom. Then at ten-fifteen come into court and give it to me. If I'm crossing the witness, just sit in the first row and wait until I notice you."

"Got it."

I closed the phone and went back into the courtroom. The jury was seated and Meehan was leading a man in a gray jumpsuit through the lockup door. Dwayne Corliss was a thin man with stringy hair that wasn't getting washed enough in the lockdown drug program at County-USC. He wore a blue plastic hospital ID band on his wrist. I recognized him. He was the man who had asked me for a business card when I interviewed Roulet in the holding cell my first day on the case.

Corliss was led by Meehan to the witness box and the court clerk swore him in. Minton took over the show from there.

"Mr. Corliss, were you arrested on March fifth of this year?"

"Yes, the police arrested me for burglary and possession of drugs."

"Are you incarcerated now?"

Corliss looked around.

"Um, no, I don't think so. I'm just in the courtroom."

I heard Kurlen's coarse laugh behind me but nobody joined in.

"No, I mean are you currently being held in jail? When you are not here in court."

"I'm in a lockdown drug treatment program in the jail ward at Los Angeles County–USC Medical Center."

"Are you addicted to drugs?"

"Yes. I'm addicted to heroin but at the moment I am straight. I haven't had any since I got arrested."

"More than sixty days."

"That's right."

"Do you recognize the defendant in this case?"

Corliss looked over at Roulet and nodded.

"Yes, I do."

"Why is that?"

"Because I met him in lockup after I got arrested."

"You are saying that after you were arrested you came into close proximity to the defendant, Louis Roulet?"

"Yes, the next day."

"How did that happen?"

"Well, we were both in Van Nuys jail but in different wards. Then, when we got bused over here to the courts, we were together, first in the bus and then in the tank and then when we were brought into the courtroom for first appearance. We were together all of that time."

"When you say 'together,' what do you mean?"

"Well, we sort of stuck close because we were the only white guys in the group we were in."

"Now, did you talk at all while you were together for all of that time?"

Corliss nodded his head and at the same time Roulet shook his. I touched my client's arm to caution him to make no demonstrations.

"Yes, we talked," Corliss said.

"About what?"

"Mostly about cigarettes. We both needed them but they don't let you smoke in the jail."

Corliss made a what-are-you-going-to-do gesture with both hands and a few of the jurors — probably smokers — smiled and nodded.

"Did you reach a point where you asked Mr. Roulet what got him into jail?" Minton asked.

"Yes, I did."

"What did he say?"

I quickly stood up and objected but just as quickly was overruled.

"What did he tell you, Mr. Corliss?" Minton prompted.

"Well, first he asked me why I was there and I told him. So then I asked him why he was in and he said, 'For giving a bitch exactly what she deserved.'"

"Those were his words?"

"Yes."

"Did he elaborate further on what he meant by that?"

"No, not really. Not on that."

I leaned forward, waiting for Minton to ask the next obvious question. But he didn't. He moved on.

"Now, Mr. Corliss, have you been promised anything by me or the district attorney's office in return for your testimony?"

"Nope. I just thought it was the right thing to do."

"What is the status of your case?"

"I still got the charges against me, but it looks like if I complete my program I'll be able to get a break on them. The drugs, at least. I don't know about the burglary yet."

"But I have made no promise of help in that regard, correct?"

"No, sir, you haven't."

"Has anyone else from the district attorney's office made any promises?"

"No, sir."

"I have no further questions."

I sat unmoving and just staring at Corliss. My pose was that of a man who was angry but didn't know exactly what to do about it. Finally, the judge prompted me into action.

"Mr. Haller, cross-examination?"

"Yes, Your Honor."

I stood up, glancing back at the door as if hoping a miracle would walk through it. I then checked the big clock on the back door and saw it was five minutes after ten. I noticed as I turned back to the witness that I had not lost Kurlen. He was still in the back row and he still had the same smirk on his face. I realized that it might have been his natural look.

I turned to the witness.

"Mr. Corliss, how old are you?"

"Forty-three."

"You go by Dwayne?"

"That's right."

"Any other names?"

"People called me D.J. when I was growing up. Everybody called me that."

"And where did you grow up?"

"Mesa, Arizona."

"Mr. Corliss, how many times have you been arrested before?"

Minton objected but the judge overruled. I knew she was going to give me a lot of room with this witness since I was the one who had supposedly been sandbagged.

"How many times have you been arrested before, Mr. Corliss?" I asked again.

"I think about seven."

"So you've been in a number of jails in your time, haven't you?"

"You could say that."

"All in Los Angeles County?"

"Mostly. But I got arrested over in Phoenix before, too."

"So you know how the system works, don't you?"

"I just try to survive."

"And sometimes surviving means ratting out your fellow inmates, doesn't it?"

"Your Honor?" Minton said, standing to object.

"Take a seat, Mr. Minton," Fullbright said. "I gave you a lot of leeway bringing this witness in. Mr. Haller gets his share of it now. The witness will answer the question."

The stenographer read the question back to Corliss.

"I suppose so."

"How many times have you snitched on another inmate?"

"I don't know. A few times."

"How many times have you testified in a court proceeding for the prosecution?"

"Would that include my own cases?"

"No, Mr. Corliss. For the prosecution. How many times have you testified against a fellow inmate for the prosecution?"

"I think this is my fourth time."

I looked surprised and aghast, although I was neither.

"So you are a pro, aren't you? You could almost say your occupation is drug-addicted jailhouse snitch."

"I just tell the truth. If people tell me things that are bad, then I feel obligated to report it."

"But you try to get people to tell you things, don't you?"

"No, not really. I guess I'm just a friendly guy."

"A friendly guy. So what you expect this jury to believe is that a man you didn't know would just come out of the blue and tell you — a perfect stranger — that he gave a bitch exactly what she deserved. Is that correct?"

"It's what he said."

"So he just mentioned that to you and then you both just went back to talking about cigarettes after that, is that right?"

"Not exactly."

"Not exactly? What do you mean by 'not exactly'?"

"He also told me he did it before. He said he got away with it before and he would get away with it now. He was bragging about it because with the other time, he said he killed the bitch and got away with it."

I froze for a moment. I then glanced at Roulet, who sat as still as a statue with surprise on his face, and then back at the witness.

"You..."

I started and stopped, acting like I was the man in the minefield who had just heard the *click* come from beneath my foot. In my peripheral vision I noticed Minton's body posture tightening.

"Mr. Haller?" the judge prompted.

I broke my stare from Corliss and looked at the judge.

"Your Honor, I have no further questions at this time."

40

Minton came up from his seat like a boxer coming out of his corner at his bleeding opponent.

"Redirect, Mr. Minton?" Fullbright asked.

But he was already at the lectern.

"Absolutely, Your Honor."

He looked at the jury as if to underline the importance of the upcoming exchange and then at Corliss.

"You said he was bragging, Mr. Corliss. How so?"

"Well, he told me about this time he actually killed a girl and got away with it."

I stood up.

"Your Honor, this has nothing to do with the case at hand and it is rebuttal to no evidence previously offered by the defense. The witness can't —"

"Your Honor," Minton cut in, "this is information brought forward by defense counsel. The prosecution is entitled to pursue it."

"I will allow it," Fullbright said.

I sat down and appeared dejected. Minton plowed ahead. He was going just where I wanted him to go.

"Mr. Corliss, did Mr. Roulet offer any of the details of this previous incident in which he said he got away with killing a woman?"

"He called the girl a snake dancer. She danced in some joint where she was like in a snake pit."

I felt Roulet wrap his fingers around my biceps and squeeze. His hot breath came into my ear.

"What the fuck is this?" he whispered.

I turned to him.

"I don't know. What the hell did you tell this guy?"

He whispered back through gritted teeth.

"I didn't tell him anything. This is a setup. You set me up!"

"Me? What are you talking about? I told you, I couldn't get to this guy in lockdown. If you didn't tell him this shit, then somebody else did. Start thinking. Who?"

I turned and looked up at Minton standing at the lectern and continuing his questioning of Corliss.

"Did Mr. Roulet say anything else about the dancer he said he murdered?" he asked.

"No, that's all he really told me."

Minton checked his notes to see if there was anything else, then nodded to himself.

"Nothing further, Your Honor."

The judge looked at me. I could almost see sympathy on her face.

"Any recross from the defense with this witness?"

Before I could answer, there was a noise from the rear of the courtroom and I turned to see Lorna Taylor entering. She hurriedly walked down the aisle toward the gate.

"Your Honor, can I have a moment to confer with my staff?"

"Hurry, Mr. Haller."

I met Lorna at the gate and took from her a videotape with a single piece of paper wrapped around it with a rubber band. As she had been told to do earlier, she whispered in my ear.

"This is where I act like I am whispering something very important into your ear," she said. "How is it going?"

I nodded as I took the rubber band off the tape and looked at the piece of paper.

"Perfect timing," I whispered back. "I'm good to go."

"Can I stay and watch?"

"No, I want you out of here. I don't want anybody talking to you after this goes down."

I nodded and she nodded and then she left. I went back to the lectern.

"No recross, Your Honor."

I sat down and waited. Roulet grabbed my arm.

"What are you doing?"

I pushed him away.

"Stop touching me. We have new information we can't bring up on cross."

I focused on the judge.

"Any other witnesses, Mr. Minton?" she asked.

"No, Your Honor. No further rebuttal."

The judge nodded.

"The witness is excused."

Meehan started crossing the courtroom to Corliss. The judge looked at me and I started to stand.

"Mr. Haller, surrebuttal?"

"Yes, Your Honor, the defense would like to call D.J. Corliss back to the stand as surrebuttal."

Meehan stopped in his tracks and all eyes were on me. I held up the tape and the paper Lorna had brought me.

"I have new information on Mr. Corliss, Your Honor. I could not have brought it up on cross."

"Very well. Proceed."

"Can I have a moment, Judge?"

"A short one."

I huddled with Roulet again.

"Look, I don't know what is going on but it doesn't matter," I whispered.

"What do you mean it doesn't matter? Are you —"

"Listen to me. It doesn't matter because I can still destroy him. Doesn't matter if he says you killed twenty women. If he's a liar, he's a liar. If I destroy him, none of it counts. You understand?"

Roulet nodded and seemed to calm as he considered this.

"Then destroy him."

"I will. But I have to know. Is there anything else he knows that could come out? Is there anything I need to stay away from?"

Roulet whispered slowly, as if explaining something to a child.

"I don't know because I never talked to him. I'm not that stupid as to have a discussion about cigarettes and murder with a total fucking stranger!"

"Mr. Haller," the judge prompted.

I looked up at her.

"Yes, Your Honor."

Carrying the tape and the paper that came with it, I stood up to go back to the lectern. On the way I took a quick glance across the gallery and saw that Kurlen was gone. I had no way of knowing how long he had stayed and what he had heard. Lankford was gone as well. Only Sobel remained and she averted her eyes from mine. I turned my attention to Corliss.

"Mr. Corliss, can you tell the jury exactly where you were when Mr. Roulet supposedly made these revelations to you about murder and assault?"

"When we were together."

"Together where, Mr. Corliss?"

"Well, on the bus ride we didn't talk because we were in different seats. But when we got to the courthouse, we were in the same holding cell with about six other guys and we sat together there and we talked."

"And those six other men all witnessed you and Mr. Roulet talking, correct?"

"They woulda had to. They were there."

"So what you are saying is that if I brought them in here one by one and asked them if they observed you and Mr. Roulet talking, they would confirm that?"

"Well, they should. But..."

"But what, Mr. Corliss?"

"It's just that they probably wouldn't talk, that's all."

"Is it because nobody likes a snitch, Mr. Corliss?"

Corliss shrugged.

"I guess so."

"Okay, so let's make sure we have all of this straight. You didn't talk with Mr. Roulet on the bus but you did talk to him when you were in the holding cell together. Anywhere else?"

"Yeah, we talked when they moved us on out into the courtroom. They stick you in this glassed-in area and you wait for your case to be called. We talked some in there, too, until his case got called. He went first."

"This is in the arraignment court where you had your first appearance before a judge?"

"That's right."

"So you two were talking in the court and this is where Mr. Roulet would have revealed his part in these crimes you described."

"That's right."

"Do you remember specifically what he told you when you were in the courtroom?"

"No, not really. Not specifics. I think that might have been when he told me about the girl who was a dancer."

"Okay, Mr. Corliss."

I held the videotape up, described it as video of Louis Roulet's first appearance, and asked to enter it as a defense exhibit. Minton tried to block it as something I had not produced during discovery, but that was easily and quickly shot down by the judge without my having to argue the point. He then objected again, citing the lack of authentication of the tape.

"I am just trying to save the court some time," I said. "If needed I can have the man who took the film here in about an hour to authenticate it. But I think that Your Honor will be able to authenticate it herself with just one look."

"I am going to allow it," the judge said. "Once we see it the prosecution can object again if so inclined."

The television and video unit I had used previously was rolled into the courtroom and placed at an angle viewable by Corliss, the jury and the judge. Minton had to move to a chair to the side of the jury box to fully see it. The tape was played. It lasted twenty minutes and showed Roulet from the moment he entered the courtroom custody area until he was led out after the bail hearing. At no time did Roulet talk to anyone but me. When the tape was over I left the television in its place in case it was needed again. I addressed Corliss with a tinge of outrage in my voice.

"Mr. Corliss, did you see a moment anywhere on that tape where you and Mr. Roulet were talking?"

"Uh, no. I—"

"Yet, you testified under oath and penalty of perjury that he confessed crimes to you while you were both in the courtroom, didn't you?"

"I know I said that but I must have been mistaken. He must have told me everything when we were in the holding cell."

"You lied to the jury, didn't you?"

"I didn't mean to. That was the way I remembered it but I guess I was wrong. I was coming off a high that morning. Things got confused."

"It would seem that way. Let me ask you, were things confused when you testified against Frederic Bentley back in nineteen eighty-nine?"

Corliss knitted his eyebrows together in concentration but didn't answer.

"You remember Frederic Bentley, don't you?"

Minton stood.

"Objection. Nineteen eighty-nine? Where is he going with this?"

"Your Honor," I said. "This goes to the veracity of the witness. It is certainly at issue here."

"Connect the dots, Mr. Haller," the judge ordered. "In a hurry."

"Yes, Your Honor."

I picked up the piece of paper and used it as a prop during my final questions of Corliss.

"In nineteen eighty-nine Frederic Bentley was convicted, with your help, of raping a sixteen-year-old girl in her bed in Phoenix. Do you remember this?"

"Barely," Corliss said. "I've done a lot of drugs since then."

"You testified at his trial that he confessed the crime to you while you were both together in a police station holding cell. Isn't that correct?"

"Like I said, it's hard for me to remember back then."

"The police put you in that holding cell because they knew you were willing to snitch, even if you had to make it up, didn't they?"

My voice was rising with each question.

"I don't remember that," Corliss responded. "But I don't make things up."

"Then, eight years later, the man who you testified had told you he did it was exonerated when a DNA test determined that the semen from the girl's attacker came from another man. Isn't that correct, sir?"

"I don't...I mean...that was a long time ago."

"Do you remember being questioned by a reporter for the *Arizona Star* newspaper following the release of Frederic Bentley?"

"Vaguely. I remember somebody calling but I didn't say anything."

"He told you that DNA tests exonerated Bentley and asked you whether you fabricated Bentley's confession, didn't he?"

"I don't know."

I held the paper I was clutching up toward the bench.

"Your Honor, I have an archival story from the *Arizona Star* newspaper here. It is dated February ninth, nineteen ninety-seven. A member of my staff came across it when she Googled the name D.J. Corliss on her office computer. I ask that it be marked as a defense exhibit and admitted into evidence as a historical document detailing an admission by silence."

My request set off a brutal clash with Minton about authenticity and proper foundation. Ultimately, the judge ruled in my favor. She was showing some of the same outrage I was manufacturing, and Minton didn't stand much of a chance.

The bailiff took the computer printout to Corliss, and the judge instructed him to read it.

"I'm not too good at reading, Judge," he said.

"Try, Mr. Corliss."

Corliss held the paper up and leaned his face into it as he read.

"Out loud, please," Fullbright barked.

Corliss cleared his throat and read in a halting voice.

" 'A man wrongly convicted of rape was released Saturday from the Arizona Correctional Institution and vowed to seek justice for other inmates falsely accused. Frederic Bentley, thirty-four, served almost eight years in prison for attacking a sixteen-year-old Tempe girl. The victim of the assault identified Bentley, a neighbor, and blood tests matched his type to semen recovered from the victim after the attack. The case was bolstered at trial by testimony from an informant who said Bentley had confessed the crime to him while they were housed together in a holding cell. Bentley always maintained his innocence during the trial and even after his conviction. Once DNA testing was accepted as valid evidence by courts in the state, Bentley hired attorneys to fight for such testing of semen collected from the victim of the attack. A judge ordered the testing earlier this year, and the resulting analysis proved Bentley was not the attacker.

" 'At a press conference yesterday at the Arizona Biltmore the newly freed Bentley railed against jailhouse informants and called for a state law that would put strict guidelines on police and prosecutors who wish to use them.

" 'The informant who claimed in sworn testimony that Bentley admitted the rape was identified as D.J. Corliss, a Mesa man who had been arrested on drug charges. When told of Bentley's exoneration and asked whether he fabricated his testimony against Bentley, Corliss declined comment Saturday. At his press conference, Bentley charged that Corliss was well known to the police as a snitch and was used in several cases to get close to suspects. Bentley claimed that Corliss's practice was to make up confessions if he could not draw them out of the suspects. The case against Bentley—' "

"Okay, Mr. Corliss," I said. "I think that is enough."

Corliss put the printout down and looked at me like a child who has opened the door of a crowded closet and sees everything about to fall out on top of him.

"Were you ever charged with perjury in the Bentley case?" I asked him.

"No, I wasn't," he said forcefully, as if that fact exonerated him of wrongdoing.

"Was that because the police were complicit with you in setting up Mr. Bentley?"

Minton objected, saying, "I am sure Mr. Corliss would have no idea what went into the decision of whether or not to charge him with perjury."

Fullbright sustained it but I didn't care. I was so far ahead on this witness that there was no catching up. I just moved on to the next question.

"Did any prosecutor or police officer ask you to get close to Mr. Roulet and get him to confide in you?"

"No, it was just luck of the draw, I guess."

"You were not told to get a confession from Mr. Roulet?"

"No, I was not."

I stared at him for a long moment with disgust in my eyes.

"I have nothing further."

I carried the pose of anger with me to my seat and dropped the tape box angrily down in front of me before sitting down.

"Mr. Minton?" the judge asked.

"I have nothing further," he responded in a weak voice.

"Okay," Fullbright said quickly. "I am going to excuse the jury for an early lunch. I would like you all back here at one o'clock sharp."

She put on a strained smile and directed it at the jurors and kept it there until they had filed out of the courtroom. It dropped off her face the moment the door was closed.

"I want to see counsel in my chambers," she said. "Immediately."

She didn't wait for any response. She left the bench so fast that her robe flowed up behind her like the black gown of the grim reaper.

41

Judge Fullbright had already lit a cigarette by the time Minton and I got back to her chambers. After one long drag she put it out against a glass paperweight and then put the butt into a Ziploc bag she had taken out of her purse. She closed the bag, folded it and replaced it in the purse. She would leave no evidence of her transgression for the night cleaners or any-one else. She exhaled the smoke toward a ceiling intake vent and then brought her eyes down to Minton's. Judging by the look in them I was glad I wasn't him.

"Mr. Minton, what the fuck have you done to my trial?"

"Your—"

"Shut up and sit down. Both of you."

We did as we were told. The judge composed herself and leaned forward across her desk. She was still looking at Minton.

"Who did the due diligence on this witness of yours?" she asked calmly. "Who did the background?"

"Uh, that would have—actually, we only did a background on him in L.A. County. There were no cautions, no flags. I checked his name on the computer but I didn't use the initials."

"How many times had he been used in this county before today?"

"Only one previous time in court. But he had given information on three other cases I could find. Nothing about Arizona came up."

"Nobody thought to check to see if this guy had been anywhere else or used variations of his name?"

"I guess not. He was passed on to me by the original prosecutor on the case. I just assumed she had checked him out."

"Bullshit," I said.

The judge turned her eyes to me. I could have sat back and watched Minton go down but I wasn't going to let him try to take Maggie McPherson with him.

"The original prosecutor was Maggie McPherson," I said. "She had the case all of about three hours. She's my ex-wife and she knew as soon as she saw me at first apps that she was gone. And you got the case that same day, Minton. Where in there was she supposed to background your witnesses, especially this guy who didn't come out from under his rock until after first appearance? She passed him on and that was it."

Minton opened his mouth to say something but the judge cut him off.

"It doesn't matter who should have done it. It wasn't done properly and, either way, putting that man on the stand in my opinion was gross prosecutorial misconduct."

"Your Honor," Minton barked. "I did—"

"Save it for your boss. He's the one you'll need to convince. What was the last offer the state made to Mr. Roulet?"

Minton seemed frozen and unable to respond. I answered for him.

"Simple assault, six months in county."

The judge raised her eyebrows and looked at me.

"And you didn't take it?"

I shook my head.

"My client won't take a conviction. It will ruin him. He'll gamble on a verdict."

"You want a mistrial?" she asked.

I laughed and shook my head.

"No, I don't want a mistrial. All that will do is give the prosecution time to clean up its mess, get it all right and then come back at us."

"Then what do you want?" she asked.

"What do I want? A directed verdict would be nice. Something with no comebacks from the state. Other than that, we'll ride it out."

The judge nodded and clasped her hands together on the desk.

"A directed verdict would be ridiculous, Your Honor," Minton said, finally finding his voice. "We're at the end of trial, anyway. We might as well take it to a verdict. The jury deserves it. Just because one mistake was made by the state, there is no reason to subvert the whole process."

"Don't be stupid, Mr. Minton," the judge said dismissively. "It's not about what the jury deserves. And as far as I am concerned, one mistake like you have made is enough. I don't want this kicked back at me by the Second and that is surely what they will do. Then I am holding the bag for your miscon—"

"I didn't know Corliss's background!" Minton said forcefully. "I swear to God I didn't know."

The intensity of his words brought a momentary silence to the chambers. But soon I slipped into the void.

"Just like you didn't know about the knife, Ted?"

Fullbright looked from Minton to me and then back at Minton.

"What knife?" she asked.

Minton said nothing.

"Tell her," I said.

Minton shook his head.

"I don't know what he's talking about," he said.

"Then you tell me," the judge said to me.

"Judge, if you wait on discovery from the DA, you might as well hang it up at the start," I said. "Witnesses disappear, stories change, you can lose a case just sitting around waiting."

"All right, so what about the knife?"

"I needed to move on this case. So I had my investigator go through the back door and get reports. It's fair game. But they were waiting for him and they phonied up a report on the knife so I wouldn't know about the initials. I didn't know until I got the formal discovery packet."

The judge formed a hard line with her lips.

"That was the police, not the DA's office," Minton said quickly.

"Thirty seconds ago you said you didn't know what he was talking about," Fullbright said. "Now suddenly you do. I don't care who did it. Are you telling me that this did in fact occur?"

Minton reluctantly nodded.

"Yes, Your Honor. But I swear, I didn't—"

"You know what this tells me?" the judge said, cutting him off. "It tells me that from start to finish the state has not played fair in this case. It doesn't matter who did what or that Mr. Haller's investigator may have been acting improperly. The state must be above that. And as evidenced today in my courtroom it has been anything but that."

"Your Honor, that's not—"

"No more, Mr. Minton. I think I've heard enough. I want you both to leave now. In half an hour I'll take the bench and announce what we'll do about this. I am not sure yet what that will be but no matter what I do, you aren't going to like what I have to say, Mr. Minton. And I am directing you to have your boss, Mr. Smithson, in the courtroom with you to hear it."

I stood up. Minton didn't move. He still seemed frozen to the seat.

"I said you can go!" the judge barked.

42

I followed Minton through the court clerk's station and into the court-room. It was empty except for Meehan, who sat at the bailiff's desk. I took my briefcase off the defense table and headed toward the gate.

"Hey, Haller, wait a second," Minton said, as he gathered files from the prosecution table.

I stopped at the gate and looked back.

"What?"

Minton came to the gate and pointed to the rear door of the courtroom.

"Let's go out here."

"My client is going to be waiting out there for me."

"Just come here."

He headed to the door and I followed. In the vestibule where I had con-fronted Roulet two days earlier Minton stopped to confront me. But he didn't say anything. He was putting words together. I decided to push him even further.

"While you go get Smithson I think I'll stop by the *Times* office on two and make sure the reporter down there knows there'll be some fireworks up here in a half hour."

"Look," Minton sputtered. "We have to work this out."

"We?"

"Just hold off on the *Times*, okay? Give me your cell number and give me ten minutes."

"For what?"

"Let me go down to my office and see what I can do."

"I don't trust you, Minton."

"Well, if you want what's best for your client instead of a cheap headline, you're going to have to trust me for ten minutes."

I looked away from his face and acted like I was considering the offer. Finally, I looked back at him. Our faces were only two feet apart.

"You know, Minton, I could've put up with all your bullshit. The knife and the arrogance and everything else. I'm a pro and I have to live with that shit from prosecutors every day of my life. But when you tried to put Corliss on Maggie McPherson in there, that's when I decided not to show you any mercy."

"Look, I did nothing to intentionally—"

"Minton, look around. There's nobody here but us. No cameras, no tape, no witnesses. Are you going to stand there and tell me you never heard of Corliss until a staff meeting yesterday?"

He responded by pointing an angry finger in my face.

"And you're going to stand there and tell me you never heard of him until this morning?"

We stared at each other for a long moment.

"I may be green but I'm not stupid," he said. "The strategy of your whole case was to push me toward using Corliss. You knew all along what you could do with him. And you probably got it from your ex."

"If you can prove that, then prove it," I said.

"Oh, don't worry, I could…if I had the time. But all I've got is a half hour."

I slowly raised my arm and checked my watch.

"More like twenty-six minutes."

"Give me your cell number."

I did and then he was gone. I waited in the vestibule for fifteen seconds before stepping through the door. Roulet was standing close to the glass wall that looked down at the plaza below. His mother and C. C. Dobbs were sitting on a bench against the opposite wall. Further down the hallway I saw Detective Sobel lingering in the hallway.

Roulet noticed me and started walking quickly toward me. Soon his mother and Dobbs followed.

"What's going on?" Roulet asked first.

I waited until they were all gathered close to me before answering.

"I think it's all about to blow up."

"What do you mean?" Dobbs asked.

"The judge is considering a directed verdict. We'll know pretty soon."

"What is a directed verdict?" Mary Windsor asked.

"It's when the judge takes it out of the jury's hands and issues a verdict of acquittal. She's hot because she says Minton engaged in misconduct with Corliss and some other things."

"Can she do that? Just acquit him."

"She's the judge. She can do what she wants."

"Oh my God!"

Windsor brought one hand to her mouth and looked like she might burst into tears.

"I said she is considering it," I cautioned. "It doesn't mean it will happen. But she did offer me a mistrial already and I turned that down flat."

"You turned it down?" Dobbs yelped. "Why on earth did you do that?"

"Because it's meaningless. The state could come right back and try Louis again — this time with a better case because they'll know our moves. Forget the mistrial. We're not going to educate the prosecution. We want something with no comebacks or we ride with this jury to a verdict today. Even if it goes against us we have solid grounds for appeal."

"Isn't that a decision for Louis to make?" Dobbs asked. "After all, he's —"

"Cecil, shut up," Windsor snapped. "Just shut up and stop second-guessing everything this man does for Louis. He's right. We're not going through this again!"

Dobbs looked like he had been slapped by her. He seemed to shrink back from the huddle. I looked at Mary Windsor and saw a different face. It was the face of the woman who had started a business from scratch and had taken it to the top. I also looked at Dobbs differently, realizing that he had probably been whispering sweet negatives about me in her ear all along.

I let it go and focused on what was at hand.

"There's only one thing the DA's office hates worse than losing a verdict," I said. "That's getting embarrassed by a judge with a directed verdict, especially after a finding of prosecutorial misconduct. Minton went down to talk to his boss and he's a guy who is very political and always has his finger in the wind. We might know something in a few minutes."

Roulet was directly in front of me. I looked over his shoulder to see that Sobel was still standing in the hallway. She was talking on a cell phone.

"Listen," I said. "All of you just sit tight. If I don't hear from the DA, then we go back into court in twenty minutes to see what the judge wants to do. So stay close. If you will excuse me, I'm going to go to the restroom."

I stepped away from them and walked down the hallway toward Sobel. But Roulet broke away from his mother and her lawyer and caught up to me. He grabbed me by the arm to stop me.

"I still want to know how Corliss got that shit he was saying," he demanded.

"What does it matter? It's working for us. That's what matters."

Roulet brought his face in close to mine.

"The guy calls me a murderer on the stand. How is that working for us?"

"Because no one believed him. And that's why the judge is so pissed, because they used a professional liar to get up there on the stand and say the worst things about you. To put that in front of the jury and then have the guy revealed as a liar, that's the misconduct. Don't you see? I had to heighten the stakes. It was the only way to push the judge into pushing the prosecution. I am doing exactly what you wanted me to do, Louis. I'm getting you off."

I studied him as he computed this.

"So let it go," I said. "Go back to your mother and Dobbs and let me go take a piss."

He shook his head.

"No, I'm not going to let it go, Mick."

He poked a finger into my chest.

"Something else is going on here, Mick, and I don't like it. You have to remember something. I have your gun. And you have a daughter. You have to—"

I closed my hand over his hand and finger and pushed it away from my chest.

"Don't you ever threaten my family," I said with a controlled but angry voice. "You want to come at me, fine, then come at me and let's do it. But if you *ever* threaten my daughter again, I will bury you so deep you will never be found. You understand me, Louis?"

He slowly nodded and a smile creased his face.

"Sure, Mick. Just so we understand each other."

I released his hand and left him there. I started walking toward the end of the hallway where the restrooms were and where Sobel seemed to be waiting while talking on a cell. I was walking blind, my thoughts of the threat to my daughter crowding my vision. But as I got close to Sobel I shook it off. She ended her call when I got there.

"Detective Sobel," I said.

"Mr. Haller," she said.

"Can I ask why you are here? Are you going to arrest me?"

"I'm here because you invited me, remember?"

"Uh, no, I don't."

She narrowed her eyes.

"You told me I ought to check out your trial."

I suddenly realized she was referring to the awkward conversation in my home office during the search of my house on Monday night.

"Oh, right, I forgot about that. Well, I'm glad you took me up on it. I saw your partner earlier. What happened to him?"

"Oh, he's around."

I tried to read something in that. She had not answered the question about whether she was going to arrest me. I gestured back up the hallway toward the courtroom.

"So what did you think?"

"Interesting. I wish I could have been a fly on the wall in the judge's chambers."

"Well, stick around. It ain't over yet."

"Maybe I will."

My cell phone started to vibrate. I reached under my jacket and pulled it off my hip. The caller ID readout said the call was coming from the district attorney's office.

"I have to take this," I said.

"By all means," Sobel said.

I opened the phone and started walking back up the hallway toward where Roulet was pacing.

"Hello?"

"Mickey Haller, this is Jack Smithson in the DA's office. How's your day going?"

"I've had better."

"Not after you hear what I'm offering to do for you."
"I'm listening."

43

The judge did not come out of chambers for fifteen minutes on top of the thirty she had promised. We were all waiting, Roulet and I at the defense table, his mother and Dobbs behind us in the first row. At the prosecution table Minton was no longer flying solo. Next to him sat Jack Smithson. I was thinking that it was probably the first time he had actually been inside a courtroom in a year.

Minton looked downcast and defeated. Sitting next to Smithson, he could have been taken as a defendant with his attorney. He looked guilty as charged.

Detective Booker was not in the courtroom and I wondered if he was working on something or simply if no one had bothered to call him with the bad news.

I turned to check the big clock on the back wall and to scan the gallery. The screen for Minton's PowerPoint presentation was gone now, a hint of what was to come. I saw Sobel sitting in the back row, but her partner and Kurlen were still nowhere to be seen. There was nobody else but Dobbs and Windsor, and they didn't count. The row reserved for the media was empty. The media had not been alerted. I was keeping my side of the deal with Smithson.

Deputy Meehan called the courtroom to order and Judge Fullbright took the bench with a flourish, the scent of lilac wafting toward the tables. I guessed that she'd had a cigarette or two back there in chambers and had gone heavy with the perfume as cover.

"In the matter of the state versus Louis Ross Roulet, I understand from my clerk that we have a motion."

Minton stood.

"Yes, Your Honor."

He said nothing further, as if he could not bring himself to speak.

"Well, Mr. Minton, are you sending it to me telepathically?"

"No, Your Honor."

Minton looked down at Smithson and got the go-ahead nod.

"The state moves to dismiss all charges against Louis Ross Roulet."

The judge nodded as though she had expected the move. I heard a sharp intake of breath behind me and knew it was from Mary Windsor. She knew

what was going to happen but had held her emotions in check until she had actually heard it in the courtroom.

"Is that with or without prejudice?" the judge asked.

"Dismiss with prejudice."

"Are you sure about that, Mr. Minton? That means no comebacks from the state."

"Yes, Your Honor, I know," Minton said with a note of annoyance at the judge's need to explain the law to him.

The judge wrote something down and then looked back at Minton.

"I believe for the record the state needs to offer some sort of explanation for this motion. We have chosen a jury and heard more than two days of testimony. Why is the state doing this at this stage, Mr. Minton?"

Smithson stood. He was a tall and thin man with a pale complexion. He was a prosecutorial specimen. Nobody wanted a fat man as district attorney and that was exactly what he hoped one day to be. He wore a charcoal gray suit with what had become his trademark: a maroon bow tie with matching handkerchief peeking from the suit's breast pocket. The word among the defense pros was that a political advisor had told him to start building a recognizable media image so that when the time came to run, the voters would think they already knew him. This was one situation where he didn't want the media carrying his image to the voters.

"If I may, Your Honor," he said.

"The record will note the appearance of Assistant District Attorney John Smithson, head of the Van Nuys Division. Welcome, Jack. Go right ahead, please."

"Judge Fullbright, it has come to my attention that in the interest of justice, the charges against Mr. Roulet should be dropped."

He pronounced Roulet's name wrong.

"Is that all the explanation you can offer, Jack?" the judge asked.

Smithson deliberated before answering. While there were no reporters present, the record of the hearing would be public and his words viewable later.

"Judge, it has come to my attention that there were some irregularities in the investigation and subsequent prosecution. This office is founded upon the belief in the sanctity of our justice system. I personally safeguard that in the Van Nuys Division and take it very, very seriously. And so it is better for us to dismiss a case than to see justice possibly compromised in any way."

"Thank you, Mr. Smithson. That is refreshing to hear."

The judge wrote another note and then looked back down at us.

"The state's motion is granted," she said. "All charges against Louis Roulet are dismissed with prejudice. Mr. Roulet, you are discharged and free to go."

"Thank you, Your Honor," I said.

"We still have a jury returning at one o'clock," Fullbright said. "I will gather them and explain that the case has been resolved. If any of you attorneys wish to come back then, I am sure they will have questions for you. However, it is not required that you be back."

I nodded but didn't say I would be back. I wouldn't be. The twelve people who had been so important to me for the last week had just dropped off the radar. They were now as meaningless to me as the drivers going the other way on the freeway. They had gone by and I was finished with them.

The judge left the bench and Smithson was the first one out of the courtroom. He had nothing to say to Minton or me. His first priority was to distance himself from this prosecutorial catastrophe. I looked over and saw Minton's face had lost all color. I assumed that I would soon see his name in the yellow pages. He would not be retained by the DA and he would join the ranks of the defense pros, his first felony lesson a costly one.

Roulet was at the rail, leaning over to hug his mother. Dobbs had a hand on his shoulder in a congratulatory gesture, but the family lawyer had not recovered from Windsor's harsh rebuke in the hallway.

When the hugs were over, Roulet turned to me and with hesitation shook my hand.

"I wasn't wrong about you," he said. "I knew you were the one."

"I want the gun," I said, deadpan, my face showing no joy in the victory just achieved.

"Of course you do."

He turned back to his mother. I hesitated a moment and then turned back to the defense table. I opened my briefcase to return all the files to it.

"Michael?"

I turned and it was Dobbs reaching a hand across the railing. I shook it and nodded.

"You did good," Dobbs said, as if I needed to hear it from him. "We all appreciate it greatly."

"Thanks for the shot. I know you were shaky about me at the start."

I was courteous enough not to mention Windsor's outburst in the hallway and what she had said about him backstabbing me.

"Only because I didn't know you," Dobbs said. "Now I do. Now I know who to recommend to my clients."

"Thank you. But I hope your kind of clients never need me."

He laughed.

"Me, too!"

Then it was Mary Windsor's turn. She extended her hand across the bar.

"Mr. Haller, thank you for my son."

"You're welcome," I said flatly. "Take care of him."

"I always do."

I nodded.

"Why don't you all go out to the hallway and I'll be out in a minute. I have to finish up some things here with the clerk and Mr. Minton."

I turned back to the table. I then went around it and approached the clerk.

"How long before I can get a signed copy of the judge's order?"

"We'll enter it this afternoon. We can send you a copy if you don't want to come back."

"That would be great. Could you also fax one?"

She said she would and I gave her the number to the fax in Lorna Taylor's condominium. I wasn't sure yet how it could be used but I had to believe that an order to dismiss could somehow help me get a client or two.

When I turned back to get my briefcase and leave I noticed that Detective Sobel had left the courtroom. Only Minton remained. He was standing and gathering his things.

"Sorry I never got the chance to see your PowerPoint thing," I said.

He nodded.

"Yeah, it was pretty good. I think it would have won them over."

I nodded.

"What are you going to do now?"

"I don't know. See if I can ride this out and somehow hold on to my job."

He put his files under his arm. He had no briefcase. He only had to go down to the second floor. He turned and gave me a hard stare.

"The only thing I know is that I don't want to cross the aisle. I don't want to become like you, Haller. I think I like sleeping at night too much for that."

With that he headed through the gate and strode out of the courtroom. I glanced over at the clerk to see if she had heard what he had said. She acted like she hadn't.

I took my time following Minton out. I picked up my briefcase and turned backwards as I pushed through the gate. I looked at the judge's empty bench and the state seal on the front panel. I nodded at nothing in particular and then walked out.

44

Roulet and his entourage were waiting for me in the hallway. I looked both ways and saw Sobel down by the elevators. She was on her cell phone and it seemed as though she was waiting for an elevator but it didn't look like the down button was lit.

"Michael, can you join us for lunch?" Dobbs said upon seeing me. "We are going to celebrate!"

I noticed that he was now calling me by my given name. Victory made everybody friendly.

"Uh…," I said, still looking down at Sobel. "I don't think I can make it."

"Why not? You obviously don't have court in the afternoon."

I finally looked at Dobbs. I felt like saying that I couldn't have lunch because I never wanted to see him or Mary Windsor or Louis Roulet again.

"I think I'm going to stick around and talk to the jurors when they come back at one."

"Why?" Roulet asked.

"Because it will help me to know what they were thinking and where we stood."

Dobbs gave me a clap on the upper arm.

"Always learning, always getting better for the next one. I don't blame you."

He looked delighted that I would not be joining them. And for good reason. He probably wanted me out of the way now so he could work on repairing his relationship with Mary Windsor. He wanted that franchise account just to himself again.

I heard the muted bong of the elevator and looked back down the hall. Sobel was standing in front of the opening elevator. She was leaving.

But then Lankford, Kurlen and Booker stepped out of the elevator and joined Sobel. They turned and started walking toward us.

"Then we'll leave you to it," Dobbs said, his back to the approaching detectives. "We have a reservation at Orso and I'm afraid we're already going to be late getting back over the hill."

"Okay," I said, still looking down the hall.

Dobbs, Windsor and Roulet turned to walk away just as the four detectives got to us.

"Louis Roulet," Kurlen announced. "You are under arrest. Turn around, please, and place your hands behind your back."

"No!" Mary Windsor shrieked. "You can't—"

"What is this?" Dobbs cried out.

Kurlen didn't answer or wait for Roulet to comply. He stepped forward and roughly turned Roulet around. As he made the forced turn, Roulet's eyes came to mine.

"What's going on, Mick?" he said in a calm voice. "This shouldn't be happening."

Mary Windsor moved toward her son.

"Take your hands off of my son!"

She grabbed Kurlen from behind but Booker and Lankford quickly moved in and detached her, handling her gently but strongly.

"Ma'am, step back," Booker commanded. "Or I will put you in jail."

Kurlen started giving Roulet the Miranda warning. Windsor stayed back but was not silent.

"How dare you? You cannot do this!"

Her body moved in place and she looked as though unseen hands were keeping her from charging at Kurlen again.

"Mother," Roulet said in a tone that carried more weight and control than any of the detectives.

Windsor's body relented. She gave up. But Dobbs didn't.

"You're arresting him for what?" he demanded.

"Suspicion of murder," Kurlen said. "The murder of Martha Renteria."

"That's impossible!" Dobbs cried. "Everything that witness Corliss said in there was proven to be a lie. Are you crazy? The judge dismissed the case because of his lies."

Kurlen broke from his recital of Roulet's rights and looked at Dobbs.

"If it was all a lie, how'd you know he was talking about Martha Renteria?"

Dobbs realized his mistake and took a step back from the gathering. Kurlen smiled.

"Yeah, I thought so," he said.

He grabbed Roulet by an elbow and turned him back around.

"Let's go," he said.

"Mick?" Roulet said.

"Detective Kurlen," I said. "Can I talk to my client for a moment?"

Kurlen looked at me, seemed to measure something in me and then nodded.

"One minute. Tell him to behave himself and it will all go a lot easier for him."

He shoved Roulet toward me. I took him by one arm and walked him a few paces away from the others so we would have privacy if we kept our voices down. I stepped close to him and began in a whisper.

"This is it, Louis. This is good-bye. I got you off. Now you're on your own. Get yourself a new lawyer."

The shock showed in his eyes. Then his face clouded over with a tightly focused anger. It was pure rage and I realized it was the same rage Regina Campo and Martha Renteria must have seen.

"I won't need a lawyer," he said to me. "You think they can make a case off of what you somehow fed to that lying snitch in there? You better think again."

"They won't need the snitch, Louis. Believe me, they'll find more. They probably already have more."

"What about you, Mick? Aren't you forgetting something? I have —"

"I know. But it doesn't matter anymore. They don't need my gun. They've already got all they need. But whatever happens to me, I'll know that I put you down. At the end, after the trial and all the appeals, when they finally stick that needle in your arm, that will be me, Louis. Remember that."

I smiled with no humor and moved in closer.

"This is for Raul Levin. You might not go down for him but make no mistake, you are going down."

I let that register for a moment and then stepped back and nodded to Kurlen. He and Booker came up on either side of Roulet and took hold of his upper arms.

"You set me up," Roulet said, somehow maintaining his calm. "You aren't a lawyer. You work for them."

"Let's go," Kurlen said.

They started moving him but he shook them off momentarily and put his raging eyes right back into mine.

"This isn't the end, Mick," he said. "I'll be out by tomorrow morning. What will you do then? Think about it. What are you going to do then? You can't protect everybody."

They took a tighter hold of him and roughly turned him toward the elevators. This time Roulet went without a struggle. Halfway down the hall toward the elevator, his mother and Dobbs trailing behind, he turned his head to look back over his shoulder at me. He smiled and it sent something right through me.

You can't protect everybody.

A cold shiver of fear pierced my chest.

Someone was waiting for the elevator and it opened just as the entourage got there. Lankford signaled the person back and took the elevator. Roulet was hustled in. Dobbs and Windsor were about to follow when they were halted by Lankford's hand extended in a stop signal. The elevator door started to close and Dobbs angrily and impotently pushed on the button next to it.

My hope was that it would be the last I would ever see of Louis Roulet, but the fear stayed locked in my chest, fluttering like a moth caught inside a porch light. I turned away and almost walked right into Sobel. I hadn't noticed that she had stayed behind the others.

"You have enough, don't you?" I said. "Tell me you wouldn't have moved so quickly if you didn't have enough to keep him."

She looked at me a long moment before answering.

"We won't decide that. The DA will. Probably depends on what they get out of him in interrogation. But up till now he's had a pretty smart lawyer. He probably knows not to say a word to us."

"Then why didn't you wait?"

"Wasn't my call."

I shook my head. I wanted to tell her that they had moved too fast. It wasn't part of the plan. I wanted to plant the seed, that's all. I wanted them to move slowly and get it right.

The moth fluttered inside and I looked down at the floor. I couldn't shake the idea that all of my machinations had failed, leaving me and my family exposed in the hard-eyed focus of a killer. *You can't protect everybody.*

It was as if Sobel read my fears.

"But we're going to try to keep him," she said. "We have what the snitch said in court and the ticket. We're working on witnesses and the forensics."

My eyes came up to hers.

"What ticket?"

A look of suspicion entered her face.

"I thought you had it figured out. We put it together as soon as the snitch mentioned the snake dancer."

"Yeah. Martha Renteria. I got that. But what ticket? What are you talking about?"

I had moved in too close to her and Sobel took a step back from me. It wasn't my breath. It was my desperation.

"I don't know if I should tell you, Haller. You're a defense lawyer. You're *his* lawyer."

"Not anymore. I just quit."

"Doesn't matter. He—"

"Look, you just took that guy down because of me. I might get disbarred because of it. I might even go to jail for a murder I didn't commit. What ticket are you talking about?"

She hesitated and I waited, but then she finally spoke.

"Raul Levin's last words. He said he found Jesus's ticket out."

"Which means what?"

"You really don't know, do you?"

"Look, just tell me. Please."

She relented.

"We traced Levin's most recent movements. Before he was murdered he had made inquiries about Roulet's parking tickets. He even pulled hard copies of them. We inventoried what he had in the office and eventually compared it with what's on the computer. He was missing one ticket. One hard copy. We didn't know if his killer took it that day or if he had just missed pulling it. So we went and pulled a copy ourselves. It was issued two years ago on the night of April eighth. It was a citation for parking in front of a hydrant in the sixty-seven-hundred block of Blythe Street in Panorama City."

It all came together for me, like the last bit of sand dropping through the middle of an hourglass. Raul Levin really had found Jesus Menendez's salvation.

"Martha Renteria was murdered two years ago on April eighth," I said. "She lived on Blythe in Panorama City."

"Yes, but we didn't know that. We didn't see the connection. You told us that Levin was working separate cases for you. Jesus Menendez and Louis Roulet were separate investigations. Levin had them filed that way, too."

"It was a discovery issue. He kept the cases separate so I wouldn't have to turn over anything on Roulet that he came up with on Menendez."

"One of your lawyer angles. Well, it stopped us from putting it together until that snitch in there mentioned the snake dancer. That connected everything."

I nodded.

"So whoever killed Raul Levin took the hard copy?"

"We think."

"Did you check Raul's phones for a tap? Somehow somebody knew he found the ticket."

"We did. They were clear. Bugs could have been removed at the time of the murder. Or maybe it was someone else's phone that was tapped."

Meaning mine. Meaning it might explain how Roulet knew so many of my moves and was even conveniently waiting for me in my home the night I had come home from seeing Jesus Menendez.

"I will have them checked," I said. "Does all of this mean I am clear on Raul's murder?"

"Not necessarily," Sobel said. "We still want to see what comes back from ballistics. We're hoping for something today."

I nodded. I didn't know how to respond. Sobel lingered, looking like she wanted to tell me or ask me something.

"What?" I said.

"I don't know. Is there anything you want to tell me?"

"I don't know. There's nothing to tell."

"Really? In the courtroom it seemed like you were trying to tell us a lot."

I was silent a moment, trying to read between the lines.

"What do you want from me, Detective Sobel?"

"You know what I want. I want Raul Levin's killer."

"Well, so do I. But I couldn't give you Roulet on Levin even if I wanted to. I don't know how he did it. And that's off the record."

"So that still leaves you in the crosshairs."

She looked down the hall at the elevators, her implication clear. If the ballistics matched, I could still have a problem on Levin. They would use it as leverage. Give up how Roulet did it or go down for it myself. I changed the subject.

"How long do you think before Jesus Menendez gets out?" I asked.

She shrugged.

"Hard to say. Depends on the case they build against Roulet — if they have a case. But I know one thing. They can't prosecute Roulet as long as another man is in prison for the same crime."

I turned and walked over to the glass wall. I put my free hand on the railing that ran along the glass. I felt a mixture of elation and dread and that moth still batting around in my chest.

"That's all I care about," I said quietly. "Getting him out. That and Raul."

She came over and stood next to me.

"I don't know what you are doing," she said. "But leave the rest for us."

"I do that and your partner will probably put me in jail for a murder I didn't commit."

"You are playing a dangerous game," she said. "Leave it alone."

I looked at her and then back down at the plaza.

"Sure," I said. "I'll leave it alone now."

Having heard what she needed to, she made a move to go.

"Good luck," she said.

I looked at her again.

"Same to you."

She left then and I stayed. I turned back to the window and looked down into the plaza. I saw Dobbs and Windsor crossing the concrete squares and heading toward the parking garage. Mary Windsor was leaning against her lawyer for support. I doubted they were still headed to lunch at Orso.

45

By that night the word had begun to spread. Not the secret details but the public story. The story that I had won the case, gotten a DA's motion to dismiss with no comebacks, only to have my client arrested for a murder in the hallway outside the courtroom where I had just cleared him. I got calls from every other defense pro I knew. I got call after call until my cell phone finally died. My colleagues were all congratulating me. In their eyes, there was no downside. Roulet was the ultimate franchise. I got schedule A fees for one trial and then I would get schedule A fees for the next one. It was a double-dip most defense pros could only dream about. And, of course, when I told them I would not be handling the defense of the new case, each one of them asked if I could refer him to Roulet.

It was the one call that came in on my home line that I wanted the most. It was from Maggie McPherson.

"I've been waiting for your call all night," I said.

I was pacing in the kitchen, tethered by the phone cord. I had checked my phones when I had gotten home and found no evidence of bugging devices.

"Sorry, I've been in the conference room," she said.

"I heard you were pulled in on Roulet."

"Yes, that's why I'm calling. They're going to cut him loose."

"What are you talking about? They're letting him go?"

"Yes. They've had him for nine hours in a room and he hasn't broken. Maybe you taught him too well not to talk, because he's a rock and they got nothing and that means they don't have enough."

"You're wrong. There is enough. They have the parking ticket and there have to be witnesses who can put him in The Cobra Room. Even Menendez can ID him there."

"You know as well as I do that Menendez is a scratch. He'd identify anybody to get out. And if there are other wits from The Cobra Room, then it's going to take some time to run them down. The parking ticket puts him in the neighborhood but it doesn't put him inside her apartment."

"What about the knife?"

"They're working on it but that's going to take time, too. Look, we want to do this right. It was Smithson's call and, believe me, he wanted to keep him, too. It would make that fiasco you created in court today a little more palatable. But it's just not there. Not yet. They're going to kick him loose and work the forensics and look for the witnesses. If Roulet's good for this, then we will get him, and your other client will get out. You don't have to worry. But we have to do it right."

I swung a fist impotently through the air.

"They jumped the gun. Damn it, they shouldn't have made the move today."

"I guess they thought nine hours in interrogation would do the trick."

"They were stupid."

"Nobody's perfect."

I was annoyed by her attitude but held my tongue on that. I needed her to keep me in the loop.

"When exactly will they let him go?" I asked.

"I don't know. This all just went down. Kurlen and Booker came over here to present it and Smithson just sent them back to the PD. When they get back, I assume they'll kick him loose."

"Listen to me, Maggie. Roulet knows about Hayley."

There was a horribly long moment of silence before she answered.

"What are you saying, Haller? You let our daughter into—"

"I didn't let anything happen. He broke into my house and saw her picture. It doesn't mean he knows where she lives or even what her name is. But he knows about her and he wants to get back at me. So you have to go home right now. I want you to be with Hayley. Get her and get out of the apartment. Just play it safe."

Something made me hold back on telling her everything, that I felt that Roulet had specifically threatened my family in the courthouse. *You can't protect everybody.* I would only use that if she refused to do what I wanted her to do with Hayley.

"I'm leaving now," she said. "And we're coming to you."

I knew she would say that.

"No, don't come to me."

"Why not?"

"Because *he* might come to me."

"This is crazy. What are you going to do?"

"I'm not sure yet. Just go get Hayley and get somewhere safe. Then call me on your cell, but don't tell me where you are. It will be better if I don't even know."

"Haller, just call the police. They can —"

"And tell them what?"

"I don't know. Tell them you've been threatened."

"A defense lawyer telling the police he feels threatened...yeah, they'll jump all over that. Probably send out a SWAT team."

"Well, you have to do something."

"I thought I did. I thought he was going to be in jail for the rest of his life. But you people moved too fast and now you have to let him go."

"I told you, it wasn't enough. Even knowing now about the possible threat to Hayley, it's still not enough."

"Then go to our daughter and take care of her. Leave the rest to me."

"I'm going."

But she didn't hang up. It was like she was giving me the chance to say something more.

"I love you, Mags," I said. "Both of you. Be careful."

I closed the phone before she could respond. Almost immediately I opened it again and called Fernando Valenzuela's cell phone number. After five rings he answered.

"Val, it's me, Mick."

"Shit. If I'd known it was you I wouldn't have answered."

"Look, I need your help."

"My help? You're asking for my help after what you asked me the other night? After you accused me?"

"Look, Val, this is an emergency. What I said the other night was out of line and I apologize. I'll pay for your TV, I'll do whatever you want, but I need your help right now."

I waited. After a pause he responded.

"What do you want me to do?"

"Roulet still has the bracelet on his ankle, right?"

"That's right. I know what happened in court but I haven't heard from the guy. One of my courthouse people said the cops picked him up again so I don't know what's going on."

"They picked him up but he's about to be kicked loose. He'll probably be calling you so he can get the bracelet taken off."

"I'm already home, man. He can find me in the morning."

"That's what I want. Make him wait."

"That ain't no favor, man."

"This is. I want you to open your laptop and watch him. When he leaves the PD, I want to know where he's going. Can you do that for me?"

"You mean right now?"

"Yeah, right now. You got a problem with that?"

"Sort of."

I got ready for another argument. But I was surprised.

"I told you about the battery alarm on the bracelet, right?" Valenzuela said.

"Yeah, I remember."

"Well, I got the twenty percent alarm about an hour ago."

"So how much longer can you track him until the battery's dead?"

"Probably about six to eight hours' active tracking before it goes on low pulse. Then he'll come up every fifteen minutes for another five hours."

I thought about all of this. I just needed to make it through the night and to know that Maggie and Hayley were safe.

"The thing is, when he is on low pulse he beeps," Valenzuela said. "You'll hear him coming. Or he'll get tired of the noise and juice the battery."

Or maybe he'll pull the Houdini act again, I thought.

"Okay," I said. "You told me that there were other alarms that you could build into the tracking program."

"That's right."

"Can you set it so you get an alarm if he comes near a specific target?"

"Yeah, like if it's on a child molester you can set an alarm if he gets close to a school. Stuff like that. It's got to be a fixed target."

"Okay."

I gave him the address of the apartment on Dickens in Sherman Oaks where Maggie and my daughter lived.

"If he comes within ten blocks of that place you call me. Doesn't matter what time, call me. That's the favor."

"What is this place?"

"It's where my daughter lives."

There was a long silence before Valenzuela responded.

"With Maggie? You think this guy's going to go there?"

"I don't know. I'm hoping that as long as he's got the tracker on his ankle he won't be stupid."

"Okay, Mick. You got it."

"Thanks, Val. And call my home number. My cell is dead."

I gave him the number and then was silent for a moment, wondering what else I could say to make up for my betrayal two nights earlier. Finally, I let it go. I had to focus on the current threat.

I moved from the kitchen and down the hallway to my office. I rolled through the Rolodex on my desk until I found a number and then grabbed the desk phone.

I dialed and waited. I looked out the window to the left of my desk and noticed for the first time that it was raining. It looked like it was going to come down hard and I wondered if the weather would affect the satellite tracking of Roulet. I dropped the thought when my call was answered by Teddy Vogel, the leader of the Road Saints.

"Speak to me."

"Ted, Mickey Haller."

"Counselor, how are you?"

"Not so good tonight."

"Then I am glad you called. What can I do for you?"

I looked out the window at the rain before answering. I knew that if I continued I would be indebted to people I never wanted to be on the hook with.

But there was no choice.

"You happen to have anybody down my way tonight?" I asked.

There was a hesitation before Vogel answered. I knew he had to be curious about his lawyer calling him for help. I was obviously asking about the kind of help that came with muscles and guns.

"Got a few guys watching things at the club. What's up?"

The club was the strip bar on Sepulveda, not too far from Sherman Oaks. I was counting on that.

"There's a threat to my family, Ted. I need some warm bodies to put up a front, maybe grab a guy if needed."

"Armed and dangerous?"

I hesitated but not too long.

"Yeah, armed and dangerous."

"Sounds like our kind of move. Where do you want them?"

He was immediately ready to act. He knew the value of having me under his thumb instead of on retainer. I gave him the address of the apartment on Dickens. I also gave him a description of Roulet and what he had been wearing in court that day.

"If he shows up at that apartment, I want him stopped," I said. "And I need your people to go now."

"Done," Vogel said.

"Thank you, Ted."

"No, thank you. We're glad to help you out, seeing as how you've helped us out so much."

Yeah, right, I thought. I hung the phone up, knowing I had just crossed one of those lines you hope to never see let alone have to step across. I looked out the window again. Outside, the rain was now coming down hard off the roof. I had no gutter in the back and it was coming down in a translucent sheet that blurred the lights out there. Nothing but rain this year, I thought. Nothing but rain.

I left the office and went back to the front of the house. On the table in the dining alcove was the gun Earl Briggs had given me. I contemplated the weapon and all the moves I had made. The bottom line was I had been flying blind and in the process had endangered more than just myself.

Panic started to set in. I grabbed the phone off the kitchen wall and called Maggie's cell. She answered right away. I could tell she was in her car.

"Where are you?"

"I'm just getting home now. I'll get some things together and we'll get out."

"Good."

"What do I tell Hayley, that her father put her life in danger?"

"It's not like that, Maggie. It's him. It's Roulet. I couldn't control him. One night I came home and he was sitting in my house. He's a real estate guy. He knows how to find places. He saw her picture on my desk. What was I —"

"Can we talk about this later? I have to go in now and get my daughter."

Not *our* daughter. *My* daughter.

"Sure. Call me when you're in a new place."

She disconnected without further word and I slowly hung the phone back on the wall. My hand was still on the phone. I leaned forward until my forehead touched the wall. I was out of moves. I could only wait on Roulet to make the next one.

The phone's ring startled me and I jumped back. The phone fell to the floor and I pulled it up by the cord. It was Valenzuela.

"You get my message? I just called."

"No, I've been on the phone. What?"

"Glad I called back, then. He's moving."

"Where?"

I shouted it too loud into the phone. I was losing it.

"He's heading south on Van Nuys. He called me and said he wanted to lose the bracelet. I told him I was already home and that he could call me tomorrow. I told him he had better juice the battery so he wouldn't start beeping in the middle of the night."

"Good thinking. Where's he now?"

"Still on Van Nuys."

I tried to build an image of Roulet driving. If he was going south on Van Nuys that meant he was heading directly toward Sherman Oaks and the neighborhood where Maggie and Hayley lived. But he could also be headed right through Sherman Oaks on his way south over the hill and to his home. I had to wait to be sure.

"How up to the moment is the GPS on that thing?" I asked.

"It's real time, man. This is where he's at. He just crossed under the one-oh-one. He might be just going home, Mick."

"I know, I know. Just wait till he crosses Ventura. The next street is Dickens. If he turns there, then he's not going home."

I stood up and didn't know what to do. I started pacing, the phone pressed tightly to my ear. I knew that even if Teddy Vogel had immediately put his men in motion they were still minutes away. They were no good to me now.

"What about the rain? Does it affect the GPS?"

"It's not supposed to."

"That's comforting."

"He stopped."

"Where?"

"Must be a light. I think that's Moorpark Avenue there."

That was a block before Ventura and two before Dickens. I heard a beeping sound come over the phone.

"What's that?"

"The ten-block alarm you asked me to set."

The beeping sound stopped.

"I turned it off."

"I'll call you right back."

I didn't wait for a response. I hung up and called Maggie's cell. She answered right away.

"Where are you?"

"You told me not to tell you."

"You're out of the apartment?"

"No, not yet. Hayley's picking the crayons and coloring books she wants to take."

"Goddamn it, get out of there! Now!"

"We're going as fast as—"

"Just get out! I'll call you back. Make sure you answer."

I hung up and called Valenzuela back.

"Where is he?"

"He's now at Ventura. Must've caught another light, because he's not moving."

"You're sure he's on the road and not just parked there?"

"No, I'm not sure. He could—never mind, he's moving. Shit, he turned on Ventura."

"Which way?"

I started pacing, the phone pressed so hard against my ear that it hurt.

"Right—uh, west. He's going west."

He was now driving parallel to Dickens, one block away, in the direction of my daughter's apartment.

"He just stopped again," Valenzuela announced. "It's not an intersection. It looks like he's in the middle of the block. I think he parked it."

I ran my free hand through my hair like a desperate man.

"Fuck it, I've gotta go. My cell's dead. Call Maggie and tell her he's heading her way. Tell her to just get in the car and get out of there!"

I shouted Maggie's number into the phone and dropped it as I headed out of the kitchen. I knew it would take me a minimum of twenty minutes to get to Dickens—and that was hitting the curves on Mulholland at sixty in the Lincoln—but I couldn't stand around shouting orders on the phone while my family was in danger. I grabbed the gun off the table and went to the door. I was shoving it into the side pocket of my jacket as I opened the door.

Mary Windsor was standing there, her hair wet from the rain.

"Mary, what —"

She raised her hand. I looked down to see the metal glint of the gun in it just as she fired.

46

The sound was loud and the flash as bright as a camera's. The impact of the bullet tearing into me was like what I imagine a kick from a horse would feel like. In a split second I went from standing still to moving backwards. I hit the wood floor hard and was propelled into the wall next to the living room fireplace. I tried to reach both hands to the hole in my gut but my right hand was hung up in the pocket of my jacket. I held myself with the left and tried to sit up.

Mary Windsor stepped forward and into the house. I had to look up at her. Through the open door behind her I could see the rain coming down. She raised the weapon and pointed it at my forehead. In a flash moment my daughter's face came to me and I knew I wasn't going to let her go.

"You tried to take my son from me!" Windsor shouted. "Did you think I could allow you to do that and just walk away?"

And then I knew. Everything crystallized. I knew she had said similar words to Raul Levin before she had killed him. And I knew that there had been no rape in an empty house in Bel-Air. She was a mother doing what she had to do. Roulet's words came back to me then. *You're right about one thing. I am a son of a bitch.*

And I knew, too, that Raul Levin's last gesture had not been to make the sign of the devil, but to make the letter *M* or *W*, depending on how you looked at it.

Windsor took another step toward me.

"You go to hell," she said.

She steadied her hand to fire. I raised my right hand, still wrapped in my jacket. She must have thought it was a defensive gesture because she didn't hurry. She was savoring the moment. I could tell. Until I fired.

Mary Windsor's body jerked backwards with the impact and she landed on her back in the threshold of the door. Her gun clattered to the floor and I heard her make a high-pitched whining noise. Then I heard the sound of running feet on the steps up to the front deck.

"Police!" a woman shouted. "Put your weapons down!"

I looked through the door and didn't see anyone.

"Put your weapons down and come out with your hands in full view!"

This time it was a man who had yelled and I recognized the voice.

I pulled the gun out of my jacket pocket and put it on the floor. I slid it away from me.

"The weapon's down," I called out, as loud as the hole in my stomach allowed me to. "But I'm shot. I can't get up. We're both shot."

I first saw the barrel of a pistol come into view in the doorway. Then a hand and then a wet black raincoat containing Detective Lankford. He moved into the house and was quickly followed by his partner, Detective Sobel. Lankford kicked the gun away from Windsor as he came in. He kept his own weapon pointed at me.

"Anybody else in the house?" he asked loudly.

"No," I said. "Listen to me."

I tried to sit up but pain shot through my body and Lankford yelled.

"Don't move! Just stay there!"

"Listen to me. My fam—"

Sobel yelled a command into a handheld radio, ordering paramedics and ambulance transport for two people with gunshot wounds.

"One transport," Lankford corrected. "She's gone."

He pointed his gun at Windsor.

Sobel shoved the radio into her raincoat pocket and came to me. She knelt down and pulled my hand away from my wound. She pulled my shirt out of my pants so she could lift it and see the damage. She then pressed my hand back down on the bullet hole.

"Press down as hard as you can. It's a bleeder. You hear me, hold your hand down tight."

"Listen to me," I said again. "My family's in danger. You have to—"

"Hold on."

She reached inside her raincoat and pulled a cell phone off her belt. She flipped it open and hit a speed-dial button. Whoever she called answered right away.

"It's Sobel. You better bring him back in. His mother just tried to hit the lawyer. He got her first."

She listened for a moment and asked, "Then, where is he?"

She listened some more and then said good-bye. I stared at her as she closed her phone.

"They'll pick him up. Your daughter is safe."

"You're watching him?"

She nodded.

"We piggy-backed on your plan, Haller. We have a lot on him but we were hoping for more. I told you, we want to clear Levin. We were hoping that if we kicked him loose he'd show us his trick, show us how he got to Levin. But the mother sort of just solved that mystery for us."

I understood. Even with the blood and life running out of the hole in my gut I was able to put it together. Releasing Roulet had been a play. They were hoping that he'd go after me, revealing the method he had used to defeat the GPS ankle bracelet when he had killed Raul Levin. Only he hadn't killed Raul. His mother had done it for him.

"Maggie?" I asked weakly.

Sobel shook her head.

"She's fine. She had to play along because we didn't know if Roulet had a tap on your line or not. She couldn't tell you that she and Hayley were safe."

I closed my eyes. I didn't know whether just to be thankful that they were okay or to be angry that Maggie had used her daughter's father as bait for a killer.

I tried to sit up.

"I want to call her. She—"

"Don't move. Just stay still."

I leaned my head back on the floor. I was cold and on the verge of shaking, yet I also felt as though I were sweating. I could feel myself getting weaker as my breathing grew shallow.

Sobel pulled the radio out of her pocket again and asked dispatch for an ETA on the paramedics. The dispatcher reported back that the medical help was still six minutes away.

"Hang in there," Sobel said to me. "You'll be all right. Depending on what the bullet did inside, you should be all right."

"Gray..."

I meant to say *great* with full sarcasm attached. But I was fading.

Lankford came up next to Sobel and looked at me. In a gloved hand he held up the gun Mary Windsor had shot me with. I recognized the pearl grips. Mickey Cohen's gun. My gun. The gun she shot Raul with.

He nodded and I took it as some sort of signal. Maybe that in his eyes I had stepped up, that he knew I had done their work by drawing the killer out. Maybe it was even the offering of a truce and maybe he wouldn't hate lawyers so much after this.

Probably not. But I nodded back at him and the small movement made me cough. I tasted something in my mouth and knew it was blood.

"Don't flatline on us now," Lankford ordered. "If we end up giving a defense lawyer mouth-to-mouth, we'll never live it down."

He smiled and I smiled back. Or tried to. Then the blackness started crowding my vision. Pretty soon I was floating in it.

PART THREE

— Postcard from Cuba

47

Tuesday, October 4

It has been five months since I was in a courtroom. In that time I have had three surgeries to repair my body, been sued in civil court twice and been investigated by both the Los Angeles Police Department and the California Bar Association. My bank accounts have been bled dry by medical expenses, living expenses, child support and, yes, even my own kind — the lawyers.

But I have survived it all and today will be the first day since I was shot by Mary Alice Windsor that I will walk without a cane or the numbing of painkillers. To me it is the first real step toward getting back. The cane is a sign of weakness. Nobody wants a defense attorney who looks weak. I must stand upright, stretch the muscles the surgeon cut through to get to the bullet, and walk on my own before I feel I can walk into a courtroom again.

I have not been in a courtroom but that does not mean I am not the subject of legal proceedings. Jesus Menendez and Louis Roulet are both suing me and the cases will likely follow me for years. They are separate claims but both of my former clients charge me with malpractice and violation of legal ethics. For all the specific accusations in his lawsuit, Roulet has not been able to learn how I supposedly got to Dwayne Jeffery Corliss at County-USC and fed him privileged information. And it is unlikely he ever will. Gloria Dayton is long gone. She finished her program, took the $25,000 I gave her and moved to Hawaii to start life again. And Corliss, who probably knows better than anyone the value of keeping one's mouth shut, has divulged nothing other than what he testified to in court — maintaining that while in custody Roulet told him about the murder of the snake dancer. He has avoided perjury charges because pursuing them would undermine the case against Roulet and be an act of self-flagellation by the DA's office. My lawyer tells me Roulet's lawsuit against me is a face-saving effort without merit and that it will eventually go away. Probably when I have no more money to pay my lawyer his fees.

But Menendez will never go away. He is the one who gets to me at night when I sit on the deck and watch the million-dollar view from my house with the million-one mortgage. He was pardoned by the governor and released from San Quentin two days after Roulet was charged with Martha

Renteria's murder. But he only traded one life sentence for another. It was revealed that he contracted HIV in prison and the governor doesn't have a pardon for that. Nobody does. Whatever happens to Jesus Menendez is on me. I know this. I live with it every day. My father was right. There is no client as scary as an innocent man. And no client as scarring.

Menendez wants to spit on me and take my money as punishment for what I did and didn't do. As far as I am concerned he is entitled. But no matter what my failings of judgment and ethical lapses were, I know that by the end, I bent things in order to do the right thing. I traded evil for innocence. Roulet is in because of me. Menendez is out because of me. Despite the efforts of his new attorneys — it has now taken the partnership of Dan Daly and Roger Mills to replace me — Roulet will not see freedom again. From what I have heard from Maggie McPherson, prosecutors have built an impenetrable case against him for the Renteria murder. They have also followed Raul Levin's steps and connected Roulet to another killing: the follow-home rape and stabbing of a woman who tended bar in a Hollywood club. The forensic profile of his knife was matched to the fatal wounds inflicted on this other woman. For Roulet, the science will be the iceberg spotted too late. His ship will founder and go down. The battle for him now lies in just staying alive. His lawyers are engaged in plea negotiations to keep him from a lethal injection. They are hinting at other murders and rapes that he would be willing to clear up in exchange for his life. Whatever the outcome, alive or dead, he is surely gone from this world and I take my salvation in that. It is what has mended me better than any surgeon.

Maggie McPherson and I are attempting to mend our wounds, too. She brings my daughter to visit me every weekend and often stays for the day. We sit on the deck and talk. We both know our daughter will be what saves us. I can no longer hold anger for being used as bait for a killer. I think Maggie no longer holds anger for the choices I have made.

The California bar looked at all of my actions and sent me on a vacation to Cuba. That's what defense pros call being suspended for conduct unbecoming an attorney. CUBA. I was shelved for ninety days. It was a bullshit finding. They could prove no specific ethical violations in regard to Corliss, so they hit me for borrowing a gun from my client Earl Briggs. I got lucky there. It was not a stolen or unregistered gun. It belonged to Earl's father, so my ethical infraction was minor.

I didn't bother contesting the bar reprimand or appealing the suspension. After taking a bullet in the gut, ninety days on the shelf didn't look so bad to me. I served the suspension during my recovery, mostly in a bathrobe while watching Court TV.

Neither the bar nor the police found ethical or criminal violation on my part in the killing of Mary Alice Windsor. She entered my home with a stolen weapon. She shot first and I shot last. From a block away Lankford and

Sobel watched her take that first shot at my front door. Self-defense, cut and dried. But what has not been so clear-cut are the feelings I have for what I did. I wanted to avenge my friend Raul Levin, but I didn't want to see it done in blood. I am a killer now. Being state sanctioned only tempers slightly the feelings that come with that.

All investigations and official findings aside, I think now that in the whole matter of Menendez and Roulet I was guilty of conduct unbecoming myself. And the penalty for that is harsher than anything the state or the bar could ever throw at me. No matter. I will carry all of it with me as I go back to work. My work. I know my place in this world and on the first day of court next year I will pull the Lincoln out of the garage, get back on the road and go looking for the underdog. I don't know where I will go or what cases will be mine. I just know I will be healed and ready to stand once again in the world without truth.

The Brass
Verdict

In memory of Terry Hansen
and Frank Morgan

PART ONE

— Rope a Dope

1992

1

Everybody lies.

Cops lie. Lawyers lie. Witnesses lie. The victims lie.

A trial is a contest of lies. And everybody in the courtroom knows this. The judge knows this. Even the jury knows this. They come into the building knowing they will be lied to. They take their seats in the box and agree to be lied to.

The trick if you are sitting at the defense table is to be patient. To wait. Not for just any lie. But for the one you can grab on to and forge like hot iron into a sharpened blade. You then use that blade to rip the case open and spill its guts out on the floor.

That's my job, to forge the blade. To sharpen it. To use it without mercy or conscience. To be the truth in a place where everybody lies.

2

I was in the fourth day of trial in Department 109 in the downtown Criminal Courts Building when I got the lie that became the blade that ripped the case open. My client, Barnett Woodson, was riding two murder charges all the way to the steel-gray room in San Quentin where they serve you Jesus juice direct through the arm.

Woodson, a twenty-seven-year-old drug dealer from Compton, was accused of robbing and killing two college students from Westwood. They had wanted to buy cocaine from him. He decided instead to take their money and kill them both with a sawed-off shotgun. Or so the prosecution said. It was a black-on-white crime and that made things bad enough for Woodson — especially coming just four months after the riots that had torn the city apart. But what made his situation even worse was that the killer had attempted to hide the crime by weighing down the two bodies and dropping them into the Hollywood Reservoir. They stayed down for four days before popping to the surface like apples in a barrel. Rotten apples. The idea of dead bodies moldering in the reservoir that was a primary source of the city's drinking water caused a collective twist in the community's guts. When Woodson was linked by phone records to the dead men and arrested, the public outrage directed toward him was almost palpable. The District Attorney's Office promptly announced it would seek the death penalty.

The case against Woodson, however, wasn't all that palpable. It was constructed largely of circumstantial evidence — the phone records — and the testimony of witnesses who were criminals themselves. And state's witness Ronald Torrance sat front and center in this group. He claimed that Woodson confessed the killings to him.

Torrance had been housed on the same floor of the Men's Central Jail as Woodson. Both men were kept in a high-power module that contained sixteen single-prisoner cells on two tiers that opened onto a dayroom. At the time, all sixteen prisoners in the module were black, following the routine but questionable jail procedure of "segregating for safety," which entailed dividing prisoners according to race and gang affiliation to avoid confrontations and violence. Torrance was awaiting trial on robbery and aggravated assault charges stemming from his involvement in looting during the riots. High-power detainees had six a.m. to six p.m. access to the dayroom, where they ate and played cards at tables and otherwise interacted under the watchful eyes of guards in an overhead glass booth. According to Torrance, it was at one of these tables that my client had confessed to killing the two Westside boys.

The prosecution went out of its way to make Torrance presentable and believable to the jury, which had only three black members. He was given a shave, his hair was taken out of cornrows and trimmed short and he was dressed in a pale blue suit with no tie when he arrived in court on the fourth day of Woodson's trial. In direct testimony elicited by Jerry Vincent, the prosecutor, Torrance described the conversation he allegedly had with Woodson one morning at one of the picnic tables. Woodson not only confessed to the killings, he said, but furnished Torrance with many of the telling details of the murders. The point made clear to the jury was that these were details that only the true killer would know.

During the testimony, Vincent kept Torrance on a tight leash with long questions designed to elicit short answers. The questions were overloaded to the point of being leading but I didn't bother objecting, even when Judge Companioni looked at me with raised eyebrows, practically begging me to jump in. But I didn't object, because I wanted the counterpoint. I wanted the jury to see what the prosecution was doing. When it was my turn, I was going to let Torrance run with his answers while I hung back and waited for the blade.

Vincent finished his direct at eleven a.m. and the judge asked me if I wanted to take an early lunch before I began my cross. I told him no, I didn't need or want a break. I said it like I was disgusted and couldn't wait another hour to get at the man on the stand. I stood up and took a big, thick file and a legal pad with me to the lectern.

"Mr. Torrance, my name is Michael Haller. I work for the Public Defender's Office and represent Barnett Woodson. Have we met before?"

"No, sir."

"I didn't think so. But you and the defendant, Mr. Woodson, you two go back a long way, correct?"

Torrance gave an "aw, shucks" smile. But I had done the due diligence on him and I knew exactly who I was dealing with. He was thirty-two years old and had spent a third of his life in jails and prisons. His schooling had ended in the fourth grade when he stopped going to school and no parent seemed to notice or care. Under the state's three-strike law, he was facing the lifetime achievement award if convicted of charges he robbed and pistol-whipped the female manager of a coin laundry. The crime had been committed during three days of rioting and looting that ripped through the city after the not-guilty verdicts were announced in the trial of four police officers accused of the excessive beating of Rodney King, a black motorist pulled over for driving erratically. In short, Torrance had good reason to help the state take down Barnett Woodson.

"Well, we go back a few months is all," Torrance said. "To high-power."

"Did you say 'higher power'?" I asked, playing dumb. "Are you talking about a church or some sort of religious connection?"

"No, high-power module. In county."

"So you're talking about jail, correct?"

"That's right."

"So you're telling me that you didn't know Barnett Woodson before that?" I asked the question with surprise in my voice.

"No, sir. We met for the first time in the jail."

I made a note on the legal pad as if this were an important concession.

"So then, let's do the math, Mr. Torrance. Barnett Woodson was transferred into the high-power module where you were already residing on the fifth of September earlier this year. Do you remember that?"

"Yeah, I remember him coming in, yeah."

"And why were you there in high-power?"

Vincent stood and objected, saying I was covering ground he had already trod in direct testimony. I argued that I was looking for a fuller explanation of Torrance's incarceration, and Judge Companioni allowed me the leeway. He told Torrance to answer the question.

"Like I said, I got a count of assault and one of robbery."

"And these alleged crimes took place during the riots, is that correct?"

With the anti-police climate permeating the city's minority communities since even before the riots, I had fought during jury selection to get as many blacks and browns on the panel as I could. But here was a chance to work on the five white jurors the prosecution had been able to get by me. I wanted them to know that the man the prosecution was hanging so much of its case on was one of those responsible for the images they saw on their television sets back in May.

"Yeah, I was out there like everybody else," Torrance answered. "Cops get away with too much in this town, you ask me."

I nodded like I agreed.

"And your response to the injustice of the verdicts in the Rodney King beating case was to go out and rob a sixty-two-year-old woman and knock her unconscious with a steel trash can? Is that correct, sir?"

Torrance looked over at the prosecution table and then past Vincent to his own lawyer, sitting in the first row of the gallery. Whether or not they had earlier rehearsed a response to this question, his legal team couldn't help Torrance now. He was on his own.

"I didn't do that," he finally said.

"You're innocent of the crime you are charged with?"

"That's right."

"What about looting? You committed no crimes during the riots?"

After a pause and another glance at his attorney, Torrance said, "I take the fifth on that."

As expected. I then took Torrance through a series of questions designed so that he had no choice but to incriminate himself or refuse to answer under the protections of the Fifth Amendment. Finally, after he took the nickel six times, the judge grew weary of the point being made over and over and prodded me back to the case at hand. I reluctantly complied.

"All right, enough about you, Mr. Torrance," I said. "Let's get back to you and Mr. Woodson. You knew the details of this double-murder case before you even met Mr. Woodson in lockup?"

"No, sir."

"Are you sure? It got a lot of attention."

"I been in jail, man."

"They don't have television or newspapers in jail?"

"I don't read no papers and the module's TV been broke since I got there. We made a fuss and they said they'd fix it but they ain't fixed shit."

The judge admonished Torrance to check his language and the witness apologized. I moved on.

"According to the jail's records, Mr. Woodson arrived in the high-power module on the fifth of September and, according to the state's discovery material, you contacted the prosecution on October second to report his alleged confession. Does that sound right to you?"

"Yeah, that sounds right."

"Well, not to me, Mr. Torrance. You are telling this jury that a man accused of a double murder and facing the possible death penalty confessed to a man he had known for less than four weeks?"

Torrance shrugged before answering.

"That's what happened."

"So you say. What will you get from the prosecution if Mr. Woodson is convicted of these crimes?"

"I don't know. Nobody has promised me nothing."

"With your prior record and the charges you currently face, you are looking at more than fifteen years in prison if you're convicted, correct?"

"I don't know about any of that."

"You don't?"

"No, sir. I let my lawyer handle all that."

"He hasn't told you that if you don't do something about this, you might go to prison for a long, long time?"

"He hasn't told me none of that."

"I see. What have you asked the prosecutor for in exchange for your testimony?"

"Nothing. I don't want nothing."

"So then, you are testifying here because you believe it is your duty as a citizen, is that correct?"

The sarcasm in my voice was unmistakable.

"That's right," Torrance responded indignantly.

I held the thick file up over the lectern so he could see it.

"Do you recognize this file, Mr. Torrance?"

"No. Not that I recall, I don't."

"You sure you don't remember seeing it in Mr. Woodson's cell?"

"Never been in his cell."

"Are you sure that you didn't sneak in there and look through his discovery file while Mr. Woodson was in the dayroom or in the shower or maybe in court sometime?"

"No, I did not."

"My client had many of the investigative documents relating to his prosecution in his cell. These contained several of the details you testified to this morning. You don't think that is suspicious?"

Torrance shook his head.

"No. All I know is that he sat there at the table and told me what he'd done. He was feeling poorly about it and opened up to me. It ain't my fault people open up to me."

I nodded as if sympathetic to the burden Torrance carried as a man others confided in — especially when it came to double murders.

"Of course not, Mr. Torrance. Now, can you tell the jury exactly what he said to you? And don't use the shorthand you used when Mr. Vincent was asking the questions. I want to hear exactly what my client told you. Give us his words, please."

Torrance paused as if to probe his memory and compose his thoughts.

"Well," he finally said, "we were sittin' there, the both of us by ourselves, and he just started talkin' about feelin' bad about what he'd done. I asked him, 'What'd you do?' and he told me about that night he killed the two fellas and how he felt pretty rough about it."

The truth is short. Lies are long. I wanted to get Torrance talking in long form, something Vincent had successfully avoided. Jailhouse snitches have something in common with all con men and professional liars. They seek to hide the con in misdirection and banter. They wrap cotton around their lies. But in all of that fluff you often find the key to revealing the big lie.

Vincent objected again, saying the witness had already answered the questions I was asking and I was simply badgering him at this point.

"Your Honor," I responded, "this witness is putting a confession in my client's mouth. As far as the defense is concerned, this is the case right here. The court would be remiss if it did not allow me to fully explore the content and context of such damaging testimony."

Judge Companioni was nodding in agreement before I finished the last sentence. He overruled Vincent's objection and told me to proceed. I turned my attention back to the witness and spoke with impatience in my voice.

"Mr. Torrance, you are still summarizing. You claim Mr. Woodson confessed to the murders. So then, tell the jury what he said to you. What were the *exact* words he said to you when he confessed to this crime?"

Torrance nodded as if he were just then realizing what I was asking for.

"The first thing he said to me was 'Man, I feel bad.' And I said, 'For what, my brother?' He said he kept thinking about those two guys. I didn't know what he was talking about 'cause, like I said, I hadn't heard nothin' about the case, you know? So I said, 'What two guys?' and he said, 'The two niggers I dumped in the reservoir.' I asked what it was all about and he told me about blasting them both with a shorty and wrappin' them up in chicken wire and such. He said, 'I made one bad mistake' and I asked him what it was. He said, 'I shoulda taken a knife and opened up their bellies so they wouldn't end up floatin' to the top the way they did.' And that was what he told me."

In my peripheral vision I had seen Vincent flinch in the middle of Torrance's long answer. And I knew why. I carefully moved in with the blade.

"Did Mr. Woodson use that word? He called the victims 'niggers'?"

"Yeah, he said that."

I hesitated as I worked on the phrasing of the next question. I knew Vincent was waiting to object if I gave him the opening. I could not ask Torrance to interpret. I couldn't use the word "why" when it came to Woodson's meaning or motivation. That was objectionable.

"Mr. Torrance, in the black community the word 'nigger' could mean different things, could it not?"

"'Spose."

"Is that a yes?"

"Yes."

"The defendant is African-American, correct?"

Torrance laughed.

"Looks like it to me."

"As are you, correct, sir?"

Torrance started to laugh again.

"Since I was born," he said.

The judge tapped his gavel once and looked at me.

"Mr. Haller, is this really necessary?"

"I apologize, Your Honor."

"Please move on."

"Mr. Torrance, when Mr. Woodson used that word, as you say he did, did it shock you?"

Torrance rubbed his chin as he thought about the question. Then he shook his head.

"Not really."

"Why weren't you shocked, Mr. Torrance?"

"I guess it's 'cause I hear it all a' time, man."

"From other black men?"

"That's right. I heard it from white folks, too."

"Well, when fellow black men use that word, like you say Mr. Woodson did, who are they talking about?"

Vincent objected, saying that Torrance could not speak for what other men were talking about. Companioni sustained the objection and I took a moment to rework the path to the answer I wanted.

"Okay, Mr. Torrance," I finally said. "Let's talk only about you, then, okay? Do you use that word on occasion?"

"I think I have."

"All right, and when you have used it, who were you referring to?"

Torrance shrugged.

"Other fellas."

"Other black men?"

"That's right."

"Have you ever on occasion referred to white men as niggers?"

Torrance shook his head.

"No."

"Okay, so then, what did you take the meaning to be when Barnett Woodson described the two men who were dumped in the reservoir as niggers?"

Vincent moved in his seat, going through the body language of making an objection but not verbally following through with it. He must have known it would be useless. I had led Torrance down the path and he was mine.

Torrance answered the question.

"I took it that they were black and he killed 'em both."

Now Vincent's body language changed again. He sank a little bit in his seat because he knew his gamble in putting a jailhouse snitch on the witness stand had just come up snake eyes.

I looked up at Judge Companioni. He knew what was coming as well.

"Your Honor, may I approach the witness?"

"You may," the judge said.

I walked to the witness stand and put the file down in front of Torrance. It was legal size, well worn and faded orange — a color used by county jailers to denote private legal documents that an inmate is authorized to possess.

"Okay, Mr. Torrance, I have placed before you a file in which Mr. Woodson keeps discovery documents provided to him in jail by his attorneys. I ask you once again if you recognize it."

"I seen a lotta orange files in high-power. It don't mean I seen that one."

"You are saying you never saw Mr. Woodson with his file?"

"I don't rightly remember."

"Mr. Torrance, you were with Mr. Woodson in the same module for thirty-two days. You testified he confided in you and confessed to you. Are you saying you never saw him with that file?"

He didn't answer at first. I had backed him into a no-win corner. I waited. If he continued to claim he had never seen the file, then his claim of a confession from Woodson would be suspect in the eyes of the jury. If he finally conceded that he was familiar with the file, then he opened a big door for me.

"What'm saying is that I seen him with his file but I never looked at what was in it."

Bang. I had him.

"Then, I'll ask you to open the file and inspect it."

The witness followed the instruction and looked from side to side at the open file. I went back to the lectern, checking on Vincent on my way. His eyes were downcast and his face was pale.

"What do you see when you open the file, Mr. Torrance?"

"One side's got photos of two bodies on the ground. They're stapled in there — the photos, I mean. And the other side is a bunch of documents and reports and such."

"Could you read from the first document there on the right side? Just read the first line of the summary."

"No, I can't read."

"You can't read at all?"

"Not really. I didn't get the schooling."

"Can you read any of the words that are next to the boxes that are checked at the top of the summary?"

Torrance looked down at the file and his eyebrows came together in concentration. I knew that his reading skills had been tested during his last stint in prison and were determined to be at the lowest measurable level — below second-grade skills.

"Not really," he said. "I can't read."

I quickly walked over to the defense table and grabbed another file and a Sharpie pen out of my briefcase. I went back to the lectern and quickly printed the word CAUCASIAN on the outside of the file in large block letters. I held the file up so that Torrance, as well as the jury, could see it.

"Mr. Torrance, this is one of the words checked on the summary. Can you read this word?"

Vincent immediately stood but Torrance was already shaking his head and looking thoroughly humiliated. Vincent objected to the demonstration without proper foundation and Companioni sustained. I expected him to. I was just laying the groundwork for my next move with the jury and I was sure most of them had seen the witness shake his head.

"Okay, Mr. Torrance," I said. "Let's move to the other side of the file. Could you describe the bodies in the photos?"

"Um, two men. It looks like they opened up some chicken wire and some tarps and they're laying there. A bunch a police is there investigatin' and takin' pictures."

"What race are the men on the tarps?"

"They're black."

"Have you ever seen those photographs before, Mr. Torrance?"

Vincent stood to object to my question as having previously been asked and answered. But it was like holding up a hand to stop a bullet. The judge sternly told him he could take his seat. It was his way of telling the prosecutor he was going to have to just sit back and take what was coming. You put the liar on the stand, you take the fall with him.

"You may answer the question, Mr. Torrance," I said after Vincent sat down. "Have you ever seen those photographs before?"

"No, sir, not before right now."

"Would you agree that the pictures portray what you described to us earlier? That being the bodies of two slain black men?"

"That's what it looks like. But I ain't seen the picture before, just what he tell me."

"Are you sure?"

"Something like these I wouldn't forget."

"You've told us Mr. Woodson confessed to killing two black men, but he is on trial for killing two white men. Wouldn't you agree that it appears that he didn't confess to you at all?"

"No, he confessed. He told me he killed those two."

I looked up at the judge.

"Your Honor, the defense asks that the file in front of Mr. Torrance be admitted into evidence as defense exhibit one."

Vincent made a lack-of-foundation objection but Companioni overruled.

"It will be admitted and we'll let the jury decide whether Mr. Torrance has or hasn't seen the photographs and contents of the file."

I was on a roll and decided to go all in.

"Thank you," I said. "Your Honor, now might also be a good time for the prosecutor to reacquaint his witness with the penalties for perjury."

It was a dramatic move made for the benefit of the jury. I was expecting I would have to continue with Torrance and eviscerate him with the blade of his own lie. But Vincent stood and asked the judge to recess the trial while he conferred with opposing counsel.

This told me I had just saved Barnett Woodson's life.

"The defense has no objection," I told the judge.

3

After the jury filed out of the box, I returned to the defense table as the courtroom deputy was moving in to cuff my client and take him back to the courtroom holding cell.

"That guy's a lying sack of shit," Woodson whispered to me. "I didn't kill two black guys. They were white."

My hope was that the deputy hadn't heard that.

"Why don't you shut the fuck up?" I whispered right back. "And next time you see that lying sack of shit in lockup, you ought to shake his hand. Because of his lies the prosecutor's about to come off of the death penalty and float a deal. I'll be back there to tell you about it as soon as I get it."

Woodson shook his head dramatically.

"Yeah, well, maybe I don't want no deal now. They put a goddamn liar on the stand, man. This whole case should go down the toilet. We can win this motherfucker, Haller. Don't take no deal."

I stared at Woodson for a moment. I had just saved his life but he wanted more. He felt entitled because the state hadn't played fair — never mind responsibility for the two kids he had just admitted to killing.

"Don't get greedy, Barnett," I told him. "I'll be back with the news as soon as I get it."

The deputy took him through the steel door that led to the holding cells attached to the courtroom. I watched him go. I had no false conceptions about Barnett Woodson. I had never directly asked him but I knew he had killed those two Westside boys. That wasn't my concern. My job was to test the state's case against him with the best of my skills — that's how the system worked. I had done that and had been given the blade. I would now use it to improve his situation significantly, but Woodson's dream of walking away from those two bodies that had turned black in the water was not in the cards. He might not have understood this but his underpaid and underappreciated public defender certainly did.

After the courtroom cleared, Vincent and I were left looking at each other from our respective tables.

"So," I said.

Vincent shook his head.

"First of all," he said. "I want to make it clear that obviously I didn't know Torrance was lying."

"Sure."

"Why would I sabotage my own case like this?"

I waved off the mea culpa.

"Look, Jerry, don't bother. I told you in pretrial that the guy had copped the discovery my client had in his cell. It's common sense. My guy wouldn't have said shit to your guy, a perfect stranger, and everybody knew it except you."

Vincent emphatically shook his head.

"I did not know it, Haller. He came forward, was vetted by one of our best investigators, and there was no indication of a lie, no matter how improbable it would seem that your client talked to him."

I laughed that off in an unfriendly way.

"Not 'talked' to him, Jerry. *Confessed* to him. A little difference there. So you better check with this prized investigator of yours because he isn't worth the county paycheck."

"Look, he told me the guy couldn't read, so there was no way he could have gotten what he knew out of the discovery. He didn't mention the photos."

"Exactly, and that's why you should find yourself a new investigator. And I'll tell you what, Jerry. I'm usually pretty reasonable about this sort of stuff. I try to go along to get along with the DA's office. But I gave you fair warning about this guy. So after the break, I'm going to gut him right there on the stand and all you're going to be able to do is sit there and watch."

I was in full outrage now, and a lot of it was real.

"It's called 'rope a dope.' But when I'm done with Torrance, he's not the only one who's going to look like a dope. That jury's going to know that you either knew this guy was a liar or you were too dumb to realize it. Either way, you're not coming off too good."

Vincent looked down blankly at the prosecution table and calmly straightened the case files stacked in front of him. He spoke in a quiet voice.

"I don't want you going forward with the cross," he said.

"Fine. Then, cut the denials and the bullshit and give me a dispo I can—"

"I'll drop the death penalty. Twenty-five to life without."

I shook my head without hesitation.

"That's not going to do it. The last thing Woodson said before they took him back was that he was willing to roll the dice. To be exact, he said, 'We can win this motherfucker.' And I think he could be right."

"Then, what do you want, Haller?"

"I'll go fifteen max. I think I can sell that to him."

Vincent emphatically shook his head.

"No way. They'll send me back to filing buy-busts if I give you that for two cold-blooded murders. My best offer is twenty-five with parole. That's it. Under current guidelines he could be out in sixteen, seventeen years. Not bad for what he did, killing two kids like that."

I looked at him, trying to read his face, looking for the tell. I decided I believed it was going to be the best he would do. And he was right, it wasn't a bad deal for what Barnett Woodson had done.

"I don't know," I said. "I think he'll say roll the dice."

Vincent shook his head and looked at me.

"Then, you'll have to sell it to him, Haller. Because I can't go lower and if you continue the cross, then my career in the DA's office is probably finished."

Now I hesitated before responding.

"Wait a minute, what are you saying, Jerry? That I have to clean your mess up for you? I catch you with your pants around your ankles and it's *my* client that has to take it in the ass?"

"I'm saying it's a fair offer to a man who is guilty as sin. More than fair. Go talk to him and work your magic, Mick. Convince him. We both know you're not long for the Public Defender's Office. You might need a favor from me someday when you're out there in the big bad world with no steady paycheck coming in."

I just stared back at him, registering the quid pro quo of the offer. I help him and somewhere down the line he helps me, and Barnett Woodson does an extra couple of years in stir.

"He'll be lucky to last five years in there, let alone twenty," Vincent said. "What's the difference to him? But you and I? We're going places, Mickey. We can help each other here."

I nodded slowly. Vincent was only a few years older than me but was trying to act like some kind of wise old sage.

"The thing is, Jerry, if I did what you suggest, then I'd never be able to look another client in the eye again. I think I'd end up being the dope that got roped."

I stood up and gathered my files. My plan was to go back and tell Barnett Woodson to roll the dice and let me see what I could do.

"I'll see you after the break," I said.

And then I walked away.

PART TWO
— Suitcase City
2007

4

It was a little early in the week for Lorna Taylor to be calling and checking on me. Usually she waited until at least Thursday. Never Tuesday. I picked up the phone, thinking it was more than a check-in call.

"Lorna?"

"Mickey, where've you been? I've been calling all morning."

"I went for my run. I just got out of the shower. You okay?"

"I'm fine. Are you?"

"Sure. What is —?"

"You got a forthwith from Judge Holder. She wants to see you — like an hour ago."

This gave me pause.

"About what?"

"I don't know. All I know is first Michaela called, then the judge herself called. That usually doesn't happen. She wanted to know why you weren't responding."

I knew that Michaela was Michaela Gill, the judge's clerk. And Mary Townes Holder was the chief judge of the Los Angeles Superior Court. The fact that she had called personally didn't make it sound like they were inviting me to the annual justice ball. Mary Townes Holder didn't call lawyers without a good reason.

"What did you tell her?"

"I just said you didn't have court today and you might be out on the golf course."

"I don't play golf, Lorna."

"Look, I couldn't think of anything."

"It's all right, I'll call the judge. Give me the number."

"Mickey, don't call. Just go. The judge wants to *see* you in chambers. She was very clear about that and she wouldn't tell me why. So just go."

"Okay, I'm going. I have to get dressed."

"Mickey?"

"What?"

"How are you really doing?"

I knew her code. I knew what she was asking. She didn't want me appearing in front of a judge if I wasn't ready for it.

"You don't have to worry, Lorna. I'm fine. I'll be fine."

"Okay. Call me and let me know what is going on as soon as you can."

"Don't worry. I will."

I hung up the phone, feeling like I was being bossed around by my wife, not my ex-wife.

5

As the chief judge of the Los Angeles Superior Court, Judge Mary Townes Holder did most of her work behind closed doors. Her courtroom was used on occasion for emergency hearings on motions but rarely used for trials. Her work was done out of the view of the public. In chambers. Her job largely pertained to the administration of the justice system in Los Angeles County. More than two hundred fifty judgeships and forty courthouses fell under her purview. Every jury summons that went into the mail had her name on it, and every assigned parking space in a courthouse garage had her approval. She assigned judges by both geography and designation of law — criminal, civil, juvenile and family. When judges were newly elected to the bench, it was Judge Holder who decided whether they sat in Beverly Hills or Compton, and whether they heard high-stakes financial cases in civil court or soul-draining divorce cases in family court.

I had dressed quickly in what I considered my lucky suit. It was an Italian import from Corneliani that I used to wear on verdict days. Since I hadn't been in court for a year, or heard a verdict for even longer, I had to take it out of a plastic bag hanging in the back of the closet. After that I sped downtown without delay, thinking that I might be headed toward some sort of verdict on myself. As I drove, my mind raced over the cases and clients I had left behind a year earlier. As far as I knew, nothing had been left open or on the table. But maybe there had been a complaint or the judge had picked up on some courthouse gossip and was running her own inquiry. Regardless, I entered Holder's courtroom with a lot of trepidation. A summons from any judge was usually not good news; a summons from the chief judge was even worse.

The courtroom was dark and the clerk's pod next to the bench was empty. I walked through the gate and was heading toward the door to the back hallway, when it opened and the clerk stepped through it. Michaela Gill was a pleasant-looking woman who reminded me of my third-grade teacher. But she wasn't expecting to find a man approaching the other side of the door when she opened it. She startled and nearly let out a shriek. I quickly identified myself before she could make a run for the panic button on the judge's bench. She caught her breath and then ushered me back without delay.

I walked down the hallway and found the judge alone in her chambers, working at a massive desk made of dark wood. Her black robe was hanging on a hat rack in the corner. She was dressed in a maroon suit with a conservative cut. She was attractive and neat, midfifties with a slim build and brown hair kept in a short, no-nonsense style.

I had never met Judge Holder before but I knew about her. She had put twenty years in as a prosecutor before being appointed to the bench by a conservative governor. She presided over criminal cases, had a few of the big ones, and was known for handing out maximum sentences. Consequently, she had been easily retained by the electorate after her first term. She had been elected chief judge four years later and had held the position ever since.

"Mr. Haller, thank you for coming," she said. "I'm glad your secretary finally found you."

There was an impatient if not imperious tone to her voice.

"She's not actually my secretary, Judge. But she found me. Sorry it took so long."

"Well, you're here. I don't believe we have met before, have we?"

"I don't think so."

"Well, this will betray my age but I actually opposed your father in a trial once. One of his last cases, I believe."

I had to readjust my estimate of her age. She would have to be at least sixty if she had ever been in a courtroom with my father.

"I was actually third chair on a case, just out of USC Law and green as can be. They were trying to give me some trial exposure. It was a murder case and they let me handle one witness. I prepared a week for my examination and your father destroyed the man on cross in ten minutes. We won the case but I never forgot the lesson. Be prepared for anything."

I nodded. Over the years I had met several older lawyers who had Mickey Haller Sr. stories to share. I had very few of my own. Before I could ask the judge about the case on which she'd met him, she pressed on.

"But that's not why I called you here," she said.

"I didn't think so, Judge. It sounded like you have something...kind of urgent?"

"I do. Did you know Jerry Vincent?"

I was immediately thrown by her use of the past tense.

"Jerry? Yes, I know Jerry. What about him?"

"He's dead."

"Dead?"

"Murdered, actually."

"When?"

"Last night. I'm sorry."

My eyes dropped and I looked at the nameplate on her desk. *Honorable*

M. T. Holder was carved in script into a two-dimensional wooden display that held a ceremonial gavel and a fountain pen and inkwell.

"How close were you?" she asked.

It was a good question and I didn't really know the answer. I kept my eyes down as I spoke.

"We had cases against each other when he was with the DA and I was at the PD. We both left for private practice around the same time and both of us had one-man shops. Over the years we worked some cases together, a couple of drug trials, and we sort of covered for each other when it was needed. He threw me a case occasionally when it was something he didn't want to handle."

I had had a professional relationship with Jerry Vincent. Every now and then we clicked glasses at Four Green Fields or saw each other at a ball game at Dodger Stadium. But for me to say we were close would have been an exaggeration. I knew little about him outside of the world of law. I had heard about a divorce a while back on the courthouse gossip line but had never even asked him about it. That was personal information and I didn't need to know it.

"You seem to forget, Mr. Haller, but I was with the DA back when Mr. Vincent was a young up-and-comer. But then he lost a big case and his star faded. That was when he left for private practice."

I looked at the judge but said nothing.

"And I seem to recall that you were the defense attorney on that case," she added.

I nodded.

"Barnett Woodson. I got an acquittal on a double murder. He walked out of the courtroom and sarcastically apologized to the media for getting away with murder. He had to rub the DA's face in it and that pretty much ended Jerry's career as a prosecutor."

"Then, why would he ever work with you or throw you cases?"

"Because, Judge, by ending his career as a prosecutor, I started his career as a defense attorney."

I left it at that but it wasn't enough for her.

"And?"

"And a couple of years later he was making about five times what he had made with the DA. He called me up one day and thanked me for showing him the light."

The judge nodded knowingly.

"It came down to money. He wanted the money."

I shrugged like I was uncomfortable answering for a dead man and didn't respond.

"What happened to your client?" the judge asked. "What became of the man who got away with murder?"

"He would've been better off taking a conviction. Woodson got killed in a drive-by about two months after the acquittal."

The judge nodded again, this time as if to say end of story, justice served. I tried to put the focus back on Jerry Vincent.

"I can't believe this about Jerry. Do you know what happened?"

"That's not clear. He was apparently found late last night in his car in the garage at his office. He had been shot to death. I am told that the police are still there at the crime scene and there have been no arrests. All of this comes from a *Times* reporter who called my chambers to make an inquiry about what will happen now with Mr. Vincent's clients—especially Walter Elliot."

I nodded. For the last twelve months I had been in a vacuum but it wasn't so airtight that I hadn't heard about the movie mogul murder case. It was just one in a string of big-time cases Vincent had scored over the years. Despite the Woodson fiasco, his pedigree as a high-profile prosecutor had set him up from the start as an upper-echelon criminal defense attorney. He didn't have to go looking for clients; they came looking for him. And usually they were clients who could pay or had something to say, meaning they had at least one of three attributes: They could pay top dollar for legal representation, they were demonstrably innocent of the charges lodged against them, or they were clearly guilty but had public opinion and sentiment on their side. These were clients he could get behind and forthrightly defend no matter what they were accused of. Clients who didn't make him feel greasy at the end of the day.

And Walter Elliot qualified for at least one of those attributes. He was the chairman/owner of Archway Pictures and a very powerful man in Hollywood. He had been charged with murdering his wife and her lover in a fit of rage after discovering them together in a Malibu beach house. The case had all sorts of connections to sex and celebrity and was drawing wide media attention. It had been a publicity machine for Vincent and now it would go up for grabs.

The judge broke through my reverie.

"Are you familiar with RPC two-three-hundred?" she asked.

I involuntarily gave myself away by squinting my eyes at the question.

"Uh...not exactly."

"Let me refresh your memory. It is the section of the California bar's rules of professional conduct referring to the transfer or sale of a law practice. We, of course, are talking about a transfer in this case. Mr. Vincent apparently named you as his second in his standard contract of representation. This allowed you to cover for him when he needed it and included you, if necessary, in the attorney-client relationship. Additionally, I have found that he filed a motion with the court ten years ago that allowed for the transfer of his practice to you should he become incapacitated or deceased. The motion has never been altered or updated, but it's clear what his intentions were."

I just stared at her. I knew about the clause in Vincent's standard contract. I had the same in mine, naming him. But what I realized was that the judge was telling me that I now had Jerry's cases. All of them, Walter Elliot included.

This, of course, did not mean I would keep all of the cases. Each client would be free to move on to another attorney of their choosing once apprised of Vincent's demise. But it meant that I would have the first shot at them.

I started thinking about things. I hadn't had a client in a year and the plan was to start back slow, not with a full caseload like the one I had apparently just inherited.

"However," the judge said, "before you get too excited about this proposition, I must tell you that I would be remiss in my role as chief judge if I did not make every effort to ensure that Mr. Vincent's clients were transferred to a replacement counsel of good standing and competent skill."

Now I understood. She had called me in to explain why I would not be appointed to Vincent's clients. She was going to go against the dead lawyer's wishes and appoint somebody else, most likely one of the high-dollar contributors to her last reelection campaign. Last I had checked, I'd contributed exactly nothing to her coffers over the years.

But then the judge surprised me.

"I've checked with some of the judges," she said, "and I am aware that you have not been practicing law for almost a year. I have found no explanation for this. Before I issue the order appointing you replacement counsel in this matter, I need to be assured that I am not turning Mr. Vincent's clients over to the wrong man."

I nodded in agreement, hoping it would buy me a little time before I had to respond.

"Judge, you're right. I sort of took myself out of the game for a while. But I just started taking steps to get back in."

"Why did you take yourself out?"

She asked it bluntly, her eyes holding mine and looking for anything that would indicate evasion of the truth in my answer. I spoke very carefully.

"Judge, I had a case a couple years ago. The client's name was Louis Roulet. He was—"

"I remember the case, Mr. Haller. You got shot. But, as you say, that was a couple years ago. I seem to remember you practicing law for some time after that. I remember the news stories about you coming back to the job."

"Well," I said, "what happened is I came back too soon. I had been gut shot, Judge, and I should've taken my time. Instead, I hurried back and the next thing I knew I started having pain and the doctors said I had a hernia. So I had an operation for that and there were complications. They did it wrong. There was even more pain and another operation and, well, to make a long story short, it knocked me down for a while. I decided the second time not to come back until I was sure I was ready."

The judge nodded sympathetically. I guessed I had been right to leave out the part about my addiction to pain pills and the stint in rehab.

"Money wasn't an issue," I said. "I had some savings and I also got a settlement from the insurance company. So I took my time coming back. But I'm ready. I was just about to take the back cover of the Yellow Pages."

"Then, I guess inheriting an entire practice is quite convenient, isn't it?" she said.

I didn't know what to say to her question or the smarmy tone in which she said it.

"All I can tell you, Judge, is that I would take good care of Jerry Vincent's clients."

The judge nodded but she didn't look at me as she did so. I knew the tell. She knew something. And it bothered her. Maybe she knew about the rehab.

"According to bar records, you've been disciplined several times," she said.

Here we were again. She was back to throwing the cases to another lawyer. Probably some campaign contributor from Century City who couldn't find his way around a criminal proceeding if his Riviera membership depended on it.

"All of it ancient history, Judge. All of it technicalities. I'm in good standing with the bar. If you called them today, then I'm sure you were told that."

She stared at me for a long moment before dropping her eyes to the document in front of her on the desk.

"Very well, then," she said.

She scribbled a signature on the last page of the document. I felt the flutter of excitement begin to build in my chest.

"Here is an order transferring the practice to you," the judge said. "You might need it when you go to his office. And let me tell you this. I am going to be monitoring you. I want an updated inventory of cases by the beginning of next week. The status of every case on the client list. I want to know which clients will work with you and which will find other representation. After that, I want biweekly status updates on all cases in which you remain counsel. Am I being clear?"

"Perfectly clear, Judge. For how long?"

"What?"

"For how long do you want me to give you biweekly updates?"

She stared at me and her face hardened.

"Until I tell you to stop."

She handed me the order.

"You can go now, Mr. Haller, and if I were you, I would get over there and protect my new clients from any unlawful search and seizure of their files by the police. If you have any problem, you can always call on me. I have put my after-hours number on the order."

"Yes, Your Honor. Thank you."

"Good luck, Mr. Haller."

I stood up and headed out of the room. When I got to the doorway of her chambers I glanced back at her. She had her head down and was working on the next court order.

Out in the courthouse hallway, I read the two-page document the judge had given me, confirming that what had just happened was real.

It was. The document I held appointed me substitute counsel, at least temporarily, on all of Jerry Vincent's cases. It granted me immediate access to the fallen attorney's office, files, and bank accounts into which client advances had been deposited.

I pulled out my cell phone and called Lorna Taylor. I asked her to look up the address of Jerry Vincent's office. She gave it to me and I told her to meet me there and to pick up two sandwiches on her way.

"Why?" she asked.

"Because I haven't had lunch."

"No, why are we going to Jerry Vincent's office?"

"Because we're back in business."

6

I was in my Lincoln driving toward Jerry Vincent's office, when I thought of something and called Lorna Taylor back. When she didn't answer I called her cell and caught her in her car.

"I'm going to need an investigator. How would you feel if I called Cisco?"

There was a hesitation before she answered. Cisco was Dennis Wojciechowski, her significant other as of the past year. I was the one who had introduced them when I used him on a case. Last I heard, they were now living together.

"Well, I have no problem working with Cisco. But I wish you would tell me what this is all about."

Lorna knew Jerry Vincent as a voice on the phone. It was she who would take his calls when he was checking to see if I could stand in on a sentence or babysit a client through an arraignment. I couldn't remember if they had ever met in person. I had wanted to tell her the news in person but things were moving too quickly for that.

"Jerry Vincent is dead."

"What?"

"He was murdered last night and I'm getting first shot at all of his cases. Including Walter Elliot."

She was silent for a long moment before responding.

"My God.... How? He was such a nice man."

"I couldn't remember if you had ever met him."

Lorna worked out of her condo in West Hollywood. All my calls and billing went through her. If there was a brick-and-mortar office for the law firm of Michael Haller and Associates, then her place was it. But there weren't any associates and when I worked, my office was the backseat of my car. This left few occasions for Lorna to meet face-to-face with any of the people I represented or associated with.

"He came to our wedding, don't you remember?"

"That's right. I forgot."

"I can't believe this. What happened?"

"I don't know. Holder said he was shot in the garage at his office. Maybe I'll find out something when I get there."

"Did he have a family?"

"I think he was divorced but I don't know if there were kids or what. I don't think so."

Lorna didn't say anything. We both had our own thoughts occupying us.

"Let me go so I can call Cisco," I finally said. "Do you know what he's doing today?"

"No, he didn't say."

"All right, I'll see."

"What kind of sandwich do you want?"

"Which way you coming?"

"Sunset."

"Stop at Dusty's and get me one of those turkey sandwiches with cranberry sauce. It's been almost a year since I've had one of those."

"You got it."

"And get something for Cisco in case he's hungry."

"All right."

I hung up and looked up the number for Dennis Wojciechowski in the address book I keep in the center console compartment. I had his cell phone. When he answered I heard a mixture of wind and exhaust blast in the phone. He was on his bike and even though I knew his helmet was set up with an earpiece and mike attached to his cell, I had to yell.

"It's Mickey Haller. Pull over."

I waited and heard him cut the engine on his 'sixty-three panhead.

"What's up, Mick?" he asked when it finally got quiet. "Haven't heard from you in a long time."

"You gotta put the baffles back in your pipes, man. Or you'll be deaf before you're forty and then you won't be hearing from anybody."

"I'm already past forty and I hear you just fine. What's going on?"

Wojciechowski was a freelance defense investigator I had used on a few cases. That was how he had met Lorna, collecting his pay. But I had known him for more than ten years before that because of his association with the Road Saints Motorcycle Club, a group for which I served as a de facto house counsel for several years. Dennis never flew RSMC colors but was considered an associate member. The group even bestowed a nickname on him, largely because there was already a Dennis in the membership—known, of course, as Dennis the Menace—and his last name, Wojciechowski, was intolerably difficult to pronounce. Riffing off his dark looks and mustache, they christened him the Cisco Kid. It didn't matter that he was one hundred percent Polish out of the south side of Milwaukee.

Cisco was a big, imposing man but he kept his nose clean while riding with the Saints. He never caught an arrest record and that paid off when he later applied to the state for his private investigator's license. Now, many years later, the long hair was gone and the mustache was trimmed and going gray. But the name Cisco and the penchant for riding classic Harleys built in his hometown had stuck for life.

Cisco was a thorough and thoughtful investigator. And he had another value as well. He was big and strong and could be physically intimidating when necessary. That attribute could be highly useful when tracking down and dealing with people who fluttered around the edges of a criminal case.

"First of all, where are you?" I asked.

"Burbank."

"You on a case?"

"No, just a ride. Why, you got something for me? You taking on a case finally?"

"A lot of cases. And I'm going to need an investigator."

I gave him the address of Vincent's office and told him to meet me there as soon as he could. I knew that Vincent would have used either a stable of investigators or just one in particular, and that there might be a loss of time as Cisco got up to speed on the cases, but all of that was okay with me. I wanted an investigator I could trust and already had a working relationship with. I was also going to need Cisco to immediately start work by running down the locations of my new clients. My experience with criminal defendants is that they are not always found at the addresses they put down on the client info sheet when they first sign up for legal representation.

After closing the phone I realized I had driven right by the building where Vincent's office was located. It was on Broadway near Third Street and there was too much traffic with cars and pedestrians for me to attempt a U-turn. I wasted ten minutes working my way back to it, catching red lights at every corner. By the time I got to the right place, I was so frustrated that I resolved to hire a driver again as soon as possible so that I could concentrate on cases instead of addresses.

Vincent's office was in a six-story structure called simply the Legal Center. Being so close to the main downtown courthouses—both criminal and civil—meant it was a building full of trial lawyers. Just the kind of place most cops and doctors—lawyer haters—probably wished would implode every time there was an earthquake. I saw the opening for the parking garage next door and pulled in.

As I was taking the ticket out of the machine, a uniformed police officer approached my car. He was carrying a clipboard.

"Sir? Do you have business in the building here?"

"That's why I'm parking here."

"Sir, could you state your business?"

"What business is it of yours, Officer?"

"Sir, we are conducting a crime scene investigation in the garage and I need to know your business before I can allow you in."

"My office is in the building," I said. "Will that do?"

It wasn't exactly a lie. I had Judge Holder's court order in my coat pocket. That gave me an office in the building.

The answer seemed to work. The cop asked to see my ID and I could've argued that he had no right to request my identification but decided that there was no need to make a federal case out of it. I pulled my wallet and gave him the ID and he wrote my name and driver's license number down on his clipboard. Then he let me through.

"At the moment there's no parking on the second level," he said. "They haven't cleared the scene."

I waved and headed up the ramp. When I reached the second floor, I saw that it was empty of vehicles except for two patrol cars and a black BMW coupe that was being hauled onto the bed of a truck from the police garage. Jerry Vincent's car, I assumed. Two other uniformed cops were just beginning to pull down the yellow crime scene tape that had been used to cordon off the parking level. One of them signaled for me to keep going. I saw no detectives around but the police weren't giving up the murder scene just yet.

I kept going up and didn't find a space I could fit the Lincoln into until I got to the fifth floor. One more reason I needed to get a driver again.

The office I was looking for was on the second floor at the front of the building. The opaque glass door was closed but not locked. I entered a reception room with an empty sitting area and a nearby counter behind which sat a woman whose eyes were red from crying. She was on the phone but when she saw me, she put it down on the counter without so much as a "hold on" to whomever she was talking to.

"Are you with the police?" she asked.

"No, I'm not," I replied.

"Then, I'm sorry, the office is closed today."

I approached the counter, pulling the court order from Judge Holder out of the inside pocket of my suit coat.

"Not for me," I said as I handed it to her.

She unfolded the document and stared at it but didn't seem to be reading it. I noticed that in one of her hands she clutched a wad of tissues.

"What is this?" she asked.

"That's a court order," I said. "My name is Michael Haller and Judge Holder has appointed me replacement counsel in regard to Jerry Vincent's clients. That means we'll be working together. You can call me Mickey."

She shook her head as if warding off some invisible threat. My name usually didn't carry that sort of power.

"You can't do this. Mr. Vincent wouldn't want this."

I took the court papers out of her hand and refolded them. I started putting the document back into my pocket.

"Actually, I can. The chief judge of Los Angeles Superior Court has directed me to do this. And if you look closely at the contracts of representation that Mr. Vincent had his clients sign, you will find my name already on them, listed as associate counsel. So, what you think Mr. Vincent would have wanted is immaterial at this point because he did in fact file the papers that named me his replacement should he become incapacitated or...dead."

The woman had a dazed look on her face. Her mascara was heavy and running beneath one eye. It gave her an uneven, almost comical look. For some reason a vision of Liza Minnelli jumped to my mind.

"If you want, you can call Judge Holder's clerk and talk about it with her," I said. "Meantime, I really need to get started here. I know this has been a very difficult day for you. It's been difficult for me—I knew Jerry going back to his days at the DA. So you have my sympathy."

I nodded and looked at her and waited for a response but I still wasn't getting one. I pressed on.

"I'm going to need some things to get started here. First of all, his calendar. I want to put together a list of all the active cases Jerry was handling. Then, I'm going to need you to pull the files for those—"

"It's gone," she said abruptly.

"What's gone?"

"His laptop. The police told me whoever did this took his briefcase out of the car. He kept everything on his laptop."

"You mean his calendar? He didn't keep a hard copy?"

"That's gone, too. They took his portfolio. That was in the briefcase."

Her eyes were staring blankly ahead. I tapped the top of the computer screen on her desk.

"What about this computer?" I asked. "Didn't he back up his calendar anywhere?"

She didn't say anything, so I asked again.

"Did Jerry back up his calendar anywhere else? Is there any way to access it?"

She finally looked up at me and seemed to take pleasure in responding.

"I didn't keep the calendar. He did. He kept it all on his laptop and he kept a hard copy in the old portfolio he carried. But they're both gone. The police made me look everywhere in here but they're gone."

I nodded. The missing calendar was going to be a problem but it wasn't insurmountable.

"What about files? Did he have any in the briefcase?"

"I don't think so. He kept all the files here."

"Okay, good. What we're going to have to do is pull all the active cases and rebuild the calendar from the files. I'll also need to see any ledgers or checkbooks pertaining to the trust and operating accounts."

She looked up at me sharply.

"You're not going to take his money."

"It's not—"

I stopped, took a deep breath, and then started again in a calm but direct tone.

"First of all, I apologize. I did this backwards. I don't even know your name. Let's start over. What is your name?"

"Wren."

"Wren? Wren what?"

"Wren Williams."

"Okay, Wren, let me explain something. It's not his money. It's his clients' money and until they say otherwise, his clients are now my clients. Do you understand? Now, I have told you that I am aware of the emotional upheaval of the day and the shock you are experiencing. I'm experiencing some of it myself. But you need to decide right now if you are with me or against me, Wren. Because if you are with me, I need you to get me the things I asked for. And I'm going to need you to work with my case manager when she gets here. If you are against me, then I need you just to go home right now."

She slowly shook her head.

"The detectives told me I had to stay until they were finished."

"What detectives? There were only a couple uniforms left out there when I drove in."

"The detectives in Mr. Vincent's office."

"You let—"

I didn't finish. I stepped around the counter and headed toward two separate doors on the back wall. I picked the one on the left and opened it.

I walked into Jerry Vincent's office. It was large and opulent and empty. I turned in a full circle until I found myself staring into the bugged eyes of a large fish mounted on the wall over a dark wood credenza next to the door I had come through. The fish was a beautiful green with a white underbelly. Its body was arched as if it had frozen solid just at the moment it had jumped out of the water. Its mouth was open so wide I could have put my fist in it.

Mounted on the wall beneath the fish was a brass plate. It said:

IF I'D KEPT MY MOUTH SHUT
I WOULDN'T BE HERE

Words to live by, I thought. Most criminal defendants talk their way into prison. Few talk their way out. The best single piece of advice I have ever given a client is to just keep your mouth shut. Talk to no one about your case, not even your own wife. You keep close counsel with yourself. You take the nickel and you live to fight another day.

The unmistakable sound of a metal drawer being rolled and then banged closed spun me back around. On the other side of the room were two more doors. Both were open about a foot and through one I could see a darkened bathroom. Through the other I could see light.

I approached the lighted room quickly and pushed the door all the way open. It was the file room, a large, windowless walk-in closet with rows of steel filing cabinets going down both sides. A small worktable was set up against the back wall.

There were two men sitting at the worktable. One old, one young. Probably one to teach and one to learn. They had their jackets off and draped over the chairs. I saw their guns and holsters and their badges clipped to their belts.

"What are you doing?" I asked gruffly.

The men looked up from their reading. I saw a stack of files on the table between them. The older detective's eyes momentarily widened in surprise when he saw me.

"LAPD," he said. "And I guess I should ask you the same question."

"Those are my files and you're going to have to put them down right now."

The older man stood up and came toward me. I started pulling the court order from my jacket again.

"My name is—"

"I know who you are," the detective said. "But I still don't know what you're doing here."

I handed him the court order.

"Then, this should explain it. I've been appointed by the chief judge of the superior court as replacement counsel to Jerry Vincent's clients. That means his cases are now my cases. And you have no right to be in here looking through files. That is a clear violation of my clients' right to protection against unlawful search and seizure. These files contain privileged attorney-client communications and information."

The detective didn't bother looking at the paperwork. He quickly flipped through it to the signature and seal on the last page. He didn't seem all that impressed.

"Vincent's been murdered," he said. "The motive could be sitting in one of these files. The identity of the killer could be in one of them. We have to—"

"No, you don't. What you have to do is get out of this file room right now."

The detective didn't move a muscle.

"I consider this part of a crime scene," he said. "It's you who has to leave."

"Read the order, Detective. I'm not going anywhere. Your crime scene is out in the garage, and no judge in L.A. would let you extend it to this office and these files. It's time for you to leave and for me to take care of my clients."

He made no move to read the court order or to vacate the premises.

"If I leave," he said, "I'm going to shut this place down and seal it."

I hated getting into pissing matches with cops but sometimes there was no choice.

"You do that and I'll have it unsealed in an hour. And you'll be standing in front of the chief judge of the superior court explaining how you trampled on the rights of every one of Vincent's clients. You know, depending on how many clients we're talking about, that might be a record — even for the LAPD."

The detective smiled at me like he was mildly amused by my threats. He held up the court order.

"You say this gives you all of these cases?"

"That's right, for now."

"The entire law practice?"

"Yes, but each client will decide whether to stick with me or find someone else."

"Well, I guess that puts you on our list."

"What list?"

"Our suspect list."

"That's ridiculous. Why would I be on it?"

"You just told us why. You inherited all of the victim's clients. That's got to amount to some sort of a financial windfall, doesn't it? He's dead and you get the whole business. Think that's enough motivation for murder? Care to tell us where you were last night between eight and midnight?"

He grinned at me again without any warmth, giving me that cop's practiced smile of judgment. His brown eyes were so dark I couldn't see the line between iris and pupil. Like shark eyes, they didn't seem to carry or reflect any light.

"I'm not even going to begin to explain how ludicrous that is," I said. "But for starters you can check with the judge and you'll find out that I didn't even know I was in line for this."

"So you say. But don't worry, we'll be checking you out completely."

"Good. Now please leave this room or I make the call to the judge."

The detective stepped back to the table and took his jacket off the chair. He carried it rather than put it on. He picked a file up off the table and brought it toward me. He shoved it into my chest until I took it from him.

"Here's one of your new files back, Counselor. Don't choke on it."

He stepped through the door, and his partner went with him. I followed them out into the office and decided to take a shot at reducing the tension. I had a feeling it wouldn't be the last time I saw them.

"Look, detectives, I'm sorry it's like this. I try to have a good relationship with the police and I am sure we can work something out. But at the moment my obligation is to the clients. I don't even know what I have here. Give me some time to—"

"We don't have time," the older man said. "We lose momentum and we lose the case. Do you understand what you're getting yourself into here, Counselor?"

I looked at him for a moment, trying to understand the meaning behind his question.

"I think so, Detective. I've only been working cases for about eighteen years but—"

"I'm not talking about your experience. I'm talking about what happened in that garage. Whoever killed Vincent was waiting for him out there. They knew where he was and just how to get to him. He was ambushed."

I nodded like I understood.

"If I were you," the detective said, "I'd watch myself with those new clients of yours. Jerry Vincent knew his killer."

"What about when he was a prosecutor? He put people in prison. Maybe one of—"

"We'll check into it. But that was a long time ago. I think the person we're looking for is in those files."

With that, he and his partner started moving toward the door.

"Wait," I said. "You have a card? Give me a card."

The detectives stopped and turned back. The older one pulled a card out of his pocket and gave it to me.

"That's got all my numbers."

"Let me just get the lay of the land here and then I'll call and set something up. There's got to be a way for us to cooperate and still not trample on anybody's rights."

"Whatever you say, you're the lawyer."

I nodded and looked down at the name on the card. Harry Bosch. I was sure I had never met the man before, yet he had started the confrontation by saying he knew who I was.

"Look, Detective Bosch," I said, "Jerry Vincent was a colleague. We weren't that close but we were friends."

"And?"

"And good luck, you know? With the case. I hope you crack it."

Bosch nodded and there was something familiar about the physical gesture. Maybe we did know each other.

He turned to follow his partner out of the office.

"Detective?"

Bosch once more turned back to me.

"Did we ever cross paths on a case before? I think I recognize you."

Bosch smiled glibly and shook his head.

"No," he said. "If we'd been on a case, you'd remember me."

7

An hour later I was behind Jerry Vincent's desk with Lorna Taylor and Dennis Wojciechowski sitting across from me. We were eating our sandwiches and about to go over what we had put together from a very preliminary survey of the office and the cases. The food was good but nobody had much of an appetite considering where we were sitting and what had happened to the office's predecessor.

I had sent Wren Williams home early. She had been unable to stop crying or objecting to my taking control of her dead boss's cases. I decided to remove the barricade rather than have to keep walking around it. The last thing she asked before I escorted her through the door was whether I was going to fire her. I told her the jury was still out on that question but that she should report for work as usual the next day.

With Jerry Vincent dead and Wren Williams gone, we'd been left stumbling around in the dark until Lorna figured out the filing system and started pulling the active case files. From calendar notations in each file, she'd been able to start to put together a master calendar — the key component in any trial lawyer's professional life. Once we had worked up a rudimentary calendar, I began to breathe a little easier and we'd broken for lunch and opened the sandwich cartons Lorna had brought from Dusty's.

The calendar was light. A few case hearings here and there but for the most part it was obvious that Vincent was keeping things clear in advance of the Walter Elliot trial, which was scheduled to begin with jury selection in nine days.

"So let's start," I said, my mouth still full with my last bite. "According to the calendar we've pieced together, I've got a sentencing in forty-five minutes. So I was thinking we could have a preliminary discussion now, and then I could leave you two here while I go to court. Then I'll come back and see how much farther we've gotten before Cisco and I go out and start knocking on doors."

They both nodded, their mouths still working on their sandwiches as well. Cisco had cranberry in his mustache but didn't know it.

Lorna was as neat and as beautiful as ever. She was a stunner with blonde hair and eyes that somehow made you think you were the center of the universe when she was looking at you. I never got tired of that. I had kept her on salary the whole year I was out. I could afford it with the insurance settlement and I didn't want to run the risk that she'd be working for another lawyer when it was time for me to come back to work.

"Let's start with the money," I said.

Lorna nodded. As soon as she had gotten the active files together and placed them in front of me, she had moved on to the bank books, perhaps the only thing as important as the case calendar. The bank books would tell us more than just how much money Vincent's firm had in its coffers. They would give us an insight into how he ran his one-man shop.

"All right, good and bad news on the money," she said. "He's got thirty-eight thousand in the operating account and a hundred twenty-nine thousand in the trust account."

I whistled. That was a lot of cash to keep in the trust account. Money taken in from clients goes into the trust account. As work for each client proceeds, the trust account is billed and the money transferred to the operating account. I always want more money in the operating account than in the trust account, because once it's moved into the operating account, the money's mine.

"There's a reason why it's so lopsided," Lorna said, picking up on my surprise. "He just took in a check for a hundred thousand dollars from Walter Elliot. He deposited it Friday."

I nodded and tapped the makeshift calendar I had on the table in front of me. It was drawn on a legal pad. Lorna would have to go out and buy a real calendar when she got the chance. She would also input all of the court appointments on my computer and on an online calendar. Lastly, and as Jerry Vincent had not done, she would back it all up on an off-site data-storage account.

"The Elliot trial is scheduled to start Thursday next week," I said. "He took the hundred up front."

Saying the obvious prompted a sudden realization.

"As soon as we're done here, call the bank," I told Lorna. "See if the check has cleared. If not, try to push it through. As soon as Elliot hears that Vincent's dead, he'll probably try to put a stop-payment on it."

"Got it."

"What else on the money? If a hundred of it's from Elliot, who's the rest for?"

Lorna opened one of the accounting books she had on her lap. Each dollar in a trust fund must be accounted for with regard to which client it is being held for. At any time, an attorney must be able to determine how much of a client's advance has been transferred to the operating fund and used and how much is still on reserve in trust. A hundred thousand of Vincent's trust account was earmarked for the Walter Elliot trial. That left only twenty-nine thousand received for the rest of the active cases. That wasn't a lot, considering the stack of files we had pulled together while going through the filing cabinets looking for live cases.

"That's the bad news," Lorna said. "It looks like there are only five or six other cases with trust deposits. With the rest of the active cases, the money's already been moved into operating or been spent or the clients owe the firm."

I nodded. It wasn't good news. It was beginning to look like Jerry Vincent was running ahead of his cases, meaning he'd been on a treadmill, bringing in new cases to keep money flowing and paying for existing cases. Walter Elliot must have been the get-well client. As soon as his hundred thousand cleared, Vincent would have been able to turn the treadmill off and catch his breath—for a while, at least. But he never got the chance.

"How many clients with payment plans?" I asked.

Lorna once again referred to the records on her lap.

"He's got two on pretrial payments. Both are well behind."

"What are the names?"

It took her a moment to answer as she looked through the records.

"Uh, Samuels is one and Henson is the other. They're both about five thousand behind."

"And that's why we take credit cards and don't put out paper."

I was talking about my own business routine. I had long ago stopped providing credit services. I took nonrefundable cash payments. I also took plastic, but not until Lorna had run the card and gotten purchase approval.

I looked down at the notes I had kept while conducting a quick review of the calendar and the active files. Both Samuels and Henson were on a sub list I had drawn up while reviewing the actives. It was a list of cases I was going to cut loose if I could. This was based on my quick review of the charges and facts of the cases. If there was something I didn't like about a case—for any reason—then it went on the sub list.

"No problem," I said. "We'll cut 'em loose."

Samuels was a manslaughter DUI case and Henson was a felony grand theft and drug possession. Henson momentarily held my interest because Vincent was going to build a defense around the client's addiction to prescription painkillers. He was going to roll sympathy and deflection defenses into one. He would lay out a case in which the doctor who overprescribed the drugs to Henson was the one most responsible for the consequences of the addiction he created. Patrick Henson, Vincent would argue, was a victim, not a criminal.

I was intimately familiar with this defense because I had employed it repeatedly over the past two years to try to absolve myself of the many infractions I had committed in my roles as father, ex-husband and friend to people in my life. But I put Henson into what I called the dog pile because I knew at heart the defense didn't hold up—at least not for me. And I wasn't ready to go into court with it for him either.

Lorna nodded and made notes about the two cases on a pad of paper.

"So what is the score on that?" she asked. "How many cases are you putting in the dog pile?"

"We came up with thirty-one active cases," I said. "Of those, I'm thinking only seven look like dogs. So that means we've got a lot of cases where there's no money in the till. I'll either have to get new money or they'll go in the dog pile, too."

I wasn't worried about having to go and get money out of the clients. Skill number one in criminal defense is getting the money. I was good at it and Lorna was even better. It was getting paying clients in the first place that was the trick, and we'd just had two dozen of them dropped into our laps.

"You think the judge is just going to let you drop some of these?" she asked.

"Nope. But I'll figure something out on that. Maybe I could claim conflict of interest. The conflict being that I like to be paid for my work and the clients don't like to pay."

No one laughed. No one even cracked a smile. I moved on.

"Anything else on the money?" I asked.

Lorna shook her head.

"That's about it. When you're in court, I'm going to call the bank and get that started. You want us both to be signers on the accounts?"

"Yeah, just like with my accounts."

I hadn't considered the potential difficulty of getting my hands on the money that was in the Vincent accounts. That was what I had Lorna for. She was good on the business end in ways I wasn't. Some days she was so good I wished we had either never gotten married or never gotten divorced.

"See if Wren Williams can sign checks," I said. "If she's on there, take her off. For now I want just you and me on the accounts."

"Will do. You may have to go back to Judge Holder for a court order for the bank."

"That'll be no problem."

My watch said I had ten minutes before I had to get going to court. I turned my attention to Wojciechowski.

"Cisco, whaddaya got?"

I had told him earlier to work his contacts and to monitor the investigation of Vincent's murder as closely as possible. I wanted to know what moves the detectives were making because it appeared from what Bosch had said that the investigation was going to be entwined with the cases I had just inherited.

"Not much," Cisco said. "The detectives haven't even gotten back to Parker Center yet. I called a guy I know in forensics and they're still processing everything. Not a lot of info on what they do have but he told me about something they don't. Vincent was shot at least two times that they could tell at the scene. And there were no shells. The shooter cleaned up."

There was something telling in that. The killer had either used a revolver or had had the presence of mind after killing a man to pick up the bullet casings ejected from his gun.

Cisco continued his report.

"I called another contact in communications and she told me the first call came in at twelve forty-three. They'll narrow down time of death at autopsy."

"Is there a general idea of what happened?"

"It looks like Vincent worked late, which was apparently his routine on Mondays. He worked late every Monday, preparing for the week ahead. When he was finished he packed his briefcase, locked up, and left. He goes to the garage, gets in his car, and gets popped through the driver's side window. When they found him the car was in park, the ignition on. The window was down. It was in the low sixties last night. He could've put the window down because he liked the chill, or he could've lowered it for somebody coming to the car."

"Somebody he knew."

"That's one possibility."

I thought about this and what Detective Bosch had said.

"Nobody was working in the garage?"

"No, the attendant leaves at six. You have to put your money in the machine after that or use your monthly pass. Vincent had a monthly."

"Cameras?"

"Only cameras are where you drive in and out. They're license plate cameras so if somebody says they lost their ticket they can tell when the car went in, that sort of thing. But from what I hear from my guy in forensics, there was nothing on tape that was useful. The killer didn't drive into the garage. He walked in either through the building or through one of the pedestrian entrances."

"Who found Jerry?"

"The security guard. They got one guard for the building and the garage. He hits the garage a couple times a night and noticed Vincent's car on his second sweep. The lights were on and it was running, so he checked it out. He thought Vincent was sleeping at first, then he saw the blood."

I nodded, thinking about the scenario and how it had gone down. The killer was either incredibly careless and lucky or he knew the garage had no cameras and he would be able to intercept Jerry Vincent there on a Monday night when the space was almost deserted.

"Okay, stay on it. What about Harry Potter?"

"Who?"

"The detective. Not Potter. I mean—"

"Bosch. Harry Bosch. I'm working on that, too. Supposedly he's one of the best. Retired a few years ago and the police chief himself recruited him back. Or so the story goes."

Cisco referred to some notes on a pad.

"Full name is Hieronymus Bosch. He has a total of thirty-three years on the job and you know what that means."

"No, what does it mean?"

"Well, under the LAPD's pension program you max out at thirty years, meaning that you are eligible for retirement with full pension and no matter how long you stay on the job, after thirty years your pension doesn't grow. So it makes no economic sense to stay."

"Unless you're a man on a mission."

Cisco nodded.

"Exactly. Anybody who stays past thirty isn't staying for the money or the job. It's more than a job."

"Wait a second," I said. "You said Hieronymus Bosch? Like the painter?"

The second question confused him.

"I don't know anything about any painter. But that's his name. Rhymes with 'anonymous,' I was told. Weird name, if you ask me."

"No weirder than Wojciechowski — if you ask me."

Cisco was about to defend his name and heritage when Lorna cut in.

"I thought you said you didn't know him, Mickey."

I looked over at her and shook my head.

"I never met him before today but the name... I know the name."

"You mean from the paintings?"

I didn't want to get into a discussion of past history so distant I couldn't be sure about it.

"Never mind," I said. "It's nothing and I've got to get going."

I stood up.

"Cisco, stay on the case and find out what you can about Bosch. I want to know how much I can trust the guy."

"You're not going to let him look at the files, are you?" Lorna asked.

"This wasn't a random crime. There's a killer out there who knew how to get to Jerry Vincent. I'll feel a lot better about things if our man with a mission can figure it out and bring the bad guy in."

I stepped around the desk and headed toward the door.

"I'll be in Judge Champagne's court. I'm taking a bunch of the active files with me to read while I'm waiting."

"I'll walk you out," Lorna said.

I saw her throw a look and nod at Cisco so that he would stay behind. We walked out to the reception area. I knew what Lorna was going to say but I let her say it.

"Mickey, are you sure you're ready for this?"

"Absolutely."

"This wasn't the plan. You were going to come back slowly, remember? Take a couple cases and build from there. Instead, you're taking on an entire practice."

"I'm not practicing."

"Look, be serious."

"I am. And I'm ready. Don't you see that this is better than the plan? The Elliot case not only brings in all that money but it's going to be like having a billboard on top of the CCB that says i'm back in big neon letters!"

"Yeah, that's great. And the Elliot case alone is going to put so much pressure on you that..."

She didn't finish but she didn't have to.

"Lorna, I'm done with all of that. I'm fine, I'm over it, and I'm ready for this. I thought you'd be happy about this. We've got money coming in for the first time in a year."

"I don't care about that. I want to make sure you are okay."

"I'm more than okay. I'm excited. I feel like in one day I've suddenly got my mojo back. Don't drag me down. Okay?"

She stared at me and I stared back and finally a reluctant smile peeked through her stern expression.

"All right," she said. "Then, go get 'em."

"Don't worry. I will."

8

Despite the assurances I had given Lorna, thoughts about all the cases and all the setup work that needed to be done played in my mind as I walked down the hallway to the bridge that linked the office building with the garage. I had forgotten that I had parked on the fifth level and ended up walking up three ramps before I found the Lincoln. I popped the trunk and put the thick stack of files I was carrying into my bag.

The bag was a hybrid I had picked up at a store called Suitcase City while I was plotting my comeback. It was a backpack with straps I could put over my shoulders on the days I was strong. It also had a handle so I could carry it like a briefcase if I wanted. And it had two wheels and a telescoping handle so I could just roll it behind me on the days I was weak.

Lately, the strong days far outnumbered the weak and I probably could have gotten by with the traditional lawyer's leather briefcase. But I liked the bag and was going to keep using it. It had a logo on it—a mountain ridgeline with the words "Suitcase City" printed across it like the Hollywood sign. Above it, skylights swept the horizon, completing the dream image of desire and hope. I think that logo was the real reason I liked the bag. Because I knew Suitcase City wasn't a store. It was a place. It was Los Angeles.

Los Angeles was the kind of place where everybody was from some-where else and nobody really dropped anchor. It was a transient place. People drawn by the dream, people running from the nightmare. Twelve million people and all of them ready to make a break for it if necessary. Figuratively, literally, metaphorically — any way you want to look at it — everybody in L.A. keeps a bag packed. Just in case.

As I closed the trunk, I was startled to see a man standing between my car and the one parked next to it. The open trunk lid had blocked my view of his approach. He was a stranger to me but I could tell he knew who I was. Bosch's warning about Vincent's killer shot through my mind and the fight-or-flight instinct gripped me.

"Mr. Haller, can I talk to you?"

"Who the hell are you, and what are you doing sneaking around people's cars?"

"I wasn't sneaking around. I saw you and cut between the other cars, that's all. I work for the *Times* and was wondering if I could talk to you about Jerry Vincent."

I shook my head and blew out my breath.

"You scared the shit out of me. Don't you know he got killed in this garage by somebody who came up to his car?"

"Look, I'm sorry. I was just —"

"Forget it. I don't know anything about the case and I have to get to court."

"But you're taking over his cases, aren't you?"

Signaling him out of the way, I moved to the door of my car.

"Who told you that?"

"Our court reporter got a copy of the order from Judge Holder. Why did Mr. Vincent pick you? Were you two good friends or something?"

I opened the door.

"Look, what's your name?"

"Jack McEvoy. I work the police beat."

"Good for you, Jack. But I can't talk about this right now. You want to give me a card, I'll call you when I can talk."

He made no move to give me a card or to indicate he'd understood what I said. He just asked another question.

"Has the judge put a gag order on you?"

"No, she hasn't put out a gag order. I can't talk to you because I don't know anything, okay? When I have something to say, I'll say it."

"Well, could you tell me why you are taking over Vincent's cases?"

"You already know the answer to that. I was appointed by the judge. I have to get to court now."

I ducked into the car but left the door open as I turned the key. McEvoy put his elbow on the roof and leaned in to continue to try to talk me into an interview.

"Look," I said, "I've got to go, so could you stand back so I can close my door and back this tank up?"

"I was hoping we could make a deal," he said quickly.

"Deal? What deal? What are you talking about?"

"You know, information. I've got the police department wired and you've got the courthouse wired. It would be a two-way street. You tell me what you're hearing and I'll tell you what I'm hearing. I have a feeling this is going to be a big case. I need any information I can get."

I turned and looked up at him for a moment.

"But won't the information you'd be giving me just end up in the paper the next day? I could just wait and read it."

"Not all of it will be in there. Some stuff you can't print, even if you know it's true."

He looked at me as though he were passing on a great piece of wisdom.

"I have a feeling you'll be hearing things before I do," I said.

"I'll take my chances. Deal?"

"You got a card?"

This time he took a card out of his pocket and handed it to me. I held it between my fingers and draped my hand over the steering wheel. I held the card up and looked at it again. I figured it wouldn't hurt to get a line on inside information on the case.

"Okay, deal."

I signaled him away again and pulled the door closed, then started the car. He was still there. I lowered the window.

"What?" I asked.

"Just remember, I don't want to see your name in the other papers or on the TV saying stuff I don't have."

"Don't worry. I know how it works."

"Good."

I dropped it into reverse but thought of something and kept my foot on the brake.

"Let me ask you a question. How tight are you with Bosch, the lead investigator on the case?"

"I know him, but nobody's really tight with him. Not even his own partner."

"What's his story?"

"I don't know. I never asked."

"Well, is he any good at it?"

"At clearing cases? Yes, he's very good. I think he's considered one of the best."

I nodded and thought about Bosch. The man on a mission.

"Watch your toes."

I backed the Lincoln out. McEvoy called out to me just as I put the car in drive.

"Hey, Haller, love the plate."

I waved a hand out the window as I drove down the ramp. I tried to remember which of my Lincolns I was driving and what the plate said. I have a fleet of three Town Cars left over from my days when I carried a full case load. But I had been using the cars so infrequently in the last year that I had put all three into a rotation to keep the engines in tune and the dust out of the pipes. Part of my comeback strategy, I guess. The cars were exact duplicates, except for the license plates, and I wasn't sure which one I was driving.

When I got down to the parking attendant's booth and handed in my stub, I saw a small video screen next to the cash register. It showed the view from a camera located a few feet behind my car. It was the camera Cisco had told me about, designed to pick up an angle on the rear bumper and license plate.

On the screen I could see my vanity plate.

IWALKEM

I smirked. I walk 'em, all right. I was heading to court to meet one of Jerry Vincent's clients for the first time. I was going to shake his hand and then walk him right into prison.

9

Judge Judith Champagne was on the bench and hearing motions when I walked into her courtroom with five minutes to spare. There were eight other lawyers cooling their heels, waiting their turn. I parked my roller bag against the rail and whispered to the courtroom deputy, explaining that I was there to handle the sentencing of Edgar Reese for Jerry Vincent. He told me the judge's motions calendar was running long but Reese would be first out for his sentencing as soon as the motions were cleared. I asked if I could see Reese, and the deputy got up and led me through the steel door behind his desk to the court-side holding cell. There were three prisoners in the cell.

"Edgar Reese?" I said.

A small, powerfully built white man came over to the bars. I saw prison tattoos climbing up his neck and felt relieved. Reese was heading back to a place he already knew. I wasn't going to be holding the hand of a wide-eyed prison virgin. It would make things easier for me.

"My name's Michael Haller. I'm filling in for your attorney today."

I didn't think there was much point in explaining to this guy what had happened to Vincent. It would only make Reese ask me a bunch of questions I didn't have the time or knowledge to answer.

"Where's Jerry?" Reese asked.

"Couldn't make it. You ready to do this?"

"Like I got a choice?"

"Did Jerry go over the sentence when you pled out?"

"Yeah, he told me. Five years in state, out in three if I behave."

It was more like four but I wasn't going to mess with it.

"Okay, well, the judge is finishing some stuff up out there and then they'll bring you out. The prosecutor will read you a bunch of legalese, you answer yes that you understand it, and then the judge will enter the sentence. Fifteen minutes in and out."

"I don't care how long it takes. I ain't got nowhere to go."

I nodded and left him there. I tapped lightly on the metal door so the deputy — bailiffs in L.A. County are sheriffs' deputies — in the courtroom would hear it but hopefully not the judge. He let me out and I sat in the first row of the gallery. I opened up my case and pulled out most of the files, putting them down on the bench next to me.

The top file was the Edgar Reese file. I had already reviewed this one in preparation for the sentencing. Reese was one of Vincent's repeat clients. It was a garden-variety drug case. A seller who used his own product, Reese was set up on a buy-bust by a customer working as a confidential informant. According to the background information in the file, the CI zeroed in on Reese because he held a grudge against him. He had previously bought cocaine from Reese and found it had been hit too hard with baby laxative. This was a frequent mistake made by dealers who were also users. They cut the product too hard, thereby increasing the amount kept for their own personal use but diluting the charge delivered by the powder they sold. It was a bad business practice because it bred enemies. A user trying to work off a charge by cooperating as a CI is more inclined to set up a dealer he doesn't like than a dealer he does. This was the business lesson Edgar Reese would have to think about for the next five years in state prison.

I put the file back in my bag and looked at what was next on the stack. The file on top belonged to Patrick Henson, the painkiller case I had told Lorna I would be dropping. I leaned over to put the file back in the bag, when I suddenly sat back against the bench and held it on my lap. I flapped it against my thigh a couple times as I reconsidered things and then opened it.

Henson was a twenty-four-year-old surfer from Malibu by way of Florida. He was a professional but at the low end of the spectrum, with limited endorsements and winnings from the pro tour. In a competition on Maui, he'd wiped out in a wave that drove him down hard into the lava bottom of Pehei. It crimped his shoulder, and after surgery to scrape it out, the doctor prescribed oxycodone. Eighteen months later Henson was a full-blown addict, chasing pills to chase the pain. He lost his sponsors and was too weak to compete anymore. He finally hit bottom when he stole a diamond necklace from a home in Malibu to which he'd been invited by a female friend. According to the sheriff's report, the necklace belonged to his friend's mother and contained eight diamonds representing her three children and five grandchildren. It was listed on the report as worth $25,000 but Henson hocked it for $400 and went down to Mexico to buy two hundred tabs of oxy over the counter.

Henson was easy to connect to the caper. The diamond necklace was recovered from the pawnshop and the film from the security camera showed him pawning it. Because of the high value of the necklace, he was hit with a full deck, dealing in stolen property and grand theft, along with illegal drug possession. It also didn't help that the lady he stole the necklace from was married to a well-connected doctor who had contributed liberally to the reelection of several members of the county board of supervisors.

When Vincent took Henson on as a client, the surfer made the initial $5,000 advance payment in trade. Vincent took all twelve of his custom-made Trick Henson boards and sold them through his liquidator to collectors and on eBay. Henson was also placed on the $1,000-a-month payment plan but had never made a single payment because he had gone into rehab the day after being bailed out of jail by his mother, who lived back in Melbourne, Florida.

The file said Henson had successfully completed rehab and was working part-time at a surf camp for kids on the beach in Santa Monica. He was barely making enough to live on, let alone pay $1,000 a month to Vincent. His mother, meanwhile, had been tapped out by his bail and the cost of his stay in rehab.

The file was replete with motions to continue and other filings as delay tactics undertaken by Vincent while he waited for Henson to come across with more cash. This was standard practice. Get your money up front, especially when the case is probably a dog. The prosecutor had Henson on tape selling the stolen merchandise. It meant the case was worse than a dog. It was roadkill.

There was a phone number in the file for Henson. One thing every lawyer drilled into nonincarcerated clients was the need to maintain a method of contact. Those facing criminal charges and the likelihood of prison often had unstable home lives. They moved around, sometimes were completely homeless. But a lawyer had to be able to reach them at a moment's notice. The number was listed in the file as Henson's cell, and if it was still good, I could call him right now. The question was, did I want to?

I looked up at the bench. The judge was still in the middle of oral arguments on a bail motion. There were still three other lawyers waiting their turn at other motions and no sign of the prosecutor who was assigned to the Edgar Reese case. I got up and whispered to the deputy again.

"I'm going out into the hallway to make a call. I'll be close."

He nodded.

"If you're not back when it's time, I'll come grab you," he said. "Just make sure you turn that phone off before coming back in. The judge doesn't like cell phones."

He didn't have to tell me that. I already knew firsthand that the judge didn't like cell phones in her court. My lesson was learned when I was making an appearance before her and my phone started playing the *William Tell* Overture — my daughter's ringtone choice, not mine. The judge slapped me with a $100-dollar fine and had taken to referring to me ever since as the Lone Ranger. That last part I didn't mind so much. I sometimes felt like I was the Lone Ranger. I just rode in a black Lincoln Town Car instead of on a white horse.

I left my case and the other files on the bench in the gallery and walked out into the hallway with only the Henson file. I found a reasonably quiet spot in the crowded hallway and called the number. It was answered after two rings.

"This is Trick."

"Patrick Henson?"

"Yeah, who's this?"

"I'm your new lawyer. My name is Mi—"

"Whoa, wait a minute. What happened to my old lawyer? I gave that guy Vincent—"

"He's dead, Patrick. He passed away last night."

"Nooooo."

"Yes, Patrick. I'm sorry about that."

I waited a moment to see if he had anything else to say about it, then started in as perfunctorily as a bureaucrat.

"My name is Michael Haller and I'm taking over Jerry Vincent's cases. I've been reviewing your file here and I see you haven't made a single payment on the schedule Mr. Vincent put you on."

"Ah, man, this is the deal. I've been concentrating on getting right and staying right and I've got no fucking money. Okay? I already gave that guy Vincent all my boards. He counted it as five grand but I know he got more. A couple of those long boards were worth at least a grand apiece. He told me that he got enough to get started but all he's been doing is delaying things. I can't get back to shit until this thing is all over."

"Are you staying right, Patrick? Are you clean?"

"As a fucking whistle, man. Vincent told me it was the only way I'd have a shot at staying out of jail."

I looked up and down the hallway. It was crowded with lawyers and defendants and witnesses and the families of those victimized or accused.

It was a football field long and everybody in it was hoping for one thing. A break. For the clouds to open and something to go their way just this one time.

"Jerry was right, Patrick. You have to stay clean."

"I'm doing it."

"You got a job?"

"Man, don't you guys see? No one's going to give a guy like me a job. Nobody's going to hire me. I'm waiting on this case and I might be in jail before it's all over. I mean, I teach water babies part-time on the beach but it don't pay me jack. I'm living out of my damn car, sleeping on a lifeguard stand at Hermosa Beach. This time two years ago? I was in a suite at the Four Seasons in Maui."

"Yeah, I know, life sucks. You still have a driver's license?"

"That's about all I got left."

I made a decision.

"Okay, you know where Jerry Vincent's office is? You ever been there?"

"Yeah, I delivered the boards there. And my fish."

"Your fish?"

"He took a sixty-pound tarpon I caught when I was a kid back in Florida. Said he was going to put it on the wall and pretend like he caught it or something."

"Yeah, well, your fish is still there. Anyway, be at the office at nine sharp tomorrow morning and I'll interview you for a job. If it goes right, then you'll start right away."

"Doing what?"

"Driving me. I'll pay you fifteen bucks an hour to drive and another fifteen toward your fees. How's that?"

There was a moment of silence before Henson responded in an accommodating voice.

"That's good, man. I can be there for that."

"Good. See you then. Just remember something, Patrick. You gotta stay clean. If you're not, I'll know. Believe me, I'll know."

"Don't worry, man. I will never go back to that shit. That shit fucked my life up for good."

"Okay, Patrick, I'll see you tomorrow."

"Hey, man, why are you doing this?"

I hesitated before answering.

"You know, I don't really know."

I closed the phone and made sure to turn it off. I went back into the courtroom wondering if I was doing something good or making the kind of mistake that would catch up and bite me on the ass.

It was perfect timing. The judge finished with the last motion as I came back in. I saw that a deputy district attorney named Don Pierce was sitting at the prosecution table, ready to go with the sentencing. He was an ex-navy guy who kept the crew cut going and was one of the regulars at cocktail hour at Four Green Fields. I quickly packed all the files back into my bag and wheeled it through the gate to the defense table.

"Well," the judge said, "I see the Lone Ranger rides again."

She said it with a smile and I smiled back at her.

"Yes, Your Honor. Nice to see you."

"I haven't seen you in quite a while, Mr. Haller."

Open court was not the place to tell her where I had been. I kept my responses short. I spread my hands as if presenting the new me.

"All I can say is, I'm back now, Judge."

"I'm glad to see that. Now, you are here in place of Mr. Vincent, is that correct?"

It was said in a routine tone. I could tell she did not know about Vincent's demise. I knew I could keep the secret and get through the sentencing with it. But then she would hear the story and wonder why I hadn't brought it up and told her. It was not a good way to keep a judge on your side.

"Unfortunately, Your Honor," I said, "Mr. Vincent passed away last night."

The judge's eyebrows arched in shock. She had been a longtime prosecutor before being a longtime judge. She was wired into the legal community and most likely knew Jerry Vincent well. I had just hit her with a major jolt.

"Oh, my, he was so young!" she exclaimed. "What happened?"

I shook my head like I didn't know.

"It wasn't a natural death, Your Honor. The police are investigating it and I don't really know a lot about it other than that he was found in his car last night at his office. Judge Holder called me in today and appointed me replacement counsel. That's why I am here for Mr. Reese."

The judge looked down and took a moment to get over her shock. I felt bad about being the messenger. I bent down and pulled the Edgar Reese file out of my bag.

"I'm very sorry to hear this," the judge finally said.

I nodded in agreement and waited.

"Very well," the judge said after another long moment. "Let's bring the defendant out."

Jerry Vincent garnered no further delay. Whether the judge had suspicions about Jerry or the life he led, she didn't say. But life would move on in the Criminal Courts Building. The wheels of justice would grind without him.

10

The message from Lorna Taylor was short and to the point. I got it the moment I turned my phone on after leaving the courtroom and seeing Edgar Reese get his five years. She told me she had just been in touch with Judge Holder's clerk about obtaining the court order the bank was requiring before putting Lorna's and my names on the Vincent bank accounts. The judge had agreed to draw up the order and I could just walk down the hallway to her chambers to pick it up.

The courtroom was once again dark but the judge's clerk was in her pod next to the bench. She still reminded me of my third-grade teacher.

"Mrs. Gill?" I said. "I'm supposed to pick up an order from the judge."

"Yes, I think she still has it with her in chambers. I'll go check."

"Any chance I could get in there and talk to her for a few minutes, too?"

"Well, she has someone with her at the moment but I will check."

She got up and went down the hallway located behind the clerk's station. At the end was the door to the judge's chambers and I watched her knock once before being summoned to enter. When she opened the door, I could see a man sitting in the same chair I had sat in a few hours earlier. I recognized him as Judge Holder's husband, a personal-injury attorney named Mitch Lester. I recognized him from the photograph on his ad. Back when he was doing criminal defense we had once shared the back of the Yellow Pages, my ad taking the top half and his the bottom. He hadn't worked criminal cases in a long time.

A few minutes later Mrs. Gill came out carrying the court order I needed. I thought this meant I wasn't going to get in to see the judge but Mrs. Gill told me I would be allowed back as soon as the judge finished up with her visitor.

It wasn't enough time to continue my review of the files in my roller bag, so I wandered the courtroom, looking around and thinking about what I was going to say to the judge. At the empty bailiff's desk, I looked down and scanned a calendar sheet from the week before. I knew the names of several of the attorneys who were listed and had been scheduled for emergency hearings and motions. One of them was Jerry Vincent on behalf of Walter Elliot. It had probably been one of Jerry's last appearances in court.

After three minutes I heard a bell tone at the clerk's station and Mrs. Gill said I was free to go back to the judge's chambers.

When I knocked on the door it was Mitch Lester who opened it. He

smiled and bid me entrance. We shook hands and he remarked that he h
just heard about Jerry Vincent.

"It's a scary world out there," he said.

"It can be," I said.

"If you need any help with anything, let me know."

He left the office and I took his seat in front of the judge's desk.

"What can I do for you, Mr. Haller? You got the order for the bank?"

"Yes, I got the order, Your Honor. Thank you for that. I wanted to update
you a little bit and ask a question about something."

She took off a pair of reading glasses and put them down on her blotter.

"Please go ahead, then."

"Well, on the update. Things are going a bit slowly because we started
without a calendar. Both Jerry Vincent's laptop computer and his hard-
copy calendar were stolen after he was killed. We had to build a new calendar after pulling the active files. We think we have that under control and,
in fact, I just came from a sentencing in Judge Champagne's in regard to
one of the cases. So we haven't missed anything."

The judge seemed unimpressed by the efforts made by my staff and me.

"How many active cases are we talking about?" she asked.

"Uh, it looks like there are thirty-one active cases — well, thirty now that
I handled that sentencing. That case is done."

"Then, I would say you inherited quite a thriving practice. What is the
problem?"

"I'm not sure there is a problem, Judge. So far I've had a conversation
with only one of the active clients and it looks like I will be continuing as
his lawyer."

"Was that Walter Elliot?"

"Uh, no, I have not talked to him yet. I plan to try to do that later today.
The person I talked to was involved in something a little less serious. A felony theft, actually."

"Okay."

She was growing impatient so I moved to the point of the meeting.

"What I wanted to ask about was the police. You were right this morning
when you warned me about guarding against police intrusion. When I got
over to the office after leaving here, I found a couple of detectives going
through the files. Jerry's receptionist was there but she hadn't tried to stop
them."

The judge's face grew hard.

"Well, I hope you did. Those officers should have known better than to
start going through files willy-nilly."

"Yes, Your Honor, they backed off once I got there and objected. In fact,
I threatened to make a complaint to you. That's when they backed off."

She nodded, her face showing pride in the power the mention of her
name had.

"Then, why are you here?"

"Well, I'm wondering now whether I should let them back in."

"I don't understand you, Mr. Haller. Let the police back in?"

"The detective in charge of the investigation made a good point. He said the evidence suggests that Jerry Vincent knew his killer and probably even allowed him to get close enough to, you know, shoot him. He said that makes it a good bet that it was one of his own clients. So they were going through the files looking for potential suspects when I walked in on them."

The judge waved one of her hands in a gesture of dismissal.

"Of course they were. And they were trampling on those clients' rights as they were doing it."

"They were in the file room and were looking through old cases. Closed cases."

"Doesn't matter. Open or closed, it still constitutes a violation of the attorney-client privilege."

"I understand that, Judge. But after they were gone, I saw they had left behind a stack of files on the table. These were the files they were either going to take or wanted to look more closely at. I looked them over and there were threats in those files."

"Threats against Mr. Vincent?"

"Yes. They were cases in which his clients weren't happy about the outcome, whether it was the verdict or the disposition or the terms of imprisonment. There were threats, and in each of the cases, he took the threats seriously enough to make a detailed record of exactly what was said and who said it. That was what the detectives were pulling together."

The judge leaned back and clasped her hands, her elbows on the arms of her leather chair. She thought about the situation I had described and then brought her eyes to mine.

"You believe we are inhibiting the investigation by not allowing the police to do their job."

I nodded.

"I was wondering if there was a way to sort of serve both sides," I said. "Limit the harm to the clients but let the police follow the investigation wherever it goes."

The judge considered this in silence again, then sighed.

"I wish my husband had stayed," she finally said. "I value his opinion greatly."

"Well, I had an idea."

"Of course you did. What is it?"

"I was thinking that I could vet the files myself and draw up a list of the people who threatened Jerry. Then I could pass it on to Detective Bosch and give him some of the details of the threats as well. This way, he would have what he needs but he wouldn't have the files themselves. He's happy, I'm happy."

"Bosch is the lead detective?"

"Yes, Harry Bosch. He's with Robbery-Homicide. I can't remember his partner's name."

"You have to understand, Mr. Haller, that even if you just give this man Bosch the names, you are still breaching client confidentiality. You could be disbarred for this."

"Well, I was thinking about that and I believe there's a way out. One of the mechanisms of relief from the client confidentiality bond is in the case of threat to safety. If Jerry Vincent knew a client was coming to kill him last night, he could have called the police and given that client's name to them. There would've been no breach in that."

"Yes, but what you are considering here is completely different."

"It's different, Judge, but not completely. I've been directly told by the lead detective on the case that it is highly likely that the identity of Jerry Vincent's killer is contained in Jerry's own files. Those files are now mine. So that information constitutes a threat to me. When I go out and start meeting these clients, I could shake hands with the killer and not even know it. You add that up any way and I feel I am in some jeopardy here, Judge, and that qualifies for relief."

She nodded her head again and put her glasses back on. She reached over and picked up a glass of water that had been hidden from my view by her desktop computer.

After drinking deeply from the glass she spoke.

"All right, Mr. Haller. I believe that if you vet the files as you have suggested, then you will be acting in an appropriate and acceptable manner. I would like you to file a motion with this court that explains your actions and the feeling of threat you are under. I will sign it and seal it and with any good luck it will be something that never sees the light of day."

"Thank you, Your Honor."

"Anything else?"

"I think that is it."

"Then, have a good day."

"Yes, Your Honor. Thank you."

I got up and headed toward the door but then remembered something and turned back to stand in front of the judge's desk.

"Judge? I forgot something. I saw your calendar from last week out there and noticed that Jerry Vincent came in on the Elliot matter. I haven't thoroughly reviewed the case file yet, but do you mind my asking what the hearing was about?"

The judge had to think for a moment to recall the hearing.

"It was an emergency motion. Mr. Vincent came in because Judge Stanton had revoked bail and ordered Mr. Elliot remanded to custody. I stayed the revocation."

"Why was it revoked?"

"Mr. Elliot had traveled to a film festival in New York without getting permission. It was one of the qualifiers of bail. When Mr. Golantz, the prosecutor, saw a picture of Elliot at the festival in *People* magazine, he asked Judge Stanton to revoke bail. He obviously wasn't happy that bail had been allowed in the first place. Judge Stanton revoked and then Mr. Vincent came to me for an emergency stay of his client's arrest and incarceration. I decided to give Mr. Elliot a second chance and to modify his freedom by making him wear an ankle monitor. But I can assure you that Mr. Elliot will not receive a third chance. Keep that in mind if you should retain him as a client."

"I understand, Judge. Thank you."

I nodded and left the chambers, thanking Mrs. Gill as I walked out through the courtroom.

Harry Bosch's card was still in my pocket. I dug it out while I was going down in the elevator. I had parked in a pay lot by the Kyoto Grand Hotel and had a three-block walk that would take me right by Parker Center. I called Bosch's cell phone as I headed to the courthouse exit.

"This is Bosch."

"It's Mickey Haller."

There was a hesitation. I thought that maybe he didn't recognize my name.

"What can I do for you?" he finally asked.

"How's the investigation going?"

"It's going, but nothing I can talk to you about."

"Then I'll just get to the point. Are you in Parker Center right now?"

"That's right. Why?"

"I'm heading over from the courthouse. Meet me out front by the memorial."

"Look, Haller, I'm busy. Can you just tell me what this is about?"

"Not on the phone, but I think it will be worth your while. If you're not there when I go by, then I'll know you've passed on the opportunity and I won't bother you with it again."

I closed the phone before he could respond. It took me five minutes to get over to Parker Center by foot. The place was in its last years of life, its replacement being built a block over on Spring Street. I saw Bosch standing next to the fountain that was part of the memorial for officers killed in the line of duty. I saw thin white wires leading from his ears to his jacket pocket. I walked up and didn't bother with a handshake or any other greeting. He pulled the earbuds out and shoved them into his pocket.

"Shutting the world out, Detective?"

"Helps me concentrate. Is there a purpose to this meeting?"

"After you left the office today I looked at the files you had stacked on the table. In the file room."

"And?"

"And I understand what you are trying to do. I want to help you but I want you to understand my position."

"I understand you, Counselor. You have to protect those files and the possible killer hiding in them because those are the rules."

I shook my head. This guy didn't want to make it easy for me to help him.

"I'll tell you what, Detective Bosch. Come back by the office at eight o'clock tomorrow morning and I will give you what I can."

I think the offer surprised him. He had no response.

"You'll be there?" I asked.

"What's the catch?" he asked right back.

"No catch. Just don't be late. I've got an interview at nine, and after that I'll probably be on the road for client conferences."

"I'll be there at eight."

"Okay, then."

I was ready to walk away but it looked like he wasn't.

"What is it?"

"I was going to ask you something."

"What?"

"Did Vincent have any federal cases?"

I thought for a moment, going over what I knew of the files. I shook my head.

"We're still reviewing everything but I don't think so. He was like me, liked to stay in state court. It's a numbers game. More cases, more fuck-ups, more holes to slip through. The feds kind of like to stack the deck. They don't like to lose."

I thought he might take the slight personally. But he had moved past it and was putting something in place. He nodded.

"Okay."

"That's it? That's all you wanted to ask?"

"That's it."

I waited for further explanation but none came.

"Okay, Detective."

I clumsily put out my hand. He shook it and appeared to feel just as awkward about it. I decided to ask a question I had been holding back on.

"Hey, there was something I was meaning to ask you, too."

"What's that?"

"It doesn't say it on your card but I heard that your full name is Hieronymus Bosch. Is that true?"

"What about it?"

"I was just wondering, where'd you get a name like that?"

"My mother gave it to me."

"Your mother? Well, what did your father think about it?"

"I never asked him. I have to get back to the investigation now, Counselor. Is there anything else?"

"No, that was it. I was just curious. I'll see you tomorrow at eight."

"I'll be there."

I left him standing there at the memorial and walked away. I headed down the block, thinking the whole time about why he had asked if Jerry Vincent had had any federal cases. When I turned left at the corner, I glanced back and saw Bosch still standing by the fountain. He was watching me. He didn't look away, but I did, and I kept walking.

11

Cisco and Lorna were still at work in Jerry Vincent's office when I got back. I handed the court order for the bank over to Lorna and told her about the two early appointments I had set for the next day.

"I thought you put Patrick Henson into the dog pile," Lorna said.

"I did. But now I moved him back."

She put her eyebrows together the way she did whenever I confounded her — which was a lot. I didn't want to explain things. Moving on, I asked if anything new had developed while I had gone to court.

"A couple things," Lorna said. "First of all, the check from Walter Elliot cleared. If he heard about Jerry it's too late to stop payment."

"Good."

"It gets better. I found the contracts file and took a look at Jerry's deal with Elliot. That hundred thousand deposited Friday for trial was only a partial payment."

She was right. It was getting better.

"How much?" I asked.

"According to the deal," she said, "Vincent took two fifty up front. That was five months ago and it looks like that is all gone. But he was going to get another two fifty for the trial. Nonrefundable. The hundred was only the first part of that. The rest is due on the first day of testimony."

I nodded with satisfaction. Vincent had made a great deal. I had never had a case with that kind of money involved. But I wondered how he had blown through the first $250,000 so quickly. Lorna would have to study the ins and outs of the accounts to get that answer.

"Okay, all of that's real good — if we get Elliot. Otherwise, it doesn't matter. What else do we have?"

Lorna looked disappointed that I didn't want to linger over the money and celebrate her discovery. She had lost sight of the fact that I still had to nail Elliot down. Technically, he was a free agent. I would get the first shot at him but I still had to secure him as a client before I could consider what it would be like to get a $250,000 trial fee.

Lorna answered my question in a monotone.

"We had a series of visitors while you were in court."

"Who?"

"First, one of the investigators Jerry used came by after hearing the news. He took one look at Cisco and almost got into it with him. Then he got smart and backed down."

"Who was it?"

"Bruce Carlin. Jerry hired him to work the Elliot case."

I nodded. Bruce Carlin was a former LAPD bull who had crossed to the dark side and did defense work now. A lot of attorneys used him because of his insider's knowledge of how things worked in the cop shop. I had used him on a case once and thought he was living off an undeserved reputation. I never hired him again.

"Call him back," I said. "Set up a time for him to come back in."

"Why, Mick? You've got Cisco."

"I know I've got Cisco but Carlin was doing work on Elliot and I doubt it's all in the files. You know how it is. If you keep it out of the file, you keep it out of discovery. So bring him in. Cisco can sit down with him and find out what he's got. Pay him for his time—whatever his hourly rate is—and then cut him loose when he's no longer useful. What else? Who else came in?"

"A real loser's parade. Carney Andrews waltzed in, thinking she was going to just pick the Elliot case up off the pile and waltz back out with it. I sent her away empty-handed. I then looked through the P and Os in the operating account and saw she was hired five months ago as associate counsel on Elliot. A month later she was dropped."

I nodded and understood. Vincent had been judge shopping for Elliot. Carney Andrews was an untalented attorney and weasel, but she was married to a superior court judge named Bryce Andrews. He had spent twenty-five years as a prosecutor before being appointed to the bench. In the view of most criminal defense attorneys who worked in the CCB, he had never left the DA's office. He was believed to be one of the toughest judges in the building, one who at times acted in concert with, if not as a direct arm of, the prosecutor's office. This created a cottage industry in which his wife made a very comfortable living by being hired as co-counsel on cases in her husband's court, thereby creating a conflict of interest that would require the reassignment of the cases to other, hopefully more lenient, judges.

It worked like a charm and the best part was that Carney Andrews never really had to practice law. She just had to sign on to a case, make an appearance as co-counsel in court and then wait until it was reassigned from her husband's calendar. She could then collect a substantial fee and move on to the next case.

I didn't have to even look into the Elliot file to see what had happened. I knew. Case assignments were generated by random selection in the chief judge's office. The Elliot case had obviously been initially assigned to Bryce Andrews's court and Vincent didn't like his chances there. For starters, Andrews would never allow bail on a double-murder case, let alone the hard line he would take against the defendant when it got to trial. So Vincent hired the judge's wife as co-counsel and the problem went away. The case was then randomly reassigned to Judge James P. Stanton, whose reputation was completely the opposite of Andrews's. The bottom line was that whatever Vincent had paid Carney, it had been worth it.

"Did you check?" I asked Lorna. "How much did he pay her?"

"She took ten percent of the initial advance."

I whistled. Twenty-five thousand dollars for nothing. That at least explained where some of the first quarter million went.

"Nice work if you can get it," I said.

"But then you'd have to sleep at night with Bryce Andrews," Lorna said. "I'm not sure that would be worth it."

Cisco laughed. I didn't but Lorna did have a point. Bryce Andrews had at least twenty years and almost two hundred pounds on his wife. It wasn't a pretty picture.

"That it on the visitors?" I asked.

"No," Lorna said. "We also had a couple of clients drop by to ask for their files after they heard on the radio about Jerry's death."

"And?"

"We stalled them. I told them that only you could turn over a file and that you would get back to them within twenty-four hours. It looked like they wanted to argue about it but with Cisco here they decided it would be better to wait."

She smiled at Cisco and the big man bowed as if to say "at your service."

Lorna handed me a slip of paper.

"Those are the names. There's contact info, too."

I looked at the names. One was in the dog pile, so I would be happily turning the file over. The other was a public indecency case that I thought I could do something with. The woman was charged when a sheriff's deputy ordered her out of the water on a Malibu beach. She was swimming nude but this was not apparent until the deputy ordered her out of the water. Because the charge was a misdemeanor, the deputy had to witness the crime to make an arrest. But by ordering her out of the water, he created the crime he arrested her for. That wouldn't fly in court. It was a case I knew I could get dismissed.

"I'll go see these two tonight," I said. "In fact, I want to hit the road with all of the cases soon. Starting with a stop at Archway Pictures. I'm going to take Cisco with me, and Lorna, I want you to gather up whatever you need from here and head on home. I don't want you being here by yourself."

She nodded but then said, "Are you sure Cisco should go with you?"

I was surprised she had asked the question in front of him. She was referring to his size and appearance—the tattoos, the earring, the boots, leather vest and so on—the overall menace his appearance projected. Her concern was that he might scare away more clients than he would help lock down.

"Yeah," I said. "He should go. When I want to be subtle he can just wait in the car. Besides, I want him driving so I can look at the files."

I looked at Cisco. He nodded and seemed fine with the arrangement. He might look foolish in his bike vest behind the wheel of a Lincoln but he wasn't complaining yet.

"Speaking of the files," I said. "We have nothing in federal court, right?"

Lorna shook her head.

"Not that I know of."

I nodded. It confirmed what I had indicated to Bosch and made me more curious about why he had asked about federal cases. I was beginning to get an idea about it and planned to bring it up when I saw him the next morning.

"Okay," I said. "I guess it's time for me to be a Lincoln lawyer again. Let's hit the road."

12

In the last decade Archway Pictures had grown from a movie industry fringe dweller to a major force. This was because of the one thing that had always ruled Hollywood. Money. As the cost of producing films grew exponentially at the same time the industry focused on the most expensive kinds of films to make, the major studios began increasingly to look for partners to share the cost and risk.

This is where Walter Elliot and Archway Pictures came in. Archway was previously an overrun lot. It was on Melrose Avenue just a few blocks from the behemoth that was Paramount Studios. Archway was built to act as the remora fish does with the great white shark. It would hover near the mouth of the bigger fish and take whatever torn scraps somehow missed being sucked into the giant maw. Archway offered production facilities and soundstages for rent when everything was booked at the big studios. It leased office space to would-be and has-been producers who weren't up to the standards of or didn't have the same deals as on-lot producers. It nurtured independent films, the movies that were less expensive to make but more risky and supposedly less likely to be hits than their studio-bred counterparts.

Walter Elliot and Archway Pictures limped along in this fashion for a decade, until luck and lightning struck twice. In a space of only three years Elliot hit gold with two of the independent films he'd backed by providing soundstages, equipment, and production facilities in exchange for a piece of the action. The films went on to defy Hollywood expectations and became huge hits — critically and financially. One even took home the Academy Award as best picture. Walter and his stepchild studio suddenly basked in the glow of huge success. More than one hundred million people heard Walter being personally thanked on the Academy Awards broadcast. And, more important, Archway's worldwide cut from the two films was more than a hundred million dollars apiece.

Walter did a wise thing with that newfound money. He fed it to the sharks, cofinancing a number of productions in which the big studios were looking for risk partners. There were some misses, of course. The business, after all, was Hollywood. But there were enough hits to keep the nest egg growing. Over the next decade Walter Elliot doubled and then tripled his stake and along the way became a player who made regular appearances on the power 100 lists in industry minds and magazines. Elliot had taken Archway from being an address associated with Hollywood pariahs to a place where there was a three-year wait for a windowless office.

All the while, Elliot's personal wealth grew commensurately. Though he had come west twenty-five years before as the rich scion of a Florida phosphate family, that money was nothing like the riches provided by Hollywood. Like many on those power 100 lists, Elliot traded in his wife for a newer model and together they started accumulating houses. First in the canyons, then down in the Beverly Hills flats, and then on out to Malibu and up to Santa Barbara. According to the information in the files I had, Walter Elliot and his wife owned seven different homes and two ranches in or around Los Angeles. Never mind how often they used each place. Real estate was a way of keeping score in Hollywood.

All those properties and top 100 lists came in handy when Elliot was charged with double murder. The studio boss flexed his political and financial muscles and pulled off something rarely accomplished in a murder case. He got bail. With the prosecution objecting all the way, bail was set at $20 million and Elliot quickly ponied it up in real estate. He'd been out of jail and awaiting trial ever since — his brief flirtation with bail revocation the week before notwithstanding.

One of the properties Elliot put up as collateral for bail was the house where the murders took place. It was a waterfront weekender on a secluded cove. On the bail escrow its value was listed at $6 million. It was there that thirty-nine-year-old Mitzi Elliot was murdered along with her lover in a twelve-hundred-square-foot bedroom with a glass wall that looked out on the big blue Pacific.

The discovery file was replete with forensic reports and color copies of the crime scene photographs. The death room was completely white — walls, carpet, furniture and bedding. Two naked bodies were sprawled on the bed and floor. Mitzi Elliot and Johan Rilz. The scene was red on white. Two large bullet holes in the man's chest. Two in the woman's chest and one in her forehead. He by the bedroom door. She on the bed. Red on white. It was not a clean scene. The wounds were large. Though the murder weapon was missing, an accompanying report said that slugs had been identified through ballistic markings as coming from a Smith & Wesson model 29, a .44 magnum revolver. Fired at close quarters, it was overkill.

Walter Elliot had been suspicious about his wife. She had announced her intentions to divorce him and he believed there was another man involved. He told the sheriff's homicide investigators that he had gone to the Malibu beach house because his wife had told him she was going to meet with the interior designer. Elliot thought that was a lie and timed his approach so that he would be able to confront her with a paramour. He loved her and wanted her back. He was willing to fight for her. He had gone to confront, he repeated, not to kill. He didn't own a .44 magnum, he told them. He didn't own any guns.

According to the statement he gave investigators, when Elliot got to Malibu he found his wife and her lover naked and already dead. It turned out that the lover was in fact the interior designer, Johan Rilz, a German national Elliot had always thought was gay.

Elliot left the house and got back in his car. He started to drive away but then thought better of it. He decided to do the right thing. He turned around and pulled back into the driveway. He called 911 and waited out front for the deputies to arrive.

The chronology and details of how the investigation proceeded from that point would be important in mounting a defense. According to the reports in the file, Elliot gave investigators an initial account of his discovery of the two bodies. He was then transported by two detectives to the Malibu substation so he would be out of the way while the investigation of the crime scene proceeded. He was not under arrest at this time. He was placed in an unlocked interview room where he waited three long hours for the two lead detectives to finally clear the crime scene and come to the substation. A videotaped interview was then conducted but, according to the transcript I reviewed, quickly crossed the line into interrogation. At this point Elliot was finally advised of his rights and asked if he wanted to continue to answer questions. Elliot wisely chose to stop talking and to ask for an attorney. It was a decision made better late than never but Elliot would have been better off if he had never said word one to the investigators. He should've just taken the nickel and kept his mouth shut.

While investigators had been working the crime scene and Elliot was cooling his heels in the substation interview room, a homicide investigator working in the sheriff's headquarters in Whittier drew up several search warrants that were faxed to a superior court judge and signed. These allowed investigators to search throughout the beach house and Elliot's car and permitted them to conduct a gunshot residue test on Elliot's hands and clothes to determine if there were gas nitrates and microscopic particles of burned gunpowder on them. After Elliot refused further cooperation, his hands were bagged in plastic at the substation and he was transported to Sheriff's Headquarters, where a criminalist conducted the GSR test in the crime lab. This consisted of wiping chemically treated disks on Elliot's hands and clothing. When the disks were processed by a lab technician, those that had been wiped on his hands and sleeves tested positive for high levels of gunshot residue.

At that point Elliot was formally arrested on suspicion of murder. With his one phone call he contacted his personal lawyer, who in turn called in Jerry Vincent, whom he had attended law school with. Elliot was eventually transported to the county jail and booked on two counts of murder. The sheriff's investigators then called the department's media office and suggested that a press conference should be set up. They had just bagged a big one.

I closed the file as Cisco stopped the Lincoln in front of Archway Studios. There were a number of picketers walking the sidewalk. They were writers on strike, holding up red-and-white signs that said WE WANT A FAIR SHARE! and WRITERS UNITED! Some signs showed a fist holding a pen. Another said YOUR FAVORITE LINE? A WRITER WROTE IT. Anchored on the sidewalk was a large blow-up figure of a pig smoking a cigar with the word producer branded on its rear end. The pig and most of the signs were well-worn clichés and I would have thought that with the protesters being writers, they would have come up with something better. But maybe that kind of creativity happened only when they were getting paid.

I had ridden in the backseat for the sake of appearances on this first stop. I was hoping that Elliot might catch a glimpse of me through his office window and take me for an attorney of great means and skill. But the writers saw a Lincoln with a rider in the back and thought I was a producer. As we turned into the studio, they descended on the car with their signs and started chanting, "Greedy Bastard! Greedy Bastard!" Cisco gunned it and plowed through, a few of the hapless scribes dodging the fenders.

"Careful!" I barked. "All I need is to run over an out-of-work writer."

"Don't worry," Cisco replied calmly. "They always scatter."

"Not this time."

When he got up to the guardhouse, Cisco pulled forward enough that my window was even with the door. I checked to make sure none of the writers had followed us onto studio property and then lowered the glass so

I could speak to the man who stepped out. His uniform was a beige color with a dark brown tie and matching epaulets. It looked ridiculous.

"Can I help you?"

"I'm Walter Elliot's attorney. I don't have an appointment but I need to see him right away."

"Can I see your driver's license?"

I got it out and handed it through the window.

"I am handling this for Jerry Vincent. That's the name Mr. Elliot's secretary will recognize."

The guard went into the booth and slid the door closed. I didn't know if this was to keep the air-conditioning from escaping or to prevent me from hearing what was said when he picked up the phone. Whatever the reason, he soon slid the door back open and extended the phone to me, his hand covering the mouthpiece.

"Mrs. Albrecht is Mr. Elliot's executive assistant. She wants to speak to you."

I took the phone.

"Hello?"

"Mr. Haller, is it? What is this all about? Mr. Elliot has dealt exclusively with Mr. Vincent on this matter and there is no appointment on his calendar."

This matter. It was a strange way of referring to double charges of murder.

"Mrs. Albrecht, I'd rather not talk about this at the front gate. As you can imagine, it's quite a delicate 'matter,' to use your word. Can I come to the office and see Mr. Elliot?"

I turned in my seat and looked out the back window. There were two cars in the guardhouse queue behind my Lincoln. They must not have been producers. The writers had let them through unmolested.

"I'm afraid that's not good enough, Mr. Haller. Can I place you on hold while I call Mr. Vincent?"

"You won't get through to him."

"He'll take a call from Mr. Elliot, I am sure."

"I am sure he won't, Mrs. Albrecht. Jerry Vincent's dead. That's why I'm here."

I looked at Cisco's reflection in the rearview mirror and shrugged as though to say I had no choice but to hit her with the news. The plan had been to finesse my way through the arch and then be the one to personally tell Elliot his lawyer was dead.

"Excuse me, Mr. Haller. Did you say Mr. Vincent is...dead?"

"That's what I said. And I'm his court-appointed replacement. Can I come in now?"

"Yes, of course."

I handed the phone back and soon the gate opened.

13

We were assigned to a prime parking space in the executive lot. I told Cisco to wait in the car and went in alone, carrying the two thick files Vincent had put together on the case. One contained discovery materials turned over so far by the prosecution, including the important investigative documents and interview transcripts, and the other contained documents and other work product generated by Vincent during the five months he had handled the case. Between the two files I was able to get a good handle on what the prosecution had and didn't have, and the direction in which the prosecutor wanted to take the trial. There was still work to be done and pieces were missing from the defense's case and strategy. Perhaps those pieces had been carried in Jerry Vincent's head, or in his laptop or on the legal pad in his portfolio, but unless the cops arrested a suspect and recovered the stolen property, whatever was there would be of no help to me.

I followed a sidewalk across a beautifully manicured lawn on the way to Elliot's office. My plan for the meeting was threefold. The first order of business was to secure Elliot as a client. That done, I would ask his approval in delaying the trial to give me time to get up to speed and prepare for it. The last part of the plan would be to see if Elliot had any of the pieces missing from the defense case. Parts two and three obviously didn't matter if I was unsuccessful with part one.

Walter Elliot's office was in Bungalow One on the far reaches of the Archway lot. "Bungalows" sounded small but they were big in Hollywood. A sign of status. It was like having your own private home on the lot. And as in any private home, activities inside could be kept secret.

A Spanish-tiled entranceway led to a step-down living room with a fireplace blowing gas flames on one wall and a mahogany wood bar set up in an opposite corner. I stepped into the middle of the room and looked around and waited. I looked at the painting over the fireplace. It depicted an armored knight on a white steed. The knight had reached up and flipped open the visor on his helmet and his eyes stared out intently. I took a few steps further into the room and realized the eyes had been painted so that they stared at the viewer of the painting from any angle in the room. They followed me.

"Mr. Haller?"

I turned as I recognized the voice from the guardhouse phone. Elliot's gatekeeper, Mrs. Albrecht, had stepped into the room from some unseen entrance. Elegance was the word that came to mind. She was an aging beauty who appeared to take the process in stride. Gray streaked through her un-dyed hair and tiny wrinkles were working their way toward her eyes and mouth, seemingly unchecked by injection or incision. Mrs. Albrecht looked like a woman who liked her own skin. In my experience, this was a rare thing in Hollywood.

"Mr. Elliot will see you now."

I followed her around a corner and down a short hallway to a reception office. She passed an empty desk—hers, I assumed—and pushed open a large door to Walter Elliot's office.

Elliot was an overly tanned man with more gray hair sprouting from his open shirt collar than from the top of his head. He sat behind a large glass worktable. No drawers beneath it and no computer on top of it, though paperwork and scripts were spread across it. It didn't matter that he was facing two counts of murder. He was staying busy. He was working and running Archway the way he always did. Maybe it was on the advice of some Hollywood self-help guru but it wasn't an unusual behavior or philosophy for the accused. Act like you are innocent and you will be perceived as innocent. Finally, you will become innocent.

There was a sitting area to the right but he chose to remain behind the worktable. He had dark, piercing eyes that seemed familiar and then I realized I had just been looking at them—the knight on the steed out in the living room was Elliot.

"Mr. Elliot, this is Mr. Haller," Mrs. Albrecht said.

She signaled me to the chair across the table from Elliot. After I sat down Elliot made a dismissive gesture without looking at Mrs. Albrecht and she left the room without another word. Over the years I had represented and been in the company of a couple dozen killers. The one rule is that there are no rules. They come in all sizes and shapes, rich and poor, humble and arrogant, regretful and cold to the bone. The percentages told me that it was most likely Elliot was a killer. That he had calmly dispatched his wife and her lover and arrogantly thought he could and would get away with it. But there was nothing about him on first meeting that told me one way or the other for sure. And that's the way it always was.

"What happened to my lawyer?" he asked.

"Well, for a detailed explanation I would have to refer you to the police. The shorthand is that somebody killed him last night in his car."

"And where does that leave me? I'm on trial for my life in a week!"

That was a slight exaggeration. Jury selection was scheduled in nine days and the DA's office had not announced that it would seek the death penalty. But it didn't hurt that he was thinking in such terms.

"That's why I'm here, Mr. Elliot. At the moment you are left with me."

"And who are you? I've never heard of you."

"You haven't heard of me because I make it a practice not to be heard of.

Celebrity lawyers bring too much attention to their clients. They feed their own celebrity by offering up their clients. I don't operate that way."

He pursed his lips and nodded. I could tell I had just scored a point.

"And you're taking over Vincent's practice?" he asked.

"Let me explain it, Mr. Elliot. Jerry Vincent had a one-man shop. Just like I do. On occasion one of us would need help with a case or need another attorney to fill in here and there. We filled that role for each other. If you look at the contract of representation you signed with him, you will find my name in a paragraph with language that allowed Jerry to discuss your case with me and to include me within the bonds of the attorney-client relationship. In other words, Jerry trusted me with his cases. And now that he is gone, I am prepared to carry on in his stead. Earlier today the chief judge of the superior court issued an order placing me in custody of Jerry's cases. Of course, you ultimately get to choose who represents you at trial. I am very familiar with your case and prepared to continue your legal representation without so much as a hiccup. But, as I said, you must make the choice. I'm only here to tell you your options."

Elliot shook his head.

"I really can't believe this. We were set for trial next week and I'm not pushing it back. I've been waiting five months to clear my name! Do you have any idea what it is like for an innocent man to have to wait and wait and wait for justice? To read all the innuendo and bullshit in the media? To have a prosecutor with his nose up my ass, waiting for me to make the move that gets my bail pulled? Look at this!"

He stretched out a leg and pulled his left pant leg up to reveal the GPS monitor Judge Holder had ordered him to wear.

"I want this over!"

I nodded in a consoling manner and knew that if I told him I wanted to delay his case, I would be looking at a quick dismissal from consideration. I decided I would bring that up in a strategy session after I closed the deal — if I closed the deal.

"I've dealt with many clients wrongly accused," I lied. "The wait for justice can be almost intolerable. But it also makes the vindication all the more meaningful."

Elliot didn't respond and I didn't let the silence last long.

"I spent most of the afternoon reviewing the files and evidence in your case. I'm confident you won't have to delay the trial, Mr. Elliot. I would be more than prepared to proceed. Another attorney, maybe not. But I would be ready."

There it was, my best pitch to him, most of it lies and exaggerations. But I didn't stop there.

"I've studied the trial strategy Mr. Vincent outlined. I wouldn't change it but I believe I can improve on it. And I'd be ready to go next week if need be. I think a delay can always be useful, but it won't be necessary."

Elliot nodded and rubbed a finger across his mouth.

"I would have to think about this," he said. "I need to talk to some people and have you checked out. Just like I had Vincent checked out before I went with him."

I decided to gamble and to try to force Elliot into a quick decision. I didn't want him checking me out and possibly discovering I had disappeared for a year. That would raise too many questions.

"It's a good idea," I said. "Take your time but don't take too much time. The longer you wait to decide, the greater the chance that the judge will find it necessary to push the trial back. I know you don't want that, but in the absence of Mr. Vincent or any attorney of record, the judge is probably already getting nervous and considering it. If you choose me, I will try to get before the judge as soon as possible and tell him we're still good to go."

I stood up and reached into my coat pocket for a card. I put it down on the glass.

"Those are all my numbers. Call anytime."

I hoped he would tell me to sit back down and we'd start planning for trial. But Elliot just reached over and picked up the card. He seemed to be studying it when I left him. Before I reached the door to the office it opened from the outside and Mrs. Albrecht stood there. She smiled warmly.

"I'm sure we will be in touch," she said.

I had a feeling that she'd heard every word that had been spoken between me and her boss.

"Thank you, Mrs. Albrecht," I said. "I certainly hope so."

14

I found Cisco leaning against the Lincoln, smoking a cigarette.

"That was fast," he said.

I opened the back door in case there were cameras in the parking lot and Elliot was watching me.

"Look at you with the encouraging word."

I got in and he did the same.

"I'm just saying that it seemed kind of quick," he said. "How'd it go?"

"I gave it my best shot. We'll probably know something soon."

"You think he did it?"

"Probably, but it doesn't matter. We've got other things to worry about."

It was hard to go from thinking about a quarter-million-dollar fee to some of the also-rans on Vincent's client list, but that was the job. I opened my bag and pulled out the other active files. It was time to decide where our next stop was going to be.

Cisco backed out of the space and started heading toward the arch.

"Lorna's waiting to hear," he said.

I looked up at him in the mirror.

"What?"

"Lorna called me while you were inside. She really wants to know what happened with Elliot."

"Don't worry, I'll call her. First let me figure out where we're going."

The address of each client—at least the address given upon signing for Vincent's services—was printed neatly on the outside of each file. I quickly checked through the files, looking for addresses in Hollywood. I finally came across the file belonging to the woman charged with indecent exposure. The client who had come to Vincent's office earlier to ask for the return of her file.

"Here we go," I said. "When you get out of here, head down Melrose to La Brea. We've got a client right there. One of the ones who came in today for her file."

"Got it."

"After that stop, I'll ride in the front seat. Don't want you to feel too much like a chauffeur."

"It ain't a bad gig. I think I could get used to it."

I got out my phone.

"Hey, Mick, I gotta tell you something," Cisco said.

I took my thumb off the speed-dial button for Lorna.

"Yeah, what?"

"I just wanted to tell you myself before you heard it somewhere else. Me and Lorna . . . we're gonna get married."

I had figured that they were headed in that direction. Lorna and I had been friends for fifteen years before we were married for one. It had been a rebound marriage for me and as ill-advised as anything I had ever done. We ended it when we realized the mistake and somehow managed to remain close. There was no one I trusted more in the world. We were no longer in love but I still loved her and would always protect her.

"That okay with you, Mick?"

I looked at Cisco in the rearview.

"I'm not part of the equation, Cisco."

"I know but I want to know if it's *okay* with you. Know what I mean?"

I looked out the window and thought a moment before answering. Then I looked back at him in the mirror.

"Yes, it's all right with me. But I'll tell you something, Cisco. She's one of the four most important people in my life. You have maybe seventy-five pounds on me—and granted, all of them in muscle. But if you hurt her, I'm going to find a way to hurt you back. That okay with you?"

He looked away from the mirror to the road ahead. We were in the exit line, moving slowly. The striking writers were massing out on the sidewalk and delaying the people trying to leave the studio.

"Yeah, Mick, I'm okay with that."

We were silent for a while after that as we inched along. Cisco kept glancing at me in the mirror.

"What?" I finally asked.

"Well, I got your daughter. That makes one. And then Lorna. I was wondering who the other two were."

Before I could answer, the electronic version of the *William Tell* Overture started to play in my hand. I looked down at my phone. It said private caller on the screen. I opened it up.

"Haller."

"Please hold for Walter Elliot," Mrs. Albrecht said.

Not much time went by before I heard the familiar voice.

"Mr. Haller?"

"I'm here. What can I do for you?"

I felt the stirring of anxiety in my gut. He had decided.

"Have you noticed something about my case, Mr. Haller?"

The question caught me off guard.

"How do you mean?"

"One lawyer. I have one lawyer, Mr. Haller. You see, I not only must win this case in court but I must also win it in the court of public opinion."

"I see," I said, though I didn't quite understand the point.

"In the last ten years I've picked a lot of winners. I'm talking about films in which I invested my money. I picked winners because I believe I have an accurate sense of public opinion and taste. I know what people like because I know what they are thinking."

"I'm sure you do, sir."

"And I think that the public believes that the more guilty you are, the more lawyers you need."

He wasn't wrong about that.

"So the first thing I said to Mr. Vincent when I hired him was, no dream team, just you. We had a second lawyer on board early on but that was temporary. She served a purpose and was gone. One lawyer, Mr. Haller. That's how I want it. The best one lawyer I can get."

"I under—"

"I've decided, Mr. Haller. You impressed me when you were in here. I would like to engage your services for trial. You will be my one lawyer."

I had to calm my voice before answering.

"I'm glad to hear that. Call me Mickey."

"And you can call me Walter. But I insist on one condition before we agree to this arrangement."

"What is that?"

"No delay. We go to trial on schedule. I want to hear you say it."

I hesitated. I wanted a delay. But I wanted the case more.

"We won't delay," I said. "We'll be ready to go next Thursday."

"Then, welcome aboard. What do we do next?"

"Well, I'm still on the lot. I could turn around and come back."

"I'm afraid I have meetings until seven and then a screening of our film for the awards season."

I thought that his trial and freedom would have trumped his meetings and movies but I let it go. I would educate Walter Elliot and bring him to reality the next time I saw him.

"Okay, then, for now you give me a fax number and I'll have my assistant send over a contract. It will have the same fee structure as you had with Jerry Vincent."

There was silence and I waited. If he was going to try to knock down the fee, this is when he would do it. But instead he repeated a fax number I could hear Mrs. Albrecht giving him. I wrote it down on the outside of one of the files.

"What's tomorrow look like, Walter?"

"Tomorrow?"

"Yes, if not tonight, then tomorrow. We need to get started. You don't want a delay; I want to be even more prepared than I am now. We need to talk and go over things. There are a few gaps in the defense case and I think you can help me fill them in. I could come back to the studio or meet you anywhere else in the afternoon."

I heard muffled voices as he conferred with Mrs. Albrecht.

"I have a four o'clock open," he finally said. "Here at the bungalow."

"Okay, I'll be there. And cancel whatever you have at five. We're going to need at least a couple hours to start."

Elliot agreed to the two hours and we were about to end the conversation, when I thought of something else.

"Walter, I want to see the crime scene. Can I get into the house in Malibu tomorrow sometime before we meet?"

Again there was a pause.

"When?"

"You tell me what will work."

Again he covered the phone and I heard his muffled conversation with Mrs. Albrecht. Then he came back on the line with me.

"How about eleven? I'll have someone meet you there to let you in."

"That'll work. See you tomorrow, Walter."

I closed the phone and looked at Cisco in the mirror.

"We got him."

Cisco hit the Lincoln's horn in celebration. It was a long blast that made the driver in front of us hold up a fist and send us back the finger. Out in the street the striking writers took the blast as a sign of support from inside the hated studio. I heard a loud cheer go up from the masses.

15

≈≈≈

Bosch arrived early the next morning. He was alone. His peace offering was the extra cup of coffee he carried and handed over to me. I don't drink coffee anymore—trying to avoid any addiction in my life—but I took it from him anyway, thinking that maybe the smell of caffeine would get me going. It was only 7:45 but I had been in Jerry Vincent's office for more than two hours already.

I led Bosch back into the file room. He looked more tired than I felt and I was pretty sure he was in the same suit he'd been wearing when I saw him the day before.

"Long night?" I asked.

"Oh, yeah."

"Chasing leads or chasing tail?"

It was a question I had once heard one detective ask another in a court-house hallway. I guess it was a question reserved for brothers of the badge because it didn't go over so well with Bosch. He made some sort of guttural noise and didn't answer.

In the file room I told him to have a seat at the small table. There was a yellow legal tablet on the table, but no files. I took the other seat and put my coffee down.

"So," I said, picking up the legal pad.

"So," Bosch said when I offered nothing else.

"So I met with Judge Holder in chambers yesterday and worked out a plan by which we can give you what you need from the files without actually giving you the files."

Bosch shook his head.

"What's wrong?" I asked.

"You should've told me this yesterday at Parker Center," he said. "I wouldn't have wasted my time."

"I thought you'd appreciate this."

"It's not going to work."

"How do you know that? How can you be sure?"

"How many homicides have you investigated, Haller? And how many have you cleared?"

"All right, point taken. You're the homicide guy. But I am certainly capable of reviewing files and discerning what constituted a legitimate threat to Jerry Vincent. Possibly because of my experience as a criminal defense attorney I could even perceive a threat that you would miss in your capacity as a detective."

"So you say."

"Yeah, I say."

"Look, all I'm pointing out here is the obvious. I'm the detective. I'm the one who should look through the files because I know what I am looking for. No offense, but you are an amateur at this. So I'm in a position here where I have to take what an amateur is giving me and trust that I'm getting everything there is to get from the files. It doesn't work that way. I don't trust the evidence unless I find it myself."

"Again, your point is well taken, Detective, but this is the way it is. This is the only method Judge Holder approved, and I gotta tell you that you're lucky to get this much. She wasn't interested in helping you out at all."

"So you're saying you went to bat for me?"

He said it in a disbelieving, sarcastic tone, as if it were some sort of a mathematical impossibility for a defense attorney to help a police detective.

"That's right," I said defiantly. "I went to bat for you. I told you yesterday, Jerry Vincent was a friend. I'd like to see you take down the person who took him down."

"You're probably worried about your own ass, too."

"I'm not denying that."

"If I were you I would be."

"Look, do you want the list or not?"

I held the legal pad up as if I were teasing a dog with a toy. He reached for it and I pulled it back, immediately regretting the move. I quickly handed it to him. It was an awkward exchange, like shaking hands had been the day before.

"There are eleven names on that list, with a brief summary of the threat each made to Jerry Vincent. We were lucky that Jerry thought it was important to memorialize an account of each threat he received. I've never done that."

Bosch didn't respond. He was reading the first page of the legal pad.

"I prioritized them," I said.

Bosch looked at me and I knew he was ready to step on me again for assuming the role of detective. I raised a hand to stop him.

"Not from the standpoint of your investigation. From the standpoint of being a lawyer. Of putting myself in Jerry Vincent's shoes and looking at these things and determining which ones would concern me the most. Like the first one on that list. James Demarco. The guy goes away on weapons charges and thinks Jerry fucked up the case. A guy like that can get a gun as soon as he gets out."

Bosch nodded and dropped his eyes back to the legal pad. He spoke without looking up from it.

"What else do you have for me?"

"What do you mean?"

He looked at me and waved the pad up and down as if it were as light as a feather and the information on it was equally so.

"I'll run these names and see where these guys are at now. Maybe your gunrunner is out and about and looking for revenge. But these are dead cases. Most likely if these threats were legit, they would've been carried out long ago. Same with any threats he got when he was a prosecutor. So this is just busywork you're giving me, Counselor."

"Busywork? Some of those guys threatened him when they were being led off to prison. Maybe some of them are out. Maybe one just got out and made good on the threat. Maybe they contracted it out from prison. There are a lot of possibilities and they shouldn't be dismissed as just busywork. I don't understand your attitude on this."

Bosch smiled and shook his head. I remembered my father doing the same thing when he was about to tell me as a five-year-old that I had misunderstood something.

"I don't really care what you think about my attitude," he said. "We'll check your leads out. But I'm looking for something a little more current. Something from Vincent's open cases."

"Well, I can't help you there."

"Sure you can. You have all the cases now. I assume you are reviewing them and meeting all your new clients. You're going to come across something or see something or hear something that doesn't fit, that doesn't seem right, that maybe scares you a little bit. That's when you call me."

I stared at him without answering.

"You never know," he said. "It might save you from..."

He shrugged and didn't finish, but the message was clear. He was trying to scare me into cooperating far more than Judge Holder was allowing, or than I felt comfortable with.

"It's one thing sharing threat information from closed cases," I said. "It's another thing entirely to do it with active cases. And besides that, I know you are asking for more than just threats. You think Jerry stumbled across something or had some knowledge that got him killed."

Bosch kept his eyes on me and slowly nodded. I was the first to look away.

"What about it being a two-way street, Detective? What do you know that you aren't telling me? What was in the laptop that was so important? What was in the portfolio?"

"I can't talk to you about an active investigation."

"You could yesterday when you asked about the FBI."

He looked at me and squinted his dark eyes.

"I didn't ask you about the FBI."

"Come on, Detective. You asked if he had any federal cases. Why would you do that unless you have some sort of federal connection? I'm guessing it was the FBI."

Bosch hesitated. I had a feeling I had guessed right and now he was in a corner. My mentioning the bureau would make him think I knew something. Now he would have to give in order to get.

"This time you go first," I prompted.

He nodded.

"Okay, the killer took Jerry Vincent's cell phone — either off his body or it was in his briefcase."

"Okay."

"I got the call records yesterday right before I saw you. On the day he was killed he got three calls from the bureau. Four days before that, there were two. He was talking to somebody over there. Or they were talking to him."

"Who?"

"I can't tell. All outgoing calls from over there register on the main number. All I know is he got calls from the bureau, no names."

"How long were the calls?"

Bosch hesitated, unsure what to divulge. He looked down at the tablet in his hand and I saw him grudgingly decide to share more. He was going to get angry when I had nothing to share back.

"They were all short calls."

"How short?"

"None of them over a minute."

"Then, maybe they were just wrong numbers."

He shook his head.

"That's too many wrong numbers. They wanted something from him."

"Anybody from there check in on the homicide investigation?"

"Not yet."

I thought about this and shrugged.

"Well, maybe they will and then you'll know."

"Yeah, and maybe they won't. It's not their style, if you know what I mean. Now your turn. What do you have that's federal?"

"Nothing. I confirmed that Vincent had no federal cases."

I watched Bosch do a slow burn as he realized I had played him.

"You're telling me you have found no federal connections? Not even a bureau business card in that office?"

"That's right. Nothing."

"There's been a rumor going around about a federal grand jury looking into corruption in the state courts. You know anything about that?"

I shook my head.

"I've been on the shelf for a year."

"Thanks for the help."

"Look, Detective, I don't get this. Why can't you just call over there and ask who was calling your victim? Isn't that how an investigation should proceed?"

Bosch smiled like he was dealing with a child.

"If they want me to know something, they'll come to me. If I call them, they'll just shine me on. If this was part of a corruption probe or they've got something else going, the chances of them talking to a local cop are between slim and none. If they're the ones who got him killed, then make it none."

"How would they get him killed?"

"I told you, they kept calling. They wanted something. They were pressuring him. Maybe someone else knew about it and thought he was a risk."

"That's a lot of conjecture about five calls that don't even add up to five minutes."

Bosch held up the yellow pad.

"No more conjecture than this list."

"What about the laptop?"

"What about it?"

"Is that what this is all about, something in his computer?"

"You tell me."

"How can I tell you when I have no idea what was in it?"

Bosch nodded the point and stood up.

"Have a good day, Counselor."

He walked out, carrying the legal pad at his side. I was left wondering whether he had been warning me or playing me the whole time he had been in the room.

16

Lorna and Cisco arrived together fifteen minutes after Bosch's departure and we convened in Vincent's office. I took a seat behind the dead lawyer's desk and they sat side by side in front of it. It was another score-keeping session in which we went over cases, what had been accomplished the previous night and what still needed to be done.

With Cisco driving, I had visited eleven of Vincent's clients the night before, signing up eight of them and giving back files to the remaining three. These were the priority cases, potential clients I hoped to keep because they could pay or their cases had garnered some form of merit in my review. They were cases I could win or be challenged by.

So it had not been a bad night. I had even convinced the woman charged with indecent exposure to keep me on as her attorney. And of course, bagging Walter Elliot was the icing on the cake. Lorna reported that she had faxed him a representation contract and it had already been signed and returned. We were in good shape there. I could start chipping away at the hundred thousand in the trust account.

We next set the plan for the day. I told Lorna that I wanted her and Wren — if she showed up — to run down the remaining clients, apprise them of Jerry Vincent's demise and set up appointments for me to discuss the options of legal representation. I also wanted Lorna to continue building the calendar and familiarizing herself with Vincent's files and financial records.

I told Cisco I wanted him to focus his attention on the Elliot case, with particular emphasis on witness maintenance. This meant that he had to take the preliminary defense witness list, which had already been compiled by Jerry Vincent, and prepare subpoenas for the law enforcement officers and other witnesses who might be considered hostile to the defense's cause. For the paid expert witness and others who were willingly going to testify at trial for the defense, he had to make contact and assure them that the trial was moving forward as scheduled, with me replacing Vincent at the helm.

"Got it," Cisco said. "What about the Vincent investigation? You still want me monitoring?"

"Yes, keep tabs on that and let me know what you find out."

"I found out that they spent last night sweating somebody but kicked him loose this morning."

"Who?"

"I don't know yet."

"A suspect?"

"They cut him loose, so whoever it was is cleared. For now."

I nodded as I thought about this. No wonder Bosch looked like he had been up all night.

"What are you going to be doing today?" Lorna asked.

"My priority starting today is Elliot. There are a few things on these other cases that I'll need to pay some attention to but for the most part I'm going to be on Elliot from here on out. We've got jury selection in eight days. Today I want to start at the crime scene."

"I should go with you," Cisco said.

"No, I just want to get a feel for the place. You can get in there with a camera and tape measure later."

"Mick, isn't there any way you can convince Elliot to delay?" Lorna asked. "Doesn't he realize that you need time to study and understand the case?"

"I told him that, but he's not interested. He made it a condition of my hire. I had to agree to go to trial next week or he'd find another lawyer who could. He says he's innocent and doesn't want to wait a single day longer to prove it."

"Do you believe him?"

I shrugged.

"Doesn't matter. He believes it. And he's got this strange confidence in it all turning out his way—like the Monday morning box office. So I either get ready to go to trial at the end of next week or I lose the client."

Just then the door to the office swung open and revealed Wren Williams standing tentatively in the doorway.

"Excuse me," she said.

"Hello, Wren," I said. "Glad you're here. Could you wait out there in reception, and Lorna will be right out to work with you?"

"No problem. You also have one of the clients waiting out here. Patrick Henson. He was already waiting when I came in."

I looked at my watch. It was five of nine. It was a good sign in regard to Patrick Henson.

"Then, send him in."

A young man walked in. Patrick Henson was smaller than I thought he would be, but maybe it was the low center of gravity that made him a good surfer. He had the requisite hardened tan but his hair was cropped short. No earrings, no white shell necklace or shark's tooth. No tattoos that I could see. He wore black cargo pants and what probably passed as his best shirt. It had a collar.

"Patrick, we spoke on the phone yesterday. I'm Mickey Haller and this is my case manager, Lorna Taylor. This big guy is Cisco, my investigator."

He stepped toward the desk and shook our hands. His grip was firm.

"I'm glad you decided to come in. Is that your fish on the wall back there?"

Without moving his feet Henson swiveled at the hips as if on a surfboard and looked at the fish hanging on the wall.

"Yeah, that's Betty."

"You gave a stuffed fish a name?" Lorna asked. "What, was it a pet?"

Henson smiled, more to himself than to us.

"No, I caught it a long time ago. Back in Florida. We hung it by the front door in the place I was sharing in Malibu. My roommates and me, we'd always say, 'Hellooo, Betty' to it when we came home. It was kind of stupid."

He swiveled back and looked at me.

"Speaking of names, do we call you Trick?"

"Nah, that was just the name my agent came up with. I don't have him anymore. You can just call me Patrick."

"Okay, and you told me you had a valid driver's license?"

"Sure do."

He reached into a front pocket and removed a thick nylon wallet. He pulled his license out and handed it to me. I studied it for a moment and then handed it to Cisco. He studied it a little longer and then nodded, giving it his official approval.

"Okay, Patrick, I need a driver," I said. "I provide the car and gas and insurance and you show up here every morning at nine to drive me wherever I need to go. I told you the pay schedule yesterday. You still interested?"

"I'm interested."

"Are you a safe driver?" Lorna asked.

"I've never had an accident." Patrick said.

I nodded my approval. They say an addict is best suited for spotting another addict. I was looking for signs that he was still using. Heavy eyelids, slow speech, avoidance of eye contact. But I didn't pick up on anything.

"When can you start?"

He shrugged.

"I don't have anything...I mean, whenever you want, I guess."

"How about we start right now? Today will be a test-drive. We'll see how you do and we can talk about it at the end of the day."

"Sounds good to me."

"Okay, well, we're going to get out of here and hit the road and I'll explain in the car how I like things to work."

"Cool."

He hooked his thumbs in his pockets and awaited the next move or instruction. He looked like he was about thirty but that was because of what the sun had done to his skin. I knew from the file that he was only twenty-four and still had a lot to learn.

Today the plan was to take him back to school.

17

We took the 10 out of downtown and headed west toward Malibu. I sat in the back and opened my computer on the fold-down table. While I waited for it to boot up I told Patrick Henson how it all worked.

"Patrick, I haven't had an office since I left the Public Defender's Office twelve years ago. My car is my office. I've got two other Lincolns just like this one. I keep them in rotation. Each one's got a printer and a fax and I've got a wireless card in my computer. Anything I have to do in an office I can do back here while I'm on the road to the next place. There are more than forty courthouses spread across L.A. County. Being mobile is the best way to do business."

"Cool," Patrick said. "I wouldn't want to be in an office either."

"Damn right," I said. "Too claustrophobic."

My computer was ready. I went to the file where I kept generic forms and motions and began to customize a pretrial motion to examine evidence.

"I'm working on your case right now, Patrick."

He looked at me in the mirror.

"What do you mean?"

"Well, I reviewed your file and there's something Mr. Vincent hadn't done that I think we need to do that may help."

"What's that?"

"Get an independent appraisal of the necklace you took. They list the value as twenty-five thousand and that bumps you up to a felony theft category. But it doesn't look like anybody ever challenged that."

"You mean like if the diamonds are bogus there's no felony?"

"It could work out like that. But I was thinking of something else, too."

"What?"

I pulled his file out of my bag so I could check a name.

"Let me ask you a few questions first, Patrick," I said. "What were you doing in that house where you took the necklace?"

He shrugged his shoulders.

"I was dating the old lady's youngest daughter. I met her on the beach and was sort of teaching her to surf. We went out a few times and hung out. One time there was a birthday party at the house and I was invited and the mother was given the necklace as a gift."

"That's when you learned its value."

"Yeah, the father said they were diamonds when he gave it to her. He was real proud of 'em."

"So then, the next time you were there at the house, you stole the necklace."

He didn't respond.

"It wasn't a question, Patrick. It's a fact. I'm your lawyer now and we need to discuss the facts of the case. Just don't ever lie to me or I won't be your lawyer anymore."

"Okay."

"So the next time you were in the house, you stole the necklace."

"Yeah."

"Tell me about it."

"We were there alone using the pool and I said I had to go to the can, only I really just wanted to check the medicine cabinet for pills. I was hurting. There weren't any in the bathroom downstairs so I went upstairs and looked around. I looked in the old lady's jewelry box and saw the necklace. I just took it."

He shook his head and I knew why. He was thoroughly embarrassed and defeated by the actions his addiction had made him take. I had been there myself and knew that looking back from sobriety was almost as scary as looking forward.

"It's all right, Patrick. Thank you for being honest. What did the guy say when you pawned it?"

"He said he'd only give me four bills because the chain was gold but he didn't think the diamonds were legit. I told him he was full of shit but what could I do? I took the money and went down to TJ. I needed the tabs and so I took what he was giving. I was so messed up on the stuff, I didn't care."

"What's the name of the girl? It's not in the file."

"Mandolin, like the instrument. Her parents call her Mandy."

"Have you talked to her since you were arrested?"

"No, man. We're done."

Now the eyes in the mirror looked sad and humiliated.

"Stupid," Henson said. "The whole thing was stupid."

I thought about things for a moment and then reached into my jacket pocket and pulled out a Polaroid photograph. I handed it over the seat and tapped Patrick on the shoulder with it.

"Take a look at that."

He took the photo and held it on top of the steering wheel while he looked at it.

"What the hell happened to you?" he asked.

"I tripped over a curb and did a nice face plant in front of my house. Broke a tooth and my nose, opened up my forehead pretty good, too. They took that picture for me in the ER. To carry around as a reminder."

"Of what?"

"I had just gotten out of my car after driving my eleven-year-old daughter home to her mother. By then I was up to three hundred twenty milligrams of OxyContin a day. Crushing and snorting first thing in the morning, except for me, the mornings were the afternoon."

I let him register that for a few moments before continuing.

"So, Patrick, you think what you did was stupid? I was driving my little girl around on three hundred twenty migs of hillbilly heroin."

Now I shook my head.

"There's nothing you can do about the past, Patrick. Except keep it there."

He was staring directly at me in the mirror.

"I'm going to help you get through the legal stuff," I said. "It's up to you to do the rest. And the rest is the hard part. But you already know that."

He nodded.

"Anyway, I see a ray of light here, Patrick. Something Jerry Vincent didn't see."

"What is it?"

"The victim's husband gave her that necklace. His name is Roger Vogler and he's a big supporter of lots of elected people in the county."

"Yeah, he's big into politics. Mandolin told me that. They hold fundraisers and stuff at the house."

"Well, if the diamonds on that necklace are phony, he's not going to want that coming up in court. Especially if his wife doesn't know."

"But how's he gonna stop it?"

"He's a contributor, Patrick. His contributions helped elect at least four members of the county board of supervisors. The county supervisors control the budget of the District Attorney's Office. The DA is prosecuting you. It's a food chain. If Dr. Vogler wants to send a message, believe me, it will be sent."

Henson nodded. He was beginning to see the light.

"The motion I'm going to file requests that we be allowed to independently examine and appraise the evidence, to wit, the diamond necklace. You never know, that word 'appraise' may stir things up. We'll just have to sit back and see what happens."

"Do we go to court to file it?"

"No. I'm going to write this thing up right now and send it to the court in an e-mail."

"That's cool!"

"The beauty of the Internet."

"Thanks, Mr. Haller."

"You're welcome, Patrick. Can I have my picture back now?"

He handed it over the seat and I took a look at it. I had a marble under my lip, and my nose was pointing in the wrong direction. There was also a bloody friction abrasion on my forehead. The eyes were the toughest part to study. Dazed and lost, staring unsteadily at the camera. This was me at my lowest point.

I put the photo back in my pocket for safekeeping.

We drove in silence for the next fifteen minutes while I finished the motion, went online, and sent it. It was definitely a shot across the prosecution's bow and it felt good. The Lincoln lawyer was back on the beat. The Lone Ranger was riding again.

I made sure I looked up from the computer when we hit the tunnel that marks the end of the freeway and dumps out onto the Pacific Coast Highway. I cracked the window open. I always loved the feeling I got when I'd swing out of the tunnel and see and smell the ocean.

We followed the PCH as it took us north to Malibu. It was hard for me to go back to the computer when I had the blue Pacific right outside my office window. I finally gave up, lowered the window all the way, and just rode.

Once we got past the mouth of Topanga Canyon I started seeing packs of surfers on the swells. I checked Patrick and saw him taking glances out toward the water.

"It said in the file you did your rehab at Crossroads in Antigua," I said.

"Yeah. The place Eric Clapton started."

"Nice?"

"As far as those places go, I suppose."

"True. Any waves there?"

"None to speak of. I didn't get much of a chance to use a board anyway. Did you do rehab?"

"Yeah, in Laurel Canyon."

"That place all the stars go to?"

"It was close to home."

"Yeah, well, I went the other way. I was as far from my friends and my home as possible. It worked."

"You thinking about going back into surfing?"

He glanced out the window before answering. A dozen surfers in wet suits were straddling their boards out there, waiting on the next set.

"I don't think so. At least not on a professional level. My shoulder's shot."

I was about to ask what he needed his shoulder for when he continued his answer.

"The paddling's one thing but the key thing is getting up. I lost my move when I fucked up my shoulder. Excuse the language."

"That's okay."

"Besides, I'm taking things one day at a time. They taught you that in Laurel Canyon, didn't they?"

"They did. But surfing's a one-day-at-a-time, one-wave-at-a-time sort of thing, isn't it?"

He nodded and I watched his eyes. They kept tripping to the mirror and looking back at me.

"What do you want to ask me, Patrick?"

"Um, yeah, I had a question. You know how Vincent kept my fish and put it on the wall?"

"Yeah."

"Well, I was, uh, wondering if he kept any of my boards somewhere."

I opened his file again and looked through it until I found the liquidator's report. It listed twelve surfboards and the prices obtained for them.

"You gave him twelve boards, right?"

"Yeah, all of them."

"Well, he gave them to his liquidator."

"What's that?"

"It's a guy he used when he took assets from clients — you know, jewelry, property, cars, mostly — and would turn them into cash to be applied toward his fee. According to the report here, the liquidator sold all twelve of them, took twenty percent and gave Vincent forty-eight hundred dollars."

Patrick nodded his head but didn't say anything. I watched him for a few moments and then looked back at the liquidator's inventory sheet. I remembered that Patrick had said in that first phone call that the two long boards were the most valuable. On the inventory, there were two boards described as ten feet long. Both were made by One World in Sarasota, Florida. One sold for $1,200 to a collector and the other for $400 on eBay, the online auction site. The disparity between the two sales made me think the eBay sale was bogus. The liquidator had probably sold the board to himself cheap. He would then turn around and sell it at a profit he'd keep for himself. Everybody's got an angle. Including me. I knew that if he hadn't resold the board yet, then I still had a shot at it.

"What if I could get you one of the long boards back?" I asked.

"That would be awesome! I just wish I had kept one, you know?"

"No promises. But I'll see what I can do."

I decided to pursue it later by putting my investigator on it. Cisco showing up and asking questions would probably make the liquidator more accommodating.

Patrick and I didn't speak for the rest of the ride. In another twenty minutes we pulled into the driveway of Walter Elliot's house. It was of Moorish design with white stone and dark brown shutters. The center facade rose into a tower silhouetted against the blue sky. A silver midlevel Mercedes was parked on the cobblestone pavers. We parked next to it.

"You want me to wait here?" Patrick asked.

"Yeah. I don't think I'll take too long."

"I know this house. It's all glass in the back. I tried to surf behind it a couple times but it closes out on the inside and the rip's really bad."

"Pop the trunk for me."

I got out and went to the back to retrieve my digital camera. I turned it on to make sure I had some battery power and took a quick shot of the front of the house. The camera was working and I was good to go.

I walked to the entrance and the front door opened before I could push the bell. Mrs. Albrecht stood there, looking as lovely as I had seen her the day before.

18

When Walter Elliot had told me he would have someone meet me at the house in Malibu, I hadn't expected it to be his executive assistant.

"Mrs. Albrecht, how are you today?"

"Very well. I just got here and thought maybe I had missed you."

"Nope. I just got here too."

"Come in, please."

The house had a two-story entry area below the tower. I looked up and saw a wrought-iron chandelier hanging in the atrium. There were cobwebs on it, and I wondered if they had formed because the house had gone unused since the murders or because the chandelier was too high up and too hard to get to with a duster.

"This way," Mrs. Albrecht said.

I followed her into the great room, which was larger than my entire home. It was a complete entertainment area with a glass wall on the western exposure that brought the Pacific right into the house.

"Beautiful," I said.

"It is indeed. Do you want to see the bedroom?"

Ignoring the question, I turned the camera on and took a few shots of the living room and its view.

"Do you know who has been in here since the Sheriff's Department relinquished control of it?" I asked.

Mrs. Albrecht thought for a moment before answering.

"Very few people. I do not believe that Mr. Elliot has been out here. But, of course, Mr. Vincent came out once and his investigator came out a couple of times, I believe. And the Sheriff's Department has come back twice since turning the property back over to Mr. Elliot. They had search warrants."

Copies of the search warrants were in the case file. Both times they were looking for only one thing—the murder weapon. The case against Elliot was all circumstantial, even with the gunshot residue on his hands. They needed the murder weapon to ice the case but they didn't have it. The notes in the file said that divers had searched the waters behind the house for two days after the murders but had also failed to come up with the gun.

"What about cleaners?" I asked. "Did someone come in and clean the place up?"

"No, no one like that. We were told by Mr. Vincent to leave things as they were in case he needed to use the place during the trial."

There was no mention in the case files of Vincent possibly using the house in any way during the trial. I wasn't sure what the thinking would have been there. My instinctive response upon seeing the place was that I wouldn't want a jury anywhere near it. The view and sheer opulence of the property would underline Elliot's wealth and serve to disconnect him from the jurors. They would understand that they weren't really a jury of his peers. They would know that he was from a completely different planet.

"Where's the master suite?" I asked.

"It comprises the entire top floor."

"Then, let's go up."

As we went up a winding white staircase with an ocean-blue banister, I asked Mrs. Albrecht what her first name was. I told her I felt uncomfortable being so formal with her, especially when her boss and I were on a first-name basis.

"My name is Nina. You can call me that if you want."

"Good. And you can call me Mickey."

The stairs led to a door that opened into a bedroom suite the size of some courtrooms I had been in. It was so big it had twin fireplaces on the north and south walls. There was a sitting area, a sleeping area, and his-and-her bathrooms. Nina Albrecht pushed a button near the door, and the curtains covering the west view silently began to split and reveal a wall of glass that looked out over the sea.

The custom-made bed was double the size of a regular king. It had been stripped of the top mattress and all linens and pillows and I assumed these had been taken for forensic analysis. In two locations in the room, six-foot-square segments of carpet had been cut out, again, I believed, for the collection and analysis of blood evidence.

On the wall next to the door, there were blood-spatter marks that had been circled and marked with letter codes by investigators. There were no other signs of the violence that had occurred in the room.

I walked to the corner by the glass wall and looked back into the room. I raised the camera and took a few shots from different angles. Nina walked into the shot a couple times but it didn't matter. The photos weren't for court. I would use them to refresh my memory of the place while I was working out the trial strategy.

A murder scene is a map. If you know how to read it, you can sometimes find your way. The lay of the land, the repose of victims in death, the angle of views and light and blood. The spatial restrictions and geometric differentiations were all elements of the map. You can't always get all of that from a police photo. Sometimes you have to see it for yourself. This is why I had come to the house in Malibu. For the map. For the geography of murder. When I understood it, I would be ready to go to trial.

From the corner, I looked at the square cut out of the white carpet near the bedroom door. This is where the male victim, Johan Rilz, had been shot down. My eyes traveled to the bed, where Mitzi Elliot had been shot, her naked body sprawled diagonally across it.

The investigative summary in the file suggested that the naked couple had heard an intruder in the house. Rilz went to the bedroom door and opened it, only to be immediately surprised by the killer. Rilz was shot down in the doorway and the killer stepped over his body and into the room.

Mitzi Elliot jumped up from the bed and stood frozen by its side, clutching a pillow in front of her naked body. The state believed that the elements of the crime suggested that she knew her killer. She might have pleaded for her life or might have known her death could not be stopped. She was shot twice through the pillow from a distance estimated at three feet and knocked back onto the bed. The pillow she had used as a shield fell to the floor. The killer then stepped forward to the bed and pressed the barrel of the gun against her forehead for the kill shot.

That was the official version anyway. Standing there in the corner of the room, I knew there were enough unfounded assumptions built into it that I would have no trouble slicing and dicing it at trial.

I looked at the glass doors that led out to a deck overlooking the Pacific. There had been nothing in the files about whether the curtain and doors had been open at the time of the murders. I was not sure it meant anything one way or the other but it was a detail I would've liked to know.

I walked over to the glass doors and found them locked. I had a hard time figuring out how to open them. Nina finally came over and helped me, holding her finger down on a safety lever while turning the bolt with her other hand. The doors opened outward and brought in the sounds of the crashing surf.

I immediately knew that if the doors had been open at the time of the murders, then the sound of the surf could have easily drowned out any noise an intruder might have made in the house. This would contradict the state's theory that Rilz was killed at the bedroom door because he had gone to the door after hearing an intruder. It would then raise a new question about what Rilz was doing naked at the door, but that didn't matter to the defense. I only needed to raise questions and point out discrepancies to plant the seed of doubt in a juror's mind. It took only one doubt in one juror's mind for me to be successful. It was the distort-or-destroy method of criminal defense.

I stepped out onto the deck. I didn't know if it was high or low tide but suspected it was somewhere in between. The water was close. The waves were coming in and washing right up to the piers on which the house was built.

There were six-foot swells but no surfers out there. I remembered what Patrick had said about attempting to surf in the cove.

I walked back inside, and as soon as I reentered the bedroom, I realized my phone was ringing but I had been unable to hear it because of the ocean noise. I checked to see who it was but it said private caller on the screen. I knew that most people in law enforcement blocked their ID.

"Nina, I have to take this. Do you mind going out to my car and asking my driver to come in?"

"No problem."

"Thank you."

I took the call.

"Hello?"

"It's me. I'm just checking to see when you're coming by."

"Me" was my first ex-wife, Maggie McPherson. Under the recently revamped custody agreement, I got to be with my daughter on Wednesday nights and every other weekend only. It was a long way from the shared custody we'd once had. But I had blown that along with the second chance I'd had with Maggie.

"Probably around seven thirty. I have a meeting with a client this afternoon and it might run a little late."

There was silence and I sensed I had given the wrong answer.

"What, you've got a date?" I asked. "What time you want me there?"

"I'm supposed to leave at seven thirty."

"Then, I'll be there before that. Who's the lucky guy?"

"That wouldn't be any of your business. But speaking of lucky, I heard you got Jerry Vincent's whole practice."

Nina Albrecht and Patrick Henson entered the bedroom. I saw Patrick looking at the missing square in the carpet. I covered the phone and asked them to go back downstairs and wait for me. I then went back to the phone conversation. My ex-wife was a deputy district attorney assigned to the Van Nuys courthouse. This put her in a position to hear things about me.

"That's right," I said. "I'm his replacement, but I don't know how lucky that makes me."

"You should get a good ride on the Elliot case."

"I'm standing in the murder house right now. Nice view."

"Well, good luck in getting him off. If anyone can, it's certainly you."

She said it with a prosecutor's sneer.

"I guess I won't respond to that."

"I know how you would anyway. One other thing. You're not going to have company over tonight, are you?"

"What are you talking about?"

"I'm talking about two weeks ago. Hayley said a woman was there. I believe her name was Lanie? She felt very awkward about it."

"Don't worry, she won't be there tonight. She's just a friend and she used the guest room. But for the record, I can have anybody I want over at my house at any time because it's *my* house, and you are free to do the same at your house."

"And I'm also free to go to the judge and say you're exposing our daughter to people who are drug addicts."

I took a deep breath before responding as calmly as I could.

"How would you know who I am exposing Hayley to?"

"Because your daughter isn't stupid and her hearing is perfect. She told me a little bit of what was said and it was quite easy to figure out that your...friend is from rehab."

"And so that's a crime, consorting with people from rehab?"

"It's not a crime, Michael. I just don't think it is best for Hayley to be exposed to a parade of addicts when she stays with you."

"Now it's a parade. I guess the one addict you're most concerned with is me."

"Well, if the shoe fits..."

I almost lost it but once again calmed myself by gulping down some of the fresh sea air. When I spoke I was calm. I knew that showing anger would only hurt me in the long run when it came time to readdress the custody arrangement.

"Maggie, this is our daughter we're talking about here. Don't hurt her by trying to hurt me. She needs her father and I need my daughter."

"And that's my point. You are doing well. Hooking up with an addict is not a good idea."

I was squeezing my phone so hard I thought it might break. I could feel the scarlet burn of embarrassment on my cheeks and neck.

"I have to go."

My words came out strangled by my own failures.

"And so do I. I'll tell Hayley you'll be there by seven thirty."

She always did that, ended the call with inferences that I would disappoint my daughter if I was late or couldn't make a scheduled pickup. She hung up before I could respond.

The living room downstairs was empty but then I saw Patrick and Nina out on the lower deck. I stepped out and over to the railing where Patrick stood staring at the waves. I tried to put the upset from the conversation with my ex-wife out of my head.

"Patrick, you said you tried surfing here but the rip was too strong?"

"That's right."

"Are you talking about a riptide?"

"Yeah, it's tough out here. The shape of the cove creates it. The energy of the waves coming in on the north side is redirected under the surface and sort of ricochets south. It follows the contour of the cove and carries it all the way down and then out. I got caught in that pipeline a couple times, man. It took me all the way out past those rocks at the south end."

I studied the cove as he described what was happening beneath the surface. If he was right and there was a riptide on the day of the murders, then the sheriff's divers had probably searched in the wrong place for the murder weapon.

And now it was too late. If the killer had thrown the gun into the surf, it could have been carried in the underwater pipeline completely out of the cove and out to sea. I began to feel confident that the murder weapon would not be making a surprise appearance at trial.

As far as my client was concerned, that was a good thing.

I stared out at the waves and thought about how beneath the beautiful surface a hidden power never stopped moving.

19

The writers had taken the day off or moved their picket line to another protest location. At Archway Studios we made it through the security checkpoint without any of the delay of the day before. It helped that Nina Albrecht was in the car in front of us and had smoothed the way.

It was late and the studio was emptying out for the day. Patrick was able to get a parking spot right in front of Elliot's bungalow. Patrick was excited because he had never been inside the gates of a movie studio. I told him he was free to look around but to keep his phone handy because I was unsure how long the meeting with my client would last and I needed to stick to a schedule for picking up my daughter.

As I followed Nina in I asked her if there was a place for me to meet with Elliot other than his office. I said I had paperwork to spread out and that the table we had sat at the day before was too small. She said she would take me to the executive boardroom and I could set up there while she went to get her boss and bring him to the meeting. I said that would be fine. But the truth was I wasn't going to spread documents out. I just wanted to meet with Elliot in a neutral spot. If I was sitting across from him at his worktable, he would have command of the meeting. That was made clear during our first encounter. Elliot was a forceful personality. But I needed to be the one in charge from here on out.

It was a big room with twelve black leather chairs around the polished oval table. There was an overhead projector and a long box on the far wall containing the drop-down screen. The other walls were hung with framed posters of the movies that had been made on the lot. I assumed that these were the films that had made the studio money.

I took a seat and pulled the case files out of my bag. Twenty-five minutes later I was looking through the state's discovery documents when the door opened and Elliot finally walked in. I didn't bother to get up or extend my hand. I tried to look annoyed as I pointed him to a chair across the table from me.

Nina trailed him into the room to see what she could get us for refreshment.

"Nothing, Nina," I said before Elliot could respond. "We're going to be fine and we need to get started. We'll let you know if we need anything."

She seemed momentarily taken aback by the issuance of orders from someone other than Elliot. She looked to him for clarification and he simply nodded. She left, closing the double doors behind her. Elliot sat down in the chair I had pointed him to.

I looked across the table at my client for a long moment before speaking.

"I can't figure you out, Walter."

"What do you mean? What's to figure out?"

"Well, for starters, you spend a lot of time protesting your innocence. But I don't think you are taking this that seriously."

"You're wrong about that."

"Am I? You understand that if you lose this trial, you are going to prison? And there won't be any bail on a double-murder conviction while you appeal. You get a bad verdict and they'll cuff you in the courtroom and take you away."

Elliot leaned a few inches toward me before responding again.

"I understand exactly the position I am in. So don't dare tell me I am not taking it seriously."

"Okay, then, when we set a meeting, let's be on time for it. There is a lot of ground to cover and not a lot of time to cover it. I know you have a studio to run but that is no longer the priority. For the next two weeks you have one priority. This case."

Now he looked at me for a long moment before responding. It may have been the first time in his life he had been chided for being late and then told what to do. Finally, he nodded.

"Fair enough," he said.

I nodded back. Our positions were now understood. We were in his boardroom and on his studio lot, but I was the alpha dog now. His future depended on me.

"Good," I said. "Now, the first thing I need to ask is whether we are speaking privately in here."

"Of course we are."

"Well, we weren't yesterday. It was pretty clear that Nina's got your office wired. That may be fine for your movie meetings but it's not fine when we're discussing your case. I'm your lawyer, and no one should hear our discussion. No one. Nina has no privilege. She could be subpoenaed to testify against you. In fact, it won't surprise me if she ends up on the prosecution's witness list."

Elliot leaned back in his padded chair and raised his face toward the ceiling.

"Nina," he said. "Mute the feed. If I need anything I will call you on the line."

He looked at me and opened his hands. I nodded that I was satisfied.

"Thank you, Walter. Now let's get to work."

"I have a question first."

"Sure."

"Is this the meeting where I tell you I didn't do it and then you tell me that it doesn't matter to you whether I did it or not?"

I nodded.

"Whether you did it or not is irrelevant, Walter. It's what the state can prove beyond a—"

"No!"

He slammed an open palm down on the table. It sounded like a shot. I was startled but hoped I didn't show it.

"I am tired of that legal bullshit! That it doesn't matter whether I did it, only what can be proved. It does matter! Don't you see? It does matter. I need to be believed, goddamnit! I need *you* to believe me. I don't care what the evidence is against me. I did *NOT* do this. Do you understand me? Do you believe me? If my own lawyer doesn't believe me or care, then I don't have a chance."

I was sure Nina was going to come charging in to see if everything was all right. I leaned back in my padded chair and waited for her and to make sure Elliot was finished.

As expected, one of the doors opened and Nina was about to step in. But Elliot dismissed her with a wave of his hand and a harsh command not to bother us. The door closed again and he locked eyes with me. I held my hand up to stop him from speaking. It was my turn.

"Walter, there are two things I have to concern myself with," I said calmly. "Whether I understand the state's case and whether I can knock it down."

I tapped a finger on the discovery file as I spoke.

"At the moment I do understand the state's case. It's straightforward prosecution one-oh-one. The state believes that they have motive and opportunity in spades.

"Let's go with motive first. Your wife was having an affair and that made you angry. Not only that, but the prenuptial agreement she signed twelve years before had vested and the only way you could get rid of her without splitting everything up was to kill her. Next is opportunity. They have the time your car left through the gate at Archway that morning. They've made the run and timed it again and again and say you could've easily been at the Malibu house at the time of the killings. That is opportunity.

"And what the state is counting on is motive and opportunity being enough to sway the jury and win the day, while the actual evidence against you is quite thin and very circumstantial. So my job is to figure out a way of making the jury understand that there is a lot of smoke here but no real fire. If I do that, then you walk away."

"I still want to know if you believe I am innocent."

I smiled and shook my head.

"Walter, I'm telling you, it doesn't matter."

"It does to me. One way or the other, I need to know."

I relented and held my hands up in surrender.

"All right, then, I'll tell you what I think, Walter. I have studied the file forwards and backwards. I've read everything in here at least twice and most of it three times. I have now been out to the beach house where this unfortunate event happened and studied the geography of these murders. I have done all of that and I can see the very real possibility that you are innocent of these charges. Does that mean that I believe that you are an innocent man? No, Walter, it doesn't. I'm sorry but I have been doing this too long, and the reality is, I haven't seen too many innocent clients. So the best I can tell you is that I don't know. If that's not good enough for you, then I am sure you will have no trouble finding a lawyer who will tell you exactly what you want to hear, whether he believes it or not."

I rocked back in my chair while awaiting his response. He clasped his hands together on the table in front of him while he chewed on my words and then he finally nodded.

"Then, I guess that is the best I can ask for," he said.

I tried to let out my breath without his noticing. I still had the case. For the moment.

"But you know what I do believe, Walter?"

"What do you believe?"

"That you're holding out on me."

"Holding out? What are you talking about?"

"There's something I don't know about this case and you are holding back on it with me."

"I don't know what you are talking about."

"You are too confident, Walter. It's like you know you are going to walk."

"I *am* going to walk. I'm innocent."

"Being innocent is not enough. Innocent men sometimes get convicted and deep down everybody knows it. That's why I've never met a truly innocent man who wasn't scared. Scared that the system won't work right, that it's built to find guilty people guilty and not innocent people innocent. That's what you're missing, Walter. You're not scared."

"I don't know what you're talking about. Why should I be scared?"

I stared across the table at him, trying to read him. I knew my instincts were right. There was something I didn't know, something that I had missed in the files or that Vincent had carried in his head instead of his files. Whatever it was, Elliot wasn't sharing it with me yet.

For now that was okay. Sometimes you don't want to know what your client knows, because once the smoke comes out of the bottle, you can't put it back in.

"All right, Walter," I said. "To be continued. Meantime, let's go to work."

Without waiting for a reply I opened the defense file and looked at the notes I had written on the inside flap.

"I think we're set in terms of witnesses and strategy when it comes to the state's case. What I have not found in the file is a solid strategy for putting forth your defense."

"What do you mean?" Elliot asked. "Jerry told me we were ready."

"Maybe not, Walter. I know it's not something you want to see or hear but I found this in the file."

I slid a two-page document across the polished table to him. He glanced at it but didn't really look at it.

"What is it?"

"That is a motion for a continuance. Jerry drew it up but hadn't filed it. But it seems clear that he wanted to delay the trial. The coding on the motion indicates he printed it out Monday—just a few hours before he was killed."

Elliot shook his head and shoved the document back across the table.

"No, we talked about it and he agreed with me to move forward on schedule."

"That was Monday?"

"Yes, Monday. The last time I talked to him."

I nodded. That covered one of the questions I had. Vincent kept billing records in each of his files, and I had noted in the Elliot file that he had billed an hour on the day of his murder.

"Was that a conference at his office or yours?"

"It was a phone call. Monday afternoon. He'd left a message earlier and I called him back. Nina can get you the exact time if you need it."

"He has it down here at three. He talked to you about a delay?"

"That's right but I told him no delay."

Vincent had billed an hour. I wondered how long he and Elliot had sparred over the delay.

"Why did he want a continuance?" I asked.

"He just wanted more time to prepare and maybe pad his bill. I told him we were ready, like I'm telling you. We are ready!"

I sort of laughed and shook my head.

"The thing is, you're not the lawyer here, Walter. I am. And that's what I'm trying to tell you, I'm not seeing much here in terms of a defense strategy. I think that's why Jerry wanted to delay the trial. He didn't have a case."

"No, it's the prosecution that doesn't have the case."

I was growing tired of Elliot and his insistence on calling the legal shots.

"Let me explain how this works," I said wearily. "And forgive me if you know all of this, Walter. It's going to be a two-part trial, okay? The prosecutor goes first and he lays out his case. We get a chance to attack it as he goes. Then we get our shot and that's when we put up our evidence and alternate theories of the crime."

"Okay."

"And what I can tell from my study of the files is that Jerry Vincent was relying more on the prosecution's case than on a defense case. There are—"

"How so?"

"What I'm saying is that he's locked and loaded on the prosecution side.

He has counter witnesses and cross-examination plans ready for every-thing the prosecution is going to put forward. But I'm missing something on the defense side of the equation. We've got no alibi, no alternate sus-pects, no alternate theories, nothing. At least nothing in the file. And that's what I mean when I say we have no case. Did he ever discuss with you how he planned to roll out the defense?"

"No. We were going to have that conversation but then he got killed. He told me that he was working all of that out. He said he had the magic bullet and the less I knew, the better. He was going to tell me when we got closer to trial but he never did. He never got the chance."

I knew the term. The "magic bullet" was your get-out-of-jail-and-go-home card. It was the witness or piece of evidence that you had in your back pocket that was going to either knock all the evidence down like dominoes or firmly and permanently fix reasonable doubt in the mind of every juror on the panel. If Vincent had a magic bullet, he hadn't noted it in the case file. And if he had a magic bullet, why was he talking about a delay on Monday?

"You have no idea what this magic bullet was?" I asked Elliot.

"Just what he told me, that he found something that was going to blow the state out of the water."

"That doesn't make sense if on Monday he was talking about delaying the trial."

Elliot shrugged.

"I told you, he just wanted more time to be prepared. Probably more time to charge me more money. But I told him, when we make a movie, we pick a date, and that movie comes out on that date no matter what. I told him we were going to trial without delay."

I nodded my head at Elliot's no-delay mantra. But my mind was on Vin-cent's missing laptop. Was the magic bullet in there? Had he saved his plan on the computer and not put it into the hard file? Was the magic bullet the reason for his murder? Had his discovery been so sensitive or dangerous that someone had killed him for it?

I decided to move on with Elliot while I had him in front of me.

"Well, Walter, I don't have the magic bullet. But if Jerry could find it, then so can I. I will."

I checked my watch and tried to give the outward appearance that I was not troubled by not knowing what was assuredly the key element in the case.

"Okay. Let's talk about an alternate theory."

"Meaning what?"

"Meaning that the state has its theory and we should have ours. The state's theory is that you were upset over your wife's infidelity and what it would cost you to divorce her. So you went out to Malibu and killed both your wife and her lover. You then got rid of the murder weapon in some way—either hid it or threw it into the ocean—and then called nine-one-one to report that you had discovered the murders. That theory gives them all they need. Motive and opportunity. But to back it up they have the GSR and almost nothing else."

"GSR?"

"Gunshot residue. Their evidentiary case—what little there is—firmly rests on it."

"That test was a false positive!" Elliot said forcefully. "I never shot any weapon. And Jerry told me he was bringing in the top expert in the country to knock it all down. A woman from John Jay in New York. She'll testify that the sheriff's lab procedures were sloppy and lax, prone to come up with the false positive."

I nodded. I liked the fervor of his denial. It could be useful if he testified.

"Yes, Dr. Arslanian—we still have her coming in," I said. "But she's no magic bullet, Walter. The prosecution will counter with their own expert saying exactly the opposite—that the lab is well run and that all procedures were followed. At best, the GSR will be a wash. The prosecution will still be leaning heavily on motive and opportunity."

"What motive? I loved her and I didn't even know about Rilz. I thought he was a faggot."

I held my hands up in a slow-it-down gesture.

"Look, do yourself a favor, Walter, and don't call him that. In court or anywhere else. If it is appropriate to reference his sexual orientation, you say you thought he was gay. Okay?"

"Okay."

"Now, the prosecution will simply say that you did know Johan Rilz was your wife's lover, and they'll trot out evidence and testimony that will indicate that a divorce forced by your wife's infidelity would cost you in excess of a hundred million dollars and possibly dilute your control of the studio. They plant all of that in the jury's minds and you start having a pretty good motivation for murder."

"And it's all bullshit."

"And I'll be able to potshot the hell out of it at trial. A lot of their positives can be turned into negatives. It will be a dance, Walter. We'll trade punches. We'll try to distort and destroy but ultimately they'll land more punches than we can block and that's why we're the underdog and why it's always good for the defense to float an alternate theory. We give the jury a plausible explanation for why these two people were killed. We throw suspicion away from you and at somebody else."

"Like the one-armed man in *The Fugitive*?"

I shook my head.

"Not exactly."

I remembered the movie and the television show before it. In both cases, there actually was a one-armed man. I was talking about a smoke screen, an alternate theory concocted by the defense because I wasn't buying into Elliot's "I-am-innocent rap"—at least not yet.

There was a buzzing sound and Elliot took a phone out of his pocket and looked at the screen.

"Walter, we have work here," I said.

He didn't take the call and reluctantly put the phone away. I continued.

"Okay, during the prosecution phase we are going to use cross-examination to make one thing crystal clear to the jury. That is, that once that GSR test came back positive on you, then —"

"False positive!"

"Whatever. The point is, once they had what they believed was a positive indication that you had very recently fired a weapon, all bets were off. A wide-open investigation became very tightly focused on one thing. You. It went from what they call a full-field investigation to a full investigation of you. So, what happened is that they left a lot of stones unturned. For example, Rilz had only been in this country four years. Not a single investigator went to Germany to check on his background and whether he had any enemies back there who wanted him dead. That's just one thing. They didn't thoroughly background the guy in L.A. either. This was a man who was allowed entry into the homes and lives of some of the wealthiest women in this city. Excuse my bluntness, but was he banging other married clients, or just your wife? Were there other important and powerful men he could have angered, or just you?"

Elliot didn't respond to the crude questions. I had asked them that way on purpose, to see if it got a rise out of him or any reaction that contradicted his statements of loving his wife. But he showed no reaction either way.

"You see what I'm getting at, Walter? The focus, from almost the very start, was on you. When it's the defense's turn, we're going to put it on Rilz. And from that we'll grow doubts like stalks in a cornfield."

Elliot nodded thoughtfully as he looked down at his reflection in the polished tabletop.

"But this can't be the magic bullet Jerry told you about," I said. "And there are risks in going after Rilz."

Elliot raised his eyes to mine.

"Because the prosecutor knows this was a deficiency when the investigators brought in the case. He's had five months to anticipate that we might go this way, and if he is good, as I am sure he is, then he's been quietly getting ready for us to go in this direction."

"Wouldn't that come out in the discovery material?"

"Not always. There is an art to discovery. Most of the time it's what is not in the discovery file that is important and that you have to watch out for. Jeffrey Golantz is a seasoned pro. He knows just what he has to put in and what he can keep for himself."

"You know Golantz? You've gone to trial against him before?"

"I don't know him and have never gone up against him. It's his reputation I know. He's never lost at trial. He's something like twenty-seven and oh."

I checked my watch. The time had passed quickly and I needed to keep things moving if I was going to pick my daughter up on time.

"Okay," I said. "There are a couple other things we need to cover. Let's talk about whether you testify."

"That's not a question. That's a given. I want to clear my name. The jury will want me to say I did not do this."

"I knew you were going to say that and I appreciate the fervor I see in your denials. But your testimony has to be more than that. It has to offer an explanation and that's where we can get into trouble."

"I don't care."

"Did you kill your wife and her lover?"

"No!"

"Then why did you go out there to the house?"

"I was suspicious. If she was there with somebody, I was going to confront her and throw him out on his ass."

"You expect this jury to believe that a man who runs a billion-dollar movie studio took the afternoon off to drive out to Malibu to spy on his wife?"

"No, I'm no spy. I had suspicions and went out there to see for myself."

"And to confront her with a gun?"

Elliot opened his mouth to speak but then hesitated and didn't respond.

"You see, Walter?" I said. "You get up there and you open yourself up to anything—most of it not good."

He shook his head.

"I don't care. It's a given. Guilty guys don't testify. Everybody knows it. I'm testifying that I did not do this."

He poked a finger at me with each syllable of the last sentence. I still liked his forcefulness. He was believable. Maybe he could survive on the stand.

"Well, ultimately it is your decision," I said. "We'll get you prepared to testify but we won't make the decision until we get into the defense phase of the trial and we see where we stand."

"It's decided now. I'm testifying."

His face began to turn a deep shade of crimson. I had to tread lightly here. I didn't want him to testify but it was unethical for me to forbid it. It was a client decision, and if he ever claimed I took it away from him or refused to let him testify, I would have the bar swarming me like angry bees.

"Look, Walter," I said. "You're a powerful man. You run a studio and make movies and put millions of dollars on the line every day. I understand all of that. You are used to making decisions with nobody questioning them. But when we go into trial, I'm the boss. And while it will be you who makes this decision, I need to know that you are listening to me and considering my counsel. There's no use going further if you don't."

He rubbed his hand roughly across his face. This was hard for him.

"Okay. I understand. We make a final decision on this later."

He said it grudgingly. It was a concession he didn't want to make. No man wants to relinquish his power to another.

"Okay, Walter," I said. "I think that puts us on the same page."

I checked my watch again. There were a few more things on my list and I still had some time.

"Okay, let's move on," I said.

"Please."

"I want to add a couple people to the defense team. They will be ex—"

"No. I told you, the more lawyers a defendant has, the guiltier he looks. Look at Barry Bonds. Tell me people don't think he's guilty. He's got more lawyers than teammates."

"Walter, you didn't let me finish. These are not lawyers I'm talking about, and when we go to trial, I promise it is going to be just you and me sitting at the table."

"Then, who do you want to add?"

"A jury-selection consultant and somebody to work with you on image and testimony, all of that."

"No jury consultant. Makes it look like you're trying to rig things."

"Look, the person I want to hire will be sitting out in the gallery. No one will notice her. She plays poker for a living and just reads people's faces and looks for tells—little giveaways. That's it."

"No, I won't pay for that mumbo jumbo."

"Are you sure, Walter?"

I spent five minutes trying to convince him, telling him that picking the jury might be the most important part of the trial. I stressed that in circumstantial cases the priority had to be in picking jurors with open minds, ones who didn't believe that just because the police or prosecution say something, it's automatically true. I told him that I prided myself on my skills in picking a jury but that I could use the help of an expert who knew how to read faces and gestures. At the end of my plea Elliot simply shook his head.

"Mumbo jumbo. I will trust your skills."

I studied him for a moment and decided we'd talked enough for the day. I would bring up the rest with him the next time. I had come to realize that while he was paying lip service to the idea that I was the trial boss, there was no doubt that he was firmly in charge of things.

And I couldn't help but believe it might lead him straight to prison.

20

By the time I dropped Patrick back at his car in downtown and headed to the Valley in heavy evening traffic, I knew I was going to be late and would tip off another confrontation with my ex-wife. I called to let her know but she didn't pick up and I left a message. When I finally got to her apartment complex in Sherman Oaks it was almost seven forty and I found mother and daughter out at the curb, waiting. Hayley had her head down and was looking at the sidewalk. I noticed she had begun to adopt this posture whenever her parents came into close proximity of one another. It was like she was just standing on the transporter circle and waiting to be beamed far away from us.

I popped the locks as I pulled to a stop, and Maggie helped Hayley into the back with her school backpack and her overnight bag.

"Thanks for being on time," she said in a flat voice.

"No problem," I said, just to see if it would put the flares in her eyes. "Must be a hot date if you're waiting out here for me."

"No, not really. Parent-teacher conference at the school."

That got through my defenses and hit me in the jaw.

"You should've told me. We could've gotten a babysitter and gone together."

"I'm not a baby," Hayley said from behind me.

"We tried that," Maggie said from my left. "Remember? You jumped on the teacher so badly about Hayley's math grade—the circumstance of which you knew nothing about—that they asked me to handle communications with the school."

The incident sounded only vaguely familiar. It had been safely locked away somewhere in my oxycodone-corrupted memory banks. But I felt the burn of embarrassment on my face and neck. I didn't have a comeback.

"I have to go," Maggie said quickly. "Hayley, I love you. Be good for your father and I'll see you tomorrow."

"Okay, Mom."

I stared out the window for a moment at my ex-wife before pulling away.

"Give 'em hell, Maggie McFierce," I said.

I pulled away from the curb and put my window up. My daughter asked me why her mother was nicknamed Maggie McFierce.

"Because when she goes into battle, she always knows she is going to win," I said.

"What battle?"

"Any battle."

We drove silently down Ventura Boulevard and stopped for dinner at DuPar's. It was my daughter's favorite place to eat dinner because I always let her order pancakes. Somehow, the kid thought ordering breakfast for dinner was crossing some line and it made her feel rebellious and brave.

I ordered a BLT with Thousand Island dressing on it and, considering my last cholesterol count, figured I was the one being rebellious and brave. We did her homework together, which was a breeze for her and taxing for me, then I asked her what she wanted to do. I was willing to do anything—a movie, the mall, whatever she wanted—but I was hoping she'd just want to go home to my place and hang out, maybe pull out some old family scrapbooks and look at the yellowed photos.

She hesitated in responding and I thought I knew why.

"There's nobody staying at my place if that's what you're worried about, Hay. The lady you met, Lanie? She doesn't visit me anymore."

"You mean like she's not your girlfriend anymore?"

"She never was my girlfriend. She was a friend. Remember when I stayed in the hospital last year? I met her there and we became friends. We try to watch out for each other, and every now and then she comes over when she doesn't want to stay home alone."

It was the shaded truth. Lanie Ross and I had met in rehab during group therapy. We continued the relationship after leaving the program but never consummated it as a romance, because we were emotionally incapable of it. The addiction had cauterized those nerve endings and they were slow to come back. We spent time with each other and were there for each other— a two-person support group. But once we were back in the real world, I began to recognize in Lanie a weakness. I instinctively knew she wasn't going to go the distance and I couldn't make the journey with her. There are three roads that can be taken in recovery. There is the clean path of sobriety and there is the road to relapse. The third way is the fast out. It is when the traveler realizes that relapse is just a slow suicide and there is no reason to wait. I didn't know which of those second two roads Lanie would go down but I couldn't follow either one. We finally went our separate ways, the day after Hayley had met her.

"You know, Hayley, you can always tell me if you don't like something or there's something I am doing that is bothering you."

"I know."

"Good."

We were silent for a few moments and I thought she wanted to say something else. I gave her the time to work up to it.

"Hey Dad?"

"What, baby?"

"If that lady wasn't your girlfriend, does that mean you and Mom might get back together?"

The question left me without words for a few moments. I could see the hope in Hayley's eyes and wanted her to see the same in mine.

"I don't know, Hay. I messed things up pretty good when we tried that last year."

Now the pain entered her eyes, like the shadows of clouds on the ocean.

"But I'm still working on it, baby," I said quickly. "We just have to take it one day at a time. I'm trying to show her that we should be a family again."

She didn't respond. She looked down at her plate.

"Okay, baby?"

"Okay."

"Did you decide what you want to do?"

"I think I just want to go home and watch TV."

"Good. That's what I want to do."

We packed up her schoolbooks and I put money down on the bill. On the drive over the hill, she said her mother had told her I had gotten an important new job. I was surprised but happy.

"Well, it's sort of a new job. I'm going back to work doing what I always did. But I have a lot of new cases and one big one. Did your mom tell you that?"

"She said you had a big case and everybody would be jealous but you would do real good."

"She said that?"

"Yeah."

I drove for a while, thinking about that and what it might mean. Maybe I hadn't entirely blown things with Maggie. She still respected me on some level. Maybe that meant something.

"Um..."

I looked at my daughter in the rearview mirror. It was dark out now but I could see her eyes looking out the window and away from mine. Children are so easy to read sometimes. If only grown-ups were the same.

"What's up, Hay?"

"Um, I was just wondering, sort of, why you can't do what Mom does."

"What do you mean?"

"Like putting bad people in jail. She said your big case is with a man who killed two people. It's like you're always working for the bad guys."

I was quiet for a moment before finding my words.

"The man I am defending is accused of killing two people, Hayley. Nobody has proved he did anything wrong. Right now he's not guilty of anything."

She didn't respond and her skepticism was almost palpably emanating from the backseat. So much for the innocence of children.

"Hayley, what I do is just as important as what your mother does. When somebody is accused of a crime in our country, they are entitled to defend themselves. What if at school you were accused of cheating and you knew that you didn't cheat? Wouldn't you want to be able to explain and defend yourself?"

"I think so."

"I think so, too. It's like that with the courts. If you get accused of a crime, you can have a lawyer like me help you explain and defend yourself. The laws are very complicated and it's hard for someone to do it by themselves when they don't know all the rules of evidence and things like that. So I help them. It doesn't mean I agree with them or what they have done — if they have done it. But it's part of the system. An important part."

The explanation felt hollow to me as I said it. On an intellectual level I understood and believed the argument, every word of it. But on a father-daughter level I felt like one of my clients, squirming on the witness stand. How could I get her to believe it when I wasn't sure I believed it anymore myself?

"Have you helped any innocent people?" my daughter asked.

This time I didn't look in the mirror.

"A few, yes."

It was the best I could honestly say.

"Mom's made a lot of bad people go to jail."

I nodded.

"Yes, she has. I used to think we were a great balancing act. What she did and what I did. Now..."

There was no need to finish the thought. I turned the radio on and hit the preset button that tuned in the Disney music channel.

The last thing I thought about on the drive home was that maybe grown-ups were just as easy to read as their children.

21

After dropping my daughter off at school Thursday morning I drove directly to Jerry Vincent's law offices. It was still early and traffic was light. When I got into the garage adjoining the Legal Center, I found that I almost had my pick of the place — most lawyers don't get into the office until closer to nine, when court starts. I had all of them beat by at least an hour. I drove up to the second level so I could park on the same floor as the office. Each level of the garage had its own entrance into the building.

I drove by the spot where Jerry Vincent had been parked when he was shot to death and parked farther up the ramp. As I walked toward the bridge that connected the garage to the Legal Center, I noticed a parked

Subaru station wagon with surfboard racks on the roof. There was a sticker on the back window that showed the silhouette of a surfer riding the nose of a board. It said one world on the sticker.

The back windows on the wagon were darkly tinted and I couldn't see in. I moved up to the front and looked into the car through the driver's side window. I could see that the backseat had been folded flat. Half the rear area was cluttered with open cardboard boxes full of clothes and personal belongings. The other half served as a bed for Patrick Henson. I knew this because he was lying there asleep, his face turned from the light into the folds of a sleeping bag. And it was only then that I remembered something he had said during our first phone conversation when I had asked if he was interested in a job as my driver. He had told me he was living out of his car and sleeping in a lifeguard stand.

I raised my fist to knock on the window but then decided to let Patrick sleep. I wouldn't need him until later in the morning. There was no need to roust him. I crossed into the office complex, made a turn, and headed down a hallway toward the door marked with Jerry Vincent's name. Standing in front of that door was Detective Bosch. He was listening to his music and waiting for me. He had his hands in his pockets and looked pensive, maybe even a little put out. I was pretty sure we had no appointment, so I didn't know what he was upset about. Maybe it was the music. He pulled out the earbuds as I approached and put them away.

"What, no coffee?" I said by way of a greeting.

"Not today. I could tell you didn't want it yesterday."

He stepped aside so I could use a key to open the door.

"Can I ask you something?" I said.

"If I said no, you'd ask anyway."

"You're probably right."

I opened the door.

"So then, just ask the question."

"All right. Well, you don't seem like an iPod sort of guy to me. Who were you listening to there?"

"Somebody I am sure you never heard of."

"I get it. It's Tony Robbins, the self-help guru?"

Bosch shook his head, not rising to take the bait.

"Frank Morgan," he said.

I nodded.

"The saxophone player? Yeah, I know Frank."

Bosch looked surprised as we entered the reception area.

"You know him," he said in a disbelieving tone.

"Yeah, I usually drop by and say hello when he plays at the Catalina or the Jazz Bakery. My father loved jazz and back in the fifties and sixties he was Frank's lawyer. Frank got into a lot of trouble before he got straight. Ended up playing in San Quentin with Art Pepper—you've heard of him, right? By the time I met Frank, he didn't need any help from a defense attorney. He was doing good."

It took Bosch a moment to recover from my surprise knowledge of Frank Morgan, the obscure heir to Charlie Parker who for two decades squandered the inheritance on heroin. We crossed the reception area and went into the main office.

"So how's the case going?" I asked.

"It's going," he said.

"I heard that before you came and saw me yesterday, you spent the night in Parker Center sweating a suspect. No arrest, though?"

I moved around behind Vincent's desk and sat down. I started pulling the files out of my bag. Bosch stayed standing.

"Who told you that?" Bosch asked.

There wasn't anything casual about the question. It was more of a demand. I acted nonchalant about it.

"I don't know," I said. "I must've heard it somewhere. Maybe a reporter. Who was the suspect?"

"That's none of your business."

"Then, what is my business with you, Detective? Why are you here?"

"I came to see if you had any more names for me."

"What happened to the names I gave you yesterday?"

"They've checked out."

"How could you check them all out already?"

He leaned down and put both hands on the desk.

"Because I'm not working this case alone, okay? I have help and we checked out every one of your names. Every one of them is in jail, dead, or was not worried about Jerry Vincent anymore. We also checked out several of the people he put away as a prosecutor. It's a dead end."

I felt a real sense of disappointment and realized that maybe I had put too much hope in the possibility of one of those names from the past belonging to the killer, and his arrest being the end of any threat to me.

"What about Demarco, the gun dealer?"

"I took that one myself and it didn't take long to scratch him off the list. He's dead, Haller. Died two years ago in his cell up at Corcoran. Internal bleeding. When they opened him up they found a toothbrush shiv lodged in the anal cavity. It was never determined whether he'd put it up there for safekeeping himself or somebody else did it for him, but it was a good lesson for the rest of the inmates. They even put up a sign. Never put sharp objects up your ass."

I leaned back in my seat, as much repelled by the story as by the loss of a potential suspect. I recovered and tried to continue in nonchalant form.

"Well, what can I tell you, Detective? Demarco was my best shot. Those names were all I had. I told you I can't reveal anything about active cases, but here's the deal: There's nothing to reveal."

He shook his head in disbelief.

"I mean it, Detective. I've been through all of the active cases. There is nothing in any of them that constitutes a threat or reason for Vincent to feel threatened. There is nothing in any of them that connects to the FBI. There is nothing in any of them that indicates Jerry Vincent stumbled onto something that put him in harm's way. Besides, when you find out bad things about your clients, they're protected. So there's nothing there. I mean, he wasn't representing mobsters. He wasn't representing drug dealers. There wasn't anything in—"

"He represents murderers."

"Accused murderers. And at the time of his death he had only one murder case—Walter Elliot—and there isn't anything there. Believe me, I've looked."

I wasn't so sure I believed it as I said it but Bosch didn't seem to notice. He finally sat down on the edge of the chair in front of the desk, and his face seemed to change. There was an almost desperate look to it.

"Jerry was divorced," I offered. "Did you check out the ex-wife?"

"They got divorced nine years ago. She's happily remarried and about to have her second kid. I don't think a woman seven months pregnant is going to come gunning for an ex-husband she hasn't talked to in nine years."

"Any other relatives?"

"A mother in Pittsburgh. The family angle is dry."

"Girlfriend?"

"He was banging his secretary but there was nothing serious there. And her alibi checks out. She was also banging his investigator. And they were together that night."

I felt my face turning red. That sordid scenario wasn't too far from my own current situation. At least Lorna, Cisco, and I had been entangled at different times. I rubbed my face as if I were tired and hoped it would account for my new coloration.

"That's convenient," I said. "That they alibi each other."

Bosch shook his head.

"It checks out through witnesses. They were with friends at a screening at Archway. That big-shot client of yours got them the invitation."

I nodded and took an educated guess at something, then threw a zinger at Bosch.

"The guy you sweated in a room that first night was the investigator, Bruce Carlin."

"Who told you that?"

"You just did. You had a classic love triangle. It would've been the place to start."

"Smart lawyer. But like I said, it didn't pan out. We spent a night on it and in the morning we were still at square one. Tell me about the money."

He'd thrown a zinger right back at me.

"What money?"

"The money in the business accounts. I suppose you're going to tell me they are protected territory, too."

"Actually, I'd probably need to talk to the judge for an opinion on that, but I don't need to bother. My case manager is one of the best accounts people I've ever run across. She's been working with the books and she tells me they're clean. Every penny Jerry took in is accounted for."

Bosch didn't respond, so I continued.

"Let me tell you something, Detective. When lawyers get into trouble, most of the time it's because of the money. The books. It's the one place where there are no gray areas. It's the one place where the California bar loves to stick its nose in. I keep the cleanest books in the business because I don't ever want to give them a reason to come after me. So I would know and Lorna, my case manager, would know if there was something in these books that didn't add up. But there isn't. I think Jerry probably paid himself a little too quickly but there is nothing technically wrong with that."

I saw Bosch's eyes light on something I had said.

"What?"

"What's that mean, he 'paid himself too quickly'?"

"It means — let me just start at the start. The way it works is you take on a client and you receive an advance. That money goes into the client trust account. It's their money but you are holding it because you want to make sure you can get it when you earn it. You follow?"

"Yeah, you can't trust your clients because they're criminals. So you get the money up front and put it in a trust account. Then you pay yourself from it as you do the work."

"More or less. Anyway, it's in the trust and as you do the work, make appearances, prepare the case and so forth, you take your fees from the trust account. You move it into the operating account. Then, from the operating account you pay your own bills and salaries. Rent, secretary, investigator, car costs, and so on and so forth. You also pay yourself."

"Okay, so how did Vincent pay himself too quickly?"

"Well, I am not exactly saying he did. It's a matter of custom and practice. But it looks from the books that he liked to keep a low balance in operating. He happened to have had a franchise client who paid a large advance up front and that money went through the trust and operating accounts pretty quickly. After costs, the rest went to Jerry Vincent in salary."

Bosch's body language indicated I was hitting on something that jibed with something else and was important to him. He had leaned slightly toward me and seemed to have tightened his shoulders and neck.

"Walter Elliot," he said. "Was he the franchise?"

"I can't give out that information but I think it's an easy guess to make."

Bosch nodded and I could see that he was working on something inside. I waited and he said nothing.

"How does this help you, Detective?" I finally asked.

"I can't give out that information but I think it's an easy guess to make." I nodded. He'd nailed me back.

"Look, we both have rules we have to follow," I said. "We're flip sides of the same coin. I'm just doing my job. And if there is nothing else I can help you with, I'll get back to it."

Bosch stared at me and seemed to be deciding something.

"Who did Jerry Vincent bribe on the Elliot case?" he finally asked.

The question came out of left field. I wasn't expecting it but in the moments after he asked it, I realized that it was the question he had come to ask. Everything else up until this point had been window dressing.

"What, is that from the FBI?"

"I haven't talked to the FBI."

"Then, what are you talking about?"

"I'm talking about a payoff."

"To who?"

"That's what I'm asking you."

I shook my head and smiled.

"Look, I told you. The books are clean. There's —"

"If you were going to bribe someone with a hundred thousand dollars, would you put it in your books?"

I thought about Jerry Vincent and the time I turned down the subtle quid pro quo on the Barnett Woodson case. I turned him down and ended up hanging a not-guilty verdict on him. It changed Vincent's life and he was still thanking me for it from the grave. But maybe it didn't change his ways in the years that followed.

"I guess you're right," I said to Bosch. "I wouldn't do it that way. So what aren't you telling me?"

"This is in confidence, Counselor. But I need your help and I think you need to know this in order to help me."

"Okay."

"Then, say it."

"Say what?"

"That you will treat this information in confidence."

"I thought I did. I will. I'll keep it confidential."

"Not even your staff. Just you."

"Fine. Just me. Tell me."

"You have Vincent's work accounts. I have his private accounts. You said he paid himself the money from Elliot quickly. He —"

"I didn't say it was Elliot. You did."

"Whatever. The point is, that five months ago he accumulated a hundred grand in a personal investment account and a week later called his broker and told him he was cashing out."

"You mean he took a hundred thousand out in cash?"

"That's what I just said."

"What happened to it?"

"I don't know. But you can't just go into a broker's and pick up a hundred grand in cash. You have to order that kind of money. It took a couple days to put it together and then he went in to pick it up. His broker asked a lot of questions to make sure there wasn't a security issue. You know, like somebody being held hostage while he went and got the money. A ransom or something like that. Vincent said everything was fine, that he needed the money to buy a boat and that if he made the deal in cash, he would get the best deal and save a lot of money."

"So where's the boat?"

"There is no boat. The story was a lie."

"Are you sure?"

"We've checked all state transactions and asked questions all over Marina del Rey and San Pedro. We can't find any boat. We've searched his home twice and reviewed his credit-card purchases. No receipts or records of boat-related expenses. No photos, no keys, no fishing poles. No coast guard registration—required on a transaction that large. He didn't buy a boat."

"What about Mexico?"

Bosch shook his head.

"This guy hadn't left L.A. in nine months. He didn't go down to Mexico and he didn't go anywhere else. I'm telling you, he didn't buy a boat. We would've found it. He bought something else and your client Walter Elliot probably knows what it was."

I tracked his logic and could see it coming to the doorway of Walter Elliot. But I wasn't going to open it with Bosch looking over my shoulder.

"I think you've got it wrong, Detective."

"I don't think so, Counselor."

"Well, I can't help you. I have no idea about this and have seen no indication of it in any of the books or records I've got. If you can connect this alleged bribe to my client, then arrest him and charge him. Otherwise, I'll tell you right now he's off limits. He's not talking to you about this or anything else."

Bosch shook his head.

"I wouldn't waste my time trying to talk to him. He used his lawyer as cover on this and I'll never be able to get past the attorney-client protection. But you should take it as a warning, Counselor."

"Yeah, how's that?"

"Simple. His lawyer got killed, not him. Think about it. And remember, that little trickle on the back of your neck and running down your spine? That's the feeling you get when you know you have to look over your shoulder. When you know you're in danger."

I smiled back at him.

"Oh, is that what that is? I thought it was the feeling I get when I know I'm being bullshitted."

"I'm only telling you the truth."

"You've been running a game on me for two days. Spinning bullshit about bribes and the FBI. You've been trying to manipulate me and it's been a waste of my time. You have to go now, Detective, because I have real work to do."

I stood up and extended a hand toward the door. Bosch stood up but didn't turn to go.

"Don't kid yourself, Haller. Don't make a mistake."

"Thanks for the advice."

Bosch finally turned and started to leave. But then he stopped and came back to the desk, pulling something from the inside pocket of his jacket as he approached.

It was a photograph. He put it down on the desk.

"You recognize that man?" Bosch asked.

I studied the photo. It was a grainy still taken off a video. It showed a man pushing out through the front door of an office building.

"This is the front entrance of the Legal Center, isn't it?"

"Do you recognize him?"

The shot was taken at a distance and blown up, spreading the pixels of the image and making it unclear. The man in the photograph looked to me to be of Latin origin. He had dark skin and hair and had a Pancho Villa mustache, like Cisco used to wear. He wore a panama hat and an open-collared shirt beneath what appeared to be a leather sport coat. As I looked more closely at the photograph, I realized why it was the frame they had chosen to take from the surveillance video. The man's jacket had pulled open as he'd pushed through the glass door. I could see what looked like the top of a pistol tucked into the belt line of his pants.

"Is that a gun? Is this the killer?"

"Look, can you answer one goddamn question without another question? Do you recognize this man? That's all I want to know."

"No, I don't, Detective. Happy?"

"That's another question."

"Sorry."

"You sure you haven't seen him before?"

"Not a hundred percent. But that's not a great photo you've got there. Where is it from?"

"A street camera on Broadway and Second. It sweeps the street and we got this guy for only a few seconds. This is the best we can do."

I knew that the city had been quietly installing street cameras on main arteries in the last few years. Streets like Hollywood Boulevard were completely visually wired. Broadway would have been a likely candidate. It was always crowded during the day with pedestrians and traffic. It was also the street used most often for protest marches organized by the underclasses.

"Well, then I guess it's better than having nothing. You think the hair and the mustache are a disguise?"

"Let me ask the questions. Could this guy be one of your new clients?"

"I don't know. I haven't met them all. Leave me the photo and I'll show it to Wren Williams. She'd know better than me if he's a client."

Bosch reached down and took the photo back.

"It's my only copy. When will she be in?"

"In about an hour."

"I'll come back later. Meantime, Counselor, watch yourself."

He pointed a finger at me like it was a gun, then turned and walked out of the room, closing the door behind him. I sat there thinking about what he had said and staring at the door, half expecting him to come back in and drop another ominous warning on me.

But when the door opened one minute later it was Lorna who entered.

"I just saw that detective in the hallway."

"Yeah, he was here."

"What did he want?"

"To scare me."

"And?"

"He did a pretty good job."

22

Lorna wanted to convene another staff meeting and update me on things that had happened while I was out of the office visiting Malibu and Walter Elliot the day before. She even said I had a court hearing scheduled later on a mystery case that wasn't on the calendar we had worked up. But I needed some time to think about what Bosch had just revealed and what it meant.

"Where's Cisco?"

"He's coming. He left early to meet one of his sources before he came into the office."

"Did he have breakfast?"

"Not with me."

"Okay, wait till he gets in and then we'll go over to the Dining Car and have breakfast. We'll go over everything then."

"I already ate breakfast."

"Then, you can do all the talking while we do all the eating."

She put a phony frown on her face but went out into the reception office and left me alone. I got up from behind the desk and started to pace the office, hands in my pockets, trying to evaluate what the information from Bosch meant.

According to Bosch, Jerry Vincent had paid a sizable bribe to a person or persons unknown. The fact that the $100,000 came out of the Walter Elliot advance would indicate the bribe was somehow linked to the Elliot case, but this was by no means conclusive. Vincent could easily have used money from Elliot to pay a debt or a bribe relating to another case or something else entirely. It could have been a gambling debt he wanted to hide. The only fact was that Vincent had diverted the $100K from his account to an unknown destination and had wanted to hide the transaction.

Next to consider was the timing of the transaction and whether it was linked to Vincent's murder. Bosch said the money transfer had gone down five months ago. Vincent's murder was just three nights before and Elliot's trial was set to begin in a week. Again there was nothing definitive. The distance between the transaction and the murder seemed to me to strain any possibility of a link between the two.

But still, I could not push the two apart, and the reason for this was Walter Elliot himself. Through the filter of Bosch's information I now began to fill in some answers and to view my client—and myself—differently. I now saw Elliot's confidence in his innocence and eventual acquittal coming possibly from his belief that it had already been bought and paid for. I now saw his unwillingness to consider delaying the trial as a timing issue relating to the bribe. And I saw his willingness to quickly allow me to carry the torch for Vincent without checking a single reference as a move made so he could get to the trial without delay. It had nothing to do with any confidence in my skills and tenacity. I had not impressed him. I had simply been the one who showed up. I was simply a lawyer who would work in the scheme of things. In fact, I was perfect. I was pulled out of the lost-and-found bin. I had been on the shelf and was hungry and ready. I could be dusted off and suited up and sent in to replace Vincent, no questions asked.

The reality jolt this sent through me was as uncomfortable as the first night in rehab. But I also understood that this self-knowledge could give me an edge. I was in the middle of some sort of play but at least now I knew it was a play. That was an advantage. I could now make it my own play.

There was a reason for the hurry-up to trial and I now thought I knew what it was. The fix was in. Money had been paid for a specific fix, and that fix was tied to the trial remaining on schedule. The next question in this string was why. Why must the trial take place as scheduled? I didn't have an answer for that yet but I was going to get it.

I walked over to the windows and split the Venetian blinds with my hand. Out on the street I saw a van from Channel 5 parked with two wheels up on the curb. A camera crew and a reporter were on the sidewalk and they were getting ready to do a live shot, offering their viewers the latest on the Vincent case — the latest being the exact same report given the morning before: no arrests, no suspects, no news.

I left the window and stepped back into the middle of the room to continue my pacing. The next thing I needed to consider was the man in the photograph Bosch showed me. There was a contradiction at work here. The early indications of evidence were that Vincent had known the person who killed him and allowed him to get close. But the man in the photograph appeared to be in disguise. Would Jerry have lowered his window for the man in the photograph? The fact that Bosch had zeroed in on this man didn't make sense when applied to what was known about the crime scene.

The calls from the FBI to Vincent's cell phone were also part of the unknown equation. What did the bureau know and why had no agent come forward to Bosch? It might be that the agency was hiding its tracks. But I also knew that it might not want to come out of the shadows to reveal an ongoing investigation. If this was the case, I would need to step more carefully than I had been. If I ended up the least bit tainted in a federal corruption probe, I would never recover from it.

The last unknown to consider was the murder itself. Vincent had paid the bribe and was ready for trial as scheduled. Why had he become a liability? His murder certainly threatened the timetable and was an extreme response. Why was he killed?

There were too many questions and too many unknowns for now. I needed more information before I could draw any solid conclusions about how to proceed. But there was a basic conclusion I couldn't stop myself from reaching. It seemed uncomfortably clear that I was being mushroomed by my own client. Elliot was keeping me in the dark about the interior machinations of the case.

But that could work both ways. I decided that I would do exactly what Bosch had asked: keep the information the detective had given me confidential. I would not share it with my staff and certainly, at this point, I would not question Walter Elliot about his knowledge of these things. I would keep my head above the dark waters of the case and keep my eyes wide open.

I shifted focus from my thoughts to what was directly in front of me. I was looking at the gaping mouth of Patrick Henson's fish.

The door opened and Lorna reentered the office to find me standing there staring at the tarpon.

"What are you doing?" she asked.

"Thinking."

"Well, Cisco's here and we've got to go. You have a busy court schedule today and I don't want to make you late."

"Then, let's go. I'm starved."

I followed her out but not before glancing back at the big beautiful fish hanging on the wall. I thought I knew exactly how he felt.

23

≈≈≈

I had Patrick drive us over to the Pacific Dining Car, and Cisco and I ordered steak and eggs while Lorna had tea and honey. The Dining Car was a place where downtown power brokers liked to gather before a day of fighting it out in the glass towers nearby. The food was overpriced but good. It instilled confidence, made the downtown warrior feel like a heavy hitter.

As soon as the waiter took our order and left us, Lorna put her silverware to the side and opened a spiral-bound At-A-Glance calendar on the table.

"Eat fast," she said. "You have a busy day."

"Tell me."

"All right, the easy stuff first."

She flipped a couple of pages back and forth in the calendar, then proceeded.

"You have a ten a.m. in chambers with Judge Holder. She wants an updated client inventory."

"She told me I had a week," I protested. "Today's Thursday."

"Yeah, well, Michaela called and said the judge wants an interim update. I think she — the judge, that is — saw in the paper that you are continuing on as Elliot's lawyer. She's afraid you're spending all your time on Elliot and none on the other clients."

"That's not true. I filed a motion for Patrick yesterday and Tuesday I took the sentencing on Reese. I mean, I haven't even met all the clients yet."

"Don't worry, I have a hard-copy inventory back at the office for you to take with you. It shows who you've met, who you signed up and calendars on all of them. Just hit her with the paperwork and she won't be able to complain."

I smiled. Lorna was the best case manager in the business.

"Great. What else?"

"Then at eleven you have an in-chambers with Judge Stanton on Elliot."

"Status conference?"

"Yes. He wants to know if you are going to be able to go next Thursday."

"No, but Elliot won't have it any other way."

"Well, the judge will get to hear Elliot say that for himself. He's requiring the defendant's presence."

That was unusual. Most status conferences were routine and quick. The fact that Stanton wanted Elliot there bumped this one up into a more important realm.

I thought of something and pulled out my cell phone.

"Did you let Elliot know? He might —"

"Put it away. He knows and he'll be there. I talked to his assistant — Mrs. Albrecht — this morning and she knows he has to show and that the judge can revoke if he doesn't."

I nodded. It was a smart move. Threaten Elliot's freedom as a means of making sure he shows up.

"Good," I said. "That it?"

I wanted to get to Cisco to ask what else he had been able to find out about the Vincent investigation and whether his sources had mentioned anything about the man in the surveillance photo Bosch had shown me.

"Not by a long shot, my friend," Lorna responded. "Now we get to the mystery case."

"Let's hear it."

"We got a call yesterday afternoon from Judge Friedman's clerk, who called Vincent's office blind to see if there was anyone there taking over the cases. When the clerk was informed that you were taking over, she asked if you were aware of the hearing scheduled before Friedman today at two. I checked our new calendar and you didn't have a two o'clock on there for today. So there is the mystery. You have a hearing at two for a case we not only don't have on calendar but don't have a file for either."

"What's the client's name?"

"Eli Wyms."

It meant nothing to me.

"Did Wren know the name?"

Lorna shook her head in a dismissive way.

"Did you check the dead cases? Maybe it was just misfiled."

"No, we checked. There is no file anywhere in the office."

"And what's the hearing? Did you ask the clerk?"

Lorna nodded.

"Pretrial motions. Wyms is charged with attempted murder of a peace officer and several other weapons-related charges. He was arrested May second at a county park in Calabasas. He was arraigned, bound over and sent out to Camarillo for ninety days. He must've been found competent because the hearing today is to set a trial date and consider bail."

I nodded. From the shorthand, I could read between the lines. Wyms had gotten into some sort of confrontation involving weapons with the Sheriff's Department, which provided law enforcement services in the unincorporated area known as Calabasas. He was sent to the state's mental evaluation center in Camarillo, where the shrinks took three months deciding whether he was a crazy man or competent to stand trial on the charges against him. The docs determined he was competent, meaning he knew right from wrong when he tried to kill a peace officer, most likely the sheriff's deputy who confronted him.

It was a bare-bones sketch of the trouble Eli Wyms was in. There would be more detail in the file but we had no file.

"Is there any reference to Wyms in the trust account deposits?" I asked.

Lorna shook her head. I should've assumed she would be thorough and check the bank accounts in search of Eli Wyms.

"Okay, so it looks like maybe Jerry took him on pro bono."

Attorneys occasionally provide legal services free of charge—pro bono—to indigent or special clients. Sometimes this is an altruistic endeavor and sometimes it's because the client just won't pay up. Either way, the lack of an advance from Wyms was understandable. The missing file was another story.

"You know what I was thinking?" Lorna said.

"What?"

"That Jerry had the file with him—in his briefcase—when he left Monday night."

"And it got taken, along with his laptop and cell phone, by the killer."

She nodded and I nodded back.

It made sense. He was spending the evening preparing for the week and he had a hearing Thursday on Wyms. Maybe he had run out of gas and thrown the file in his briefcase to look at later. Or maybe he kept the file with him because it was important in a way I couldn't see yet. Maybe the killer wanted the Wyms file and not the laptop or the cell phone.

"Who's the prosecutor on the case?"

"Joanne Giorgetti, and I'm way ahead of you. I called her yesterday and explained our situation and asked if she wouldn't mind copying the discovery again for us. She said no problem. You can pick it up after your eleven with Judge Stanton and then have a couple hours to familiarize yourself with it before the hearing at two."

Joanne Giorgetti was a top-flight prosecutor who worked in the crimes-against-law-officers section of the DA's Office. She was also a longtime friend of my ex-wife's and was my daughter's basketball coach in the YMCA league. She had always been cordial and collegial with me, even after Maggie and I split up. It didn't surprise me that she would run off a copy of the discovery materials for me.

"You think of everything, Lorna," I said. "Why don't you just take over Vincent's practice and run with it? You don't need me."

She smiled at the compliment and I saw her eyes flick in the direction of Cisco. The read I got was that she wanted him to realize her value to the law firm of Michael Haller and Associates.

"I like working in the background," she said. "I'll leave center stage for you."

Our plates were served and I spread a liberal dose of Tabasco sauce on both my steak and the eggs. Sometimes hot sauce was the only way I knew I was still alive.

I was finally able to hear what Cisco had come up with on the Vincent investigation but he dug into his meal and I knew better than to try to keep him from his food. I decided to wait and asked Lorna how things were working out with Wren Williams. She answered in a low voice, as if Wren were sitting nearby in the restaurant and listening.

"She's not a lot of help, Mickey. She seems to have no idea of how the office worked or where Jerry put things. She'd be lucky to remember where she parked her car this morning. If you ask me, she was working there for some other reason."

I could have told her the reason—as it had been told to me by Bosch—but decided to keep it to myself. I didn't want to distract Lorna with gossip.

I looked over and saw Cisco mopping up the steak juice and hot sauce on his plate with a piece of toast. He was good to go.

"What do you have going today, Cisco?"

"I'm working on Rilz and his side of the equation."

"How's that going?"

"I think there'll be a couple things you can use. You want to hear about it?"

"Not yet. I'll ask when I need it."

I didn't want to be given any information about Rilz that I might have to turn over to the prosecution in discovery. At the moment, the less I knew, the better. Cisco understood this and nodded.

"I also have the Bruce Carlin debriefing this afternoon," Cisco added.

"He wants two hundred an hour," Lorna said. "Highway robbery, if you ask me."

I waved off her protest.

"Just pay it. It's a onetime expense and he probably has information we can use, and that might save Cisco some time."

"Don't worry, we're paying him. I'm just not happy about it. He's gouging us because he knows he can."

"Technically, he's gouging Elliot and I don't think he's going to care."

I turned back to my investigator.

"You have anything new on the Vincent case?"

Cisco updated me with what he had. It consisted mostly of forensic details, suggesting that the source he had inside the investigation came from that side of the equation. He said Vincent had been shot twice, both times in the area of the left temple. The spread on the entry wounds was less than an inch, and powder burns on the skin and hair indicated the weapon was nine to twelve inches away when fired. Cisco said this indicated that the killer had fired two quick shots and was fairly skilled. It was unlikely that an amateur would fire twice quickly and be able to cluster the impacts.

Additionally, Cisco said, the slugs never left the body and were recovered during the autopsy conducted late the day before.

"They were twenty-fives," he said.

I had handled countless cross-examinations of tool marks and ballistics experts. I knew my bullets and I knew a .25 caliber round came out of a small weapon but could do great damage, especially if fired into the cranial vault. The slugs would ricochet around inside. It would be like putting the victim's brain in a blender.

"They know the exact weapon yet?"

I knew that by studying the markings — lands and grooves — on the slugs they would be able to tell what kind of gun fired the rounds. Just as with the Malibu murders, in which the investigators knew what gun had been used, even though they didn't have it.

"Yeah. A twenty-five caliber Beretta Bobcat. Nice and small, you could almost hide it in your hand."

A completely different weapon than the one used to kill Mitzi Elliot and Johan Rilz.

"So what's all of this tell us?"

"It's a hitter's gun. You take it when you know it's going to be a head shot."

I nodded my agreement.

"So this was planned. The killer knew just what he was going to do. He waits in the garage, sees Jerry come out, and comes right up to the car. The window goes down or it was already down, and the guy pops Jerry twice in the head, then reaches in for the briefcase that has the laptop, the cell phone, the portfolio and, we think, the Eli Wyms file."

"Exactly."

"Okay, what about the suspect?"

"The guy they sweated the first night?"

"No, that was Carlin. They cut him loose."

Cisco looked surprised.

"How'd you find out it was Carlin?"

"Bosch told me this morning."

"Are you saying they have another suspect?"

I nodded.

"He showed me a photo of a guy coming out of the building at the time of the shooting. He had a gun and was wearing an obvious disguise."

I saw Cisco's eyes flare. It was a point of professional pride that he provide me with information like that. He didn't like it happening the other way around.

"He didn't have a name, just the photo," I said. "He wanted to know if I had ever seen the guy before or if it was one of the clients."

Cisco's eyes darkened as he realized that his inside source was holding out on him. If I'd told him about the FBI calls, he probably would have picked the table up and thrown it through the window.

"I'll see what I can find out," he said quietly through a tight jaw.

I looked at Lorna.

"Bosch said he was coming back later to show the photo to Wren."

"I'll tell her."

"Make sure you look at it, too. I want everybody to be on alert for this guy."

"Okay, Mickey."

I nodded. We were finished. I put a credit card on the tab and pulled out my cell phone to call Patrick. Calling my driver reminded me of something.

"Cisco, there's one other thing I want you to try to do today."

Cisco looked at me, happy to move on from the idea that I had a better source on the investigation than he did.

"Go to Vincent's liquidator and see if he's sitting on one of Patrick's surfboards. If he is, I want it back for Patrick."

Cisco nodded.

"I can do that. No problem."

24

Waylaid by the slow-moving elevators in the CCB, I was four minutes late when I walked into Judge Holder's courtroom and hustled through the clerk's corral toward the hallway leading to her chambers. I didn't see anyone and the door was closed. I knocked lightly and I heard the judge call for me to enter.

She was behind her desk and wearing her black robe. This told me she probably had a hearing in open court scheduled soon and my being late was not a good thing.

"Mr. Haller, our meeting was set for ten o'clock. I believe you were given proper notice of this."

"Yes, Your Honor, I know. I'm sorry. The elevators in this building are —"

"All lawyers take the same elevators and most seem to be on time for meetings with me."

"Yes, Your Honor."

"Did you bring your checkbook?"

"I think so, yes."

"Well, we can do this one of two ways," the judge said. "I can hold you in contempt of court, fine you, and let you explain yourself to the California bar, or we can go informal and you take out your checkbook and make a donation to the Make-A-Wish Foundation. It's one of my favorite charities. They do good things for sick children."

This was incredible. I was being fined for being four minutes late. The arrogance of some judges was amazing. I somehow was able to swallow my outrage and speak.

"I like the idea of helping out sick children, Your Honor," I said. "How much do I make it out for?"

"As much as you want to contribute. And I will even send it in for you."

She pointed to a stack of paperwork on the left side of her desk. I saw two other checks, most likely stroked out by two other poor bastards who had run afoul of the judge this week. I leaned down and rummaged through the front pocket of my backpack until I found my checkbook. I wrote a check for $250 to Make-A-Wish, tore it out, and handed it across the desk. I watched the judge's eyes as she looked at the amount I was donating. She nodded approvingly and I knew I was all right.

"Thank you, Mr. Haller. They'll be sending you a receipt for your taxes in the mail. It will go to the address on the check."

"Like you said, they do good work."

"Yes, they do."

The judge put the check on top of the two others and then turned her attention back to me.

"Now, before we go over the cases, let me ask you a question," she said. "Do you know if the police are making any headway on the investigation of Mr. Vincent's death?"

I hesitated a moment, wondering what I should be telling the chief judge of the superior court.

"I'm not really in the loop on that, Judge," I said. "But I was shown a photograph of a man I assume they're looking at as a suspect."

"Really? What kind of photo?"

"Like a surveillance shot from out on the street. A guy, and it looks like he has a gun. I think they matched it up timewise to the shooting in the garage."

"Did you recognize the man?"

I shook my head.

"No, the shot was too grainy. It looked like he might have had a disguise on anyway."

"When was this?"

"The night of the shooting."

"No, I mean, when was it that you were shown this photo?"

"Just this morning. Detective Bosch came to the office with it."

The judge nodded. We were quiet for a moment and then the judge got to the point of the meeting.

"Okay, Mr. Haller, why don't we talk about clients and cases now?"

"Yes, Your Honor."

I reached down and unzipped my bag, taking out the scorecard Lorna had prepared for me.

Judge Holder kept me at her desk for the next hour while I went over every case and client, detailing the status and conversations I'd had with each. By the time she finally let me go, I was late for my eleven o'clock hearing in Judge Stanton's chambers.

I left Holder's court and didn't bother with the elevators. I hit the exit stairs and charged up two flights to the floor where Stanton's courtroom was located. I was running eight minutes late and wondered if it was going to cost me another donation to another judge's favorite charity.

The courtroom was empty but Stanton's clerk was in her corral. She pointed with a pen to the open door to the hallway leading to the judge's chambers.

"They're waiting for you," she said.

I quickly moved by her and down the hall. The door to the chambers was open and I saw the judge sitting behind his desk. To his left rear side was a stenographer and across the desk from him were three chairs. Walter Elliot was sitting in the chair to the right, the middle chair was empty, and Jeffrey Golantz was in the third. I had never met the prosecutor before but he was recognizable because I had seen his face on TV and in the newspapers. In the last few years, he had successfully handled a series of high-profile cases and was making a name for himself. He was the undefeated up-and-comer in the DA's Office.

I loved going up against undefeated prosecutors. Their confidence often betrayed them.

"Sorry I'm late, Your Honor," I said as I slid into the empty seat. "Judge Holder called me into a hearing and she ran long."

I hoped that mentioning the chief judge as the reason for my tardiness would keep Stanton from further assaulting my checkbook and it seemed to work.

"Let's go on the record now," he said.

The stenographer leaned forward and put her fingers on the keys of her machine.

"In the matter of *California versus Walter Elliot*, we are in chambers today for a status conference. Present is the defendant, along with Mr. Golantz for the state and Mr. Haller, who is here in the late Mr. Vincent's stead."

The judge had to break there to give the stenographer the proper spellings of all the names. He spoke in an authoritative voice that a decade on the bench often gives a jurist. The judge was a handsome man with a full head of bristly gray hair. He was in good shape, the black robe doing little to disguise his well-developed shoulders and chest.

"So," he then said, "we're scheduled in this matter for voir dire next Thursday—a week from today—and I notice, Mr. Haller, that I have received no motion from you to continue the matter while you get up to speed on the case."

"We don't want a delay," Elliot said.

I reached over and put my hand on my client's forearm and shook my head.

"Mr. Elliot, in this session I want you to let your lawyer do the talking," the judge said.

"Sorry, Your Honor," I said. "But the message is the same whether from me or directly from Mr. Elliot. We want no delay. I have spent the week getting up to speed and I will be prepared to begin jury selection next Thursday."

The judge squinted his eyes at me.

"You sure about that, Mr. Haller?"

"Absolutely. Mr. Vincent was a good lawyer and he kept thorough records. I understand the strategy he built and will be ready to go on Thursday. The case has my full attention. That of my staff as well."

The judge leaned back in his high-backed chair and swiveled side to side as he thought. He finally looked at Elliot.

"Mr. Elliot, it turns out you do get to speak after all. I would like to hear directly from you that you are in full agreement with your new attorney here and that you understand the risk you run, bringing in a fresh lawyer so close to the start of trial. It's your freedom at stake here, sir. Let's hear what you have to say about it."

Elliot leaned forward and spoke in a defiant tone.

"Judge, first of all, I am in complete agreement. I want to get this thing to trial so I can blow the district attorney here right out of the water. I am an innocent man being persecuted and prosecuted for something I did not do. I don't want to spend a single extra day as the accused, sir. I loved my wife and I'll miss her forever. I didn't kill her and it pierces my heart when I hear the people on TV saying these vile things about me. What hurts the most is knowing that the real killer is out there someplace. The sooner Mr. Haller gets to prove my innocence to the world, the better."

It was O.J. 101 but the judge studied Elliot and nodded thoughtfully, then turned his attention to the prosecutor.

"Mr. Golantz? What is the state's view of this?"

The deputy district attorney cleared his throat. The word to describe him was telegenic. He was handsome and dark and his eyes seemed to carry the very wrath of justice in them.

"Your Honor, the state is prepared for trial and has no objection to proceeding on schedule. But I would ask that, if Mr. Elliot is so sure about proceeding without delay, he formally waive any appellate redress in this regard should things not go as he predicts in trial."

The judge swiveled his chair so that his focus could go back on me.

"What about that, Mr. Haller?"

"Your Honor, I don't think it's necessary for my client to waive any protections that might be afforded to —"

"I don't mind," Elliot said, cutting in on me. "I'll waive whatever you damn well please. I want to go to trial."

I looked sharply at him. He looked at me and shrugged.

"We're going to win this thing," he explained.

"You want to take a moment in the corridor, Mr. Haller?" the judge asked.

"Thank you, Judge."

I got up and signaled Elliot up.

"Come with me."

We walked out into the short hallway that led to the courtroom. I closed the door behind us. Elliot spoke before I could, underlining the problem.

"Look, I want this thing over and I —"

"Shut up!" I said in a forced whisper.

"What?"

"You heard me. Shut the fuck up. You understand? I am sure you are quite used to talking whenever you want and having everybody listen to every brilliant word you say. But you are not in Hollywood anymore, Walter. You aren't talking make-believe movies with this week's mogulito. You understand what I'm saying? This is real life. You don't speak unless you are spoken to. If you have something to say otherwise, then you whisper it into my ear and if I think it is worth repeating, then I — not you — will say it to the judge. You got it?"

It took Elliot a long time to answer. His face turned dark and I understood that I might be about to lose the franchise. But in that moment I didn't care. What I had said needed to be said. It was a welcome-to-my-world speech that was long overdue.

"Yes," he finally said, "I get it."

"Good, then remember it. Now, let's go back in there and see if we can avoid giving away your right to appeal if you happen to get convicted because I fucked up by being unprepared for trial."

"That won't happen. I have faith in you."

"I appreciate that, Walter. But the truth is, you have no basis for that faith. And whether you do or don't, it doesn't mean we have to give anything away. Let's go back in now, and let me do the talking. That's why I get the big bucks, right?"

I clapped him on the shoulder. We went in and sat back down. And Walter didn't say another word. I argued that he shouldn't have to give away his right to appellate review just because he wanted the speedy trial he was entitled to. But Judge Stanton sided with Golantz, ruling that if Elliot declined the offer to delay the trial, he couldn't come complaining after a conviction that his attorney hadn't had enough time to prepare. Faced with the ruling, Elliot stuck to his guns and declined the delay, as I knew he would. That was okay with me. Under the Byzantine rules of law, almost nothing was safe from appeal. I knew that if necessary, Elliot would still be able to appeal the ruling the judge had just made.

We moved on to what the judge called housekeeping after that. The first order of business was to have both sides sign off on a motion from Court TV to be allowed to broadcast segments of the trial live on its daily programming. Neither I nor Golantz objected. After all, it was free advertising — me for new clients, Golantz to further his political aspirations. And as far as Walter Elliot was concerned, he whispered to me that he wanted the cameras there to record his not-guilty verdict.

Next the judge outlined the schedule for submitting final discovery and witness lists. He gave us until Monday on the discovery materials and the witness lists were due the day after that.

"No exceptions, gentlemen," he said. "I look dimly on surprise additions after deadline."

This was not going to be a problem from the defense's side of the aisle. Vincent had already made two previous discovery filings and there was very little new since then for me to share with the prosecution. Cisco Wojciechowski was doing a good job of keeping me in the dark as to what he was finding out about Rilz. And what I didn't know I couldn't put in the discovery file.

When it comes to witnesses, my plan was to give Golantz the usual runaround. I would be submitting a list of potential witnesses, naming every law officer and forensic tech mentioned in the sheriff's reports. That was standard operating procedure. Golantz would have to puzzle over who I really would call to testify and who was important to the defense's case.

"All right, guys, I've probably got a courtroom full of lawyers out there waiting for me," Stanton finally said. "Are we clear on everything?"

Golantz and I nodded our heads. I couldn't help but wonder if either the judge or the prosecutor was the recipient of the bribe. Was I sitting with the man who would turn the case my client's way? If so, he had done nothing to give himself away. I finished the meeting thinking that Bosch had it all wrong. There was no bribe. There was a hundred-thousand-dollar boat somewhere in a harbor in San Diego or Cabo and it had Jerry Vincent's name on the title.

"Okay, then," the judge said. "We'll get this going next week. We can talk about ground rules Thursday morning. But I want to make it clear right now, I'm going to run this trial like a well-oiled machine. No surprises, no shenanigans, no funny stuff. Again, are we clear?"

Golantz and I both agreed once more that we were clear. But the judge swiveled his chair and looked directly at me. He squinted his eyes in suspicion.

"I'm going to hold you to that," he said.

It seemed to be a message intended only for me, a message that would never show on the stenographer's record.

How come, I wondered, it's always the defense attorney who gets the judicial squint?

25

I got to Joanne Giorgetti's office shortly before the noon break. I knew that getting there a minute after twelve would be too late. The DA's Offices literally empty during the lunch hour, the inhabitants seeking sunlight, fresh air, and sustenance outside the CCB. I told the receptionist I had an appointment with Giorgetti and she made a call. Then she buzzed the door lock and told me to go back.

Giorgetti had a small, windowless office with most of the floor space taken up by cardboard file boxes. It was the same way in every prosecutor's office I had ever been in, big or small. She was at her desk but was hidden behind a wall of stacked motions and files. I carefully reached over the wall to shake her hand.

"How's it going, Joanne?"

"Not bad, Mickey. How about you?"

"I'm doing okay."

"You just got a lot of cases, I hear."

"Yeah, quite a few."

The conversation was stilted. I knew she and Maggie were tight, and there was no telling whether my ex-wife had opened up to her about my difficulties in the past year.

"So you're here for Wyms?"

"That's right. I didn't even know I had the case till this morning."

She handed me a file with an inch-thick stack of documents in it.

"What do you think happened to Jerry's file?" she asked.

"I think maybe the killer took it."

She made a cringing face.

"Weird. Why would the killer take this file?"

"Probably unintended. The file was in Jerry's briefcase along with his laptop, and the killer just took the whole thing."

"Hmmm."

"Well, is there anything unusual about this case? Anything that would have made Jerry a target?"

"I don't think so. Just your usual everyday crazy-with-a-gun sort of thing."

I nodded.

"Have you heard anything about a federal grand jury taking a look at the state courts?"

She knitted her eyebrows.

"Why would they be looking at this case?"

"I'm not saying they were. I've been out of the loop for a while. I was wondering what you've heard."

She shrugged.

"Just the usual rumors on the gossip circuit. Seems like there's always a federal investigation of something."

"Yeah."

I said nothing else, hoping she would fill me in on the rumor. But she didn't and it was time to move on.

"The hearing today is to set a trial date?" I asked.

"Yes, but I assume you'll want a continuance so you can get up to speed."

"Well, let me go look at the file during lunch and I'll let you know if that's what the plan is."

"Okay, Mickey. But just so you know. I won't oppose a continuance, considering what happened with Jerry."

"Thanks, CoJo."

She smiled as I used the name her young basketball players called her by at the Y.

"You seen Maggie lately?" she asked.

"Saw her last night when I went to pick up Hayley. She seems to be doing okay. Have you seen her?"

"Just at basketball practice. But she usually sits there with her nose in a file. We used to go out after with the girls to Hamburger Hamlet but Maggie's been too busy."

I nodded. She and Maggie had been foxhole buddies since day one, coming up through the ranks of the prosecutor's office. Competitors but not competitive with each other. But time goes by and distances work their way into any relationship.

"Well, I'll take this and look it all over," I said. "The hearing's with Friedman at two, right?"

"Yeah, two. I'll see you then."

"Thanks for doing this, Joanne."

"No problem."

I left the DA's Office and waited ten minutes to get on an elevator with the lunch crowd. The last one on, I rode down with my face two inches from the door. I hated the elevators more than anything else in the entire Criminal Courts Building.

"Hey, Haller."

It was a voice from behind me. I didn't recognize it but it was too crowded for me to turn around to see who it was.

"What?"

"Heard you scored all of Vincent's cases."

I wasn't going to discuss my business in a crowded elevator. I didn't respond. We finally hit bottom, and the doors spread open. I stepped out and looked back for the person who had spoken.

It was Dan Daly, another defense attorney who was part of a coterie of lawyers who took in Dodgers games occasionally and martinis routinely at Four Green Fields. I had missed the last season of booze and baseball.

"How ya doin', Dan?"

We shook hands, an indication of how long it had been since we'd seen each other.

"So, who'd you grease?"

He said it with a smile but I could tell there was something behind it. Maybe a dose of jealousy over my scoring the Elliot case. Every lawyer in town knew it was a franchise case. It could pay top dollar for years — first the trial and then the appeals that would come after a conviction.

"Nobody," I said. "Jerry put me in his will."

We started walking toward the exit doors. Daly's ponytail was longer and grayer. But what was most notable was that it was intricately braided. I hadn't seen that before.

"Then, lucky you," Daly said. "Let me know if you need a second chair on Elliot."

"He wants only one lawyer at the table, Dan. He said no dream team."

"Well, then keep me in mind as a writer in regard to the rest."

This meant he was available to write appeals on any convictions my new set of clients might incur. Daly had forged a solid reputation as an expert appeals man with a good batting average.

"I'll do that," I said. "I'm still reviewing everything."

"Good enough."

We came through the doors and I could see the Lincoln at the curb, waiting. Daly was going the other way. I told him I'd keep in touch.

"We miss you at the bar, Mick," he said over his shoulder.

"I'll drop by," I called back.

But I knew I wouldn't drop by, that I had to stay away from places like that.

I got in the back of the Lincoln — I tell my drivers never to get out and open the door for me — and told Patrick to take me over to Chinese Friends on Broadway. I told him to drop me and go get lunch on his own. I needed to sit and read and didn't want any conversation.

I got to the restaurant between the first and second waves of patrons and waited no more than five minutes for a table. Wanting to get to work immediately, I ordered a plate of the fried pork chops right away. I knew they would be perfect. They were paper-thin and delicious and I'd be able to eat them with my fingers without taking my eyes off the Wyms documents.

I opened the file Joanne Giorgetti had given me. It contained copies only of what the prosecutor had turned over to Jerry Vincent under the rules of discovery—primarily sheriff's documents relating to the incident, arrest, and follow-up investigation. Any notes, strategies, or defense documents that Vincent had generated were lost with the original file.

The natural starting point was the arrest report, which included the initial and most basic summary of what had transpired. As is often the case, it started with 911 calls to the county communications-and-dispatch center. Multiple reports of gunfire came in from a neighborhood next to a park in Calabasas. The calls fell under Sheriff's Department jurisdiction because Calabasas was in an unincorporated area north of Malibu and near the western limits of the county.

The first deputy to respond was listed on the report as Todd Stallworth. He worked the night shift out of the Malibu substation and had been dispatched at 10:21 p.m. to the neighborhood off Las Virgenes Road. From there he was directed into the nearby Malibu Creek State Park, where the shots were being fired. Now hearing shots himself, Stallworth called for backup and drove into the park to investigate.

There were no lights in the rugged mountain park, as it was posted CLOSED AT SUNSET. As Stallworth entered on the main road, the headlights of his patrol car picked up a reflection, and the deputy saw a vehicle parked in a clearing ahead. He put on his spotlight and illuminated a pickup truck with its tailgate down. There was a pyramid of beer cans on the tailgate and what looked like a gun bag with several rifle barrels protruding from it.

Stallworth stopped his car eighty yards from the pickup and decided to wait until backup arrived. He was on the radio to the Malibu station, describing the pickup truck and saying that he was not close enough to read its license plate, when suddenly there was a gunshot and the searchlight located above the side-view mirror exploded with the bullet's impact. Stallworth killed the rest of the car's lights and bailed out, crawling into the cover of some bushes that lined the clearing. He used his handheld radio to call for additional backup and the special weapons and tactics team.

A three-hour standoff ensued, with the gunman hidden in the wooded terrain near the clearing. He fired his weapon repeatedly but apparently his aim was at the sky. No deputies were struck by bullets. No other vehicles were damaged. Finally, a deputy in black SWAT gear worked his way close enough to the pickup truck to read the license plate by using high-powered binoculars equipped with night-vision lenses. The plate number led to the name Eli Wyms, which in turn led to a cell-phone number. The shooter answered on the first ring and a SWAT team negotiator began a conversation.

The shooter was indeed Eli Wyms, a forty-four-year-old housepainter from Inglewood. He was characterized in the arrest report as drunk, angry, and suicidal. Earlier in the day, he had been kicked out of his home by his wife, who informed him that she was in love with another man. Wyms had driven to the ocean and then north to Malibu and then over the mountains to Cala-basas. He saw the park and thought it looked like a good place to stop the truck and sleep, but he drove on by and bought a case of beer at a gas station near the 101 Freeway. He then turned around and went back to the park.

Wyms told the negotiator that he started shooting because he heard noises in the dark and was afraid. He believed he was shooting at rabid coyotes that wanted to eat him. He said he could see their red eyes glowing in the dark. He said he shot out the spotlight on the first patrol car that arrived because he was afraid the light would give his position away to the animals. When asked about the shot from eighty yards, he said he had qualified as an expert marksman during the first war in Iraq.

The report estimated that Wyms fired at least twenty-seven times while deputies were on the scene and dozens of times before that. Investigators eventually collected a total of ninety-four spent bullet casings.

Wyms did not surrender that night until he ran out of beer. Shortly after crushing the last empty in his hand, he told the cell-phone negotiator that he would trade one rifle for a six-pack of beer. He was turned down. He then announced that he was sorry and ready for the incident and every-thing else to be over, that he was going to kill himself and literally go out with a bang. The negotiator tried to talk him out of it and kept the conver-sation going while a two-man SWAT unit moved through the heavy terrain toward his position in a dense stand of eucalyptus trees. But soon the negotiator heard snoring on the cell line. Wyms had passed out.

The SWAT team moved in and Wyms was captured without a shot being fired by law enforcement. Order was restored. Since Deputy Stallworth had taken the initial call and was the one fired upon, he was given the collar. The gunman was placed in Stallworth's squad car and transported to the Malibu substation and jailed.

Other documents in the file continued the Eli Wyms saga. At his arraign-ment the morning after his arrest, Wyms was declared indigent and assigned a public defender. The case moved slowly in the system, with Wyms being held in the Men's Central Jail. But then Vincent stepped in and offered his services pro bono. His first order of business was to ask for and receive a competency evaluation of his client. This had the effect of slowing the case down even further as Wyms was carted off to the state hospital in Camarillo for a ninety-day psych evaluation.

That evaluation period was over and the reports were now in. All of the doctors who examined, tested, and talked to Wyms in Camarillo had agreed that he was competent and ready to stand trial.

In the hearing scheduled before Judge Mark Friedman at two, a trial date would be set and the case clock would begin to tick again. To me it was all a formality. One read of the case documents and I knew there would be no trial. What the day's hearing would do was set the time period I would have to negotiate a plea agreement for my client.

It was a cut-and-dried case. Wyms would enter a plea and probably face a year or two of incarceration and mental-health counseling. The only question I got from my survey of the file was why Vincent had taken the case in the first place. It didn't fall into line with the kinds of cases he usually handled, with paying or higher-profile clients. There didn't seem to be much of a challenge to the case either. It was routine and Wyms's crime wasn't even unusual. Was it simply a case Jerry took on to satisfy a need for pro bono work? It seemed to me if that was the case that Vincent could have found something more interesting, which would pay off in other ways, such as publicity. The Wyms case had initially drawn media attention because of the public spectacle in the park. But when it came to trial or disposition of the case, it would likely fly well below the media radar.

My next thought was to suspect that there was a connection to the Elliot case. Vincent had found some sort of link.

But on first read I couldn't nail it down. There were two general connections in that the Wyms incident had happened less than twelve hours before the beach house murders and both crimes had occurred in the Sheriff's Department's Malibu district. But those connections didn't hold up to further scrutiny. In terms of topography they weren't remotely connected. The murders were on the beach and the Wyms shooting spree took place far inland, in the county park on the other side of the mountains. As far as I could recall, none of the names in the Wyms file were mentioned in the Elliot materials I had reviewed. The Wyms incident happened on the night shift; the Elliot murders on the day shift.

I couldn't nail down any specific connection and in great frustration closed the file with the question unanswered. I checked my watch and saw I had to get back to the CCB if I wanted time to meet my client in lockup before the two o'clock hearing.

I called Patrick to come get me, paid for lunch, and stepped out to the curb. I was on my cell, talking with Lorna, when the Lincoln pulled up and I jumped into the back.

"Has Cisco met with Carlin yet?" I asked her.

"No, that's at two."

"Have Cisco ask him about the Wyms case, too."

"Okay, what about it?"

"Ask him why Vincent even took it."

"You think they're connected? Elliot and Wyms?"

"I think it but I don't see it."

"Okay, I'll tell him."

"Anything else going on?"

"Not at the moment. You're getting a lot of calls from the media. Who's this guy Jack McEvoy?"

The name rang a bell but I couldn't place it.

"I don't know. Who is he?"

"He works at the *Times*. He called up all huffy about not hearing from you, saying you had an exclusive deal with him."

Now I remembered. The two-way street.

"Don't worry about him. I haven't heard from him either. What else?"

"Court TV wants to sit down and talk about Elliot. They're going to carry live coverage throughout the trial, making it their feature, and so they're hoping to get daily commentary from you at the end of court each day."

"What do you think, Lorna?"

"I think it's like free national advertising. You better do it. They told me they're giving the trial its own logo wrap at the bottom of the screen. 'Murder in Malibu,' they're calling it."

"Then, set it up. What else?"

"Well, while we're on the subject, I got a notice a week ago that your bus bench contract expires at the end of the month. I was just going to let it go because there was no money, but now you're back and you've got money. Should we renew?"

For the past six years I had advertised on bus benches strategically located in high-crime and-traffic locations around the city. Although I had dropped out for the past year, the benches still spawned a steady stream of calls, all of which Lorna deferred or referred.

"That's a two-year contract, right?"

"Yes."

I made a quick decision.

"Okay, renew it. Anything else?"

"That's it from here. Oh, wait. One other thing. The landlord for the building came in today. Called herself the leasing agent, which is just a fancy way of saying landlord. She wants to know if we're going to keep the office. Jerry's death is a lease breaker if we want it to be. I got the feeling there's a waiting list on the building and this is an opportunity to jack the rent up for the next lawyer who comes in here."

I looked out the window of the Lincoln as we cruised across the 101 overpass and back into the civic center area. I could see the newly built Catholic cathedral and past that, the waving steel skin of the Disney Concert Hall. It caught the sunlight and took on a warm orange glow.

"I don't know, Lorna, I like working from the backseat here. It's never boring. What do you think?"

"I'm not particularly fond of putting on makeup every morning."

Meaning she liked working out of her condo more than she liked getting ready and driving downtown to an office each day. As usual, we were on the same page.

"Something to think about," I said. "No makeup. No office overhead. No fighting for a spot in the parking garage."

She didn't respond. It was going to be my call. I looked ahead and saw we were a block from my drop-off point in front of the CCB.

"Let's talk about it later," I said. "I gotta jump out."

"Okay, Mickey. Be safe."

"You, too."

26

Eli Wyms was still doped up from the three months he'd spent in Camarillo. He'd been sent back to county with a prescription for a drug therapy that wasn't going to help me defend him, let alone help him answer any questions about possible connections to the murders on the beach. It took me less than two minutes in courtside lockup to grasp the situation and to decide to submit a motion to Judge Friedman, requesting that all drug therapy be halted. I went back to the courtroom and found Joanne Giorgetti at her place at the prosecution table. The hearing was scheduled to start in five minutes.

She was writing something on the inside flap of a file when I walked up to the table. Without looking up she somehow knew it was me.

"You want a continuance, don't you?"

"And a cease-and-desist on the drugs. The guy's a zombie."

She stopped writing and looked up at me.

"Considering he was potshotting my deputies, I'm not sure I object to his being in that condition."

"But Joanne, I've got to be able to ask the guy basic questions in order to defend him."

"Really?"

She said it with a smile but the point was taken. I shrugged and crouched down so we were on an even eye line.

"You're right, I don't think we're talking about a trial here," I said. "I'd be happy to listen to any offers."

"Your client shot at an occupied sheriff's car. The state is interested in sending a message on this one. We don't like people doing that."

She folded her arms to signal the state's unwillingness to compromise on this. She was an attractive and athletically built woman. She drummed her fingers on one of her biceps and I couldn't help but notice the red fingernail polish. As long as I could remember dealing with Joanne Giorgetti, her nails were always painted bloodred. She did more than represent the state. She represented cops who had been shot at, assaulted, ambushed, and spit on. And she wanted the blood of every miscreant who had the bad luck to be prosecuted by her.

"I would argue that my client, panicked as he was by the coyotes, was shooting at the light on the car, not into the car. Your own documents say he was an expert marksman in the U.S. Army. If he wanted to shoot the deputy, he could have. But he didn't."

"He was discharged from the army fifteen years ago, Mickey."

"Right, but some skills never go away. Like riding a bike."

"Well, that's an argument you could surely make to the jury."

My knees were about to give out. I reached over to one of the chairs at the defense table, wheeled it over, and sat down.

"Sure, I can make that argument but it is probably in the state's best interest to bring this case to a close, get Mr. Wyms off the street and into some sort of therapy that will help prevent this from ever happening again. So what do you say? Should we go off into a corner someplace and work this out, or go at it in front of a jury?"

She thought for a moment before responding. It was the classic prosecutor's dilemma. It was a case she could easily win. She had to decide whether to pad her stats or do what might be the right thing.

"As long as I get to pick the corner."

"That's fine with me."

"Okay, I won't oppose a continuance if you make the motion."

"Sounds good, Joanne. What about the drug therapy?"

"I don't want this guy acting out again, even in Men's Central."

"Look, wait till they bring him out. You'll see, he's a zombie. You don't want this to go down and then have him challenge the deal because the state made him incompetent to make a decision. Let's get his head clear, do the deal, and then you can have them pump him up with whatever you want."

She thought about it, saw the logic, and finally nodded.

"But if he acts out in jail one time, I'm going to blame you and take it out on him."

I laughed. The idea of blaming me was absurd.

"Whatever."

I got up and started to push the chair back to the defense table. But then I turned back to the prosecutor.

"Joanne, let me ask you something else. Why did Jerry Vincent take on this case?"

She shrugged and shook her head.

"I don't know."

"Well, did it surprise you?"

"Sure. It was kind of strange, him showing up. I knew him from way back when, you know?"

Meaning when he was a prosecutor.

"Yeah, so what happened?"

"One day — a few months ago — I got notice of a competency motion on

Wyms, and Jerry's name was on it. I called him up and said, 'What the hell,' you know? 'You don't even call to say, I'm taking over the case?' And he just said he wanted to get some pro bono in and asked the PD for a case. But I know Angel Romero, the PD who had the case originally. A couple months back, I ran into him on one of the floors and he asked me what was happening on Wyms. And in the course of the conversation, he told me that Jerry didn't just come in asking for a PB referral. He went to Wyms first in Men's Central, signed him up, and then came in and told Angel to turn over the file."

"Why do you think he took the case?"

I've learned over the years that sometimes if you ask the same question more than once you get different responses.

"I don't know. I specifically asked him that and he didn't really answer. He changed the subject to something else and it was all kind of awkward. I remember thinking there was something else here, like maybe he had a connection to Wyms. But then when he sent him off to Camarillo, I knew he wasn't doing the guy any favors."

"What do you mean?"

"Look, you just spent a couple hours with the case and you know how it's going to go. This is a plea. Jail time, counseling, and supervision. That's what it was before he was sent to Camarillo. So Wyms's time there wasn't really necessary. Jerry just prolonged the inevitable."

I nodded. She was right. Sending a client to the psych ward at Camarillo wasn't doing him any favors. The mystery case was getting more mysterious. Only, my client was in no condition to tell me why. His lawyer — Vincent — had kept him drugged up and locked away for three months.

"Okay, Joanne. Thanks. Let's —"

I was interrupted by the clerk, who called court into session, and I looked up to see Judge Friedman taking the bench.

27

Angel Romero was one of those human interest stories you read in the paper every now and then. The story about the gangbanger who grew up hard on the streets of East L.A. but fought his way through to an education and even law school, then turned around and gave back to the community. Angel's way to give back was to go into the Public Defender's Office and represent the underdogs of society. He was a lifer in the PD and had seen many young lawyers — myself included — come and go on their way to private practice and the supposed big bucks that came with it.

After the Wyms hearing — in which the judge granted the motion to continue in order to give Giorgetti and me time to work out a plea — I went down to the PD's office on the tenth floor and asked for Romero. I knew he was a working lawyer, not a supervisor, and that most likely meant he was in a courtroom somewhere in the building. The receptionist typed something into her computer and looked at the screen.

"Department one-twenty-four," she said.

"Thank you," I said.

Department 124 was Judge Champagne's courtroom on the thirteenth floor, the same floor I had just come from. But that was life in the CCB. It seemed to run in circles. I took the elevator back up and walked down the hall to 124, powering my phone down as I approached the double doors. Court was in session and Romero was in front of the judge, arguing a motion to reduce bail. I slid into the back row of the gallery and hoped for a quick ruling so I could get to Romero without a long wait.

My ears perked up when I heard Romero mention his client by name, calling him Mr. Scales. I slid further down the bench so I had a better visual angle on the defendant sitting next to Romero. He was a white guy in an orange jail jumpsuit. When I saw his profile, I knew it was Sam Scales, a con man and former client. The last I remembered of Scales, he had gone off to prison on a plea deal I'd obtained for him. That was three years ago. He obviously had gotten out and gotten right back into trouble — only this time he hadn't called me.

After Romero finished his bail argument, the prosecutor stood up and vigorously opposed bail, outlining in his argument the new charges against Scales. When I had represented him, he had been accused in a credit-card fraud in which he ripped off people donating to a tsunami relief organization. This time it was worse. He was once more charged with fraud but in this case the victims were the widows of military servicemen killed in Iraq. I shook my head and almost smiled. I was glad Sam hadn't called me. The public defender could have him.

Judge Champagne ruled quickly after the prosecutor finished. She called Scales a predator and a menace to society and kept his bail at a million dollars. She noted that if she'd been asked, she probably would have raised it. It was then that I remembered it had been Judge Champagne who had sentenced Scales in the earlier fraud. There was nothing worse for a defendant than coming back and facing the same judge for another crime. It was almost as if the judges took the failings of the justice system personally.

I slouched in my seat and used another observer in the gallery as a blind so that Scales couldn't see me when the court deputy stood him up, cuffed him, and took him back into lockup. After he was gone, I straightened back up and was able to catch Romero's eye. I signaled him out into the hallway and he flashed five fingers at me. Five minutes. He still had some business to take care of in the court.

I went out into the hallway to wait for him and turned my phone back on. No messages. I was calling Lorna to check in when I heard Romero's voice behind me. He was four minutes early.

"Eenie, meenie, minie, moe, catch a killer by the toe. If his lawyer's Haller, let him go. Eenie, meenie, minie, moe. Hey bro."

He was smiling. I closed the phone and we bumped fists. I hadn't heard that homespun jingle since I was with the PD's Office. Romero had made it up after I had gotten the not-guilty verdict in the Barnett Woodson case back in 'ninety-two.

"What's up?" Romero asked.

"I'll tell you what's up. You're guzzling my clients, man. Sam Scales used to be mine."

I said it with a knowing smile and Romero smiled right back.

"You want him? You can have him. That's one dirty white boy. As soon as the media gets wind of this case, they're going to lynch his ass for what he's done."

"Taking war widows' money, huh?"

"Stealing government death benefits. I tell you, I've repped a lot of bad guys who did a lot of bad things, but I put Scales up there with the baby rapers, man. I can't stand the guy."

"Yeah, what are you doing with a white boy anyway? You work gang crimes."

Romero's face turned serious and he shook his head.

"Not anymore, man. They thought I was getting too close to the customers. You know, once a vato always a vato. So they took me off gangs. After nineteen years, I'm off gangs."

"Sorry to hear that, buddy."

Romero had grown up in Boyle Heights in a neighborhood ruled by a gang called Quatro Flats. He had the tattoos to prove it, if you could ever see his arms. It didn't matter how hot a day it was, he always wore long sleeves when he was working. And when he represented a banger accused of a crime, he did more than defend him in court. He worked to spring the man from the clutches of gang life. To pull him away from gang cases was an act of stupidity that could only happen in a bureaucracy like the justice system.

"What do you want with me, Mick? You didn't really come here to take Scales from me, right?"

"No, you get to keep Scales, Angel. I wanted to ask you about another client you had for a while earlier this year. Eli Wyms."

I was about to give the details of the case as a prompt but Romero immediately recognized the case and nodded.

"Yeah, Vincent took that one off me. You got it now with him being dead?"

"Yeah, I got all of Vincent's cases. I just found out about Wyms today."

"Well, good luck with them, bro. What do you need to know about Wyms? Vincent took it off me three months ago, at least."

I nodded.

"Yeah, I know. I got a handle on the case. What I'm curious about is Vincent taking it. According to Joanne Giorgetti, he went after it. Is that right?"

Romero checked the memory banks for a few moments before answering. He raised a hand and rubbed his chin as he did so. I could see faint scars across his knuckles from where he'd had tattoos removed.

"Yeah, he went down to the jail and talked Wyms into it. Got a signed discharge letter and brought it in. After that, the case was his. I gave him my file and I was done, man."

I moved in closer to him.

"Did he say why he wanted the case? I mean, he didn't know Wyms, did he?"

"I don't think so. He just wanted the case. He gave me the big wink, you know?"

"No, what do you mean? What's the 'big wink'?"

"I asked him why he was taking on a Southside homeboy who went up there in white-people country and shot the place up. Pro bono, no less. I thought he had some sort of racial angle on it or something. Something that would get him a little publicity. But he just sort of gave me the wink, like there was something else."

"Did you ask him what?"

Romero took an involuntary step back as I pressed his personal space.

"Yeah, man, I asked. But he wouldn't tell me. He just said that Wyms had fired the magic bullet. I didn't know what the hell he meant and I didn't have any more time to play games with him. I gave him the file and I went on to the next one."

There it was again. The magic bullet. I was getting close to something here and I could feel the blood in my veins start to move with high velocity.

"Is that it, Mick? I gotta get back inside."

My eyes focused on Romero and I realized he was looking at me strangely.

"Yeah, Angel, thanks. That's all. Go back in there and give 'em hell."

"Yeah, man, that's what I do."

Romero went back toward the door to Department 124 and I headed off quickly to the elevators. I knew what I would be doing for the rest of the day and into the night. Tracing a magic bullet.

28

I entered the office and blew right by Lorna and Cisco, who were at the reception desk, looking at the computer. I spoke without stopping on my way to the inner sanctum.

"If you two have any updates for me or anything else I should know, then come in now. I'm about to go into lockdown."

"And hello to you, too," Lorna called after me.

But Lorna knew well what was about to happen. Lockdown was when I closed all the doors and windows, drew the curtains, and killed the phones and went to work on a file and a case with total concentration and absorption. Lockdown for me was the ultimate DO NOT DISTURB sign hanging on the door. Lorna knew that once I was in lockdown mode, there was no getting me out until I had found what I was looking for.

I moved around Jerry Vincent's desk and dropped into the seat. I opened my bag on the floor and started pulling out the files. I viewed what I needed to do here as me against them. Somewhere in the files, I would find the key to Jerry Vincent's last secret. I would find the magic bullet.

Lorna and Cisco came into the office soon after I was settled.

"I didn't see Wren out there," I said before either could speak.

"And you never will again," Lorna said. "She quit."

"That was kind of abrupt."

"She went out to lunch and never came back."

"Did she call?"

"Yeah, she finally called. She said she got a better offer. She's going to be Bruce Carlin's secretary now."

I nodded. That seemed to make a certain amount of sense.

"Now, before you go into lockdown, we need to go over some things," Lorna said.

"That's what I said when I came in. What've you got?"

Lorna sat down in one of the chairs in front of the desk. Cisco stayed standing, more like pacing, behind her.

"All right," Lorna said. "Couple things while you were in court. First, you must've touched a nerve with that motion you filed on the evidence in Patrick's case."

"What happened?" I asked.

"The prosecutor's called three times today, wanting to talk about a dispo."

I smiled. The motion to examine the evidence had been a long shot but it looked like it might come through and I would be able to help Patrick.

"What's going on with that?" Lorna asked. "You didn't tell me you filed motions."

"From the car yesterday. And what's going on is that I think Dr. Vogler gave his wife phony diamonds for her birthday. Now, to make sure she never knows it, they're going to float a deal to Patrick if I withdraw my request to examine the evidence."

"Good. I think I like Patrick."

"I hope he gets the break. What's next?"

Lorna looked at the notes on her steno pad. I knew she didn't like to be rushed but I was rushing her.

"You're still getting a lot of calls from the local media. About Jerry Vincent or Walter Elliot or both. You want to go over them?"

"No. I don't have the time for any media calls."

"Well, that's what I've been telling them but it's not making them happy. Especially that guy from the *Times*. He's being an asshole."

"So what if they're not happy? I don't care."

"Well, you better be careful, Mickey. Hell hath no fury like the media scorned."

It was a good point. The media can love you one day and bury you the next. My father had spent twenty years as a media darling. But toward the end of his professional life, he had become a pariah because the reporters had grown weary of him getting guilty men off. He became the embodiment of a justice system that had different rules for well-heeled defendants with powerful attorneys.

"I'll try to be more accommodating," I said. "Just not now."

"Fine."

"Anything else to report?"

"I think that's — I told you about Wren, so that's all I have. You'll call the prosecutor on Patrick's case?"

"Yes, I will call him."

I looked over Lorna's shoulder at Cisco, who was still standing.

"Okay, Cisco, your turn. What've you got?"

"Still working on Elliot. Mostly in regard to Rilz and some hand-holding with our witnesses."

"I have a question about witnesses," Lorna interrupted. "Where do you want to put up Dr. Arslanian?"

Shamiram Arslanian was the gunshot residue authority Vincent had scheduled to bring in from New York as an expert witness to knock down the state's expert witness at trial. She was the best in the field and, with Walter Elliot's financial reserves, Vincent was going with the best money could buy. I wanted her close to the downtown CCB but the choice of hotels was limited.

"Try Checkers first," I said. "And get her a suite. If they're booked, then try the Standard and then the Kyoto Grand. But get a suite so we have room to work."

"Got it. And what about Muniz? You want him in close, too?"

Julio Muniz was a freelance videographer who lived in Topanga Canyon. Because of his home's proximity to Malibu he had been the first member of the media to respond to the crime scene after hearing the call out for homicide investigators on the sheriff's radio band. He had shot video of Walter Elliot with the sheriff's deputies outside the beach house. He was a valuable witness because his videotape and his own recollections could be used to confirm or contradict testimony offered by sheriff's deputies and investigators.

"I don't know," I said. "It can take anywhere from an hour to three hours to get from Topanga to downtown. I'd rather not risk it. Cisco, is he willing to come in and stay at a hotel?"

"Yeah, just as long as we're paying and he can order room service."

"Okay, then bring him in. Also, where's the video? There are only notes on it in the file. I don't want the first time I look at the video to be in court."

Cisco looked puzzled.

"I don't know. But if it's not around here, I can have Muniz dub off a copy."

"Well, I haven't seen it around here. So get me a copy. What else?"

"Couple other things. First, I got with my source on the Vincent thing and he didn't know anything about a suspect or this photo Bosch showed you this morning."

"Nothing?"

"Nada."

"What do you think? Does Bosch know your guy's the leak and is shutting him out?"

"I don't know. But everything I was telling him about this photo was news to him."

I took a few moments to consider what this meant.

"Did Bosch ever come back and show the photo to Wren?"

"No," Lorna said. "I was with her all morning. Bosch never came in then or after lunch."

I wasn't sure what any of this meant but I couldn't become bogged down with it. I had to get to the files.

"What was the second thing?" I asked Cisco.

"What?"

"You said you had a couple other things to tell me. What was the second thing?"

"Oh, yeah. I called Vincent's liquidator and you had that right. He's still got one of Patrick's long boards."

"What's he want for it?"

"Nothing."

I looked at Cisco and raised my eyebrows, asking where the catch was.

"Let's just say he'd like to do you the favor. He lost a good client in Vincent. I think he's hoping you'll use him for future liquidations. And I didn't dissuade him from the idea or tell him you usually don't barter property for services with your clients."

I understood. The surfboard would not come with any real strings attached.

"Thanks, Cisco. Did you take it with you?"

"No, he didn't have it at the office. But he made a call and somebody was supposed to bring it in to him this afternoon. I could go back and get it if you want."

"No, just get me an address and I'll have Patrick pick it up. What happened with Bruce Carlin? Didn't you debrief him today? Maybe he's got the Muniz tape."

I was anxious to hear about Bruce Carlin on several levels. Most important, I wanted to know if he had worked for Vincent on the Eli Wyms case. If so, he might be able to lead me to the magic bullet.

But Cisco didn't answer my question. Lorna turned and they looked at each other as if wondering which one of them should deliver the bad news.

"What's wrong?" I asked.

Lorna turned back to me.

"Carlin's fucking with us," she said.

I could see the angry set of her jaw. And I knew she reserved that kind of language for special occasions. Something had gone wrong with Carlin's debriefing and she was particularly upset.

"How so?"

"Well, he never showed up at two like he said he would. Instead, he called at two—right after Wren called and quit—and gave us the new parameters of his deal."

I shook my head in annoyance.

"His deal? How much does he want?"

"Well, I guess he realized that at two hundred dollars an hour he wouldn't make much, since he was probably going to bill only two or three hours tops. That's all Cisco would need with him. So he called up and said he wanted a flat fee or we could figure out things on our own."

"Like I said, how much?"

"Ten thousand dollars."

"You gotta be fucking kidding me."

"My words exactly."

I looked from her to Cisco.

"This is extortion. Isn't there a state agency that regulates you guys? Can't we come down on his shit somehow?"

Cisco shook his head.

"There are all kinds of regulatory agencies but this is a shady area."

"Yeah, I know it's shady. He's shady. I've thought that for years."

"What I mean is, he had no deal with Vincent. We can't find any contract. So he's not required to give us anything. We simply need to hire him and he's setting his price at ten grand. It's a bullshit rip-off but it's probably legal. I mean, you're the lawyer. You tell me."

I thought about it for a few moments and then tried to push it aside. I was still riding on the adrenaline charge I'd picked up in the courthouse. I didn't want it to dissipate with distractions.

"All right, I'll ask Elliot if he wants to pay it. Meantime, I'm going to hit all the files again tonight, and if I get lucky and crack through, then we won't need him. We say fuck you and are done with him."

"Asshole," Lorna muttered.

I was pretty sure that was directed at Bruce Carlin and not me.

"Okay, is that it?" I asked. "Anything else?"

I looked from one face to the other. Nobody had anything else to bring up.

"Okay, then, thank you both for all you've been putting up with and doing this week. Go out and have a good night."

Lorna looked at me curiously.

"You're sending us home?" she asked.

I checked my watch.

"Why not?" I said. "It's almost four thirty and I'm going to dive into the files and I don't want any distractions. You two go on home, have a good night, and we'll start again tomorrow."

"You're going to work here alone tonight?" Cisco asked.

"Yeah, but don't worry. I'll lock the door and I won't let anybody in — even if I know him."

I smiled. Lorna and Cisco didn't. I pointed to the open door to the office. It had a slide bolt that could be used to lock it at the top of the doorframe. If necessary I would be able to secure both outside and inside perimeters. It gave new meaning to the idea of going into lockdown.

"Come on, I'll be fine. I've got work to do."

They slowly, reluctantly, started to make their way out of my office.

"Lorna," I called after them. "Patrick should be out there. Tell him to keep hanging. I might have something to tell him after I make that call."

29

I opened the Patrick Henson file on my desk and looked up the prosecutor's number. I wanted to get this out of the way before I went to work on the Elliot case.

The prosecutor was Dwight Posey, a guy I had dealt with before on cases and never liked. Some prosecutors deal with defense attorneys as though they are only one step removed from their clients. As pseudocriminals, not as educated and experienced professionals. Not as necessary cogs in the winding gears of the justice system. Most cops have this view and I can live with it. But it bothers me when fellow lawyers adopt the pose. Unfortunately, Dwight Posey was one of these, and if I could've gone through the rest of my life without ever having to talk to him, I would have been a happy man. But that was not going to be the case.

"So, Haller," he said after taking the call, "they've got you walking in a dead man's shoes, don't they?"

"What?"

"They gave you all of Jerry Vincent's cases, right? That's how you ended up with Henson."

"Yeah, something like that. Anyway, I'm returning your call, Dwight. Actually, your three calls. What's up? You get the motion I filed yesterday?"

I reminded myself that I had to step carefully here if I wanted to get everything I could out of the phone call. I couldn't let my distaste for the prosecutor affect the outcome for my client.

"Yes, I got the motion. It's sitting right here on my desk. That's why I've been calling."

He left it open for me to step in.

"And?"

"And, uh, well, we're not going to do that, Mick."

"Do what, Dwight?"

"Put our evidence out there for examination."

It was looking more and more like I had struck a major nerve with my motion.

"Well, Dwight, that's the beauty of the system, right? You don't get to make that decision. A judge does. That's why I didn't ask you. I put it in a motion and asked the judge."

Posey cleared his throat.

"No, actually, we do this time," he said. "We're going to drop the theft charge and just proceed with the drug charge. So you can withdraw your motion or we can inform the judge that the point is moot."

I smiled and nodded. I had him. I knew then that Patrick was going to walk.

"Only problem with that, Dwight, is that the drug charge came out of the theft investigation. You know that. When they popped my client, the warrant was for the theft. The drugs were found during the arrest. So you don't have one without the other."

I had the feeling that he knew everything I was saying and that the call was simply following a script. We were going where Posey wanted us to go and that was fine with me. This time I wanted to go there, too.

"Then, maybe we can just talk about a disposition on the matter," he said as if the idea had just occurred to him.

And there we were. We had come to the place Posey had wanted to get to from the moment he'd answered the call.

"I'm open to it, Dwight. You should know that my client voluntarily entered a rehab program after his arrest. He has completed the program, has full-time employment, and has been clean for four months. He'll give his piss anytime, anywhere, to prove it."

"That is really good to hear," Posey said with false enthusiasm. "The DA's Office, as well as the courts, always looks favorably upon voluntary rehabilitation."

Tell me something I don't know, I almost said.

"The kid is doing good. I can vouch for that. What do you want to do for him?"

I knew how the script would read now. Posey would turn it into a good-will gesture from the prosecution. He would make it seem as though the DA's Office were giving out the favor here, when the truth was that the prosecution was acting to insulate an important figure from political and personal embarrassment. That was fine with me. I didn't care about the political ends of the deal as long as my client got what I wanted him to get.

"Tell you what, Mick. Let's make it go away, and maybe Patrick can use this opportunity to move ahead with being a productive member of society."

"Sounds like a plan to me, Dwight. You're making my day. And his."

"Okay, then get me his rehab records and we'll put it into a package for the judge."

Posey was talking about making it a pretrial intervention case. Patrick would have to take biweekly drug tests and in six months the case would go away if he kept clean. He would still have an arrest on his record but no conviction. Unless...

"You willing to expunge his record?" I asked.

"Uh...that's asking a lot, Mickey. He did, after all, break in and steal the diamonds."

"He didn't break in, Dwight. He was invited in. And the alleged diamonds are what this is all about, right? Whether or not he actually did steal any diamonds."

Posey must have realized he had misspoken by bringing up the diamonds. He folded his tent quickly.

"All right, fine. We'll put it into the package."

"You're a good man, Dwight."

"I try to be. You will withdraw your motion now?"

"First thing tomorrow. When do we go to court? I have a trial starting the end of next week."

"Then we'll go for Monday. I'll let you know."

I hung up the phone and called the reception desk on the intercom. Luckily, Lorna answered.

"I thought you were sent home," I said.

"We're about to go through the door. I'm going to leave my car here and go with Cisco."

"What, on his *donor*cycle?"

"Excuse me, *Dad*, but I don't think you have anything to say about that."

I groaned.

"But I do have a say over who works as my investigator. If I can keep you two apart, maybe I can keep you alive."

"Mickey, don't you dare!"

"Can you just tell Cisco I need that address for the liquidator?"

"I will. And I'll see you tomorrow."

"Hope so. Wear a helmet."

I hung up and Cisco came in, carrying a Post-it in one hand and a gun in a leather holster in the other. He walked around the desk, put the Post-it down in front of me, then opened a drawer and put the weapon in it.

"What are you doing?" I asked. "You can't give me a gun."

"It's totally legal and registered to me."

"That's great but you can't give it to me. That's il—"

"I'm not giving it to you. I'm just storing it here because I'm done work for the day. I'll get it in the morning, okay?"

"Whatever. I think you two are overreacting."

"Better than underreacting. See you tomorrow."

"Thank you. Will you send Patrick in before you go?"

"You got it. And by the way, I always make her wear a helmet."

I looked at him and nodded.

"That's good, Cisco."

He left the room, and Patrick soon came in.

"Patrick, Cisco talked to Vincent's liquidator and he still has one of your long boards. You can go by and pick it up. Just tell him you are picking it up for me and to call me if there is any problem."

"Oh man, thank you!"

"Yeah, well, I've got even better news than that on your case."

"What happened?"

I went over the phone call I'd just had with Dwight Posey. As I told Patrick that he would do no jail time if he stayed clean, I watched his eyes gain a little light. It was as if I could see the burden drop off his shoulders. He could look once again at the future.

"I have to call my mom," he said. "She's gonna be so happy."

"Yeah, well, I hope you are, too."

"I am, I am."

"Now, the way I figure it, you owe me a couple thousand for my work on this. That's about two and a half weeks of driving. If you want, you can stick with me until it's paid off. After that, we can talk about it and see where we're at."

"That sounds good. I like the job."

"Good, Patrick, then it's a deal."

Patrick smiled broadly and was turning to go.

"One other thing, Patrick."

He turned back to me.

"I saw you sleeping in your car in the garage this morning."

"Sorry. I'll find another spot."

He looked down at the floor.

"No, *I'm* sorry," I said. "I forgot that you told me when we talked on the phone the first time that you were living in your car and sleeping on a lifeguard stand. I just don't know how safe it is to be sleeping in the same garage where a guy got shot the other night."

"I'll find someplace else."

"Well, if you want, I can give you an advance on your pay. Would that help you maybe get a motel room or something?"

"Um, I guess."

I was glad to help him out but I knew that living out of a weekly motel was almost as depressing as living out of a car.

"I'll tell you what," I said. "If you want, you could stay with me for a couple weeks. Until you get some money in your pocket and maybe get a better plan going."

"At your place?"

"Yeah, you know, temporarily."

"With you?"

I realized my mistake.

"Nothing like that, Patrick. I've got a house and you'd have your own room. In fact, on Wednesday nights and every other weekend, it would be better if you stayed with a friend or in a motel. That's when I have my daughter."

He thought about it and nodded.

"Yeah, I could do that."

I reached across the desk and signaled him to give me back the Post-it with the liquidator's address on it. I wrote my own address on it while I spoke.

"Why don't you go pick up your board and then head over to my place at this second address. Fareholm is right off Laurel Canyon, one street before Mount Olympus. You go up the stairs to the front porch and there's a table and chairs out there and an ashtray. The extra key's under the ashtray. The guest bedroom is right next to the kitchen. Just make yourself at home."

"Thanks."

He took the Post-it back and looked at the address I'd written.

"I probably won't get there till late," I told him. "I've got a trial starting next week and a lot of work to do before then."

"Okay."

"Look, we're only talking about a few weeks. Till you get on your feet again. Meantime, maybe we can help each other out. You know, like if one of us starts to feel the pull, maybe the other one will be there to talk about it. Okay?"

"Okay."

We were quiet for a moment, probably both of us thinking about the deal. I didn't tell Patrick that he might end up helping me more than I would help him. In the past forty-eight hours, the pressure of the new caseload had begun to weigh on me. I could feel myself being pulled back, feel the desire to go to the cotton-wrapped world the pills could give me. The pills opened the space between where I was and the brick wall of reality. I was beginning to crave that distance.

Up front and deep down I knew I didn't want that again, and maybe Patrick could help me avoid it.

"Thanks, Mr. Haller."

I looked up at him from my thoughts.

"Call me Mickey," I said. "And I should be the one saying thanks."

"Why are you doing all of this for me?"

I looked at the big fish on the wall behind him for a moment, then back at him.

"I'm not sure, Patrick. But I'm hoping that if I help you, then I'll be helping myself."

Patrick nodded like he knew what I was talking about. That was strange because I wasn't sure myself what I had meant.

"Go get your board, Patrick," I said. "I'll see you at the house. And make sure you remember to call your mother."

30

After I was finally alone in the office, I started the process the way I always do, with clean pages and sharp points. From the supply closet I retrieved two fresh legal pads and four Black Warrior pencils. I sharpened their points and got down to work.

Vincent had broken the Elliot case into two files. One file contained the state's case, and the second, thinner file contained the defense case. The weight of the defense file was not of concern to me. The defense played by the same rules of discovery as the prosecution. Anything that went into the second file went to the prosecutor. A seasoned defense attorney knew to keep the file thin. Keep the rest in your head, or hidden on a microchip in your computer if it is safe. I had neither Vincent's head nor his laptop. But I was sure the secrets Jerry Vincent kept were hidden somewhere in the hard copy. The magic bullet was there. I just had to find it.

I began with the thicker file, the prosecution's case. I read straight through, every page and every word. I took notes on one legal pad and drew a time-and-action flowchart on the other. I studied the crime scene photographs with a magnifying glass I took from the desk drawer. I drew up a list of every single name I encountered in the file.

From there, I moved on to the defense file and again read every word on every page. The phone rang two different times but I didn't even look up to see what name was on the screen. I didn't care. I was in relentless pursuit and cared about only one thing. Finding the magic bullet.

When I was finished with the Elliot files, I opened the Wyms case and read every document and report it contained, a time-consuming process. Because Wyms was arrested following a public incident that had drawn several uniform and SWAT deputies, this file was thick with reports from the various units involved and personnel at the scene. It was stuffed with transcriptions of the conversations with Wyms, as well as weapons and ballistics reports, a lengthy evidence inventory, witness statements, dispatch records, and patrol deployment reports.

There were a lot of names in the file and I checked every one of them against the list of names from the Elliot files. I also cross-referenced every address.

I had this client once. I don't even know her name because I was sure that the name she was under in the system was not her own. She was in on a first offense but she knew the system too well to be a virgin. In fact, she knew everything too well. Whatever her name was, she had somehow rigged the system and it had her down as someone she wasn't.

The charge was burglary of an occupied dwelling. But there was so much more than that behind the one charge. This woman liked to target hotel rooms where men with large amounts of money slept. She knew how to pick them, follow them, then finesse the door locks and the room safes while they slept. In one candid moment — probably the only one in our relationship — she told me of the white-hot adrenaline high she got every time the last digit fell into place and she heard the electronic gears of the hotel safe start to move and unlock. Opening the safe and finding what was inside was never as good as that magic moment when the gears began to grind and she felt the velocity of her blood moving in her veins. Nothing before or after was as good as that moment. The jobs weren't about the money. They were about the velocity of blood.

I nodded when she told me all of this. I had never broken into a hotel room while some guy was snoring on the bed. But I knew about the moment when the gears began to grind. I knew about the velocity.

I found what I was looking for an hour into my second run at the files. It had been there in front of me the whole time. First in Elliot's arrest report and then on the time-and-action chart I had drawn myself. I called the chart the Christmas tree. It always started basic and unadorned. Just the bare-bones facts of the case. Then, as I continued to study and make the case my own, I started hanging lights and ornaments on it. Details and witness statements, evidence and lab results. Soon the tree was lit up and bright. Everything about the case was there for me to see in the context of time and action.

I had paid particular attention to Walter Elliot as I had drawn the Christmas tree. He was the tree trunk and all branches came from him. I had his movements, statements, and actions noted by time.

12:40 p.m. — WE arrives at beach house
12:50 p.m. — WE discovers bodies
 1:05 p.m. — WE calls 911
 1:24 p.m. — WE calls 911 again
 1:28 p.m. — Deputies arrive on scene
 1:30 p.m. — WE secured
 2:15 p.m. — Homicide arrives
 2:40 p.m. — WE taken to Malibu station
 4:55 p.m. — WE interviewed, advised
 5:40 p.m. — WE transported to Whittier
 7:00 p.m. — GSR testing
 8:00 p.m. — Second interview attempt, declined, arrested
 8:40 p.m. — WE transported to Men's Central

Some of the times I estimated but most came directly from the arrest report and other documents in the file. Law enforcement in this country is as much about the paperwork as anything else. I could always count on the prosecution file for reconstructing a time line.

On the second go-round I used both the pencil point and eraser and started adding decorations to the tree.

12:40 p.m. — WE arrives at beach house front door unlocked
12:50 p.m. — WE discovers bodies balcony door open
 1:05 p.m. — WE calls 911 waits outside
 1:24 p.m. — WE calls 911 again what's the holdup?
 1:28 p.m. — Deputies arrive on scene
               Murray (4-alpha-1) and Harber (4-alpha-2)
 1:30 p.m. — WE secured placed in patrol car
               Murray/Harber search house
 2:15 p.m. — Homicide arrives
               first team: Kinder (#14492) and Ericsson (#21101)
               second team: Joshua (#22234) and Toles (#15154)
 2:30 p.m. — WE taken inside house, describes discovery
 2:40 p.m. — WE taken to Malibu station
               Joshua and Toles transport
 4:55 p.m. — WE interviewed, advised Kinder takes lead in
               interview
 5:40 p.m. — WE transported to Whittier Joshua/Toles
 7:00 p.m. — GSR testing
               F.T. Anita Sherman
               Lab Transport, Sherman
 8:00 p.m. — Second interview, Ericsson in lead, WE declines got smart
 8:40 p.m. — WE transported to Men's Central Joshua/Toles

As I had constructed the Christmas tree, I kept a separate list on another page of every human being mentioned in the sheriff's reports. I knew this would become the witness list I would turn over to the prosecution the following week. As a rule I blanket the case, subpoenaing anybody mentioned in the investigative record just to be safe. You can always cut down a witness list at trial. Sometimes adding to it can be a problem.

From the witness list and the Christmas tree, I would be able to infer how the prosecution would roll out its case. I would also be able to determine which witnesses the prosecution team was avoiding and possibly why. It was while I was studying my work and thinking in these terms that I felt the gears begin to grind and the cold finger of revelation went down my spine. Everything became clear and bright and I found Jerry Vincent's magic bullet.

Walter Elliot had been taken from the crime scene to the Malibu station so that he would be out of the way and secured while the lead detectives continued their on-site investigation. One short interview was conducted at the station before Elliot ended it. He was then transported to sheriff's headquarters in Whittier, where a gunshot residue test was conducted and his hands tested positive for nitrates associated with gunpowder. Afterward, Kinder and Ericsson took another stab at interviewing their suspect but he wisely declined. He was then formally placed under arrest and booked into county jail.

It was standard procedure and the arrest report documented the chain of Elliot's custody. He was handled solely by the homicide detectives as he was moved from crime scene to substation to headquarters to jail. But it was how he was handled previous to their arrival that caught my eye. It was here that I saw something I had missed earlier. Something as simple as the designations of the uniform deputies who first responded to the call. According to the records, deputies Murray and Harber had the designations 4-alpha-1 and 4-alpha-2 after their names. And I had seen at least one of those designations in the Wyms file.

Jumping from case to case and from file to file, I found the Wyms arrest report and quickly scanned the narrative, not stopping until my eyes came to the first reference to the 4-alpha-1 designation.

Deputy Todd Stallworth had the designation written after his name. He was the deputy originally called to investigate the report of gunfire at Malibu Creek State Park. He was the deputy driving the car Wyms fired upon, and at the end of the standoff he was the deputy who formally placed Wyms under arrest and took him to jail.

I realized that 4-alpha-1 did not refer to a specific deputy but to a specific patrol zone or responsibility. The Malibu district covered the huge unincorporated areas of the west county, from the beaches of Malibu up over the mountains and into the communities of Thousand Oaks and Calabasas. I assumed that this was the fourth district and alpha was the specific designation for a patrol unit — a specific car. It seemed to be the only way to explain why deputies who worked different shifts would share the same designation on different arrest reports.

Adrenaline crashed into my veins and my blood took off running as everything came together. All in a moment I realized what Vincent had been up to and what he had been planning. I didn't need his laptop or his legal pads anymore. I didn't need his investigator. I knew exactly what the defense strategy was.

At least I thought I did.

I pulled my cell phone and called Cisco. I skipped the pleasantries.

"Cisco, it's me. Do you know any sheriff's deputies?"

"Uh, a few. Why?"

"Any of them work out of the Malibu station?"

"I know one guy who used to. He's in Lynwood now. Malibu was too boring."

"Can you call him tonight?"

"Tonight? Sure, I guess. What's up?"

"I need to know what the patrol designation four-alpha-one means. Can you get that?"

"Shouldn't be a problem. I'll call you back. But hold on a sec for Lorna. She wants to talk to you."

I waited while she was given the phone. I could hear TV noise in the background. I had interrupted a scene of domestic bliss.

"Mickey, are you still there at the office?"

"I'm here."

"It's eight-thirty. I think you should go home."

"I think I should, too. I'm going to wait to hear back from Cisco — he's checking something out for me — and then I think I'm going over to Dan Tana's to have steak and spaghetti."

She knew I went to Dan Tana's when I had something to celebrate. Usually a good verdict.

"You had steak for breakfast."

"Then I guess this will make it a perfect day."

"Things went well tonight?"

"I think so. Real well."

"You're going alone?"

She said it with sympathy in her voice, like now that she had hooked up with Cisco, she was starting to feel sorry for me, alone out there in the big bad world.

"Craig or Christian will keep me company."

Craig and Christian worked the door at Dan Tana's. They took care of me whether I came in alone or not.

"I'll see you tomorrow, Lorna."

"Okay, Mickey. Have fun."

"I already am."

I hung up and waited, pacing in the room and thinking it all through again. The dominoes went down one after the other. It felt good and it all fit. Vincent had not taken on the Wyms case out of any obligation to the law or the poor or the disenfranchised. He was using Wyms as camouflage. Rather than move the case toward the obvious plea agreement, he had stashed Wyms out at Camarillo for three months, thereby keeping the case alive and active. Meantime, he gathered information under the flag of the Wyms defense that he would use in the Elliot case, thereby hiding his moves and strategy from the prosecution.

Technically, he was probably acting within bounds, but ethically it was underhanded. Eli Wyms had spent ninety days in a state facility so Vincent could build a defense for Elliot. Elliot got the magic bullet while Wyms got the zombie cocktail.

The good thing was, I didn't have to worry about the sins of my predecessor. Wyms was out of Camarillo, and besides, they weren't my sins. I could just take the benefit of Vincent's discoveries and go to trial.

It didn't take too long before Cisco called back.

"I talked to my guy in Lynwood. Four-alpha is Malibu's lead car. The four is for the Malibu station and the alpha is for...alpha. Like the alpha dog. The leader of the pack. Hot shots—the priority calls—usually go to the alpha car. Four-alpha-one would be the driver, and if he's riding with a partner, then the partner would be four-alpha-two."

"So the alpha car covers the whole fourth district?"

"That's what he told me. Four-alpha is free to roam the district and scoop the cream off the top."

"What do you mean?"

"The best calls. The hot shots."

"Got it."

My theory was confirmed. A double murder and shots fired near a residential neighborhood would certainly be alpha-car calls. One designation but different deputies responding. Different deputies responding but one car. The dominoes clicked and fell.

"Does that help, Mick?"

"It does, Cisco. But it also means more work for you."

"On the Elliot case?"

"No, not Elliot. I want you to work on the Eli Wyms case. Find out everything you can about the night he was arrested. Get me details."

"That's what I'm here for."

31

The night's discovery pushed the case off the paper and into my imagination. I was starting to get courtroom images in my head. Scenes of examinations and cross-examinations. I was laying out the suits I would wear to court and the postures I would take in front of the jury. The case was coming alive inside and this was always a good thing. It was a momentum thing. You time it right and you go into trial with the inescapable conviction that you will not lose. I didn't know what had happened to Jerry Vincent, how his actions might have brought about his demise, or whether his death was linked at all to the Elliot case, but I felt as though I had a head on things. I had velocity and I was getting battle ready.

My plan was to sit in a corner booth at Dan Tana's and sketch out some of the key witness examinations, listing the baseline questions and probable answers for each. I was excited about getting to it, and Lorna need not have worried about me. I wouldn't be alone. I would have my case with me. Not Jerry Vincent's case. Mine.

After quickly repacking the files and adding fresh pencils and legal pads, I killed the lights and locked the office door. I headed down the hallway and then across the bridge to the parking garage. Just as I was entering the garage, I saw a man walking up the ramp from the first floor. He was fifty yards away and it was only a few moments and a few strides before I recognized him as the man in the photograph Bosch had shown me that morning.

My blood froze in my heart. The fight-or-flight instinct stabbed into my brain. The rest of the world didn't matter. There was just this moment and I had to make a choice. My brain assessed the situation faster than any computer IBM ever made. And the result of the computation was that I knew the man coming toward me was the killer and that he had a gun.

I swung around and started to run.

"Hey!" a voice called from behind me.

I kept running. I moved back across the bridge to the glass doors leading back into the building. One clear, single thought fired through every synapse in my brain. I had to get inside and get to Cisco's gun. I had to kill or be killed.

But it was after hours and the doors had locked behind me as I had left the building. I shot my hand into my pocket in search of the key, then jerked it out, bills, coins and wallet flying out with it.

As I jammed the key into the lock, I could hear running steps coming up quickly behind me. *The gun! Get the gun!*

I finally yanked the door open and bolted down the hallway toward the office. I glanced behind me and saw the man catch the door just before it closed and locked. He was still coming.

Key still in my hand, I reached the office door and fumbled the key while getting it into the lock. I could feel the killer closing in. Finally getting the door open, I entered, slammed it shut, and threw the lock. I hit the light switch, then crossed the reception area and charged into Vincent's office.

The gun Cisco left for me was there in the drawer. I grabbed it, yanked it out of its holster, and went back out to the reception area. Across the room I could see the killer's shape through the frosted glass. He was trying to open the door. I raised the gun and pointed at the blurred image.

I hesitated and then raised the gun higher and fired two shots into the ceiling. The sound was deafening in the closed room.

"That's right!" I yelled. "Come on in!"

The image on the other side of the glass door disappeared. I heard footsteps

moving away in the hallway and then the door to the bridge opening and closing. I stood stock-still and listened for any other sound. There was nothing.

Without taking my eyes off the door, I stepped over to the reception desk
and picked up the phone. I called 911 and it was answered right away, but I
got a recording that told me my call was important and that I needed to
hold on for the next available emergency dispatcher.

I realized I was shaking, not with fear but with the overload of adrenaline. I put the gun on the desk, checked my pocket, and found that I hadn't
lost my cell phone. With the office phone in one hand, I used the other to
open the cell and call Harry Bosch. He answered on the first ring.

"Bosch! That guy you showed me was just here!"

"Haller? What are you talking about? Who?"

"The guy in the photo you showed me today! The one with the gun!"

"All right, calm down. Where is he? Where are you?"

I realized that the stress of the moment had pulled my voice tight and
sharp. Embarrassed, I took a deep breath and tried to calm myself before
answering.

"I'm at the office. Vincent's office. I was leaving and I saw him in the
garage. I ran back inside and he ran in after me. He tried to get into the
office. I think he's gone but I'm not sure. I fired a couple of shots and then —"

"You have a gun?"

"Goddamn right I do."

"I suggest you put it away before somebody gets hurt."

"If that guy's still out there, he'll be the one getting hurt. Who the hell is
he?"

There was a pause before he answered.

"I don't know yet. Look, I'm still downtown and was just heading home
myself. I'm in the car. Sit tight and I'll be there in five minutes. Stay in the
office and keep the door locked."

"Don't worry, I'm not moving."

"And don't shoot me when I get there."

"I won't."

I reached over and hung up the office phone. I didn't need 911 if Bosch
was coming. I picked the gun back up.

"Hey, Haller?"

"What?"

"What did he want?"

"What?"

"The guy. What did he come there for?"

"That's a good goddamn question. But I don't have the answer."

"Look, stop fucking around and tell me!"

"I'm telling you! I don't know what he's after. Now quit talking and get
over here!"

I involuntarily squeezed my hands into fists as I yelled and put an accidental shot into the floor. I jumped as though I had been shot at by someone else.

"Haller!" Bosch yelled. "What the hell was that?"

I pulled in a deep breath and took my time composing myself before answering.

"Haller? What's going on?"

"Get over here and you'll find out."

"Did you hit him? Did you put him down?"

Without answering I closed the phone.

32

Bosch made it in six minutes but it felt like an hour. A dark image appeared on the other side of the glass and he knocked sharply.

"Haller, it's me, Bosch."

Carrying the gun at my side, I unlocked the door and let him in. He, too, had his gun out and at his side.

"Anything since we were on the phone?" he asked.

"Haven't seen or heard him. I guess I scared his ass away."

Bosch holstered his gun and threw me a look, as if to say my tough-guy pose was convincing no one except maybe myself.

"What was that last shot?"

"An accident."

I pointed toward the hole in the floor.

"Give me that gun before you get yourself killed."

I handed it over and he put it into the waistband of his pants.

"You don't own a gun — not legally. I checked."

"It's my investigator's. He leaves it here at night."

Bosch scanned the ceiling, until he saw the two holes I had put there. He then looked at me and shook his head.

He went over to the blinds and checked the street. Broadway was dead out there this time of night. A couple of nearby buildings had been converted into residential lofts but Broadway still had a way to go before recapturing the nightlife it had had eighty years before.

"Okay, let's sit down," he said.

He turned from the window to see me standing behind him.

"In your office."

"Why?"

"Because we're going to talk about this."

I moved into the office and took a seat behind the desk. Bosch sat down across from me.

"First of all, here's your stuff. I found it out there on the bridge."

From the pocket of his jacket he pulled my wallet and loose bills. He put it all on the desk and then reached back in for the coins.

"Okay, now what?" I asked as I put my property back in my pocket.

"Now we talk," Bosch said. "First off, do you want to file a report on this?"

"Why bother? You know about it. It's your case. Why don't you know who this guy is?"

"We're working on it."

"That's not good enough, Bosch! He came after me! Why can't you ID him?"

Bosch shook his head.

"Because we think he's a hitter brought in from out of town. Maybe out of the country."

"That's fucking fantastic! Why did he come back here?"

"Obviously, because of you. Because of what you know."

"Me? I don't know anything."

"You've been in here for three days. You must know something that makes you a danger to him."

"I'm telling you, I've got nothing."

"Then, you have to ask yourself, why did that guy come back? What did he leave behind or forget the first time?"

I just stared at him. I actually wanted to help. I was tired of being under the gun — in more ways than one — and if I could've given Bosch just one answer, I would have.

I shook my head.

"I can't think of a single —"

"Come on, Haller!" Bosch barked at me. "Your life is threatened here! Don't you get it? What've you got?"

"I told you!"

"Who did Vincent bribe?"

"I don't know and I couldn't tell you if I did."

"What did the FBI want with him?"

"I don't know that, either!"

He started pointing at me.

"You fucking hypocrite. You're hiding behind the protections of the law, while the killer is out there waiting. Your ethics and rules won't stop a bullet, Haller. Tell me what you've got!"

"I told you! I don't have anything and don't point your fucking finger at me. This isn't my job. It's your job. And maybe if you would get it done, people around here would feel —"

"Excuse me?"

The voice came from behind Bosch. In one fluid move he turned and pivoted out of his chair, drawing his gun and aiming it at the door.

A man holding a trash bag stood there, his eyes going wide in fright.

Bosch immediately lowered his weapon, and the office cleaner looked like he might faint.

"Sorry," Bosch said.

"I come back later," the man said in a thick accent from Eastern Europe. He turned and disappeared quickly through the door.

"Goddamn it!" Bosch cursed, clearly unhappy about pointing his gun at an innocent man.

"I doubt we'll ever get our trash cans emptied again," I said.

Bosch went over to the door and closed and bolted it. He came back to the desk and looked at me with angry eyes. He sat back down, took a deep breath, and proceeded in a much calmer voice.

"I'm glad you can keep your sense of humor, Counselor. But enough with the fucking jokes."

"All right, no jokes."

Bosch looked like he was struggling internally with what to say or do next. His eyes swept the room and then held on me.

"All right, look, you're right. It is my job to catch this guy. But you had him right here. Right goddamn here! And so it stands to reason that he was here with a purpose. He came to either kill you, which seems unlikely, since he apparently doesn't even know you, or he came to get something from you. The question is, what is it? What is in this office or in one of your files that could lead to the identity of the killer?"

I tried to match him with an even-tempered voice of my own.

"All I can tell you is that I have had my case manager in here since Tuesday. I've had my investigator in here, and Jerry Vincent's own receptionist was in here up until lunchtime today, when she quit. And none of us, Detective, *none of us*, has been able to find the smoking gun you're so sure is here. You tell me that Vincent paid somebody a bribe. But I can find no indication in any file or from any client that that is true. I spent the last three hours in here looking at the Elliot file and I saw no indication — not one — that he paid anybody off or bribed somebody. In fact, I found out that he didn't *need* to bribe anybody. Vincent had a magic bullet and he had a shot at winning the case fair and square. So when I tell you I have nothing, I mean it. I'm not playing you. I'm not holding back. I have nothing to give you. Nothing."

"What about the FBI?"

"Same answer. Nothing."

Bosch didn't respond. I saw true disappointment cloud his face. I continued.

"If this mustache man is the killer, then, of course there is a reason that brought him back here. But I don't know it. Am I concerned about it? No, not concerned. I'm fucking scared shitless about it. I'm fucking scared shitless that this guy thinks I have something, because if I have it, I don't even know I have it, and that is not a good place to be."

Bosch abruptly stood up. He pulled Cisco's gun out of his waistband and put it down on the desk.

"Keep it loaded. And if I were you, I would stop working at night."

He turned and headed toward the door.

"That's it?" I called after him.

He spun in his tracks and came back to the desk.

"What else do you want from me?"

"All you want is information from me. Most of the time information I can't give. But you in turn give nothing back, and that's half the reason I'm in danger."

Bosch looked like he might be about to jump over the desk at me. But then I saw him calm himself once more. All except for the palpitation high on his cheek near his left temple. That didn't go away. That was his tell, and it was a tell that once again gave me a sense of familiarity.

"Fuck it," he finally said. "What do you want to know, Counselor? Go ahead. Ask me a question — any question — and I'll answer it."

"I want to know about the bribe. Where did the money go?"

Bosch shook his head and laughed in a false way.

"I give you a free shot and I say to myself that I'll answer your question, no matter what it is, and you go and ask me the question I don't have an answer to. You think if I knew where the money went and who got the bribe that I'd be here right now with you? Uh-uh, Haller, I'd be booking a killer."

"So you're sure one thing had to do with the other? That the bribe — if there was a bribe — is connected to the killing."

"I'm going with the percentages."

"But the bribe — if there was a bribe — went down five months ago. Why was Jerry killed now? Why's the FBI calling him now?"

"Good questions. Let me know if you come up with any answers. Meantime, anything else I can do for you, Counselor? I was heading home when you called."

"Yeah, there is."

He looked at me and waited.

"I was on my way out, too."

"What, you want me to hold your hand on the way to the garage? Fine, let's go."

I closed the office once again and we proceeded down the hall to the bridge to the garage. Bosch had stopped talking and the silence was nerve-racking. I finally broke it.

"I was going to go have a steak. You want to come? Maybe we'll solve the world's problems over some red meat."

"Where, Musso's?"

"I was thinking Dan Tana's."

Bosch nodded.

"If you can get us in."

"Don't worry. I know a guy."

33

Bosch followed me but when I slowed on Santa Monica Boulevard to pull into the valet stop in front of the restaurant, he kept going. I saw him drive by and turn right on Doheny.

I went in by myself and Craig sat me in one of the cherished corner booths. It was a busy night but things were tapering off. I saw the actor James Woods finishing dinner in a booth with a movie producer named Mace Neufeld. They were regulars and Mace gave me a nod. He had once tried to option one of my cases for a film but it didn't work out. I saw Corbin Bernsen in another booth, the actor who had given the best approximation of an attorney I had ever seen on television. And then in another booth, the man himself, Dan Tana, was having a late dinner with his wife. I dropped my eyes to the checkered tablecloth. Enough who's who. I had to prepare for Bosch. During the drive, I had thought long and hard about what had just happened back at the office and now I only wanted to think about how best to confront Bosch about it. It was like preparing for the cross-examination of a hostile witness.

Ten minutes after I was seated, Bosch finally appeared in the doorway and Craig led him to me.

"Get lost?" I asked as he squeezed into the booth.

"I couldn't find a parking space."

"I guess they don't pay you enough for valet."

"No, valet's a beautiful thing. But I can't give my city car to a valet. Against the rules."

I nodded, guessing that it was probably because he packed a shotgun in the trunk.

I decided to wait until after we ordered to make a play with Bosch. I asked if he wanted to look at the menu and he said he was ready to order. When the waiter came, we both ordered the Steak Helen with spaghetti and red sauce on the side. Bosch ordered a beer and I asked for a bottle of flat water.

"So," I said, "where's your partner been lately?"

"He's working on other aspects of the investigation."

"Well, I guess it's good to hear there are other aspects to it."

Bosch studied me for a long moment before replying.

"Is that supposed to be a crack?"

"Just an observation. Doesn't seem from my end to be much happening."

"Maybe that's because your source dried up and blew away."

"My source? I don't have any source."

"Not anymore. I figured out who was feeding your guy and that ended today. I just hope you weren't paying him for the information because IAD will take him down for that."

"I know you won't believe me, but I have no idea who or what you are talking about. I get information from my investigator. I don't ask him how he gets it."

Bosch nodded.

"That's the best way to do it, right? Insulate yourself and then you don't get any blowback in your face. In the meantime, if a police captain loses his job and pension, those are the breaks."

I hadn't realized Cisco's source was so highly placed.

The waiter brought our drinks and a basket of bread. I drank some of the water as I contemplated what to say next. I put the glass down and looked at Bosch. He raised his eyebrows like he was expecting something.

"How'd you know when I was leaving the office tonight?"

Bosch looked puzzled.

"What do you mean?"

"I figure it was the lights. You were out there on Broadway, and when I killed the lights, you sent your guy into the garage."

"I don't know what you are talking about."

"Sure you do. The photo of the guy with the gun coming out of the building. It was a phony. You set it up — choreographed it — and used it to smoke out your leak, then you tried to scam me with it."

Bosch shook his head and looked out of the booth as if he were looking for someone to help him interpret what I was saying. It was a bad act.

"You set up the phony picture and then you showed it to me because you knew it would come back around through my investigator to your leak. You'd know that whoever asked you about the photo was the leak."

"I can't discuss any aspect of the investigation with you."

"And then you used it to try to play me. To see if I was hiding something and to scare it out of me."

"I told you, I can't—"

"Well, you don't have to, Bosch. I know it's what you did. You know what your mistakes were? First of all, not coming back like you said you would to show the photo to Vincent's secretary. If the guy in the picture was legit, you would've shown it to her because she knows the clients better than me. Your second mistake was the gun in the waistband of your hit man. Vincent was shot with a twenty-five — too small for a waistband. I missed that when you showed me the photo, but I've got it now."

Bosch looked toward the bar in the middle of the restaurant. The overhead TV was showing sports highlights. I leaned across the table closer to him.

"So who's the guy in the photo? Your partner with a stick-on mustache? Some clown from vice? Don't you have better things to do than to be running a game on me?"

Bosch leaned back and continued to look around the place, his eyes moving everywhere but to me. He was contemplating something and I gave him all the time he needed. Finally, he looked at me.

"Okay, you got me. It was a scam. I guess that makes you one smart lawyer, Haller. Just like the old man. I wonder why you're wasting it defending scumbags. Shouldn't you be out there suing doctors or defending big tobacco or something noble like that?"

I smiled.

"Is that how you like to play it? You get caught being underhanded, so you respond by accusing the other guy of being underhanded?"

Bosch laughed, his face colored red as he turned away from me. It was a gesture that struck me as familiar, and his mention of my father brought him to mind. I had a vague memory of my father laughing uneasily and looking away as he leaned back at the dinner table. My mother had accused him of something I was too young to understand.

Bosch put both arms on the table and leaned toward me.

"You've heard of the first forty-eight, right?"

"What are you talking about?"

"The first forty-eight. The chances of clearing a homicide diminish by almost half each day if you don't solve it in the first forty-eight hours."

He looked at his watch before continuing.

"I'm coming up on seventy-two hours and I've got nothing," he said. "Not a suspect, not a viable lead, nothing. And I was hoping that tonight I might be able to scare something out of you. Something that would point me in the right direction."

I sat there, staring at him, digesting what he had said. Finally, I found my voice.

"You actually thought I knew who killed Jerry and wasn't telling?"

"It was a possibility I had to consider."

"Fuck you, Bosch."

Just then the waiter came with our steaks and spaghetti. As the plates were put down, Bosch looked at me with a knowing smile on his face. The waiter asked what else he could get for us and I waved him away without breaking eye contact.

"You're an arrogant son of a bitch," I said. "You can just sit there with a smile on your face after accusing me of hiding evidence or knowledge in a murder. A murder of a guy I knew."

Bosch looked down at his steak, picked up his knife and fork, and cut into it. I noticed he was left-handed. He put a chunk of meat into his mouth and stared at me while he ate it. He rested his fists on either side of his plate, fork and knife in his grips, as if guarding the food from poachers. A lot of my clients who had spent time in prison ate the same way.

"Why don't you take it easy there, Counselor," he said. "You have to understand something. I'm not used to being on the same side of the line as the defense lawyer, okay? It has been my experience that defense attorneys have tried to portray me as stupid, corrupt, bigoted, you name it. So with that in mind, yes, I tried to run a game on you in hopes that it would help me solve a murder. I apologize all to hell and back. If you want, I will have them wrap up my steak and I'll take it to go."

I shook my head. Bosch had a talent for trying to make me feel guilty for his transgressions.

"Maybe now you should be the one who takes it easy," I said. "All I'm saying is that from the start, I have acted openly and honestly with you. I have stretched the ethical bounds of my profession. And I have told you what I could tell you, when I could tell you. I didn't deserve to have the shit scared out of me tonight. And you're damn lucky I didn't put a bullet in your man's chest when he was at the office door. He made a beautiful target."

"You weren't supposed to have a gun. I checked."

Bosch started eating again, keeping his head down as he worked on the steak. He took several bites and then moved to the side plate of spaghetti. He wasn't a twirler. He chopped at the pasta with his fork before putting a bite into his mouth. He spoke after he swallowed his food.

"So now that we have that out of the way, will you help me?"

I blew out my breath in a laugh.

"Are you kidding? Have you heard a single thing I've said here?"

"Yeah, I heard it all. And no, I'm not kidding. When all is said and done, I still have a dead lawyer — your colleague — on my hands and I could still use your help."

I started cutting my first piece of steak. I decided he could wait for me to eat, like I had waited for him.

Dan Tana's was considered by many to serve the best steak in the city. Count me as one of the many. I was not disappointed. I took my time, savoring the first bite, then put my fork down.

"What kind of help?"

"We draw out the killer."

"Great. How dangerous will it be?"

"Depends on a lot of things. But I'm not going to lie to you. It could get dangerous. I need you to shake some things up, make whoever's out there think there's a loose end, that you might be dangerous to them. Then we see what happens."

"But you'll be there. I'll be covered."

"Every step of the way."

"How do we shake things up?"

"I was thinking a newspaper story. I assume you've been getting calls from the reporters. We pick one and give them the story, an exclusive, and we plant something in there that gets the killer thinking."

I thought about this and remembered what Lorna had warned about playing fair with the media.

"There's a guy at the *Times*," I said. "I kind of made a deal with him to get him off my back. I told him that when I was ready to talk, I would talk to him."

"That's a perfect setup. We'll use him."

I didn't say anything.

"So, are you in?"

I picked up my fork and knife and remained silent while I cut into the steak again. Blood ran onto the plate. I thought about my daughter getting to the point of asking me the same questions her mother asked and that I could never answer. *It's like you're always working for the bad guys.* It wasn't as simple as that but knowing this didn't take away the sting or the look I remembered seeing in her eyes.

I put the knife and fork down without taking a bite. I suddenly was no longer hungry.

"Yeah," I said. "I'm in."

PART THREE
—To Speak the Truth

34

Everybody lies.

Cops lie. Lawyers lie. Clients lie. Even jurors lie.

There is a school of belief in criminal law that says every trial is won or lost in the choosing of the jury. I've never been ready to go all the way to that level but I do know that there is probably no phase in a murder trial more important than the selection of the twelve citizens who will decide your client's fate. It is also the most complex and fleeting part of the trial, reliant on the whims of fate and luck and being able to ask the right question of the right person at the right time.

And yet we begin each trial with it.

Jury selection in the case of *California v. Elliot* began on schedule in Judge James P. Stanton's courtroom at ten a.m. Thursday. The courtroom was packed, half filled with the venire — the eighty potential jurors called randomly from the jury pool on the fifth floor of the CCB — and half filled with media, courthouse professionals, well-wishers, and just plain gawkers who had been able to squeeze in.

I sat at the defense table alone with my client — fulfilling his wish for a legal team of just one. Spread in front of me was an open but empty manila file, a Post-it pad, and three different markers, red, blue and black. Back at the office, I had prepared the file by using a ruler to draw a grid across it. There were twelve blocks, each the size of a Post-it. Each block was for one of the twelve jurors who would be chosen to sit in judgment of Walter Elliot. Some lawyers use computers to track potential jurors. They even have software that can take information revealed during the selection process, filter it through a sociopolitical pattern–recognition program, and spit out instant recommendations on whether to keep or reject a juror. I had been using the old-school grid system since I had been a baby lawyer in the Public Defender's Office. It had always worked well for me and I wasn't changing now. I didn't want to use a computer's instincts when it came to picking a jury. I wanted to use my own. A computer can't hear how someone gives an answer. It can't see someone's eyes when they lie.

The way it works is that the judge has a computer-generated list from which he calls the first twelve citizens from the venire, and they take seats in the jury box. At that point each is a member of the jury. But they get to keep their seats only if they survive voir dire — the questioning of their background and views and understanding of the law. There is a process.

The judge asks them a series of basic questions and then the lawyers get the chance to follow up with a more narrow focus.

Jurors can be removed from the box in one of two ways. They can be rejected for cause if they show through their answers or demeanor or even their life's circumstances that they cannot be fair judges of credibility or hear the case with an open mind. There is no limit to the number of challenges for cause at the disposal of the attorneys. Oftentimes the judge will make a dismissal for cause before the prosecutor or defense attorney even raises an objection. I have always believed that the quickest way off a jury panel is to announce that you are convinced that all cops lie or all cops are always right. Either way, a closed mind is a challenge for cause.

The second method of removal is the peremptory challenge, of which each attorney is given a limited supply, depending on the type of case and charges. Because this trial involved charges of murder, both the prosecution and defense would have up to twenty peremptory challenges each. It is in the judicious and tactful use of these peremptories that strategy and instinct come into play. A skilled attorney can use his challenges to help sculpt the jury into a tool of the prosecution or defense. A peremptory challenge lets the attorney strike a juror for no reason other than his instinctual dislike of the individual. An exception to this would be the obvious use of peremptories to create a bias on the jury. A prosecutor who continually removed black jurors, or a defense attorney who did the same with white jurors, would quickly run afoul of the opposition as well as the judge.

The rules of voir dire are designed to remove bias and deception from the jury. The term itself comes from the French phrase "to speak the truth." But this of course is contradictory to each side's cause. The bottom line in any trial is that I want a biased jury. I want them biased against the state and the police. I want them predisposed to be on my side. The truth is that a fair-minded person is the last person I want on my jury. I want somebody who is already on my side or can easily be pushed there. I want twelve lemmings in the box. Jurors who will follow my lead and act as agents for the defense.

And, of course, the man sitting four feet from me in the courtroom wanted to achieve a diametrically opposite result out of jury selection. The prosecutor wanted his own lemmings and would use his challenges to sculpt the jury his way, and at my expense.

By ten fifteen the efficient Judge Stanton had looked at the printout from the computer that randomly selected the first twelve candidates and had welcomed them to the jury box by calling out code numbers issued to them in the jury-pool room on the fifth floor. There were six men and six women. We had three postal workers, two engineers, a housewife from Pomona, an out-of-work screenwriter, two high school teachers, and three retirees.

We knew where they were from and what they did. But we didn't know their names. It was an anonymous jury. During all pretrial conferences the judge had been adamant about protecting the jurors from public attention and scrutiny. He had ordered that the truTV camera be mounted on the wall over the jury box so that the jurors would not be seen in its view of the courtroom. He had also ruled that the identities of all prospective jurors be withheld from even the lawyers and that each be referred to during voir dire by their seat number.

The process began with the judge asking each prospective juror questions about what they did for a living and the area of Los Angeles County they lived in. He then moved on to basic questions about whether they had been victims of crime, had relatives in prison, or were related to any police officers or prosecutors. He asked what their knowledge of the law and court procedures was. He asked who had prior jury experience. The judge excused three for cause: a postal employee whose brother was a police officer; a retiree whose son had been the victim of a drug-related murder; and the screenwriter because although she had never worked for Archway Studios, the judge felt she might harbor ill will toward Elliot because of the contentious relationship between screenwriters and studio management in general.

A fourth prospective juror — one of the engineers — was dismissed when the judge agreed with his plea for a hardship dismissal. He was a self-employed consultant and two weeks spent in a trial were two weeks with no income other than the five bucks a day he made as a juror.

The four were quickly replaced with four more random selections from the venire. And so it went. By noon I had used two of my peremptories on the remaining postal workers and would have used a third to strike the second engineer from the panel but decided to take the lunch hour to think about it before making my next move. Meanwhile, Golantz was holding fast with a full arsenal of challenges. His strategy was obviously to let me use my strikes up and then he would come in with the final shaping of the jury.

Elliot had adopted the pose of CEO of the defense. I did the work in front of the jury but he insisted that he be allowed to sign off on each of my peremptory challenges. It took extra time because I needed to explain to him why I wanted to dump a juror and he would always offer his opinion. But each time, he ultimately nodded his approval like the man in charge, and the juror was struck. It was an annoying process but one I could put up with, just as long as Elliot went along with what I wanted to do.

Shortly after noon, the judge broke for lunch. Even though the day was devoted to jury selection, technically it was the first day of my first trial in over a year. Lorna Taylor had come to court to watch and show her support. The plan was to go to lunch together and then she would go back to the office and start packing it up.

As we entered the hallway outside the courtroom, I asked Elliot if he wanted to join us but he said he had to make a quick run to the studio to check on things. I told him not to be late coming back. The judge had given us a very generous ninety minutes for the lunch break and he would not look kindly on any late returns.

Lorna and I hung back and let the prospective jurors crowd onto the elevators. I didn't want to ride down with them. Inevitably when you do that, one of them opens their mouth and asks something that is improper and you then have to go through the motions of reporting it to the judge.

When one of the elevators opened, I saw the reporter Jack McEvoy push his way out past the jurors, scan the hallway, and zero in on me.

"Great," I said. "Here comes trouble."

McEvoy came directly toward me.

"What do you want?" I said.

"To explain."

"What, you mean explain why you're a liar?"

"No, look, when I told you it was going to run Sunday, I meant it. That's what I was told."

"And here it is Thursday and no story in the paper, and when I've tried to call you about it, you don't call me back. I've got other reporters interested, McEvoy. I don't need the *Times*."

"Look, I understand. But what happened was that they decided to hold it so it would run closer to the trial."

"The trial started two hours ago."

The reporter shook his head.

"You know, the real trial. Testimony and evidence. They're running it out front this coming Sunday."

"The front page on Sunday. Is that a promise?"

"Monday at the latest."

"Oh, now it's Monday."

"Look, it's the news business. Things change. It's supposed to run out front on Sunday but if something big happens in the world, they might kick it over till Monday. It's either-or."

"Whatever. I'll believe it when I see it."

I saw that the area around the elevators was clear. Lorna and I could go down now and not encounter any prospective jurors. I took Lorna by the arm and started leading her that way. I pushed past the reporter.

"So we're okay?" McEvoy said. "You'll hold off?"

"Hold off on what?"

"Talking to anyone else. On giving away the exclusive."

"Whatever."

I left him hanging and headed toward the elevators. When we got out of the building, we walked a block over to City Hall and I had Patrick pick us up there. I didn't want any prospective jurors who might be hanging around the courthouse to see me getting into the back of a chauffeured Lincoln. It might not sit well with them. Among my pretrial instructions to

Elliot had been a directive for him to eschew the studio limo and drive himself to court every day. You never know who might see what outside the courtroom and what the effect might be.

I told Patrick to take us over to the French Garden on Seventh Street. I then called Harry Bosch's cell phone and he answered right away.

"I just talked to the reporter," I said.

"And?"

"And it's finally running Sunday or Monday. On the front page, he says, so be ready."

"Finally."

"Yeah. You going to be ready?"

"Don't worry about it. I'm ready."

"I have to worry. It's my — Hello?"

He was gone already. I closed the phone.

"What was that?" Lorna asked.

"Nothing."

I realized that I had to change the subject.

"Listen, when you go back to the office today, I want you to call Julie Favreau and see if she can come to court tomorrow."

"I thought Elliot didn't want a jury consultant."

"He doesn't have to know we're using her."

"Then, how will you pay her?"

"Take it out of general operating. I don't care. I'll pay her out of my own pocket if I have to. But I'm going to need her and I don't care what Elliot thinks. I already burned through two strikes and have a feeling that by tomorrow I'm going to have to make whatever I have left count. I'll want her help on the final chart. Just tell her the bailiff will have her name and will make sure she gets a seat. Tell her to sit in the gallery and not to approach me when I'm with my client. Tell her she can text me on the cell when she has something important."

"Okay, I'll call her. Are you doing all right, Mick?"

I must've been talking too fast or sweating too much. Lorna had picked up on my agitation. I was feeling a little shaky and I didn't know if it was because of the reporter's bullshit or Bosch's hanging up or the growing realization that what I had been working toward for a year would soon be upon me. Testimony and evidence.

"I'm fine," I said sharply. "I'm just hungry. You know how I get when I'm hungry."

"Sure," she said. "I understand."

The truth was, I wasn't hungry. I didn't even feel like eating. I was feeling the weight on me. The burden of a man's future.

And it wasn't my client's future I was thinking of.

35

By three o'clock on the second day of jury selection, Golantz and I had traded peremptory and cause challenges for more than ten hours of court time. It had been a battle. We had quietly savaged each other, identifying each other's must-have jurors and striking them without care or conscience. We had gone through almost the entire venire, and my jury seating chart was covered in some spots with as many as five layers of Post-its. I had two peremptory challenges left. Golantz, at first judicious with his challenges, had caught up and then passed me and was down to his final peremptory. It was zero hour. The jury box was about to be complete.

In its current composition, the panel now included an attorney, a computer programmer, two new postal service employees and three new retirees, as well as a male nurse, a tree trimmer, and an artist.

From the original twelve seated the morning before, there were still two prospective jurors remaining. The engineer in seat seven and one of the retirees, in seat twelve, had somehow gone the distance. Both were white males and both, in my estimation, leaning toward the state. Neither was overtly on the prosecution's side, but on my chart I had written notes about each in blue ink — my code for a juror whom I perceived as being cold to the defense. But their leanings were so slight that I had still not used a precious challenge on either.

I knew I could take them both out in my final flourish and use of peremptory strikes, but that was the risk of voir dire. You strike one juror because of blue ink and the replacement might end up being neon blue and a greater risk to your client than the original was. It was what made jury selection such an unpredictable proposition.

The latest addition to the box was the artist who took the opening in seat number eleven after Golantz had used his nineteenth peremptory to remove a city sanitation worker who I'd had down as a red juror. Under the general questioning of Judge Stanton, the artist revealed that she lived in Malibu and worked in a studio off the Pacific Coast Highway. Her medium was acrylic paint and she had studied at the Art Institute of Philadelphia before coming to California for the light. She said she didn't own a television and didn't regularly read any newspapers. She said she knew nothing about the murders that had taken place six months earlier in the beach house not far from where she lived and worked.

Almost from the start I had taken notes about her in red and grew happier and happier with her on my jury as the questions progressed. I knew that Golantz had made a tactical error. He had eliminated the sanitation worker with one challenge and had ended up with a juror seemingly even more detrimental to his cause. He would now have to live with the mistake or use his final challenge to remove the artist and run the same risk all over again.

When the judge finished his general inquiries, it was the lawyers' turn. Golantz went first and asked a series of questions he hoped would draw out a bias so that the artist could be removed for cause instead of through the use of his last peremptory. But the woman held her own, appearing very honest and open-minded.

Four questions into the prosecutor's effort, I felt a vibration in my pocket and reached in for my cell. I held it down below the defense table between my legs and at an angle where it could not be seen by the judge. Julie Favreau had been texting me all day.

FAVREAU: She's a keeper.

I sent her one back immediately.

HALLER: I know. What about 7, 8, and 10? Which one next?

Favreau, my secret jury consultant, had been in the fourth row of the gallery during both the morning and afternoon sessions. I had also met her for lunch while Walter Elliot had once again gone back to the studio to check on things, and I had allowed her to study my chart so that she could make up her own. She was a quick study and knew exactly where I was with my codes and challenges.

I got a response to my text message almost immediately. That was one thing I liked about Favreau. She didn't overthink things. She made quick, instinctive decisions based solely on visual tells in relation to verbal answers.

FAVREAU: Don't like 8. Haven't heard enough from 10. Kick 7 if you have to.

Juror eight was the tree trimmer. I had him in blue because of some of the answers he gave when questioned about the police. I also thought he was too eager to be on the jury. This was always a flag in a murder case. It signaled to me that the potential juror had strong feelings about law and order and wasn't hesitant about the idea of sitting in judgment of another person. The truth was, I was suspicious of anybody who liked to sit in judgment of another. Anybody who relished the idea of being a juror was blue ink all the way.

Judge Stanton was allowing us a lot of leeway. When it came time to question a prospective juror, the attorneys were allowed to trade their time to question anyone else on the panel. He was also allowing the liberal use of back strikes, meaning it was acceptable to use a peremptory challenge to strike out anybody on the panel, even if they had already been questioned and accepted.

When it was my turn to question the artist, I walked to the lectern and told the judge I accepted her on the jury at this time without further questioning. I asked to be allowed instead to make further inquiries of juror number eight, and the judge allowed me to proceed.

"Juror number eight, I just want to clarify a couple of your views on things. First, let me ask you, at the end of this trial, after you've heard all the testimony, if you think my client might be guilty, would you vote to convict him?"

The tree trimmer thought for a moment before answering.

"No, because that wouldn't be beyond a reasonable doubt."

I nodded, letting him know that he had given the right answer.

"So you don't equate 'might've' with 'beyond a reasonable doubt'?"

"No, sir. Not at all."

"Good. Do you believe that people get arrested in church for singing too loud?"

A puzzled look spread across the tree trimmer's face, and there was a murmur of laughter in the gallery behind me.

"I don't understand."

"There's a saying that people don't get arrested in church for singing too loud. In other words, where there's smoke there's fire. People don't get arrested without good reason. The police usually have it right and arrest the right people. Do you believe that?"

"I believe that everybody makes mistakes from time to time — including the police — and you have to look at each case individually."

"But do you believe that the police *usually* have it right?"

He was cornered. Any answer would raise a flag for one side or the other.

"I think they probably do — they're the professionals — but I would look at every case individually and not think that just because the police usually get things right, they automatically got the right man in this case."

That was a good answer. From a tree trimmer, no less. Again I gave him the nod. His answers were right but there was something almost practiced about his delivery. It was smarmy, holier-than-thou. The tree trimmer wanted very badly to be on the jury and that didn't sit well with me.

"What kind of car do you drive, sir?"

The unexpected question was always good for a reaction. Juror number eight leaned back in his seat and gave me a look like he thought I was trying to trick him in some way.

"My car?"

"Yes, what do you drive to work?"

"I have a pickup. I keep my equipment and stuff in it. It's a Ford one-fifty."

"Do you have any bumper stickers on the back?"

"Yeah...a few."

"What do they say?"

He had to think a long moment to remember his own bumper stickers.

"Uh, I got the NRA sticker on there, and then I got another that says, If you can read this, then back off. Something like that. Maybe it doesn't say it that nice."

There was laughter from his fellow members of the venire, and number eight smiled proudly.

"How long have you been a member of the National Rifle Association?" I asked. "On the juror information sheet you didn't list that."

"Well, I'm not really. Not a member, I mean. I just have the sticker on there."

Deception. He was either lying about being a member and leaving it off his info sheet, or he wasn't a member and was using his bumper sticker to hold himself out as something he was not, or as part of an organization he believed in but didn't want to officially join. Either way it was deceptive and it confirmed everything I was feeling. Favreau was right. He had to go. I told the judge I was finished with my questioning and sat back down.

When the judge asked if the prosecution and defense accepted the panel as composed, Golantz attempted to challenge the artist for cause. I opposed this and the judge sided with me. Golantz had no choice but to use his last peremptory to remove her. I then used my second-to-last challenge to remove the tree trimmer. The man looked angry as he made the long walk out of the courtroom.

Two more names were called from the venire and a real-estate agent and one more retiree took seats eight and eleven in the box. Their answers to the questions from the judge put them right down the middle of the road. I coded them black and heard nothing that raised a flag. Halfway through the judge's voir dire I got another text from Favreau.

FAVREAU: Both of them +/– if you ask me. Both lemmings.

In general, having lemmings on the panel was good. Jurors with no indication of forceful personality and with middle-of-the-road convictions could oftentimes be manipulated during deliberations. They look for someone to follow. The more lemmings you have, the more important it is to have a juror with a strong personality and one who you believe is predisposed to be for the defense. You want somebody in the deliberations room who will pull the lemmings with him.

Golantz, in my view, had made a basic tactical error. He had exhausted his peremptory challenges before the defense and, far worse, had left an attorney on the panel. Juror three had made it through and my gut instinct was that Golantz had been saving his last peremptory for him. But the artist got that and now Golantz was stuck with a lawyer on the panel.

Juror number three didn't practice criminal law but he'd had to study it to get his ticket and from time to time must have flirted with the idea of practicing it. They didn't make movies and TV shows about real-estate lawyers. Criminal law had the pull and juror three would not be immune to this. In my view, that made him an excellent juror for the defense. He was lit up all red on my chart and was my number-one choice for the panel. He would go into the trial and the deliberations that come after it knowing the law and the absolute underdog status of the defense. It not only made him sympathetic to my side but it made him the obvious candidate as foreman — the juror elected by the panel to make communications with the judge and to speak for the entire panel. When the jury got back in there to begin deliberations, the person they would all turn to first would be the lawyer. If he was red, then he was going to pull and push many of his fellow jurors toward a not-guilty. And at minimum, his ego as an attorney would insist that his verdict was correct, and he would hold out for it. He alone could be the one who hung the jury and kept my client from a conviction.

It was a lot to bank on, considering juror number three had answered questions from the judge and the lawyers for less than thirty minutes. But that was what jury selection came down to. Quick, instinctual decisions based on experience and observation.

The bottom line was that I was going to let the two lemmings ride on the panel. I had one peremptory left and I was going to use it on juror seven or juror ten. The engineer or the retiree.

I asked the judge for a few moments to confer with my client. I then turned to Elliot and slid my chart over in front of him.

"This is it, Walter. We're down to our last bullet. What do you think? I think we need to get rid of seven and ten but we can get rid of only one."

Elliot had been very involved. Since the first twelve were seated the morning before, he had expressed strong and intuitive opinions about each juror I wanted to strike. But he had never picked a jury before. I had. I put up with his comments but ultimately made my own choices. This last choice, however, was a toss-up. Either of the jurors could be damaging to the defense. Either could turn out to be a lemming. It was a tough call and I was tempted to let my client's instincts be the deciding factor.

Elliot tapped a finger on the block for juror ten on my grid. The retired technical writer for a toy manufacturer.

"Him," he said. "Get rid of him."

"You sure?"

"Absolutely."

I looked at the grid. There was a lot of blue on block ten, but there was an equal amount on block seven. The engineer.

I had a hunch that the technical writer was like the tree trimmer. He wanted badly to be on the jury but probably for a wholly different set of reasons. I thought maybe his plan was to use his experience as research for a book or maybe a movie script. He had spent his career writing instruction manuals for toys. In retirement, he had acknowledged during voir dire, he was trying to write fiction. There would be nothing like a front-row seat on a murder trial to help stimulate the imagination and creative process. That was fine for him but not for Elliot. I didn't want anybody who relished the idea of sitting in judgment — for any reason — on my jury.

Juror seven was blue for another reason. He was listed as an aerospace engineer. The industry he worked in had a large presence in Southern California and consequently I had questioned several engineers during voir dire over the years. In general, engineers were conservative politically and religiously, two very blue attributes, and they worked for companies that relied on huge government contracts and grants. A vote for the defense was a vote against the government, and that was a hard leap for them to make.

Last, and perhaps most important, engineers exist in a world of logic and absolutes. These are things you often cannot apply to a crime or crime scene or even to the criminal justice system as a whole.

"I don't know," I said. "I think the engineer should go."

"No, I like him. I've liked him since the beginning. He's given me good eye contact. I want him to stay."

I turned from Elliot and looked over at the box. My eyes traveled from juror seven to juror ten and then back again. I was hoping for some sign, some tell that would reveal the right choice.

"Mr. Haller," Judge Stanton said. "Do you wish to use your last challenge or accept the jury as it is now composed? I remind you, it is getting late in the day and we still have to choose our alternate jurors."

My phone was buzzing while the judge addressed me.

"Uh, one more moment, Your Honor."

I turned back toward Elliot and leaned into him as if to whisper something. But what I really was doing was pulling my phone.

"Are you sure, Walter?" I whispered. "The guy's an engineer. That could be trouble for us."

"Look, I make my living reading people and rolling the dice," Elliot whispered back. "I want that man on my jury."

I nodded and looked down between my legs where I was holding the phone. It was a text from Favreau.

FAVREAU: Kick 10. I see deception. 7 fits prosecution profile but I see good eye contact and open face. He's interested in your story. He likes your client.

Eye contact. That settled it. I slipped the phone back into my pocket and stood up. Elliot grabbed me by the sleeve of my jacket. I bent down to hear his urgent whisper.

"What are you doing?"

I shook off his grasp because I didn't like his public display of attempting control over me. I straightened back up and looked up at the judge.

"Your Honor, the defense would like to thank and excuse juror ten at this time."

While the judge dismissed the technical writer and called a new candidate to the tenth chair in the box, I sat down and turned to Elliot.

"Walter, don't ever grab me like that in front of the jury. It makes you look like an asshole and I'm already going to have a tough enough time convincing them you're not a killer."

I turned so that my back was to him as I watched the latest and most likely the last juror take the open seat in the box.

PART FOUR

— Fillet of Soul

Walking in a Dead Man's Shoes

Attorney Takes Over for Murdered Colleague

First Case; The Trial of the Decade

BY JACK McEVOY, Times Staff Writer

It wasn't the 31 cases dropped in his lap that were the difficulty. It was the big one with the big client and highest stakes attached to it. Defense Attorney Michael Haller stepped into the shoes of the murdered Jerry Vincent two weeks ago and now finds himself at the center of this year's so-called Trial of the Decade.

Today testimony is scheduled to begin in the trial of Walter Elliot, the 54-year-old chairman of Archway Studios, charged with murdering his wife and her alleged lover six months ago in Malibu. Haller stepped into the case after Vincent, 45, was found shot to death in his car in downtown Los Angeles.

Vincent had made legal provisions that allowed Haller to step into his practice in the event of his death. Haller, who had been at the end of a year-long sabbatical from practicing law, went to sleep one night with zero cases and woke up the next day with 31 new clients to handle.

"I was excited about coming back to work but I wasn't expecting anything like this," said Haller, the 42-year-old son of the late Michael Haller Sr., one of Los Angeles's storied defense attorneys in the 50's and 60's. "Jerry Vincent was a friend and colleague and, of course, I would gladly go back to having no cases if he could be alive today."

The investigation of Vincent's murder is ongoing. There have been no arrests, and detectives say there are no suspects. He was shot twice in the head while sitting in his car in the garage next to the building where he kept his office, in the 200 block of Broadway.

Following Vincent's death, the fallen attorney's entire law practice was turned over to Haller. His job was to cooperate with investigators within the bounds of attorney-client protections, inventory the cases, and make contact with all active clients. There was an immediate surprise. One of Vincent's clients was due in court the day after the murder.

"My staff and I were just beginning to put all the cases together when we saw that Jerry—and now, of course, I—had a sentencing with a client," Haller said. "I had to drop all of that, race over to the Criminal Courts Building, and be there for the client."

That was one down and 30 other active cases to go. Every client on that list had to be quickly contacted, informed of Vincent's death, and given the option of hiring a new lawyer or continuing with Haller handling the case.

A handful of clients decided to seek other representation but the vast majority of cases remain with Haller. By far the biggest of these is the "Murder in Malibu" case. It has drawn wide public attention. Portions of the trial are scheduled to be broadcast live nationally on Court TV. Dominick Dunne, the premier chronicler of courts and crime for *Vanity Fair,* is among members of the media who have requested seats in the courtroom.

The case came to Haller with one big condition. Elliot would agree to keep Haller as his attorney only if Haller agreed not to delay the trial.

"Walter is innocent and has insisted on his innocence since day one," Haller told the *Times* in his first interview since taking on the case. "There were early delays in the case and he has waited six months for his day in court and the opportunity to clear his name. He wasn't interested in another delay in justice and I agreed with him. If you're innocent, why wait? We've been working almost around the clock to be ready and I think we are."

It wasn't easy to be ready. Whoever killed Vincent also stole his briefcase from his car. It contained Vincent's laptop computer and his calendar.

"It was not too difficult to rebuild the calendar but the laptop was a big loss," Haller said. "It was really the central storage point for case information and strategy. The hard files we found in the office were incomplete. We needed the laptop and at first I thought we were dead in the water."

But then Haller found something the killer had not taken. Vincent backed his computer up on a digital flash drive attached to his key chain. Wading through the megabytes of data, Haller began to find bits and pieces of strategy for the Elliot trial. Jury selection took place last week and when the testimony begins today, he said he will be fully prepared.

"I don't think Mr. Elliot is going to have any drop-off in his defense whatsoever," Haller said. "We're locked and loaded and ready to go."

Elliot did not return calls for comment for this story and has avoided speaking to the media, except for one press conference after his arrest, in which he vehemently denied involvement in the murders and mourned the loss of his wife.

Prosecutors and investigators with the Los Angeles County Sheriff's Department said Elliot killed his wife, Mitzi, 39, and Johan Rilz, 35, in a fit of rage after finding them together at a weekend home owned by the Elliots on the beach in Malibu. Elliot called deputies to the scene and was arrested following the crime scene investigation. Though the murder weapon has never been found, forensic tests determined that Elliot had recently fired a weapon. Investigators said he also gave inconsistent statements while initially interviewed at the crime scene and afterwards. Other evidence against the movie mogul is expected to be revealed at trial.

Elliot remains free on $20 million bail, the highest amount ever ordered for a suspect in a crime in Los Angeles County history.

Legal experts and courthouse observers say it is expected that the defense will attack the handling of evidence in the investigation and the testing procedures that determined that Elliot had fired a gun.

Deputy Dist. Atty. Jeffrey Golantz, who is prosecuting the case, declined comment for this story. Golantz has never lost a case as a prosecutor and this will be his eleventh murder case.

36

The jury came out in a single-file line like the Lakers taking the basketball court. They weren't all wearing the same uniform but the same feeling of anticipation was in the air. The game was about to begin. They split into two lines and moved down the two rows of the jury box. They carried steno pads and pens. They took the same seats they were in on Friday when the jury was completed and sworn in.

It was almost ten a.m. Monday and a later-than-expected start. But earlier, Judge Stanton had had the lawyers and the defendant back in chambers for almost forty minutes while he went over last-minute ground rules and took the time to give me the squint and express his displeasure over the story published on the front page of the morning's *Los Angeles Times*. His chief concern was that the story was weighted heavily on the defense side and cast me as a sympathetic underdog. Though on Friday afternoon he had admonished the new jury not to read or watch any news reports on the case or trial, the judge was concerned that the story might have slipped through.

In my own defense, I told the judge that I had given the interview ten days earlier for a story I had been told would run at least a week before the trial started. Golantz smirked and said my explanation suggested I was trying to affect jury selection by giving the interview earlier but was now tainting the trial instead. I countered by pointing out that the story clearly stated that the prosecution had been contacted but refused to comment. If the story was one-sided, that was why.

Stanton grumpily seemed to accept my story but cautioned us about talking to the media. I knew then that I had to cancel my agreement to give commentary to Court TV at the end of each day's trial session. The publicity would've been nice but I didn't want to be on the wrong side of the judge.

We moved on to other things. Stanton was very interested in budgeting time for the trial. Like any judge, he had to keep things moving. He had a backlog of cases, and a long trial only backed things up further. He wanted to know how much time each side expected to take putting forth his case. Golantz said he would take a minimum of a week and I said I needed the same, though realistically I knew I would probably take much less time. Most of the defense case would be made, or at least set up, during the prosecution phase.

Stanton frowned at the time estimates and suggested that both the prosecution and defense think hard about streamlining. He said he wanted to get the case to the jury while their attention was still high.

I studied the jurors as they took their seats and looked for indications of biases or anything else. I was still happy with the jury, especially with juror three, the lawyer. A few others were questionable but I had decided over the weekend that I would make my case to the lawyer and hope that he would pull and push the others along with him when he voted for acquittal.

The jurors all kept their eyes to themselves or looked up at the judge, the alpha dog of the courtroom. As far as I could tell, no juror even glanced at the prosecution or defense table.

I turned and looked back at the gallery. The courtroom once again was packed with members of the media and the public, as well as those with a blood link to the case.

Directly behind the prosecution's table sat Mitzi Elliot's mother, who had flown in from New York. Next to her sat Johan Rilz's father and two brothers, who had traveled all the way from Berlin. I noticed that Golantz had positioned the grieving mother on the end of the aisle, where she and her constant flow of tears would be fully visible to the jury.

The defense had five seats on reserve in the first row behind me. Sitting there were Lorna, Cisco, Patrick, and Julie Favreau—the last on hand because I had hired her to ride through the trial and observe the jury for me. I couldn't watch the jurors at all times, and sometimes they revealed themselves when they thought none of the lawyers were watching.

The empty fifth seat had been reserved for my daughter. My hope had been that over the weekend I would convince my ex-wife to allow me to take Hayley out of school for the day so she could go with me to court. She had never seen me at work before and I thought opening statements would be the perfect time. I felt very confident in my case. I felt bulletproof and I wanted my daughter to see her father this way. The plan was for her to sit with Lorna, whom she knew and liked, and watch me operate in front of the jury. In my argument I had even employed the Margaret Mead line about taking her out of school so that she could get an education. But it was a case I ultimately couldn't win. My ex-wife refused to allow it. My daughter went to school and the reserved seat went unused.

Walter Elliot had no one in the gallery. He had no children and no relatives he was close to. Nina Albrecht had asked me if she would be allowed to sit in the gallery to show her support, but because she was listed on both the prosecution and defense witness lists, she was excluded from watching the trial until her testimony was completed. Otherwise, my client had no one. And this was by design. He had plenty of associates, well-wishers, and hangers-on who wanted to be there for him. He even had A-list movie actors willing to sit behind him and show their support. But I told him that if he had a Hollywood entourage or his corporate lawyers in the seats behind him, he would be broadcasting the wrong message and image to the jury. It is all about the jury, I told him. Every move that is made — from the choice of tie you wear to the witnesses you put on the stand — is made in deference to the jury. Our anonymous jury.

After the jurors were seated and comfortable, Judge Stanton went on the record and began the proceedings by asking if any jurors had seen the story in the morning's *Times*. None raised their hands and Stanton responded with another reminder about not reading or watching reports on the trial in the media.

He then told jurors that the trial would begin with opening statements from the opposing attorneys.

"Ladies and gentlemen, remember," he said, "these are statements. They are not evidence. It's up to each side to present the evidence that backs the statements up. And you will be the ones at the end of the trial who decide if they have done that."

With that, he gestured to Golantz and said the prosecution would go first. As outlined in a pretrial conference, each side would have an hour for its opening statement. I didn't know about Golantz but I wouldn't take close to that.

Handsome and impressive-looking in a black suit, white shirt and maroon tie, Golantz stood up and addressed the jury from the prosecution table. For the trial he had a second chair, an attractive young lawyer named

Denise Dabney. She sat next to him and kept her eyes on the jury the whole time he spoke. It was a way of double-teaming, two pairs of eyes constantly sweeping across the faces of the jurors, doubly conveying the seriousness and gravity of the task at hand.

After introducing himself and his second, Golantz got down to it.

"Ladies and gentleman of the jury, we are here today because of unchecked greed and anger. Plain and simple. The defendant, Walter Elliot, is a man of great power, money, and standing in our community. But that was not enough for him. He did not want to divide his money and power. He did not want to turn the cheek on betrayal. Instead, he lashed out in the most extreme way possible. He took not just one life, but two. In a moment of high anger and humiliation, he raised a gun and killed both his wife, Mitzi Elliot, and Johan Rilz. He believed his money and power would place him above the law and save him from punishment for these heinous crimes. But that will not be the case. The state will prove to you beyond any reasonable doubt that Walter Elliot pulled the trigger and is responsible for the deaths of two innocent human beings."

I was turned in my seat, half to obscure the jury's view of my client and half to keep a view of Golantz and the gallery rows behind him. Before his first paragraph was completed, the tears were flowing from Mitzi Elliot's mother, and that was something I would need to bring up with the judge out of earshot of the jury. The theatrics were prejudicial and I would ask the judge to move the victim's mother to a seat that was less of a focal point for the jury.

I looked past the crying woman and saw hard grimaces on the faces of the men from Germany. I was very interested in them and how they would appear to the jury. I wanted to see how they handled emotion and the surroundings of an American courtroom. I wanted to see how threatening they could be made to look. The grimmer and more menacing they looked, the better the defense strategy would work when I focused on Johan Rilz. Looking at them now, I knew I was off to a good start. They looked angry and mean.

Golantz laid his case out to the jurors, telling them what he would be presenting in testimony and evidence and what he believed it meant. There were no surprises. At one point I got a one-line text from Favreau, which I read below the table.

FAVREAU: They are eating this up. You better be good.

Right, I thought. Tell me something I don't know.

There was an unfair advantage to the prosecution built into every trial. The state has the power and the might on its side. It comes with an assumption of honesty and integrity and fairness. An assumption in every juror's and onlooker's mind that we wouldn't be here if smoke didn't lead to a fire.

It is that assumption that every defense has to overcome. The person on trial is supposed to be presumed innocent. But anybody who has ever stepped foot into a courtroom as a lawyer or defendant knows that presumed innocence is just one of the idealistic notions they teach in law school. There was no doubt in my mind or anybody else's that I started this trial with a defendant who was presumed guilty. I had to find a way to either prove him innocent or prove the state guilty of malfeasance, ineptitude, or corruption in its preparation of the case.

Golantz lasted his entire allotted hour, seemingly leaving no secrets about his case hidden. He showed typical prosecutorial arrogance; put it all out there and dare the defense to try to contradict it. The prosecution was always the six-hundred-pound gorilla, so big and strong it didn't have to worry about finesse. When it painted its picture, it used a six-inch brush and hung it on the wall with a sledgehammer and spike.

The judge had told us in the pretrial session that we would be required to remain at our tables or to use the lectern placed between them while addressing witnesses during testimony. But opening statements and closing arguments were an exception to this rule. During these bookend moments of the trial, we would be free to use the space in front of the jury box — a spot the veterans of the defense bar called the "proving grounds" because it was the only time during a trial when the lawyers spoke directly to the jury and either made their case or didn't.

Golantz finally moved from the prosecution table to the proving grounds when it was time for his big finish. He stood directly in front of the midpoint of the box and held his hands wide, like a preacher in front of his flock.

"I'm out of time here, folks," he said. "So in closing, I urge you to take great care as you listen to the evidence and the testimony. Common sense will lead you. I urge you not to get confused or sidetracked by the roadblocks to justice the defense will put before you. Keep your eyes on the prize. Remember, two people had their lives stolen from them. Their future was ripped away. That is why we are here today. For them. Thank you very much."

The old keep-your-eyes-on-the-prize opener. That one had been kicking around the courthouse since I was a public defender. Nevertheless, it was a solid beginning from Golantz. He wouldn't win any orator-of-the-year trophies but he had made his points. He'd also addressed the jurors as "folks" at least four times by my count, and that was a word I would never use with a jury.

Favreau had texted me twice more during the last half hour of his delivery with reports of declining jury interest. They might have been eating it up at the start but now they were apparently full. Sometimes you can go on too long. Golantz had trudged through a full fifteen rounds like a heavyweight boxer. I was going to be a welterweight. I was interested in quick jabs. I was going to get in and get out, make a few points, plant a few seeds, and raise a few questions. I was going to make them like me. That was the main thing. If they liked me, they would like my case.

Once the judge gave me the nod, I stood up and immediately moved into the proving grounds. I wanted nothing between me and the jury. I was also aware that this put me right in front and in focus of the Court TV camera mounted on the wall above the jury box.

I faced the jury without physical gesture except for a slight nod of my head.

"Ladies and gentlemen, I know the judge already introduced me but I would like to introduce myself and my client. I am Michael Haller, the attorney representing Walter Elliot, whom you see here sitting at the table by himself."

I pointed to Elliot and by prior design he nodded somberly, not offering any form of a smile that would appear as falsely ingratiating as calling the jurors folks.

"Now, I am not going to take a lot of time here, because I want to get to the testimony and the evidence — what little there is of it — and get this show on the road. Enough talk. It's time to put up or shut up. Mr. Golantz wove a big and complicated picture for you. It took him a whole hour just to get it out. But I am here to tell you that this case is not that complicated. What the prosecution's case amounts to is a labyrinth of smoke and mirrors. And when we blow away the smoke and get through the labyrinth, you will understand that. You will find that there is no fire, that there is no case against Walter Elliot. That there is more than reasonable doubt here, that there is outrage that this case was ever brought against Walter Elliot in the first place."

Again I turned and pointed to my client. He sat with his eyes cast downward on the pad of paper he was now writing notes on — again, by prior design, depicting my client as busy, actively involved in his own defense, chin up, and not worried about the terrible things the prosecutor had just said about him. He had right on his side, and right was might.

I turned back to the jury and continued.

"I counted six times that Mr. Golantz mentioned the word 'gun' in his speech. Six times he said Walter took a gun and blew away the woman he loved and a second, innocent bystander. Six times. But what he didn't tell you six times is that there is no gun. He has no gun. The Sheriff's Department has no gun. They have no gun and have no link between Walter and a gun because he has never owned or had such a weapon.

"Mr. Golantz told you that he will introduce indisputable evidence that Walter fired a gun, but let me tell you to hold on to your hats. Keep that promise in your back pocket and let's see at the end of this trial whether that so-called evidence is indisputable. Let's just see if it is even left standing."

As I spoke, my eyes washed back and forth across the jurors like the spotlights sweeping the sky over Hollywood at night. I remained in constant but calm motion. I felt a certain rhythm in my thoughts and cadence, and I instinctively knew I was holding the jury. Each one of them was riding with me.

"I know that in our society we want our law enforcement officers to be professional and thorough and the best they can possibly be. We see crime on the news and in the streets and we know that these men and women are the thin line between order and disorder. I mean, I want that as much as you do. I've been the victim of a violent crime myself. I know what that is like. And we want our cops to step in and save the day. After all, that's what they are there for."

I stopped and swept the whole jury box, holding every set of eyes for a brief moment before continuing.

"But that's not what happened here. The evidence—and I'm talking about the state's own evidence and testimony—will show that from the start the investigators focused on one suspect, Walter Elliot. The evidence will show that once Walter became that focus, then all other bets were off. All other avenues of investigation were halted or never even pursued. They had a suspect and what they believed was a motive, and they never looked back. They never looked anywhere else either."

For the first time I moved from my position. I stepped forward to the railing in front of juror number one. I slowly walked along the front of the box, hand sliding along the railing.

"Ladies and gentlemen, this case is about tunnel vision. The focus on one suspect and the complete lack of focus on anything else. And I will promise you that when you come out of the prosecution's tunnel, you're going to be looking at one another and squinting your eyes against the bright light. And you're going to be wondering where the hell their case is. Thank you very much."

My hand trailed off the railing and I headed back to my seat. Before I sat down, the judge recessed court for lunch.

37

Once more my client eschewed lunch with me so he could get back to the studio and make his business-as-usual appearance in the executive offices. I was beginning to think he viewed the trial as an annoying inconvenience in his schedule. He was either more confident than I was in the defense's case, or the trial simply wasn't a priority.

Whatever the reason, that left me with my entourage from the first row. We went over to Traxx in Union Station because I felt it was far enough away from the courthouse to avoid our ending up in the same place as one of the jurors. Patrick drove and I had him valet the Lincoln and join us so that he would feel like part of the team.

They gave us a table in a quiet enclosure next to a window that looked out on the train station's huge and wonderful waiting room. Lorna had made the seating arrangements and I ended up next to Julie Favreau. Ever since Lorna had hooked up with Cisco, she had decided that I needed to be with someone and had endeavored to be something of a matchmaker. This effort coming from an ex-wife—an ex-wife I still cared for on many levels—was decidedly uncomfortable and it felt clumsy when Lorna overtly pointed me to the chair next to my jury consultant. I was in the middle of day one of a trial and the possibility of romance was the last thing I was thinking about. Besides that, I was incapable of a relationship. My addiction had left me with an emotional distance from people and things that I was only now beginning to close. As such, I had made it my priority to reconnect with my daughter. After that, I would worry about finding a woman to spend time with.

Romance aside, Julie Favreau was wonderful to work with. She was an attractive, diminutive woman with delicate facial features and raven hair that fell around her face in curls. A spray of youthful freckles across her nose made her look younger than she was. I knew she was thirty-three years old. She had once told me her story. She'd come to Los Angeles by way of London to act in film and had studied with a teacher who believed that internal thoughts of character could be shown externally through facial tells, tics, and body movements. It was her job as an actor to bring these giveaways to the surface without making them obvious. Her student exercises became observation, identification, and interpretation of these tells in others. Her assignments took her anywhere from the poker rooms in the south county, where she learned to read the faces of people trying not to give anything away, to the courtrooms of the CCB, where there were always lots of faces and giveaways to read.

After seeing her in the gallery for three days straight of a trial in which I was defending an accused serial rapist, I approached her and asked who she was. Expecting to find out she was a previously unknown victim of the man at the defense table, I was surprised to hear her story and to learn she was simply there to practice reading faces. I took her to lunch, got her number, and the next time I picked a jury, I hired her to help me. She had been dead-on in her observations and I had used her several times since.

"So," I said as I spread a black napkin on my lap. "How is my jury doing?"

I thought it was obvious that the question was directed at Julie but Patrick spoke up first.

"I think they want to throw the book at your guy," he said. "I think they think he's a stuck-up rich guy who thinks he can get away with murder."

I nodded. His take probably wasn't too far off.

"Well, thanks for the encouraging word," I said. "I'll make sure I tell Walter to not be so stuck-up and rich from now on."

Patrick looked down at the table and seemed embarrassed.

"I was just saying, is all."

"No, Patrick, I appreciate it. Any and all opinions are welcome and they all matter. But some things you can't change. My client is rich beyond anything any of us can imagine and that gives him a certain style and image. An off-putting countenance that I'm not sure I can do anything about. Julie, what do you think of the jury so far?"

Before she could answer, the waiter came and took our drink orders. I stuck with water and lime, while the others ordered iced tea and Lorna asked for a glass of Mad Housewife Chardonnay. I gave her a look and she immediately protested.

"What? I'm not working. I'm just watching. Plus, I'm celebrating. You're in trial again and we're back in business."

I grudgingly nodded.

"Speaking of which, I need you to go to the bank."

I pulled an envelope out of my jacket pocket and handed it across the table to her. She smiled because she knew what was in it: a check from Elliot for $150,000, the remainder of the agreed-upon fee for my services.

Lorna put the envelope away and I turned my attention back to Julie.

"So what are you seeing?"

"I think it's a good jury," she said. "Overall, I see a lot of open faces. They are willing to listen to your case. At least right now. We all know they are predisposed to believe the prosecution, but they haven't shut the door on anything."

"You see any change from what we talked about Friday? I still present to number three?"

"Who is number three?" Lorna asked before Julie could answer.

"Golantz's slip-up. Three's a lawyer, and the prosecution should've never left him in the box."

"I still think he's a good one to present to," Julie said. "But there are others. I like eleven and twelve, too. Both retirees and sitting right next to each other. I have a feeling that they're going to bond and almost work as a team when it gets to deliberations. You win one over and you win them both."

I loved her English accent. It wasn't upper-crust at all. It had a street-smarts tone to it that gave what she said validity. She had not been very successful as an actress so far, and she had once told me that she got a lot of audition calls for period pieces requiring a dainty English accent that she hadn't quite mastered. Her income was primarily earned in the poker rooms, where she now played for keeps, and from jury reading for me and the small group of lawyers I had introduced her to.

"What about juror seven?" I asked. "During selection he was all eyes. Now he won't look at me."

Julie nodded.

"You noticed that. Eye contact has completely dropped off the chart. Like something changed between Friday and today. I would have to say at this point that that's a sign he's in the prosecution's camp. While you're present-ing to number three, you can bet Mr. Undefeated's going to number seven."

"So much for listening to my client," I said under my breath.

We ordered lunch and told the waiter to hurry the order because we needed to get back to court. While we waited I checked with Cisco on our witnesses and he said we were good to go in that department. I then asked him to hang around after court and see if he could follow the Germans out of the courthouse and stay with them until they reached their hotel. I wanted to know where they were staying. It was just a precaution. Before the trial was over, they were not going to be very happy with me. It was good strategy to know where your enemies were.

I was halfway through my grilled-chicken salad when I glanced through the window into the waiting room. It was a grand mixture of architectural designs but primarily it had an art deco vibe to it. There were rows and rows of big leather chairs for travelers to wait in and huge chandeliers hanging above. I saw people sleeping in chairs and others sitting with their suitcases and belongings gathered close around them.

And then I saw Bosch. He was sitting alone in the third row from my window. He had his earbuds in. Our eyes held for a moment and then he looked away. I put my fork down and reached into my pocket for my cash. I had no idea how much Mad Housewife cost per glass but Lorna was into her second round. I put five twenties down on the table and told the others to finish eating while I stepped out to make a phone call.

I left the restaurant and called Bosch's cell. He pulled his plugs and answered it as I was approaching the third row of seats.

"What?" he said by way of a greeting.

"Frank Morgan again?"

"Actually, Ron Carter. Why are you calling me?"

"What did you think of the story?"

I sat in the open seat across from him, gave him a glance but acted like I was talking to someone far away from me.

"This is kind of stupid," Bosch said.

"Well, I didn't know whether you wanted to stay undercover or—"

"Just hang up."

We closed our phones and looked at each other.

"Well?" I asked. "Are we in play?"

"We won't know until we know."

"What's that mean?"

"The story is out there. I think it did what we wanted it to do. Now we wait and see. If something happens, then, yes, we're in play. We won't know we're in play until we're in play."

I nodded, even though what he had said made no sense to me.

"Who's the woman in black?" he asked. "You didn't tell me you had a girlfriend. We should probably put coverage on her, too."

"She's my jury reader, that's all."

"Oh, she helps you pick out the cop haters and antiestablishment types?"

"Something like that. Is it just you here? Are you watching me by yourself?"

"You know, I had a girlfriend once. She always asked questions in bunches. Never one at a time."

"Did you ever answer any of her questions? Or did you just cleverly deflect them like you are doing now?"

"I'm not alone, Counselor. Don't worry. You have people around you that you'll never see. I've got people on your office whether you are there or not."

And cameras. They had been installed ten days earlier, when we had thought that the *Times* story was imminent.

"Yeah, good, but we won't be there for long."

"I noticed. Where are you moving to?"

"Nowhere. I work out of my car."

"Sounds like fun."

I studied him a moment. He had been sarcastic in his tone as usual. He was an annoying guy but somehow he had gotten me to entrust my safety to him.

"Well, I've got to get to court. Is there something I should be doing? Any particular way you want me to act or place you want me to go?"

"Just do what you always do. But there is one thing. Keeping an eye on you in motion takes a lot of people. So, at the end of the day, when you are home for the night, call me and tell me so I can release some people."

"Okay. But you'll still have somebody watching, right?"

"Don't worry. You'll be covered twenty-four-seven. Oh, and one other thing."

"What?"

"Don't ever approach me again like this."

I nodded. I was being dismissed.

"Got it."

I stood up and looked toward the restaurant. I could see Lorna counting the twenties I had left and putting them down on the check. It looked like she was using them all. Patrick had left the table and gone to get the car from the valet.

"See ya, Detective," I said without looking at him.

He didn't respond. I walked away and caught up with my party as they were coming out of the restaurant.

"Was that Detective Bosch you were with?" Lorna asked.

"Yeah, I saw him out there."

"What was he doing?"

"He said he likes to come over here for lunch, sit in those big, comfortable chairs and just think."

"That's a coincidence that we were here too."

Julie Favreau shook her head.

"There are no coincidences," she said.

38

After lunch Golantz began to present his case. He went with what I called the "square one" presentation. He started at the very beginning — the 911 call that brought the double murder to public light — and proceeded in linear fashion from there. The first witness was an emergency operator with the county's communications center. She was used to introduce the tape recordings of Walter Elliot's calls for help. I had sought in a pretrial motion to thwart the playing of the two tapes, arguing that printed transcripts would be clearer and more useful to the jurors, but the judge had ruled in the prosecution's favor. He ordered Golantz to provide transcripts so jurors could read along with the audio when the tapes were played in court.

I had tried to halt the playing of the tapes because I knew they were prejudicial to my client. Elliot had calmly spoken to the dispatcher in the first call, reporting that his wife and another person had been murdered. In that calm demeanor was room for an interpretation of calculated coldness that I didn't want the jury to make. The second tape was worse from a defense standpoint. Elliot sounded annoyed and also indicated he knew and disliked the man who had been killed with his wife.

Tape 1 — 13:05 — 05/02/07

Dispatcher: Nine-one-one. Do you have an emergency?

Walter Elliot: I . . . well, they look dead. I don't think anybody can help them.

Dispatcher: Excuse me, sir. Who am I talking to?

Walter Elliot: This is Walter Elliot. This is my house.

Dispatcher: Yes, sir. And you say somebody is dead?

Walter Elliot: I found my wife. She's shot. And there's a man here. He's shot, too.

Dispatcher: Hold on a moment, sir. Let me type this in and get help going to you.

—break—

Dispatcher: Okay, Mr. Elliot, I have paramedics and deputies on their way.

Walter Elliot: It's too late for them. The paramedics, I mean.

Dispatcher: I have to send them, sir. You said they are shot? Are you in danger?

Walter Elliot: I don't know. I just got here. I didn't do this thing. Are you recording this?

Dispatcher: Yes, sir. Everything is recorded. Are you in the house right now?

Walter Elliot: I'm in the bedroom. I didn't do it.

Dispatcher: Is there anybody else in the house besides you and the two people who are shot?

Walter Elliot: I don't think so.

Dispatcher: Okay, I want you to step outside so the deputies will see you when they pull up. Stand out where they can see you.

Walter Elliot: Okay, I'm going out.

—end—

The second tape involved a different dispatcher but I allowed Golantz to play it. I had lost the big argument about whether the tapes could be played at all. I saw no sense in wasting the court's time by making the prosecutor bring in the second dispatcher to establish and introduce the second tape.

This one was made from Elliot's cell phone. He was outside, and the slight sound of the ocean's waves could be heard in the background.

Tape 2 — 13:24 — 05/02/07

Dispatcher: Nine-one-one, what is your emergency?

Walter Elliot: Yeah, I called before. Where is everybody?

Dispatcher: You called nine-one-one?

Walter Elliot: Yeah, my wife's shot. So's the German. Where is everybody?

Dispatcher: Is this the call in Malibu on Crescent Cove Road?

Walter Elliot: Yeah, that's me. I called at least fifteen minutes ago and nobody's here.

Dispatcher: Sir, my screen shows our alpha unit has an ETA of less than one minute. Hang up the phone and stand out front so they will see you when they arrive. Will you do that, sir?

Walter Elliot: I'm already standing out here.
Dispatcher: Then wait right there, sir.
Walter Elliot: If you say so. Good-bye.

— end —

Elliot not only sounded annoyed in the second call by the delay but said the word "German" with almost a sneer in his voice. Whether or not guilt could be extrapolated from his verbal tones didn't matter. The tapes helped set the prosecution's theme of Walter Elliot's being arrogant and believing he was above the law. It was a good start for Golantz.

I passed on questioning the dispatcher because I knew there was nothing to be gained for the defense. Next up for the prosecution was sheriff's deputy Brendan Murray, who was driving the alpha car that first responded to the 911 call. In a half hour of testimony, in minute detail Golantz led the deputy through his arrival and discovery of the bodies. He paid special attention to Murray's recollections of Elliot's behavior, demeanor, and statements. According to Murray, the defendant showed no emotions when leading them up the stairs to the bedroom where his wife lay shot to death and naked on the bed. He calmly stepped over the legs of the dead man in the doorway and pointed to the body on the bed.

"He said, 'That's my wife. I'm pretty sure she's dead,' " Murray testified.

According to Murray, Elliot also said at least three times that he had not killed the two people in the bedroom.

"Well, was that unusual?" Golantz asked.

"Well, we're not trained to get involved in murder investigations," Murray said. "We're not supposed to. So I never asked Mr. Elliot if he did it. He just kept telling us he didn't."

I had no questions for Murray either. He was on my witness list and I would be able to recall him during the defense phase if I needed to. But I wanted to wait for the prosecution's next witness, Christopher Harber, who was Murray's partner and a rookie in the Sheriff's Department. I thought that if either of the deputies was to make a mistake that might help the defense, it would be the rookie.

Harber's testimony was shorter than Murray's and he was used primarily to confirm his partner's testimony. He heard the same things Murray heard. He saw the same things as well.

"Just a few questions, Your Honor," I said when Stanton inquired about cross-examination.

While Golantz had been conducting his direct examination from the lectern, I remained at the defense table for the cross. This was a ploy. I wanted the jury, the witness, and the prosecutor to think I was just going through the motions and asking a few questions on cross. The truth was I was about to plant what would be a key point in the defense's case.

"Now, Deputy Harber, you are a rookie, correct?"

"That is correct."

"Have you ever testified in court before?"

"Not in a murder case."

"Well, don't be nervous. Despite what Mr. Golantz may have told you, I don't bite."

There was a polite murmur of laughter in the courtroom. Harber's face turned a little pink. He was a big man with sandy hair cut military-short, the way they like it in the Sheriff's Department.

"Now, when you and your partner arrived at the Elliot house, you said you saw my client standing out front in the turnaround. Is that correct?"

"That is correct."

"Okay, what was he doing?"

"Just standing there. He had been told to wait there for us."

"Okay, now, what did you know about the situation when the alpha car pulled in there?"

"We only knew what dispatch had told us. That a man named Walter Elliot had called from the house and said that two people were dead inside. They had been shot."

"Had you ever had a call like that before?"

"No."

"Were you scared, nervous, jacked-up, what?"

"I would say that the adrenaline was flowing, but we were pretty calm."

"Did you draw your weapon when you got out of your car?"

"Yes, I did."

"Did you point it at Mr. Elliot?"

"No, I carried it at my side."

"Did your partner draw his weapon?"

"I believe so."

"Did he point it at Mr. Elliot?"

Harber hesitated. I always liked it when witnesses for the prosecution hesitated.

"I don't recall. I wasn't really looking at him. I was looking at the defendant."

I nodded like that made sense to me.

"You had to be safe, correct? You didn't know this guy. You just knew that there supposedly were two dead people inside."

"That's right."

"So it would be correct to say you approached Mr. Elliot cautiously?"

"That's right."

"When did you put your weapon away?"

"That was after we had searched and secured the premises."

"You mean after you went inside and confirmed the deaths and that there was no one else inside?"

"Correct."

"Okay, so when you were doing this, Mr. Elliot was with you the whole time?"

"Yes, we needed to keep him with us so he could show us where the bodies were."

"Now was he under arrest?"

"No, he was not. He volunteered to show us."

"But you handcuffed him, didn't you?"

Harber's second hesitation followed the question. He was in uncharted water and probably remembering the lines he'd rehearsed with Golantz or his young second chair.

"He had voluntarily agreed to be handcuffed. We explained to him that we were not arresting him but that we had a volatile situation inside the house and that it would be best for his safety and ours if we could handcuff him until we secured the premises."

"And he agreed."

"Yes, he agreed."

In my peripheral vision I saw Elliot shake his head. I hoped the jury saw it too.

"Were his hands cuffed behind his back or in the front?"

"In the back, according to procedure. We are not allowed to handcuff a subject in the front."

"A subject? What does that mean?"

"A subject can be anybody involved in an investigation."

"Someone who is arrested?"

"Including that, yes. But Mr. Elliot was not under arrest."

"I know you are new on the job, but how often have you handcuffed someone who was not under arrest?"

"It's happened on occasion. But I don't recall the number of times."

I nodded but I hoped it was clear that I wasn't nodding because I believed him.

"Now, your partner testified and you have testified that Mr. Elliot on three occasions told you both that he was not responsible for the killings in that house. Right?"

"Right."

"You heard those statements?"

"Yes, I did."

"Was that when you were outside or inside or where?"

"That was inside, when we were up in the bedroom."

"So that means that he made these supposedly uninvited protestations of his innocence while he was handcuffed with his arms behind his back and you and your partner had your weapons drawn and ready, is that correct?"

The third hesitation.

"Yes, I believe that would be so."

"And you are saying he was not under arrest at this time?"

"He was not under arrest."

"Okay, so what happened after Mr. Elliot led you inside and up to the bodies and you and your partner determined that there was no one else in the house?"

"We took Mr. Elliot back outside, we sealed the house, and we called detective services for a homicide call-out."

"Was that all according to sheriff's procedure, too?"

"Yes, it was."

"Good. Now, Deputy Harber, did you take the handcuffs off of Mr. Elliot then, since he was not under arrest?"

"No, sir, we didn't. We placed Mr. Elliot in the back of the car, and it is against procedure to place a subject in a sheriff's car without handcuffs."

"Again, there's that word 'subject.' Are you sure Mr. Elliot wasn't under arrest?"

"I am sure. We did not arrest him."

"Okay, how long was he in the backseat of that car?"

"Approximately one half hour while we waited for the homicide team."

"And what happened when the team arrived?"

"When the investigators arrived, they looked in the house first. Then they came out and took custody of Mr. Elliot. I mean, took him out of the car."

There was a slip I dove into.

"He was in custody at that time?"

"No, I made a mistake there. He voluntarily agreed to wait in the car and then they arrived and took him out."

"You are saying he voluntarily agreed to be handcuffed in the back of a patrol car?"

"Yes."

"If he had wanted to, could he have opened the door and gotten out?"

"I don't think so. The back doors have security locks. You can't open them from inside."

"But he was in there voluntarily."

"Yes, he was."

Even Harber didn't look like he believed what he was saying. His face had turned a deeper shade of pink.

"Deputy Harber, when did the handcuffs finally come off of Mr. Elliot?"

"When the detectives removed him from the car, they took the cuffs off and gave them back to my partner."

"Okay."

I nodded like I was finished and flipped up a few pages on my pad to check for questions I missed. I kept my eyes down on the pad when I spoke.

"Oh, Deputy? One last thing. The first call to nine-one-one went out at one-oh-five according to the dispatch log. Mr. Elliot had to call again nineteen minutes later to make sure he hadn't been forgotten about, and then you and your partner finally arrived four minutes after that. A total of twenty-three minutes to respond."

I now looked up at Harber.

"Deputy, why did it take so long to respond to what must've been a priority call?"

"The Malibu district is our largest geographically. We had to come all the way over the mountain from another call."

"Wasn't there another patrol car that was closer and also available?"

"My partner and I were in the alpha car. It's a rover. We handle the priority calls and we accepted this one when it came in from dispatch."

"Okay, Deputy, I have nothing further."

On redirect Golantz followed the misdirection I'd set up. He asked Harber several questions that revolved around whether Elliot had been under arrest or not. The prosecutor sought to diffuse this idea, as it would play into the defense's tunnel-vision theory. That was what I wanted him to think I was doing and it had worked. Golantz spent another fifteen minutes eliciting testimony from Harber that underlined that the man he and his partner had handcuffed outside the scene of a double murder was not under arrest. It defied common sense but the prosecution was sticking with it.

When the prosecutor was finished, the judge adjourned for the afternoon break. As soon as the jury had cleared the courtroom, I heard a whispered voice call my name. I turned around and saw Lorna, who pointed her finger toward the back of the courtroom. I turned further to look back, and there were my daughter and her mother, squeezed into the back row of the gallery. My daughter surreptitiously waved to me and I smiled back.

39

I met them in the hallway outside the courtroom, away from the clot of reporters who surrounded the other principals of the trial as they exited. Hayley hugged me and I was overwhelmed that she had come. I saw an empty wooden bench and we sat down.

"How long were you guys in there?" I asked. "I didn't see you."

"Unfortunately, not that long," Maggie said. "Her last period today was

PE, so I decided to take the afternoon off, pull her out early, and come on down. We saw most of your cross with the deputy."

I looked from Maggie to our daughter, who was sitting between us. She had her mother's looks; dark hair and eyes, skin that held a tan long into the winter.

"What did you think, Hay?"

"Um, I thought it was really interesting. You asked him a lot of questions. He looked like he was getting mad."

"Don't worry, he'll get over it."

I looked over her head and winked at my ex-wife.

"Mickey?"

I turned around and saw it was McEvoy from the *Times*. He had come over, his pad and pen ready.

"Not now," I said.

"I just had a quick—"

"And I just said, not now. Leave me alone."

McEvoy turned and walked back to one of the groups circling Golantz.

"Who was that?" Hayley asked.

"A newspaper reporter. I'll talk to him later."

"Mom said there was a big story about you today."

"It wasn't really about me. It was about the case. That's why I was hoping you could come see some of it."

I looked at my ex-wife again and nodded my thanks. She had put aside any anger she had toward me and placed our daughter first. No matter what else, I could always count on her for that.

"Do you go back in there?" Hayley asked.

"Yes, this is just a little break so people can get something to drink or use the bathroom. We have one more session and then we'll go home and start it all over tomorrow."

She nodded and looked down the hall toward the courtroom door. I followed her eyes and saw that people were starting to go back in.

"Um, Daddy? Did that man in there kill somebody?"

I looked at Maggie and she shrugged as if to say, *I didn't tell her to ask the question.*

"Well, honey, we don't know. He is accused of that, yes. And a lot of people think he did. But nothing has been proven yet and we're going to use this trial to decide that. That's what the trial is for. Remember how I explained that to you?"

"I remember."

"Mick, is this your family?"

I looked over my shoulder and froze when I looked into the eyes of Walter Elliot. He was smiling warmly, expecting an introduction. Little did he know who Maggie McFierce was.

"Uh, hi, Walter. This is my daughter, Hayley, and this is her mom, Maggie McPherson."

"Hi," Hayley said shyly.

Maggie nodded and looked uncomfortable.

Walter made the mistake of thrusting his hand out to Maggie. If she could have acted more stiffly, I couldn't imagine it. She shook his hand once and then quickly pulled away from his grasp. When his hand moved toward Hayley, Maggie literally jumped up, put her arms on our daughter's shoulders, and pulled her from the bench.

"Hayley, let's go into the restroom real quick before court starts again."

She hustled Hayley off toward the restroom. Walter watched them go and then looked at me, his hand still held out and empty. I stood up.

"Sorry, Walter, my ex-wife's a prosecutor. She works for the DA."

His eyebrows climbed his forehead.

"Then, I guess I understand why she's an ex-wife."

I nodded just to make him feel better. I told him to go on back into the courtroom and that I would be along shortly.

I walked toward the restrooms and met Maggie and Hayley as they were coming out.

"I think we're going to head home," Maggie said.

"Really?"

"She's got a lot of homework and I think she's seen enough for today."

I could've argued that last point but I let it go.

"Okay," I said. "Hayley, thanks for coming. It means a lot to me."

"Okay."

I bent down and kissed her on the top of her head, then pulled her in close for a hug. It was only at times like this with my daughter that the distance I had opened in my life came closed. I felt connected to something that mattered. I looked up at Maggie.

"Thanks for bringing her."

She nodded.

"For what it's worth, you're doing good in there."

"It's worth a lot. Thank you."

She shrugged and let a small smile slip out. And that was nice, too.

I watched them walk toward the elevator alcove, knowing they weren't going home to my house and wondering how it was that I had messed up my life so badly.

"Hayley!" I called after them.

My daughter looked back at me.

"See you Wednesday. Pancakes!"

She was smiling as they joined the crowd waiting for an elevator. I noticed that my former wife was smiling, too. I pointed at her as I walked back toward the courtroom.

"And you can come, too."

She nodded.

"We'll see," she said.

An elevator opened and they moved toward it. "We'll see." Those two words seemed to cover it all for me.

40

In any murder trial, the main witness for the prosecution is always the lead investigator. Because there are no living victims to tell the jury what happened to them, it falls upon the lead to tell the tale of the investigation as well as to speak for the dead. The lead investigator brings the hammer. He puts everything together for the jury, makes it clear and makes it sympathetic. The lead's job is to sell the case to the jury and, like any exchange or transaction, it is often just as much about the salesman as it is about the goods being sold. The best homicide men are the best salesmen. I've seen men as hard as Harry Bosch on the stand shed a tear when they've described the last moments a murder victim spent on earth.

Golantz called the case's lead investigator to the stand after the afternoon break. It was a stroke of genius and master planning. John Kinder would hold center stage until court was adjourned for the day, and the jurors would go home with his words to consider over dinner and then into the night. And there was nothing I could do about it but watch.

Kinder was a large, affable black man who spoke with a fatherly baritone. He wore reading glasses slipped down to the end of his nose when referring to the thick binder he'd carried with him to the stand. Between questions he would look over the rims at Golantz or the jury. His eyes seemed comfortable, kind, alert, and wise. He was the one witness I didn't have a comeback for.

With Golantz's precise questioning and a series of blowups of crime scene photos — which I had been unsuccessful in keeping out on the grounds they were prejudicial — Kinder led the jury on a tour of the murder scene and what the evidence told the investigative team. It was purely clinical and methodical but it was supremely interesting. With his deep, authoritative voice, Kinder came off as something akin to a professor, teaching Homicide 101 to every person in the courtroom.

I objected here and there when I could in an effort to break the Golantz/Kinder rhythm, but there was little I could do but nut it out and wait. At one point I got a text on my phone from the gallery and it didn't help ease my concerns.

FAVREAU: They love this guy! Isn't there anything you can do?

Without turning to glance back at Favreau I simply shook my head while looking down at the phone's screen under the defense table.

I then glanced at my client and it appeared that he was barely paying attention to Kinder's testimony. He was writing notes on a legal pad but they weren't about the trial or the case. I saw a lot of numbers and the heading FOREIGN DISTRIBUTION underlined on the page. I leaned over and whispered to him.

"This guy's killing us up there," I said. "Just in case you're wondering."

A humorless smile bent his lips and Elliot whispered back.

"I think we're doing fine. You've had a good day."

I shook my head and turned back to watch the testimony. I had a client who wasn't concerned by the reality of his situation. He was well aware of my trial strategy and that I had the magic bullet in my gun. But nothing is a sure thing when you go to trial. That's why ninety percent of all cases are settled by disposition before trial. Nobody wants to roll the dice. The stakes are too high. And a murder trial is the biggest gamble of them all.

But from day one, Walter Elliot didn't seem to get this. He just went about the business of making movies and working out foreign distribution and seemingly believed that there was no question that he would walk at the end of the trial. I felt my case was bulletproof but not even I had that kind of confidence.

After the basics of the crime scene investigation were thoroughly covered with Kinder, Golantz moved the testimony toward Elliot and the investigator's interaction with him.

"Now, you have testified that the defendant remained in Deputy Murray's patrol car while you initially surveyed the crime scene and sort of got the lay of the land, correct?"

"Yes, that is correct."

"When did you first speak with Walter Elliot?"

Kinder referred to a document in the binder open on the shelf at the front of the witness stand.

"At approximately two thirty, I came out of the house after completing my initial survey of the crime scene and I asked the deputies to take Mr. Elliot out of the car."

"And then what did you do?"

"I told one of deputies to take the handcuffs off him because I didn't think that was necessary any longer. There were several deputies and investigators on the scene by this point and the premises were very secure."

"Well, was Mr. Elliot under arrest at that point?"

"No, he wasn't and I explained that to him. I told him that the guys — the deputies — had been taking every precaution until they knew what they had. Mr. Elliot said he understood this. I asked if he wanted to continue to cooperate and show the members of my team around inside and he said, yes, he would do it."

"So you took him back inside the house?"

"Yes. We had him put on booties first so as not to contaminate anything and then we went back inside. I had Mr. Elliot retrace the exact steps he said he had taken when he came in and found the bodies."

I made a note about the booties being a bit late, since Elliot had already shown the first deputies around inside. I'd potshot Kinder with that on cross.

"Was there anything unusual about the steps he said he had taken or anything inconsistent in what he told you?"

I objected to the question, saying that it was too vague. The judge agreed. Score one inconsequential point for the defense. Golantz simply rephrased and got more specific.

"Where did Mr. Elliot lead you in the house, Detective Kinder?"

"He walked us in and we went straight up the stairs to the bedroom. He told us this was what he had done when he entered. He said he then found the bodies and called nine-one-one from the phone next to the bed. He said the dispatcher told him to leave the house and go out front to wait and that's what he did. I asked him specifically if he had been anywhere else in the house and he said no."

"Did that seem unusual or inconsistent to you?"

"Well, first of all, I thought it was odd if true that he'd gone inside and directly up to the bedroom without initially looking around the first level of the house. It also didn't jibe with what he told us when we got back outside the house. He pointed at his wife's car, which was parked in the circle out front, and said that was how he knew she had somebody with her in the house. I asked him what he meant and he said that she parked out front so that Johan Rilz, the other victim, could use the one space available in the garage. They had stored a bunch of furniture and stuff in there and that left only one space. He said the German had hidden his Porsche in there and his wife had to park outside."

"And what was the significance of that to you?"

"Well, to me it showed deception. He'd told us that he hadn't been anywhere in the house but the bedroom upstairs. But it was pretty clear to me he had looked in the garage and seen the second victim's Porsche."

Golantz nodded emphatically from the lectern, driving home the point about Elliot being deceptive. I knew I would be able to handle this point on cross but I wouldn't get the chance until the next day, after it had percolated in the brains of the jury for almost twenty-four hours.

"What happened after that?" Golantz asked.

"Well, there was still a lot of work to do inside the house. So I had a couple members of my team take Mr. Elliot to the Malibu substation so he could wait there and be comfortable."

"Was he arrested at this time?"

"No, once again I explained to him that we needed to talk to him and if he was still willing to be cooperative, we were going to take him to an interview room at the station, and I said that I would get there as soon as possible. Once again he agreed."

"Who transported him?"

"Investigators Joshua and Toles took him in their car."

"Why didn't they go ahead and interview him once they got to the Malibu station?"

"Because I wanted to know more about him and the crime scene before we talked to him. Sometimes you get only one chance, even with a cooperating witness."

"You used the word 'witness.' Wasn't Mr. Elliot a suspect at this time?"

It was a cat-and-mouse game with the truth. It didn't matter how Kinder answered, everybody in the courtroom knew that they had drawn a bead on Elliot.

"Well, to some extent anybody and everybody is a suspect," Kinder answered. "You go into a situation like that and you suspect everybody. But at that point, I didn't know a lot about the victims, I didn't know a lot about Mr. Elliot, and I didn't know exactly what we had. So at that time, I was viewing him more as a very important witness. He found the bodies and he knew the victims. He could help us."

"Okay, so you stashed him at the Malibu station while you went to work at the crime scene. What were you doing?"

"My job was to oversee the documentation of the crime scene and the gathering of any evidence in that house. We were also working the phones and the computers and confirming the identities and backgrounding the parties involved."

"What did you learn?"

"We learned that neither of the Elliots had a criminal record or had any guns legally registered to them. We learned that the other victim, Johan Rilz, was a German national and appeared to have no criminal record or own any weapons. We learned that Mr. Elliot was the head of a studio and very successful in the movie business, things like that."

"At some point did a member of your team draw up search warrants in the case?"

"Yes, we did. Proceeding with an abundance of caution, we drew up and had a judge sign off on a series of search warrants so we had the authority to continue the investigation and take it wherever it led."

"Is it unusual to take such steps?"

"Perhaps. The courts have granted law enforcement wide leeway in the gathering of evidence. But we determined that because of the parties involved in this case, we would go the extra mile. We went for the search warrants even though we might not need them."

"What specifically were the search warrants for?"

"We had warrants for the Elliot house and for the three cars, Mr. Elliot's, his wife's, and the Porsche in the garage. We also had a search warrant granting us permission to conduct tests on Mr. Elliot and his clothing to determine if he had discharged a gun in recent hours."

The prosecutor continued to lead Kinder through the investigation up until he cleared the crime scene and interviewed Elliot at the Malibu station. This set up the introduction of a videotape of the first sit-down interview with Elliot. This was a tape I had viewed several times during preparation for trial. I knew it was unremarkable in terms of the content of what Elliot told Kinder and his partner, Roland Ericsson. What was important to the prosecution about the tape was Elliot's demeanor. He didn't look like somebody who had just discovered the naked body of his dead wife with a bullet hole in the center of her face and two more in her chest. He appeared as calm as a summer sunset, and that made him look like an ice-cold killer.

A video screen was set up in front of the jury box and Golantz played the tape, often stopping it to ask Kinder a question and then starting it again. The taped interview lasted ten minutes and was nonconfrontational. It was simply an exercise in which the investigators locked in Elliot's story. There were no hard questions. Elliot was asked broadly about what he did and when. It ended with Kinder presenting a search warrant to Elliot that the investigator explained granted the Sheriff's Department access to test his hands, arms, and clothing for gunshot residue.

Elliot smiled slightly as he replied.

"Have at it, gentlemen," he said. "Do what you have to do."

Golantz checked the clock on the back wall of the courtroom and then used a remote to freeze the image of Elliot's half smile on the video screen. That was the image he wanted the jurors to take with them. He wanted them to think about that catch-me-if-you-can smile as they drove home in five o'clock traffic.

"Your Honor," he said. "I think now would be a good time to break for the day. I will be moving with Deputy Kinder in a new direction after this and maybe we should start that tomorrow morning."

The judge agreed, adjourning court for the day after once more admonishing the jurors to avoid all media reports on the trial.

I stood at the defense table and watched the jurors file into the deliberation room. I was pretty sure that the prosecution had won the first day, but that was to be expected. We still had our shots coming. I looked over at my client.

"Walter, what do you have going tonight?" I asked.

"A small dinner party with friends. They've invited Dominick Dunne. Then I am going to watch the first cut of a film my studio is producing with Johnny Depp playing a detective."

"Well, call your friends and call Johnny and cancel it all. You're having dinner with me. We're going to work."

"I don't understand."

"Yes, you do. You've been ducking me since the trial began. That was okay because I didn't want to know what I didn't need to know. Now it's different. We're in trial, we're past discovery, and I need to know. Everything, Walter. So, we're going to talk tonight, or you're going to have to hire another lawyer in the morning."

I saw his face grow tight with checked anger. In that moment, I knew he could be a killer, or at least someone who could order it done.

"You wouldn't dare," he said.

"Try me."

We stared at each other for a moment and I saw something about his face relax.

"Make your calls," I finally said. "We'll take my car."

41

Since I had insisted on the meeting, Elliot insisted on the place. With a thirty-second phone call he got us a private booth at the Water Grill over by the Biltmore and had a martini waiting on the table for him when we got there. As we sat down, I asked for a bottle of flat water and some sliced lemons.

I sat across from my client and watched him study the fresh fish menu. For the longest time I had wanted to be in the dark about Walter Elliot. Usually the less you know about your client, the better able you are to provide a defense. But we were past that time now.

"You called it a dinner meeting," Elliot said without taking his eyes from the menu. "Aren't you going to look?"

"I'm having what you're having, Walter."

He put the menu to the side and looked at me.

"Fillet of sole."

"Sounds good."

He signaled a waiter who had been standing nearby but too intimidated to approach the table. Elliot ordered for us both, adding a bottle of Chardonnay to come with the fish, and told the waiter not to forget about my flat water and lemon. He then clasped his hands on the table and looked expectantly at me.

"I could be dining with Dominick Dunne," he said. "This better be good."

"Walter, this *is* going to be good. This is going to be where you stop hiding from me. This is where you tell me the whole story. The true story. You see, if I know what you know, then I'm not going to get sandbagged by the prosecution. I am going to know what moves Golantz is going to make before he makes them."

Elliot nodded as though he agreed it was time to deliver the goods.

"I did not kill my wife or her Nazi friend," he said. "I have told you that from day one."

I shook my head.

"That's not good enough. I said I want the story. I want to know what really happened, Walter. I want to know what's going on or I'm going to be moving on."

"Don't be ridiculous. No judge is going to let you walk away in the middle of a trial."

"You want to bet your freedom on that, Walter? If I want off this case, I will find a way off it."

He hesitated and studied me before answering.

"You should be careful what you ask for. Guilty knowledge could be a dangerous thing."

"I'll risk it."

"But I'm not sure I can."

I leaned across the table to him.

"What does that mean, Walter? What is going on? I'm your lawyer. You can tell me what you've done and it stays with me."

Before he could speak, the waiter brought a bottle of European water to the table and a side plate of sliced lemons. Enough for everybody in the restaurant. Elliot waited until he had filled my glass and moved away and out of earshot before responding.

"What is going on is that you have been hired to present my defense to the jury. In my estimation you have done an excellent job so far and your preparations for the defense phase are on the highest level. All of this in two weeks. Astonishing!"

"Drop the bullshit!"

I said it too loud. Elliot looked outside the booth and stared down a woman at a nearby table who had heard the expletive.

"You'll have to keep your voice down," he said. "The bond of attorney-client confidentiality ends at this table."

I looked at him. He was smiling but I also knew he was reminding me of what I had already assured him of, that what was said here stayed here. Was it a signal that he was willing to finally talk? I played the only ace I had.

"Tell me about the bribe Jerry Vincent paid," I said.

At first I detected a momentary shock in his eyes. Then came a knowing look as the wheels turned inside and he put something together. Then I thought I saw a quick flash of regret. I wished Julie Favreau had been sitting next to me. She could have read him better than I could.

"That is a very dangerous piece of information to be in possession of," he said. "How did you get it?"

I obviously couldn't tell my client I got it from a police detective I was now cooperating with.

"I guess you could say it came with the case, Walter. I have all of Vincent's records, including his financials. It wasn't hard to figure out that he funneled a hundred thousand of your advance to an unknown party. Is the bribe what got him killed?"

Elliot raised his martini glass with two fingers clenching the delicate stem and drank what was left in it. He then nodded to someone unseen over my shoulder. He wanted another. Then he looked at me.

"I think it is safe to say a confluence of events led to Jerry Vincent's death."

"Walter, I'm not fucking around with you. I need to know — not only to defend you, but to protect myself."

He put his empty glass to the side of the table and someone whisked it away within two seconds. He nodded as if in agreement with me and then he spoke.

"I think you may have found the reason for his death," he said. "It was in the file. You even mentioned it to me."

"I don't understand. What did I mention?"

Elliot responded in an impatient tone.

"He planned to delay the trial. You found the motion. He was killed before he could file it."

I tried to put it together but I didn't have enough of the parts.

"I don't understand, Walter. He wanted to delay the trial and that got him killed? Why?"

Elliot leaned across the table toward me. He spoke in a tone just above a whisper.

"Okay, you asked for it and I'll tell you. But don't blame me when you wish you didn't know what you know. Yes, there was a bribe. He paid it and everything was fine. The trial was scheduled and all we had to do was be ready to go. We had to stay on schedule. No delays, no continuances. But then he changed his mind and wanted to delay."

"Why?"

"I don't know. I think he actually thought he could win the case without the fix."

It appeared that Elliot didn't know about the FBI's phone calls and apparent interest in Vincent. If he did know, now would have been the time to mention it. The FBI's focus on Vincent would have been as good a reason as any to delay a trial involving a bribery scheme.

"So delaying the trial got him killed?"

"That's my guess, yes."

"Did you kill him, Walter?"

"I don't kill people."

"You had him killed."

Elliot shook his head wearily.

"I don't *have* people killed either."

A waiter moved up to the booth with a tray and a stand and we both leaned back to let him work. He deboned our fish, plated them, and put them down on the table along with two small serving pitchers with beurre blanc sauce in them. He then placed Elliot's fresh martini down along with two wineglasses. He uncorked the bottle Elliot had ordered and asked if he wanted to taste the wine yet. Elliot shook his head and told the waiter to go away.

"Okay," I said when we were left alone. "Let's go back to the bribe. Who was bribed?"

Elliot took down half his new martini in one gulp.

"That should be obvious when you think about it."

"Then I'm stupid. Help me out."

"A trial that cannot be delayed. Why?"

My eyes stayed on him but I was no longer looking at him. I went inside to work the riddle until it came to me. I ticked off the possibilities — judge, prosecutor, cops, witnesses, jury...I realized that there was only one place where a bribe and an unmovable trial intersected. There was only one aspect that would change if the trial were delayed and rescheduled. The judge, prosecutor, and all the witnesses would remain the same no matter when it was scheduled. But the jury pool changes week to week.

"There's a sleeper on the jury," I said. "You got to somebody."

Elliot didn't react. He let me run with it and I did. My mind swept along the faces in the jury box. Two rows of six. I stopped on juror number seven.

"Number seven. You wanted him in the box. You knew. He's the sleeper. Who is he?"

Elliot nodded slightly and gave me that half smile. He took his first bite of fish before answering my question as calmly as if we were talking about the Lakers' chances at the playoffs and not the rigging of a murder trial.

"I have no idea who he is and don't really care to know. But he's ours. We were told that number seven would be ours. And he's no sleeper. He's a persuader. When it gets to deliberations, he will go in there and turn the tide for the defense. With the case Vincent built and you're delivering, it probably won't take more than a little push. I'm banking on us getting our verdict. But at minimum he will hold out for acquittal and we'll have a hung jury. If that happens, we just start all over and do it again. They will never convict me, Mickey. Never."

I pushed my plate aside. I couldn't eat.

"Walter, no more riddles. Tell me how this went down. Tell me from the start."

"From the start?"

"From the start."

Elliot chuckled at the thought of it and poured himself a glass of wine without first tasting from the bottle. A waiter swooped in to take over the operation but Elliot waved him away with the bottle.

"This is a long story, Mickey. Would you like a glass of wine to go with it?"

He held the mouth of the bottle poised over my empty glass. I was tempted but I shook my head.

"No, Walter, I don't drink."

"I'm not sure I can trust someone who doesn't take a drink from time to time."

"I'm your lawyer. You can trust me."

"I trusted the last one, too, and look what happened to him."

"Don't threaten me, Walter. Just tell me the story."

He drank heavily from his wineglass and then put it down too hard on the table. He looked around to see if anyone in the restaurant had noticed and I got the sense that it was all an act. He was really checking to see if we were being watched. I scanned the angles I had without being obvious. I didn't see Bosch or anyone else I pegged as a cop in the restaurant.

Elliot began his story.

"When you come to Hollywood, it doesn't matter who you are or where you come from as long as you've got one thing in your pocket."

"Money."

"That's right. I came here twenty-five years ago and I had money. I put it in a couple of movies first and then into a half-assed studio nobody gave two shits about. And I built that place into a contender. Another five years and it will no longer be the Big Four they talk about. It will be the Big Five. Archway will be right up there with Paramount and Warner's and the rest."

I wasn't anticipating going back twenty-five years when I told him to start the story from the beginning.

"Okay, Walter, I get all of that about your success. What are you saying?"

"I'm saying it wasn't my money. When I came here, it wasn't my money."

"I thought the story was that you came from a family that owned a phosphate mine or shipping operation in Florida."

He nodded emphatically.

"All true, but it depends on your definition of family."

It slowly came to me.

"Are you talking about the mob, Walter?"

"I am talking about an organization in Florida with a tremendous cash flow that needed legitimate businesses to move it through and legitimate front men to operate those businesses. I was an accountant. I was one of those men."

It was easy to put together. Florida twenty-five years ago. The heyday of the uninhibited flow of cocaine and money.

"I was sent west," Elliot said. "I had a story and I had suitcases full of money. And I loved movies. I knew how to pick 'em and put 'em together. I took Archway and turned it into a billion-dollar enterprise. And then my wife..."

A sad look of regret crossed his face.

"What, Walter?"

He shook his head.

"On the morning after our twelfth anniversary—after the prenuptial agreement was vested—she told me she was leaving. She was going to get a divorce."

I nodded. I understood. With the prenup vested, Mitzi Elliot would be entitled to half of Walter Elliot's holdings in Archway Studios. Only he was just a front. His holdings actually belonged to the organization and it wasn't the type of organization that would allow half of its investment to walk out the door in a skirt.

"I tried to change her mind," Elliot said. "She wouldn't listen. She was in love with that Nazi bastard and thought he could protect her."

"The organization had her killed."

It sounded so strange to say those words out loud. It made me look around and sweep my eyes across the restaurant.

"I wasn't supposed to be there that day," Elliot said. "I was told to stay away, to make sure I had a rock-solid alibi."

"Why'd you go, then?"

His eyes held on mine before he answered.

"I still loved her in some way. Somehow I still did and I wanted her. I wanted to fight for her. I went out there to try to stop it, maybe be the hero, save the day, and win her back. I don't know. I didn't have a plan. I just didn't want it to happen. So I went out there... but I was too late. They were both dead when I got there. Terrible..."

Elliot was staring at the memory, perhaps the scene in the bedroom in Malibu. I dropped my eyes down to the white tablecloth in front of me. A defense attorney never expects his client to tell him the whole truth. Parts of the truth, yes. But never the cold, hard, and complete truth. I had to think that there were things Elliot had left out. But what he had told me was enough for now. It was time to talk about the bribe.

"And then came Jerry Vincent," I prompted.

His eyes came back into focus and he looked at me.

"Yes."

"Tell me about the bribe."

"I don't have a lot to tell. My corporate attorney hooked me up with Jerry and he was fine. We worked out the fee arrangement and then he came to me—this was early on, at least five months ago—and he said he had been approached by someone who could salt the jury. You know, put someone on the jury who would be for us. No matter what happened he would be a holdout for acquittal but he would also work for the defense on the inside — during deliberations. He would be a talker, a skilled persuader — a con man. The catch was that once it was in play, the trial would have to stay on schedule so that this person would end up on my jury."

"And you and Jerry took the offer."

"We took it. This was five months ago. At the time, I didn't have much of a defense. I didn't kill my wife but it seemed the odds were stacked against me. We had no magic bullet...and I was scared. I was innocent but could see that I was going to be convicted. So we took the offer."

"How much?"

"A hundred thousand up front. Like you found out, Jerry paid it through his fees. He inflated his fee and I paid him and then he paid for the juror. Then it was going to be another hundred for a hung jury and two-fifty for an acquittal. Jerry told me that these people had done it before."

"You mean fixed a jury?"

"Yes, that's what he said."

I thought maybe the FBI had gotten wind of the earlier fixes and that was why they had come to Vincent.

"Were they Jerry's trials that were fixed before?" I asked.

"He didn't say and I didn't ask."

"Did he ever say anything about the FBI sniffing around your case?"

Elliot leaned back, as if I had just said something repulsive.

"No. Is that what's going on?"

He looked very concerned.

"I don't know, Walter. I'm just asking questions here. But Jerry told you he was going to delay the trial, right?"

Elliot nodded.

"Yes. That Monday. He said we didn't need the fix. He had the magic bullet and he was going to win the trial without the sleeper on the jury."

"And that got him killed."

"It had to be. I don't think these kinds of people just let you change your mind and pull out of something like this."

"What kind of people? The organization?"

"I don't know. Just these kinds of people. Whoever does this sort of thing."

"Did you tell anyone that Jerry was going to delay the case?"

"No."

"You sure?"

"Of course I'm sure."

"Then, who did Jerry tell?"

"I wouldn't know."

"Well, who did Jerry make the deal with? Who did he bribe?"

"I don't know that either. He wouldn't tell me. Said it would be better if I didn't know names. Same thing I'm telling you."

It was a little late for that. I had to end this and get away by myself to think. I glanced at my untouched plate of fish and wondered if I should take it to go for Patrick or if someone back in the kitchen would eat it.

"You know," Elliot said, "not to put any more pressure on you, but if I get convicted, I'm dead."

I looked at him.

"The organization?"

He nodded.

"A guy gets busted and he becomes a liability. Normally, they wipe him out before he even gets to court. They don't take the chance that he'll try to cut a deal. But I still have control of their money, you see. They wipe me out and they lose it all. Archway, the real estate, everything. So they're hanging back and watching. If I get off, then we go back to normal and everything's good. If I get convicted, I'm too much of a liability and I won't last two nights in prison. They'll get to me in there."

It's always good to know exactly what the stakes are but I probably could have gone without the reminder.

"We're dealing with a higher authority here," Elliot continued. "It goes way beyond things like attorney-client confidentiality. That's small change, Mick. The things I've told you tonight can go no further than this table. Not into court or anywhere else. What I've told you here could get you killed in a heartbeat. Just like Jerry. Remember that."

Elliot had spoken matter-of-factly and concluded the statement by calmly draining the wine from his glass. But the threat was implicit in every word he had said. I would have no trouble remembering it.

Elliot waved down a waiter and asked for the check.

42

I was thankful that my client liked his martinis before dinner and his Chardonnay with it. I wasn't sure I would have gotten what I got from Elliot without the alcohol smoothing the way and loosening his tongue. But afterward I didn't want him running the risk of getting pulled over on a DUI in the middle of a murder trial. I insisted that he not drive home. But Elliot insisted he wasn't going to leave his $400,000 Maybach overnight in a downtown garage. So I had Patrick take us to the car and then I drove Elliot home while Patrick followed.

"This car cost four hundred grand?" I asked him. "I'm scared to drive it."

"A little less, actually."

"Yeah, well, do you have anything else to drive? When I told you not to take the limo, I didn't expect you'd be tooling up to your murder trial in one of these. Think about the impressions you are putting out there, Walter. This doesn't look good. Remember what you told me the first day we met? About having to win outside of the courtroom too? A car like this doesn't help you with that."

"My other car is a Carrera GT."

"Great. What's that worth?"

"More than this one."

"Tell you what, why don't you borrow one of my Lincolns. I even have one that has a plate that says not guilty. You can drive that."

"That's okay. I have access to a nice modest Mercedes. Is that all right?"

"Perfect. Walter, despite everything you told me tonight, I'm going to do my best for you. I think we have a good shot at this."

"Then, you believe I'm innocent."

I hesitated.

"I believe you didn't shoot your wife and Rilz. I'm not sure that makes you innocent, but put it this way: I don't think you're guilty of the charges you're facing. And that's all I need."

He nodded.

"Maybe that's the best I can ask for. Thank you, Mickey."

After that we didn't talk much as I concentrated on not wrecking the car, which was worth more than most people's houses.

Elliot lived in Beverly Hills in a gated estate in the flats south of Sunset. He pushed a button on the car's ceiling that opened the steel entry gate and we slipped through, Patrick coming in right behind me in the Lincoln. We got out and I gave Elliot his keys. He asked if I wanted to come in for another drink and I reminded him that I didn't drink. He stuck out his hand and I shook it and it felt awkward, as if we were sealing some sort of deal on what had been revealed earlier. I said good night and got into the back of my Lincoln.

The internal gears were working all the way back to my house. Patrick had been a quick study of my nuances and seemed to know that it was not the time to interrupt with small talk. He let me work.

I sat leaning against the door, my eyes gazing out the window but not seeing the neon world go by. I was thinking about Jerry Vincent and the deal he had made with a party unknown. It wasn't hard to figure out how it was done. The question of who did it was another matter.

I knew that the jury system relied on random selection on multiple levels. This helped ensure the integrity and cross-social composition of juries. The initial pool of hundreds of citizens summoned to jury duty each week was drawn randomly from voter registrations as well as property and public utility records. Jurors culled from this larger group for the jury selection process in a specific trial were again chosen randomly — this time by a courthouse computer. The list of those prospective jurors was given to the judge presiding over the trial, and the first twelve names or code numbers on the list were called to take the seats in the box for the initial round of voir dire. Again, the order of names or numbers on the list was determined by computer-generated random selection.

Elliot told me that after a trial date had been set in his case, Jerry Vincent was approached by an unknown party and told that a sleeper could be placed on the jury. The catch was that there could be no delays. If the trial moved, the sleeper couldn't move with it. All of this told me that this unknown party had full access to all levels of the random processes of the jury system: the initial summons to show for jury duty at a specific courthouse on a specific week; the random selection of the venire for the trial; and the random selection of the first twelve jurors to go into the box.

Once the sleeper was in the box, it was up to him to stay there. The defense would know not to oust him with a peremptory strike, and by appearing to be pro-prosecution he would avoid being challenged by the prosecution. It was simple enough, as long as the trial's date didn't change.

Stepping it out this way gave me a better understanding of the manipulation involved and who might have engineered it. It also gave me a better understanding of the ethical predicament I was in. Elliot had admitted several crimes to me over dinner. But I was his lawyer and these admissions would remain confidential under the bonds of the attorney-client relationship. The exception to this rule was if I were endangered by my knowledge or had knowledge of a crime that was planned but had not yet occurred. I knew that someone had been bribed by Vincent. That crime had already occurred. But the crime of jury tampering had not yet occurred. That crime wouldn't take place until deliberations began, so I was duty-bound to report it. Elliot apparently didn't know of this exception to the rules of client confidentiality or was convinced that the threat of my meeting the same end as Jerry Vincent would keep me in check.

I thought about all of this and realized there was one more exception to consider. I would not have to report the intended jury tampering if I were to stop the crime from happening.

I straightened up and looked around. We were on Sunset coming into West Hollywood. I looked ahead and saw a familiar sign.

"Patrick, pull over up here in front of Book Soup. I want to run in for a minute."

Patrick pulled the Lincoln to the curb in front of the bookstore. I told him to wait in front and I jumped out. I went in the store's front door and back into the stacks. Although I loved the store, I wasn't there to shop. I needed to make a phone call and I didn't want Patrick to hear it.

The mystery aisle was too crowded with customers. I went further back and found an empty alcove where big coffee-table books were stacked heavily on the shelves and tables. I pulled my phone and called my investigator.

"Cisco, it's me. Where are you?"

"At home. What's up?"

"Lorna there?"

"No, she went to a movie with her sister. She should be back in —"

"That's all right. I wanted to talk to you. I want you to do something and you may not want to do it. If you don't, I understand. Either way, I don't want you to talk about it with anybody. Including Lorna."

There was a hesitation before he answered.

"Who do I kill?"

We both started to laugh and it relieved some of the tension that had been building through the night.

"We can talk about that later but this might be just as dicey. I want you to shadow somebody for me and find out everything you can about him. The catch is, if you get caught, we'll both probably get our tickets pulled."

"Who is it?"

"Juror number seven."

43

As soon as I got back in the Lincoln, I started to regret what I was doing. I was walking a fine gray line that could lead me into big trouble. On the one hand, it is perfectly reasonable for an attorney to investigate a report of jury misconduct and tampering. But on the other hand, that investigation could be viewed as tampering in itself. Judge Stanton had taken steps to ensure the anonymity of the jury. I had just asked my investigator to subvert that. If it blew up in our faces, Stanton would be more than upset and would do more than give me the squint. This wasn't a Make-A-Wish infraction. Stanton would complain to the bar, the chief judge, and all the way up the line to the Supreme Court if he could get them to listen. He would see to it that the Elliot trial was my last.

Patrick drove up Fareholm and pulled the car into the garage below my house. We walked out and then up the stairs to the front deck. It was almost ten o'clock and I was beat after a fourteen-hour day. But my adrenaline kicked in when I saw a man sitting in one of the deck chairs, his face in silhouette with the lights of the city behind him. I put my arm out to stop

Patrick from advancing, the way a parent would stop a child from stepping blindly into the street.

"Hello, Counselor."

Bosch. I recognized the voice and the greeting. I relaxed and let Patrick continue. We stepped up onto the porch and I unlocked the door to let Patrick go in. I then closed the door and turned to Bosch.

"Nice view," he said. "Defending scumbags got you this place?"

I was too tired to do the dance with him.

"What are you doing here, Detective?"

"I figured you might be heading home after the bookstore," he said. "So I just went on ahead and waited for you up here."

"Well, I'm done for the night. You can give your team the word, if there really is a team."

"What makes you think there's not?"

"I don't know. I just haven't seen anybody. I hope you weren't bullshitting me, Bosch. I've got my ass way out in the wind on this."

"After court you had dinner with your client at Water Grill. You both had the fillet of sole and both of you raised your voices at times. Your client drank liberally, which resulted in you driving him home in his car. On your way back from there you stopped into Book Soup and made a phone call you obviously didn't want your driver to hear."

I was impressed.

"Okay, then, never mind that. I get it. They're out there. What do you want, Bosch? What's going on?"

Bosch stood up and approached me.

"I was going to ask you the same thing," he said. "What was Walter Elliot so hot and bothered about tonight at dinner? And who'd you call in the back of the bookstore?"

"First of all, Elliot's my client and I'm not telling you what we talked about. I'm not crossing that line with you. And as far as the call in the bookstore goes, I was ordering pizza because, as you and your colleagues might have noticed, I didn't eat my dinner tonight. Stick around if you want a slice."

Bosch looked at me with that half smile of his, the knowing look with his flat dead eyes.

"So that's how you want to play it, Counselor?"

"For now."

We didn't speak for a long moment. We just sort of stood there, waiting for the next clever line. It didn't come and I decided I really was tired and hungry.

"Good night, Detective Bosch."

I went in and closed the door, leaving Bosch out there on the deck.

44

My turn at Detective Kinder did not come until late on Tuesday, after the prosecutor had spent several more hours drawing the details of the investigation out on direct examination. This worked in my favor. I thought the jury — and Julie Favreau confirmed this by text message — was getting bored by the minutiae of the testimony and would welcome a new line of questions.

The direct testimony primarily regarded the investigative efforts that took place after Walter Elliot's arrest. Kinder described at length his delving into the defendant's marriage, the discovery of a recently vested prenuptial agreement, and the efforts Elliot made in the weeks before the murders to determine how much money and control of Archway Studios he would lose in a divorce. With a time chart he was also able to establish through Elliot's statements and documented movements that the defendant had no credible alibi for the estimated time of the murders.

Golantz also took the time to question Kinder about all the dead ends and offshoots of the investigation that proved to be ancillary. Kinder described the many unfounded leads that were called in and dutifully checked out, the investigation of Johan Rilz in an effort to determine if he had been the main target of the killer, and the comparison of the double murder to other cases that were similar and unsolved.

In all, Golantz and Kinder appeared to have done a thorough job of nailing my client to the murders in Malibu, and by midafternoon the young prosecutor was satisfied enough to say, "No more questions, Your Honor."

It was now finally my turn and I had decided to go after Kinder in a cross-examination that would stay tightly focused on just three areas of his direct testimony, and then surprise him with an unexpected punch to the gut. I moved to the lectern to conduct the questioning.

"Detective Kinder, I know we will be hearing from the medical examiner later in the trial, but you testified that you were informed after the autopsy that the time of death of Mrs. Elliot and Mr. Rilz was estimated to be between eleven a.m. and noon on the day of the murders."

"That is correct."

"Was it closer to eleven or closer to noon?"

"It's impossible to tell for sure. That is just the time frame in which it happened."

"Okay, and once you had that frame, you then proceeded to make sure that the man you had already arrested had no alibi, correct?"

"I would not put it that way, no."

"Then, how would you put it?"

"I would say that it was my obligation to continue to investigate the case and prepare it for trial. Part of that due diligence would be to keep an open mind to the possibility that the suspect had an alibi for the murders. In carrying out that obligation, I determined according to multiple interviews as well as records kept at the gate at Archway Studios that Mr. Elliot left the studio, driving by himself, at ten forty that morning. This gave him plenty of time to —"

"Thank you, Detective. You've answered the question."

"I haven't finished my answer."

Golantz stood and asked the judge if the witness could finish his answer, and Stanton allowed it. Kinder continued in his Homicide 101 tone.

"As I was saying, this gave Mr. Elliot plenty of time to get to the Malibu house within the parameters of the estimated time of death."

"Did you say plenty of time to get there?"

"Enough time."

"Earlier you described making the drive yourself several times. When was that?"

"The first time was exactly one week after the murders. I left the gate-house at Archway at ten forty in the morning and drove to the Malibu house. I arrived at eleven forty-two, well within the murder window."

"How did you know that you were taking the same route that Mr. Elliot would have taken?"

"I didn't. So I just took what I considered the most obvious and quickest route that somebody would take. Most people don't take the long cut. They take the short cut — the shortest amount of time to their destination. From Archway I took Melrose to La Brea and then La Brea down to the ten. At that point I headed west to the Pacific Coast Highway."

"How did you know that the traffic you encountered would be the same that Mr. Elliot encountered?"

"I didn't."

"Traffic in Los Angeles can be a very unpredictable thing, can it not?"

"Yes."

"Is that why you drove the route several times?"

"One reason, yes."

"Okay, Detective Kinder, you testified that you drove the route a total of five times and got to the Malibu house each time before your so-called murder window closed, right?"

"Correct."

"In regard to these five driving tests, what was the earliest time you got to the house in Malibu?"

Kinder looked at his notes.

"That would have been the first time, when I got there at eleven forty-two."

"And what was the worst time?"

"The worst?"

"What was the longest drive time you recorded during your five trips?"

Kinder checked his notes again.

"The latest I got there was eleven fifty-one."

"Okay, so your best time was still in the last third of the window the medical examiner set for the time of these murders, and your worst time would have left Mr. Elliot less than ten minutes to sneak into his house and murder two people. Correct?"

"Yes, but it could have been done."

"Could have? You don't sound very confident, Detective."

"I am very confident that the defendant had the time to commit these murders."

"But only if the murders took place at least forty-two minutes after the killing window opened, correct?"

"If you want to look at it that way."

"It's not how I am looking at it, Detective. I'm working with what the medical examiner has given us. So, in summary for the jury, you are saying that Mr. Elliot left his studio at ten forty and got all the way out to Malibu, snuck into his house, surprised his wife and her lover in the upstairs bedroom and killed them both, all before that window slammed shut at noon. Do I have all of that right?"

"Essentially. Yes."

I shook my head as if it was a lot to swallow.

"Okay, Detective, let's move on. Please tell the jury how many times you began the driving route to Malibu but broke it off when you knew that you weren't going to make it before that window closed at noon."

"That never happened."

But there had been a slight hesitation in Kinder's response. I was sure the jury picked up on it.

"Yes or no, Detective, if I were to produce records and even video that showed you started at the Archway gate at ten forty in the morning seven times and not five, then those records would be false?"

Kinder's eyes flicked to Golantz and then back to me.

"What you're suggesting happened didn't happen," he said.

"And you're not answering the question, Detective. Once again, yes or no: If I introduced records that showed you conducted your driving study at least seven times but have only testified to five times, would those records be false?"

"No, but I didn't —"

"Thank you, Detective. I only asked for a yes or no response."

Golantz stood and asked the judge to allow the witness to fully answer the question but Stanton told him he could take it up on redirect. But now I hesitated. Knowing that Golantz would go after Kinder's explanation on redirect, I had the opportunity to get it now and possibly still control it and turn the admission to my advantage. It was a gamble because at the moment, I felt I had dinged him pretty good, and if I went with him until court adjourned for the day, then the jurors would go home with police suspicion percolating in their brains. That was never a bad thing.

I decided to risk it and try to control it.

"Detective, tell us how many of these test drives you broke off before reaching the house in Malibu."

"There were two."

"Which ones?"

"The second time and the last time — the seventh."

I nodded.

"And you stopped these because you knew you would never make it to the house in Malibu within the murder window, correct?"

"No, that's very incorrect."

"Then, what was the reason you stopped the test drives?"

"One time, I was called back to the office to conduct an interview of somebody waiting there, and the other time, I was listening to the radio and I heard a deputy call for backup. I diverted to back him up."

"Why didn't you document these in your report on your driving time investigation?"

"I didn't think they were germane, because they were incomplete tests."

"So these incompletes were not documented anywhere in that thick file of yours?"

"No, they were not."

"And so we have only your word about what caused you to stop them before reaching the Elliot house in Malibu, correct?"

"That would be correct."

I nodded and decided I had flogged him enough on this front. I knew Golantz could rehabilitate Kinder on redirect, maybe even come up with documentation of the calls that pulled Kinder off the Malibu route. But I hoped that I had raised at least a question of trust in the minds of the jurors. I took my small victory and moved on.

I next hammered Kinder on the fact that there was no murder weapon recovered and that his six-month investigation of Walter Elliot had never linked him to a gun of any sort. I hit this from several angles so that Kinder had to repeatedly acknowledge that a key part of the investigation and prosecution was never located, even though if Elliot was the killer, he'd had little time to hide the weapon.

Finally, in frustration, Kinder said, "Well, it's a big ocean out there, Mr. Haller."

It was an opening I was waiting for.

"A big ocean, Detective? Are you suggesting that Mr. Elliot had a boat and dumped the gun out in the middle of the Pacific?"

"No, nothing like that."

"Then, like what?"

"I am just saying the gun could have ended up in the water and the currents took it away before our divers got out there."

"It *could have* ended up out there? You want to take Mr. Elliot's life and livelihood away from him on a '*could have*,' Detective Kinder?"

"No, that's not what I am saying."

"What you are saying is that you don't have a gun, you can't connect a gun to Mr. Elliot, but you have never wavered in believing he is your man, correct?"

"We had a gunshot residue examination that came back positive. In my mind that connected Mr. Elliot to a gun."

"What gun was that?"

"We don't have it."

"Uh-huh, and can you sit there and say to a scientific certainty that Mr. Elliot fired a gun on the day his wife and Johan Rilz were murdered?"

"Well, not to a scientific certainty, but the test—"

"Thank you, Detective Kinder. I think that answers the question. Let's move on."

I flipped the page on my notepad and studied the next set of questions I had written the night before.

"Detective Kinder, in the course of your investigation, did you determine when Johan Rilz and Mitzi Elliot became acquainted?"

"I determined that she hired him for his interior decorating services in the fall of two thousand five. If she was acquainted with him before that, I do not know."

"And when did they become lovers?"

"That was impossible for us to determine. I do know that Mr. Rilz's appointment book showed regular appointments with Mrs. Elliot at one home or the other. The frequency increased about six months before her death."

"Was he paid for each one of those appointments?"

"Mr. Rilz kept very incomplete books. It was hard to determine if he was paid for specific appointments. But in general, the payments to Mr. Rilz from Mrs. Elliot increased when the frequency of the appointments increased."

I nodded like this answer fit with a larger picture I was seeing.

"Okay, and you have also testified that you learned that the murders occurred just thirty-two days after the prenuptial agreement between Walter and Mitzi Elliot vested, thereby giving Mrs. Elliot a full shot at the couple's financial holdings in the event of a divorce."

"That's right."

"And that is your motive for these killings."

"In part, yes. I call it an aggravating factor."

"Do you see any inconsistency in your theory of the crime, Detective Kinder?"

"No, I do not."

"Was it not obvious to you from the financial records and the appointment frequency that there was some sort of romantic or at least a sexual relationship going on between Mr. Rilz and Mrs. Elliot?"

"I wouldn't say it was obvious."

"You wouldn't?"

I said it with surprise. I had him in a little corner. If he said the affair was obvious, he would be giving me the answer he knew I wanted. If he said it was not obvious, then he came off as a fool because everyone else in the courtroom thought it was obvious.

"In retrospect it might look obvious but at the time I think it was hidden."

"Then how did Walter Elliot find out about it?"

"I don't know."

"Doesn't the fact that you were unable to find a murder weapon indicate that Walter Elliot planned these murders?"

"Not necessarily."

"Then it's easy to hide a weapon from the entire Sheriff's Department?"

"No, but like I told you, it could have simply been thrown into the ocean off the back deck and the currents took over from there. That wouldn't take a lot of planning."

Kinder knew what I wanted and where I was trying to go. I couldn't get him there so I decided to use a shove.

"Detective, didn't it ever occur to you that if Walter Elliot knew about his wife's affair, it would have made better sense just to divorce her before the prenuptial agreement vested?"

"There was no indication of when he learned of the affair. And your question does not take into account things like emotions and rage. It was possible that the money had nothing to do with it as a motivating factor. It could have just been betrayal and rage, pure and simple."

I hadn't gotten what I wanted. I was annoyed with myself and chalked it up to rust. I was prepared for the cross but it was the first time I had gone head-to-head with a seasoned and cagey witness in a year. I decided to back off here and to hit Kinder with the punch he wouldn't see coming.

45

I asked the judge for a moment and then went to the defense table. I bent down to my client's ear.

"Just nod like I am telling you something really important," I whispered.

Elliot did as instructed and then I picked up a file and went back to the lectern. I opened the file and then looked at the witness stand.

"Detective Kinder, at what point in your investigation did you determine that Johan Rilz was the primary target of this double murder?"

Kinder opened his mouth to respond immediately, then closed it and sat back and thought for a moment. It was just the kind of body language I was hoping the jury would pick up on.

"At no point did I ever determine that," Kinder finally responded.

"At no point was Johan Rilz front and center in your investigation?"

"Well, he was the victim of a homicide. That made him front and center the whole time in my book."

Kinder seemed pretty proud of that answer but I didn't give him much time to savor it.

"Then his being front and center explains why you went to Germany to investigate his background, correct?"

"I did not go to Germany."

"What about France? His passport indicates he lived there before coming to the United States."

"I didn't go there."

"Then, who on your team did?"

"No one. We didn't believe it was necessary."

"Why wasn't it necessary?"

"We had asked Interpol for a background check on Johan Rilz and it came back clean."

"What is Interpol?"

"It stands for International Criminal Police Organization. It's an organization that links the police in more than a hundred countries and facilitates cross-border cooperation. It has several offices throughout Europe and enjoys total access and cooperation from its host countries."

"That's nice but it means you didn't go directly to the police in Berlin, where Rilz was from?"

"No, we did not."

"Did you directly check with police in Paris, where Rilz lived five years ago?"

"No, we relied on our Interpol contacts for background on Mr. Rilz."

"The Interpol background pretty much was a check of a criminal arrest record, correct?"

"That was included, yes."

"What else was included?"

"I'm not sure what else. I don't work for Interpol."

"If Mr. Rilz had worked for the police in Paris as a confidential informant on a drug case, would Interpol have given you this information?"

Kinder's eyes widened for a split second before he answered. It was clear he wasn't expecting the question, but I couldn't get a read on whether he knew where I was heading or if it was all new to him.

"I don't know whether they would have given us that information or not."

"Law enforcement agencies usually don't give out the names of their confidential informants willy-nilly, do they?"

"No, they don't."

"Why is that?"

"Because it might put the informants in danger."

"So being an informant in a criminal case can be dangerous?"

"On occasion, yes."

"Detective, have you ever investigated the murder of a confidential informant?"

Golantz stood up before Kinder could answer and asked the judge for a sidebar conference. The judge signaled us up. I grabbed the file off the lectern and followed Golantz up. The court reporter moved next to the bench with her steno machine. The judge rolled his chair over and we huddled.

"Mr. Golantz?" the judge prompted.

"Judge, I would like to know where this is going, because I'm feeling like I'm being sandbagged here. There has been nothing in any of the defense's discovery that even hints at what Mr. Haller is asking the witness about."

The judge swiveled in his chair and looked at me.

"Mr. Haller?"

"Judge, if anybody is being sandbagged, it's my client. This was a sloppy investigation that—"

"Save it for the jury, Mr. Haller. Whaddaya got?"

I opened the file and put a computer printout down in front of the judge, which positioned it upside down to Golantz.

"What I've got is a story that ran in *Le Parisien* four and a half years ago. It names Johan Rilz as a witness for the prosecution in a major drug case. He was used by the Direction de la Police Judiciaire to make buys and get inside knowledge of the drug ring. He was a CI, Your Honor, and these guys over here never even looked at him. It was tunnel vision from the—"

"Mr. Haller, again, save your argument for the jury. This printout is in French. Do you have the translation?"

"Sorry, Your Honor."

I took the second of three sheets out of the file and put it down on top of the first, again in the direction of the judge. Golantz was twisting his head awkwardly as he tried to read it.

"How do we know this is the same Johan Rilz?" Golantz said. "It's a common name over there."

"Maybe in Germany, but not in France."

"So how do we know it's him?" the judge asked this time. "This is a translated newspaper article. This isn't any kind of official document."

I pulled the last sheet from the file and put it down.

"This is a photocopy of a page from Rilz's passport. I got it from the state's own discovery. It shows that Rilz left France for the United States in March, two thousand three. One month after this story was published. Plus, you've got the age. The article has his age right and it says he was making drug buys for the cops out of his business as an interior decorator. It obviously is him, Your Honor. He betrayed a lot of people over there and put them in jail, then he comes here and starts over."

Golantz started shaking his head in a desperate sort of way.

"It's still no good," he said. "This is a violation of the rules of discovery and is inadmissible. You can't sit on this and then sucker punch the state with it."

The judge swiveled his view to me and this time gave me the squint as well.

"Your Honor, if anybody sat on anything, it was the state. This is stuff the prosecution should've come up with and given to me. In fact, I think the witness did know about this and *he* sat on it."

"That is a serious accusation, Mr. Haller," the judge intoned. "Do you have evidence of that?"

"Judge, the reason I know about this at all is by accident. On Sunday I was reviewing my investigator's prep work and noticed that he had run all the names associated with this case through the Lexis-Nexis search engine. He had used the computer and account I inherited with Jerry Vincent's law practice. I checked the account and noticed that the default setting was for English-language search only. Having looked at the photocopy of Rilz's passport in the discovery file and knowing of his background in Europe, I did the search again, this time including French and German languages. I came up with this French newspaper article in about two minutes, and I find it hard to believe that I found something that easily that the entire Sheriff's Department, the prosecution, and Interpol didn't know about. So Judge, I don't know if that is evidence of anything but the defense is certainly feeling like the party that's been damaged here."

I couldn't believe it. The judge swiveled to Golantz and gave him the squint. The first time ever. I shifted to my right so that a good part of the jury had an angle on it.

"What about that, Mr. Golantz?" the judge asked.

"It's absurd, Your Honor. We have sat on nothing, and anything that we have found has gone into the discovery file. And I would like to ask why Mr. Haller didn't alert us to this yesterday when he just admitted that he made this discovery Sunday and the printout is dated then as well."

I stared deadpan at Golantz when I answered.

"If I had known you were fluent in French I would have given it to you, Jeff, and maybe you could've helped out. But I'm not fluent and I didn't know what it said and I had to get it translated. I was handed that translation about ten minutes before I started my cross."

"All right," the judge said, breaking up the stare-down. "This is still a printout of a newspaper article. What are you going to do about verifying the information it contains, Mr. Haller?"

"Well, as soon as we break, I'm going to put my investigator on it and see if we can contact somebody in the Police Judiciaire. We're going to be doing the job the Sheriff's Department should have done six months ago."

"We're obviously going to verify it as well," Golantz added.

"Rilz's father and two brothers are sitting in the gallery. Maybe you can start with them."

The judge held up a hand in a calming gesture like he was a parent quelling an argument between two brothers.

"Okay," he said. "I am going to stop this line of cross-examination. Mr. Haller, I will allow you to lay the foundation for it during the presentation of the defense. You can call the witness back then, and if you can verify the report and the identity, then I will give you wide latitude in pursuing it."

"Your Honor, that puts the defense at a disadvantage," I protested.

"How so?"

"Because now that the state's been made aware of this information, it can take steps to hinder my verification of it."

"That's absurd," Golantz said.

But the judge nodded.

"I understand your concern and I am putting Mr. Golantz on notice that if I find any indication of that, then I will become...shall we say, very agitated. I think we are done here, gentlemen."

The judge rolled back into position and the lawyers returned to theirs. On my way back, I checked the clock on the back wall of the courtroom. It was ten minutes until five. I figured if I could stall for a few more minutes, the judge would recess for the day and the jurors would have the French connection to mull over for the night.

I stood at the lectern and asked the judge for a few moments. I then acted like I was studying my notepad, trying to decide if there was anything else I wanted to ask Kinder about.

"Mr. Haller, how are we doing?" the judge finally prompted.

"We're doing fine, Judge. And I look forward to exploring Mr. Rilz's activities in France more thoroughly during the defense phase of the trial. Until then, I have no further questions for Detective Kinder."

I returned to the defense table and sat down. The judge then announced that court was recessed for the day.

I watched the jury file out of the courtroom and picked up no read from any of them. I then glanced behind Golantz to the gallery. All three of the Rilz men were staring at me with hardened, dead eyes.

46

Cisco called me at home at ten o'clock. He said he was nearby in Hollywood and that he could come right over. He said he already had some news about juror number seven.

After hanging up I told Patrick that I was going out on the deck to meet privately with Cisco. I put on a sweater because there was a chill in the air outside, grabbed the file I'd used in court earlier, and went out to wait for my investigator.

The Sunset Strip glowed like a blast furnace fire over the shoulder of the hills. I'd bought the house in a flush year because of the deck and the view it offered of the city. It never ceased to entrance me, day or night. It never ceased to charge me and tell me the truth. That truth being that anything was possible, that anything could happen, good or bad.

"Hey, boss."

I jumped and turned. Cisco had climbed the stairs and come up behind me without my even hearing him. He must've come up the hill on Fairfax and then killed the engine and freewheeled down to my house. He knew I'd be upset if his pipes woke up everybody in the neighborhood.

"Don't scare me like that, man."

"What are you so jumpy about?"

"I just don't like people sneaking up on me. Sit down out here."

I pointed him to the small table and chairs positioned under the roof's eave and in front of the living room window. It was uncomfortable outdoor furniture I almost never used. I liked to contemplate the city from the deck and draw the charge. The only way to do that was standing.

The file I'd brought out was on the table. Cisco pulled out a chair and was about to sit down when he stopped and used a hand to sweep the smog dust and crud off the seat.

"Man, don't you ever spray this stuff off?"

"You're wearing jeans and a T-shirt, Cisco. Just sit down."

He did and I did and I saw him look through the translucent window shade into the living room. The television was on and Patrick was in there watching the extreme-sports channel on cable. People were doing flips on snowmobiles.

"Is that a sport?" Cisco asked.

"To Patrick, I guess."

"How's it working out with him?"

"It's working. He's only staying a couple weeks. Tell me about number seven?"

"Down to business. Okay."

He reached behind him and pulled a small journal out of his back pocket.

"You got any light out here?"

I got up, went to the front door, and reached in to turn on the deck light. I glanced at the TV and saw the medical staff attending to a snowmobile driver who apparently had failed to complete his flip and had three hundred pounds of sled land on him.

I closed the door and sat back down across from Cisco. He was studying something in his journal.

"Okay," he said. "Juror number seven. I haven't had much time on this but I've got a few things I wanted to get right to you. His name is David McSweeney and I think almost everything he put on his J-sheet is false."

The J-sheet was the single-page form each juror fills out as part of the voir dire process. The sheets carry the prospective juror's name, profession, and area of residence by zip code as well as a checklist of basic questions designed to help attorneys form opinions about whether they want the individual on their jury. In this case the name would've been excised but all the other information was on the sheet I had given Cisco to start with.

"Give me some examples."

"Well, according to the zip on the sheet, he lives down in Palos Verdes. Not true. I followed him from the courthouse directly to an apartment off of Beverly over there behind CBS."

Cisco pointed south in the general direction of Beverly Boulevard and Fairfax Avenue, where the CBS television studio was located.

"I had a friend run the plate on the pickup he drove home from court and it came back to David McSweeney on Beverly, same address I saw him go into. I then had my guy run his DL and shoot me over the photo. I looked at it on my phone and McSweeney is our guy."

The information was intriguing but I was more concerned with how Cisco was conducting his investigation of juror number seven. We had already blown up one source on the Vincent investigation.

"Cisco, man, your prints are going to be all over this. I told you I can't have any blowback on this."

"Chill, man. There's no fingerprints. My guy isn't going to go volunteering that he did a search for me. It's illegal for a cop to do an outside search.

He'd lose his job. And if somebody comes looking, we still don't need to worry, because he doesn't use his terminal or user ID when he does these for me. He cadged an old lieutenant's password. So there are no prints, okay? No trails. We're safe on this."

I reluctantly nodded. Cops stealing from cops. Why didn't that surprise me?

"All right," I said. "What else?"

"Well, for one thing, he's got an arrest record and he checked the box on the sheet that said he'd never been popped before."

"What was the arrest for?"

"Two arrests. ADW in 'ninety-seven and conspiracy to commit fraud in ' ninety-nine. No convictions but that is all I know for right now. When the court opens I can get more if you want."

I wanted to know more, especially about how arrests for fraud and assault with a deadly weapon could result in no convictions, but if Cisco pulled records on the case, then he'd have to show ID and that would leave a trail.

"Not if you have to sign out the files. Let it go for now. You got anything else?"

"Yeah, I'm telling you, I think it's all phony. On the sheet he says he's an engineer with Lockheed. As far as I can tell, that's not true. I called Lockheed and they don't have a David McSweeney in the phone directory. So unless the guy's got a job with no phone, then..."

He raised his hands palm up, as if to say there was no explanation but deception.

"I've only had t'night on this, but everything's coming up phony and that probably includes the guy's name."

"What do you mean?"

"Well, we don't officially know his name, do we? It was blacked out on the J-sheet."

"Right."

"So I followed juror number seven and IDed him as David McSweeney, but who's to say that's the same name that was blacked out on the sheet. Know what I mean?"

I thought for a moment and then nodded.

"You're saying that McSweeney could've hijacked a legitimate juror's name and maybe even his jury summons and is masquerading as that person in the courthouse."

"Exactly. When you get a summons and show up at the juror check-in window, all they do is check your DL against the list. These are minimum-wage court clerks, Mick. It would not be difficult to get a dummy DL by one of them, and we both know how easy it is to get a dummy."

I nodded. Most people want to get out of jury duty. This was a scheme to get into it. Civic duty taken to extreme.

Cisco said, "If you can somehow get me the name the court has for number seven, I would check it, and I'm betting I find out there *is* a guy at Lockheed with that name."

I shook my head.

"There's no way I can get it without leaving a trail."

Cisco shrugged.

"So what's going on with this, Mick? Don't tell me that fucking prosecutor put a sleeper on the jury."

I thought a moment about telling him but decided against it.

"At the moment it's better if I don't tell you."

"Down periscope."

It meant that we were taking the submarine—compartmentalizing so if one of us sprang a leak it wouldn't sink the whole sub.

"It's best this way. Did you see this guy with anybody? Any KAs of interest?"

"I followed him over to the Grove tonight and he met somebody for a coffee in Marmalade, one of the restaurants they've got over there. It was a woman. It looked like a casual thing, like they sort of ran into each other unplanned and sat down together to catch up. Other than that, I've got no known associates so far. I've really only been with the guy since five, when the judge cut the jury loose."

I nodded. He had gotten me a lot in a short amount of time. More than I'd anticipated.

"How close did you get to him and the woman?"

"Not close. You told me to take all precautions."

"So you can't describe her?"

"I just said I didn't get close, Mick. I can describe her. I even got a picture of her on my camera."

He had to stand up to get his big hand into one of the front pockets of his jeans. He pulled out a small, black, non-attention-getting camera and sat back down. He turned it on and looked at the screen on the back. He clicked some buttons on the top and then handed it across the table to me.

"They start there and you can scroll through till you get to the woman."

I manipulated the camera and scrolled through a series of digital photos showing juror number seven at various times during the evening. The last three shots were of him sitting with a woman in Marmalade. She had jet-black hair that hung loose and shadowed her face. The photos also weren't very crisp because they had been taken from long distance and without a flash.

I didn't recognize the woman. I handed the camera back to Cisco.

"Okay, Cisco, you did good. You can drop it now."

"Just drop it?"

"Yeah, and go back to this."

I slid the file across the table to him. He nodded and smiled slyly as he took it.

"So what did you tell the judge up there at the sidebar?"

I had forgotten he had been in the courtroom, waiting to start his tail of juror seven.

"I told him I realized that you had done the original background search on the English-language default so I redid it to include French and German. I even printed the story out again Sunday so I would have a fresh date on it."

"Nice. But I look like a fuckup."

"I had to come up with something. If I'd told him you came across it a week ago and I'd been sitting on it since, we wouldn't be having this conversation. I'd probably be in lockup for contempt. Besides, the judge thinks Golantz is the fuckup for not finding it before the defense."

That seemed to placate Cisco. He held up the file.

"So then, what do you want me to do with it?" he asked.

"Where's the translator you used on the printout?"

"Probably in her dorm over in Westwood. She's an exchange student I came up with on the Net."

"Well, call her up and pick her up because you're going to need her tonight."

"I have a feeling Lorna isn't going to like this. Me and a twenty-year-old French girl."

"Lorna doesn't speak French, so she will understand. They're what, nine hours ahead over there in Paris?"

"Yeah, nine or ten. I forget."

"Okay, then I want you to get with the translator and at midnight start working the phones. Call all the gendarmes, or whatever they call themselves, who worked that drug case and get one of them on a plane over here. At least three of them are named in that article. You can start there."

"Just like that? You think one of those guys is going to just jump on a plane for us?"

"They'll probably be stabbing one another in the back, trying to get the ticket. Tell them we'll fly first class and put whoever comes out in the hotel where Mickey Rourke stays."

"Yeah, what hotel's that?"

"I don't know but I hear he's big over there. They think he's like a genius or something. Anyway, look, what I'm saying is, just tell them whatever they want to hear. Spend whatever needs to be spent. If two want to come, then bring over two and we vet them and put the best one on the stand. Just get somebody over here. It's Los Angeles, Cisco. Every cop in the world wants to see this place and then go back home and tell everybody what and who he saw."

"Okay, I'll get somebody on a plane. But what if he can't leave right away?"

"Then get him going as soon as possible and let me know. I can stretch things in court. The judge wants to hurry everything along but I can slow it down if I need to. Probably next Tuesday or Wednesday is as far as I can go. Get somebody here by then."

"You want me to call you tonight when I have it set up?"

"No, I need my beauty rest. I'm not used to being on my toes in court all day and I'm wiped out. I'm going to bed. Just call me in the morning."

"Okay, Mick."

He stood up and so did I. He slapped me on the shoulder with the file and then tucked it into the waistband at the back of his jeans. He descended the steps and I walked to the edge of the deck to look down on him as he mounted his horse by the curb, dropped it into neutral, and silently started to glide down Fareholm toward Laurel Canyon Boulevard.

I then looked up and out at the city and thought about the moves I was making, my personal situation, and my professional deceit in front of the judge in court. I didn't ponder it all too long and I didn't feel guilty about any of it. I was defending a man I believed was innocent of the murders he was charged with but complicit in the reason they had occurred. I had a sleeper on the jury whose placement was directly related to the murder of my predecessor. And I had a detective watching over me whom I was holding back on and couldn't be sure was considering my safety ahead of his own desire to break open the case.

I had all of that and I didn't feel guilty or fearful about anything. I felt like a guy flipping a three-hundred-pound sled in midair. It might not be a sport but it was dangerous as hell and it did what I hadn't been able to do in more than a year's time. It shook off the rust and put the charge back in my blood.

It gave it a fierce momentum.

I heard the sound of the pipes on Cisco's panhead finally fire up. He had made it all the way down to Laurel Canyon before kicking over the engine. The throttle roared deeply as he headed into the night.

PART FIVE

—Take the Nickel

47

On Monday morning I had my Corneliani suit on. I was sitting next to my client in the courtroom and was ready to begin to present his defense. Jeffrey Golantz, the prosecutor, sat at his table, ready to thwart my efforts. And the gallery behind us was maxed out once again. But the bench in front of us was empty. The judge was sequestered in his chambers and running almost an hour behind his own nine-o'clock start time. Something was wrong or something had come up, but we had not yet been informed. We had seen sheriff's deputies escort a man I didn't recognize into chambers and then out again but there had been no word on what was going on.

"Hey, Jeff, what do you think?" I finally asked across the aisle.

Golantz looked over at me. He was wearing his nice black suit, but he had been wearing it every other day to court and it wasn't as impressive anymore. He shrugged.

"No idea," he said.

"Maybe he's back there reconsidering my request for a directed verdict."

I smiled. Golantz didn't.

"I'm sure he is," he said with his best prosecutorial sarcasm.

The prosecution's case had strung out through the entire previous week. I had helped with a couple of protracted cross-examinations but for the most part it had been Golantz engaging in overkill. He kept the medical examiner who had conducted the autopsies on Mitzi Elliot and Johan Rilz on the witness stand for nearly an entire day, describing in excruciating detail how and when the victims died. He kept Walter Elliot's accountant on the stand for half a day, explaining the finances of the Elliot marriage and how much Walter stood to lose in a divorce. And he kept the sheriff's forensic tech on for nearly as long, explaining his finding of high levels of gunshot residue on the defendant's hands and clothes.

In between these anchor witnesses he conducted shorter examinations of lesser witnesses and then finally finished his case Friday afternoon with a tearjerker. He put Mitzi Elliot's lifelong best friend on the stand. She testified about Mitzi confiding in her the plans to divorce her husband as soon as the prenuptial agreement vested. She told of the fight between husband and wife when the plan was revealed and of seeing bruises on Mitzi Elliot's arms the next day. She never stopped crying during her hour on the stand and continually veered into hearsay testimony that I objected to.

As is routine, I asked the judge as soon as the prosecution rested for a directed verdict of acquittal. I argued that the state had not come close to establishing a prima facie case against Elliot. But as is also routine, the judge flatly denied my motion and said the trial would move to the defense phase promptly at nine a.m. the following Monday. I spent the weekend strategizing and preparing my two anchor witnesses: Dr. Shamiram Arslanian, my GSR expert, and a jet-lagged French police captain named Malcolm Pepin. It was now Monday morning and I was locked and loaded and ready to go. But there was no judge on the bench to let me.

"What's going on?" Elliot whispered to me.

I shrugged.

"Your guess is as good as mine. Most times when the judge doesn't come out, it has nothing to do with the case at hand. Usually, it's about the next trial on his calendar."

Elliot wasn't appeased. A deep furrow had settled into the center of his brow. He knew something was up. I turned and looked back into the gallery. Julie Favreau was sitting three rows back with Lorna. I gave them a wink and Lorna sent back a thumbs-up. I swept the rest of the gallery and noticed that behind the prosecution table, there was a gap in the shoulder-to-shoulder spectators. No Germans. I was about to ask Golantz where Rilz's family members were, when a uniformed sheriff's deputy walked up to the rail behind the prosecutor.

"Excuse me."

Golantz turned and the deputy beckoned him with a document he was holding.

"Are you the prosecutor?" the deputy said. "Who do I talk to about this?"

Golantz got up and walked over to the rail. He took a quick look at the document and handed it back.

"It's a defense subpoena. Are you Deputy Stallworth?"

"That's right."

"Then you're in the right spot."

"No, I'm not. I didn't have anything to do with this case."

Golantz took the subpoena back and studied it. I could see the wheels begin turning, but it was going to be too late when he figured things out.

"You weren't on the scene at the house? What about the perimeter or traffic control?"

"I was home asleep, man. I work midnight shift."

"Hold it a second."

Golantz went back to his desk and opened a file. I saw him check the final witness list I had submitted two weeks before.

"What is this, Haller?"

"What's what? He's on there."

"This is bullshit."

"No, it's not. He's been on there for two weeks."

I got up and went to the rail. I held out my hand.

"Deputy Stallworth, I'm Michael Haller."

Stallworth refused to shake my hand. Embarrassed in front of the whole gallery, I pressed on.

"I'm the one who summoned you. If you wait out in the hall, I'll try to get you in and out as soon as court starts. There's some sort of delay with the judge. But sit tight and I'll get to you."

"No, this is wrong. I didn't have anything to do with this case. I just got off duty and I'm going home."

"Deputy Stallworth, there is no mistake here and even if there were, you can't walk out on a subpoena. Only the judge can release you at my request. You go home and you're going to make him mad. I don't think you want him mad at you."

The deputy huffed like he was being put out in a big way. He looked over at Golantz for help but the prosecutor was holding a cell phone to his ear and whispering into it. I had a feeling it was an emergency call.

"Look," I said to Stallworth, "just go out into the hall and I'll—"

I heard my name along with the prosecutor's called from the front of the courtroom. I turned and saw the clerk signaling us to the door that led to the judge's chambers. Finally, something was happening. Golantz ended his call and got up. I turned from Stallworth and followed Golantz toward the judge's chambers.

The judge was sitting behind his desk in his black robe. He appeared ready to go as well, but something was holding him back.

"Gentlemen, sit down," he said.

"Judge, did you want the defendant in here?" I asked.

"No, I don't think that's necessary. Just have a seat and I'll tell you what's going on."

Golantz and I sat side by side in front of the judge. I could tell that Golantz was silently steaming over the Stallworth subpoena and what it might mean. Stanton leaned forward and clasped his hands together on top of a folded piece of paper on the desk in front of him.

"We have an unusual situation involving juror misconduct," he said. "It is still . . . developing and I apologize for keeping you out there in the dark."

He stopped there and we both looked at him, wondering if we were supposed to leave now and go back to the courtroom, or if we could ask questions. But Stanton continued after a moment.

"My office received a letter Thursday addressed personally to me. Unfortunately, I didn't get a chance to open it until after court on Friday—kind of an end-of-the-week catch-up session after everybody was sent home. The letter said—well, here is the letter. I've already handled it but don't either of you touch it."

He unfolded the piece of paper he'd weighted with his hands and allowed us to read it. I stood up so I could lean over the desk. Golantz was tall enough—even sitting down—that he didn't have to.

Judge Stanton, you should know that juror number seven is not who you think he is and not who he says he is. Check Lockheed and check his prints. He's got an arrest record.

The letter looked like it had come out of a laser printer. There were no other markings on the page other than the two creases from where it had been folded.

I sat back down.

"Did you keep the envelope it came in?" I asked.

"Yes," Stanton said. "No return address and the postmark is Hollywood. I'm going to have the sheriff's lab take a look at the note and the envelope."

"Judge, I hope you haven't spoken to this juror," Golantz said. "We should be present and part of any questioning. This could just be a ploy by someone to get that juror off the panel."

I expected Golantz to rush to the juror's defense. As far as he was concerned, number seven was a blue juror.

I rushed to my own defense.

"He's talking about this being a ploy by the defense and I object to the accusation."

The judge quickly held his hands up in a calming gesture.

"Just hold your horses, both of you. I didn't talk to number seven yet. I spent the weekend thinking about how to proceed with it when I came to court today. I conferred with a few other judges on the matter and I was fully prepared to bring it up with counsel present this morning. The only problem is, juror number seven didn't show up today. He's not here."

That brought a pause to both Golantz and me.

"He's not here?" Golantz said. "Did you send deputies to—?"

"Yes, I sent court deputies to his home, and his wife told them that he was at work but she didn't know anything about court or a trial or anything like that. They went over to Lockheed and found the man and brought him here a few minutes ago. It wasn't him. He was not juror number seven."

"Judge, you're losing me," I said. "I thought you said they found him at work."

The judge nodded.

"I know. I did. This is beginning to sound like Laurel and Hardy and that 'Who's on first?' thing."

"Abbott and Costello," I said.

"What?"

"Abbott and Costello. They did the 'Who's on first?' thing."

"Whichever. The point is, juror number seven was not juror number seven."

"I'm still not following you, Judge," I said.

"We had number seven down in the computer as Rodney L. Banglund, engineer from Lockheed, resident of Palos Verdes. But the man who has been sitting for two weeks in seat number seven is not Rodney Banglund. We don't know who he was and now he's missing."

"He took Banglund's place but Banglund didn't know about it," Golantz said.

"Apparently," the judge said. "Banglund — the real one — is being interviewed about it now, but when he was in here he didn't seem to know anything about this. He said he never got a jury summons in the first place."

"So his summons was sort of hijacked and used by this unknown person?" I said.

The judge nodded.

"So it appears. The question is why, and the sheriff's department will hopefully get that answered."

"What does this do to the trial?" I asked. "Do we have a mistrial?"

"I don't think so. I think we bring the jury out, we explain that number seven's been excused for reasons they don't need to know about, we drop in the first alternate and go from there. Meantime, the sheriff's department quietly makes damn sure everybody else in that box is exactly who they are supposed to be. Mr. Golantz?"

Golantz nodded thoughtfully before speaking.

"This is all rather shocking," he said. "But I think the state would be prepared to continue — as long as we find out that this whole thing stops at juror number seven."

"Mr. Haller?"

I nodded my approval. The session had gone as I had hoped.

"I've got witnesses from as far as Paris in town and ready to go. I don't want a mistrial. My client doesn't want a mistrial."

The judge sealed the deal with a nod.

"Okay, go on back out there and we'll get this thing going in ten minutes."

On the way down the hall to the courtroom Golantz whispered a threat to me.

"He's not the only one who's going to investigate this, Haller."

"Yeah, what's that supposed to mean?"

"It means when we find this bastard we're also going to find out what he was doing on the jury. And if there is any tie to the defense, then I'm go —"

I pushed by him toward the door to the courtroom. I didn't need to listen to the rest.

"Good for you, Jeff," I said as I entered the courtroom.

I didn't see Stallworth and hoped the deputy had gone out into the hallway as I had instructed and was waiting. Elliot was all over me when I got to the defense table.

"What happened? What's going on?"

I used my hand to signal him to keep his voice down. I then whispered to him.

"Juror number seven didn't show up today and the judge looked into it and found out he was a phony."

Elliot stiffened and looked like somebody had just pressed a letter opener two inches into his back.

"My God, what does this mean?"

"For us, nothing. The trial continues with an alternate juror in his place. But there will be an investigation of who number seven was, and hopefully, Walter, it doesn't come to your door."

"I don't see how it could. But we can't go on now. You have to stop this. Get a mistrial."

I looked at the pleading look on my client's face and realized he'd never had any faith in his own defense. He had been counting solely on the sleeping juror.

"The judge said no on a mistrial. We go with what we've got."

Elliot rubbed a shaking hand over his mouth.

"Don't worry, Walter. You're in good hands. We're going to win this thing fair and square."

Just then the clerk called the courtroom to order and the judge bounded up the steps to the bench.

"Okay, back on the record with *California versus Elliot*," he said. "Let's bring in our jury."

48

The first witness for the defense was Julio Muniz, the freelance videographer from Topanga Canyon who got the jump on the rest of the local media and arrived ahead of the pack at the Elliot house on the day of the murders. I quickly established through my questions how Muniz made his living. He worked for no network or local news channel. He listened to police scanners in his home and car and picked up addresses for crime scenes and active police situations. He responded to these scenes with his video camera and took film he then sold to the local news broadcasts that had not responded. In regard to the Elliot case, it began for him when he heard a call-out for a homicide team on his scanner and went to the address with his camera.

"Mr. Muniz, what did you do when you arrived there?" I asked.

"Well, I got my camera out and started shooting. I noticed that they had somebody in the back of the patrol car and I thought that was probably a suspect. So I shot him and then I shot the deputies stringing crime scene tape across the front of the property, things like that."

I then introduced the digital videocassette Muniz used that day as the first defense exhibit and rolled the video screen and player in front of the jury. I put in the cassette and hit "play." It had been previously spooled to begin at the point that Muniz began shooting outside the Elliot house. As the video played, I watched the jurors paying close attention to it. I was already familiar with the video, having watched it several times. It showed Walter Elliot sitting in the back passenger seat of the patrol car. Because the video had been shot at an angle above the car, the 4a designation painted on its roof was clearly visible.

The video jumped from the car to scenes of the deputies cordoning off the house and then jumped back again to the patrol car. This time it showed Elliot being removed from the car by detectives Kinder and Ericsson. They uncuffed him and led him into the house.

Using a remote, I stopped the video and rewound it back to a point where Muniz had come in close on Elliot in the backseat of the patrol car. I started the video forward again and then froze the image so the jury could see Elliot leaning forward because his hands were cuffed behind his back.

"Okay, Mr. Muniz, let me draw your attention to the roof of the patrol car. What do you see painted there?"

"I see the car's designation painted there. It is four-A, or four alpha, as they say on the sheriff's radio."

"Okay, and did you recognize that designation? Had you seen it before?"

"Well, I listen to the scanner a lot and so I am familiar with the four-alpha designation. And I had actually seen the four-alpha car earlier that day."

"And what were the circumstances of that?"

"I had been listening to the scanner and I heard about a hostage situation in Malibu Creek State Park. I went out to shoot that, too."

"What time was this?"

"About two a.m."

"So, about ten hours before you were videoing the activities at the Elliot house you went out to shoot video at this hostage situation, correct?"

"That's correct."

"And the four-alpha car was involved also in this earlier incident?"

"Yes, when the suspect was finally captured, he was transported in four-alpha. The same car."

"About what time did that occur?"

"That wasn't until almost five in the morning. It was a long night."

"Did you shoot video of this?"

"Yes, I did. That footage comes earlier on the same tape."

He pointed to the frozen image on the screen.

"Then, let's see," I said.

I hit the "rewind" button on the remote. Golantz immediately stood, objected, and asked for a sidebar. The judge waved us up and I brought along the witness list I had submitted to the court two weeks earlier.

"Your Honor," Golantz said angrily. "The defense is once again sandbagging. There has been no indication in discovery or otherwise of Mr. Haller's intent to explore some other crime with this witness. I object to this being introduced."

I calmly slid the witness list in front of the judge. Under the rules of discovery, I had to list each witness I intended to call and give a brief summary of what their testimony was expected to include. Julio Muniz was on my list. The summary was brief but all-inclusive.

"It clearly says he would testify about video he shot on May second, the day of the murders," I said. "The video he shot at the park was shot on the day of the murders, May two. It's been on there for two weeks, Judge. If anybody is sandbagging, then it's Mr. Golantz sandbagging himself. He could have talked to this witness and checked out his videos. He apparently didn't."

The judge studied the witness list for a moment and nodded.

"Objection overruled," he said. "You may proceed, Mr. Haller."

I went back and rewound the video and started to play it. The jury continued to pay maximum interest. It was a night shoot and the images were more grainy and the scenes seemed to jump around more than in the first sequence.

Finally, it came to footage showing a man with his hands cuffed behind his back being placed in a patrol car. A deputy closed the door and slapped the roof twice. The car drove off and came directly by the camera. As it was going by I froze the image.

The screen showed a grainy shot of the patrol car. The light of the camera illuminated the man sitting in the backseat as well as the roof of the car.

"Mr. Muniz, what's the designation on the roof of that car?"

"Again it's four-A or four-alpha."

"And the man being transported, where is he sitting?"

"In the rear right passenger seat."

"Is he handcuffed?"

"Well, he was when they put him in the car. I shot it."

"His hands were cuffed behind his back, correct?"

"Correct."

"Now, is he in the same position and seat in the patrol car that Mr. Elliot was in when you videotaped him about eight hours later?"

"Yes, he is. Exact same position."

"Thank you, Mr. Muniz. No further questions."

Golantz passed on cross-examination. There was nothing about the direct that could be attacked and the video didn't lie. Muniz stepped down. I told the judge I wanted to leave the video screen in place for my next witness and I called Deputy Todd Stallworth to the stand.

Stallworth looked angrier as he came into the courtroom. This was good. He also looked beat and his uniform looked like it had wilted on his body. One of the sleeves of his shirt had a black scuff mark on it, presumably from some struggle during the night.

I quickly established Stallworth's identity and that he was driving the alpha car in the Malibu district during the first shift on the day of the murders in the Elliot house. Before I could ask another question, Golantz once more objected and asked for another sidebar. When we got there, he raised his hands palms up in a *What's this?* gesture. His style was getting old with me.

"Judge, I object to this witness. The defense hid him on the witness list among the many deputies who were on the scene and have no bearing on the case."

Once again I had the witness list ready. This time I slapped it down in front of the judge with frustration, then ran my finger down the column of names until I reached Todd Stallworth. It was there in the middle of a list of five other deputies, all of whom had been on the scene at the Elliot house.

"Judge, if I was hiding Stallworth, I was hiding him in plain sight. He's clearly listed there under law enforcement personnel. The explanation is the same as before. It says he'll testify about his activities on May 2. That's all I put down because I never talked to him. I'm hearing what he has to say for the first time right now."

Golantz shook his head and tried to maintain his composure.

"Judge, from the start of this trial, the defense has relied on trickery and deception to—"

"Mr. Golantz," the judge interrupted, "don't say something you can't back up and that will get you in trouble. This witness, just like the first one Mr. Haller called, has been on this list for two weeks. Right there in black-and-white. You had every opportunity to find out what these people were going to say. If you didn't take that opportunity, then that was your decision. But this is not trickery or deception. You better watch yourself."

Golantz stood with his head bowed for a moment before speaking.

"Your Honor, the state requests a brief recess," he finally said in a quiet voice.

"How brief?"

"Until one o'clock."

"I wouldn't call two hours brief, Mr. Golantz."

"Your Honor," I cut in. "I object to any recess. He just wants to grab my witness and turn his testimony."

"Now *that* I object to," Golantz said.

"Look, no recess, no delay, and no more bickering," the judge said. "We've already lost most of the morning. Objection overruled. Step back."

We returned to our places and I played a thirty-second cut of the video showing the handcuffed man being placed in the back of the 4-alpha car at Malibu Creek State Park. I froze the image in the same spot as before, just as the car was speeding by the camera. I left it on the screen as I continued my direct examination.

"Deputy Stallworth, is that you driving that car?"

"Yes, it is."

"Who is the man in the backseat?"

"His name is Eli Wyms."

"I noticed that he was handcuffed before being placed in the car. Is that because he was under arrest?"

"Yes, he was."

"What was he arrested for?"

"For trying to kill me, for one. He was also charged with unlawful discharge of a weapon."

"How many counts of unlawful discharge of a weapon?"

"I can't recall the exact number."

"How about ninety-four?"

"That sounds about right. It was a lot. He shot the place up out there."

Stallworth was tired and subdued but unhesitant in his answers. He had no idea how they fit into the Elliot case and didn't seem to care about trying to protect the prosecution with short, nonresponsive answers. He was probably mad at Golantz for not getting him out of testifying.

"So you arrested him and took him to the nearby Malibu station?"

"No, I transported him all the way to the county jail in downtown, where he could be placed on the psych level."

"How long did that take? The drive, I mean."

"About an hour."

"And then you drove back to Malibu?"

"No, first I had four-alpha repaired. Wyms had fired a shot that took out the side lamp. While I was downtown, I went to the motor pool and had it replaced. That took up the rest of my shift."

"So when did the car return to Malibu?"

"At shift change. I turned it over to the day-watch guys."

I looked down at my notes.

"That would have been deputies...Murray and Harber?"

"That's right."

Stallworth yawned and there was murmured laughter in the courtroom.

"I know we have you past your bedtime, Deputy. I won't take too much longer. When you turn the car over from shift to shift, do you clean it out or disinfect the car in any way?"

"You're supposed to. Realistically, unless you've got puke in the backseat, nobody does that. The cars get taken out of rotation once or twice a week and the motor guys clean them up."

"Did Eli Wyms puke in your car?"

"No, I would've known."

More murmured laughter. I looked down from the lectern at Golantz and he wasn't smiling at all.

"Okay, Deputy Stallworth, let me see if I got this right. Eli Wyms was arrested for shooting at you and firing at least ninety-three other shots that morning. He was arrested, his hands were cuffed behind his back, and he was transported by you downtown. Do I have all of that right?"

"Sounds right to me."

"In the video, Mr. Wyms can be seen in the rear passenger side seat. Did he stay there for the whole hour-long ride downtown?"

"Yes, he did. I had him belted in."

"Is it standard procedure to place someone who is in custody on the passenger side?"

"Yes, it is. You don't want him behind you when you're driving."

"Deputy, I also noticed on the tape that you did not place Mr. Wyms's hands in plastic bags or anything of that nature before placing him in your patrol car. Why is that?"

"Didn't think it was necessary."

"Why?"

"Because it was not going to be an issue. The evidence was overwhelming that he had fired the weapons in his possession. We weren't worried about gunshot residue."

"Thank you, Deputy Stallworth. I hope you can go get some sleep now."

I sat down and left the witness for Golantz. He slowly got up and took the lectern. He knew exactly where I was going now but there was little he was going to be able to do to stop me. But I had to give him credit. He found a small crack in my direct and tried his best to exploit it.

"Deputy Stallworth, approximately how long did you wait for your car to be repaired at the downtown motor hub?"

"About two hours. They only have a couple guys work midnight watch and they were juggling jobs down there."

"Did you stay with the car for those two hours?"

"No, I grabbed a desk in the office and wrote up the arrest report on Wyms."

"And you testified earlier that no matter what the procedure is supposed to be, you generally rely on the motor pool to keep the fleet cars clean, is that correct?"

"Yes, correct."

"Do you make a formal request or do people working in the motor hub just take it upon themselves to clean and maintain the car?"

"I've never made a formal request. It just gets done, I guess."

"Now, during those two hours that you were away from the car and writing the report, do you know if the employees in the motor hub cleaned or disinfected the car?"

"No, I do not."

"They could have and you wouldn't necessarily know about it, right?"

"Right."

"Thank you, Deputy."

I hesitated but got up for redirect.

"Deputy Stallworth, you said it took them two hours to repair the car because they were short-handed and busy, correct?"

"Correct."

He said it in a boy-am I getting-tired-of-this tone.

"So it is unlikely that these guys would have taken the time to clean your car if you didn't ask, right?"

"I don't know. You'd have to ask them."

"Did you specifically ask them to clean the car?"

"Nope."

"Thank you, Deputy."

I sat down and Golantz passed on another round.

It was now almost noon. The judge adjourned for lunch but gave the jury and lawyers only a forty-five-minute break as he sought to make up for time lost during the morning. That was fine with me. My star witness was next and the sooner I got her on the stand, the closer my client was going to be to a verdict of acquittal.

49

Dr. Shamiram Arslanian was a surprise witness. Not in terms of her presence at the trial — she had been on the witness list longer than I had been on the case. But in terms of her physical appearance and personality. Her name and pedigree in forensics conjured an image of a woman deep, dark, and scientific. A white lab coat and hair ironed back in a knot. But she was none of that. She was a vivacious, blue-eyed blonde with a cheerful disposition and easy smile. She wasn't just photogenic. She was telegenic. She was articulate and confident but never came close to being arrogant. The one-word description for her was the one-word description every lawyer wants for every one of his witnesses: likable. And it was rare to get that in a witness delivering your forensic case.

I had spent most of the weekend with Shami, as she preferred to be called. We had gone over the gunshot residue evidence in the Elliot case and the testimony she would give for the defense, as well as the cross-examination she could expect to receive from Golantz. This had been delayed until so late in the game to avoid discovery issues. What my expert didn't know she couldn't reveal to the prosecutor. So she was kept in the dark about the magic bullet until the last possible moment.

There was no doubt that she was a celebrity gun for hire. She had once hosted a show about her own exploits on Court TV. She was asked twice for her autograph when I took her to dinner at the Palm and was on a first-name basis with a couple of TV execs who visited the table. She charged a celebrity-level fee as well. For four days in Los Angeles to study, prepare, and testify she would receive a flat rate of $10,000 plus expenses. Nice work if you could get it, and she could. She was known to study the many requests for her time and to choose only those in which she steadfastly believed there had been a grievous error committed or a miscarriage of justice. It also didn't hurt if you had a case that was getting the attention of the national media.

I knew after spending the first ten minutes with her that she was going to be worth every penny Elliot would pay her. She would be double trouble for the prosecution. Her personality was going to win over the jury, and her facts were going to seal the deal. So much of trial work comes down to who is testifying, not what the testimony actually reveals. It's about selling your case to the jury, and Shami could sell burnt matches. The state's forensic witness was a lab geek with the personality of a test tube. My witness had hosted a television show called *Chemically Dependent*.

I heard the low hum of recognition in the courtroom as my big-haired witness made her entrance from the back, holding all eyes as she walked up the center aisle, through the gate, and across the proving grounds to the witness stand. She wore a navy blue suit that fit her curves snugly and accentuated the cascade of blonde curls over her shoulders. Even Judge Stanton seemed infatuated. He asked the courtroom deputy to get her a glass of water before she had even taken the oath. He hadn't asked the state's forensic geek if he had wanted jack shit.

After she gave her name and spelled it and took the oath to tell nothing but the truth, I got up with my legal pad and went to the lectern.

"Good afternoon, Dr. Arslanian. How are you?"

"I'm doin' just fine. Thanks for asking."

There was a slight trace of a southern accent in her voice.

"Before we go over your curriculum vitae, I want to get something out of the way up front. You are a paid consultant to the defense, is that correct?"

"Yes, that is correct. I'm paid to be here, not paid to testify to anything other than my own opinion — whether it's in line with the defense or not. That's my deal and I never change it."

"Okay, tell us where you are from, Doctor."

"I live in Ossining, New York, right now. I was born and raised in Florida and spent a lot of years in the Boston area, going to different schools here and there."

"Shamiram Arslanian. That doesn't sound like a Florida name."

She smiled brilliantly.

"My father is one hundred percent Armenian. So I guess that makes me half Armenian and half Floridian. My father said I was Armageddian when I was a girl."

Many in the courtroom chuckled politely.

"What is your background in forensic sciences?" I asked.

"Well, I've got two related degrees. I got my master's at MIT—the Massachusetts Institute of Technology—and that is in chemical engineering. I then got a PhD in criminology and that was awarded to me from John Jay College in New York."

"When you say 'awarded,' does that mean it's an honorary degree?"

"Hell, no," she said forcefully. "I worked my butt off two years to get that sucker."

This time laughter broke out across the courtroom and I noticed that even the judge smiled before politely tapping his gavel one time for order.

"I saw on your résumé that you have two undergraduate degrees as well. Is that true?"

"I've got two of everything, it seems. Two kids. Two cars. I've even got two cats at home, named Wilbur and Orville."

I glanced over at the prosecution table and saw that Golantz and his second were staring straight forward and had not so much as cracked a smile. I then checked the jury and saw all twenty-four eyes holding on my witness with rapt attention. She had them eating out of her hand and she hadn't even started yet.

"What are your undergraduate degrees?"

"I got one from Harvard in engineering and one from the Berklee College of Music. I went to both schools at the same time."

"You have a music degree?" I said with feigned surprise.

"I like to sing."

More laughter. The hits kept coming. One surprise after another. Shami Arslanian was the perfect witness.

Golantz finally stood and addressed the judge.

"Your Honor, the state would ask that the witness provide testimony regarding forensics and not music or pet names or things not germane to the serious nature of this trial."

The judge grudgingly asked me to keep my examination on point. Golantz sat down. He had won the point but lost the position. Everybody in the room now viewed him as a spoilsport, stealing what little levity there was in such a serious matter.

I asked a few more questions, which revealed that Dr. Arslanian currently worked as a teacher and researcher at John Jay. I covered her history and limited availability as an expert witness and finally brought her testimony to her study of the gunshot residue found on Walter Elliot's body and clothing on the day of the murders in Malibu. She testified that she reviewed the procedures and results of the sheriff's lab and conducted her own evaluations and modeling. She said she also reviewed all videotapes submitted to her by the defense in conjunction with her studies.

"Now, Dr. Arslanian, the state's forensic witness testified earlier in this trial that the tabs wiped on Mr. Elliot's hands and sleeves and jacket tested positive for elevated levels of certain elements associated with gunshot residue. Do you agree with that conclusion?"

"Yes, I do," my witness said.

A low vibration of surprise rolled through the room.

"You are saying that your studies concluded that the defendant had gunshot residue on his hands and clothes?"

"That is correct. Elevated levels of barium, antimony, and lead. In combination, these are indications of gunshot residue."

"What does 'elevated levels' mean?"

"It just means that some of these materials you would find on a person's body whether they had fired or handled a weapon or not. Just from everyday life."

"So it is elevated levels of all three materials that are required for a positive result in gunshot residue testing, correct?"

"Yes, that and concentration patterns."

"Can you explain what you mean by 'concentration patterns'?"

"Sure. When a gun discharges — in this case we think we're talking about a handgun — there is an explosion in the chamber that gives the bullet its energy and velocity. That explosion sends gases out the barrel with the bullet as well as out any little crack and opening in the gun. The breech — that is, the part at the rear of the gun's barrel — comes open after a shot has been fired. The escaping gases propel these microscopic elements we're talking about backward onto the shooter."

"And that's what happened in this case, correct?"

"No, not correct. Based on the totality of my investigation I cannot say that."

I raised my eyebrows in feigned surprise.

"But Doctor, you just said you agreed with the state's conclusion that there was gunshot residue on the defendant's hands and sleeves."

"I do agree with the state's conclusion that there was GSR on the defendant. But that wasn't the question you asked."

I took a moment as if to retrace my question.

"Dr. Arslanian, are you saying that there could be an alternate explanation for the gunshot residue on Mr. Elliot?"

"Yes, I am."

We were there. We had finally arrived at the crux of the defense's case. It was time to shoot the magic bullet.

"Did your study of the materials provided to you over the weekend by the defense lead you to an alternate explanation for the gunshot residue on Walter Elliot's hands and clothing?"

"Yes, they did."

"And what is that explanation?"

"It is very highly likely, in my opinion, that the residue on Mr. Elliot's hands and clothes was transferred there."

"Transferred? Are you suggesting someone intentionally planted GSR on him?"

"No, I am not. I am suggesting that it occurred inadvertently by happenstance or mistake. Gunshot residue is basically microscopic dust. It moves. It can be transferred by contact."

"What does 'transferred by contact' mean?"

"It means the material we are talking about lights on a surface after it is discharged from the firearm. If that surface comes into contact with another, some of the material will transfer. It will rub off, is what'm saying. This is why there are law enforcement protocols for safeguarding against this. The victims and suspects in gun crimes often have their clothes removed for preservation and study. Some agencies put evidence bags over people's hands to preserve and guard against transference."

"Can this material be transferred more than once?"

"Yes, it can, with depreciating levels. This is a solid material. It's not a gas. It doesn't dissipate like a gas. It is microscopic but solid and it has to be someplace at the end of the day. I have conducted numerous studies of this and found that transference can repeat and repeat."

"But in the case of repeated transference, wouldn't the amount of material depreciate with each transfer until negligible?"

"That's right. Each new surface will hold less than the prior surface. So it's all a matter of how much you start with. The more you start with, the greater the amount that can be transferred."

I nodded and took a small break by flipping up pages on my pad as if I were looking for something. I wanted there to be a clear line between the discussion of theory and the specific case at hand.

"Okay, Doctor," I finally said. "With these theories in mind, can you tell us what happened in the Elliot case?"

"I can tell you *and* show you," Dr. Arslanian said. "When Mr. Elliot was handcuffed and placed in the back of the four-alpha patrol car, he was literally placed in a hotbed of gunshot residue. That is where and when the transference took place."

"How so?"

"His hands, arms, and clothing were placed in direct contact with gunshot residue from another case. Transfer to him would have been inevitable."

Golantz quickly objected, saying I had not laid the groundwork for such an answer. I told the judge I intended to do that right now and asked permission to set the video equipment up in front of the jury again.

Dr. Arslanian had taken the video shot by my first witness, Julio Muniz, and edited it into one demonstration video. I introduced it as a defense exhibit over Golantz's failed objection. Using it as a visual aid, I carefully walked my witness through the defense's theory of transference. It was a demonstration that took nearly an hour and was one of the most thorough presentations of alternate theory I had ever been involved in.

We started with Eli Wyms's arrest and his placement in the backseat of the alpha car. We then cut to Elliot being placed in the same patrol car less than ten hours later. The same car and the same seat. Both men's hands cuffed behind their backs. She was stunningly authoritative in her conclusion.

"A man who had fired weapons at least ninety-four times was placed in that seat," she said. "Ninety-four times! He would have literally been reeking of gunshot residue."

"And is it your expert opinion that gunshot residue would have transferred from Eli Wyms to that car seat?" I asked.

"Most definitely."

"And is it your expert opinion that the gunshot residue on that seat could then have been transferred to the next person who sat there?"

"Yes, it is."

"And is it your expert opinion that this was the origin of the gunshot residue on Walter Elliot's hands and clothes?"

"Again, with his hands behind his back like that, he came in direct contact with a transfer surface. Yes, in my expert opinion, I do believe that this is how he got the gunshot residue on his hands and clothes."

I paused again to drive home the expert's conclusions. If I knew anything about reasonable doubt, I knew I had just embedded it in every juror's consciousness. Whether they would later vote their conscience was another matter.

50

It was now time to bring in the big prop to drive Dr. Arslanian's testimony home.

"Doctor, did you draw any other conclusions from your analysis of the GSR evidence that supported the theory of transference you have outlined here?"

"Yes, I did."

"And what was that?"

"Can I use my mannequin to demonstrate?"

I asked the judge for permission to allow the witness to use a mannequin for demonstration purposes and he granted it without objection from Golantz. I then stepped through the clerk's corral to the hallway leading to the judge's chambers. I had left Dr. Arslanian's mannequin here until it had been ruled admissible. I wheeled it out to the center of the proving grounds in front of the jury—and the Court TV camera. I signaled to Dr. Arslanian to come down from the witness stand to make her demonstration.

The mannequin was a full-body model with fully manipulating limbs, hands, and even fingers. It was made of white plastic and had several smudges of gray on its face and hands from experiments and demonstrations conducted over the years. It was dressed in blue jeans and a dark blue collared shirt beneath a windbreaker with a design on the back commemorating a University of Florida national football championship earlier in the year. The mannequin was suspended two inches off the ground on a metal brace and wheeled platform.

I realized I had forgotten something and went over to my rolling bag. I quickly pulled out the wooden dummy gun and collapsing pointer. I handed them both to Dr. Arslanian and then went back to the lectern.

"Okay, what do we have here, Doctor?"

"This is Manny, my demonstration mannequin. Manny, this is the jury."

There was a bit of laughter and one juror, the lawyer, even nodded his hello to the dummy.

"Manny's a Florida Gator fan?"

"Uh, he is today."

Sometimes the messenger can obscure the message. With some witnesses you want that because their testimony isn't all that helpful. But that was not the case with Dr. Arslanian. I knew I had been walking a tightrope with her: too cute and entertaining on one side; solid scientific evidence on the other. The proper balance would make her and her information leave the strongest impression on the jury. I knew it was now time to get back to serious testimony.

"Why do we need Manny here, Doctor?"

"Because an analysis of the SEMS tabs collected by the sheriff's forensic expert can show us why the gunshot residue on Mr. Elliot did not come from his firing of a weapon."

"I know the state's expert explained these procedures to us last week but I would like you to refresh us. What is a SEMS tab?"

"The GSR test is conducted with round tabs or disks that have a peel-off sticky side. The tabs are patted on the area to be tested and they collect all the microscopic material on the surface. The tab then goes into a scanning electron microscope, or SEMS, as we call it. Through the microscope, we see or don't see the three elements we have been talking about here. Barium, antimony, and lead."

"Okay, then, do you have a demonstration for us?"

"Yes, I do."

"Please explain it to the jury."

Dr. Arslanian extended her pointer and faced the jury. Her demonstration had been carefully planned and rehearsed, right down to my always referring to her as 'doctor' and her always referring to the state's forensic man as 'mister.'

"Mr. Guilfoyle, the Sheriff's Department forensic expert, took eight different samples from Mr. Elliot's body and clothes. Each tab was coded so that the location it sampled would be known and charted."

She used the pointer on the mannequin as she discussed the locations of the samples. The mannequin stood with its arms down at its sides.

"Tab A was the top of the right hand. Tab B was the top of the left hand. Tab C was the right sleeve of Mr. Elliot's windbreaker and D was the left sleeve. Then we have tabs E and F being the right-and left-front panels of the jacket, and G and H being the chest and torso portions of the shirt Mr. Elliot wore beneath the open jacket."

"Are these the clothes he was wearing that day?"

"No, they are not. These are exact duplicates of what he was wearing, right down to the size and manufacturer."

"Okay, what did you learn from your analysis of the eight tabs?"

"I've prepared a chart for the jurors so they can follow along."

I presented the chart as a defense exhibit. Golantz had been given a copy of it that morning. He now stood and objected, saying his late receipt of the chart violated the rules of discovery. I told the judge the chart had only been composed the night before after my meetings with Dr. Arslanian on Saturday and Sunday. The judge agreed with the prosecutor, saying that the direction of my examination of the witness was obvious and well prepared and that I therefore should have drawn the chart sooner. The objection was sustained, and Dr. Arslanian now had to wing it on her own. It had been a gamble but I didn't regret the move. I would rather have my witness talking to the jurors without a net than have had Golantz in possession of my strategy in advance of its implementation.

"Okay, Doctor, you can still refer to your notes and the chart. The jurors just need to follow along. What did you learn from your analysis of the eight SEMS tabs?"

"I learned that the levels of gunshot residue on the different tabs greatly differed."

"How so?"

"Well, tabs A and B, which came from Mr. Elliot's hands, were where the highest levels of GSR were found. From there we get a steep drop-off in the GSR levels: tabs C, D, E and F with much lower levels, and no GSR reading at all on tabs G and H."

Again she used the pointer to illustrate.

"What did that tell you, Doctor?"

"That the GSR on Mr. Elliot's hands and clothes did not come from firing a weapon."

"Can you illustrate why?"

"First, comparable readings coming from both hands indicate that the weapon was fired in a two-handed grip."

She went to the mannequin and raised its arms, forming a V by pulling the hands together out front. She bent the hands and fingers around the wooden gun.

"But a two-handed grip would also have to result in higher levels of GSR on the sleeves of the jacket in particular and the rest of the clothes as well."

"But the tabs processed by the sheriff's department don't show that, am I right?"

"You're right. They show the opposite. While a drop-off from the readings on the hands is expected, it is not expected to be of this rate."

"So in your expert opinion, what does it mean?"

"A compound-transfer exposure. The first exposure occurred when he was placed with his hands and arms behind his back in the four-alpha car. After that, the material was on his hands and arms, and some of it was then transferred for a second time onto the front panels of his jacket during normal hand and arm movement. This would have occurred continuously until the clothing was collected from him."

"What about the zero reading on the tabs from the shirt beneath the jacket?"

"We discount that because the jacket could have been zipped closed during the commission of the shooting."

"In your expert opinion, Doctor, is there any way that Mr. Elliot could have gotten this pattern of GSR on his hands and clothing by discharging a firearm?"

"No, there is not."

"Thank you, Doctor Arslanian. No further questions."

I returned to my seat and leaned over to whisper into Walter Elliot's ear.

"If we didn't just give them reasonable doubt, then I don't know what it is."

Elliot nodded and whispered back to me.

"The best ten thousand dollars I've ever spent."

I didn't think I had done so badly myself but I let it go. Golantz asked the judge for the midafternoon break before cross-examination of the witness began and the judge agreed. I noticed what I believed to be a higher energy in the verbal buzz of the courtroom after the adjournment. Shami Arslanian had definitely given the defense momentum.

In fifteen minutes I would see what Golantz had in his arsenal for impeaching my witness's credibility and testimony but I couldn't imagine he had much. If he had something, he wouldn't have asked for the break. He would have gotten up and charged right after her.

After the jury and the judge had vacated the courtroom and the observers were pushing out into the hallway, I sauntered over to the prosecutor's table. Golantz was writing out questions on a legal pad. He didn't look up at me.

"What?" he said.

"The answer's no."

"To what question?"

"The one you were going to ask about my client taking a plea agreement. We're not interested."

Golantz smirked.

"You're funny, Haller. So what, you've got an impressive witness. The trial's a long way from over."

"And I've got a French police captain who's going to testify tomorrow that Rilz ratted out seven of the most dangerous, vindictive men he's ever investigated. Two of them happened to get out of prison last year and they disappeared. Nobody knows where they are. Maybe they were in Malibu last spring."

Golantz put his pen down and finally looked up at me.

"Yeah, I talked to your Inspector Clouseau yesterday. It's pretty clear he's saying whatever you want him to say, as long as you fly him first class. At the end of the depo, he pulled out one of those star maps and asked me if I could show him where Angelina Jolie lives. He's one serious witness you came up with."

I had told Captain Pepin to cool it with the star map stuff. He apparently hadn't listened. I needed to change the subject.

"So, where are the Germans?" I asked.

Golantz checked behind him as if to make sure Johan Rilz's family members weren't there.

"I told them that they had to be prepared for your strategy of building a defense by shitting all over the memory of their son and brother," he said. "I told them you were going to take Johan's problems in France five years ago and use them to try to get his killer off. I told them that you were going to depict him as a German gigolo who seduced rich clients, men and women, all over Malibu and the west side. You know what the father said to me?"

"No, but you'll tell me."

"He said that they'd had enough of American justice and were going back home."

I tried to retort with a clever and cynical comeback line. But I came up empty.

"Don't worry," Golantz said. "Up or down, I'll call them and tell them the verdict."

"Good."

I left him there and went out into the hallway to look for my client. I saw him in the center of a ring of reporters. Feeling cocky after the success of Dr. Arslanian's testimony, he was now working the big jury—public opinion.

"All this time they've concentrated on coming after me, the real killer's been out there running around free!"

A nice concise sound bite. He was good. I was about to push through the crowd to grab him, when Dennis Wojciechowski intercepted me first.

"Come with me," he said.

We walked down the hallway away from the crowd.

"What's up, Cisco? I was wondering where you've been."

"I've been busy. I got the report from Florida. Do you want to hear it?"

I had told him what Elliot had told me about fronting for the so-called organization. Elliot's story had seemed sincere enough but in the light of day I reminded myself of a simple truism — everybody lies — and told Cisco to see what he could do about confirming it.

"Give it to me," I said.

"I used a PI in Fort Lauderdale who I've worked with before. Tampa's on the other side of the state but I wanted to go with a guy I knew and trusted."

"I understand. What did he come up with?"

"Elliot's grandfather founded a phosphate-shipping operation seventy-eight years ago. He worked it, then Elliot's father worked it, and then Elliot himself worked it. Only he didn't like getting his hands dirty in the phosphate business and he sold it a year after his father died of a heart attack. It was a privately owned company, so the record of the sale is not public. Newspaper articles at the time put the sale at about thirty-two million."

"What about organized crime?"

"My guy couldn't find a whiff of it. Looked to him like it was a good, clean operation — legally, that is. Elliot told you he was a front and he was sent out here to invest their money. He didn't say anything about him selling his own company and bringing the money out here. The man's lying to you."

I nodded.

"Okay, Cisco, thanks."

"You need me in court? I've got a few things I'm still working on. I heard juror number seven went missing this morning."

"Yeah, he's in the wind. And I don't need you in court."

"Okay, man, I'll talk to you."

He headed off toward the elevators and I was left to stare at my client holding forth with the reporters. A slow burn started in me and it gained heat as I waded into the crowd to get to him.

"Okay, that's all, people," I said. "No further comment. No further comment."

I grabbed Elliot by the arm, pulled him out of the crowd, and walked him down the hall. I shooed a couple of trailing reporters away until we were finally far enough from all other ears and could speak privately.

"Walter, what were you doing?"

He was smiling gleefully. He made a fist and pumped it into the air.

"Sticking it up their asses. The prosecutor and the sheriffs, all of them."

"Yeah, well, you better wait on that. We've still got a ways to go. We may have won the day but we haven't won the war yet."

"Oh, come on. It's in the bag, Mick. She was fucking outstanding in there. I mean, I want to marry her!"

"Yeah, that's nice but let's see how she does on cross before you buy the ring, okay?"

Another reporter came up and I told her to take a hike, then turned back to my client.

"Listen, Walter, we need to talk."

"Okay, talk."

"I had a private investigator check your story out in Florida and I just found out it was bullshit. You lied to me, Walter, and I told you never to lie to me."

Elliot shook his head and looked annoyed with me for taking the wind out of his sails. To him, being caught in the lie was a minor inconvenience, an annoyance that I would even bring it up.

"Why did you lie to me, Walter? Why'd you spin that story?"

He shrugged and looked away from me when he spoke.

"The story? I read it in a script once. I turned the project down, actually. But I remembered the story."

"But why? I'm your lawyer. You can tell me anything. I asked you to tell me the truth and you lied to me. Why?"

He finally looked me in the eyes.

"I knew I had to light a fire under you."

"What fire? What are you talking about?"

"Come on, Mickey. Let's not get—"

He was turning to go back to the courtroom but I grabbed him roughly by the arm.

"No, I want to hear. What fire did you light?"

"Everybody's going back in. The break is over and we should be in there."

I gripped him even harder.

"What fire, Walter?"

"You're hurting my arm."

I relaxed my grip but didn't let go. And I didn't take my eyes off his.

"What fire?"

He looked away from me and put an "aw, shucks" grin on his face. I finally let go of his arm.

"Look," he said. "From the start I needed you to believe I didn't do it. It was the only way for me to know you would bring your best game. That you would be goddamn relentless."

I stared at him and saw the smile become a look of pride.

"I told you I could read people, Mick. I knew you needed something to believe in. I knew if I was a little bit guilty but not guilty of the big crime, then it would give you what you needed. It would give you your fire back."

They say the best actors in Hollywood are on the wrong side of the camera.

At that moment I knew that was true. I knew that Elliot had killed his wife and her lover and was even proud of it. I found my voice and spoke.

"Where'd you get the gun?"

"Oh, I'd had it. Bought it under the table at a flea market back in the seventies. I was a big Dirty Harry fan and I wanted a forty-four mag. I kept it out at the beach house for protection. You know, a lot of drifters down on the beach."

"What really happened in that house, Walter?"

He nodded like it was his plan all along to take this moment to tell me.

"What happened was I went out there to confront her and whoever she was fucking every Monday like clockwork. But when I got there, I realized it was Rilz. She'd passed him off in front of me as a faggot, had him to dinners and parties and premieres with us, and they probably laughed all about it later. Laughed about me, Mick.

"It got me mad. Enraged, actually. I got the gun out of the cabinet, put on rubber gloves from under the sink, and I went upstairs. You should have seen the look on their faces when they saw that big gun."

I stared at him for a long moment. I'd had clients confess to me before. But usually they were crying, wringing their hands, battling the demons their crimes had created inside. But not Walter Elliot. He was cold to the bone.

"How'd you get rid of the gun?"

"I hadn't gone out there alone. I had somebody with me and they took the gun, the gloves, and my first set of clothes, then walked down the beach, got back up to the PCH, and caught a cab. Meantime, I washed up and changed, then I dialed nine-one-one."

"Who was it that helped you?"

"You don't need to know that."

I nodded. Not because I agreed with him. I nodded because I already knew. I had a flash vision of Nina Albrecht easily unlocking the door to the deck when I couldn't figure it out. It showed a familiarity with her boss's bedroom that had struck me the moment I saw it.

I looked away from my client and down at the floor. It had been scuffed by a million people who had trod a million miles for justice.

"I never counted on the transference, Mick. When they said they wanted to do the test, I was all for it. I thought I was clean and they would see that and it would be the end of it. No gun, no residue, no case."

He shook his head at such a close call.

"Thank God for lawyers like you."

I jerked my eyes up to his.

"Did you kill Jerry Vincent?"

Elliot looked me in the eye and shook his head.

"No, I didn't. But it was a lucky break because I ended up with a better lawyer."

I didn't know how to respond. I looked down the hall to the courtroom door. The deputy was there. He waved to me and signaled me into the courtroom. The break was over and the judge was ready to start. I nodded and held up one finger. Wait. I knew the judge wouldn't take the bench until he was told the lawyers were in place.

"Go back in," I said to Elliot. "I have to use the restroom."

Elliot calmly walked toward the waiting deputy. I quickly stepped into the nearby restroom and went to one of the sinks. I splashed cold water on my face, spotting my best suit and shirt but not caring at all.

51

That night I sent Patrick to the movies because I wanted the house to myself. I wanted no television or conversation. I wanted no interruption and no one watching me. I called Bosch and told him I was in for the night. It was not so that I could prepare for what likely would be the last day of the trial. I was more than ready for that. I had the French police captain primed and ready to deliver another dose of reasonable doubt to the jury.

And it was not because I now knew that my client was guilty. I could count the truly innocent clients I'd had over the years on one hand. Guilty people were my specialty. But I was feeling bruised because I had been used so well. And because I had forgotten the basic rule: Everybody lies.

And I was feeling bruised because I knew that I, too, was guilty. I could not stop thinking about Rilz's father and brothers, about what they had told Golantz about their decision to go home. They were not waiting to see the verdict if it first meant seeing their dead loved one dragged through the sewers of the American justice system. I had spent the good part of twenty years defending guilty and sometimes evil men. I had always been able to accept that and deal with it. But I didn't feel very good about myself or the work that I would perform the next day.

It was in these moments that I felt the strongest desire to return to old ways. To find that distance again. To take the pill for the physical pain that I knew would numb me to the internal pain. It was in these moments that I realized that I had my own jury to face and that the coming verdict was guilty, that there would be no more cases after this one.

I went outside to the deck, hoping the city could pull me out of the abyss into which I had fallen. The night was cool and crisp and clear. Los Angeles spread out in front of me in a carpet of lights, each one a verdict on a dream somewhere. Some people lived the dream and some didn't. Some people cashed in their dreams a dime on the dollar and some kept them close and as sacred as the night. I wasn't sure if I even had a dream left. I felt like I only had sins to confess.

After a while a memory washed over me and somehow I smiled. It was one of my last clear memories of my father, the greatest lawyer of his time. An antique glass ball—an heirloom from Mexico passed down through my mother's family—had been found broken beneath the Christmas tree. My mother brought me to the living room to view the damage and to give me the chance to confess my guilt. By then my father was sick and wasn't going to get better. He had moved his work—what was left of it—home to the study next to the living room. I didn't see him through the open door but from that room I heard his voice in a sing-song nursery rhyme.

In a pickle, take the nickel . . .

I knew what it meant. Even at five years old I was my father's son in blood and the law. I refused to answer my mother's questions. I refused to incriminate myself.

Now I laughed out loud as I looked at the city of dreams. I leaned down, elbows on the railing, and bowed my head.

"I can't do this anymore," I whispered to myself.

The song of the Lone Ranger suddenly burst from the open door behind me. I stepped back inside and looked at the cell phone left on the table with my keys. The screen said PRIVATE NUMBER. I hesitated, knowing exactly how long the song would play before the call went to message.

At the last moment I took the call.

"Is this Michael Haller, the lawyer?"

"Yes, who is this?"

"This is Los Angeles police officer Randall Morris. Do you know an individual named Elaine Ross, sir?"

I felt a fist grip my guts.

"Lanie? Yes. What happened? What's wrong?"

"Uh, sir, I have Miss Ross up here on Mulholland Drive and she shouldn't be driving. In fact, she sort of passed out after she handed me your card."

I closed my eyes for a moment. The call seemed to confirm my fears about Lanie Ross. She had fallen back. An arrest would put her back into the system and probably cost her another stay in jail and rehab.

"Which jail are you taking her to?" I asked.

"I gotta be honest, Mr. Haller. I'm code seven in twenty minutes. If I take her down to book her, I'm looking at two more hours and I'm tapped on my overtime allowance this month. I was going to say, if you can come get her or send somebody for her, I'm willing to give her the break. You know what I mean?"

"Yes, I do. Thank you, Officer Morris. I'll come get her if you give me the address."

"You know where the overlook is above Fryman Canyon?"

"Yes, I do."

"We're right here. Make it quick."

"I'll be there in less than fifteen minutes."

Fryman Canyon was only a few blocks from the converted garage guest-house where a friend allowed Lanie to live rent free. I could get her home, walk back to the park, and retrieve her car afterward. It would take me less than an hour and it would keep Lanie out of jail and her car out of the tow lot.

I left the house and drove Laurel Canyon up the hill to Mulholland. When I reached the top, I took a left and headed west. I lowered the windows and let the cool air in as I felt the first pulls of fatigue from the day grab me. I followed the serpentine road for half a mile, slowing once when my headlights washed across a scruffy coyote standing vigil on the side of the road.

My cell phone buzzed as I had been expecting it to.

"What took you so long to call, Bosch?" I said by way of a greeting.

"I've been calling but there's no cell coverage in the canyon," Bosch said. "Is this some kind of test? Where the hell are you going? You called and said you were done for the night."

"I got a call. A...client of mine got busted on a deuce up here. The cop's giving her a break if I drive her home."

"From where?"

"The Fryman Canyon overlook. I'm almost there."

"Who was the cop?"

"Randall Morris. He didn't say whether he was Hollywood or North Hollywood."

Mulholland was a boundary between the two police divisions. Morris could work out of either one.

"Okay, pull over until I can check it out."

"Pull over? Where?"

Mulholland was a winding two-lane road with no pull-over spots except for the overlooks. If you pulled over anywhere else, you would get plowed into by the next car to come around the bend.

"Then, slow down."

"I'm already here."

The Fryman Canyon overlook was on the Valley side. I took a right to turn in and drove right by the sign that said that the parking area was closed after sunset.

I didn't see Lanie's car or a police cruiser. The parking area was empty. I checked my watch. It had been only twelve minutes since I had told Officer Morris that I would be there in less than fifteen.

"Damn!"

"What?" Bosch asked.

I hit the heel of my palm on the steering wheel. Morris hadn't waited. He'd gone ahead and taken Lanie to jail.

"What?" Bosch repeated.

"She's not here," I said. "And neither is the cop. He took her to jail."

I would now have to figure out which station Lanie had been transported to and probably spend the rest of the night arranging bail and getting her home. I'd be wrecked in court the next day.

I put the car in park and got out and looked around. The lights of the Valley spread out below the precipice for miles and miles.

"Bosch, I gotta go. I have to try to find—"

I saw movement in my peripheral vision to the left. I turned and saw a crouching figure coming out of the tall brush next to the parking clearing. At first I thought coyote but then I saw that it was a man. He was dressed in black and a ski mask was pulled down over his face. As he straightened from the crouch, I saw that he was raising a gun at me.

"Wait a minute," I said. "What is—"

"Drop the fucking phone!"

I dropped the phone and raised my hands.

"Okay, okay, what is this? Are you with Bosch?"

The man moved quickly toward me and shoved me backwards. I stumbled to the ground and then felt him grab the back of my jacket's collar.

"Get up!"

"What is—?"

"Get up! Now!"

He started pulling me up.

"Okay, okay. I'm getting up."

The moment I was on my feet I was shoved forward and crossed through the lights at the front of my car.

"Where are we going? What is—?"

I was shoved again.

"Who are you? Why are you—?"

"You ask too many questions, lawyer."

He grabbed the back of my collar and shoved me toward the precipice. I knew it was almost a sheer drop-off at the edge. I was going to end up in somebody's backyard hot tub — after a three-hundred-foot high dive.

I tried to dig my heels in and slow my forward momentum but that resulted in an even harder shove. I had velocity now and the man in the mask was going to run me off the edge into the blackness of the abyss.

"You can't—"

Suddenly there was a shot. Not from behind me. But from the right and from a distance. Almost simultaneously, there was a metal snapping sound from behind me and the man in the mask yelped and fell into the brush to the left.

Then came voices and shouting.

"Drop your weapon! Drop your weapon!"

"Get on the ground! Get down on the ground!"

I dove facedown to the dirt at the edge of the precipice and put my hands over my head for protection. I heard more yelling and the sound of running. I heard engines roaring and vehicles crunching across the gravel. When I opened my eyes, I saw blue lights flashing in repeated patterns off the dirt and brush. Blue lights meant cops. It meant I was safe.

"Counselor," a voice said from above me. "You can get up now."

I craned my neck to look up. It was Bosch, his shadowed face silhouetted by the stars above him.

"You cut that one pretty close," he said.

52

The man in the black mask groaned in pain as they cuffed his hands behind his back.

"My hand! Jesus, you assholes, my hand is broken!"

I climbed to my feet and saw several men in black windbreakers moving about like ants on a hill. Some of the plastic raid jackets said lapd on them but most had fbi printed across the back. Soon a helicopter came overhead and lit the entire parking clearing with a spotlight.

Bosch stepped over to the FBI agents huddling over the man in the mask.

"Was he hit?" he asked.

"There is no wound," an agent said. "The round must have hit the gun, but that still hurts like a son of a bitch."

"Where is the gun?"

"We're still looking," the agent said.

"It may have gone over the side," another agent said.

"If we don't find it tonight, we find it in daylight," said a third.

They pulled the man up into a standing position. Two of the FBI agents stood on either side of him, holding him at the elbows.

"Let's see who we've got," Bosch said.

The ski mask was unceremoniously yanked off and a flashlight was aimed point-blank at the man's face. Bosch turned and looked back at me.

"Juror number seven," I said.

"What are you talking about?"

"Juror number seven from the trial. He didn't show up today and the Sheriff's Department was looking for him."

Bosch turned back to the man I knew was named David McSweeney.

"Hold him right there."

He then turned and signaled to me to follow him. He walked out of the circle of activity and into the parking clearing near my car. He stopped and turned back to me. But I got my question in first.

"What just happened?"

"What just happened was we just saved your life. He was going to push you over the side."

"I know that, but what *happened?* Where did you and everybody else come from? You said you would let people go at night after I was tucked in. Where did all of these cops come from? And what's the FBI doing here?"

"Things were different tonight. Things happened."

"What things happened? What changed?"

"We can go over that later. Let's talk about what we've got here first."

"I don't know what we've got here."

"Tell me about juror number seven. Why didn't he show up today?"

"Well, you should probably ask him that. All I can tell you is that this morning the judge called us into chambers and said he got an anonymous letter saying number seven was a phony and he lied about having a record. The judge planned to question him but he didn't show up. The sheriffs were sent to his house and his job and they brought back a guy who wasn't juror number seven."

Bosch raised his hand like a traffic cop.

"Hold on, hold on. You're not making sense. I know you just had a scare but—"

He stopped when one of the men in an LAPD jacket came over to address him.

"You want us to call paramedics? He says he thinks his hand is broken."

"No, just hold him there. We'll have him checked after we book him."

"You sure?"

"Fuck him."

The man nodded and went back to the spot where they were holding McSweeney.

"Yeah, fuck him," I said.

"Why did he want to kill you?" Bosch asked.

I raised my empty hands.

"I don't know. Maybe because of the story we planted. Wasn't that the plan, to draw him out?"

"I think you're holding out on me, Haller."

"Look, I've told you what I could tell you all along. You're the one holding out and playing games. What's the FBI doing here?"

"They've been in it from the start."

"Right, and you just forgot to tell me."

"I told you what you needed to know."

"Well, I need to know it all now or my cooperation with you ends now. That includes being any sort of witness against that man over there."

I waited a moment and he said nothing. I turned to walk toward my car and Bosch put his hand on my arm. He smiled in frustration and shook his head.

"Come on, man, cool your jets. Don't be throwing empty threats around."

"You think it's an empty threat? Why don't we see how empty it is when I start stringing out the federal grand jury subpoena I know is going to come out of this. I can argue client confidentiality all the way to the Supreme Court—I bet that will only take about two years—and your newfound pals over in the bureau are going to wish you had just come clean with me when you had the chance."

Bosch thought a moment and pulled me by the arm.

"All right, tough guy, come over here."

We walked to a spot in the parking area even further from the law enforcement ant hill. Bosch started to talk.

"The bureau contacted me a few days after the Vincent murder and said that he had been a person of interest to them. That's all. A person of interest. He was one of the lawyers whose names came up in their look at the state courts. Nothing specific, just based on rumors, things he had supposedly told clients he could get done, connections he claimed to have, that sort of thing. They'd drawn up a list of lawyers they heard might be bent and Vincent was on it. They invited him in as a cooperating witness and he declined. They were increasing the pressure on him when he got hit."

"So they tell you all of this and you join forces. Isn't that wonderful? Thanks for telling me."

"Like I said, you didn't need to know."

A man in an FBI jacket crossed the parking area behind Bosch, and his face was momentarily lit from above. He looked familiar to me but I couldn't place him. But then I imagined a mustache on him.

"Hey, there's the asshole you sent after me the other night," I said loud enough for the passing agent to hear. "He's lucky I didn't put a bullet in his face at the door."

Bosch put his hands on my chest and pushed me back a few steps.

"Calm down, Counselor. If it weren't for the bureau, I wouldn't have had the manpower to keep the watch on you. And right now you could be lying down there at the bottom of the mountain."

I pushed his hands off me but settled down. My anger dissipated as I accepted the reality of what Bosch had just said. And the reality that I had been used as a pawn from the beginning. By my client and now by Bosch and the FBI. Bosch took the moment to signal over another agent, who was standing nearby watching.

"This is Agent Armstead. He's been running the bureau's side of things and he's got some questions for you."

"Why not?" I said. "Nobody answers mine. I might as well answer yours."

Armstead was a young, clean-cut agent with a precision military haircut.

"Mr. Haller, we'll get to your questions as soon as we can," he said. "Right now we have a fluid situation here and your cooperation will be greatly appreciated. Is juror number seven the man Vincent paid the bribe to?"

I looked at Bosch with a "who is this guy?" expression.

"Man, how would I know that? I wasn't part of this thing. You want an answer to that, go ask him."

"Don't worry. We will be asking him a lot of questions. What were you doing up here, Mr. Haller?"

"I told you people. I told Bosch. I got a call from somebody who said he was a cop. He said he had a woman I know personally up here and she was under the influence and that I could come up and drive her home and save her the trouble of getting booked on a deuce."

"We checked that name you gave me on the phone," Bosch said. "There is one Randall Morris in the department. He's on gang detail in South Bureau."

I nodded.

"Yeah, well, I think it's pretty clear now that it was a fake call. But he knew my friend's name and he had my cell. It seemed convincing at the time, all right?"

"How did he get the woman's name?" Armstead asked.

"Good question. I had a relationship with her—a platonic relationship—but I haven't talked to her in almost a month."

"Then, how would he know about her?"

"Man, you're asking me shit I don't know. Go ask McSweeney."

I immediately realized I had slipped up. I wouldn't know that name unless I had been investigating juror number seven.

Bosch looked at me curiously. I didn't know if he realized the jury was supposed to be anonymous, even to the lawyers on the case. Before he could come up with a question, I was saved by someone yelling from the brush where I had almost been pushed over the side.

"I've got the gun!"

Bosch pointed a finger at my chest.

"Stay right here."

I watched Bosch and Armstead trot over and join a few of the others as they studied the found weapon under a flashlight beam. Bosch didn't touch the weapon but bent down into the light to examine it closely.

The *William Tell* Overture started to play behind me. I turned around and saw my phone lying on the gravel, its tiny square screen glowing like a beacon. I went over and picked it up. It was Cisco and I took the call.

"Cisco, I gotta call you back."

"Make it quick. I've got some good shit for you. You're going to want to know this."

I closed the phone and watched as Bosch finished his study of the weapon and then stepped over to McSweeney. He leaned close to him and whispered something into his ear. He didn't wait for a response. He just turned and walked back toward me. I could tell even in the dim moonlight that he was excited. Armstead was following behind him.

"The gun's a Beretta Bobcat, like we were looking for on Vincent," he said. "If the ballistics match, then we've got that guy locked in a box. I'll make sure you get a commendation from City Hall."

"Good. I'll frame it."

"Put this together for me, Haller, and you can start with him being the one who killed Vincent. Why did he want to kill you, too?"

"I don't know."

"The bribe," Armstead asked. "Is he the one who got the money?"

"Same answer I gave you five minutes ago. I don't know. But it makes sense, doesn't it?"

"How did he know your friend's name on the phone?"

"I don't know that either."

"Then, what good are you?" Bosch asked.

It was a good question and the immediate answer didn't sit well with me.

"Look, Detective, I—"

"Don't bother, man. Why don't you just get in your car and get the fuck out of here? We'll take it from here."

He turned and started walking away and Armstead followed. I hesitated and then called out to Bosch. I waved him back. He said something to the FBI agent and came back to me alone.

"No bullshit," he said impatiently. "I don't have the time."

"Okay, this is the thing," I said. "I think he was going to make it look like I jumped."

Bosch considered this and then shook his head.

"Suicide? Who would believe that? You've got the case of the decade, man. You're hot. You're on TV. And you've got a kid to worry about. Suicide wouldn't sell."

I nodded.

"Yes, it would."

He looked at me and said nothing, waiting for me to explain.

"I'm a recovering addict, Bosch. You know anything about that?"

"Why don't you tell me?"

"The story would go that I couldn't take the pressure of the big case and all the attention, and I either had or was about to relapse. So I jumped instead of going back to that. It's not an uncommon thing, Bosch. They call it the fast out. And it makes me think that..."

"What?"

I pointed across the clearing toward juror number seven.

"That he and whoever he was doing this for knew a lot about me. They did a deep background. They came up with my addiction and rehab and Lanie's name. Then they came up with a solid plan for getting rid of me because they couldn't just shoot down another lawyer without bringing down massive scrutiny on what it is they've got going. If I went down as a suicide, there'd be a lot less pressure."

"Yeah, but why did they need to get rid of you?"

"I guess they think I know too much."

"Do you?"

Before I could answer, McSweeney started yelling from the other side of the clearing.

"Hey! Over there with the lawyer. I want to make a deal. I can give you some big people, man! I want to make a deal!"

Bosch waited to see if there was more but that was it.

"My tip?" I said. "Go over there and strike while the iron's hot. Before he remembers he's entitled to a lawyer."

Bosch nodded.

"Thanks, Coach," he said. "But I think I know what I'm doing."

He started to head across the clearing.

"Hey, Bosch, wait," I called. "You owe me something before you go over there."

Bosch stopped and signaled to Armstead to go to McSweeney. He then came back to me.

"What do I owe you?"

"One answer. Tonight I called you and told you I was in for the night. You were supposed to cut the surveillance down to one car. But this is the whole enchilada up here. What changed your mind?"

"You haven't heard, have you?"

"Heard what?"

"You get to sleep late tomorrow, Counselor. There's no trial anymore."

"Why not?"

"Because your client's dead. Somebody — probably our friend over there who wants to make a deal — took Elliot and his girlfriend out tonight when they came home from dinner. His electric gate wouldn't open and when he got out to push it open, somebody came up and put a bullet in the back of his head. Then he hit the woman in the car."

I took a half step back in shock. I knew the gate Bosch was talking about. I had been to Elliot's mansion in Beverly Hills just the other night. And as far as the girlfriend went, I also thought I knew who that would be. I'd had Nina Albrecht figured for that position ever since Elliot told me he'd had help on the day of the murders in Malibu.

Bosch didn't let the stunned look on my face keep him from continuing.

"I got tipped from a friend in the medical examiner's office and figured that somebody might be out there cleaning the slate tonight. I figured I ought to call the team back and see what happens at your place. Lucky for you I did."

I stared right through Bosch when I answered.

"Yeah," I said. "Lucky for me."

53

There was no longer a trial but I went to court on Tuesday morning to see the case through to its official end. I took my place next to the empty seat Walter Elliot had occupied for the past two weeks. The news photographers who had been allowed access to the courtroom seemed to like that empty chair. They took a lot of photos of it.

Jeffrey Golantz sat across the aisle. He was the luckiest prosecutor on earth. He had left court one day, thinking he was facing a career-hobbling loss, and came back the next day with his perfect record intact. His upward trajectory in the DA's office and city politics was safe for now. He had nothing to say to me as we sat and waited for the judge.

But there was a lot of talk in the gallery. People were buzzing with news of the murders of Walter Elliot and Nina Albrecht. No one made mention of the attempt on my life and the events at the Fryman Canyon overlook. For the moment, that was all secret. Once McSweeney told Bosch and Armstead that he wanted to deal, the investigators had asked me to keep quiet so they could move slowly and carefully with their cooperating suspect. I was happy to cooperate with that myself. To a point.

Judge Stanton took the bench promptly at nine. His eyes were puffy and he looked like he'd had very little sleep. I wondered if he knew as many details of what had transpired the night before as I did.

The jury was brought in and I studied their faces. If any of them knew what had happened, they weren't showing it. I noticed several of them check out the empty seat beside me as they took their own.

"Ladies and gentlemen, good morning," the judge said. "At this time I am going to discharge you from service in this trial. As I am sure you can see, Mr. Elliot is not in his seat at the defense table. This is because the defendant in this trial was the victim of a homicide last night."

Half of the jurors' mouths dropped open in unison. The others expressed their surprise with their eyes. A low murmur of excited voices went through the courtroom and then a slow and deliberate clapping began from behind the prosecution table. I turned to see Mitzi Elliot's mother applauding the news of Elliot's demise.

The judge brought his gavel down harshly just as Golantz jumped from his seat and rushed to her, grabbing her hands gently and stopping her from continuing. I saw tears rolling down her cheeks.

"There will be no demonstrations from the gallery," the judge said harshly.

"I don't care who you are or what connection you might have to the case, everyone in here will show respect to the court or I will have you removed."

Golantz returned to his seat but the tears continued to flow from the mother of one of the victims.

"I know that to all of you, this is rather shocking news," Stanton told the jurors. "Be assured that the authorities are investigating the matter thoroughly and hopefully will soon bring the individual or individuals responsible to justice. I am sure you will learn all about it when you read the paper or watch the news, as you are now free to do. As far as today goes, I want to thank you for your service. I know you all were very attentive to the presentation of the prosecution and defense cases and I hope your time here was a positive experience. You are free now to go back to the deliberation room to gather your things and go home. You are excused."

We stood one last time for the jury and I watched them file through the doorway to the deliberation room. After they were gone, the judge thanked Golantz and me for our professional demeanor during trial, thanked his staff, and quickly adjourned court. I hadn't bothered to unpack any files from my bag, so I stood motionless for the longest time after the judge left the courtroom. My reverie wasn't broken until Golantz approached me with his hand out. Without thinking I reached out and shook it.

"No hard feelings on anything, Mickey. You're a damn good lawyer."

Was, I thought.

"Yeah," I said. "No hard feelings."

"You going to hang around and talk to jurors, see which way they were leaning?" he asked.

I shook my head.

"No, I'm not interested."

"Me neither. Take care of yourself."

He clapped me on the shoulder and pushed out through the gate. I was sure there would be a throng of media out in the hall waiting and he'd tell them that in some strange way he felt that justice had been served. Live by the gun, die by the gun. Or words to that effect.

I'd leave the media for him. Instead, I gave him a good lead and then followed him out. The reporters were already surrounding him and I was able to hug the wall and escape notice. All except for Jack McEvoy from the *Times*. He spotted me and started trailing. He caught me as I got to the stairwell entrance.

"Hey, Mick!"

I glanced at him but didn't stop walking. I knew from experience not to. If one member of the media downed you, the rest of the pride would catch up and pile on. I didn't want to be devoured. I hit the stairwell door and started down.

"No comment."

He stayed with me, stride for stride.

"I'm not writing about the trial. I'm covering the new murders. I thought maybe you and I could have the same deal again. You know, trade informa—"

"No deal, Jack. And no comment. Catch you later."

I put my hand out and stopped him on the first landing. I left him there, went down two more landings, and then went out into the hallway. I walked down to Judge Holder's courtroom and entered.

Michaela Gill was in the clerk's pod and I asked if I could see the judge for a few minutes.

"But I don't have you down for an appointment," she said.

"I know that, Michaela, but I think the judge will want to see me. Is she back there? Can you tell her I only want ten minutes? Tell her it's about the Vincent files."

The clerk picked up the phone, punched a button, and gave the judge my request. Then she hung up and told me I could go right back to her chambers.

"Thank you."

The judge was behind her desk with her half-glasses on, a pen poised in her hand as if I had interrupted her in the middle of signing an order.

"Well, Mr. Haller," she said. "It's certainly been an eventful day. Have a seat."

I sat in the familiar chair in front of her.

"Thank you for seeing me, Judge."

"What can I do for you?"

She asked the question without looking at me. She started scribbling signatures on a series of documents.

"I just wanted you to know I will be resigning as counsel on the rest of the Vincent cases."

She put the pen down and looked over her glasses at me.

"What?"

"I'm resigning. I came back too soon or probably should never have come back at all. But I'm finished."

"That's absurd. Your defense of Mr. Elliot has been the talk of this court-house. I watched parts of it on television. You clearly were schooling Mr. Golantz and I don't think there were many observers who would have bet against an acquittal."

I waved the compliments away.

"Anyway, Judge, it doesn't matter. It's not really why I'm here."

She took her glasses off and put them down on the desk. She looked hesitant but then asked the next question.

"Then, why are you here?"

"Because, Judge, I wanted you to know that I know. And soon enough everybody else will as well."

"I am sure I don't know what you are talking about. What do you know, Mr. Haller?"

"I know that you are for sale and that you tried to have me killed."

She barked out a laugh but there was no mirth in her eyes, only daggers.

"Is this some kind of joke?"

"No, it's no joke."

"Then, Mr. Haller, I suggest you calm down and compose yourself. If you go around this courthouse making these kinds of outlandish accusations, then there will be consequences for you. Severe consequences. Maybe you are right. You are feeling the stress of coming back too soon from rehab."

I smiled and I could tell by her face that she immediately realized her mistake.

"Slipped up there, didn't you, Judge? How'd you know I was in rehab? Better yet, how did juror number seven know how to lure me away from home last night? The answer is, you had me backgrounded. You set me up and sent McSweeney out to kill me."

"I don't know what you are talking about and I don't know this man you say tried to kill you."

"Well, I think he knows you, and the last time I saw him he was about to start playing *Let's Make a Deal* with the federal government."

It hit her like a punch in the gut. I knew revealing it to her wasn't going to endear me to Bosch or Armstead, but I didn't care. Neither of them was the guy who had been used like a pawn and had nearly taken the high dive off Mulholland. I was that guy and that entitled me to confront the person I knew was behind it.

"I put it together without having to make a deal with anybody," I said. "My investigator traced McSweeney. Nine years ago he was arrested for an ADW and who was his attorney? Mitch Lester, your husband. The next year he was popped again for fraud and once again it was Mitch Lester on the case. There's the connection. It makes a nice little triangle, doesn't it? You have access to and control of the jury pool and the selection process. You can get into the computers and it was you who planted the sleeper on my jury. Jerry Vincent paid you but then he changed his mind after the FBI came sniffing around. You couldn't run the risk that Jerry might get jammed up with the FBI and try to deal a judge to them. So you sent McSweeney.

"Then, when it all turned to shit yesterday, you decided to clean house. You sent McSweeney—juror number seven—after Elliot and Albrecht, and then me. How am I doing, *Judge*? I miss anything so far?"

I said the word "judge" like it had the same meaning as garbage. She stood up.

"This is insane. You have no evidence connecting me to anyone but my husband. And making the leap from one of his clients to me is completely absurd."

"You're right, Judge. I don't have evidence but we're not in court here. This is just you and me. I just have my gut instincts and they tell me that this all comes back to you."

"I want you to leave now."

"But the feds, on the other hand? They have McSweeney."

I could see it strike fear in her eyes.

"Guess you haven't heard from him, have you? Yeah, I don't think they're letting him make any calls while they debrief him. You better hope he doesn't have any of that evidence. Because if he puts you in that triangle, then you'll be trading your black robe for an orange jumpsuit."

"Get out or I will call courthouse security and have you arrested!"

She pointed toward the door. I calmly and slowly stood up.

"Sure, I'll go. And you know something? I may never practice law again in this courthouse. But I promise you that I'll come back to watch you be prosecuted. You and your husband. Count on it."

The judge stared at me, her arm still extended toward the door, and I saw the anger in her eyes slowly change to fear. Her arm drooped a little and then she let it drop all the way. I left her standing there.

I took the stairs all the way down because I didn't want to get on a crowded elevator. Eleven flights down. At the bottom I pushed through the glass doors and left the courthouse. I pulled my phone and called Patrick and told him to pull the car around. Then I called Bosch.

"I decided to light a fire under you and the bureau," I told him.

"What do you mean? What did you do?"

"I didn't want to wait around while the bureau took its usual year and a half to make a case. Sometimes justice can't wait, Detective."

"What did you do, Haller?"

"I just had a conversation with Judge Holder — yes, I figured it out without McSweeney's help. I told her the feds had McSweeney and he was cooperating. If I were you and the bureau, I'd hurry the fuck up with your case and in the meantime keep tabs on her. She doesn't seem like a runner to me, but you never know. Have a good day."

I closed the phone before he could protest my actions. I didn't care. He had used me the whole time. It felt good to turn the tables on him, make him and the FBI do the dancing at the end of the string.

PART SIX

—The Last Verdict

54

Bosch knocked on my door early Thursday morning. I hadn't combed my hair yet but I was dressed. He, on the other hand, looked like he had pulled an all-nighter.

"I wake you?" he asked.

I shook my head.

"I have to get my kid ready for school."

"That's right. Wednesday nights and every other weekend."

"What's up, Detective?"

"I've got a couple of questions and I thought you might be interested in knowing where things stand on everything."

"Sure. Let's sit out here. I don't want her hearing this."

I patted down my hair as I walked toward the table.

"I don't want to sit," Bosch said. "I don't have a lot of time."

He turned to the railing and leaned his elbows down on it. I changed directions and did the same thing right next to him.

"I don't like to sit when I'm out here either."

"I have the same sort of view at my place," he said. "Only it's on the other side."

"I guess that makes us flip sides of the same mountain."

He turned his eyes from the view to me for a moment.

"Something like that," he said.

"So, what's happening? I thought you'd be too angry with me to ever tell me what was going on."

"Truth is, I think the bureau moves too slowly myself. They didn't like what you did very much but I didn't mind. It got things rolling."

Bosch straightened up and leaned back on the railing, the view of the city behind him.

"So then, what's happening?" I asked.

"The grand jury came back with indictments last night. Holder, Lester, Carlin, McSweeney, and a woman who's a supervisor in the jury office and was the one who gave them access to the computers. We're taking them all down simultaneously this morning. So keep it under your hat until we have everybody hooked up."

It was nice that he trusted me enough to tell me before the arrests. I thought it might be even nicer to go down to the CCB and watch them take Holder out of there in handcuffs.

"Is it solid?" I asked. "Holder *is* a judge, you know. You better have it nailed down."

"It's solid. McSweeney gave it all up. We've got phone records, money transfers. He even taped her husband during some of the conversations."

I nodded. It sounded like the typical federal package. One reason I never took on federal cases when I was practicing was that when the Big G made a case, it usually stayed made. Victories for the defense were rare. Most times you just got flattened like roadkill.

"I didn't know Carlin was hooked up in this," I said.

"He's right at the center. He goes way back with the judge and she used him to approach Vincent in the first place. Vincent used him to deliver the money. Then when Vincent started getting cold feet because the FBI was sniffing around, Carlin got wind of it and told the judge. She thought the best thing to do was get rid of the weak link. She and her husband sent McSweeney to take care of Vincent."

"Got wind of it how? Wren Williams?"

"Yeah, we think. He got close to her to keep tabs on Vincent. We don't think she knew what was going on. She's not smart enough."

I nodded and thought about how all the pieces fit together.

"What about McSweeney? He just did what he was told? The judge tells him to hit a guy and he just does it?"

"First of all, McSweeney was a con man before he was a killer. So I don't for a minute think we're getting the whole truth out of him. But he says the judge can be very persuasive. The way she explained it to him, either Vincent went down or they all went down. There was no choice. Besides, she also promised to increase his cut after he went through with the trial and tipped the case."

I nodded.

"So what are the indictments?"

"Conspiracy to commit murder, corruption. This is only the first wave. There will be more down the road. This wasn't the first time. McSweeney told us he'd been on four juries in the last seven years. Two acquittals and two hangers. Three different courthouses."

I whistled as I thought of some of the big cases that had ended in shocking acquittals or hung juries in recent years.

"Robert Blake?"

Bosch smiled and shook his head.

"I wish," he said. "O.J., too. But they weren't in business back then for that one. We just lost those cases on our own."

"Doesn't matter. This is going to be huge."

"Biggest one I've ever had."

He folded his arms and glanced over his shoulder at the view.

"You've got the Sunset Strip and I've got Universal," he said.

I heard the door open and looked back to see Hayley peeking out.

"Dad?"

"What's up, Hay?"

"Is everything all right?"

"Everything's fine. Hayley, this is Detective Bosch. He's a policeman."

"Hello, Hayley," Bosch said.

I think it was the only time I had ever seen him put a real smile on his face.

"Hi," my daughter said.

"Hayley, did you eat your cereal?" I asked.

"Yes."

"Okay, then you can watch TV until it's time to go."

She disappeared inside and closed the door. I checked my watch. She still had ten minutes before we had to leave.

"She's a cute kid," Bosch said.

I nodded.

"I gotta ask you a question," he said. "You started this whole thing tumbling, didn't you? You sent that anonymous letter to the judge."

I thought for a moment before answering.

"If I say yes, am I going to become a witness?"

I had not been called to the federal grand jury after all. With McSweeney giving everything up, they apparently didn't need me. And I didn't want to change that now.

"No, it's just for me," Bosch said. "I just want to know if you did the right thing."

I considered not telling him but ultimately I wanted him to know.

"Yeah, that was me. I wanted to get McSweeney off the jury and then win the case fair and square. I didn't expect Judge Stanton to take the letter and consult other judges about it."

"He called up the chief judge and asked her advice."

I nodded.

"It's gotta be what happened," I said. "He calls her, not knowing she was behind the whole thing. She then tipped McSweeney and told him not to show up for court, then used him to try to clean up the mess."

Bosch nodded as though I was confirming things he already knew.

"And you were part of the mess. She must've figured you sent the letter to Judge Stanton. You knew too much and had to go — just like Vincent. It wasn't about the story we planted. It was about you tipping Judge Stanton."

I shook my head. My own actions had almost brought about my own demise in the form of a high dive off Mulholland.

"I guess I was pretty stupid."

"I don't know about that. You're still standing. After today none of them will be."

"There's that. What kind of deal did McSweeney cut?"

"No death penalty and consideration. If everybody goes down, then he'll probably get fifteen. In the federal system that means he'll still do thirteen."

"Who's his lawyer?"

"He's got two. Dan Daly and Roger Mills."

I nodded. He was in good hands. I thought about what Walter Elliot had told me, that the guiltier you were, the more lawyers you needed.

"Pretty good deal for three murders," I said.

"One murder," Bosch corrected.

"What do you mean? Vincent, Elliot, and Albrecht."

"He didn't kill Elliot and Albrecht. Those two didn't match up."

"What are you talking about? He killed them and then he tried to kill me."

Bosch shook his head.

"He did try to kill you but he didn't kill Elliot and Albrecht. It was a different weapon. On top of that, it didn't make sense. Why would he ambush them and then try to make you look like a suicide? It doesn't connect. McSweeney is clean on Elliot and Albrecht."

I was stunned silent for a long moment. For the last three days I had believed that the man who killed Elliot and Albrecht was the same man who had tried to kill me and that he was safely locked in the hands of the authorities. Now Bosch was telling me there was a second killer somewhere out there.

"Does Beverly Hills have any ideas?" I finally asked.

"Oh, yeah, they're pretty sure they know who did it. But they'll never make a case."

The hits kept coming. One surprise after another.

"Who?"

"The family."

"You mean like the Family, with a capital *F*? Organized crime?"

Bosch smiled and shook his head.

"The family of Johan Rilz. They took care of it."

"How do they know that?"

"Lands and grooves. The bullets they dug out of the two victims were nine-millimeter Parabellums. Brass jacket and casing and manufactured in Germany. BHPD took the bullet profile and matched them to a C-ninety-six Mauser, also manufactured in Germany."

He paused to see if I had any questions. When I didn't, he continued.

"Over at BHPD they're thinking it's almost like somebody was sending a message."

"A message from Germany."

"You got it."

I thought of Golantz telling the Rilz family how I was going to drag Johan through the mud for a week. They had left rather than witness that. And Elliot was killed before it could happen.

"Parabellum," I said. "You know your Latin, Detective?"

"Didn't go to law school. What's it mean?"

"Prepare for war. It's part of a saying. 'If you want peace, prepare for war.' What will happen with the investigation now?"

Bosch shrugged.

"I know a couple of Beverly Hills detectives who'll get a nice trip to Germany out of it. They fly their people business class with the seats that fold down into beds. They'll go through the motions and the due diligence. But if the hit was done right, nothing will ever happen."

"How'd they get the gun over here?"

"It could be done. Through Canada or Der FedEx if it absolutely, positively has to be there on time."

I didn't smile. I was thinking about Elliot and the equilibrium of justice. Somehow Bosch seemed to know what I was thinking.

"Remember what you said to me when you told me you had told Judge Holder you knew she was behind all of this?"

I shrugged.

"What did I say?"

"You said sometimes justice can't wait."

"And?"

"And you were right. Sometimes it doesn't wait. In that trial, you had the momentum and Elliot looked like he was going to walk. So somebody decided not to wait for justice and he delivered his own verdict. Back when I was riding patrol, you know what we called a killing that came down to simple street justice?"

"What?"

"The brass verdict."

I nodded. I understood. We were both silent for a long moment.

"Anyway, that's all I know," Bosch finally said. "I gotta go and get ready to put people in jail. It's going to be a good day."

Bosch pushed his weight off the railing, ready to go.

"It's funny you coming here today," I said. "Last night I decided I was going to ask you something the next time I saw you."

"Yeah, what's that?"

I thought about it for a moment and then nodded. It was the right thing to do.

"Flip sides of the same mountain.... Do you know you look a lot like your father?"

He said nothing. He just stared at me for a moment, then nodded once and turned to the railing. He cast his gaze out at the city.

"When did you put that together?" he asked.

"Technically last night, when I was looking at old photos and scrapbooks with my daughter. But I think on some level I've known it for a long time. We were looking at photos of my father. They kept reminding me of somebody and then I realized it was you. Once I saw it, it seemed obvious. I just didn't see it at first."

I walked to the railing and looked out at the city with him.

"Most of what I know about him came from books," I said. "A lot of different cases, a lot of different women. But there are a few memories that aren't in books and are just mine. I remember coming into the office he had set up at home when he started to get sick. There was a painting framed on the wall — a print actually, but back then I thought it was a real painting. *The Garden of Earthly Delights.* Weird, scary stuff for a little kid...

"The memory I have is of him holding me on his lap and making me look at the painting and telling me that it wasn't scary. That it was beautiful. He tried to teach me to say the painter's name. Hieronymus Bosch. Rhymes with 'anonymous,' he told me. Only back then, I don't think I could say 'anonymous' either."

I wasn't seeing the city out there. I was seeing the memory. I was quiet for a while after that. It was my half brother's turn. Eventually, he leaned his elbows down on the railing and spoke.

"I remember that house," he said. "I visited him once. Introduced myself. He was on the bed. He was dying."

"What did you say to him?"

"I just told him I'd made it through. That's all. There wasn't really anything else to say."

Like right now, I thought. What was there to say? Somehow, my thoughts jumped to my own shattered family. I had little contact with the siblings I knew I had, let alone Bosch. And then there was my daughter, whom I saw only eight days a month. It seemed like the most important things in life were the easiest to break apart.

"You've known all these years," I finally said. "Why didn't you ever make contact? I have another half brother and three half sisters. They're yours, too, you know."

Bosch didn't say anything at first, then he gave an answer I guessed he had been telling himself for a few decades.

"I don't know. I guess I didn't want to rock anybody's boat. Most of the time people don't like surprises. Not like this."

For a moment I wondered what my life would've been like if I had known about Bosch. Maybe I would've been a cop instead of a lawyer. Who knows?

"I'm quitting, you know."

I wasn't sure why I had said it.

"Quitting what?"

"My job. The law. You could say the brass verdict was my last verdict."

"I quit once. It didn't take. I came back."

"We'll see."

Bosch glanced at me and then put his eyes back out on the city. It was a beautiful day with low-flying clouds and a cold-air front that had compressed the smog layer to a thin amber band on the horizon. The sun had just crested the mountains to the east and was throwing light out on the Pacific. We could see all the way out to Catalina.

"I came to the hospital that time you got shot," he said. "I wasn't sure why. I saw it on the news and they said it was a gut shot and I knew those could go either way. I thought maybe if they needed blood or something, I could...I figured we matched, you know? Anyway, there were all these reporters and cameras. I ended up leaving."

I smiled and then I started to laugh. I couldn't help it.

"What's so funny?"

"You, a cop, volunteering to give blood to a defense attorney. I don't think they would've let you back into the clubhouse if they knew about that."

Now Bosch smiled and nodded.

"I guess I didn't think about that."

And just like that, both our smiles disappeared and the awkwardness of being strangers returned. Eventually Bosch checked his watch.

"The warrant teams are meeting in twenty minutes. I gotta roll."

"Okay."

"I'll see you around, Counselor."

"I'll see you around, Detective."

He went down the steps and I stayed where I was. I heard his car start up, then pull away and go down the hill.

55

I stayed out on the deck after that and looked out at the city as the light moved across it. Many different thoughts filtered through my head and flew off into the sky like the clouds up there, remotely beautiful and untouchable. Distant. I was left feeling that I would never see Bosch again. That he would have his side of the mountain and I would have mine and that's all there would be.

After a while I heard the door open and steps on the deck. I felt my daughter's presence by my side and I put my hand on her shoulder.

"What are you doing, Dad?"

"Just looking."

"Are you all right?"

"I'm fine."

"What did that policeman want?"

"Just to talk. He's a friend of mine."

We were both silent for a moment before she moved on.

"I wish Mom had stayed with us last night," she said.

I looked down at her and squeezed the back of her neck.

"One thing at a time, Hay," I said. "We got her to have pancakes with us last night, didn't we?"

She thought about it and gave me the nod. She agreed. Pancakes were a start.

"I'm going to be late if we don't go," she said. "One more time and I'll get a conduct slip."

I nodded.

"Too bad. The sun's just about to hit the ocean."

"Come on, Dad. That happens every day."

I nodded.

"Somewhere, at least."

I went in for the keys, then locked up, and we went down the steps to the garage. By the time I backed the Lincoln out and had it pointed down the hill, I could see the sun was spinning gold on the Pacific.

The Reversal

To Shannon Byrne
with many thanks

PART ONE

—The Perp Walk

1

The last time I'd eaten at the Water Grill I sat across the table from a client who had coldly and calculatedly murdered his wife and her lover, shooting both of them in the face. He had engaged my services to not only defend him at trial but fully exonerate him and restore his good name in the public eye. This time I was sitting with someone with whom I needed to be even more careful. I was dining with Gabriel Williams, the district attorney of Los Angeles County.

It was a crisp afternoon in midwinter. I sat with Williams and his trusted chief of staff—read political advisor—Joe Ridell. The meal had been set for 1:30 P.M., when most courthouse lawyers would be safely back in the CCB, and the DA would not be advertising his dalliance with a member of the dark side. Meaning me, Mickey Haller, defender of the damned.

The Water Grill was a nice place for a downtown lunch. Good food and atmosphere, good separation between tables for private conversation, and a wine list hard to top in all of downtown. It was the kind of place where you kept your suit jacket on and the waiter put a black napkin across your lap so you needn't be bothered with doing it yourself. The prosecution team ordered martinis at the county taxpayers' expense and I stuck with the free water the restaurant was pouring. It took Williams two gulps of gin and one olive before he got to the reason we were hiding in plain sight.

"Mickey, I have a proposition for you."

I nodded. Ridell had already said as much when he had called that morning to set up the lunch. I had agreed to the meet and then had gone to work on the phone myself, trying to gather any inside information I could on what the proposition would be. Not even my first ex-wife, who worked in the district attorney's employ, knew what was up.

"I'm all ears," I said. "It's not every day that the DA himself wants to give you a proposition. I know it can't be in regard to any of my clients—they wouldn't merit much attention from the guy at the top. And at the moment I'm only carrying a few cases anyway. Times are slow."

"Well, you're right," Williams said. "This is not about any of your clients. I have a case I would like you to take on."

I nodded again. I understood now. They all hate the defense attorney until they need the defense attorney. I didn't know if Williams had any children but he would have known through due diligence that I didn't do juvy work. So I was guessing it had to be his wife. Probably a shoplifting grab or a DUI he was trying to keep under wraps.

"Who got popped?" I asked.

Williams looked at Ridell and they shared a smile.

"No, nothing like that," Williams said. "My proposition is this. I would like to hire you, Mickey. I want you to come work at the DA's office."

Of all the ideas that had been rattling around in my head since I had taken Ridell's call, being hired as a prosecutor wasn't one of them. I'd been a card-carrying member of the criminal defense bar for more than twenty years. During that time I'd grown a suspicion and distrust of prosecutors and police that might not have equaled that of the gangbangers down in Nickerson Gardens but was at least at a level that would seem to exclude me from ever joining their ranks. Plain and simple, they wouldn't want me and I wouldn't want them. Except for that ex-wife I mentioned and a half brother who was an LAPD detective, I wouldn't turn my back on any of them. Especially Williams. He was a politician first and a prosecutor second. That made him even more dangerous. Though briefly a prosecutor early in his legal career, he spent two decades as a civil rights attorney before running for the DA post as an outsider and riding into office on a tide of anti-police and -prosecutor sentiment. I was employing full caution at the fancy lunch from the moment the napkin went across my lap.

"Work for you?" I asked. "Doing what exactly?"

"As a special prosecutor. A onetime deal. I want you to handle the Jason Jessup case."

I looked at him for a long moment. First I thought I would laugh out loud. This was some sort of cleverly orchestrated joke. But then I understood that couldn't be the case. They don't take you out to the Water Grill just to make a joke.

"You want me to prosecute Jessup? From what I hear there's nothing to prosecute. That case is a duck without wings. The only thing left to do is shoot it and eat it."

Williams shook his head in a manner that seemed intended to convince himself of something, not me.

"Next Tuesday is the anniversary of the murder," he said. "I'm going to announce that we intend to retry Jessup. And I would like you standing next to me at the press conference."

I leaned back in my seat and looked at them. I've spent a good part of my adult life looking across courtrooms and trying to read juries, judges, witnesses and prosecutors. I think I've gotten pretty good at it. But at that table I couldn't read Williams or his sidekick sitting three feet away from me.

Jason Jessup was a convicted child killer who had spent nearly twenty-four years in prison until a month earlier, when the California Supreme Court reversed his conviction and sent the case back to Los Angeles County for either retrial or a dismissal of the charges. The reversal came after a two-decade-long legal battle staged primarily from Jessup's cell and with his own pen. Authoring appeals, motions, complaints and whatever legal challenges he could research, the self-styled lawyer made no headway with state and federal courts but did finally win the attention of an organization of lawyers known as the Genetic Justice Project. They took over his cause and his case and eventually won an order for genetic testing of semen found on the dress of the child Jessup had been convicted of strangling.

Jessup had been convicted before DNA analysis was used in criminal trials. The analysis performed these many years later determined that the semen found on the dress had not come from Jessup but from another unknown individual. Though the courts had repeatedly upheld Jessup's conviction, this new information tipped the scales in Jessup's favor. The state's supreme court cited the DNA findings and other inconsistencies in the evidence and trial record and reversed the case.

This was pretty much the extent of my knowledge of the Jessup case, and it was largely information gathered from newspaper stories and courthouse scuttlebutt. While I had not read the court's complete order, I had read parts of it in the *Los Angeles Times* and knew it was a blistering decision that echoed many of Jessup's long-held claims of innocence as well as police and prosecutorial misconduct in the case. As a defense attorney, I can't say I wasn't pleased to see the DA's office raked over the media coals with the ruling. Call it underdog schadenfreude. It didn't really matter that it wasn't my case or that the current regime in the DA's office had nothing to do with the case back in 1986, there are so few victories from the defense side of the bar that there is always a sense of communal joy in the success of others and the defeat of the establishment.

The supreme court's ruling was announced the week before, starting a sixty-day clock during which the DA would have to retry or discharge Jessup. It seemed that not a day had gone by since the ruling that Jessup was not in the news. He gave multiple interviews by phone and in person at San Quentin, proclaiming his innocence and potshotting the police and prosecutors who put him there. In his plight, he had garnered the support of several Hollywood celebrities and professional athletes and had already launched a civil claim against both the city and county, seeking millions of dollars in damages for the many long years during which he was falsely incarcerated. In this day of nonstop media cycles, he had a never-ending forum and was using it to elevate himself to folk hero status. When he finally walked out of prison, he, too, would be a celebrity.

Knowing as little as I did about the case in the details, I was of the impression that he was an innocent man who had been subjected to a quarter century of torture and that he deserved whatever he could get for it. I did, however, know enough about the case to understand that with the DNA evidence cutting Jessup's way, the case was a loser and the idea of retrying Jessup seemed to be an exercise in political masochism unlikely to come from the brain trust of Williams and Ridell.

Unless...

"What do you know that I don't know?" I asked. "And that the *Los Angeles Times* doesn't know."

Williams smiled smugly and leaned forward across the table to deliver his answer.

"All Jessup established with the help of the GJP is that his DNA was not on the victim's dress," he said. "As the petitioner, it was not up to him to establish who it did come from."

"So you ran it through the data banks."

Williams nodded.

"We did. And we got a hit."

He offered nothing else.

"Well, who was it?"

"I'm not going to reveal that to you unless you come aboard on the case. Otherwise, I need to keep it confidential. But I will say that I believe our findings lead to a trial tactic that could neutralize the DNA question, leaving the rest of the case — and the evidence — pretty much intact. DNA was not needed to convict him the first time. We won't need it now. As in nineteen eighty-six, we believe Jessup is guilty of this crime and I would be delinquent in my duties if I did not attempt to prosecute him, no matter the chances of conviction, the potential political fallout and the public perception of the case."

Spoken as if he were looking at the cameras and not at me.

"Then why don't you prosecute him?" I asked. "Why come to me? You have three hundred able lawyers working for you. I can think of one you've got stuck up in the Van Nuys office who would take this case in a heartbeat. Why come to me?"

"Because this prosecution can't come from within the DA's office. I am sure you have read or heard the allegations. There's a taint on this case and it doesn't matter that there isn't one goddamn lawyer working for me who was around back then. I still need to bring in an outsider, an independent to take it to court. Somebody —"

"That's what the attorney general's office is for," I said. "You need an independent counsel, you go to him."

Now I was just poking him in the eye and everybody at the table knew it. There was no way Gabriel Williams was going to ask the state AG to come in on the case. That would cross the razor-wire line of politics. The AG post was an elected office in California and was seen by every political pundit in town as Williams's next stop on his way to the governor's mansion or some other lofty political plateau. The last thing Williams would be willing to do was hand a potential political rival a case that could be used against him, no matter how old it was. In politics, in the courtroom, in life, you don't give your opponent the club with which he can turn around and clobber you.

"We're not going to the AG with this one," Williams said in a matter-of-fact manner. "That's why I want you, Mickey. You're a well-known and respected criminal defense attorney. I think the public will trust you to be independent in this matter and will therefore trust and accept the conviction you'll win in this case."

While I was staring at Williams a waiter came to the table to take our order. Without ever breaking eye contact with me, Williams told him to go away.

"I haven't been paying a lot of attention to this," I said. "Who's Jessup's defense attorney? I would find it difficult to go up against a colleague I know well."

"Right now all he's got is the GJP lawyer and his civil litigator. He hasn't hired defense counsel because quite frankly he's expecting us to drop this whole thing."

I nodded, another hurdle cleared for the moment.

"But he's got a surprise coming," Williams said. "We're going to bring him down here and retry him. He did it, Mickey, and that's all you really need to know. There's a little girl who's still dead, and that's all any prosecutor needs to know. Take the case. Do something for your community and for yourself. Who knows, you might even like it and want to stay on. If so, we'll definitely entertain the possibility."

I dropped my eyes to the linen tablecloth and thought about his last words. For a moment, I involuntarily conjured the image of my daughter sitting in a courtroom and watching me stand for the People instead of the accused. Williams kept talking, unaware that I had already come to a decision.

"Obviously, I can't pay you your rate, but if you take this on, I don't think you'll be doing it for the money anyway. I can give you an office and a secretary. And I can give you whatever science and forensics you need. The very best of every—"

"I don't want an office in the DA's office. I would need to be independent of that. I have to be completely autonomous. No more lunches. We make the announcement and then you leave me alone. I decide how to proceed with the case."

"Fine. Use your own office, just as long as you don't store evidence there. And, of course, you make your own decisions."

"And if I do this, I pick second chair and my own investigator out of the LAPD. People I can trust."

"In or outside my office for your second?"

"I would need someone inside."

"Then I assume we're talking about your ex-wife."

"That's right—if she'll take it. And if somehow we get a conviction out of this thing, you pull her out of Van Nuys and put her downtown in Major Crimes, where she belongs."

"That's easier said than—"

"That's the deal. Take it or leave it."

Williams glanced at Ridell and I saw the supposed sidekick give an almost imperceptible nod of approval.

"All right," Williams said, turning back to me. "Then I guess I'll take it. You win and she's in. We have a deal."

He reached his hand across the table and I shook it. He smiled but I didn't.

"Mickey Haller for the People," he said. "Has a nice ring to it."

For the People. It should have made me feel good. It should have made me feel like I was part of something that was noble and right. But all I had was the bad feeling that I had crossed some sort of line within myself.

"Wonderful," I said.

2

Friday, February 12, 10:00 A.M.

Harry Bosch stepped up to the front counter of the District Attorney's Office on the eighteenth floor of the Criminal Courts Building. He gave his name and said he had a ten A.M. appointment with District Attorney Gabriel Williams.

"Actually, your meeting is in conference room A," said the receptionist after checking a computer screen in front of her. "You go through the door, turn right and go to the end of the hall. Right again and conference room A is on the left. It's marked on the door. They're expecting you."

The door in the paneled-wood wall behind her buzzed free and Bosch went through, wondering about the fact that *they* were waiting for him. Since he had received the summons from the DA's secretary the afternoon before, Bosch had been unable to determine what it was about. Secrecy was expected from the DA's Office but usually some information trickled out. He hadn't even known he would be meeting with more than one person until now.

Following the prescribed trail, Bosch came to the door marked CONFERENCE ROOM A, knocked once and heard a female voice say, "Come in."

He entered and saw a woman seated by herself at an eight-chaired table, a spread of documents, files, photos and a laptop computer in front of her. She looked vaguely familiar but he could not place her. She was attractive with dark, curling hair framing her face. She had sharp eyes that followed him as he entered, and a pleasant, almost curious smile. Like she knew something he didn't. She wore the standard female prosecutor's power suit in navy blue. Harry might not have been able to place her but he assumed she was a DDA.

"Detective Bosch?"

"That's me."

"Come in, have a seat."

Bosch pulled out a chair and sat across from her. On the table he saw a crime scene photograph of a child's body in an open Dumpster. It was a girl and she was wearing a blue dress with long sleeves. Her feet were bare and she was lying on a pile of construction debris and other trash. The white edges of the photo were yellowed. It was an old print.

The woman moved a file over the picture and then offered her hand across the table.

"I don't think we've ever met," she said. "My name is Maggie McPherson."

Bosch recognized the name but he couldn't remember from where or what case.

"I'm a deputy district attorney," she continued, "and I'm going to be second chair on the Jason Jessup prosecution. First chair —"

"Jason Jessup?" Bosch asked. "You're going to take it to trial?"

"Yes, we are. We'll be announcing it next week and I need to ask you to keep it confidential until then. I am sorry that our first chair is late coming to our meet —"

The door opened and Bosch turned. Mickey Haller stepped into the room. Bosch did a double take. Not because he didn't recognize Haller. They were half brothers and he easily knew him on sight. But seeing Haller in the DA's office was one of those images that didn't quite make sense. Haller was a criminal defense attorney. He fit in at the DA's office about as well as a cat did at the dog pound.

"I know," Haller said. "You're thinking, What in the hell is this?"

Smiling, Haller moved to McPherson's side of the table and started pulling out a chair. Then Bosch remembered how he knew McPherson's name.

"You two...," Bosch said. "You were married, right?"

"That's right," Haller said. "Eight wonderful years."

"And what, she's prosecuting Jessup and you're defending him? Isn't that a conflict of interest?"

Haller's smile became a broad grin.

"It would only be a conflict if we were opposing each other, Harry. But we're not. We're prosecuting him. Together. I'm first chair. Maggie's second. And we want you to be our investigator."

Bosch was completely confused.

"Wait a minute. You're not a prosecutor. This doesn't —"

"I'm an appointed independent prosecutor, Harry. It's all legit. I wouldn't be sitting here if it weren't. We're going after Jessup and we want you to help us."

"From what I heard, this case is beyond help. Unless you're telling me Jessup rigged the DNA test."

"No, we're not telling you that," McPherson said. "We did our own testing and matching. His results were correct. It wasn't his DNA on the victim's dress."

"But that doesn't mean we've lost the case," Haller quickly added.

Bosch looked from McPherson to Haller and then back again. He was clearly missing something.

"Then whose DNA was it?" he asked.

McPherson glanced sideways at Haller before answering.

"Her stepfather's," she said. "He's dead now but we believe there is an explanation for why his semen was found on his stepdaughter's dress."

Haller leaned urgently across the table.

"An explanation that still leaves room to reconvict Jessup of the girl's murder."

Bosch thought for a moment and the image of his own daughter flashed in his mind. He knew there were certain kinds of evil in the world that had to be contained, no matter the hardship. A child killer was at the top of that list.

"Okay," he said. "I'm in."

3

Tuesday, February 16, 1:00 P.M.

The DA's Office had a press conference room that had not been updated since the days they'd used it to hold briefings on the Charles Manson case. Its faded wood-paneled walls and drooping flags in the corner had been the backdrop of a thousand press briefings and they gave all proceedings there a threadbare appearance that belied the true power and might of the office. The state prosecutor was never the underdog in any undertaking, yet it appeared that the office did not have the money for even a fresh coat of paint.

The setting, however, served the announcement on the Jessup decision well. For possibly the first time in these hallowed halls of justice, the prosecution would indeed be the underdog. The decision to retry Jason Jessup was fraught with peril and the realistic likelihood of failure. As I stood at the front of the room next to Gabriel Williams and before a phalanx of video cameras, bright lights and reporters, it finally dawned on me what a terrible mistake I had made. My decision to take on the case in hopes of currying favor with my daughter, ex-wife and myself was going to be met with disastrous consequences. I was going to go down in flames.

It was a rare moment to witness firsthand. The media had gathered to report the end of the story. The DA's Office would assuredly announce that Jason Jessup would not be subjected to a retrial. The DA might not offer an apology but would at the very least say the evidence was not there. That there was no case against this man who had been incarcerated for so long. The case would be closed and in the eyes of the law as well as the public Jessup would finally be a free and innocent man.

The media is rarely fooled in complete numbers and usually doesn't react well when it happens. But there was no doubt that Williams had punked them all. We had moved stealthily in the last week, putting together the team and reviewing the evidence that was still available. Not a word had leaked, which must've been a first in the halls of the CCB. While I could see the first inkling of suspicion creasing the brows of the reporters who recognized me as we entered, it was Williams who delivered the knockout punch when he wasted no time in stepping before a lectern festooned with microphones and digital recorders.

"On a Sunday morning twenty-four years ago today, twelve-year-old Melissa Landy was taken from her yard in Hancock Park and brutally murdered. An investigation quickly led to a suspect named Jason Jessup. He was arrested, convicted at trial and sentenced to life in prison without parole. That conviction was reversed two weeks ago by the state supreme court and remanded to my office. I am here to announce that the Los Angeles County District Attorney's Office will retry Jason Jessup in the death of Melissa Landy. The charges of abduction and murder stand. This office intends once again to prosecute Mr. Jessup to the fullest extent of the law."

He paused to add appropriate gravity to the announcement.

"As you know, the supreme court found that irregularities occurred during the first prosecution—which, of course, occurred more than two decades before the current administration. To avoid political conflicts and any future appearance of impropriety on the part of this office, I have appointed an independent special prosecutor to handle the case. Many of you know of the man standing here to my right. Michael Haller has been a defense counselor of some note in Los Angeles for two decades. He is a fair-minded and respected member of the bar. He has accepted the appointment and has assumed responsibility for the case as of today. It has been the policy of this department not to try cases in the media. However, Mr. Haller and I are willing to answer a few questions as long as they don't tread on the specifics and evidence of the case."

There was a booming chorus of voices calling questions out at us. Williams raised his hands for calm in the room.

"One at a time, people. Let's start with you."

He pointed to a woman sitting in the first row. I could not remember her name but I knew she worked for the *Times*. Williams knew his priorities.

"Kate Salters from the *Times*," she said helpfully. "Can you tell us how you came to the decision to prosecute Jason Jessup again after DNA evidence cleared him of the crime?"

Before coming into the room, Williams had told me that he would handle the announcement and all questions unless specifically addressed to me. He made it clear that this was going to be his show. But I decided to make it clear from the outset that it was going to be my case.

"I'll answer that," I said as I leaned toward the lectern and the microphones. "The DNA test conducted by the Genetic Justice Project only concluded that the bodily fluid found on the victim's clothing did not come from Jason Jessup. It did not clear him of involvement in the crime. There is a difference. The DNA test only provides additional information for a jury to consider."

I straightened back up and caught Williams giving me a don't-fuck-with-me stare.

"Whose DNA was it?" someone called out.

Williams quickly leaned forward to answer.

"We're not answering questions about evidence at this time."

"Mickey, why are you taking the case?"

The question came from the back of the room, from behind the lights, and I could not see the owner of the voice. I moved back to the microphones, angling my body so Williams had to step back.

"Good question," I said. "It's certainly unusual for me to be on the other side of the aisle, so to speak. But I think this is the case to cross over for. I'm an officer of the court and a proud member of the California bar. We take an oath to seek justice and fairness while upholding the Constitution and laws of this nation and state. One of the duties of a lawyer is to take a just cause without personal consideration to himself. This is such a cause. Someone has to speak for Melissa Landy. I have reviewed the evidence in this case and I think I'm on the right side of this one. The measure is proof beyond a reasonable doubt. I think that such proof exists here."

Williams moved in and put a hand on my arm to gently move me off the microphone stand.

"We do not want to go any further than that in regard to the evidence," he said quickly.

"Jessup's already spent twenty-four years in prison," Salters said. "Anything less than a conviction for first-degree murder and he will probably walk on time served. Mr. Williams, is it really worth the expense and effort of retrying this man?"

Before she was finished asking the question, I knew she and Williams had a deal working. She lobbed softballs and he hit them out of the park, looking good and righteous on the eleven o'clock news and in the morning paper. Her end of the deal would come with inside scoops on the evidence and trial strategy. I decided in that moment that it was *my case, my trial, my deal.*

"None of that matters," I said loudly from my position to the side.

All eyes turned to me. Even Williams turned.

"Can you talk into the microphones, Mickey?"

It was the same voice from behind the line of lights. He knew to call me Mickey. I once again moved to the microphones, boxing Williams out like a power forward going for the rebound.

"The murder of a child is a crime that must be prosecuted to the full extent of the law, no matter what the possibilities or risks are. There is no guarantee of victory here. But that was not part of the decision. The measure is reasonable doubt and I believe we surpass that. We believe that the totality of evidence shows that this man committed this horrible crime and it doesn't matter how much time has gone by or how long he has been incarcerated. He must be prosecuted.

"I have a daughter only a little older than Melissa was.... You know, people forget that in the original trial, the state sought the death penalty but the jury recommended against it and the judge imposed a life sentence. That was then and this is now. We will once again be seeking the death penalty on this case."

Williams put his hand on my shoulder and pulled me away from the microphones.

"Uh, let's not get ahead of ourselves here," he said quickly. "My office has not yet made a determination in regard to whether we will be seeking the death penalty. That will come at a later time. But Mr. Haller makes a very valid and sad point. There can be no worse crime in our society than the murder of a child. We must do all that is within our power and our reach to seek justice for Melissa Landy. Thank you for being here today."

"Wait a minute," called a reporter from one of the middle seats. "What about Jessup? When will he be brought here for trial?"

Williams put his hands on both sides of the lectern in a casual move designed to keep me from the microphones.

"Earlier this morning Mr. Jessup was taken into custody by the Los Angeles police and is being transported from San Quentin. He will be booked into the downtown jail and the case will proceed. His conviction was reversed but the charges against him remain in place. We have nothing further at this time."

Williams stepped back and signaled me toward the door. He waited until I started moving and was clear of the microphones. He then followed, coming up behind me and whispering into my ear as we went through the door.

"You do that again and I'll fire you on the spot."

I turned to look back at him while I walked.

"Do what? Answer one of your setup questions?"

We moved into the hallway. Ridell was waiting there with the office's media spokesman, a guy named Fernandez. But Williams turned me down the hall away from them. He was still whispering when he spoke.

"You went off the script. Do it again and we're done."

I stopped and turned and Williams almost walked into me.

"Look, I'm not your puppet," I said. "I'm an independent contractor, remember? You treat me otherwise and you're going to be holding this hot potato without an oven mitt."

Williams just glared at me. I obviously wasn't getting through.

"And what was this shit about the death penalty?" he asked. "We haven't even gotten there and you didn't have the go-ahead to say it."

He was bigger than me, taller. He had used his body to crowd my space and back me up against the wall.

"It will get back to Jessup and keep him thinking," I said. "And if we're lucky, he comes in for a deal and this whole thing goes away, including the civil action. It'll save you all that money. That's really what this is about, right? The money. We get a conviction and he's got no civil case. You and the city save a few million bucks."

"That's got nothing to do with this. This is about justice and you still should have told me what you were doing. You don't sandbag your own boss."

The physical intimidation got old real fast. I put my palm on his chest and backed him off me.

"Yeah, well, you're not my boss. I don't have a boss."

"Is that right? Like I said, I could fire your ass right here right now."

I pointed down the hall to the door to the press conference room.

"Yeah, that'll look good. Firing the independent prosecutor *you* just hired. Didn't Nixon do that during the Watergate mess? Worked real well for him. Why don't we go back in and tell them? I'm sure there are still a few cameras in there."

Williams hesitated, realizing his predicament. I had backed him against the wall without even moving. He would look like a complete and unelectable fool if he fired me, and he knew it. He leaned in closer and his whisper dropped lower as he used the oldest threat in the mano a mano handbook. I was ready for it.

"Do not fuck with me, Haller."

"Then don't fuck with my case. This isn't a campaign stop and it's not about money. This is murder, boss. You want me to get a conviction, then get out of my way."

I threw him the bone of calling him boss. Williams pressed his mouth into a tight line and stared at me for a long moment.

"Just so we understand each other," he finally said.

I nodded.

"Yeah, I think we do."

"Before you talk to the media about this case, you get it approved by my office first. Understand?"

"Got it."

He turned and headed down the hall. His entourage followed. I remained in the hallway and watched them go. The truth was, there was nothing in the law that I objected to more than the death penalty. It was not that I had ever had a client executed or even tried such a case. It was simply a belief in the idea that an enlightened society did not kill its own.

But somehow that didn't stop me from using the threat of the death penalty as an edge in the case. As I stood there alone in the hallway, I thought that maybe that made me a better prosecutor than I had imagined I could be.

Tuesday, February 16, 2:43 P.M.

It usually was the best moment of a case. The drive downtown with a suspect handcuffed in the backseat. There was nothing better. Sure there was the eventual payoff of a conviction down the line. Being in the courtroom when the verdict is read — watching the reality shock and then deaden the eyes of the convicted. But the drive in was always better, more immediate and personal. It was always the moment Bosch savored. The chase was over and the case was about to morph from the relentless momentum of the investigation to the measured pace of the prosecution.

But this time was different. It had been a long two days and Bosch wasn't savoring anything. He and his partner, David Chu, had driven up to Corta Madera the day before, checking into a motel off the 101 and spending the night. In the morning they drove over to San Quentin, presented a court order that transferred custody of Jason Jessup to them, and then collected their prisoner for the drive back to Los Angeles. Seven hours each way with a partner who talked too much. Seven hours on the return with a suspect who didn't talk enough.

They were now at the top of the San Fernando Valley and an hour from the City Jail in downtown L.A. Bosch's back hurt from so many hours behind the wheel. His right calf muscle ached from applying pressure to the gas pedal. The city car did not have cruise control.

Chu had offered to drive but Bosch had said no. Chu religiously stuck to the speed limit, even on the freeway. Bosch would take the backache over an extra hour on the freeway and the anxiety it would create.

All of this aside, he drove in uneasy silence, brooding about a case that seemed to be proceeding backwards. He had been on it for only a few days, hadn't had the opportunity to even become acquainted with all the facts, and here he was with the suspect hooked up and in the backseat. To Bosch it felt like the arrest was coming first and the investigation wouldn't really start until after Jessup was booked.

He checked his watch and knew the scheduled press conference must be over by now. The plan was for him to meet with Haller and McPherson at four to continue kicking around the case. But by the time Jessup was booked he would be late. He also needed to go by LAPD archives to pick up two boxes that were waiting for him.

"Harry, what's wrong?"

Bosch glanced at Chu.

"Nothing's wrong."

He wasn't going to talk in front of the suspect. Besides, he and Chu had been partnered for less than a year. It was a little soon for Chu to be making reads off of Bosch's demeanor. Harry didn't want him to know that he had accurately deduced that he was uncomfortable.

Jessup spoke from the backseat, his first words since asking for a bathroom break outside of Stockton.

"What's wrong is that he doesn't have a case. What's wrong is that he knows this whole thing is bullshit and he doesn't want to be part of it."

Bosch checked Jessup in the rearview mirror. He was slightly hunched forward because his hands were cuffed and locked to a chain that went to a set of shackles around his ankles. His head was shaved, a routine prison practice among men hoping to intimidate others. Bosch guessed that with Jessup it had probably worked.

"I thought you didn't want to talk, Jessup. You invoked."

"Yeah, that's right. I'll just shut the fuck up and wait for my lawyer."

"He's in San Francisco, I wouldn't hold my breath."

"He's calling somebody. The GJP's got people all over the country. We were ready for this."

"Really? You were ready? You mean you packed your cell up because you thought you were being transferred? Or was it because you thought you were going home?"

Jessup didn't have an answer for that one.

Bosch merged onto the 101, which would take them through the Cahuenga Pass and into Hollywood before they reached downtown.

"How'd you get hooked up with the Genetic Justice Project, Jessup?" he asked, trying once again to get something going. "You go to them or they come to you?"

"Website, man. I sent in my appeal and they saw the bullshit going on in my case. They took it over and here I am. You people are totally fucked if you think you're going to win this. I was railroaded by you motherfuckers once before. Ain't gonna happen again. In two months, this'll all be over. I've been in twenty-four years. What's two more months? Just makes my book rights more valuable. I guess I should be thanking you and the district attorney for that."

Bosch glanced at the mirror again. Normally, he would love a talkative suspect. Most times they talked themselves right into prison. But Jessup was too smart and too cagey. He chose his words carefully, stayed away from talking about the crime itself, and wouldn't be making a mistake that Bosch could use.

In the mirror now, Bosch could see Jessup staring out the window. No telling what he was thinking about. His eyes looked dead. Bosch could see the top of a prison ink tattoo on his neck, just breaking the collar line. It looked like part of a word but he couldn't tell for sure.

"Welcome to L.A., Jessup," Chu said without turning around. "Guess it's been a while, huh?"

"Fuck you, you chink motherfucker," Jessup retorted. "This'll all be over soon and then I'll be out and on the beach. I'm going to get a longboard and ride some tasty waves."

"Don't count on it, killer," Chu said. "You're going down. We got you by the balls."

Bosch knew Chu was trying to provoke a response, a slip of the tongue. But he was coming off as an amateur and Jessup was too wise for him.

Harry grew tired of the back-and-forth, even after six hours of almost complete silence. He turned on the car's radio and caught the tail end of a report on the DA's press conference. He turned it up so Jessup would hear, and Chu would keep quiet.

"Williams and Haller refused to comment on the evidence but indicated they were not as impressed with the DNA analysis as the state's supreme court was. Haller acknowledged that the DNA found on the victim's dress did not come from Jessup. But he said the findings did not clear him of involvement in the crime. Haller is a well-known defense attorney and will be prosecuting a murder case for the first time. It did not sound this morning as though he has any hesitation. 'We will once again be seeking the death penalty on this case.'"

Bosch flicked the volume down and checked the mirror. Jessup was still looking out the window.

"How about that, Jessup? He's going for the Jesus juice."

Jessup responded tiredly.

"Asshole's posturing. Besides, they don't execute anybody in this state anymore. You know what *death row* means? It means you get a cell all to yourself and you control what's on the TV. It means better access to phone, food and visitors. Fuck it, I hope he does go for it, man. But it won't matter. This is bullshit. This whole thing is bullshit. It's all about the money."

The last line floated out there for a long moment before Bosch finally bit.
"What money?"

"My money. You watch, man, they'll come at me with a deal. My lawyer told me. They'll want me to take a deal and plead to time served so they don't have to pay me the money. That's all this fucking is and you two are just the deliverymen. Fuckin' FedEx."

Bosch was silent. He wondered if it could be true. Jessup was suing the city and county for millions. Could it be that the retrial was simply a political move designed to save money? Both government entities were self-insured. Juries loved hitting faceless corporations and bureaucracies with obscenely large judgments. A jury believing prosecutors and police had corruptly imprisoned an innocent man for twenty-four years would be beyond generous. A hit from an eight-figure judgment could be devastating to both city and county coffers, even if they were splitting the bill.

But if they jammed Jessup and maneuvered him into a deal in which he acknowledged guilt to gain his freedom, then the lawsuit would go away. So would all the book and movie money he was counting on.

"Makes a lot of sense, doesn't it?" Jessup said.

Bosch checked the mirror and realized that now Jessup was studying him. He turned his eyes back to the road. He felt his phone vibrate and pulled it out of his jacket.

"You want me to take it, Harry?" Chu asked.

A reminder that it was illegal to talk on a phone while driving an automobile. Bosch ignored him and took the call. It was Lieutenant Gandle.

"Harry, you close?"

"Getting off the one-oh-one."

"Good. I just wanted to give you a heads-up. They're lining up at intake. Comb your hair."

"Got it, but maybe I'll give my partner the airtime."

Bosch glanced over at Chu but didn't explain.

"Either way," Gandle said. "What's next?"

"He invoked so we just book him. Then I have to go back to the war room and meet with the prosecutors. I've got questions."

"Harry, do they have this guy or not?"

Bosch checked Jessup in the mirror. He was back to looking out the window.

"I don't know, Lieutenant. When I know, you'll know."

A few minutes later they pulled into the rear lot of the jail. There were several television cameras and their operators lined up on a ramp leading to the intake door. Chu sat up straight.

"Perp walk, Harry."

"Yeah. You take him in."

"Let's both do it."

"Nah, I'll hang back."

"You sure?"

"I'm sure. Just don't forget my cuffs."

"Okay, Harry."

The lot was clogged with media vans with their transmitters cranked to full height. But they had left the space in front of the ramp open. Bosch pulled in and parked.

"Okay, you ready back there, Jessup?" Chu asked. "Time to sell tickets."

Jessup didn't respond. Chu opened the door and got out, then opened the rear door for Jessup.

Bosch watched the ensuing spectacle from the confines of the car.

5

Tuesday, February 16, 4:14 P.M.

One of the very best things about having previously been married to Maggie McPherson was that I never had to face her in court. The marital split created a conflict of interest that saved me professional defeat and humiliation at her hands on more than one occasion. She was truly the best prosecutor I'd ever seen step into the well and they didn't call her Maggie McFierce for no reason.

Now, for the first time, we would be on the same team in court, sitting side by side at the same table. But what had seemed like such a good idea — not to mention such a positive potential payoff for Maggie — was already manifesting itself as something jagged and rusty. Maggie was having issues with being second chair. And for good reason. She was a professional prosecutor. From drug dealers and petty thieves to rapists and murderers, she had put dozens of criminals behind bars. I had appeared in dozens of trials myself but never as a prosecutor. Maggie would have to play backup to a novice and that realization wasn't sitting well with her.

We sat in conference room A with the case files spread out before us on the big table. Though Williams had said I could run the case from my own independent office, the truth was, that wasn't practical at the moment. I didn't have an office outside my home. I primarily used the backseat of my Lincoln Town Car as my office and that wouldn't do for *The People versus Jason Jessup*. I had my case manager setting up a temporary office in downtown but we were at least a few days away from that. So temporarily there we sat, eyes down and tensions up.

"Maggie," I said, "when it comes to prosecuting bad guys, I will readily admit that I couldn't carry your lunch. But the thing is, when it comes to politics *and* prosecuting bad guys, the powers that be have put me in the first chair. That's the way it is and we can either accept it or not. I took this job and asked for you. If you don't think we —"

"I just don't like the idea of carrying your briefcase through this whole thing," Maggie said.

"You won't be. Look, press conferences and outward appearances are one thing, but I fully assume that we'll be working as a tag team. You'll be conducting just as much of the investigation as I will be, probably more. The trial should be no different. We'll come up with a strategy and choreograph it together. But you have to give me a little credit. I know my way around a courtroom. I'll just be sitting at the other table this time."

"That's where you're wrong, Mickey. On the defense side you have a responsibility to one person. Your client. When you are a prosecutor, you represent the people and that is a lot more responsibility. That's why they call it the *burden of proof.*"

"Whatever. If you're saying I shouldn't be doing this, then I'm not the guy you should be complaining to. Go down the hall and talk to your boss. But if he kicks me off the case, you get kicked as well, and then you go back to Van Nuys for the rest of your career. Is that what you want?"

She didn't answer and that was an answer in itself.

"Okay, then," I said. "Let's just try to get through this without pulling each other's hair out, okay? Remember, I'm not here to count convictions and advance my career. For me, it's one and done. So we both want the same thing. Yes, you will have to help me. But you will also be helping —"

My phone started vibrating. I had left it out on the table. I didn't recognize the number on the screen but took the call, just to get away from the conversation with Maggie.

"Haller."

"Hey, Mick, how'd I do?"

"Who is this?"

"Sticks."

Sticks was a freelance videographer who fed footage to the local news channels and sometimes even the bigs. I had known him so long I didn't even remember his real name.

"How'd you do at what, Sticks? I'm busy here."

"At the press conference. I set you up, man."

I realized that it had been Sticks behind the lights, throwing the questions to me.

"Oh, yeah, yeah, you did good. Thanks for that."

"Now you're going to take care of me on the case, right? Give me the heads-up if there's something for me, right? Something exclusive."

"Yeah, no need to worry, Sticks. I got you covered. But I gotta go."

I ended the call and put the phone back on the table. Maggie was typing something into her laptop. It looked like the momentary discontent had passed and I was hesitant to touch it again.

"That was a guy who works for the news stations. He might be useful to us at some point."

"We don't want to do anything underhanded. The prosecution is held to a much higher standard of ethics than the defense."

I shook my head. I couldn't win.

"That's bullshit and I am not talking about doing anything un—"

The door opened and Harry Bosch stepped in, pushing the door with his back because he was carrying two large boxes in his hands.

"Sorry, I'm late," he said.

He put the boxes down on the table. I could tell the larger one was a carton from evidence archives. I guessed that the smaller one contained the police file on the original investigation.

"It took them three days to find the murder box. It was on the 'eighty-five aisle instead of 'eighty-six."

He looked at me and then at Maggie and then back at me.

"So what'd I miss? War break out in the war room?"

"We were talking about prosecutorial tactics and it turns out we have opposing views."

"Imagine that."

He took the chair at the end of the table. I could tell he was going to have more to say. He lifted the top off the murder box and pulled out three accordion files and put them on the table. He then moved the box to the floor.

"You know, Mick, while we're airing out our differences...I think before you pulled me into this little soap opera, you should've told me a few things up front."

"Like what, Harry?"

"Like that this whole goddamn thing is about money and not murder."

"What are you talking about? What money?"

Bosch just stared at me without responding.

"You're talking about Jessup's lawsuit?" I asked.

"That's right," he said. "I had an interesting discussion with Jessup today on the drive down. Got me thinking and it crossed my mind that if we jam this guy into a deal, the lawsuit against the city and county goes away because a guy who admits to murder isn't going to be able to sue and claim he was railroaded. So I guess what I want to know is what we're really doing here. Are we trying to put a murder suspect on trial or are we just trying to save the city and county a few million bucks?"

I noticed Maggie's posture straighten as she considered the same thing.

"You gotta be kidding me," she said. "If that—"

"Hold on, hold on," I interjected. "Let's be cool about this. I don't think that's the case here, okay? It's not that I haven't thought about it but Williams didn't say one word about going for a dispo on this case. He told me to take it to trial. In fact, he assumes it will go to trial for the same reason you just mentioned. Jessup will never take a dispo for time served or anything else because there is no pot of gold in that. No book, no movie, no payout from the city. If he wants the money, he's got to go to trial and win."

Maggie nodded slowly as if weighing a valid supposition. Bosch didn't seem appeased at all.

"But how would you know what Williams is up to?" he asked. "You're an outsider. They could've brought you in, wound you up and pointed you in the right direction and then sat back to watch you go."

"He's right," Maggie added. "Jessup doesn't even have a defense attorney. As soon as he does he'll start talking deal."

I raised my hands in a calming gesture.

"Look, at the press conference today. I threw out that we were going for the death penalty. I just did that to see how Williams would react. He didn't expect it and afterward he pressed me in the hallway. He told me that it wasn't a decision I got to make. I told him it was just strategy, that I wanted Jessup to start thinking about a deal. And it gave Williams pause. He didn't see it. If he was thinking of a deal just to blow up the civil action, I would have been able to read it. I'm good at reading people."

I could tell I still hadn't quite won Bosch over.

"Remember last year, with the two men from Hong Kong who wanted your ass on the next plane to China? I read them right and I played them right."

In his eyes I saw Bosch relent. That China story was a reminder that he owed me one and I was collecting.

"Okay," he said. "So what do we do?"

"We assume Jessup's going to go to trial. As soon as he lawyers up, we'll know for sure. But we start preparing for it now, because if I was going to represent him, I would refuse to waive speedy trial. I would try to jam the prosecution on time to prepare and make the people put up or shut up."

I checked the date on my watch.

"If I'm right, that gives us forty-eight days till trial. We've got a lot of work to do between now and then."

We looked at one another and sat in silence for a few moments before I threw the lead to Maggie.

"Maggie has spent the better part of the last week with the prosecution file on this. Harry, I know what you just brought in will have a lot of overlap. But why don't we start here by having Mags go through the case as presented at trial in 'eighty-six? I think that will give us a good starting point of looking at what we need to do this time out."

Bosch nodded his approval and I signaled for Maggie to begin. She pulled her laptop over in front of her.

"Okay, a couple of basics first. Because it was a death penalty case, jury selection was the longest part of the trial. Almost three weeks. The trial itself lasted seven days and then there were three days of deliberation on the initial verdicts, then the death penalty phase went another two weeks. But seven days of testimony and arguments — that to me is fast for a capital murder case. It was pretty cut-and-dried. And the defense...well, there wasn't much of a defense."

She looked at me as if I were responsible for the poor defense of the accused, even though I hadn't even gotten out of law school by 'eighty-six.

"Who was his lawyer?" I asked.

"Charles Barnard," she said. "I checked with the California bar. He won't be handling the retrial. He's listed as deceased as of 'ninety-four. The prosecutor, Gary Lintz, is also long gone."

"Don't remember either of them. Who was the judge?"

"Walter Sackville. He's long retired but I do remember him. He was tough."

"I had a few cases with him," Bosch added. "He wouldn't take any shit from either side."

"Go on," I said.

"Okay, so the prosecution's story was this. The Landy family — that was our victim, Melissa, who was twelve, her thirteen-year-old sister, Sarah, mother, Regina, and stepfather, Kensington — lived on Windsor Boulevard in Hancock Park. The home was about a block north of Wilshire and in the vicinity of the Trinity United Church of God, which on Sundays back then drew about six thousand people to its two morning services. People parked their cars all over Hancock Park to go to the church. That is, until the residents there got tired of their neighborhood being overrun every Sunday with traffic and parking issues and went to City Hall about it. They got the neighborhood turned into a residential parking zone during weekend hours. You had to have a sticker to park on the streets, including Windsor. This opened the door to city-contracted tow truck operators patrolling the neighborhood like sharks on Sunday morning. Any cars without the proper resident sticker on the windshield were fair game. They got towed. Which finally brings us to Jason Jessup, our suspect."

"He drove a tow truck," I said.

"Exactly. He was a driver for a city contractor named Aardvark Towing. Cute name, got them to the front of the listings in the phone book back when people still used phone books."

I glanced at Bosch and could tell by his reaction that he was somebody who still used the phone book instead of the Internet. Maggie didn't notice and continued.

"On the morning in question Jessup was working the Hancock Park patrol. At the Landy house, the family happened to be putting a pool in the backyard. Kensington Landy was a musician who scored films and was doing quite well at the time. So they were putting in a pool and there was a large open hole and giant piles of dirt in the backyard. The parents didn't want the girls playing back there. Thought it was dangerous, plus on this morning the girls were in their church dresses. The house has a large front yard. The stepfather told the girls to play outside for a few minutes before the family was planning to go off to church themselves. The older one, Sarah, was told to watch over Melissa."

"Did they go to Trinity United?" I asked.

"No, they went to Sacred Heart in Beverly Hills. Anyway, the kids were only out there about fifteen minutes. Mother was still upstairs getting ready and the stepfather, who was also supposed to be keeping an eye on the girls, was watching television inside. An overnight sports report on ESPN or whatever they had back then. He forgot about the girls."

Bosch shook his head, and I knew exactly how he felt. It was not in judgment of the father but in understanding of how it could have happened and in the dread of any parent who knows how a small mistake could be so costly.

"At some point, he heard screaming," Maggie continued. "He ran out the front door and found the older girl, Sarah, in the yard. She was screaming that a man took Melissa. The stepfather ran up the street looking for her but there was no sign. Like that, she was gone."

My ex-wife stopped there for a moment to compose herself. Everyone in the room had a young daughter and could understand the shearing of life that happened at that moment for every person in the Landy family.

"Police were called and the response was quick," she continued. "This was Hancock Park, after all. The first bulletins were out in a matter of minutes. Detectives were dispatched right away."

"So this whole thing went down in broad daylight?" Bosch asked.

Maggie nodded.

"It happened about ten-forty. The Landys were going to an eleven o'clock service."

"And nobody else saw this?"

"You gotta remember, this was Hancock Park. A lot of tall hedges, a lot of walls, a lot of privacy. People there are good at keeping the world out. Nobody saw anything. Nobody heard anything until Sarah started screaming, and by then it was too late."

"Was there a wall or a hedge at the Landy house?"

"Six-foot hedges down the north and south property lines but not on the street side. It was theorized at the time that Jessup drove by in his tow truck and saw the girl alone in the yard. Then he acted impulsively."

We sat in silence for a few moments as we thought about the wrenching serendipity of fate. A tow truck goes by a house. The driver sees a girl, alone and vulnerable. All in a moment he figures he can grab her and get away with it.

"So," Bosch finally said, "how did they get him?"

"The responding detectives were on the scene in less than an hour. The lead was named Doral Kloster and his partner was Chad Steiner. I checked. Steiner is dead and Kloster is retired and has late-stage Alzheimer's. He's no use to us now."

"Damn," Bosch said.

"Anyway, they got there quickly and moved quickly. They interviewed Sarah and she described the abductor as being dressed like a garbage man. Further questioning revealed this to mean that he was wearing dirty coveralls like the city garbage crews used. She said she heard the garbage truck in the street but couldn't see it through a bush where she had hidden from her sister during a game of hide-and-seek. Problem is that it was a Sunday. There was no garbage pickup on Sundays. But the stepfather hears this and puts it together, mentions the tow trucks that run up and down the street on Sunday mornings. That becomes their best lead. The detectives get the list of city contractors and they start visiting tow yards.

"There were three contractors who worked the Wilshire corridor. One of them is Aardvark, where they go and are told they have three trucks working in the field. The drivers are called in and Jessup is one of them. The other two guys are named Derek Wilbern and William Clinton — really. They're separated and questioned but nothing comes up suspicious. They run 'em through the box and Jessup and Clinton are clean but Wilbern has an arrest but no conviction on an attempted rape two years before. That would be good enough to get him a ride downtown for a lineup, but the girl is still missing and there's no time for formalities, no time to put together a lineup."

"They probably took him back to the house," Bosch said. "They had no choice. They had to keep things moving."

"That's right. But Kloster knew he was on thin ice. He might get the girl to ID Wilbern but then he'd lose it in court for being unduly suggestive — you know, 'Is this the guy?' So he did the next best thing he could. He took all three drivers in their overalls back to the Landy house. Each was a white man in his twenties. They all wore the company overalls. Kloster broke procedure for the sake of speed, hoping to have a chance to find the girl alive. Sarah Landy's bedroom was on the second floor in the front of the house. Kloster takes the girl up to her room and has her look out the window to the street. Through the venetian blinds. He radios his partner, who has the three guys get out of two patrol cars and stand in the street. But Sarah doesn't ID Wilbern. She points to Jessup and says that's the guy."

Maggie looked through the documents in front of her and checked an investigative chronology before continuing.

"The ID is made at one o'clock. That is really quick work. The girl's only been gone a little over two hours. They start sweating Jessup but he doesn't give up a thing. Denies it all. They are working on him and getting nowhere when the call comes in. A girl's body has been found in a Dumpster behind the El Rey Theatre on Wilshire. That was about ten blocks from Windsor and the Landy house. Cause of death would later be determined to be manual strangulation. She was not raped and there was no semen in the mouth or throat."

Maggie stopped her summary there. She looked at Bosch and then me and solemnly nodded, giving the dead her moment.

6

≈≈≈

Tuesday, February 16, 4:48 P.M.

Bosch liked watching her and listening to the way she talked. He could tell the case was already under her skin. Maggie McFierce. Of course that was what they called her. More important, it was what she thought about herself. He had been on the case with her for less than a week but he understood this within the first hour of meeting her. She knew the secret. That it wasn't about code and procedure. It wasn't about jurisprudence and strategy. It was about taking that dark thing that you knew was out there in the world and bringing it inside. Making it yours. Forging it over an internal fire into something sharp and strong that you could hold in your hands and fight back with.

Relentlessly.

"Jessup asked for a lawyer and gave no further statement," McPherson said, continuing her summary. "The case was initially built around the older sister's identification and evidence found in Jessup's tow truck. Three strands of the victim's hair found in the seat crack. It was probably where he strangled her."

"There was nothing on the girl?" Bosch asked. "Nothing from Jessup or the truck?"

"Nothing usable in court. The DNA was found on her dress while it was being examined two days later. It was actually the older girl's dress. The younger girl borrowed it that day. One small deposit of semen was found on the front hem. It was typed but of course there was no DNA in criminal prosecutions back then. A blood type was determined and it was A-positive, the second-most popular type among humans, accounting for thirty-four percent of the population. Jessup matched but all it did was include him in the suspect pool. The prosecutor decided not to introduce it at trial because it would've just given the defense the ability to point out to the jury that the donor pool was more than a million men in Los Angeles County alone."

Bosch saw her throw another look at her ex-husband. As if he were responsible for the courtroom obfuscations of all defense attorneys everywhere. Harry was starting to get an idea about why their marriage didn't work out.

"It's amazing how far we've come," Haller said. "Now they make and break cases on the DNA alone."

"Moving on," McPherson said. "The prosecution had the hair evidence and the eyewitness. It also had opportunity—Jessup knew the neighborhood and was working there the morning of the murder. As far as motivation went, their backgrounding of Jessup produced a history of physical abuse by his father and psychopathic behavior. A lot of this came out on the record during the death penalty phase, too. But—and I will say this before you jump on it, Haller—no criminal convictions."

"And you said no sexual assault?" Bosch asked.

"No evidence of penetration or sexual assault. But this was no doubt a sexually motivated crime. The semen aside, it was a classic control crime. The perpetrator seizing momentary control in a world where he felt he controlled very little. He acted impulsively. At the time, the semen found on her dress was a piece of the same puzzle. It was theorized that he killed the girl and then masturbated, cleaning up after himself but leaving one small deposit of semen on the dress by mistake. The stain had the appearance of a transfer deposit. It wasn't a drop. It was a smear."

"The hit we just got on the DNA helps explain that," Haller said.

"Possibly," McPherson responded. "But let's discuss new evidence later. Right now, I'm talking about what they had and what they knew in nineteen eighty-six."

"Fine. Go on."

"That's it on the evidence but not on the prosecution's case. Two months before trial they get a call from the guy who's in the cell next to Jessup at County. He—"

"Jailhouse snitches," Haller said, interrupting. "Never met one who told the truth, never met a prosecutor who didn't use them anyway."

"Can I continue?" McPherson asked indignantly.

"Please do," Haller responded.

"Felix Turner, a repeat drug offender who was in and out of County so often that they made him a jail orderly because he knew the day-to-day operations as well as the deputies. He delivered meals to inmates in high-power lockdown. He tells investigators that Jessup provided him with details that only the killer would know. He was interviewed and he did indeed have details of the crime that were not made public. Like that the victim's shoes were removed, that she was not sexually assaulted, that he had wiped himself off on her dress."

"And so they believed him and made him the star witness," Haller said.

"They believed him and put him on the stand at trial. Not as a star witness. But his testimony was significant. Nevertheless, four years later, the *Times* comes out with a front-page exposé on Felix 'The Burner' Turner, professional jailhouse snitch who had testified for the prosecution in sixteen different cases over a seven-year period, garnering significant reductions in charges and jail time, and other perks like private cells, good jobs and large quantities of cigarettes."

Bosch remembered the scandal. It rocked the DA's office in the early nineties and resulted in changes in the use of jailhouse informants as trial witnesses. It was one of many black eyes local law enforcement suffered in the decade.

"Turner was discredited in the newspaper investigation. It said he used a private investigator on the outside to gather information on crimes and then to feed it to him. As you may remember, it changed how we used information that comes to us through the jails."

"Not enough," Haller said. "It didn't end the entire use of jailhouse snitches and it should have."

"Can we just focus on our case here?" McPherson said, obviously tired of Haller's posturing.

"Sure," Haller said. "Let's focus."

"Okay, well, by the time the *Times* came out with all of this, Jessup had long been convicted and was sitting in San Quentin. He of course launched an appeal citing police and prosecutorial misconduct. It went nowhere fast, with every appellate panel agreeing that while the use of Turner as a witness was egregious, his impact on the jury was not enough to have changed the verdict. The rest of the evidence was more than enough to convict."

"And that was that," Haller said. "They rubber-stamped it."

"An interesting note is that Felix Turner was found murdered in West Hollywood a year after the *Times* exposé," McPherson said. "The case was never solved."

"Had it coming as far as I'm concerned," Haller added.

That brought a pause to the discussion. Bosch used it to steer the meeting back to the evidence and to step in with some questions he had been considering.

"Is the hair evidence still available?"

It took McPherson a moment to drop Felix Turner and go back to the evidence.

"Yes, we still have it," she said. "This case is twenty-four years old but it was always under challenge. That's where Jessup and his jailhouse lawyering actually helped us. He was constantly filing writs and appeals. So the trial evidence was never destroyed. Of course, that eventually allowed him to get the DNA analysis off the swatch cut from the dress, but we still have all trial evidence and will be able to use it. He has claimed since day one that the hair in the truck was planted by the police."

"I don't think his defense at retrial will be much different from what was presented at his first trial and in his appeals," Haller said. "The girl made the wrong ID in a prejudicial setting, and from then on it was a rush to judgment. Facing a monumental lack of physical evidence, the police planted hair from the victim in his tow truck. It didn't play so well before a jury in 'eighty-six, but that was before Rodney King and the riots in 'ninety-two, the O.J. Simpson case, the Rampart scandal and all the other controversies that have engulfed the police department since. It's probably going to play really well now."

"So then, what are our chances?" Bosch asked.

Haller looked across the table at McPherson before answering.

"Based on what we know so far," he said, "I think I'd have a better chance if I were on the other side of the aisle on this one."

Bosch saw McPherson's eyes grow dark.

"Well then, maybe you should cross back over."

Haller shook his head.

"No, I made a deal. It may have been a bad deal but I'm sticking to it. Besides, it's not often I get to be on the side of might and right. I could get used to that — even in a losing cause."

He smiled at his ex-wife but she didn't return the sentiment.

"What about the sister?" Bosch asked.

McPherson swung her gaze toward him.

"The witness? That's our second problem. If she's alive, then she's thirty-seven now. Finding her is the problem. No help from the parents. Her real father died when she was seven. Her mother committed suicide on her sister's grave three years after the murder. And the stepfather drank himself into liver failure and died while waiting for a transplant six years ago. I had one of the investigators here do a quick rundown on her on the computer and Sarah Landy's trail drops off in San Francisco about the same time her stepfather died. That same year she also cleared a probation tail for a controlled substance conviction. Records show she's been married and divorced twice, arrested multiple times for drugs and petty crimes. And then, like I said, she dropped off the grid. She either died or cleaned up her act. Even if she changed names, her prints would have left a trail if she'd been popped again in the past six years. But there's nothing."

"I don't think we have much of a case if we don't have her," Haller said. "We're going to need a real live person to point the finger across twenty-four years and say he did it."

"I agree," McPherson said. "She's key. The jury will need to hear the woman tell them that as a girl she did not make a mistake. That she was sure then and she is sure now. If we can't find her and get her to do that, then we have the victim's hair to go with and that's about it. They'll have the DNA and that will trump everything."

"And we will go down in flames," Haller said.

McPherson didn't respond, but she didn't have to.

"Don't worry," Bosch said. "I'll find her."

The two lawyers looked at him. It wasn't a time for empty rah-rah speeches. He meant it.

"If she's alive," he said, "I'll find her."

"Good," Haller said. "That'll be your first priority."

Bosch took out his key chain and opened the small penknife attached to it. He used it to cut the red seal on the evidence box. He had no idea what would be in the box. The evidence that had been introduced at trial twenty-four years earlier was still in the possession of the DA's Office. This box would contain other evidence that was gathered but not presented at trial.

Bosch put on a set of latex gloves from his pocket and then opened the box. On top was a paper bag that contained the victim's dress. It was a surprise. He had assumed that the dress had been introduced at trial, if only for the sympathetic response it would get from the jurors.

Opening the bag brought a musty smell to the room. He lifted the dress out, holding it up by the shoulders. All three of them were silent. Bosch was holding up a dress that a little girl had been wearing when she was murdered. It was blue with a darker blue bow in the front. A six-inch square had been cut out of the front hem, the location of the semen stain.

"Why is this here?" Bosch asked. "Wouldn't they have presented this at trial?"

Haller said nothing. McPherson leaned forward and looked closely at the dress as she considered a response.

"I think...they didn't show it because of the cutout. Showing the dress would let the defense ask about the cutout. That would lead to the blood-typing. The prosecution chose not to get into it during the presentation of the evidence. They probably relied on crime scene photos that showed the girl in the dress. They left it to the defense to introduce it and they never did."

Bosch folded the dress and put it down on the table. Also in the box was a pair of black patent leather shoes. They seemed very small and sad to him. There was a second paper bag, which contained the victim's underwear and socks. An accompanying lab report stated that the items had been checked for bodily fluids as well as hair and fiber evidence but no such evidence had been found.

At the bottom of the box was a plastic bag containing a silver necklace with a charm on it. He looked at it through the plastic and identified the figure on the charm as Winnie the Pooh. There was also a bag containing a bracelet of aqua-blue beads on an elastic string.

"That's it," he said.

"We should have forensics take a fresh look at it all," McPherson said. "You never know. Technology has advanced quite a bit in twenty-four years."

"I'll get it done," Bosch said.

"By the way," McPherson asked, "where were the shoes found? They're not on the victim's feet in the crime scene photos."

Bosch looked at the property report that was taped to the inside of the box's top.

"According to this they were found underneath the body. They must've come off in the truck, maybe when she was strangled. The killer threw them into the Dumpster first, then dropped in her body."

The images conjured by the items in the box had brought a decidedly somber mood to the prosecution team. Bosch started to carefully return everything to the box. He put the envelope containing the necklace in last.

"How old was your daughter when she left Winnie the Pooh behind?" he asked.

Haller and McPherson looked at each other. Haller deferred.

"Five or six," McPherson said. "Why?"

"Mine, too, I think. But this twelve-year-old had it on her necklace. I wonder why."

"Maybe because of where it came from," Haller said. "Hayley — our daughter — still wears a bracelet I got for her about five years ago."

McPherson looked at him as if challenging the assertion.

"Not all the time," Haller said quickly. "But on occasion. Sometimes when I pick her up. Maybe the necklace came from her real father before he died."

A low chime came from McPherson's computer and she checked her e-mail. She studied the screen for a few moments before speaking.

"This is from John Rivas, who handles afternoon arraignments in Department one hundred. Jessup's now got a criminal defense attorney and John's working on getting Jessup on the docket for a bail hearing. He's coming over on the last bus from City Jail."

"Who's the lawyer?" Haller asked.

"You'll love this. Clever Clive Royce is taking the case pro bono. It's a referral from the GJP."

Bosch knew the name. Royce was a high-profile guy who was a media darling who never missed a chance to stand in front of a camera and say all the things he wasn't allowed to say in court.

"Of course he's taking it pro bono," Haller said. "He'll make it up on the back end. Sound bites and headlines, that's all Clive cares about."

"I've never gone up against him," McPherson said. "I can't wait."

"Is Jessup actually on the docket?"

"Not yet. But Royce is talking to the clerk. Rivas wants to know if we want him to handle it. He'll oppose bail."

"No, we'll take it," Haller said. "Let's go."

McPherson closed her computer at the same time Bosch put the top back on the evidence box.

"You want to come?" Haller asked him. "Get a look at the enemy?"

"I just spent seven hours with him, remember?"

"I don't think he was talking about Jessup," McPherson said.

Bosch nodded.

"No, I'll pass," he said. "I'm going to take this stuff over to SID and get to work on tracking down our witness. I'll let you know when I find her."

7

Tuesday, February 16, 5:30 P.M.

Department 100 was the largest courtroom in the CCB and reserved for morning and evening arraignment court, the twin intake points of the local justice system. All those charged with crimes had to be brought before a judge within twenty-four hours, and in the CCB this required a large courtroom with a large gallery section where the families and friends of the accused could sit. The courtroom was used for first appearances after arrest, when the loved ones were still naive about the lengthy, devastating and difficult journey the defendant was embarking upon. At arraignment, it was not unusual to have mom, dad, wife, sister-in-law, aunt, uncle and even a neighbor or two in the courtroom in a show of support for the defendant and outrage at his arrest. In another eighteen months, when the case would grind to a finale at sentencing, the defendant would be lucky to have even dear old mom still in attendance.

The other side of the gate was usually just as crowded, with lawyers of all stripes. Grizzled veterans, bored public defenders, slick cartel reps, wary prosecutors and media hounds all mingled in the well or stood against the glass partition surrounding the prisoner pen and whispered to their clients.

Presiding over this anthill was Judge Malcolm Firestone, who sat with his head down and his sharp shoulders jutting up and closer to his ears with each passing year. His black robe gave them the appearance of folded wings and the overall image was one of Firestone as a vulture waiting impatiently to dine on the bloody detritus of the justice system.

Firestone handled the evening arraignment docket, which started at three P.M. and went as far into the night as the list of detainees required. Consequently, he was a jurist who liked to keep things moving. You had to act fast in one hundred or risk being run over and left behind. In here, justice was an assembly line with a conveyor belt that never stopped turning. Firestone wanted to get home. The lawyers wanted to get home. Everybody wanted to get home.

I entered the courtroom with Maggie and immediately saw the cameras being set up in a six-foot corral to the left side, across the courtroom from the glass pen that housed defendants brought in six at a time. Without the glare of spotlights this time, I saw my friend Sticks setting the legs of the tool that provided his nickname, his tripod. He saw me and gave me a nod and I returned it.

Maggie tapped me on the arm and pointed toward a man seated at the prosecution table with three other lawyers.

"That's Rivas on the end."

"Okay. You go talk to him while I check in with the clerk."

"You don't have to check in, Haller. You're a prosecutor, remember?"

"Oh, cool. I forgot."

We headed over to the prosecution table and Maggie introduced me to Rivas. The prosecutor was a baby lawyer, probably no more than a few years out of a top-ranked law school. My guess was that he was biding his time, playing office politics and waiting to make a move up the ladder and out of the hellhole of arraignment court. It didn't help that I had come from across the aisle to grab the golden ring of the office's current caseload. By his body language I registered his wariness. I was at the wrong table. I was the fox in the henhouse. And I knew that before the hearing was over, I was going to confirm his suspicions.

After the perfunctory handshake, I looked around for Clive Royce and found him seated against the railing, conferring with a young woman who was probably his associate. They were leaning toward each other, looking into an open folder with a thick sheaf of documents in it. I approached with my hand out.

"Clive 'The Barrister' Royce, how's it hanging, old chap?"

He looked up and a smile immediately creased his well-tanned face. Like a perfect gentleman, he stood up before accepting my hand.

"Mickey, how are you? I'm sorry it looks like we're going to be opposing counsel on this one."

I knew he was sorry but not too sorry. Royce had built his career on picking winners. He would not risk going pro bono and stepping into a heavy media case if he didn't think it would amount to free advertising and another victory. He was in it to win it and behind the smile was a set of sharp teeth.

"Me, too. And I am sure you will make me regret the day I crossed the aisle."

"Well, I guess we're both fulfilling our public duty, yes? You helping out the district attorney and me taking on Jessup on the cuff."

Royce still carried an English accent even though he had lived more than half his fifty years in the United States. It gave him an aura of culture and distinction that belied his practice of defending people accused of heinous crimes. He wore a three-piece suit with a barely discernible chalk line in the gabardine. His bald pate was well tanned and smooth, his beard dyed black and groomed to the very last hair.

"That's one way of looking at it," I said.

"Oh, where are my manners? Mickey, this is my associate Denise Graydon. She'll be assisting me in the defense of Mr. Jessup."

Graydon stood up and shook my hand firmly.

"Nice to meet you," I said.

I looked around to see if Maggie was standing nearby and could be introduced but she was huddled with Rivas at the prosecution table.

"Well," I said to Royce. "Did you get your client on the docket?"

"I did indeed. He'll be first in the group after this one. I've already gone back and visited and we'll be ready to make a motion for bail. I was wondering, though, since we have a few minutes, could we step out into the corridor for a word?"

"Sure, Clive. Let's do it now."

Royce told his associate to wait in the courtroom and retrieve us when the next group of defendants was brought into the glass cage. I followed Royce through the gate and down the aisle between the crowded rows of the gallery. We went through the mantrap and into the hallway.

"You want to get a cup of tea?" Royce asked.

"I don't think there's time. What's up, Clive?"

Royce folded his arms and got serious.

"I must tell you, Mick, that I am not out to embarrass you. You are a friend and colleague in the defense bar. But you have gotten yourself into a no-win situation here, yes? What are we going to do about it?"

I smiled and glanced up and down the crowded hallway. Nobody was paying attention to us.

"Are you saying that your client wants to plead this out?"

"On the contrary. There will be no plea negotiation on this matter. The district attorney has made the wrong choice and it's very clear what maneuver he is undertaking here and how he is using you as a pawn in the process. I must put you on notice that if you insist on taking Jason Jessup to trial, then you are going to embarrass yourself. As a professional courtesy, I just thought I needed to tell you this."

Before I could answer, Graydon came out of the courtroom and headed quickly toward us.

"Somebody in the first group is not ready, so Jessup's been moved up and was just brought out."

"We'll be in straightaway," Royce said.

She hesitated and then realized her boss wanted her to go back into the courtroom. She went back through the doors and Royce turned his attention back to me. I spoke before he could.

"I appreciate your courtesy and concern, Clive. But if your client wants a trial, he'll get a trial. We'll be ready and we'll see who gets embarrassed and who goes back to prison."

"Brilliant, then. I look forward to the contest."

I followed him back inside. Court was in session and on my way down the aisle I saw Lorna Taylor, my office manager and second ex-wife, sitting at the end of one of the crowded rows. I leaned over to whisper.

"Hey, what are you doing here?"

"I had to come see the big moment."

"How did you even know? I just found out fifteen minutes ago."

"I guess so did KNX. I was already down here to look at office space and heard it on the radio that Jessup was going to appear in court. So I came."

"Well, thanks for being here, Lorna. How is the search going? I really need to get out of this building. Soon."

"I have three more showings after this. That'll be enough. I'll let you know my final choices tomorrow, okay?"

"Yeah, that's—"

I heard Jessup's name called by the clerk.

"Look, I gotta get in there. We'll talk later."

"Go get 'em, Mickey!"

I found an empty seat waiting for me next to Maggie at the prosecution table. Rivas had moved to the row of seats against the gate. Royce had moved to the glass cage, where he was whispering to his client. Jessup was wearing an orange jumpsuit—the jail uniform—and looked calm and subdued. He was nodding to everything Royce whispered in his ear. He somehow seemed younger than I had thought he would. I guess I expected all of those years in prison to have taken their toll. I knew he was forty-eight but he looked no older than forty. He didn't even have a jailhouse pallor. His skin was pale but it looked healthy, especially next to the overtanned Royce.

"Where did you go?" Maggie whispered to me. "I thought I was going to have to handle this myself."

"I was just outside conferring with defense counsel. Do you have the charges handy? In case I have to read them into the record."

"You won't have to enter the charges. All you have to do is stand up and say that you believe Jessup is a flight risk and a danger to the community. He—"

"But I don't believe he's a flight risk. His lawyer just told me they're ready to go and that they're not interested in a disposition. He wants the money and the only way he'll get it is to stick around and go to trial—and win."

"So?"

She seemed astonished and looked down at the files stacked in front of her.

"Mags, your philosophy is to argue everything and give no quarter. I don't think that's going to work here. I have a strategy and—"

She turned and leaned in closer to me.

"Then I'll just leave you and your strategy and your bald buddy from the defense bar to it."

She pushed back her chair and got up, grabbing her briefcase from the floor.

"Maggie..."

She charged through the gate and headed toward the rear door of the courtroom. I watched her go, knowing that while I didn't like the result, I had needed to set the lines of our prosecutorial relationship.

Jessup's name was called and Royce identified himself for the record. I then stood and said the words I never expected I would say.

"Michael Haller for the People."

Even Judge Firestone looked up from his perch, peering at me over a pair of reading glasses. Probably for the first time in weeks something out of the ordinary had occurred in his courtroom. A dyed-in-the-wool defense attorney had stood for the People.

"Well, gentlemen, this is an arraignment court and I have a note here saying you want to talk about bail."

Jessup was charged twenty-four years ago with murder and abduction. When the supreme court reversed his conviction it did not throw out the charges. That had been left to the DA's Office. So he still stood accused of the crimes and his not-guilty plea of twenty-four years ago remained in place. The case now had to be assigned to a courtroom and a judge for trial. A motion to discuss bail would usually be delayed until that point, except that Jessup, through Royce, was pushing the issue forward by coming to Firestone.

"Your Honor," Royce said, "my client was already arraigned twenty-four years ago. What we would like to do today is discuss a motion for bail and to move this case along to trial. Mr. Jessup has waited a long time for his freedom and for justice. He has no intention of waiving his right to a speedy trial."

I knew it was the move Royce would make, because it was the move I would have made. Every person accused of a crime is guaranteed a speedy trial. Most often trials are delayed at the defense's request or acquiescence as both sides want time to prepare. As a pressure tactic, Royce was not going to suspend the speedy-trial statute. With a case and evidence twenty-four years old, not to mention a primary witness whose whereabouts were at the moment unknown, it was not only prudent but a no-brainer to put the prosecution on the clock. When the supreme court reversed the conviction, that clock started ticking. The People had sixty days from that point to bring Jessup to trial. Twelve of them had already gone by.

"I can move the case to the clerk for assignment," Firestone said. "And I would prefer that the assigned judge handle the question of bail."

Royce composed his thoughts for a moment before responding. In doing so he turned his body slightly so the cameras would have a better angle on him.

"Your Honor, my client has been falsely incarcerated for twenty-four years. And those aren't just my words, that's the opinion of the state supreme court. Now they have pulled him out of prison and brought him down here so he can face trial once again. This is all part of an ongoing scheme that has nothing to do with justice, and everything to do with money and politics. It's about avoiding responsibility for corruptly taking a man's freedom. To put this over until another hearing on another day would continue the travesty of justice that has beset Jason Jessup for more than two decades."

"Very well."

Firestone still seemed put out and annoyed. The assembly line had thrown a gear. He had a docket that had probably started with more than seventy-five names on it and a desire to get through them in time to get home for dinner before eight. Royce was going to slow things down immeasurably with his request for a full debate on whether Jessup should be allowed his release while awaiting trial. But Firestone, like Royce, was about to get the surprise of the day. If he didn't make it home in time for dinner, it wouldn't be because of me.

Royce asked the judge for an OR, meaning Jessup would have to put up no money as bail and simply be released on his own recognizance. This was just his opener. He fully expected there to be a financial figure attached to Jessup's freedom, if he was successful at all. Murder suspects didn't get OR'ed. In the rare instance when bail was granted in a murder case, it usually came with a steep price tag. Whether Jessup could raise the money through his supporters or from the book and movie deals he was supposedly negotiating was not germane to the discussion.

Royce closed his request by arguing that Jessup should not be considered a flight risk for the very same reason I had outlined to Maggie. He had no interest in running. His only interest was in fighting to clear his name after twenty-four years of wrongful imprisonment.

"Mr. Jessup has no other purpose at this time than to stay put and prove once and for all that he is innocent and that he has paid a nightmarish price for the mistakes and misconduct of this District Attorney's Office."

The whole time Royce spoke I watched Jessup in the glass cage. He knew the cameras were on him and he maintained a pose of rightful indignation. Despite his efforts, he could not disguise the anger and hate in his eyes. Twenty-four years in prison had made that permanent.

Firestone finished writing a note and then asked for my response. I stood and waited until the judge looked up at me.

"Go ahead, Mr. Haller," he prompted.

"Judge, providing that Mr. Jessup can show documentation of residence, the state does not oppose bail at this time."

Firestone stared at me for a long moment as he computed that my response was diametrically opposite to what he thought it would be. The hushed sounds of the courtroom seemed to get even lower as the impact of my response was understood by every lawyer in the room.

"Did I get that right, Mr. Haller?" Firestone said. "You are not objecting to an OR release in a murder case?"

"That is correct, Your Honor. We are fully expecting Mr. Jessup to show for trial. There's no money in it for him if he doesn't."

"Your Honor!" Royce cried. "I object to Mr. Haller infecting the record with such prejudicial pap directed solely at the media in attendance. My client has no other purpose at this point than —"

"I understand, Mr. Royce," Firestone interjected. "But I think you did a fair amount of playing to the cameras yourself. Let's just leave it at that. Without objection from the prosecution, I am releasing Mr. Jessup on his own recognizance once he provides the clerk with documentation of residence. Mr. Jessup is not to leave Los Angeles County without permission of the court to which his case is assigned."

Firestone then referred the case to the clerk of the court's office for reassignment to another department for trial. We were now finally out of Judge Firestone's orbit. He could restart the assembly line and get home for dinner. I picked up the files Maggie had left behind and left the table. Royce was back at the seat at the railing, dumping files into a leather briefcase. His young associate was helping him.

"How did it feel, Mick?" he asked me.

"What, being a prosecutor?"

"Yes, crossing the aisle."

"Not too much different, to tell you the truth. It was all procedure today."

"You will be raked over the coals for letting my client walk out of here."

"Fuck 'em if they can't take a joke. Just make sure he stays clean, Clive. If he doesn't, then my ass really will be thrown on the fire. And so will his."

"No problem there. We'll take care of him. He's the least of your worries, you know."

"How's that, Clive?"

"You don't have much in the way of evidence, can't find your main witness, and the DNA is a case killer. You're captain of the *Titanic*, Mickey, and Gabriel Williams put you there. Makes me wonder what he's got on you."

Out of all that he said, I only wondered about one thing. How did he know about the missing witness? I, of course, didn't ask him or respond to his jab about what the DA might have on me. I played it like all the overconfident prosecutors I had ever gone up against.

"Tell your client to enjoy himself while he's out there, Clive. Because as soon as the verdict comes in, he's going back inside."

Royce smiled as he snapped his case closed. He changed the subject.

"When can we talk about discovery?"

"We can talk about it whenever you like. I'll start putting a file together in the morning."

"Good. Let's talk soon, Mick, yes?"

"Like I said, anytime, Clive."

He headed over to the court deputy's desk, most likely to see about his client's release. I pushed through the gate and connected with Lorna and we left the courtroom together. Waiting for me outside was a small gathering of reporters and cameras. The reporters shouted questions about my not objecting to bail and I told them no comment and walked on by. They waited in place for Royce to come out next.

"I don't know, Mickey," Lorna confided. "How do you think the DA is going to respond to the no bail?"

Just as she asked it my phone started beeping in my pocket. I realized I had forgotten to turn it off in the courtroom. That was an error that could have proven costly, depending on Firestone's view of electronic interruptions while court was in session.

Looking at the screen, I said to Lorna, "I don't know but I think I'm about to find out."

I held up the phone so she could see that the caller ID said LADA.

"You take it. I'm going to run. Be careful, Mickey."

She kissed me on the cheek and headed off to the elevator alcove. I connected to the call. I had guessed right. It was Gabriel Williams.

"Haller, what the hell are you doing?"

"What do you mean?"

"One of my people said you allowed Jessup to walk on an OR."

"That's right."

"Then I'll ask again, What the hell are you doing?"

"Look, I—"

"No, you look. I don't know if you were just giving one of your buddies in the defense bar what he wanted or you are just stupid, but you *never* let a murderer walk. You understand me? Now, I want you to go back in there and ask for a new hearing on bail."

"No, I'm not going to do that."

There was a hard silence for at least ten seconds before Williams came back.

"Did I just hear you right, Haller?"

"I don't know what you heard, Williams, but I'm not going back for a rehearing. You have to understand something. You gave me a bag of shit for a case and I have to do the best I can with it. What evidence we do have is twenty-four years old. We have a big hole blown in the side of the case with the DNA and we have an eyewitness we can't find. So that tells me I have to do whatever I can do to make this case."

"And what's that got to do with letting this man out of jail?"

"Don't you see, man? Jessup has been in prison for twenty-four years. It was no finishing school. Whatever he was when he went in? He's worse now. If he's on the outside, he'll fuck up. And if he fucks up, that only helps us."

"So in other words, you are putting the general public at risk while this guy is out there."

"No, because you are going to talk to the LAPD and get them to watch this guy. So nobody gets hurt and they are able to step in and grab him the minute he acts out."

Another silence followed but this time I could hear muffled voices and I figured that Williams was talking it over with his advisor, Joe Ridell. When his voice came back to me, it was stern but had lost the tone of outrage.

"Okay, this is what I want you to do. When you want to make a move like this, you come to me first. You understand?"

"That's not going to happen. You wanted an independent prosecutor. That's what you've got. Take it or leave it."

There was a pause and then he hung up without further word. I closed my phone and watched for a few moments as Clive Royce exited the courtroom and waded into the crowd of reporters and cameras. Like a seasoned expert, he waited a moment for everyone to get their positions set and their lenses focused. He then proceeded with the first of what would be many impromptu but carefully scripted press briefings.

"I think the District Attorney's Office is running scared," he began.

It was what I knew he would say. I didn't need to listen to the rest. I walked away.

8

Wednesday, February 17, 9:48 A.M.

Some people don't want to be found. They take measures. They drag the branch behind them to confuse the trail. Some people are just running and they don't care what they leave in their wake. What's important is that the past is behind them and that they keep moving away from it.

Once he back-checked the DA investigator's work, it took Bosch only two hours to find a current name and address for their missing witness, Melissa Landy's older sister, Sarah. She hadn't dragged a branch. She had used the things that were close and just kept moving. The DA's investigator who lost the trail in San Francisco had not looked backwards for clues. That was his mistake. He had looked forward and he'd found an empty trail.

Bosch had started as his predecessor had, typing the name Sarah Landy and birth date April 14, 1972, into the computer. The department's various search engines provided myriad points of impact with law enforcement and society.

First there were arrests on drug charges in 1989 and 1990—handled discreetly and sympathetically by the Division of Children's Services. But she was beyond the reach and understanding of DYS for similar charges in late 1991 and two more times in 1992. There was probation and a period of rehabilitation and this was followed by a few years during which she left no digital fingerprints at all. Another search site provided Bosch with a series of addresses for her in Los Angeles in the early nineties. Harry recognized these as marginal neighborhoods where rents were probably low and drugs close by and easy to acquire. Sarah's illegal substance of choice was crystal meth, a drug that burned away brain cells by the billions.

The trail on Sarah Landy, the girl who had hidden behind the bushes and watched her younger sister get taken by a killer, ended there.

Bosch opened the first file he had retrieved from the murder box and looked at the witness information sheet for Sarah. He found her Social Security number and fed that along with the DOB into the search engine. This gave him two new names: Sarah Edwards, beginning in 1991, and Sarah Witten in 1997. With women changes of last names only were usually an indicator of marriage, and the DA's investigator had reported finding records of two marriages.

Under the name Sarah Edwards, the arrests continued, including two pops for property crimes and a tag for soliciting for prostitution. But the arrests were spread far enough apart and perhaps her story was sad enough that once again she never saw any jail time.

Bosch clicked through the mug shots for these arrests. They showed a young woman with changing hairstyles and colors but the unwavering look of hurt and defiance in her eyes. One mug shot showed a deep purple bruise under her left eye and open sores along her jawline. The photos seemed to tell the story best. A downward spiral of drugs and crime. An internal wound that never healed, a guilt never assuaged.

Under the name Sarah Witten, the arrests didn't change, only the location. She had probably realized she was wearing thin on the prosecutors and judges who had repeatedly given her breaks — most likely after reading the summary of her life contained in the presentencing investigations. She moved north to San Francisco and once again had frequent encounters with the law. Drugs and petty crime, charges that often go hand in hand. Bosch checked the mug shots and saw a woman who looked old beyond her years. She looked like she was forty before she was yet thirty.

In 2003 she did her first significant jail time when she was sentenced to six months in San Mateo County Jail after pleading guilty to a possession charge. The records showed that she served four months in jail followed by a lockdown rehab program. It was the last marker on the system for her. No one with any of her names or Social Security number had been arrested since or applied for a driver's license in any of the fifty states.

Bosch tried a few other digital maneuvers he had learned while working in the Open-Unsolved Unit, where Internet tracing was raised to an art form, but could not pick up the trail. Sarah was gone.

Putting the computer aside, Bosch took up the files from the murder box. He started scanning the documents, looking for clues that might help him track her. He got more than a clue when he found a photocopy of Sarah's birth certificate. It was then that he remembered that she had been living with her mother and stepfather at the time of her sister's murder.

The birth name on the certificate was Sarah Ann Gleason. He entered it into the computer along with her birth date. He found no criminal history under the name but he did find a Washington State driver's license that had been established six years earlier and renewed just two months before. He pulled up the photo and it was a match. But barely. Bosch studied it for a long time. He would have sworn that Sarah Ann Gleason was getting younger.

His guess was that she had left the hard life behind. She had found something that made her change. Maybe she had taken the cure. Maybe she had a child. But something had changed her life for the better.

Bosch next ran her name through another search engine and got utility and satellite hookups under her name. The addresses matched the one on her driver's license. Bosch was sure he had found her. Port Townsend. He went onto Google and typed it in. Soon he was looking at a map of the Olympic Peninsula in the northwest corner of Washington. Sarah Landy had changed her name three times and had run to the farthest tip of the continental United States, but he had found her.

The phone rang as he was reaching for it. It was Lieutenant Stephen Wright, commander of the LAPD's Special Investigation Section.

"I just wanted you to know that as of fifteen minutes ago we're fully deployed on Jessup. The full unit's involved and we'll get you surveillance logs each morning. If you need anything else or want to ride along at any point, you call me."

"Thank you, Lieutenant. I will."

"Let's hope something happens."

"That would be nice."

Bosch disconnected. And made the call to Maggie McPherson.

"Couple things. First, SIS is in place now on Jessup. You can let Gabriel Williams know."

He thought he heard a small chuckle before she responded.

"Ironic, huh?"

"Yeah. Maybe they'll end up killing Jessup and we won't have to worry about a trial."

The Special Investigation Section was an elite surveillance squad that had existed for more than forty years despite a kill rate higher than that of any other unit in the department, including SWAT. The SIS was used to clandestinely watch apex predators — individuals suspected in violent crimes who would not cease until caught in the act and stopped by the police. Masters of surveillance, SIS officers waited to observe suspects committing new crimes before moving in to make arrests, often with fatal consequences.

The irony McPherson mentioned was that Gabriel Williams was a civil rights attorney before running for and winning the DA's post. He had sued the department over SIS shootings on multiple occasions, claiming that the unit's strategies were designed to draw suspects into deadly confrontations with police. He had gone so far as to call the unit a "death squad" while announcing a lawsuit over an SIS shooting that had left four robbers dead outside a Tommy's fast-food franchise. That same death squad was now being used in a gambit that might help win the case against Jessup and further Williams's political rise.

"You'll be informed of his activities?" McPherson asked.

"Every morning I'll get the surveillance log. And they'll call me out if anything good happens."

"Perfect. Was there something else? I'm in a bit of a rush. I'm working on one of my preexisting cases and have a hearing about to start."

"Yeah, I found our witness."

"You're brilliant! Where is she?"

"Up in Washington on the northern tip of the Olympic Peninsula. A place called Port Townsend. She's using her birth name, Sarah Ann Gleason, and it appears that she's been living clean up there for about six years."

"That's good for us."

"Maybe not."

"How so?"

"It looks to me like most of her life has been spent trying to get away from what happened that Sunday in Hancock Park. If she's finally gotten past it and is living the clean life up there in Port Townsend, she might not be interested in picking at old scabs, if you know what I mean."

"Not even for her sister?"

"Maybe not. We're talking about twenty-four years ago."

McPherson was quiet for a long moment and then finally responded.

"That's a cynical view of the world, Harry. When are you planning on going up there?"

"As soon as I can. But I have to make arrangements for my daughter. She stayed with a friend when I went up to get Jessup at San Quentin. It didn't turn out so good and now I have to hit the road again."

"Sorry to hear that. I want to go up with you."

"I think I can handle it."

"I know you can handle it. But it might be good to have a woman and a prosecutor with you. More and more, I think she's going to be the key to this whole thing and she's going to be my witness. Our approach to her will be very important."

"I've been approaching witnesses for about thirty years. I think I—"

"Let me have the travel office here make the arrangements. That way we can go up together. Talk out the strategy."

Bosch paused. He knew he wasn't going to be able to change her mind.

"Whatever you say."

"Good. I'll tell Mickey and contact travel. We'll book a morning flight. I'm clear tomorrow. Is that too soon for you? I'd hate to wait on this till next week."

"I'll make it work."

Bosch had had a third reason to call her but now decided to hold back. Her taking over the trip to Washington made him gun-shy about discussing his investigative moves.

They hung up and he was left drumming his fingers on the edge of his desk as he contemplated what he would say to Rachel Walling.

After a few moments he pulled out his cell phone and used it to make the call. He had Walling's number in its memory. To his surprise, she answered right away. He had envisioned her seeing his name on the ID and letting him go to the message. They'd had a relationship that was long over but still left a trail of intense feelings.

"Hello, Harry."

"Hello, Rachel. How are you?"

"I'm fine. And you?"

"Pretty good. I'm calling about a case."

"Of course. Harry Bosch never goes through channels. He goes direct."

"There are no channels for this. And you know I call you because I trust you and more than anything else respect your opinion. I go through channels and I get some profiler in Quantico who's just a voice on the phone. And not only that, he doesn't call me back with anything for two months. What would you do if you were me?"

"Oh... probably the same thing."

"Besides that, I don't want the bureau's official involvement. I am just looking for your opinion and advice, Rachel."

"What's the case?"

"I think you're going to like it. It's a twenty-four-year-old murder of a twelve-year-old girl. A guy went down for it back then and now we have to retry him. I was thinking a profile of the crime might be helpful to the prosecutor."

"Is this that Jessup case that's in the news?"

"That's right."

He knew she would be interested. He could hear it in her voice.

"All right, well, bring by whatever you've got. How much time are you giving me? I've got my regular job, you know."

"No hurry this time. Not like with that Echo Park thing. I'll probably be out of town tomorrow. Maybe longer. I think you can have a few days with the file. You still in the same place above the Million Dollar Theater?"

"That's it."

"Okay, I'll drop the box by."

"I'll be here."

9

Wednesday, February 17, 3:18 P.M.

The holding cell next to Department 124 on the thirteenth floor of the CCB was empty except for my client Cassius Clay Montgomery. He sat morosely on the bench in the corner and didn't get up when he saw me come back.

"Sorry I'm late."

He didn't say anything. He didn't acknowledge my presence.

"Come on, Cash. It's not like you'd be going anywhere. What's it matter if you were waiting here or back in County?"

"They got TV in County, man," he said, looking up at me.

"Okay, so you missed *Oprah*. Can you come over here so I don't have to shout our business across the room?"

He got up and came over to the bars. I stood on the other side, beyond the red line marking the three-foot threshold.

"Doesn't matter if you shout our business. There ain't nobody left to hear it."

"I told you, I'm sorry. I've been having a busy day."

"Yeah, and I guess I'm just a no-count nigger when it comes to being on TV and turnin' into the man."

"What's that supposed to mean?"

"I saw you on the news, dog. Now you a prosecutor? What kinda shit is that?"

I nodded. Obviously, my client was more concerned with me being a turncoat than with waiting until the last hearing of the day.

"Look, all I can tell you is that I took the job reluctantly. I am not a prosecutor. I am a defense attorney. I'm your defense attorney. But every now and then they come to you and they want something. And it's hard to say no."

"So what happens to me?"

"Nothing happens to you. I'm still your lawyer, Cash. And we have a big decision to make here. This hearing is going to be short and sweet. It's to set a trial date and that's it. But Mr. Hellman, the prosecutor, says the offer he made to you is good only until today. If we tell Judge Champagne we're ready to go to trial today, then the deal disappears and we go to trial. Have you thought about it some more?"

Montgomery leaned his head in between two bars and didn't speak. I realized he couldn't pull the trigger on a decision. He was forty-seven and had already spent nine years of his life in prison. He was charged with armed robbery and assault with great bodily injury and was looking at a big fall.

According to the police, Montgomery had posed as a buyer at a drive-through drug market in the Rodia Gardens projects. But instead of paying, he pulled a gun and demanded the dealer's drugs and money roll. The dealer went for the gun and it went off. Now the dealer, a gang member named Darnell Hicks, was in a wheelchair for the rest of his life.

As is usual in the projects, no one cooperated with the investigation. Even the victim said he didn't remember what happened, choosing in his silence to trust that his fellow Crips would handle justice in the matter. But investigators made a case anyway. Picking up my client's car on a video camera at the entrance to the projects, they found the car and matched blood on the door to the victim.

It wasn't a strong case but it was solid enough for us to entertain an offer from the prosecution. If Montgomery took the deal he'd be sentenced to three years in prison and would likely serve two and a half. If he gambled and took a conviction at the end of a trial, then he'd be looking at a mandatory minimum of fifteen years inside. The add-on of GBI and use of a firearm in the commission of a robbery were the killers. And I knew first-hand that Judge Judith Champagne wasn't soft on gun crimes.

I had recommended to my client that he take the deal. It was a no-brainer to me but then I wasn't the one who had to do the time. Montgomery couldn't decide. It wasn't so much about the prison time. It was the fact that the victim, Hicks, was a Crip and the street gang had a long reach into every prison in the state. Even taking the three-year sentence could be a death penalty. Montgomery wasn't sure he would make it.

"I don't know what to tell you," I said. "It's a good offer. The DA doesn't want to go to trial on this. He doesn't want to put a victim on the stand who doesn't want to be there and may hurt the case more than help it. So he's gone as low as he can go. But it's up to you. Your decision. You've had a couple weeks now and this is it. We have to go out there in a couple minutes."

Montgomery tried to shake his head but his forehead was pressed between the two bars.

"What's that mean?" I asked.

"It means shit. Can't we win this case, man? I mean, you a prosecutor now. Can't you get a good word in for me on this?"

"They're two different matters, Cash. I can't do anything like that. You got your choice. Take the three or we go to trial. And like I told you before, we can certainly do some stuff at trial. They've got no weapon and a victim who won't tell the story, but they still got his blood on the door of your car and they got video of you driving it out of Rodia right after the shooting. We can try to play it the way you said it went down. Self-defense. You were there to buy a rock and he saw *your* roll and tried to rip *you* off. The jury might believe it, especially if he won't testify. And they might believe it even if he does testify because I'll make him take the fifth so many times they'll think he's Al Capone before he gets off the stand."

"Who's Al Capone?"

"You're kidding me, right?"

"No, man, who is he?"

"Never mind, Cash. What do you want to do?"

"You're cool if we go to trial?"

"I'm cool with it. It's just that there is that gap, you know?"

"Gap?"

"There is a wide gap between what they're offering you right now and what you could get if we lose at trial. We're talking about a minimum twelve-year swing, Cash. That's a lot of time to gamble with."

Montgomery backed away from the bars. They had left twin impressions on both sides of his forehead. He now gripped the bars in his hands.

"The thing is, three years, fifteen years, I ain't going to make it either way. They got hit men in every prison. But in County, they got the system and ev'rybody is separated and locked up tight. I'm okay there."

I nodded. But the problem was that any sentence over a year had to be served in a state prison. The county system was a holding system for those awaiting trial or sentenced to short terms.

"Okay, then I guess we go to trial."

"I guess we do."

"Sit tight. They'll be coming back for you soon."

I knocked quietly on the courtroom door and the deputy opened it. Court was in session and Judge Champagne was holding a status conference on another case. I saw my prosecutor sitting against the rail and went over to confer. This was the first case I'd had with Philip Hellman and I had found him to be extremely reasonable. I decided to test the limits of that reason one last time.

"So, Mickey, I hear we are now colleagues," he said with a smile.

"Temporarily," I said. "I don't plan to make it a career."

"Good, I don't need the competition. So what are we going to do here?"

"I think we are going to put it over one more time."

"Mickey, come on, I've been very generous. I can't keep—"

"No, you're right. You've been completely generous, Phil, and I appreciate that. My client appreciates that. It's just that he can't take a deal because anything that puts him in a state prison is a death penalty. We both know that the Crips will get him."

"First of all, I don't know that. And second of all, if that's what he thinks, then maybe he shouldn't have tried to rip off the Crips and shoot one of their guys."

I nodded in agreement.

"That's a good point but my client maintains it was self-defense. Your vic drew first. So I guess we go to trial and you've got to ask a jury for justice for a victim who doesn't want it. Who will testify only if you force him to and will then claim he doesn't remember shit."

"Maybe he doesn't. He did get shot, after all."

"Yeah, and maybe the jury will buy that, especially when I bring out his pedigree. I'll ask him what he does for a living for starters. According to what Cisco, my investigator, has found out, he's been selling drugs since he was twelve years old and his mother put him on the street."

"Mickey, we've already been down this road. What do you want? I'm getting ready to just say fuck it, let's go to trial."

"What do I want? I want to make sure you don't fuck up the start of your brilliant career."

"What?"

"Look, man, you are a young prosecutor. Remember what you just said about not wanting the competition? Well, another thing you don't want is to risk putting a loss on your ledger. Not this early in the game. You just want this to go away. So here's what I want. A year in County and restitution. You can name your price on restitution."

"Are you kidding me?"

He said it too loud and drew a look from the judge. He then spoke very quietly.

"Are you fucking kidding me?"

"Not really. It's a good solution when you think about it, Phil. It works for everybody."

"Yeah, and what's Judge Judy going to say when I present this? The victim is in a wheelchair for life. She won't sign off on this."

"We ask to go back to chambers and we both sell it to her. We tell her that Montgomery wants to go to trial and claim self-defense and that the state has real reservations because of the victim's lack of cooperation and status as a high-ranking member of a criminal organization. She was a prosecutor before she was a judge. She'll understand this. And she'll probably have more sympathy for Montgomery than she does for your drug-dealing victim."

Hellman thought for a long moment. The hearing before Champagne ended and she instructed the courtroom deputy to bring Montgomery out. It was the last case of the day.

"Now or never, Phil," I prompted.

"Okay, let's do it," he finally said.

Hellman stood up and moved to the prosecution table.

"Your Honor," he intoned, "before we bring the defendant out, could counsel discuss this case in chambers?"

Champagne, a veteran judge who had seen everything at least three times, creased her brow.

"On the record, gentlemen?"

"That's probably not necessary," Hellman said. "We would like to discuss the terms of a disposition in the case."

"Then by all means. Let's go."

The judge stepped down from the bench and headed back toward her chambers. Hellman and I started to follow. As we got to the gate next to the clerk's pod, I leaned forward to whisper to the young prosecutor.

"Montgomery gets credit for time served, right?"

Hellman stopped in his tracks and turned back to me.

"You've got to be—"

"Just kidding," I quickly said.

I held my hands up in surrender. Hellman frowned and then turned back around and headed toward the judge's chambers. I had thought it was worth a try.

10

Thursday, February 18, 7:18 A.M.

It was a silent breakfast. Madeline Bosch poked at her cereal with her spoon but managed to put very little of it into her stomach. Bosch knew that his daughter wasn't upset because he was going away for the night. And she wasn't upset because she wasn't going. He believed she had come to enjoy the breaks his infrequent travels gave her. The reason she was upset was the arrangements he had made for her care while he was gone. She was fourteen going on twenty-four and her first choice would have been to simply be left alone to fend for herself. Her second choice would have been to stay with her best friend up the street, and her last choice would have been to have Mrs. Bambrough from the school stay at the house with her.

Bosch knew she was perfectly capable of fending for herself but he wasn't there yet. They had been living together for only a few months and it had been only those few months since she had lost her mother. He just wasn't ready to turn her loose, no matter how fervently she insisted she was ready.

He finally put down his spoon and spoke.

"Look, Maddie, it's a school night and last time when you stayed with Rory you both stayed up all night, slept through most of your classes and had your parents and all your teachers mad at both of you."

"I told you we wouldn't do that again."

"I just think we need to wait on that a little bit. I'll tell Mrs. Bambrough that it's all right if Rory comes over, just not till midnight. You guys can do your homework together or something."

"Like she's really going to want to come here when I'm being watched by the assistant principal. Thanks for that, Dad."

Bosch had to concentrate on not laughing. This issue seemed so simple compared with what she had faced in October after coming to live with him. She still had regular therapy sessions and they seemed to go a long way toward helping her cope with her mother's death. Bosch would take a dispute over child care over those other deeper issues any day.

He checked his watch. It was time to go.

"If you're done playing with your food you can put your bowl in the sink. We have to get going."

"*Finished*, Dad. You should use the correct word."

"Sorry about that. Are you *finished* playing with your cereal?"

"Yes."

"Good. Let's go."

He got up from the table and went back to his room to grab his overnight bag off the bed. He was traveling light, expecting the trip to last one night at the most. If they got lucky, they might even catch a late flight home tonight.

When he came back out, Maddie was standing by the door, her backpack over one shoulder.

"Ready?"

"No, I'm just standing here for my health."

He walked up to her and kissed the top of her head before she could move away from him. She tried, though.

"Gotcha."

"Daaaad!"

He locked the door behind them and put his bag in the backseat of the Mustang.

"You have your key, right?"

"Yes!"

"Just making sure."

"Can we go? I don't want to be late."

They drove down the hill in silence after that. When they got to the school, he saw Sue Bambrough working the drop-off lane, getting the slow-moving kids out of the cars and into the school, keeping things moving.

"You know the routine, Mads. Call me, text me, vid me, let me know you're doing okay."

"I'll get out here."

She opened the door early, before they got to where the assistant principal was stationed. Maddie got out and then reached back in to grab her bag. Bosch waited for it, the sign that everything was really okay.

"Be safe, Dad."

There it was.

"You, too, baby."

She closed the door. He lowered the window and drove down to Sue Bambrough. She leaned into the open window.

"Hey, Sue. She's a little upset but she'll get over it by the end of the day. I told her that Aurora Smith could come by but not to make it late. Who knows, maybe they'll do some homework."

"She'll be fine, Harry."

"I left the check on the kitchen counter and there's some cash there for anything you guys'll need."

"Thanks, Harry. Just let me know if you think it will be more than one night. No problem on my end."

Bosch checked the rearview. He wanted to ask a question but didn't want to hold people up.

"What is it, Harry?"

"Uh, to say you're done doing something, is that wrong? You know, bad English?"

Sue tried to hide a smile.

"If she's correcting you, that's the natural course of things. Don't take it personally. We drill it into them here. They go home and want to drill somebody else. It would be proper to say you *finished* doing something. But I know what you meant."

Bosch nodded. Somebody in the line behind him tapped the horn — Bosch assumed it was a man hurrying to make drop-off and then get to work. He waved his thanks to Sue and pulled out.

Maggie McFierce had called Bosch the night before and told him that there was nothing out of Burbank, so they were taking a direct flight out of LAX. That meant it would be a brutal drive in morning traffic. Bosch lived on a hillside right above the Hollywood Freeway but it was the one freeway that wouldn't help him get to the airport. Instead, he took Highland down into Hollywood and then cut over to La Cienega. It bottlenecked through the oil fields near Baldwin Hills and he lost his cushion of time. He took La Tijera from there and when he got to the airport he was forced to park in one of the expensive garages close in because he didn't have time to ride a shuttle bus in from an economy lot.

After filling out the Law Enforcement Officer forms at the counter and being walked through security by a TSA agent, he finally got to the gate while the plane was in the final stages of loading its passengers. He looked for McPherson but didn't see her and assumed she was already on the plane.

He boarded and went through the required meet-and-greet, stepping into the cockpit, showing his badge and shaking the hands of the flight crew. He then made his way toward the back of the plane. He and McPherson had exit-row seats across the aisle from each other. She was already in place, a tall Starbucks cup in hand. She had obviously arrived early for the flight.

"Thought you weren't going to make it," she said.

"It was close. How'd you get here so early? You have a daughter just like me."

"I dropped her with Mickey last night."

Bosch nodded.

"Exit row, nice. Who's your travel agent?"

"We've got a good one. That's why I wanted to handle it. We'll send LAPD the bill for you."

"Yeah, good luck with that."

Bosch had put his bag in an overhead compartment so he would have room to extend his legs. After he sat down and buckled in, he saw that McPherson had shoved two thick files into the seat pocket in front of her. He had nothing out to prep with. His files were in his bag but he didn't feel like getting them out. He pulled his notebook out of his back pocket and was about to lean across the aisle to ask McPherson a question when a flight attendant came down the aisle and stooped down to whisper to him.

"You're the detective, right?"

"Uh, yes. Is there a —"

Before he could finish the Dirty Harry line, the flight attendant informed him that they were upgrading him to an unclaimed seat in the first-class section.

"Oh, that's nice of you and the captain, but I don't think I can do that."

"There's no charge. It's —"

"No, it's not that. See, I'm with this lady here and she's my boss and I — I mean we — need to talk and go over our investigation. She's a prosecutor, actually."

The attendant took a moment to track his explanation and then nodded and said she'd go back to the front of the plane and inform the powers that be.

"And I thought chivalry was dead," McPherson said. "You gave up a first-class seat to sit with me."

"Actually, I should've told her to give it to you. That would have been real chivalry."

"Uh-oh, here she comes back."

Bosch looked up the aisle. The same smiling attendant was headed back to them.

"We're moving some people around and we have room for you both. Come on up."

They got up and headed forward, Bosch grabbing his bag out of the overhead and following McPherson. She looked back at him, smiled and said, "My tarnished knight."

"Right," Bosch said.

The seats were side by side in the first row. McPherson took the window. Soon after they were resituated, the plane took off for its three-hour flight to Seattle.

"So," McPherson said, "Mickey told me our daughter has never met your daughter."

Bosch nodded.

"Yeah, I guess we need to change that."

"Definitely. I hear they're the same age and you guys compared photos and they even look alike."

"Well, her mother sort of looked like you. Same coloring."

And fire, Bosch thought. He pulled out his phone and turned it on. He showed her a photo of Maddie.

"That's remarkable," McPherson said. "They could be sisters."

Bosch looked at his daughter's photo as he spoke.

"It's just been a tough year for her. She lost her mother and moved across an ocean. Left all her friends behind. I've been kind of letting her move at her own pace."

"All the more reason she should know her family here."

Bosch just nodded. In the past year he had fended off numerous calls from his half brother seeking to get their daughters together. He wasn't sure if his hesitation was about the potential relationship between the two cousins or the two half brothers.

Sensing that angle of conversation was at an end, McPherson unfolded her table and pulled out her files. Bosch turned his phone off and put it away.

"So we're going to work?" he asked.

"A little. I want to be prepared."

"How much do you want to tell her up front? I was thinking we just talk about the ID. Confirm it and see if she's willing to testify again."

"And not bring up the DNA?"

"Right. That could turn a yes into a no."

"But shouldn't she know everything she's going to be getting into?"

"Eventually, yes. It's been a long time. I did the trace. She hit some hard times and rough spots but it looks like she might've come out okay. I guess we'll see when we get up there."

"Let's play it by ear, then. I think if it feels right, we need to tell her everything."

"You make the call."

"The one thing that's good is that she'll only have to do it once. We don't have to go through a preliminary hearing or a grand jury. Jessup was held over for trial in 'eighty-six and that is not what the supreme court reversed. So we just go directly to trial. We'll need her one time and that will be it."

"That's good. And you'll be handling her."

"Yes."

Bosch nodded. The assumption was that she was a better prosecutor than Haller. After all, it was Haller's first case. Harry was happy to hear she would be handling the most important witness at trial.

"What about me? Which one of you will take me?"

"I don't think that's been decided. Mickey anticipates that Jessup will actually testify. I know he's waiting for that. But we haven't talked about who will take you. My guess is that you'll be doing a lot of read-backs to the jury of sworn testimony from the first trial."

She closed the file and it looked like that was it for work.

They spent the rest of the flight small-talking about their daughters and looking through the magazines in their seat pockets. The plane landed early at SeaTac and they picked up a rental car and started north. Bosch did the driving. The car came equipped with a GPS system but the DA travel assistant had also provided McPherson with a full package of directions to Port Townsend. They drove up to Seattle and then took a ferry across Puget Sound. They left the car and went up for coffee on the concessions deck, finding an open table next to a set of windows. Bosch was staring out the window when McPherson surprised him with an observation.

"You're not happy, are you, Harry?"

Bosch looked at her and shrugged.

"It's a weird case. Twenty-four years old and we start with the bad guy already in prison and we take him out. It doesn't make me unhappy, it's just kind of strange, you know?"

She had a half smile on her face.

"I wasn't talking about the case. I was talking about you. You're not a happy man."

Bosch looked down at the coffee he held on the table with two hands. Not because of the ferry's movement, but because he was cold and the coffee was warming him inside and out.

"Oh," he said.

A long silence opened up between them. He wasn't sure what he should reveal to this woman. He had known her for only a week and she was making observations about him.

"I don't really have time to be happy right now," he finally said.

"Mickey told me what he felt he could about Hong Kong and what happened with your daughter."

Bosch nodded. But he knew Maggie didn't know the whole story. Nobody did except for Madeline and him.

"Yeah," he said. "She caught some bad breaks there. That's the thing, I guess. I think if I can make my daughter happy, then I'll be happy. But I am not sure when that will be."

He brought his eyes up to hers and saw only sympathy. He smiled.

"Yeah, we should get the two cousins together," he said, moving on.

"Absolutely," she said.

11

Thursday, February 18, 1:30 P.M.

The *Los Angeles Times* carried a lengthy story on Jason Jessup's first day of freedom in twenty-four years. The reporter and photographer met him at dawn on Venice Beach, where the forty-eight-year-old tried his hand at his boyhood pastime of surfing. On the first few sets, he was shaky on a borrowed longboard but soon he was up and riding the break. A photo of Jessup standing upright on the board and riding a curl with his arms outstretched, his face turned up to the sky, was the centerpiece photo on the newspaper's front page. The photo showed off what two decades of lifting prison iron will do. Jessup's body was roped with muscle. He looked lean and mean.

From the beach the next stop was an In-N-Out franchise in Westwood for hamburgers and French fries with all the catsup he wanted. After lunch Jessup went to Clive Royce's storefront office in downtown, where he attended a two-hour meeting with the battery of attorneys representing him in both criminal and civil matters. This meeting was not open to the *Times*.

Jessup rounded out the afternoon by watching a movie called *Shutter Island* at the Chinese theater in Hollywood. He bought a tub of buttered popcorn large enough to feed a family of four and ate every puffed kernel. He then returned to Venice, where he had a room in an apartment near the beach courtesy of a high-school surfing buddy. The day ended at a beach barbecue with a handful of supporters who had never wavered in their belief in his innocence.

I sat at my desk studying the color photos of Jessup that graced two inside pages of the A section. The paper was going all-out on the story, as it had all along, surely smelling the journalistic honors to be gathered at the end of Jessup's journey to complete freedom. Springing an innocent man from prison was the ultimate newspaper story and the *Times* was desperately trying to take credit for Jessup's release.

The largest photo showed Jessup's unabashed delight at the red plastic tray sitting in front of him at a table at In-N-Out. The tray contained a fully loaded double-double with fries smothered in catsup and melted cheese. The caption said

Why Is This Man Smiling? 12:05 — Jessup eats his first Double-Double in 24 years. "I've been thinking about this forever!"

The other photos carried similarly lighthearted captions below shots of Jessup at the movies with his bucket of popcorn, hoisting a beer at the barbecue and hugging his high-school pal, walking through a glass door that said ROYCE AND ASSOCIATES, ATTORNEYS-AT-LAW. There was no indication in the tone of the article or photos that Jason Jessup was a man who happened to still be accused of murdering a twelve-year-old girl.

The story was about Jessup relishing his freedom while being unable to plan his future until his "legal issues" were resolved. It was a nice turn of phrase, I thought, calling abduction and murder charges and a pending trial merely legal issues.

I had the paper spread wide on the desk Lorna had rented for me in my new office on Broadway. We were on the second floor of the Bradbury Building and only three blocks from the CCB.

"I think you need to put something up on the walls."

I looked up. It was Clive Royce. He had walked through the reception room unannounced because I had sent Lorna over to Philippe's to get us lunch. Royce gestured to the empty walls of the temporary office. I flipped the newspaper closed and held up the front page.

"I just ordered a twenty-by-twenty shot of Jesus on the surfboard here. I'm going to hang him on the wall."

Royce stepped up to the desk and took the paper, studying the photo on the front as if for the first time, which we both knew was not the case. Royce had been deeply involved in the generation of the story, the payoff being the photo of the office door with his firm's name on the glass.

"Yes, they did a good job with it, didn't they?"

He handed it back.

"I guess so, if you like your killers happy-go-lucky."

Royce didn't respond, so I continued.

"I know what you're doing, Clive, because I would do it, too. But as soon as we get a judge, I'm going to ask him to stop you. I'm not going to let you taint the jury pool."

Royce frowned as if I had suggested something completely untoward.

"It's a free press, Mick. You can't control the media. The man just got out of prison, and like it or not, it's a news story."

"Right, and you can give exclusives in exchange for display. Display that might plant a seed in a potential juror's mind. What do you have planned for today? Jessup co-hosting the morning show on Channel Five? Or is he judging the chili cook-off at the state fair?"

"As a matter of fact, NPR wanted to hang with him today but I showed restraint. I said no. Make sure you tell the judge that as well."

"Wow, you actually said no to NPR? Was that because most people who listen to NPR are the kind of people who can get out of jury duty, or because you got something better lined up?"

Royce frowned again, looking as though I had impaled him with an integrity spear. He looked around, grabbed the chair from Maggie's desk and pulled it over so he could sit in front of mine. Once he was seated with his legs crossed and had arranged his suit properly he spoke.

"Now, tell me, Mick, does your boss think that housing you in a separate building is really going to make people think you are acting independently of his direction? You're having us on, right?"

I smiled at him. His effort to get under my skin was not going to work.

"Let me state once again for the record, Clive, that I have no boss in this matter. I am working independently of Gabriel Williams."

I gestured to the room.

"I'm here, not in the courthouse, and all decisions on this case will be made from this desk. But at the moment my decisions aren't that important. It's you who has the decision, Clive."

"And what would that be? A disposition, Mick?"

"That's right. Today's special, good until five o'clock only. Your boy pleads guilty, I'll come down off the death penalty and we both roll the dice with the judge on sentencing. You never know, Jessup could walk away with time served."

Royce smiled cordially and shook his head.

"I am sure that would make the powers that be in this town happy, but I'm afraid I must disappoint you, Mick. My client remains absolutely uninterested in a plea. And that is not going to change. I was actually hoping that by now you would have seen the uselessness of going to trial and would simply drop the charges. You can't win this thing, Mick. The state has to bend over on this one and you unfortunately are the fool who volunteered to take it in the arse."

"Well, I guess we'll see, won't we?"

"We will indeed."

I opened the desk's center drawer and removed a green plastic case containing a computer disc. I slid it across the desk to him.

"I wasn't expecting you to come by for it yourself, Clive. Thought you'd send an investigator or a clerk. You gotta bunch of them working for you, don't you? Along with that full-time publicist."

Royce slowly collected the disc. The plastic case was marked DEFENSE DIS-COVERY 1.

"Well, aren't we snarky today? Seems that only two weeks ago you were one of us, Mick. A lowly member of the defense bar."

I nodded my contrition. He had nailed me there.

"Sorry, Clive. Perhaps the power of the office is getting to me."

"Apology accepted."

"And sorry to waste your time coming over here. As I told you on the phone, that's got everything we have up until this morning. Mostly the old files and reports. I won't play discovery games with you, Clive. I've been on the wrong end of that too many times to count. So when I get it, you get it. But right now that's all I've got."

Royce tapped the disc case on the edge of the desk.

"No witness list?"

"There is but as of now it's essentially the same list from the trial in 'eighty-six. I've added my investigator and subtracted a few names — the parents, other people no longer alive."

"No doubt Felix Turner has been redacted."

I smiled like the Cheshire cat.

"Thankfully you won't get the chance to bring him up at trial."

"Yes, a pity. I would have loved the opportunity to shove him up the state's ass."

I nodded, noting that Royce had come off the English colloquialisms and was hitting me with pure Americana now. It was a symptom of his frustration over Turner, and as a longtime counsel for the defense I certainly felt it. In the retrial, there would be no mention of any aspect of the first trial. The new jurors would have no knowledge of what had transpired before. And that meant the state's use of the fraudulent jailhouse informant — no matter how grievous a prosecutorial sin — would not hurt the current prosecution.

I decided to move on.

"I should have another disc for you by the end of the week."

"Yes, I can't wait to see what you come up with."

Sarcasm noted.

"Just remember one thing, Clive. Discovery is a two-way street. You go beyond thirty days and we'll go see the judge."

The rules of evidence required that each side complete its discovery exchange no later than thirty days before the start of trial. Missing this deadline could lead to sanctions and open the door to a trial delay as the judge would grant the offended party more time to prepare.

"Yes, well, as you can imagine, we weren't expecting the turn of events that has transpired here," Royce said. "Consequently, our defense is in its infancy. But I won't play games with you either, Mick. A disc will be along to you in short order—provided that we have any discovery to give."

I knew that as a practical matter the defense usually had little in the way of discovery to give unless the plan was to mount an extensive defense. But I sounded the warning because I was leery of Royce. In a case this old, he might try to dig up an alibi witness or something else out of left field. I wanted to know about it before it came up in court.

"I appreciate that," I said.

Over his shoulder I saw Lorna enter the office. She was carrying two brown bags, one of which contained my French dip sandwich.

"Oh, I didn't realize..."

Royce turned around in his seat.

"Ah, the lovely Lorna. How are you, my darling?"

"Hello, Clive. I see you got the disc."

"Indeed. Thank you, Lorna."

I had noticed that Royce's English accent and formal parlance became more pronounced at times, especially in front of attractive women. I wondered if that was a conscious thing or not.

"I have two sandwiches here, Clive," Lorna said. "Would you like one?"

It was the wrong time for Lorna to be magnanimous.

"I think he was just about to leave," I said quickly.

"Yes, love, I must go. But thank you for the most gracious offer."

"I'll be out here if you need me, Mickey."

Lorna went back to the reception room, closing the door behind her. Royce turned back to me and spoke in a low voice.

"You know you should never have let that one go, Mick. She was the keeper. And now, joining forces with the first Mrs. Haller to deprive an innocent man of his long-deserved freedom, there is something incestuous about the whole thing, isn't there?"

I just looked at him for a long moment.

"Is there anything else, Clive?"

He held up the disc.

"I think this should do it for today."

"Good. I have to get back to work."

I walked him out through reception and closed the door after him. I turned and looked at Lorna.

"Feels weird, doesn't it?" she said. "Being on this side of it—the prosecution side."

"It does."

She held up one of the sandwich bags.

"Can I ask you something?" I said. "Whose sandwich were you going to give him, yours or mine?"

She looked at me with a straight face, then a smile of guilt leaked out.

"I was being polite, okay? I thought you and I could share."

I shook my head.

"Don't be giving my French dip sandwich to anybody. Especially a defense lawyer."

I snatched the bag from her hand.

"Thank you, love," I said in my best British accent.

She laughed and I headed back into my office to eat.

12

Thursday, February 18, 3:31 P.M.

After driving off the ferry at Port Townsend, Bosch and McPherson followed directions from the rental car's GPS to the address on Sarah Ann Gleason's driver's license. The trail led them through the small Victorian sea village and then out into a more rural area of large and isolated properties. Gleason's house was a small clapboard house that failed to keep the nearby town's Victorian theme. The detective and the prosecutor stood on the porch and knocked but got no response.

"Maybe she's at work or something," McPherson said.

"Could be."

"We could go back into town and get rooms, then come back after five."

Bosch checked his watch. He realized that school was just over and Maddie was probably heading home with Sue Bambrough. He guessed that his daughter was giving the assistant principal the silent treatment.

He stepped off the porch and started walking toward the corner of the house.

"Where are you going?"

"To check the back. Hold on."

But as soon as Bosch turned the corner he could see that a hundred yards beyond the house there was another structure. It was a windowless barn or garage. What stood out was that it had a chimney. He could see heat waves but no smoke rising from the two black pipes that extended over the roofline. There were two cars and a van parked in front of the closed garage doors.

Bosch stood there watching for so long that McPherson finally came around the corner as well.

"What's taking—?"

Bosch held up his hand to silence her, then pointed toward the outbuilding.

"What is it?" McPherson whispered.

Before Bosch could answer, one of the garage doors slid open a few feet and a figure stepped out. It looked like a young man or a teenager. He was wearing a full-length black apron over his clothes. He took off heavy elbow-length gloves so he could light a cigarette.

"Shit," McPherson whispered, answering her own question.

Bosch stepped back to the corner of the house to use it as a blind. He pulled McPherson with him.

"All her arrests — her drug of choice was meth," he whispered.

"Great," McPherson whispered back. "Our main witness is a meth cook."

The young smoker turned when apparently called from within the barn. He threw down his cigarette, stepped on it, and went back inside. He yanked the door closed behind him but it slid to a stop six inches before closing.

"Let's go," Bosch said.

He started to move but McPherson put her hand on his arm.

"Wait, what are you talking about? We need to call Port Townsend police and get some backup, don't we?"

Bosch looked at her a moment without responding.

"I saw the police station when we went through town," McPherson said, as if to assure him that backup was waiting and willing.

"If we call for backup they're not going to be very cooperative, since we didn't bother to check in when we got to town in the first place," Bosch said. "They'll arrest her and then we have a main witness awaiting trial on drug charges. How do you think that will work with Jessup's jury?"

She didn't answer.

"Tell you what," he said. "You hold back here and I'll go check it out. Three vehicles, probably three cooks. If I can't handle it, we call backup."

"They're probably armed, Harry. You —"

"They're probably not armed. I'll check it out and if it looks like a situation we'll call Port Townsend."

"I don't like this."

"It could work to our favor."

"What? How?"

"Think about it. Watch for my signal. If something goes wrong, get in the car and get out of here."

He held up the car keys and she reluctantly took them. He could tell she was thinking about what he had said. The advantage. If they caught their witness in a compromising situation, it could give them the leverage they needed to assure her cooperation and testimony.

Bosch left McPherson there and headed on foot down the crushed-shell drive to the barn. He didn't attempt to hide in case they had a lookout. He put his hands in his pocket to try to convey he was no threat, somebody just lost and looking for directions.

The crushed shell made it impossible for him to make a completely silent approach. But as he got closer he heard loud music coming from the barn. It was rock and roll but he could not identify it. Something heavy on the guitar and with a pounding beat. It had a retro feel to it, like he had heard the song a long time ago, maybe in Vietnam.

Bosch was twenty feet from the partially opened door when it moved open another two feet and the same young man stepped out again. Seeing him closer, Bosch pegged his age at twenty one or so. In the moment he stepped out Bosch realized he should have expected that he'd be back out to finish his interrupted smoke. Now it was too late and the smoker saw him.

But the young man didn't hesitate or sound an alarm of any sort. He looked at Bosch curiously as he started tapping a cigarette out of a soft pack. He was sweating profusely.

"You parked up at the house?" he asked.

Bosch stopped ten feet from him and took his hands out of his pockets. He didn't look back toward the house, choosing instead to keep his eyes on the kid.

"Uh, yes, is that a problem?" he asked.

"No, but most people just drive on down to the barn. Sarah usually tells them to."

"Oh, I didn't get that message. Is Sarah here?"

"Yeah, inside. Go on in."

"You sure?"

"Yeah, we're almost done for the day."

Bosch was getting the idea that he had walked into something that was not what he thought it was. He now glanced back and saw McPherson peering around the corner of the house. This wasn't the best way to do this but he turned and headed toward the open door.

The heat hit him the moment he entered. The inside of the barn was like an oven and for good reason. The first thing Bosch saw was the open door of a huge furnace that was glowing orange with flames.

Standing eight feet from the heat source was another young man and an older woman. They also wore full-length aprons and heavy gloves. The man was using a pair of iron tongs to hold steady a large piece of molten glass attached to the end of an iron pipe. The woman was shaping it with a wooden block and a pair of pliers.

They were glassmakers, not drug cooks. The woman wore a welder's mask over her face as protection. Bosch could not identify her but he was pretty sure he was looking at Sarah Ann Gleason.

Bosch stepped back through the door and signaled to McPherson. He gave the okay sign but was unsure she would be able to identify it from the distance. He waved her in.

"What's going on, man?" the smoker asked.

"That's Sarah Gleason in there, you said?" Bosch responded.

"Yeah, that's her."

"I need to talk to her."

"You're going to have to wait until she's set the piece. She can't stop while it's soft. We've been working it for almost four hours."

"How much longer?"

"Maybe an hour. You can probably talk to her while she's working. You want a piece made?"

"That's okay, I think we can wait."

McPherson drove up in the rental car and got out. Bosch opened the door for her and explained quietly that they had read wrong what they had seen. He told her the barn was a glassmaking studio. He told her how he wanted to play it until they could get Gleason into a private setting. McPherson shook her head and smiled.

"What if we had gone in there with backup?"

"I guess we would've broken some glass."

"And had one pissed-off witness."

She got out of the car and Bosch reached in for the file he had put on the dashboard. He put it inside his jacket and under his arm so he could carry it unseen.

They entered the studio and Gleason was waiting for them, with her gloves off and her mask folded up to reveal her face. She had obviously been told by the smoker that they were potential customers and Bosch initially did nothing to dissuade her of that interpretation. He didn't want to reveal their true business until they were alone with her.

"I'm Harry and this is Maggie. Sorry to barge in like this."

"Oh, no problem. We like it when people get a chance to see what we do. In fact, we're right in the middle of a project right now and need to get back to it. You're welcome to stay and watch and I can tell you a little bit about what we're doing."

"That would be great."

"You just have to stay back. We're dealing with very hot material here."

"Not a problem."

"Where are you from? Seattle?"

"No, actually we're all the way up from California. We're pretty far from home."

If the mention of her native state caused Gleason any concern, she didn't show it. She pulled the mask back down over a smile, put her gloves on and went back to work. Over the next forty minutes Bosch and McPherson watched Gleason and her two assistants finish the glass piece. Gleason provided a steady narration as she worked, explaining that the three members of her team had different duties. One of the young men was a blower and the other was a blocker. Gleason was the gaffer, the one in charge. The piece they were sculpting was a four-foot-long grape leaf that would be part of a larger piece commissioned to hang in the lobby of a business in Seattle called Rainier Wine.

Gleason also filled in some of her recent history. She said she started her own studio only two years ago after spending three years apprenticing with a glass artist in Seattle. It was useful information to Bosch. Both hearing her talk about herself and watching her work the soft glass. *Gathering color,* as she called it. Using heavy tools to manipulate something beautiful and fragile and glowing with red-hot danger all at the same time.

The heat from the furnace was stifling and both Bosch and McPherson took off their jackets. Gleason said the oven burned at 2,300 degrees and Bosch marveled at how the artists could spend so many hours working so close to the source. The glory hole, the small opening into which they repeatedly passed the sculpture to reheat and add layers, glowed like the gateway to Hell.

When the day's work was completed and the piece was placed in the finishing kiln, Gleason asked the assistants to clean up the studio before heading home. She then invited Bosch and McPherson to wait for her in the office while she got cleaned up herself.

The office doubled as a break room. It was sparely furnished with a table and four chairs, a filing cabinet, a storage locker and a small kitchenette. There was a binder on the table containing plastic sleeves with photos of glass pieces made previously in the studio. McPherson studied these and seemed taken with several. Bosch took out the file he had been carrying inside his jacket and put it down on the table ready to go.

"It must be nice to be able to make something out of nothing," McPherson said. "I wish I could."

Bosch tried to think of a response but before he could come up with anything the door opened and Sarah Gleason entered. The bulky mask, apron and gloves were gone and she was smaller than Bosch had expected. She barely crested five feet and he doubted there were more than ninety pounds on her tiny frame. He knew that childhood trauma sometimes stunted growth. So it was no wonder Sarah Gleason looked like a woman in a child's body.

Her auburn hair was down now instead of tied into a knot behind her head. It framed a weary face with dark blue eyes. She wore blue jeans, clogs and a black T-shirt that said *Death Cab* on it. She headed directly to the refrigerator.

"Can I get you something? Don't have any alcohol in here but if you need something cold..."

Bosch and McPherson passed. Harry noticed she had left the door to the office open. He could hear someone sweeping in the studio. He stepped over and closed it.

Gleason turned from the refrigerator with a bottle of water. She saw Bosch closing the door and a look of apprehension immediately crossed her face. Bosch raised one hand in a calming gesture as he pulled his badge with the other.

"Ms. Gleason, everything is okay. We're from Los Angeles and just need to speak privately with you."

He opened his badge wallet and held it up to her.

"What is this?"

"My name is Harry Bosch and this is Maggie McPherson. She is a prosecutor with the L.A. County District Attorney's Office."

"Why did you lie?" she said angrily. "You said you wanted a piece made."

"No, actually we didn't. Your assistant, the blocker, just assumed that. We never said why we were here."

Her guard was clearly up and Bosch thought they had blown their approach and with that the opportunity to secure her as a witness. But then Gleason stepped forward and grabbed the badge wallet out of his hand. She studied it and the facing ID card. It was an unusual move, taking the badge from him. No more than the fifth time that had ever happened to Bosch in his long career as a cop. He saw her eyes hold on the ID card and he knew she had noticed the discrepancy between what he had said his name was and what was on the ID.

"You said *Harry* Bosch?"

"Harry for short."

"Hieronymus Bosch. You're named after the artist?"

Bosch nodded.

"My mother liked the paintings."

"Well, I like them, too. I think he knew something about inner demons. Is that why your mother liked him?"

"I think so, yeah."

She handed the badge wallet back to him and Bosch sensed a calmness come over her. The moment of anxiety and apprehension had passed, thanks to the painter whose name Bosch carried.

"What do you want with me? I haven't been to L.A. in more than ten years."

Bosch noted that if she was telling the truth, then she had not returned when her stepfather was ill and dying.

"We just want to talk," he said. "Can we sit down?"

"Talk about what?"

"Your sister."

"My sister? I don't — look, you need to tell me what this is —"

"You don't know, do you?"

"Know what?"

"Sit down and we'll tell you."

Finally, she moved to the lunch table and took a seat. She pulled a soft pack of cigarettes out of her pocket and lit one.

"Sorry," she said. "It's my one remaining addiction. And you two showing up like this — I need a smoke."

For the next ten minutes Bosch and McPherson traded off the story and walked her through the short version of Jason Jessup's journey to freedom. Gleason showed almost no reaction to the news. No tears, no outrage. And she didn't ask questions about the DNA test that had sprung him from prison. She only explained that she had no contact with anyone in California, owned no television and never read newspapers. She said they were distractions from work as well as from her recovery from addiction.

"We're going to retry him, Sarah," McPherson said. "And we're here because we're going to need your help."

Bosch could see Sarah turn inward, to start to measure the impact of what they were telling her.

"It was so long ago," she finally responded. "Can't you just use what I said from the first trial?"

McPherson shook her head.

"We can't, Sarah. The new jury can't even know there was an earlier trial because that could influence how they weigh the evidence. It would prejudice them against the defendant and a guilty verdict wouldn't stand. So in situations where witnesses from the first trial are dead or mentally incompetent, we read their earlier testimony into the trial record without telling the jury where it's from. But where that's not the case, like with you, we need the person to come to court and testify."

It wasn't clear whether Gleason had even registered McPherson's response. She sat staring at something far away. Even as she spoke, her eyes didn't come off their distant focus.

"I've spent my whole life since then trying to forget about that day. I tried different things to make me forget. I used drugs to make a big bubble with me in the middle of it. I made...Never mind, the point is, I don't think I'm going to be much help to you."

Before McPherson could respond, Bosch stepped in.

"I'll tell you what," he said. "Let's just talk here for a few minutes about what you can remember, okay? And if it's not going to work, then it won't work. You were a victim, Sarah, and we don't want to victimize you all over again."

He waited a moment for Gleason to respond but she sat mute, staring at the water bottle in front of her on the table.

"Let's start with that day," Bosch said. "I don't need you at this point to go through the horrible moments of your sister's abduction, but do you remember making the identification of Jason Jessup for the police?"

She slowly nodded.

"I remember looking through the window. Upstairs. They opened the blinds a little bit so I could look out. They weren't supposed to be able to see me. The men. He was the one with the hat. They made him take it off and that's when I saw it was him. I remember that."

Bosch was encouraged by the detail of the hat. He didn't recall seeing that in the case records or hearing it in McPherson's summary but the fact that Gleason remembered it was a good sign.

"What kind of hat was he wearing?" he asked.

"A baseball cap," Gleason said. "It was blue."

"A Dodgers cap?"

"I'm not sure. I don't think I knew back then either."

Bosch nodded and moved in.

"Do you think if I showed you a photo lineup, you would be able to identify the man who took your sister?"

"You mean the way he looks now? I doubt it."

"No, not now," McPherson said. "What we would need to do in trial is confirm the identification you made back then. We would show you photos from back then."

Gleason hesitated and then nodded.

"Sure. Through everything I've done to myself over the years, I've never been able to forget that man's face."

"Well, let's see."

While Bosch opened the file on the table, Gleason lit a new cigarette off the end of her old one.

The file contained a lineup of six black-and-white booking photos of men of the same age, build and coloring. A 1986 photo of Jessup was included in the spread. Harry knew that this was the make-or-break moment of the case.

The photos were displayed in two rows of three. Jessup's shot was in the middle window on the bottom row. The five hole. It had always been the lucky spot for Bosch.

"Take your time," he said.

Gleason drank some water and then put the bottle to the side. She leaned over the table, bringing her face within twelve inches of the photos. It didn't take her long. She pointed to the photo of Jessup without hesitation.

"I wish I could forget him," she said. "But I can't. He's always there in the back of my mind. In the shadows."

"Do you have any doubt about the photo you have chosen?" Bosch asked.

Gleason leaned down and looked again, then shook her head.

"No. He was the man."

Bosch glanced at McPherson, who made a slight nod. It was a good ID and they had handled it right. The only thing that was missing was a show of emotion on Gleason's part. But maybe twenty-four years had drained her of everything. Harry took out a pen and handed it to Gleason.

"Would you put your initials and the date below the photo you chose, please?"

"Why?"

"It confirms your ID. It just helps make it more solid when it comes up in court."

Bosch noted that she had not asked if she had chosen the right photo. She didn't have to and that was a secondary confirmation of her recall. Another good sign. After she handed the pen back to Bosch he closed the file and slid it to the side. He glanced at McPherson again. Now came the hard part. By prior agreement, Maggie was going to make the call here on whether to bring up the DNA now or to wait until Gleason was more firmly onboard as a witness.

McPherson decided not to wait.

"Sarah, there is a second issue to discuss now. We told you about the DNA that allowed this man to get this new trial and what we hope is only his temporary freedom."

"Yes."

"We took the DNA profile and checked it against the California data bank. We got a match. The semen on the dress your sister was wearing came from your stepfather."

Bosch watched Sarah closely. Not even a flicker of surprise showed on her face or in her eyes. This information was not news to her.

"In two thousand four the state started taking DNA swabs from all suspects in felony arrests. That same year your father was arrested for a felony hit-and-run with injuries. He ran a stop sign and hit —"

"Stepfather."

"Excuse me?"

"You said 'your father.' He wasn't my father. He was my stepfather."

"My mistake. I'm sorry. The bottom line is Kensington Landy's DNA was in the data bank and it's a match with the sample from the dress. What could not be determined is how long that sample was on the dress at the time of its discovery. It could have been deposited on the dress the day of the murder or the week before or maybe even a month before."

Sarah started flying on autopilot. She was there but not there. Her eyes were fixed on a distance that was far beyond the room they were in.

"We have a theory, Sarah. The autopsy that was conducted on your sister determined that she had not been sexually abused by her killer or anyone else prior to that day. We also know the dress she wore happened to be yours and Melissa was borrowing it that morning because she liked it."

McPherson paused but Sarah said nothing.

"When we get to trial we're going to have to explain the semen found on the dress. If we can't explain it, the assumption will be that it came from the killer and that killer was your stepfather. We will lose the case and Jessup, the real killer, will walk away free. I'm sure you don't want that, do you, Sarah? There are some people out there who think twenty-four years in prison is enough time served for the murder of a twelve-year-old girl.

They don't know why we're doing this. But I want you to know that I don't think that, Sarah. Not by a long shot."

Sarah Gleason didn't answer at first. Bosch expected tears but none came and he began to wonder if her emotions had been cauterized by the traumas and depravities of her life. Or maybe she simply had an internal toughness that her diminutive stature camouflaged. Either way, when she finally responded, it was in a flat, emotionless voice that belied the heart-felt words she spoke.

"You know what I always thought?" she said.

McPherson leaned forward.

"What, Sarah?"

"That that man killed three people that day. My sister, then my mother...and then me. None of us got away."

There was a long moment of silence. McPherson slowly reached out and put her hand on Gleason's arm, a gesture of comfort where no comfort could exist.

"I'm sorry, Sarah," McPherson whispered.

"Okay," Gleason said. "I'll tell you everything."

13

Thursday, February 18, 8:15 P.M.

My daughter was already missing her mother's cooking—and she'd only been gone one day. I was dropping her half-eaten sandwich into the garbage and wondering how the hell I could've messed up a grilled cheese when my cell phone's ring interrupted. It was Maggie checking in from the road.

"Tell me something good," I said by way of greeting.

"You get to spend the evening with our beautiful daughter."

"Yes, that's something good. Except she doesn't like my cooking. Now tell me something else that's good."

"Our primary witness is good to go. She'll testify."

"She made the ID?"

"She did."

"She told you about the DNA and it fits with our theory?"

"She did and it does."

"And she'll come down here and testify to all of it at the trial?"

"She will."

I felt a twelve-volt charge go through my body.

"That's actually a lot of good things, Maggie. Is there any downside?"

"Well…"

I felt the wind go out of the sails. I was about to learn that Sarah was still a drug addict or there was some other issue that would prevent me from using her at trial.

"Well, what?"

"Well, there are going to be challenges to her testimony, of course, but she's pretty solid. She's a survivor and it shows. There's really only one thing missing: emotions. She's been through a lot in her life and she basically seems to be a bit burned out—emotionally. No tears, no laughter, just straight down the middle."

"We can work on that. We can coach her."

"Yeah, well, we just have to be careful with that. I am not saying she isn't fine the way she is. I'm just saying that she's sort of a flat line. Everything else is good. I think you're going to like her and I think she'll help us put Jessup back in prison."

"That's fantastic, Maggie. Really. And you're still all right handling her at trial, right?"

"I've got her."

"Royce will attack her on the meth—memory loss and all of that. Her lifestyle…you'll have to be ready for anything and everything."

"I will be. That leaves you with Bosch and Jessup. You still think he'll testify?"

"Jessup? Yes, he's got to. Clive knows he can't do that to a jury, not after twenty-four years. So, yes, I've got him and I've got Bosch."

"At least with Harry you don't have to worry about any baggage."

"That Clive knows about yet."

"And what's that supposed to mean?"

"It means don't underestimate Clever Clive Royce. See, that's what you prosecutors always do. You get overconfident and it makes you vulnerable."

"Thank you, F. Lee Bailey. I'll keep that in mind."

"How was Bosch today?"

"He was Bosch. What happened on your end?"

I checked through the door of the kitchen. Hayley was sitting on the couch with her homework spread out on the coffee table.

"Well, for one thing, we've got a judge. Breitman, Department one-twelve."

Maggie considered the case assignment for a moment before responding.

"I would call that a no-win for either side. She's straight down the middle. Never a prosecutor, never a defense attorney. Just a good, solid civil trial lawyer. I think neither side gets an advantage with her."

"Wow, a judge who's going to be impartial and fair. Imagine that."

She didn't respond.

"She set the first status conference in chambers. Wednesday morning at eight before court starts. You read anything into that?"

This meant the judge wanted to meet the lawyers and discuss the case in chambers, starting things off informally and away from the lens of the media.

"I think that's good. She's probably going to set the rules with media and procedure. It sounds to me like she's going to run a tight ship."

"That was what I was thinking. You're free Wednesday to be there?"

"I'll have to check my calendar but I think so. I'm trying to clear everything except for this."

"I gave Royce the first bit of discovery today. It was mostly composed of material from the first trial."

"You know you could have held off on that until the thirty-day marker."

"Yeah, but what's the point?"

"The point is strategy. The earlier you give it to him, the more time he has to be ready for it. He's trying to put the squeeze on us by not waiving speedy trial. You should put the squeeze right back on him by not showing our hand until we have to. Thirty days before trial."

"I'll remember that with the next round. But this was pretty basic stuff."

"Was Sarah Gleason on the witness list?"

"Yes, but under the name Sarah Landy — as it was in 'eighty-six. And I gave the office as the address. Clive doesn't know we found her."

"We need to keep it that way until we have to reveal it. I don't want her harassed or feeling threatened."

"What did you tell her about coming down for the trial?"

"I told her she would probably be needed for two days in trial. Plus the travel."

"And that's not going to be a problem?"

"Well...she runs her own business and has been at it only a couple years. She has one big, ongoing project but otherwise said that things are slow. My guess is we can get her down when we need her."

"Are you still in Port Townsend?"

"Yes, we just got finished with her about an hour ago. We grabbed dinner and checked in at a hotel. It's been a long day."

"And you're coming back tomorrow?"

"We were planning on it. But our flight's not till two. We have to take a ferry — it's a journey just to the airport."

"Okay, call me in the morning before you leave. Just in case I think of something involving the witness."

"Okay."

"Did either of you take notes?"

"No, we thought it might freeze her."

"Did you record it?"

"No, same reason."

"Good. I want to keep as much of this out of discovery as possible. Tell

Bosch not to write anything up. We can copy Royce on the six-pack she made the ID off of, but that's it."

"Right. I'll tell Harry."

"When, tonight or tomorrow?"

"What's that supposed to mean?"

"Nothing, never mind. Anything else?"

"Yes."

I braced for it. My petty jealousy had slipped out for one small moment.

"I would like to say good night to my daughter now."

"Oh," I said, relief bursting through my body. "I'll put her on."

I took the phone out to Hayley.

"It's your mother."

PART TWO

— The Labyrinth

14

Tuesday, February 23, 8:45 P.M.

Each of them worked in silence. Bosch at one end of the dining room table, his daughter at the other. He with the first batch of SIS surveillance logs, she with her homework, her school books and laptop computer spread out in front of her. They were close in proximity but not in much else. The Jessup case had become all-encompassing with Bosch tracing old witnesses and trying to find new ones. He had spent little time with her in recent days. Like her parents, Maddie was good at holding grudges and had not let go of the perceived slight of having been left for a night in the care of an assistant school principal. She was giving Harry the silent treatment and already at fourteen she was an expert at it.

The SIS logs were another frustration to Bosch. Not because of what they contained but because of their delay in reaching him. They had been sent through bureaucratic channels, from the SIS office to the RHD office and then to Bosch's supervisor, where they had sat in an in basket for three days before finally being dropped on Bosch's desk. The result was he had logs from the first three days of the surveillance of Jason Jessup and he was looking at them three to six days after the fact. That process was too slow and Bosch was going to have to do something about it.

The logs were terse accounts of the surveillance subject's movements by date, time and location. Most entries carried only a single line of description. The logs came with an accompanying set of photos as well, but most of the shots were taken at a significant distance so the followers could avoid detection. These were grainy images of Jessup as he moved about the city as a free man.

Bosch read through the reports and quickly surmised that Jessup was already leading separate public and private lives. By day his movements were in concert with the media as he very publicly reacquainted himself with life outside a prison cell. It was about learning to drive again, to choose off a menu, to go for a three-mile run without having to make a turn. But by night a different Jessup emerged. Unaware that he was still being watched by eyes and cameras, he went out cruising alone in his borrowed car. He went to all corners of the city. He went to bars, strip clubs, a prostitute's trick pad.

Of all his activities, one was most curious to Bosch. On his fourth night of freedom, Jessup had driven up to Mulholland Drive, the winding road atop the crest of the Santa Monica Mountains, which cut the city in half. Day or night, Mulholland offered some of the best views of the city. It was no surprise that Jessup would go up there. There were overlooks that offered north and south views of the shimmering lights of the city. They could be invigorating and even majestic. Bosch had gone to these spots himself in the past.

But Jessup didn't go to any of the overlooks. He pulled his car off the road near the entrance to Franklin Canyon Park. He got out and then entered the closed park, sneaking around a gate.

This caused a surveillance issue for the SIS team because the park was empty and the watchers were at risk of being seen if they got too close. The report here was briefer than most entries in the log:

```
02/20/10-01:12. Subject entered Franklin Canyon
Park. Observed at picnic table area, northeast
corner, blind man trailhead.

02/20/10-02:34. Subject leaves park, proceeds west
on Mulholland to 405 freeway and then south.
```

After that, Jessup returned to the apartment where he was living in Venice and stayed in for the rest of the night.

There was a printout of an infrared photograph taken of Jessup in the park. It showed him sitting at a picnic table in the dark. Just sitting there.

Bosch put the photo print down on the table and looked at his daughter. She was left-handed like he was. It looked like she was writing out a math problem on a work sheet.

"What?"

She had her mother's radar.

"Uh, are you online there?"

"Yes, what do you need?"

"Can you pull up a map of Franklin Canyon Park? It's off of Mulholland Drive."

"Let me finish this."

He waited patiently for her to complete her computations on a mathematical problem he knew would be light-years beyond his understanding. For the past four months he had lived in fear that his daughter would ask him for help with her homework. She had passed by his skills and knowledge long ago. He was useless in this area and had tried to concentrate on mentoring her in other areas, observation and self-protection chief among them.

"Okay."

She put her pencil down and pulled her computer front and center. Bosch checked his watch. It was almost nine.

"Here."

Maddie slid the computer down the table, turning the screen toward him.

The park was larger than Bosch had thought, running south of Mulholland and west of Coldwater Canyon Boulevard. A key in the corner of the map said it was 605 acres. Bosch hadn't realized that there was such a large public reserve in this prime section of the Hollywood Hills. He noticed that the map had several of the hiking trails and picnic areas marked. The picnic area in the northeast section was off of Blinderman Trail. He assumed it had been misspelled in the SIS log as "blind man trailhead."

"What is it?"

Harry looked at his daughter. It was her first attempt at conversation in two days. He decided not to miss it.

"Well, we've been watching this guy. The Special Investigations Section. They're the department's surveillance experts and they're watching this guy who just got out of prison. He killed a little girl a long time ago. And for some reason he went to this park and just sat there at a picnic table."

"So? Isn't that what people do at parks?"

"Well, this was in the middle of the night. The park was closed and he snuck in...and then he sort of just sat there."

"Did he grow up near the park? Maybe he's checking out the places where he grew up."

"I don't think so. We have him growing up out in Riverside County. He used to come to L.A. to surf but I haven't found any connection to Mulholland."

Bosch studied the map once more and noticed there was an upper and lower entrance to the park. Jessup had gone in through the upper entrance. This would have been out of his way unless that picnic area and Blinderman Trail were specific destinations for him.

He slid the computer back to his daughter. And checked his watch again.

"Are you almost done your work?"

"*Finished,* Dad. Are you almost finished? Or you could say 'done *with.*'"

"Sorry. Are you almost finished?"

"I have one more math problem."

"Good. I have to make a quick call."

Lieutenant Wright's cell number was on the surveillance log. Bosch expected him to be home and annoyed with the intrusion but decided to make the call anyway. He got up and walked into the living room so he would not disturb Maddie on her last problem. He punched the number into his cell.

"Wright, SIS."

"Lieutenant, it's Harry Bosch."

"What's up, Bosch?"

He didn't sound annoyed.

"Sorry to intrude on you at home. I just wanted —"

"I'm not at home, Bosch. I'm with your guy."

Bosch was surprised.

"Is something wrong?"

"No, the night shift is just more interesting."

"Where is he right now?"

"We're with him at a bar on Venice Beach called the Townhouse. You know it?"

"I've been there. Is he alone?"

"Yes and no. He came alone but he got recognized. He can't buy a drink in there and probably has his pick of the skanks. Like I said, more interesting at night. Are you calling to check up on us?"

"Not really. I just have a couple of things I need to ask. I'm looking at the logs and the first thing is, how can I get them sooner? I'm looking at stuff from three days ago or longer. The other thing is Franklin Canyon Park. What can you tell me about his stop there?"

"Which one?"

"He's been there twice?"

"Actually, three times. He's gone there the last two nights after the first stop four days ago."

This information was very intriguing to Bosch, mostly because he had no idea what it meant.

"What did he do the last two times?"

Maddie got up from the dining room table and came into the living room. She sat on the couch and listened to Bosch's side of the conversation.

"The same thing he did the first night," Wright said. "He sneaks in there and goes to the same picnic area. He just sits there, like he's waiting for something."

"For what?"

"You tell me, Bosch."

"I wish I could. Did he go at the same time each night?"

"Give or take a half hour or so."

"Does he go in through the Mulholland entrance each time?"

"That's right. He sneaks in and picks up the same trail that takes him to the picnic area."

"I wonder why he doesn't go in the other entrance. It would be easier for him to get to."

"Maybe he likes driving on Mulholland and seeing the lights."

That was a good point and Bosch needed to consider it.

"Lieutenant, can you have your people call me the next time he goes there? I don't care what time it is."

"I can have them call you but you're not going to be able to get in there and get close. It's too risky. We don't want to expose the surveillance."

"I understand, but have them call me. I just want to know. Now, what about these logs? Is there a way for me to get them a little quicker?"

"You can come by SIS and pick one up every morning if you want. As you probably noticed, the logs run six P.M. to six P.M. Each daily log is posted by seven the following morning."

"Okay, LT, I'll do that. Thanks for the info."

"Have a good one."

Bosch closed the phone, wondering about Jessup in Franklin Canyon and what he was doing on his visits there.

"What did he say?" Maddie asked.

Bosch hesitated, wondering for the hundredth time whether he should be telling her as much as he did about his cases.

"He said my guy's gone back to that park the last two nights. Each time, he just sits there and waits."

"For what?"

"Nobody knows."

"Maybe he just wants to be somewhere where he's completely by himself and away from everybody."

"Maybe."

But Bosch doubted it. He believed there was a plan to almost everything Jessup did. Bosch just had to figure out what it was.

"I'm finished with my homework," Maddie said. "You want to watch *Lost*?"

They had been slowly going through the DVDs of the television show, catching up on five years' worth of episodes. The show was about several people who survived a plane crash on an uncharted island in the South Pacific. Bosch had trouble keeping track of things from show to show but watched because his daughter had been completely taken in by the story.

He had no time to watch television right now.

"Okay, one episode," he said. "Then you have to go to bed and I have to get back to work."

She smiled. This made her happy and for the moment Bosch's grammatical and parental transgressions seemed forgotten.

"Set it up," Bosch said. "And be prepared to remind me what's happening."

Five hours later, Bosch was on a jet that was shaking with wild turbulence. His daughter was sitting across the aisle from him rather than in the open seat next to him. They reached across the aisle to each other to hold hands but the bouncing of the plane kept knocking them apart. He couldn't grab her hand.

Just as he turned in his seat to see the tail section break off and fall away, he was awakened by a buzzing sound. He reached to the bed table and grabbed his phone. He struggled to find his voice as he answered.

"This is Bosch."

"This is Shipley, SIS. I was told to call."

"Jessup's at the park?"

"He's in a park, yeah, but tonight it's a different one."

"Where?"

"Fryman Canyon off Mulholland."

Bosch knew Fryman Canyon. It was about ten minutes away from Franklin Canyon.

"What's he doing?"

"He's just sort of walking on one of the trails. Just like at the other park. He walks the trail and then he sits down. He doesn't do anything after that. He just sits for a while and then leaves."

"Okay."

Bosch looked at the glowing numbers on the clock. It was two o'clock exactly.

"Are you coming out?" Shipley asked.

Bosch thought about his daughter asleep in her bedroom. He knew he could leave and be back before she woke up.

"Uh...no, I have my daughter here and I can't leave her."

"Suit yourself."

"When does your shift end?"

"About seven."

"Can you call me then?"

"If you want."

"I'd like you to call me every morning when you are getting off. To tell me where he's been."

"Uh...all right, I guess. Can I ask you something? This guy killed a girl, right?"

"That's right."

"And you're sure about that? I mean, no doubt, right?"

Bosch thought about the interview with Sarah Gleason.

"I have no doubt."

"Okay, well, that's good to know."

Bosch understood what he was saying. He was looking for assurance. If circumstances dictated the use of deadly force against Jessup, it was good to know who and what they would be shooting at. Nothing else needed to be said about it.

"Thanks, Shipley," Bosch said. "I'll talk to you later."

Bosch disconnected and put his head back on the pillow. He remembered the dream about the plane. About reaching out to his daughter but being unable to grab her hand.

15

≋

Judge Diane Breitman welcomed us into her chambers and offered a pot of coffee and a plate of shortbread cookies, an unusual move for a criminal courts judge. In attendance were myself and my second chair, Maggie McPherson, and Clive Royce, who was without his second but not without his temerity. He asked the judge if he could have hot tea instead.

"Well, this is nice," the judge said once we were all seated in front of her desk, cups and saucers in hand. "I have not had the opportunity to see any of you practice in my courtroom. So I thought it would be good for us to start out a bit informally in chambers. We can always step out into the courtroom to go on the record if necessary."

She smiled and none of the rest of us responded.

"Let me start by saying that I have a deep respect for the decorum of the courtroom," Breitman continued. "And I insist that the lawyers who practice before me do as well. I am expecting this trial to be a spirited contest of the evidence and facts of the case. But I won't stand for any acting out or crossing of the lines of courtesy and jurisprudence. I hope that is clearly understood."

"Yes, Your Honor," Maggie responded while Royce and I nodded.

"Good, now let's talk about media coverage. The media is going to be hovering over this case like the helicopters that followed O.J. down the freeway. That is clearly a given. I have requests here from three local network affiliates, a documentary filmmaker and *Dateline NBC*. They all want to film the trial in its entirety. While I see no problem with that, as long as proper protections of the jury are put in place, my concern is in the extracurricular activity that is bound to occur outside the courtroom. Do any of you have any thoughts in this regard?"

I waited a beat and when no one spoke up, I did.

"Judge, I think because of the nature of this case—a retrial of a case twenty-four years old—there has already been too much media attention and we're going to have a difficult time seating twelve people and two alternates who aren't aware of the case through the filter of the media. I mean, we've had the accused surfing on the front page of the *Times* and sitting courtside at the Lakers. How are we going to get an impartial jury out of this? The media, with no lack of help from Mr. Royce, is presenting this guy as this poor, persecuted innocent man and they don't have the slightest idea what the evidence is against him."

"Your Honor, I object," Royce said.

"You can't object," I said. "This isn't a court hearing."

"You *used* to be a defense attorney, Mick. Whatever happened to innocent until proven guilty?"

"He already has been."

"In a trial the top court in this state termed a travesty. Is that what you want to stand on?"

"Listen, Clive, I'm an attorney and *innocent until proven guilty* is a measure you apply in court, not on *Larry King Live*."

"We haven't been on *Larry King Live* — yet."

"See what I mean, Judge? He wants to —"

"Gentlemen, please!" Breitman said.

She waited a moment until she was certain our debate had subsided.

"This is a classic situation where we need to balance the public's right to know with safeguards that will provide us an untainted jury, an unimpeded trial and a just result."

"But, Your Honor," Royce said quickly, "we can't forbid the media to examine this case. Freedom of the press is the cornerstone of American democracy. And, further, I draw your attention to the very ruling that granted this retrial. The court found serious deficiencies in the evidence and castigated the District Attorney's Office for the corrupt manner in which it has prosecuted my client. Now you are going to prohibit the media from looking at this?"

"Oh, please," Maggie said dismissively. "We're not talking about prohibiting the media from looking at anything, and your lofty defense of the freedom of the press aside, that's not what this is about. You are clearly trying to influence voir dire with your pretrial manipulation of the media."

"That is absolutely untrue!" Royce howled. "I have responded to media requests, yes. But I am not trying to influence anything. Your Honor, this is an —"

There was a sharp crack from the judge's desk. She had grabbed a gavel from a decorative pen set and brought it down hard on the wood surface.

"Let's cool down here," Breitman said. "And let's hold off on the personal attacks. As I indicated before, there has to be a happy medium. I am not inclined to muzzle the press, but I will issue a gag order against the lawyers in my court if I believe they are not acting in a manner that is responsible to the case at hand. I am going to start off by leaving each of you to determine what is reasonable and responsible interaction with the media. But I will warn you now that the consequences for a transgression in this area will be swift and possibly detrimental to one's cause. No warnings. You cross the line and that's it."

She paused and waited for a comeback. No one said anything. She placed the gavel back in its special holder next to the gold pen. Her voice returned to its friendly tone.

"Good," she said. "I think that's understood, then."

She said she wanted to move on to other matters germane to the trial and her first stop was the trial date. She wanted to know if both sides would be ready to proceed to trial as scheduled, less than six weeks away. Royce said once again that his client would not waive the speedy trial statute.

"The defense will be ready to go on April fifth, provided that the prosecution doesn't continue to play games with discovery."

I shook my head. I couldn't win with this guy. I had gone out of my way to get the discovery pipeline going, but he had decided to take a shot at making me look like a cheater in front of the judge.

"Games?" I said. "Judge, I've already turned over to Mr. Royce an initial discovery file. But as you know, it's a two-way street and the prosecution has received nothing in return from him."

"He turned over the discovery file from the first trial, Judge Breitman, complete with a nineteen eighty-six witness list. It completely subverts the spirit and the rules of discovery."

Breitman looked at me and I could see that Royce had successfully scored a hit.

"Is this true, Mr. Haller?" she asked.

"Hardly, Your Honor, the witness list was both subtracted from and added to. Additionally, I turned over—"

"One name," Royce interjected. "He added one name and it was his own investigator. Big deal, like I didn't know his investigator might be a witness."

"Well, that's the only new name I have at the moment."

Maggie jumped into the fray with both feet.

"Your Honor, the prosecution is duty-bound to turn over all discovery materials thirty days prior to trial. By my count we are still forty days out. Mr. Royce is complaining about a good-faith effort on the part of the prosecution to provide him with discovery material before it even has to. It seems that no good deed goes unpunished with Mr. Royce."

The judge held up her hand to stop commentary while she looked at the calendar hanging on the wall to the left of her desk.

"I think Ms. McPherson makes a good point," she said. "Your complaint is premature, Mr. Royce. All discovery materials are due to both sides by this Friday, March fifth. If you have a problem then, we will take this up again."

"Yes, Your Honor," Royce said meekly.

I wanted to reach over, raise Maggie's hand in the air and shake it in victory but I didn't think that would be appropriate. Still, it felt good to win at least one point against Royce.

After discussion of a few more routine pretrial issues, the meeting ended and we walked out through the judge's courtroom. I stopped there to talk small talk with the judge's clerk. I didn't really know her that well but I didn't want to walk out of the courtroom with Royce. I was afraid I might lose my temper, which would be exactly what he'd want.

After he went through the double doors at the back of the courtroom I cut off the conversation and headed out with Maggie at my side.

"You kicked his ass, Maggie McFierce," I said to her. "Verbally."

"Doesn't matter unless we kick it at trial."

"Don't worry, we will. I want you to take over discovery fulfillment. Go ahead and do what you prosecutors do. Haystack everything. Give him so much material he'll never see what and who's important."

She smiled as she turned and used her back to push through the door.

"Now you're getting it."

"I hope so."

"What about Sarah? He's got to figure we found her and if he's smart he won't wait for discovery. He probably has his own guy looking. She can be found. Harry proved that."

"There's not a whole lot we can do about it. Speaking of Harry, where is he this morning?"

"He called me and said he had some things to check out. He'll be around later. You didn't really answer my question about Sarah. What should —?"

"Tell her that she might have another visitor, somebody working for the defense, but that she doesn't have to talk to anybody unless she wants to."

We headed out into the hallway and then went left toward the elevator bank.

"If she doesn't talk to them, Royce will complain to the judge. She's the key witness, Mickey."

"So? The judge won't be able to make her talk if she doesn't want to talk. Meantime, Royce loses prep time. He wants to play games like he did with the judge in there, then we'll play games, too. In fact, how about this? We put every convict Jessup ever shared a prison cell with on the witness list. That should keep his investigators out of the way for a while."

A broad smile broke across Maggie's face.

"You really *are* getting it, aren't you?"

We squeezed onto the crowded elevator. Maggie and I were close enough to kiss. I looked down into her eyes as I spoke.

"That's because I don't want to lose."

16

Wednesday, February 24, 8:45 A.M.

After school drop-off Bosch turned his car around and headed back up Woodrow Wilson, past his house, and to what those in the neighborhood called the upper crossing with Mulholland Drive. Both Mulholland and Woodrow Wilson were long and winding mountain roads. They intersected twice, at the bottom and top of the mountain, thus the local description of upper and lower crossings.

At the top of the mountain Bosch turned right onto Mulholland and followed it until it crossed Laurel Canyon Boulevard. He then pulled off the road to make a call on his cell. He punched in the number Shipley had given him for the SIS dispatch sergeant. His name was Willman and he would know the current status of any SIS surveillance. At any given time, SIS could be working four or five unrelated cases. Each was given a code name in order to keep them in order and so that the real names of suspects did not ever go out over the radio. Bosch knew that the Jessup surveillance had been termed Operation Retro because it involved an old case and a retrial.

"This is Bosch, RHD. I'm lead on the Retro case. I want to get a location on the suspect because I'm about to pull into one of his favorite haunts. I want to make sure I don't run into him."

"Hold one."

Bosch could hear the phone being put down, then a radio conversation in which the duty sergeant asked for Jessup's location. The response was garbled with static by the time it reached Bosch over the phone. He waited for the sergeant's official response.

"Retro is in pocket right now," he promptly reported to Bosch. "They think he's catching Zs."

In pocket meant he was at home.

"Then I'm clear," Bosch said. "Thank you, Sergeant."

"Any time."

Bosch closed the phone and pulled the car back onto Mulholland. A few curves later he reached Fryman Canyon Park and turned in. Bosch had talked to Shipley early that morning as he was passing surveillance off to the day team. He reported that Jessup had once again visited both Franklin and Fryman canyons. Bosch was becoming consumed with curiosity about what Jessup was up to and this was only increased by the report that Jessup had also driven by the house on Windsor where the Landy family had once lived.

Fryman was a rugged, inclined park with steep trails and a flat-surface parking and observation area on top and just off Mulholland. Bosch had been there before on cases and was familiar with its expanse. He pulled to a stop with his car pointing north and the view of the San Fernando Valley spread before him. The air was pretty clear and the vista stretched all the way across the valley to the San Gabriel Mountains. The brutal week of storms that had ended January had cleared the skies out and the smog was only now climbing back into the valley's bowl.

After a few minutes Bosch got out and walked over to the bench where Shipley had told him Jessup had sat for twenty minutes while looking out at the lights below. Bosch sat down and checked his watch. He had an eleven o'clock appointment with a witness. That gave him more than an hour.

Sitting where Jessup had sat brought no vibe or insight into what the suspect was doing on his frequent visits to the mountainside parks. Bosch decided to move on down Mulholland to Franklin Canyon.

But Franklin Canyon Park offered him the same thing, a large natural respite in the midst of a teeming city. Bosch found the picnic area Shipley and the SIS reports had described but once again didn't understand the pull the park had for Jessup. He found the terminus of Blinderman Trail and walked it until his legs started to hurt because of the incline. He turned around and headed back to the parking and picnic area, still puzzled by Jessup's activities.

On his return Bosch passed a large old sycamore that the trail had been routed around. He noticed a buildup of a grayish-white material at the base of the tree between two fingers of exposed roots. He looked closer and realized it was wax. Somebody had burned a candle.

There were signs all over the park warning against smoking or the use of matches, as fire was the park's greatest threat. But somebody had lit a candle at the base of the tree.

Bosch wanted to call Shipley to ask if Jessup could have lit a candle while in the park the night before, but knew it was the wrong move. Shipley had just come off a night of surveillance and was probably in his bed asleep. Harry would wait for the evening to make the call.

He looked around the tree for any other signs that Jessup had possibly been in the area. It looked like an animal had burrowed recently in a few spots under the tree. But otherwise there was no sign of activity.

As he came off the trail and into the clearing where the picnic area was located, Bosch saw a city parks ranger looking into a trash can from which he had removed the top. Harry approached him.

"Officer?"

The man whipped around, still holding the top of the trash can away from his body.

"Yes, sir!"

"Sorry, I didn't mean to sneak up on you. I was...I was walking up on that trail and there's a big tree there—I think a sycamore—and it looks like somebody burned a candle down at its base. I was wondering—"

"Where?"

"Up on Blinderman Trail."

"Show me."

"Actually, I'm not going to go all the way back up there. I don't have the right shoes. It's the big tree in the middle of the trail. I'm sure you can find it."

"You can't light fires in the park!"

The ranger put the top back on the trash can, banging it loudly to underline his statement.

"I know. That's why I was reporting it. But I wanted to ask you, is there anything special about that tree that would make somebody do that?"

"Every tree is special here. The whole park is special."

"Yes, I get that. Can you just tell—"

"Can I see some ID, please?"

"Excuse me?"

"ID. I want to see some ID. A man in a shirt and tie walking the trails with 'the wrong shoes' is a little bit suspicious to me."

Bosch shook his head and pulled out his badge wallet.

"Yeah, here's my ID."

He opened it and held it out and gave the ranger a few moments to study it. Bosch saw the nameplate on his uniform said Brorein.

"Okay?" Bosch said. "Can we get to my questions now, Officer Brorein?"

"I'm a city ranger, not an officer," Brorein said. "Is this part of an investigation?"

"No, it's part of a situation where you just answer my questions about the tree up on that trail."

Bosch pointed in the direction he had come from.

"You get it now?" he asked.

Brorein shook his head.

"I'm sorry but you're on my turf here and it's my obligation to—"

"No, pal, you're actually on my turf. But thanks for all the help. I'll make a note of it in the report."

Bosch walked away from him and headed back toward the parking clearing. Brorein called after him.

"As far as I know, there's nothing special about that tree. It's just a tree, Detective Borsh."

Bosch waved without looking back. He added poor reading skills to the list of things he didn't like about Brorein.

17

≈≈≈

Wednesday, February 24, 2:15 P.M.

My successes as a defense attorney invariably came when the prosecution was unprepared for and surprised by my moves. The entire government grinds along on routine. Prosecuting violators of the government's laws is no different. As a newly minted prosecutor I took this to heart and vowed not to succumb to the comfort and dangers of routine. I promised myself that I would be more than ready for clever Clive Royce's moves. I would anticipate them. I would know them before Royce did. And I would be like a sniper in a tree, waiting to skillfully pick them off from a distance, one by one.

This promise brought Maggie McFierce and me together in my new office for frequent strategy sessions. And on this afternoon the discussion was focused on what would be the centerpiece of our opponent's pretrial defense. We knew Royce would be filing a motion to dismiss the case. That was a given. What we were discussing were the grounds on which he would make the motion. I wanted to be ready for each one. It is said that in war the sniper ambushes an enemy patrol by first taking out the commander, the radioman and the medic. If he accomplishes this, the remaining members of the patrol panic and scatter. This was what I hoped to quickly do when Royce filed his motion. I wanted to move swiftly and thoroughly with demoralizing arguments and answers that would put the defendant on strong notice that he was in trouble. If I panicked Jessup, I might not even have to go to trial. I might get a disposition. A plea. And a plea was a conviction. That was as good as a win on this side of the aisle.

"I think one thing he's going to argue is that the charges are no longer valid without a preliminary hearing," Maggie said. "This will give him two bites out of the apple. He'll first ask the judge to dismiss but at the very least to order a new prelim."

"But the verdict of the trial was what was reversed," I said. "It goes back to the trial and we have a new trial. The prelim is not what was challenged."

"Well, that's what we'll argue."

"Good, you get to handle that one. What else?"

"I'm not going to keep throwing out angles if you keep giving them back to me to be prepared for. That's the third one you've given me and by my scorecard you've only taken one."

"Okay, I'll take the next one sight unseen. What do you have?"

Maggie smiled and I realized I had just walked into my own ambush. But before she could pull the trigger, the office door opened and Bosch entered without knocking.

"Saved by the bell," I said. "Harry, what's up?"

"I've got a witness I think you two should hear. I think he's going to be good for us and they didn't use him in the first trial."

"Who?" Maggie asked.

"Bill Clinton," Bosch said.

I didn't recognize the name as belonging to anyone associated with the case. But Maggie, with her command of case detail, brought it together.

"One of the tow truck drivers who worked with Jessup."

Bosch pointed at her.

"Right. He worked with Jessup back then at Aardvark Towing. Now he owns an auto repair shop on LaBrea near Olympic. It's called Presidential Motors."

"Of course it is," I said. "What does he do for us as a witness?"

Bosch pointed toward the door.

"I got him sitting out there with Lorna. Why don't I bring him in and he can tell you himself?"

I looked at Maggie, and seeing no objection, I told Bosch to bring Clinton in. Before stepping out Bosch lowered his voice and reported that he had run Clinton through the crime databases and he had come up clean. He had no criminal record.

"Nothing," Bosch said. "Not even an unpaid parking ticket."

"Good," Maggie said. "Now let's see what he has to say."

Bosch went out to the reception room and came back with a short man in his midfifties who was wearing blue work pants and a shirt with an oval patch above the breast pocket. It said Bill. His hair was neatly combed and he didn't wear glasses. I saw grease under his fingernails but figured that could be remedied before he ever appeared in front of a jury.

Bosch pulled a chair away from the wall and placed it in the middle of the room and facing my desk.

"Why don't you sit down here, Mr. Clinton, and we'll ask you some questions," he said.

Bosch then nodded to me, passing the lead.

"First of all, Mr. Clinton, thank you for agreeing to come in and talk to us today."

Clinton nodded.

"That's okay. Things are kind of slow at the shop right now."

"What kind of work do you do at the shop? Is there a specialty?"

"Yeah, we do restoration. Mostly British cars. Triumphs, MGs, Jags, collectibles like that."

"I see. What's a Triumph TR Two-Fifty go for these days?"

Clinton looked up at me, surprised by my apparent knowledge of one of the cars he specialized in.

"Depends on the shape. I sold a beauty last year for twenty-five. I put almost twelve into the restoration. That and a lot of man-hours."

I nodded.

"I had one in high school. Wish I'd never sold it."

"They only made them for one year. 'Sixty-eight. Makes it one of the most collectible."

I nodded. We had just covered everything I knew about the car. I just liked it because of its wooden dashboard and the drop top. I used to cruise up to Malibu in it on weekends, hang out on the surf beaches even though I didn't know how to surf.

"Well, let's jump from 'sixty-eight to 'eighty-six, okay?"

Clinton shrugged.

"Fine by me."

"If you don't mind, Ms. McPherson is going to take notes."

Clinton shrugged again.

"So then, let's start. How well do you remember the day that Melissa Landy was murdered?"

Clinton spread his hands.

"Well, see, I remember it real well because of what happened. That little girl getting killed and it turning out I was working with the guy who did it."

"Must've been pretty traumatic."

"Yeah, it was for a while there."

"And then you put it out of your mind?"

"No, not exactly...but I stopped thinking about it all the time. I started my business and everything."

I nodded. Clinton seemed genuine enough and honest. It was a start. I looked at Bosch. I knew he had pulled some nugget from Clinton that he believed was gold. I wanted him to take over.

"Bill," Bosch said. "Tell them a little about what was going on with Aardvark at the time. About how business was bad."

Clinton nodded.

"Yeah, well, back then we weren't doing so hot. What happened was they passed a law that nobody could park on the side streets off of Wilshire without a resident sticker, you know? Anybody else, we got to tow. So we would go in the neighborhoods on a Sunday morning and hook up cars right and left on account of the church services. In the beginning. Mr. Korish was the owner and we were getting so many cars that he hired another driver and even started paying us for our overtime. It was fun because there were a couple other companies with the same contract, so we were all competing for tows. It was like keeping score and we were a team."

Clinton looked at Bosch to see if he was telling the right story. Harry nodded and told him to keep going.

"So then it all kind of went bad. The people started getting wise and they stopped parking over there. Somebody said the church was even making announcements: 'Don't park north of Wilshire.' So we went from having too much to do to not enough. So Mr. Korish said he had to cut back on costs and one of us was going to have to go, and maybe even two of us. He said he was going to watch our performance levels and make his decision based on that."

"When did he tell you this in relation to the day of the murder?" Bosch asked.

"It was right before. Because all three of us were still there. See, he didn't fire anybody yet."

Taking over the questioning, I asked him what the new edict did to the competition among tow truck drivers.

"Well, it made it rough, you know. We were all friends and then all of a sudden we didn't like each other because we wanted to keep our jobs."

"How was Jason Jessup to work with then?"

"Well, Jason was real cutthroat."

"The pressure got to him?"

"Yeah, because he was in last place. Mr. Korish put up a tote board to keep track of the tows and he was last place."

"And he wasn't happy about it?"

"No, not happy. He became a real prick to work with, excuse my French."

"Do you remember how he acted on the day of the murder?"

"A little bit. Like I told Detective Bosch, he started claiming streets. Like saying Windsor was all his. And Las Palmas and Lucerne. Like that. And me and Derek — he was the other driver — we told him there were no rules like that. And he said, 'Fine, try hooking a car on one of those streets and see what happens.' "

"He threatened you."

"Yeah, you could say that. Definitely."

"Do you remember specifically that Windsor was one of the streets he claimed was his?"

"Yes, I do. He claimed Windsor."

This was all good information. It would go to the state of mind of the defendant. It would be a challenge getting it on the record if there wasn't additional corroboration from Wilbern or Korish, if either was still alive and available.

"Did he ever act on that threat in any way?" Maggie asked.

"No," Clinton said. "But that was the same day as the girl. So he got arrested and that was that. I can't say I was too upset about seeing him go. Turned out Mr. Korish then laid off Derek 'cause he lied about not having a record. I was the last man standing. I worked there another four years — till I saved up the money to start my place."

A regular American success story. I waited to see if Maggie had a follow but she didn't. I did.

"Mr. Clinton, did you ever talk about any of this with the police or prosecutors twenty-four years ago?"

Clinton shook his head.

"Not really. I mean I spoke to the detective who was in charge back then. He asked me questions. But I wasn't ever brought to court or anything like that."

Because they didn't need you back then, I thought. But I'm going to need you now.

"What makes you so sure that this threat from Jessup occurred on the day of the murder?"

"I just know it was that day. I remember that day because it's not every day that a guy you're working with gets arrested for murder."

He nodded as if to underscore the point.

I looked at Bosch to see if we had missed anything. Bosch took the cue and took back the lead.

"Bill, tell them what you told me about being in the police car with Jessup. On the way to Windsor."

Clinton nodded. He could be led easily and I took that as another good sign.

"Well, what happened was they really thought that Derek was the guy. The police did. He had a criminal record and lied about it and they found out. So that made him suspect numero uno. So they put Derek in the back of one patrol car and then me and Jason in another."

"Did they say where they were taking you?"

"They said they had additional questions, so we thought we were going to the police station. There were two officers in the car with us and we heard them talking about all of us being in a lineup. Jason asked them about it and they said it was no big thing, they just wanted guys in overalls because they wanted to see if a witness could pick out Derek."

Clinton stopped there and looked expectantly from Bosch to me and then to Maggie.

"So what happened?" I asked.

"Well, first Jason told the two cops that they couldn't just take us and put us in a lineup like that. They just said that they were following orders. So we go over to Windsor and pull up in front of a house. The cops got out and went and talked to the lead detective, who was standing there with some other detectives. Jason and I were watching out the windows but didn't see any witness or anything. Then the detective in charge goes inside the house and doesn't come back out. We don't know what's going on, and then Jason says to me he wants to borrow my hat."

"Your hat?" Maggie asked.

"Yeah, my Dodgers hat. I was wearing it like I always did and Jason said he needed to borrow it because he recognizes one of the other cops that was already standing there at the house when we pulled up. He said that he got in a fight with the guy over a tow and if he sees him there's going to be trouble. He goes on like that and says, let me have your hat."

"What did you do?" I asked.

"Well, I didn't think it was a big deal on account of I didn't know what I knew later, you know what I mean? So I gave him my hat and he put it on. Then when the cops came back to get us out of the car, they didn't seem to notice that the hat was switched. They made us get out of the car and we had to go over and stand next to Derek. We were standing there and then one of the cops gets a call on the radio — I remember that — and he turns and tells Jason to take off the hat. He did and then a few minutes later they're all of a sudden surrounding Jason and putting the cuffs on him, and it wasn't Derek, it was him."

I looked from Clinton to Bosch and then to Maggie. I could see in her expression that the hat story was significant.

"You know the funny thing?" Clinton asked.

"No, what?" I said.

"I never got that hat back."

He smiled and I smiled back.

"Well, we'll have to get you a new hat when this is all said and done. Now let me ask you the key question. What you have told us here, are you willing to testify to all of it at Jason Jessup's trial?"

Clinton seemed to think about it for a few seconds before nodding.

"Yeah, I could do that," he said.

I stood up and came around the desk, extending my hand.

"Then it looks like we've got ourselves a witness. Many thanks to you, Mr. Clinton."

We shook hands and then I gestured to Bosch.

"Harry, I should have asked you, did we cover everything?"

Bosch stood up as well.

"I think so. For now. I'll take Mr. Clinton back to his shop."

"Excellent. Thank you again, Mr. Clinton."

Clinton stood up.

"Please call me Bill."

"We will, I promise. We'll call you Bill and we'll call you as a witness."

Everybody laughed in that phony way and then Bosch shepherded Clinton out of the office. I went back to my desk and sat down.

"So tell me about the hat," I said to Maggie.

"It's a good connection," she said. "When we interviewed Sarah she remembered that Kloster radioed from the bedroom down to the street and had them make Jessup take off his hat. That was when she made the ID. Harry then looked through the case file and found a property list from Jessup's arrest. The Dodgers hat was on there. We're still trying to track his property — hard to do after twenty-four years. But it might have gone up to San Quentin. Either way, if we don't have the hat, we have the list."

I nodded. This was good on a number of levels. It showed witnesses independently corroborating each other, put a crack in any sort of defense contention that memories cannot be trusted after so many years and, last but not least, showed state of mind of the defendant. Jessup knew he was somehow in danger of being identified. Someone had seen him abduct the girl.

"All right, good," I said. "What do you think about the initial stuff, about how there was competition between them and somebody was going to get laid off? Maybe two of them."

"Again, it's good state-of-mind material. Jessup was under pressure and he acted out. Maybe this whole thing was about that. Maybe we should put a shrink on the witness list."

I nodded.

"Did you tell Bosch to find and interview Clinton?"

She shook her head.

"He did it on his own. He's good at this."

"I know. I just wish he'd tell me a little more about what he's up to."

18

Thursday, February 25, 11 A.M.

Rachel Walling wanted to meet at an office in one of the glass towers in downtown. Bosch went to the address and took the elevator up to the thirty-fourth floor. The door to the offices of Franco, Becerra & Itzuris, attorneys-at-law, was locked and he had to knock. Rachel answered promptly and invited him into a luxurious suite of offices that was empty of lawyers, clerks and anybody else. She led him to the firm's boardroom, where he saw the box and files he had given her the week before on a large oval table. They entered and he walked over to the floor-to-ceiling windows that looked out over downtown.

Bosch couldn't remember being up so high in downtown. He could see all the way to Dodger Stadium and beyond. He checked out the civic center and saw the glass-sided PAB sitting next to the *Los Angeles Times* building. His eyes then scanned toward Echo Park and he remembered a day there with Rachel Walling. They had been a team then, in more ways than one. But now that seemed so long ago.

"What is this place?" he said, still staring out and with his back to her. "Where is everybody?"

"There isn't anybody. We just used this in a money-laundering sting. So it's been empty. Half of this building is empty. The economy. This was a real law office but it went out of business. So we just sort of borrowed it. The management was happy for the government subsidy."

"They were washing money from drugs? Guns?"

"You know I can't say, Harry. I am sure you'll read about it in a few months. You'll put it together then."

Bosch nodded as he remembered the firm's name on the door. Franco, Becerra & Itzuris: FBI. Clever.

"I wonder if management will tell the next tenants that this place was used by the bureau to take down some bad people. Friends of those bad people could come looking."

She didn't respond to that. She just invited him to sit down at the table. He did, taking a good look at her as she sat across from him. Her hair was down, which was unusual. He had seen her that way before but not while she was on duty. The dark ringlets framed her face and helped direct attention to her dark eyes.

"The firm's refrigerator is empty or I'd offer you something to drink."

"I'm fine."

She opened the box and started taking out the files he had given her.

"Rachel, I really appreciate this," Bosch said. "I hope it didn't disrupt your life too much."

"The work, no. I enjoyed it. But you, Harry, you coming back into my life was a disruption."

Bosch wasn't expecting that.

"What do you mean?"

"I'm in a relationship and I'd told him about you. About the single-bullet theory, all of that. So he wasn't happy that I've been spending my nights off working this up for you."

Bosch wasn't sure about how to respond. Rachel Walling always hid deeper messages in the things she said. He wasn't sure if there was more to be considered than what she had just said out loud.

"I'm sorry," he finally said. "Did you tell him it was only work, that I just wanted your professional opinion? That I went to you because I can trust you and you're the best at this?"

"He knows I'm the best at it, but it doesn't matter. Let's just do this."

She opened a file.

"My ex-wife is dead," he said. "She was killed last year in Hong Kong."

He wasn't sure why he'd blurted it out like that. She looked up at him sharply and he knew she hadn't known.

"Oh my God, I'm so sorry."

Bosch just nodded, deciding not to tell her the details.

"What about your daughter?"

"She lives with me now. She's doing okay but it's been pretty tough on her. It's only been four months."

She nodded and then seemed to lose her grounding as she took in what had just been said.

"What about you? I assume it's been rough for you, too."

He nodded but couldn't think of the right words. He had his daughter fully in his life now, but at a terrible cost. He realized that he had brought the subject up but couldn't talk about it.

"Look," he said, "that was weird. I don't know why I just laid that on you. You mentioned the single bullet and I remember I told you about her. We can talk about it some other time. I mean, if you want. Let's just get to the case now. Is that okay?"

"Yes, sure. I was just thinking about your daughter. To lose her mother and then have to move so far from the place she knows. I mean, I know living with you will be fine, but it's...quite an adjustment."

"Yeah, but they say kids are resilient because they actually are. She's got a lot of friends already and is doing well in school. It's been a major adjustment for both of us but I think she'll come out okay."

"And how will you come out?"

Bosch held her eyes for a moment before answering.

"I've already come out ahead. I have my daughter with me and she's the best thing in my life."

"That's good, Harry."

"It is."

She broke eye contact and finished removing the files and photos from the box. Bosch could see the transformation. She was now all business, an FBI profiler ready to report her findings. He reached into his pocket and pulled out his notebook. It was in a folding leather case with a detective shield embossed on the cover. He opened it and got ready to write.

"I want to start with the photos," she said.

"Fine."

She spread out four photos of Melissa Landy's body in the Dumpster, turning them to face him. She then added two photos from the autopsy in a row above these. Photos of a dead child were never easy to look at for Bosch. But these were particularly difficult. He stared for a long moment before coming to the realization that the clutch in his gut was due to the setting of the body in a Dumpster. For the girl to be disposed of like that seemed almost like a statement about the victim and an added insult to those who loved her.

"The Dumpster," he said. "You think that was chosen as a statement?"

Walling paused as if considering it for the first time.

"I'm actually going at it from a different standpoint. I think that it was an almost spontaneous choice. That it wasn't part of a plan. He needed a place to dump the body where he wouldn't be seen and it wouldn't be immediately found. He knew about that Dumpster behind that theater and he used it. It was a convenience, not a statement."

Bosch nodded. He leaned forward and wrote a note on his pad to remind himself to go back to Clinton and ask about the Dumpster. The El Rey was in the Wilshire corridor the Aardvark drivers worked. It might have been familiar to them.

"Sorry, I didn't mean to start things off in the wrong direction," he said as he wrote.

"That's okay. The reason I wanted to start with the photos of the girl is that I believe that this crime may have been misunderstood from the very beginning."

"Misunderstood?"

"Well, it appears that the original investigators took the crime scene at face value and looked at it as the result of the suspect's kill plan. In other words, Jessup grabbed this girl, and his plan was to strangle her and leave her in the Dumpster. This is evidenced by the profile that was drawn up of the crime and submitted to the FBI and the California Department of Justice for comparison to other crimes on record."

She opened a file and pulled out the lengthy profile and submission forms prepared by Detective Kloster twenty-four years earlier.

"Detective Kloster was looking for similar crimes that he might be able to attach Jessup to. He got zero hits and that was the end of that."

Bosch had spent several days studying the original case file and knew everything that Walling was telling him. But he let her run with it without interruption because he had a feeling she would take him somewhere new. That was her beauty and art. It didn't matter that the FBI didn't recognize it and use her to the best of her abilities. He always would.

"I think what happened was that this case had a faulty profile from the beginning. Add to that the fact that back then the data banks were obviously not as sophisticated or as inclusive as they are now. This whole angle was misdirected and wrong and so no wonder they hit a dead end with it."

Bosch nodded and wrote a quick note.

"You tried to rebuild the profile?" he asked.

"As much as I could. And the starting point is right here. The photos. Take a look at her injuries."

Bosch leaned across the table and over the first row of photographs. He actually didn't see injuries to the girl. She had been dropped haphazardly into the almost full trash bin. There must have been stage building or a renovation project going on inside the theater, because the bin contained mostly construction refuse. Sawdust, paint buckets, small pieces of cut and broken wood. There were small cuts of wallboard and torn plastic sheeting. Melissa Landy was faceup near one of the corners of the Dumpster. Bosch didn't see a drop of blood on her or her dress.

"What injuries are we talking about?" he asked.

Walling stood up in order to lean over. She used the point of a pen to outline the places she wanted Bosch to look on each of the photos. She circled discolorations on the victim's neck.

"Her neck injuries," she said. "If you look you see the oval-shaped bruising on the right side of the neck, and on the other side you have a larger corresponding bruise. This evidence makes it clear that she was choked to death with one hand."

She used the pen to illustrate what she was saying.

"The thumb here on her right side and the four fingers on the left. One-handed. Now, why one-handed?"

She sat back down and Bosch leaned back away from the photos himself. The idea that Melissa had been strangled with one hand was not new to Bosch. It was in Kloster's original profile of the murder.

"Twenty-four years ago, it was suggested that Jessup strangled the girl with his right hand while he masturbated with his left. This theory was built on one thing—the semen collected from the victim's dress. It was deposited by someone with the same blood type as Jessup and so it was assumed to have come from him. You follow all of this?"

"I'm with you."

"Okay, so the problem is, we now know that the semen didn't come from Jessup and so the basic profile or theory of the crime in nineteen eighty-six is wrong. It is further demonstrated as being wrong because Jessup is right-handed according to a sample of his writing in the files, and studies have shown that with right-handers masturbation is almost always carried out by the dominant hand."

"They've done studies on that?"

"You'd be surprised. I sure was when I went online to look for this."

"I knew there was something wrong with the Internet."

She smiled but was not a bit embarrassed by the subject matter of their discussion. It was all in a day's work.

"They've done studies on everything, including which hand people use to wipe their butts. I actually found it to be fascinating reading. But the point here is that they had this wrong from the beginning. This murder did not occur during a sex act. Now let me show you a few other photos."

She reached across the table and slid all of the photos together in one stack and then put them to the side. She then spread out photos taken of the inside of the tow truck Jessup was driving on the day of the murder. The truck actually had a name, which was stenciled on the dashboard.

"Okay, so on the day in question, Jessup was driving Matilda," Walling said.

Bosch studied the three photos she had spread out. The cab of the tow truck was in neat order. Thomas Brothers maps—no GPS back then—were neatly stacked on top of the dashboard and a small stuffed animal that Bosch presumed was an aardvark hung from the rearview mirror. A cup holder on the center console held a Big Gulp from 7-Eleven and a sticker on the glove compartment door read *Grass or Ass — Nobody Rides for Free*.

With her trusty pen, Walling circled a spot on one of the photos. It was a police scanner mounted under the dashboard.

"Did anybody consider what this means?"

Bosch shrugged.

"Back then, I don't know. What's it mean now?"

"Okay, Jessup worked for Aardvark, which was a towing company licensed by the city. However, it wasn't the only one. There was competition among tow companies. The drivers listened to scanners, picking up police calls about accidents and parking infractions. It gave them the jump on the competition, right? Except that every tow truck had a scanner and everybody was listening and trying to get the jump on everyone else."

"Right. So what's it mean?"

"Well, let's look at the abduction first. It is pretty clear from the witness testimony and everything else that this was not a crime of great planning and patience. This was an impulse crime. That much they've had right from the beginning. We can talk about the motivating factors at length in a little while, but suffice it to say, something caused Jessup to act out in an almost uncontrollable way."

"I think I might have motivating factors covered," Bosch said.

"Good, I'm eager to hear about it. But for now, we will assume that some sort of internal pressure led Jessup to act on an undeniable impulse and he grabbed the girl. He took her back to the truck and took off. He obviously didn't know about the sister hiding in the bushes and that she would sound the alarm. So he completes the abduction and drives away, but within minutes he hears the report about the abduction on the police scanner he has in the truck. That brings home to him the reality of what he's done and what his predicament is. He never imagined things would move so fast. He more or less comes to his senses. He realizes he must abandon his plan now and move into preservation mode. He needs to kill the girl to eliminate her as a witness and then hide her body in order to prevent his arrest."

Bosch nodded as he understood her theory.

"So what you're saying is, the crime that occurred was not the crime that he intended."

"Correct. He abandoned the true plan."

"So when Kloster went to the bureau looking for similars, he was looking for the wrong thing."

"Right again."

"But could there actually have been a plan? You just said yourself that it was a crime of compulsion. He saw an opportunity and within a few seconds acted on it. What plan could there have been?"

"Actually, it is more than likely that he had a complex and complete plan. Killers like these have a paraphilia—a set construct of the perfect psychosexual experience. They fantasize about it in great detail. And as you can expect, it often involves torture and murder. The paraphilia is part of their daily fantasy life and it builds to the point where the desire becomes the urge which eventually becomes a compulsion to act out. When they do cross that line and act out, the abduction of the victim may be completely unplanned and improvisational, but the killing sequence is not. The victim is unfortunately dropped into a set construct that has played over and over in the killer's mind."

Bosch looked at his notebook and realized he had stopped taking notes.

"Okay, but you're saying that didn't happen here," he said. "He abandoned the plan. He heard the abduction report on the scanner, and that took him from fantasy to reality. He realized that they could be closing in on him. He killed her and dumped her, hoping to avoid detection."

"Exactly. And therefore, as you just noted, when investigators attempted to compare elements of this murder to others', they were comparing apples and oranges. They found nothing that matched and believed that this was a onetime crime of opportunity and compulsion. I don't think it was."

Bosch looked up from the photos to Rachel's eyes.

"You think he did this before."

"I think the idea that he had acted out before in this way is compelling. It would not surprise me if you were to find that he was involved in other abductions."

"You're talking about more than twenty-four years ago."

"I know. And since there was no linking of Jessup to known unsolved murders, we are probably talking about missing children and runaways. Cases where there was never a crime scene established. The girls were never found."

Bosch thought of Jessup's middle-of-the-night visits to the parks along Mulholland Drive. He thought he might now know why Jessup would light a candle at the base of a tree.

Then a more stunning and scary thought pushed through.

"Do you think a guy like this would use those crimes from so long ago to feed his fantasy now?"

"Of course he would. He's been in prison, what other choice did he have?"

Bosch felt an urgency take hold inside. An urgency that came with the growing certainty that they weren't dealing with an isolated instance of murder. If Walling's theory was correct, and he had no reason to doubt it, Jessup was a repeater. And though he had been on ice for twenty-four years, he was now roaming the city freely. It would not be long now before he became vulnerable to the pressures and urges that had driven him to deadly action before.

Bosch came to a fast resolve. The next time Jessup was seized by the pressures of his life and overcome by the compulsion to kill, Bosch was going to be there to destroy him.

His eyes refocused and he realized Rachel was looking at him oddly.

"Thank you for all of this, Rachel," he said. "I think I need to go."

19

≈≈≈

Thursday, March 4, 9 A.M.

It was only a hearing on pretrial motions but the courtroom was packed. Lots of courthouse gadflies and media, and a fair number of trial lawyers were sitting in as well. I sat at the prosecution table with Maggie and we were going over our arguments once again. All issues before Judge Breitman had already been argued and submitted on paper. This would be when the judge could ask further questions and then announce her rulings. I had a growing sense of anxiety. The motions submitted by Clive Royce were all pretty routine and Maggie and I had submitted solid responses. We were also ready with oral arguments to back them, but a hearing like this was also a time for the unexpected. On more than one occasion I had sandbagged the prosecution in a pretrial hearing. And sometimes the case is won or lost before the trial begins with a ruling in one of these hearings.

I leaned back and looked behind us and then took a quick glance around the courtroom. I gave a phony smile and nod to a lawyer I saw in the spectator section, then turned back to Maggie.

"Where's Bosch?" I asked.

"I don't think he's going to be here."

"Why not? He's completely disappeared in the last week."

"He's been working on something. He called yesterday and asked if he had to be here for this and I said he didn't."

"He'd better be working on something related to Jessup."

"He tells me it is and that he's going to bring it to us soon."

"That's nice of him. The trial starts in four weeks."

I wondered why Bosch had chosen to call her instead of me, the lead prosecutor. I realized that this made me upset with Maggie as well as Bosch.

"Listen, I don't know what happened between you two on your little trip to Port Townsend, but he should be calling me."

Maggie shook her head as if dealing with a petulant child.

"Look, you don't have to worry. He knows you're the lead prosecutor. He probably figures you are too busy for the day-to-day updates on what he's doing. And I'm going to forget what you said about Port Townsend. This one time. You make another insinuation like that and you and I are going to have a real problem."

"Okay, I'm sorry. It's just that—"

My attention was drawn across the aisle to Jessup, who was sitting at the defense table with Royce. He was staring at me with a smirk on his face and I realized he had been watching Maggie and me, maybe even listening.

"Excuse me a second," I said.

I got up and walked over to the defense table. I leaned over him.

"Can I help you with something, Jessup?"

Before Jessup could say a word his lawyer cut in.

"Don't talk to my client, Mick," Royce said. "If you want to ask him something, then you ask me."

Now Jessup smiled again, emboldened by his attorney's defensive move.

"Just go sit down," Jessup said. "I got nothing to say to you."

Royce held his hand up to quiet him.

"I'll handle this. You be quiet."

"He threatened me. You should complain to the judge."

"I said be quiet and that I would handle this."

Jessup folded his arms and leaned back in his chair.

"Mick, is there a problem here?" Royce asked.

"No, no problem. I just don't like him staring at me."

I walked back to the prosecution table, annoyed with myself for losing my calm. I sat down and looked at the pool camera set up in the jury box. Judge Breitman had approved the filming of the trial and the various hearings leading up to it, but only through the use of a pool camera, which would provide a universal feed that all channels and networks could use.

A few minutes later the judge took the bench and called the hearing to order. One by one we went through the defense motions, and the rulings mostly fell our way without much further argument. The most important one was the routine motion to dismiss for lack of evidence, which the judge rejected with little comment. When Royce asked to be heard, she said that it wasn't necessary to discuss the issue further. It was a solid rebuke and I loved it even though outwardly I acted as though it were routine and boring.

The only ruling the judge wanted to discuss in detail was the oddball request by Royce to allow his client to use makeup during trial to cover the tattoos on his neck and fingers. Royce had argued in his motion that the tattoos were all prison tattoos applied while he was falsely incarcerated for twenty-four years. He said the tattoos could be prejudicial when noticed by jurors. His client intended to cover these with skin-tone makeup and he wanted to bar the prosecution from addressing it in front of the jury.

"I have to admit I have not had a motion like this come before me," the judge said. "I'm inclined to allow it and hold the prosecution from drawing attention to it but I see the prosecution has objected to the motion, saying that it contains insufficient information about the content and history of these tattoos. Can you shed some light on the subject, Mr. Royce?"

Royce stood and addressed the court from his place at the defense table. I looked over and my eyes were drawn to Jessup's hands. I knew the tattoos across his knuckles were Royce's chief concern. The neck markings could largely be covered with a collared shirt, which he would wear with a suit at trial. But the hands were difficult to hide. Across the four digits of each hand he had inked the sentiment FUCK THIS and Royce knew that I would make sure it was seen by jurors. That sentiment was probably the chief impediment to having Jessup testify in his defense, because Royce knew I would find a way either casually or specifically to make sure the jury got his message.

"Your Honor, it is the defense's position that these tattoos were administered to Mr. Jessup's body while he was falsely imprisoned and are a product of that harrowing experience. Prison is a dangerous place, Judge, and inmates take measures to protect themselves. Sometimes it is through tattooing that is designed to be intimidating or to show an association the prisoner might not actually have or believe in. It would certainly be prejudicial for the jury to see, and therefore we ask for relief. This, I might add, is merely a tactic by the prosecution to delay the trial, and the defense firmly stands by its decision to not delay justice in this case."

Maggie stood up quickly. She had handled this motion on paper and therefore it was hers to handle in court.

"Your Honor, may I be heard on the defense's accusation?"

"One moment, Ms. McPherson, I want to be heard myself. Mr. Royce, can you explain your last statement?"

Royce bowed politely.

"Yes, of course, Judge Breitman. The defendant has begun to go through a tattoo removal process. But this takes time and will not be completed by trial. By objecting to our simple request to use makeup, the prosecution is trying to push the trial back until this removal process is completed. It's an effort to subvert the speedy trial statute which since day one the defense, to the prosecution's consternation, has refused to waive."

The judge turned her gaze to Maggie McFierce. It was her turn.

"Your Honor, this is simply a defense fabrication. The state has not once asked for a delay or opposed the defense's request for a speedy trial. In fact, the prosecution is ready for trial. So this statement is outlandish and objectionable. The true objection on the part of the prosecution to this motion is to the idea of the defendant being allowed to disguise himself. A trial is a search for truth, and allowing him to use makeup to cover up who he really is would be an affront to the search for truth. Thank you, Your Honor."

"Judge, may I respond?" Royce, still standing, said immediately.

Breitman paused for a moment while she wrote a few notes from Maggie's brief.

"That won't be necessary, Mr. Royce," she finally said. "I'm going to make a ruling on this and I will allow Mr. Jessup to cover his tattoos. If he chooses to testify on his behalf, the prosecution will not address this issue with him in front of the jury."

"Thank you, Your Honor," Maggie said.

She sat down without showing any outward sign of disappointment. It was just one ruling among many others and most had gone the prosecution's way. This loss was minor at worst.

"Okay," the judge said. "I think we have covered everything. Anything else from counsel at this time?"

"Yes, Your Honor," Royce said as he stood again. "Defense has a new motion we would like to submit."

He stepped away from the defense table and brought copies of the new motion first to the judge and then to us, giving Maggie and me individual copies of a one-page motion. Maggie was a fast reader, a skill she had genetically passed on to our daughter, who was reading two books a week on top of her homework.

"This is bullshit," she whispered before I had even finished reading the title of the document.

But I caught up quickly. Royce was adding a new lawyer to the defense team and the motion was to disqualify Maggie from the prosecution because of a conflict of interest. The new lawyer's name was David Bell.

Maggie quickly turned around to scan the spectator seats. My eyes followed and there was David Bell, sitting at the end of the second row. I knew him on sight because I had seen him with Maggie in the months after our marriage had ended. One time I had come to her apartment to pick up my daughter and Bell had opened the door.

Maggie turned back and started to stand to address the court but I put my hand on her shoulder and held her in place.

"I'm taking this," I said.

"No, wait," she whispered urgently. "Ask for a ten-minute recess. We need to talk about this."

"Exactly what I was going to do."

I stood and addressed the judge.

"Your Honor, like you, we just got this. We can take it with us and submit but we would rather argue it right now. If the court could indulge us with a brief recess, I think we would be ready to respond."

"Fifteen minutes, Mr. Haller? I have another matter holding. I could handle it and come back to you."

"Thank you, Your Honor."

This meant we had to leave the table while another prosecutor handled his business before the judge. We pushed our files and Maggie's laptop to the back of the table to make room, then got up and walked toward the back door of the courtroom. As we passed Bell he raised a hand to get Maggie's attention but she ignored him and walked by.

"You want to go upstairs?" Maggie asked as we came through the double doors. She was suggesting that we go up to the DA's office.

"There isn't time to wait for an elevator."

"We could take the stairs. It's only three flights."

We walked through the door into the building's enclosed stairwell but then I grabbed her arm.

"This is good enough right here," I said. "Tell me what we do about Bell."

"That piece of shit. He's never defended a criminal case, let alone a murder, in his life."

"Yeah, you wouldn't have made the same mistake twice."

She looked pointedly at me.

"What's that supposed to mean?"

"Never mind, bad joke. Let's just stay on point."

She had her arms folded tightly against her chest.

"This is the most underhanded thing I've ever seen. Royce wants me off the case so he goes to Bell. And Bell...I can't believe he would do something like this to me."

"Yeah, well, he's probably in it for a dip into the pot of gold at the end of the rainbow. We probably should have seen something like this coming."

It was a defense tactic I had used myself before, but not with such obviousness. If you didn't like the judge or the prosecutor, one way of getting them off the case was to bring someone onto your team who has a conflict of interest with them. Since the defendant is constitutionally guaranteed the defense counsel of his choice, it is usually the judge or prosecutor who must be disqualified from the trial. It was a shrewd move by Royce.

"You see what he's doing, right?" Maggie said. "He is trying to isolate you. He knows I'm the one person you would trust as second chair and he's trying to take that away from you. He knows that without me you are going to lose."

"Thanks for your confidence in me."

"You know what I mean. You've never prosecuted a case. I'm there to help you through it. If he gets me kicked off the table, then who are you going to have? Who would you trust?"

I nodded. She was right.

"Okay, give me the facts. How long were you with Bell?"

"With him? I wasn't. We went out briefly seven years ago. No more than two months and if he says differently he's a liar."

"Is the conflict that you had the relationship or is there something else, something you did or said, something he has knowledge of that creates the conflict?"

"There's nothing. We went out and it just didn't take."

"Who dropped who?"

She paused and looked down at the floor.

"He did."

I nodded.

"Then there's the conflict. He can claim you carry a grudge."

"A woman scorned, is that it? This is such bullshit. You men are—"

"Hold on, Maggie. Hold on. I'm saying that is their argument. I am not agreeing. In fact, I want—"

The door to the stairwell opened and the prosecutor who took our places when we had gotten up for the recess entered and started up the steps. I checked my watch. Only eight minutes had gone by.

"She went back into chambers," he said as he passed. "You guys are fine."

"Thanks."

I waited until I heard his steps on the next landing before continuing in a quiet tone with Maggie.

"Okay, how do I fight this?"

"You tell the judge that this is an obvious attempt to sabotage the prosecution. They've hired an attorney for the sole reason that he had a relationship with me, not because of any skill he brings to the table."

I nodded.

"Okay. What else?"

"I don't know. I can't think... it was remote in time, no strong emotional attachment, no effect on professional judgment or conduct."

"Yeah, yeah, yeah... and what about Bell? Does he have something or know something I have to watch out for?"

She looked at me like I was some sort of traitor.

"Maggie, I need to know so there's no surprise on top of the surprise, okay?"

"Fine, there's nothing. He must really be hard up if he's taking a fee just to knock me off the case."

"Don't worry, two can play this game. Let's go."

We went back into the courtroom and as we went through the gate I nodded to the clerk so she could call the judge back from chambers. Instead of going to the prosecution table, I diverted to the defense side where Royce was sitting next to his client. David Bell was now seated at the table on the other side of Jessup. I leaned over Royce's shoulder and whispered just loud enough that his client would hear.

"Clive, when the judge comes out, I'll give you the chance to withdraw this motion. If you don't, number one, I'm going to embarrass you in front of the camera and it will be digitally preserved forever. And number two, the release-and-remuneration offer I made to your client last week is withdrawn. Permanently."

I watched Jessup's eyebrows rise a few centimeters. He hadn't heard anything about an offer involving money and freedom. This was because I hadn't made one. But now it would be up to Royce to convince his client that he had not withheld anything from him. Good luck with that.

Royce smiled like he was pleased with my comeback. He leaned back casually and tossed his pen on his legal pad. It was a Montblanc with gold trim and that was no way to treat it.

"This is really going to get good, yes, Mick?" he said. "Well, I'll tell you. I'm not withdrawing the motion and I think if you had made me an offer involving release and remuneration I would've remembered it."

So he had called my bluff. He'd still have to convince his client. I saw the judge step out from the door of her chambers and start up the three steps to the bench. I took one more whispered shot at Royce.

"Whatever you paid Bell you wasted."

I stepped over to the prosecution table and remained standing. The judge brought the courtroom to order.

"Okay, back on the record in *California versus Jessup*. Mr. Haller, do you want to respond to the defendant's latest motion or take it on submission."

"Your Honor, the prosecution wishes to respond right now to...this motion."

"Go right ahead, then."

I tried to build a good tone of outrage into my voice.

"Judge, I am as cynical as the next guy but I have to say I am surprised by the defense's tactics here with this motion. In fact, this isn't a motion. This is very plainly an attempt to subvert the trial system by denying the People of Cal—"

"Your Honor," Royce interjected, jumping to his feet, "I strenuously object to the character assassination Mr. Haller is putting on the record and before the media. This is nothing more than grand—"

"Mr. Royce, you will have an opportunity to respond *after* Mr. Haller responds to your motion. Please be seated."

"Yes, Your Honor."

Royce sat down and I tried to remember where I was.

"Go ahead, Mr. Haller."

"Yes, Your Honor, as you know, the prosecution turned over all discovery materials to the defense on Tuesday. What you have before you now is a very disingenuous motion spawned by Mr. Royce's realization of what he will be up against at trial. He thought the state was going to roll over on this case. He now knows that it is not going to do so."

"But what does this have to do with the motion at hand, Mr. Haller?" the judge asked impatiently.

"Everything," I said. "You've heard of judge shopping? Well, Mr. Royce is prosecutor shopping. He knows through his examination of discovery materials that Margaret McPherson is perhaps the most important part of the prosecution team. Rather than take on the evidence at trial, he is attempting to undercut the prosecution by splintering the team that has assembled that evidence. Here we are, just four weeks before trial and he makes a move against my second chair. He has hired an attorney with little to no experience in criminal defense, not to mention defending a murder case. Why would he do that, Judge, other than for the purpose of concocting this supposed conflict of interest?"

"Your Honor?"

Royce was on his feet again.

"Mr. Royce," the judge said, "I told you, you will have your chance."

The warning was very clear in her voice.

"But, Your Honor, I can't—"

"*Sit down.*"

Royce sat down and the judge put her attention back on me.

"Judge, this is a cynical move made by a desperate defense. I would hope that you would not allow him to subvert the intentions of the Constitution."

Like two men on a seesaw, I went down and Royce immediately popped up.

"One moment, Mr. Royce," the judge said, holding up her hand and signaling him back down to his seat. "I want to talk to Mr. Bell."

Now it was Bell's turn to stand up. He was a well-dressed man with sandy hair and a ruddy complexion, but I could see the apprehension in his eyes. Whether he had come to Royce or Royce had come to him, it was clear that he had not anticipated having to stand in front of a judge and explain himself.

"Mr. Bell, I have not had the pleasure of seeing you practice in my courtroom. Do you handle criminal defense, sir?"

"Uh, no, ma'am, not ordinarily. I am a trial attorney and I have been lead counsel in more than thirty trials. I do know my way around a courtroom, Your Honor."

"Well, good for you. How many of those trials were murder trials?"

I felt total exhilaration as I watched what I had set in motion take on its own momentum. Royce looked mortified as he watched his plan shatter like an expensive vase.

"None of them were murder trials per se. But several were wrongful death cases."

"Not the same thing. How many criminal trials do you have under your belt, Mr. Bell?"

"Again, Judge, none were criminal cases."

"What do you bring to the defense of Mr. Jessup?"

"Your Honor, I bring a wealth of trial experience but I don't think that my résumé is on point here. Mr. Jessup is entitled to counsel of his choice and—"

"What exactly is the conflict you have with Ms. McPherson?"

Bell looked perplexed.

"Did you understand the question?" the judge asked.

"Yes, Your Honor, the conflict is that we had an intimate relationship and now we would be opposing each other at trial."

"Were you married?"

"No, Your Honor."

"When was this intimate relationship and how long did it last?"

"It was seven years ago and it lasted about three months."

"Have you had contact with her since then?"

Bell raised his eyes to the ceiling as if looking for an answer. Maggie leaned over and whispered in my ear.

"No, Your Honor," Bell said.

I stood up.

"Your Honor, in the interest of full disclosure, Mr. Bell has sent Ms. McPherson a Christmas card for the past seven years. She has not responded likewise."

There was a murmur of laughter in the courtroom. The judge ignored it and looked down at something in front of her. She looked like she had heard enough.

"Where is the conflict you are worried about, Mr. Bell?"

"Uh, Judge, this is a bit difficult to speak of in open court but I was the one who ended the relationship with Ms. McPherson and my concern is that there could be some lingering animosity there. And that's the conflict."

The judge wasn't buying this and everyone in the courtroom knew it. It was becoming uncomfortable even to watch.

"Ms. McPherson," the judge said.

Maggie pushed back her chair and stood.

"Do you hold any lingering animosity toward Mr. Bell?"

"No, Your Honor, at least not before today. I moved on to better things."

I could hear another low rumble from the seats behind me as Maggie's spear struck home.

"Thank you, Ms. McPherson," the judge said. "You can sit. And so can you, Mr. Bell."

Bell thankfully dropped into his chair. The judge leaned forward and spoke matter-of-factly into the bench's microphone.

"The motion is denied."

Royce stood up immediately.

"Your Honor, I was not heard before the ruling."

"It was your motion, Mr. Royce."

"But I would like to respond to some of the things Mr. Haller said about—"

"Mr. Royce, I've made my ruling on it. I don't see the need for further discussion. Do you?"

Royce realized his defeat could get even worse. He cut his losses.

"Thank you, Your Honor."

He sat down. The judge then ended the hearing and we packed up and headed toward the rear doors. But not as quickly as Royce. He and his client and supposed co-counsel split the courtroom like men who had to catch the last train on a Friday night. And this time Royce didn't bother stopping outside the courtroom to chat with the media.

"Thanks for sticking up for me," Maggie said when we got to the elevators. I shrugged.

"You stuck up for yourself. Did you really mean that, what you said about moving on from Bell to better things?"

"From him, yes. Definitely."

I looked at her but couldn't read her beyond the spoken line. The elevator doors opened, and there was Harry Bosch waiting to step off.

20

Thursday, March 4, 10:40 A.M.

Bosch stepped off the elevator and almost walked right into Haller and McPherson.

"Is it over?" he asked.

"You missed it," Haller said.

Bosch quickly turned and hit one of the bumpers on the elevator doors before it could close.

"Are you going down?"

"That's the plan," Haller said in a tone that didn't hide his annoyance with Bosch. "I thought you weren't coming to the hearing."

"I wasn't. I was coming to get you two."

They rode the elevator down and Bosch convinced them to walk with him a block over to the Police Administration Building. He signed them in as visitors and they went up to the fifth floor, where Robbery-Homicide Division was located.

"This is the first time I've been here," McPherson said. "It's as quiet as an insurance office."

"Yeah, I guess we lost a lot of the charm when we moved," Bosch replied.

The PAB had been in operation for only six months. It had a quiet and sterile quality about it. Most of the building's denizens, including Bosch, missed the old headquarters, Parker Center, even though it was beyond decrepit.

"I've got a private room over here," he said, pointing to a door on the far side of the squad room.

He used a key to unlock the door and they walked into a large space with a boardroom-style table at center. One wall was glass that looked out on the squad room but Bosch had lowered and closed the blinds for privacy. On the opposite wall was a large whiteboard with a row of photos across the top margin and numerous notes written beneath each shot. The photos were of young girls.

"I've been working on this nonstop for a week," Bosch said. "You probably have been wondering where I disappeared to so I figured it was time to show you what I've got."

McPherson stopped just a few steps inside the door and stared, squinting her eyes and revealing to Bosch her vanity. She needed glasses but he'd never seen her wearing them.

Haller stepped over to the table, where there were several archival case boxes gathered. He slowly pulled out a chair to sit down.

"Maggie," Bosch prompted. "Why don't you sit down?"

McPherson finally broke from her stare and took the chair at the end of the table.

"Is this what I think it is?" she asked. "They all look like Melissa Landy."

"Well," Bosch said. "Let me just go over it and you'll draw your own conclusions."

Bosch stayed on his feet. He moved around the table to the whiteboard. With his back to the board he started to tell the story.

"Okay, I have a friend. She's a former profiler. I've never —"

"For whom?" Haller asked.

"The FBI, but does it matter? What I'm saying is that I've never known anybody who was better at it. So, shortly after I came into this I asked her informally to take a look at the case files and she did. Her conclusions were that back in 'eighty-six this case was read all wrong. And where the original investigators saw a crime of impulse and opportunity, she saw something different. To keep it short, she saw indications that the person who killed Melissa Landy may have killed before."

"Here we go," Haller said.

"Look, man, I don't know why you're giving me the attitude," Bosch said. "You pulled me in as investigator on this thing and I'm investigating. Why don't you just let me tell you what I know? Then you can do with it whatever you want. You think it's legit, then run with it. You don't, then shitcan it. I will have done my job by bringing it to you."

"I'm not giving you any attitude, Harry. I'm just thinking out loud. Thinking about all the things that can complicate a trial. Complicate discovery. You realize that everything you are telling us has to be turned over to Royce now?"

"Only if you intend to use it."

"What?"

"I thought you'd know the rules of discovery better than me."

"I know the rules. Why did you bring us here for this dog and pony show if you don't think we should use it?"

"Why don't you just let him tell the story," McPherson said. "And then maybe we'll understand."

"Then, go ahead," Haller said. "Anyway, all I said was 'Here we go,' which I think is a pretty common phrase indicating surprise and change of direction. That's all. Continue, Harry. Please."

Bosch glanced back at the board for a moment and then turned back to his audience of two and continued.

"So my friend the profiler thinks Jason Jessup killed before he killed Melissa Landy, and most likely was successful in hiding his involvement in these previous crimes."

"So you went looking," McPherson said.

"I did. Now, remember our original investigator, Kloster, was no slouch. He went looking, too. Only problem was he was using the wrong profile. They had semen on the dress, strangulation and a body dump in an accessible location. That was the profile, so that is what he went looking for and he found no similars, or at least no cases that connected. End of story, end of search. They believed Jessup acted out this one time, was exceedingly disorganized and sloppy, and got caught."

Harry turned and gestured to the row of photographs on the whiteboard behind him.

"So I went a different way. I went looking for girls who were reported missing and never showed up again. Girls reported as runaways as well as possible abductions. Jessup is from Riverside County so I expanded the search to include Riverside and L.A. counties. Since Jessup was twenty-four when he was arrested I went back to when he was eighteen, putting the search limits from nineteen eighty to 'eighty-six. As far as victim profile, I went Caucasian aged twelve to eighteen."

"Why did you go as old as eighteen?" McPherson asked. "Our victim was twelve."

"Rachel said—I mean, the profiler said that sometimes starting out, these people pick from their own peer group. They learn how to kill and then they start to define their targets according to their paraphilias. A paraphilia is—"

"I know what it is," McPherson said. "You did all of this work yourself? Or did this Rachel help you?"

"No, she just worked up the profile. I had some help from my partner pulling all of this together. But it was tough because not all the records are complete, especially on cases that never got above runaway status, and a lot was cleared out. Most of the runaway files from back then are gone."

"They didn't digitize?" McPherson asked.

Bosch shook his head.

"Not in L.A. County. They prioritized when they switched over to computerized records and went back and captured records for major crimes. No runaway cases unless there was the possibility of abduction involved. Riverside County was different. Fewer cases out there so they archived everything digitally. Anyway, for that time period in these two counties, we came up with twenty-nine cases over the six-year period we're looking at. Again, these were unresolved cases. In each the girl disappeared and never came home. We pulled what records we could find and most didn't fit because of witness statements or other issues. But I couldn't rule out these eight."

Bosch turned to the board and looked at the photos of eight smiling girls. All of them long gone over time.

"I'm not saying that Jessup had anything to do with any of these girls dropping off the face of the earth, but he could have. As Maggie already noticed, they all have a resemblance to one another and to Melissa Landy. And by the way, the resemblance extends to body type as well. They're all within ten pounds and two inches of one another and our victim."

Bosch turned back to his audience and saw McPherson and Haller transfixed by the photographs.

"Beneath each photo I've put the particulars," he said. "Physical descriptors, date and location of disappearance, the basic stuff."

"Did Jessup know any of them?" Haller asked. "Is he connected in any way to any of them?"

That was the bottom line, Bosch knew.

"Nothing really solid — I mean, not that I've found so far," he said. "The best connection that we have is this girl."

He turned and pointed to the first photo on the left.

"The first girl. Valerie Schlicter. She disappeared in nineteen eighty-one from the same neighborhood in Riverside that Jessup grew up in. He would've been nineteen and she was seventeen. They both went to Riverside High but because he dropped out early, it doesn't look like they were there at the same time. Anyway, she was counted as a runaway because there were problems in her home. It was a single-parent home. She lived with her mother and a brother and then one day about a month after graduating from high school, she split. The investigation never rose above a missing persons case, largely because of her age. She turned eighteen a month after she disappeared. In fact, I wouldn't even call it an investigation. They more or less waited to see if she'd come home. She didn't."

"Nothing else?"

Bosch turned back and looked at Haller.

"So far that's it."

"Then discovery is not an issue. There's nothing here. There's no connection between Jessup and any of these girls. The closest one you have is this Riverside girl and she was five years older than Melissa Landy. This whole thing seems like a stretch."

Bosch thought he detected a note of relief in Haller's voice.

"Well," he said, "there's still another part to all of this."

He stepped over to the case boxes at the end of the table and picked up a file. He walked it down and put it in front of McPherson.

"As you know, we've had Jessup under surveillance since he was released."

McPherson opened the file and saw the stack of 8 × 10 surveillance shots of Jessup.

"With Jessup they've learned that there is no routine schedule, so they stick with him twenty-four/seven. And what they're documenting is that he has two remarkably different lives. The public one, which is carried in the media as his so-called journey to freedom. Everything from smiling for the cameras and eating hamburgers to surfing Venice Beach to the talk-show circuit."

"Yes, we're well aware," Haller said. "And most of it orchestrated by his attorney."

"And then there's the private side," Bosch said. "The bar crawls, the late-night cruising and the middle-of-the-night visits."

"Visits where?" McPherson asked.

Bosch went to his last visual aid, a map of the Santa Monica Mountains. He unfolded it on the table in front of them.

"Nine different times since his release Jessup has left the apartment where he stays in Venice and in the middle of the night driven up to Mulholland on top of the mountains. From there he has visited one or two of the canyon parks up there per night. Franklin Canyon is his favorite. He's been there six times. But he also has hit Stone Canyon, Runyon Canyon and the overlook at Fryman Canyon a few times each."

"What's he doing at these places?" McPherson asked.

"Well, first of all, these are public parks that are closed at dusk," Bosch replied. "So he's sneaking in. We're talking two, three o'clock in the morning. He goes in and he just sort of sits. He communes. He lit candles a couple times. Always the same spots in each of the parks. Usually on a trail or by a tree. We don't have photos because it's too dark and we can't risk getting in close. I've gone out with the SIS a couple times this week and watched. It looks like he just sort of meditates."

Bosch circled the four parks on the map. Each was off Mulholland and close to the others.

"Have you talked to your profiler about all this?" Haller asked.

"Yeah, I did, and she was thinking what I was thinking. That he's visiting graves. Communing with the dead...his victims."

"Oh, man...," Haller said.

"Yeah," Bosch said.

There was a long pause as Haller and McPherson considered the implications of Bosch's investigation.

"Harry, has anybody done any digging in any of these spots?" McPherson asked.

"No, not yet. We didn't want to go too crazy with the shovels, because he keeps coming back. He'd know something was up and we don't want that yet."

"Right. What about—"

"Cadaver dogs. Yeah, we brought them out there undercover yesterday. We—"

"How do you make a dog go undercover?" Haller asked.

Bosch started to laugh and it eased some of the tension in the room.

"What I mean is, there were two dogs and they weren't brought out in official vehicles and handled by people in uniforms. We tried to make it look like somebody walking their dog, but even that was a problem because the park doesn't allow dogs on these trails. Anyway, we did the best we could and got in and got out. I checked with SIS to make sure Jessup wasn't anywhere near Mulholland when we went in. He was surfing."

"And?" McPherson asked impatiently.

"These dogs are the type that just lie down on the ground when they pick up the scent of human decay. Supposedly they can pick it up through the ground after even a hundred years. Anyway, at three of the four places Jessup's gone in these parks, the dogs didn't react. But at one spot one of the two dogs did."

Bosch watched McPherson swivel in her seat and look at Haller. He looked back at her and there was some sort of silent communication there.

"It should also be noted that this particular dog has a history of being wrong—that is, giving a false positive—about a third of the time," Bosch said. "The other dog didn't react to the same spot."

"Great," Haller said. "So what does that tell us?"

"Well, that's why I invited you over," Bosch said. "We've reached the point where maybe we should start digging. At least in that one spot. But if we do, we run the risk that Jessup will find out and he'll know we've been following him. And if we dig and we find human remains, do we have enough here to charge Jessup?"

McPherson leaned forward while Haller leaned back, clearly deferring to his second chair.

"Well, I see no legal embargo on digging," she finally said. "It's public property and there is nothing that would stop you legally. No need for a search warrant. But do you want to dig right now based on this one dog with what seems like a high false-positive rate, or do we wait until after the trial?"

"Or maybe even during the trial," Haller said.

"The second question is the more difficult," McPherson said. "For the sake of argument, let's say there are remains buried in one or even all of those spots. Yes, Jessup's activities seem to form an awareness of what is below the earth in the places he visits in the middle of the night. But does that prove he's responsible? Hardly. We could charge him, yes, but he could mount a number of defenses based on what we know right now. You agree, Michael?"

Haller leaned forward and nodded.

"Suppose you dig and you find the remains of one of these girls. Even if you can confirm the ID—and that's going to be a big if—you still don't have any evidence connecting her death to Jessup. All you have is his guilty knowledge of the burial spot. That is very significant but is it enough to go into court with? I don't know. I think I'd rather be defense counsel than prosecutor on that one. I think Maggie's right, there are any number of defenses that he could employ to explain his knowledge of the burial sites. He could invent a straw man—somebody else who did the killings and told him about them or forced him to take part in the burials. Jessup's spent twenty-four years in prison. How many other convicts has he been exposed to? Thousands? Tens of thousands? How many of them were murderers? He could lay this whole thing on one of them, say that he heard in prison about these burial spots and he decided to come and pray for the souls of the victims. He could make up anything."

He shook his head again.

"The bottom line is, there are a lot of ways to go with a defense like this. Without any sort of physical evidence connecting him or a witness, I think you would have a problem."

"Maybe there is physical evidence in the graves that connects him," Bosch offered.

"Maybe, but what if there isn't?" Haller shot right back. "You never know, you could also pull a confession out of Jessup. But I doubt that, too."

McPherson took it from there.

"Michael mentioned the big if, the remains. Can they be IDed? Will we be able to establish how long they were in the ground? Remember, Jessup has an ironclad alibi for the last twenty-four years. If you pull up a set of bones and we can't say for sure that they've been down there since at least 'eighty-six, then Jessup would walk."

Haller got up and went to the whiteboard, grabbing a marker off the ledge. In a clear spot he drew two circles side by side.

"Here's what we've got so far. One is our case and one is this whole new thing you've come up with. They're separate. We have the case with the trial about to go and then we have your new investigation. When they're separate like this we're fine. Your investigation has no bearing on our trial, so we can keep the two circles separate. Understand?"

"Sure," Bosch said.

Haller grabbed the eraser off the ledge and wiped the two circles off the board. He then drew two new circles, but this time they overlapped.

"Now if you go out there and start digging and you find bones? This is what happens. Our two circles become connected. And that's when your thing becomes our thing and we have to reveal this to the defense and the whole wide world."

McPherson nodded in agreement.

"So then, what do we do?" Bosch asked. "Drop it?"

"No, we don't drop it," Haller said. "We just be careful and we keep them separate. You know what is universally held as the best trial strategy? Keep it simple, stupid. So let's not complicate things. Let's keep our circles separate and go to trial and get this guy for killing Melissa Landy. And when we're done that, we go up to Mulholland with shovels."

"Done *with*."

"What?"

"When we're done *with* that."

"Whatever, Professor."

Bosch's eyes moved from Haller's connected circles on the board to the row of faces. All his instincts told him that at least some of those girls did not get any older than they were in the photos. They were in the ground and had been buried there by Jason Jessup. He hated the idea of them spending another day in the dirt but knew that they would have to wait a little longer.

"Okay," he said. "I'll keep working it on the side. For now. But there's also one other thing from the profiler that you should know."

"The other shoe drops," McPherson said. "What?"

Haller had returned to his seat. Bosch pulled out a chair and sat down himself.

"She said a killer like Jessup doesn't reform in prison. The dark matter inside doesn't go away. It stays. It waits. It's like a cancer. And it reacts to outside pressures."

"He'll kill again," McPherson said.

Bosch slowly nodded.

"He can visit the graves of his past victims for only so long before he'll feel the need for...fresh inspiration. And if he feels under pressure, the chances are good he'll move in that direction even sooner."

"Then we'd better be ready," Haller said. "I'm the guy who let him out. If you have any doubts about him being covered, then I want to hear them."

"No doubts," Bosch said. "If Jessup makes a move, we'll be on him."

"When are you planning on going out with the SIS again?" McPherson asked.

"Whenever I can. But I've got my daughter, so it's whenever she's on a sleepover or I can get somebody to come in."

"I want to go once."

"Why?"

"I want to see the real Jessup. Not the one in the papers and on TV."

"Well..."

"What?"

"Well, there are no women on the team and they're constantly moving with this guy. There won't be any bathroom breaks. They piss in bottles."

"Don't worry, Harry, I think I can handle it."

"Then I'll set it up."

21

Friday, March 19, 10:50 A.M.

I checked my watch when I heard Maggie say hello to Lorna in the reception room. She entered the office and dropped her case on her desk. It was one of those slim and stylish Italian leather laptop totes that she never would have bought for herself. Too expensive and too red. I wanted to know who gave it to her like I wanted to know a lot of things she would never tell me.

But the origin of her red briefcase was the least of my worries. In thirteen days we would start picking jurors in the Jessup case and Clive Royce had finally landed his best pretrial punch. It was an inch thick and sat in front of me on my desk.

"Where have you been?" I said with a clear note of annoyance in my voice. "I called your cell and got no answer."

She came over to my desk, dragging the extra chair with her.

"More like, where were you?"

I glanced at my calendar blotter and saw nothing in the day's square.

"What are you talking about?"

"My phone was turned off because I was at Hayley's honors assembly. They don't like cell phones ringing when they are calling the kids up to get their pins."

"Ah, shit!"

She had told me and copied me on the e-mail. I printed it out and put it on the refrigerator. But not on my desk blotter or into my phone's calendar. I blew it.

"You should've been there, Haller. You would've been proud."

"I know, I know. I messed up."

"It's all right. You'll get other chances. To mess up or stand up."

That hurt. It would've been better if she had chewed my ass out like she used to. But the passive-aggressive approach always got deeper under the skin. And she probably knew that.

"I'll be at the next one," I said. "That's a promise."

She didn't sarcastically say *Sure, Haller,* or *I've heard that one before.* And somehow that made it worse. Instead, she just got down to business.

"What is that?"

She nodded at the document in front of me.

"This is Clive Royce's last best stand. It's a motion to exclude the testimony of Sarah Ann Gleason."

"And of course he drops it off on a Friday afternoon three weeks before trial."

"More like seventeen days."

"My mistake. What's he say?"

I turned the document around and slid it across the desk to her. It was held together with a large black clip.

"He's been working on this one since the start because he knows the case comes down to her. She's our primary witness and without her none of the other evidence matters. Even the hair in the truck is circumstantial. If he takes out Sarah he takes out our case."

"I get that. But how's he trying to get rid of her?"

She started flipping through the pages.

"It was delivered at nine and is eighty-six pages long so I haven't had the time to completely digest it. But it's a two-pronged effort. He's attacking her original identification from when she was a kid. Says the setup was prejudicial. And he—"

"That was already argued, accepted by the trial court and it held up on appeal. He's wasting the court's time."

"He's got a new angle this time. Remember, Kloster's got Alzheimer's and is no good as a witness. He can't tell us about the investigation and he can't defend himself. So this time out Royce alleges that Kloster told Sarah which man to identify. He pointed Jessup out for her."

"And what is his backup? Supposedly only Sarah and Kloster were in the room."

"I don't know. There's no backup but my guess is he's riffing on the radio call Kloster made telling them to make Jessup take off his hat."

"It doesn't matter. The lineup was put together to see if Sarah could identify Derek Wilbern, the other driver. Any argument that he then told her to put the finger on Jessup is ridiculous. That ID came quite unexpectedly but naturally and convincingly. This is nothing to get worked up about. Even without Kloster we'll tear this one up."

I knew she was right but the first attack wasn't really what I was most worried about.

"That's just his opening salvo," I said. "That's nothing compared with part two. He also seeks to exclude her entire testimony based on unreliable memory. He's got her whole drug history laid out in the motion, seemingly down to every chip of meth she ever smoked. He's got arrest records, jail records, witnesses who detail her consumption of drugs, multiple-partner sex and what they term her belief in out-of-body experiences — I guess she forgot to mention that part up in Port Townsend. And to top it all off, he's got experts on memory loss and false memory creation as a by-product of meth addiction. So in all, you know what he's got? He's got us fucked coming and going."

Maggie didn't respond as she was scanning the summary pages at the end of Royce's motion.

"He's got investigators here and up in San Francisco," I added. "It's thorough and exhaustive, Mags. And you know what? It doesn't even look like he's gone up to Port Townsend to interview her yet. He says he doesn't have to because it doesn't matter what she says now. It can't be relied upon."

"He'll have his experts and we'll have ours on rebuttal," she said calmly. "We expected this part and I've already been lining ours up. At worst, we can turn this into a wash. You know that."

"The experts are only a small part of it."

"We'll be fine," she insisted. "And look at these witnesses. Her ex-husbands and boyfriends. I see Royce conveniently didn't bother to include their own arrest records here. They're all tweakers themselves. We'll make them look like pimps and pedophiles with grudges against her because she left them in the dust when she got straight. She married the first one when she was eighteen and he was twenty-nine. She told us. I'd love to get him in the chair in front of the judge. I really think you are overreacting to this, Haller. We can argue this. We can make him put some of these so-called witnesses in front of the judge and we can knock every one of them out of the box. You're right about one thing, though. This is Royce's last best stand. It's just not going to be good enough."

I shook my head. She was seeing only what was on paper and what could be blocked or parried with our own swords. Not what was not written.

"Look, this is about Sarah. He knows the judge is not going to want to chop our main witness. He knows we'll get by this. But he's putting the judge on notice that this is what he is going to put Sarah through if she takes the stand. Her whole life, every sordid detail, every pipe and dick she ever smoked, she's going to have to sit up there and take it. Then he'll trot out some PhD who'll put pictures of a melted brain on the screen and say this is what meth does. Do we want that for her? Is she strong enough to take it? Maybe we have to go to Royce, offer a deal for time served and some kind of payout from the city. Something everybody can live with."

Maggie flopped the motion onto the desk.

"Are you kidding me? You're running scared because of this?"

"I'm not running scared. I'm being realistic. I didn't go up to Washington. I have no feel for this woman. I don't know if she can stand up to this or not. Besides, we can always take a second bite of the apple with those cases Bosch has been working."

Maggie leaned back in her chair.

"There's no guarantee that anything will come out of those other cases. We have to put everything we have into this one, Haller. I could go back up there and hold Sarah's hand a little bit. Tell her more about what to expect. Get her ready. She already understood it wasn't going to be pretty."

"To put it mildly."

"I think she's strong enough. I think in some weird way she might need it. You know, get it all out there, expiate her sins. It's about redemption with her, Michael. You know about that."

We held each other's eyes for a long moment.

"Anyway, I think she'll be more than strong and the jury will see it," she said. "She's a survivor and everybody likes a survivor."

I nodded.

"You have a way of convincing people, Mags. It's a gift. We both know you should be lead on this, not me."

"Thank you for saying that."

"All right, go up there and get her prepped for this. Next week, maybe. By then we should have a witness schedule and you can tell her when we'll be bringing her down."

"Okay," she said.

"Meantime, how's your weekend looking? We have to put together an answer to this."

I pointed at the defense motion on the desk.

"Well, Harry finally got me a ride-along with the SIS tomorrow night. He's going, too — I think his daughter has a sleepover. Other than that, I'm around."

"Why are you going to spend all that time watching Jessup? The police have that covered."

"Like I said before, I want to see Jessup out there when he doesn't think anyone is watching. I would suggest that you come, too, but you've got Hayley."

"I wouldn't waste the time. But when you see Bosch, can you give him a copy of this motion? We're going to need him to run down some of these witnesses and statements. Not all of them were in Royce's discovery package."

"Yeah, he played it smart. He keeps them off his witness list until they show up here. If the judge shoots down the motion, saying Gleason's credibility is a jury question, he'll come back with an amended witness list, saying, okay, I need to put these people in front of the jury in regard to credibility."

"And she'll allow it or she'll be contradicting her own ruling. Clever Clive. He knows what he's doing."

"Anyway, I'll get a copy to Harry, but I think he's still chasing those old cases."

"Doesn't matter. The trial is the priority. We need complete backgrounds on these people. You want to deal with him or do you want me to?"

In our divvying up of pretrial duties I had given Maggie the responsibility of prepping for defense witnesses. All except Jessup. If he testified, he was still mine.

"I'll talk to him," she said.

She furrowed her brow. It was a habit I'd seen before.

"What?"

"Nothing. I'm just thinking about how to attack this. I think we throw in a motion *in limine*, seeking to limit Royce on the impeachable stuff. We argue that the events of her life in between are not relevant to credibility if her identification of Jessup now matches her identification back then."

I shook my head.

"I would argue that you're infringing on my client's sixth amendment right to cross-examine his accuser. The judge might limit some of this stuff if it's repetitive, but don't count on her disallowing it."

She pursed her lips as she recognized that I was right.

"It's still worth a try," I said. "Everything is worth a try. In fact, I want to drown Royce in paper. Let's hit him back with a phonebook to wade through."

She looked at me and smiled.

"What?"

"I like it when you get all angry and righteous."

"You haven't seen anything yet."

She looked away before it went a step further.

"Where do you want to set up shop this weekend?" she asked. "Remember, you have Hayley. She's not going to like it if we work the entire weekend."

I had to think about that for a moment. Hayley loved museums. To the point that I was tired of going to the same museums over and over. She also loved movies. I would need to check and see if a new movie was out.

"Bring her to my house in the morning and be prepared to work on our response. We can maybe trade off. I'll take her to a movie or something in the afternoon and then you go on and do your thing with the SIS. We'll make it work."

"Okay, that's a deal."

"Or..."

"Or what?"

"You could bring her over tonight and we could have a little dinner celebrating our kid making second honors. And we might even get a little work on this done."

"And I stay over, is that what you mean?"

"Sure, if you want."

"You wish, Haller."

"I do."

"By the way, it was first honors. You better have it right when you see her tonight."

I smiled.

"Tonight? You mean that?"

"I think so."

"Then don't worry. I'll have everything right."

22

Saturday, March 20, 8:00 P.M.

Because Bosch had mentioned that a prosecutor wanted to join the SIS surveillance, Lieutenant Wright arranged his schedule to work Saturday night and be the driver of the car the visitors were assigned to. The pickup point was in Venice at a public parking lot six blocks off the beach. Bosch met McPherson there and then he put a radio call in to Wright, saying they were ready and waiting. Fifteen minutes later a white SUV entered the lot and drove up to them. Bosch gave McPherson the front seat and he climbed into the back. He wasn't being chivalrous. The long bench seat would allow him to stretch out during the long night of surveillance.

"Steve Wright," the lieutenant said, offering McPherson his hand.

"Maggie McPherson. Thanks for letting me come along."

"No sweat. We always like it when the District Attorney's Office takes an interest. Let's hope tonight is worth your while."

"Where's Jessup now?"

"When I left he was at the Brig on Abbot Kinney. He likes crowded places, which works in our favor. I have a couple guys inside and a few more on the street. We're kind of used to his rhythm now. He hits a place, waits to be recognized and for people to start buying him drinks, then he moves on — quickly if he isn't recognized."

"I guess I'm more interested in his late-night travels than his drinking habits."

"It's good that he's out drinking," Bosch said from the backseat. "There's a causal relationship. The nights he takes in alcohol are usually the nights he goes up to Mulholland."

Wright nodded in agreement and headed the SUV out of the lot. He was a perfect surveillance man because he didn't look like a cop. In his late fifties with glasses, a thinning hairline and always two or three pens in his shirt pocket, he looked more like an accountant. But he had been with the SIS for more than two decades and had been in on several of the squad's kills. Every five years or so the *Times* did a story on the SIS, usually analyzing its kill record. In the last exposé Bosch remembered reading, the paper had labeled Wright "SIS's unlikely chief gunslinger." While the reporters and editors behind the story probably viewed that as an editorial putdown, Wright wore it like a badge of honor. He had the sobriquet printed below his name on his business card. In quotes, of course.

Wright drove down Abbot Kinney Boulevard and past the Brig, which was located in a two-story building on the east side of the street. He went two blocks down and made a U-turn. He came back up the street and pulled to the curb in front of a fire hydrant a half block from the bar.

The lighted sign outside the Brig depicted a boxer in a ring, his red gloves up and ready. It was an image that seemed at odds with the name of the bar, but Bosch knew the story behind it. As a much younger man he had lived in the neighborhood. He knew the sign with the boxer was put up by a former owner who had bought out the original owners. The new man was a retired fighter and had decorated the interior with a boxing motif. He also put the sign up out front. There was still a mural on the side of the building that depicted the fighter and his wife, but they were long gone now.

"This is Five," Wright said. "What's our status?"

He was talking to the microphone clipped to the sun visor over his head. Bosch knew there was a foot button on the floor that engaged it. The return speaker was under the dash. The radio setup in the cars allowed the surveillance cops to keep their hands free while driving and, more important, helped them maintain their cover. Talking into a handheld rover was a dead giveaway. The SIS was too good for that.

"Three," a voice said over the radio. "Retro is still in the location along with One and Two."

"Roger that," Wright said.

"Retro?" McPherson said.

"Our name for him," Wright said. "Our freqs are pretty far down the bandwidth and on the FCC registry they're listed as DWP channels, but you never know who might be listening. We don't use the names of people or locations on the air."

"Got it."

It wasn't even nine yet. Bosch wasn't expecting Jessup to leave anytime soon, especially if people were buying him drinks. As they settled in, Wright seemed to like McPherson and liked informing her about procedures and the art of high-level surveillance. She might have been bored with it but she never let on.

"See, once we establish a subject's rhythms and routines we can react much better. Take this place, for example. The Brig is one of three or four places Retro hits sort of regularly. We've assigned different guys to different bars so they can go in while he's in the location and be like regulars. The two guys I've got right now in the Brig are the same two guys that always go in there. And two other guys would go into Townhouse when he's there and two others have James Beach. It goes like that. If Retro notices them he'll think it's because he's seen them in there before and they're regulars in the place. Now if he saw the same guy at two different places, he'd start getting suspicious."

"I understand, Lieutenant. Sounds like the smart way to do it."

"Call me Steve."

"Okay, Steve. Can your people inside communicate?"

"Yes, but they're deaf."

"Deaf?"

"We've all got body mikes. You know, like the Secret Service? But we don't put in the earpieces when we're in play inside a place like a bar. Too obvious. So they call in their positions when possible but they don't hear anything coming back unless they pull the receiver up from under their collar and put it in. Unfortunately, it's not like TV where they just put the bean in their ear and there's no wire."

"I see. And do your men actually drink while in a bar on a surveillance?"

"A guy in a place like that ordering a Coke or a glass of water is going to stand out as suspicious. So they order booze. But then they nurse it. Luckily, Retro likes to go to crowded places. Makes it easier to maintain cover."

While the small talk continued in the front seat, Bosch pulled his phone and started what some would consider a conversation of small talk himself. He texted his daughter. Though he knew there were several sets of eyes on the Brig and even inside on Jessup, he looked up and checked the door of the bar every few seconds.

Howzit going? Having fun?

Madeline was staying overnight at her friend Aurora Smith's house. It was only a few blocks from home but Bosch would not be nearby if she needed him. It was several minutes before she grudgingly answered the text. But they had a deal. She must answer his calls and texts, or her freedom — what she called her leash — would be shortened.

Everything's fine. You don't have to check on me.

Yes I do. I'm your father. Don't stay up too late.

K.

And that was it. A child's shorthand in a shorthand relationship. Bosch knew he needed help. There was so much he didn't know. At times they seemed fine and everything appeared to be perfect. Other times he was sure she was going to sneak out the door and run away. Living with his daughter had resulted in his love for her growing more than he thought was possible. Thoughts of her safety as well as hopes for her happy future invaded his mind at all times. His longing to make her life better and take her far past her own history had at times become a physical ache in his chest. Still, he couldn't seem to reach across the aisle. The plane was bouncing and he kept missing.

He put his phone away and checked the front of the Brig again. There was a crowd of smokers standing outside. Just then a voice and the sharp crack of billiard balls colliding in the background came over the radio speaker.

"Coming out. Retro is coming out."

"This seems early," Wright said.

"Does he smoke?" McPherson asked. "Maybe he's just—"

"Not that we've seen."

Bosch kept his eyes on the door and soon it pushed open. A man he recognized even from a distance as Jessup stepped out and headed along the sidewalk. Abbot Kinney slashed in a northwesterly direction across Venice. He was heading that way.

"Where did he park?" Bosch asked.

"He didn't," Wright said. "He only lives a few blocks from here. He walked over."

They watched in silence after that. Jessup walked two blocks on Abbot Kinney, passing a variety of restaurants, coffee shops and galleries. The sidewalk was busy. Almost every place was still open for Saturday-night business. He stepped into a coffee shop called Abbot's Habit. Wright got on the radio and assigned one of his men to enter it but before that could happen, Jessup stepped back out, coffee in hand, and proceeded on foot again.

Wright started the SUV and pulled into traffic going the opposite direction. He made a U-turn when he was two blocks further down and away from Jessup's view, should he happen to turn around. All the while he maintained constant radio contact with the other followers. Jessup had an invisible net around him. Even if he knew it was there he couldn't lose it.

"He's heading home," a radio voice reported. "Might be an early night."

Abbot Kinney, named for the man who built Venice more than a century earlier, became Brooks Avenue, which then intersected with Main Street. Jessup crossed Main and headed down one of the walk streets where automobiles could not travel. Wright was ready for this and directed two of the tail cars over to Pacific Avenue so they could pick him up when he came through.

Wright pulled to a stop at Brooks and Main and waited for the report that Jessup had passed through and was on Pacific. After two minutes he started to get anxious and went to the radio.

"Where is he, people?"

There was no response. No one had Jessup. Wright quickly sent somebody in.

"Two, you go in. Use the twenty-three."

"Got it."

McPherson looked over the seatback at Bosch and then at Wright.

"The twenty-three?"

"We have a variety of tactics we use. We don't describe them on the air."

He pointed through the windshield.

"That's the twenty-three."

Bosch saw a man wearing a red windbreaker and carrying an insulated pizza bag cut across Main and into the walk street named Breeze Avenue. They waited and finally the radio burst to life.

"I'm not seeing him. I walked all the way through and he's not—"

The transmission cut off. Wright said nothing. They waited and then the same voice came back in a whisper.

"I almost walked into him. He came out between two houses. He was pulling up his zipper."

"Okay, did he make you?" Wright asked.

"That's a negative. I asked for directions to Breeze Court and he said this was Breeze Avenue. We're cool. He should be coming through now."

"This is Four. We got him. He's heading toward San Juan."

The fourth car was one of the vehicles Wright had put on Pacific. Jessup was living in an apartment on San Juan Avenue between Speedway and the beach.

Bosch felt the momentary tension in his gut start to ease. Surveillance work was sometimes tough to take. Jessup had ducked between two houses to take a leak and it had caused a near panic.

Wright redirected the teams to the area around San Juan Avenue between Pacific and Speedway. Jessup used a key to enter the second-floor apartment where he was staying and the teams quickly moved into place. It was time to wait again.

Bosch knew from past surveillance gigs that the main attribute a good watcher needed was a comfort with silence. Some people are compelled to fill the void. Harry never was and he doubted anyone in the SIS was. He was curious to see how McPherson would do, now that the surveillance 101 lesson from Wright was over and there was nothing left but to wait and watch.

Bosch pulled his phone to see if he had missed a text from his daughter but it was clear. He decided not to pester her with another check-in and put the phone away. The genius of his giving McPherson the front seat now came into play. He turned and put his legs up and across the seat, stretching himself into a lounging position with his back against the door. McPherson glanced back and smiled in the darkness of the car.

"I thought you were being a gentleman," she said. "You just wanted to stretch out."

Bosch smiled.

"You got me."

Everyone was silent after that. Bosch thought about what McPherson had said while they had waited in the parking lot to be picked up by Wright. First she handed him a copy of the latest defense motion, which he locked in the trunk of his car. She told him he needed to start vetting the witnesses and their statements, looking for ways to turn their threats to the case into advantages for the prosecution. She said she and Haller had worked all day crafting a response to the attempt to disqualify Sarah Ann Gleason from testifying. The judge's ruling on the issue could decide the outcome of the trial.

It always bothered Bosch when he saw justice and the law being manipulated by smart lawyers. His part in the process was pure. He started at a crime scene and followed the evidence to a killer. There were rules along the way but at least the route was clear most of the time. But once things moved into the courthouse, they took on a different shape. Lawyers argued over interpretations and theories and procedures. Nothing seemed to move in a straight line. Justice became a labyrinth.

How could it be, he wondered, that an eyewitness to a horrible crime would not be allowed to testify in court against the accused? He had been a cop more than thirty-five years and he still could not explain how the system worked.

"This is Three. Retro's on the move."

Bosch was jarred out of his thoughts. A few seconds went by and the next report came from another voice.

"He's driving."

Wright took over.

"Okay, we get ready for an auto tail. One, get out to Main and Rose, Two, go down to Pacific and Venice. Everybody else, sit tight until we have his direction."

A few minutes later they had their answer.

"North on Main. Same as usual."

Wright redirected his units and the carefully orchestrated mobile surveillance began moving with Jessup as he took Main Street to Pico and then made his way to the entrance of the 10 Freeway.

Jessup headed east and then merged onto the northbound 405, which was crowded with cars even at the late hour. As expected, he was heading toward the Santa Monica Mountains. The surveillance vehicles ranged from Wright's SUV to a black Mercedes convertible to a Volvo station wagon with two bikes on a rear rack to a pair of generic Japanese sedans. The only thing missing for a surveillance in the Hollywood Hills was a hybrid. The teams employed a surveillance procedure called the *floating box*. Two outriders on either side of the target car, another car up front and one behind, all moving in a choreographed rotation. Wright's SUV was the floater, running backup behind the box.

The whole way Jessup stayed at or below the speed limit. As the freeway rose to the crest of the mountains Bosch looked out his window and saw the Getty Museum rising in the mist at the top like a castle, the sky black behind it.

Anticipating that Jessup was heading to his usual destinations on Mulholland Drive, Wright told two teams to break off from the box and move ahead. He wanted them already up and on Mulholland ahead of Jessup. He wanted a ground team with night vision goggles in Franklin Canyon Park before Jessup went in.

True to form, Jessup took the Mulholland exit and was soon heading east on the winding, two-lane snake that runs the spine of the mountain chain. Wright explained that this was when the surveillance was most vulnerable to exposure.

"You need a bee to properly do this up here but that's not in the budget," he said.

"A bee?" McPherson asked.

"Part of our code. Means helicopter. We could sure use one."

The first surprise of the night came five minutes later when Jessup drove by Franklin Canyon Park without stopping. Wright quickly recalled his ground team from the park as Jessup continued east.

Jessup passed Coldwater Canyon Boulevard without slowing and next drove by the overlook above Fryman Canyon. When he passed through the intersection of Mulholland and Laurel Canyon Boulevard he was taking the surveillance team into new territory.

"What are the chances he's made us?" Bosch asked.

"None," Wright said. "We're too good. He's got something new on his mind."

For the next ten minutes the follow continued east toward the Cahuenga Pass. The command car was well behind the surveillance, and Wright and his two passengers had to rely on radio reports to know what was happening.

One car was moving in front of Jessup while all the rest were behind. The rear cars followed a continual rotation of turning off and moving up so the headlight configurations would keep changing in Jessup's rearview. Finally, a radio report came in that made Bosch move forward in his seat, as if closer proximity to the source of the information would make things clearer.

"There's a stop sign up here and Retro turned north. It's too dark to see the street sign but I had to stay on Mulholland. Too risky. Next up turn left at the stop."

"Roger that. We got the left."

"Wait!" Bosch said urgently. "Tell him to wait."

Wright checked him in the mirror.

"What do you have in mind?" he asked.

"There's only one stop on Mulholland. Woodrow Wilson Drive. I know it. It winds down and reconnects with Mulholland at the light down at Highland. The lead car can pick him up there. But Woodrow Wilson is too tight. If you send a car down there he may know he's being followed."

"You sure?"

"I'm sure. I live on Woodrow Wilson."

Wright thought for a moment and then went on the radio.

"Cancel that left. Where's the Volvo?"

"We're holding up until further command."

"Okay, go on up and make the left on the two wheelers. Watch for oncoming. And watch for our guy."

"Roger that."

Soon Wright's SUV got to the intersection. Bosch saw the Volvo pulled off to the side. The bike rack was empty. Wright pulled over to wait, checking the teams on the radio.

"One, are you in position?"

"That's a roger. We're at the light at the bottom. No sign of Retro yet."

"Three, you up?"

There was no response.

"Okay, everybody hold till we hear."

"What do you mean?" Bosch asked. "What about the bikes?"

"They must've gone down deaf. We'll hear when they—"

"This is Three," a voice said in a whisper. "We came up on him. He'd closed his eyes and went to sleep."

Wright translated for his passengers.

"He killed his lights and stopped moving."

Bosch felt his chest start to tighten.

"Are they sure he's in the car?"

Wright communicated the question over the radio.

"Yeah, we can see him. He's got a candle burning on the dashboard."

"Where exactly are you, Three?"

"About halfway down. We can hear the freeway."

Bosch leaned all the way forward between the two front seats.

"Ask him if he can pick a number off the curb," he said. "Get me an address."

Wright relayed the request and almost a minute went by before the whisper came back.

"It's too dark to see the curbs here without using a flash. But we got a light next to the door of the house he's parked in front of. It's one of those cantilever jobs hanging its ass out over the pass. From here it looks like seventy-two-oh-three."

Bosch slid back and leaned heavily against the seat. McPherson turned to look at him. Wright used the mirror to look back.

"You know that address?" Wright asked.

Bosch nodded in the darkness.

"Yeah," he said. "It's my house."

23

Sunday, March 21, 6:40 A.M.

My daughter liked to sleep in on Sundays. Normally I hated losing the time with her. I only had her every other weekend and Wednesdays. But this Sunday was different. I was happy to let her sleep while I got up early to go back to work on the motion to save my chief witness's testimony. I was in the kitchen pouring the first cup of coffee of the day when I heard knocking on my front door. It was still dark out. I checked the peep before opening it and was relieved to see it was my ex-wife with Harry Bosch standing right behind her.

But that relief was short-lived. The moment I turned the knob they pushed in and I could immediately feel a bad energy enter with them.

"We've got a problem," Maggie said.

"What's wrong?" I asked.

"What's wrong is that Jessup camped outside my house this morning," Bosch said. "And I want to know how he found it and what the hell he's doing."

He came up too close to me when he said it. I didn't know which was worse, his breath or the accusatory tone of his words. I wasn't sure what he was thinking but I realized all the bad energy was coming from him.

I stepped back from him.

"Hayley's still asleep. Let me just go close her bedroom door. There's fresh decaf in the kitchen and I can brew some fully leaded if you need it."

I went down the hall and checked on my daughter. She was still down. I closed the door and hoped the voices that were bound to get loud would not wake her.

My two visitors were still standing when I got back to the living room. Neither had gone for coffee. Bosch was silhouetted by the big picture window that looked out upon the city — the view that made me buy the house. I could see streaks of light entering the sky behind his shoulders.

"No coffee?"

They just stared at me.

"Okay, let's sit down and talk about this."

I gestured toward the couch and chairs but Bosch seemed frozen in his stance.

"Come on, let's figure it out."

I walked past them and sat down in the chair by the window. Finally,

Bosch started to move. He sat down on the couch next to Hayley's school backpack. Maggie took the other chair. She spoke first.

"I've been trying to convince Harry that we didn't put his home address on the witness list."

"Absolutely not. We gave no personal addresses in discovery. For you, I listed two addresses. Your office and mine. I even gave the general number for the PAB. Didn't even give a direct line."

"Then how did he find my house?" Bosch asked, the accusatory tone still in his voice.

"Look, Harry, you're blaming me for something I had nothing to do with. I don't know how he found your house but it couldn't have been that hard. I mean, come on. Anybody can find anybody on the Internet. You own your house, right? You pay property taxes, have utility accounts, and I bet you're even registered to vote — Republican, I'm sure."

"Independent."

"Fine. The point is, people can find you if they want. Added to that, you have a singular name. All anybody would have to do is punch in —"

"You gave them my full name?"

"I had to. It's what's required and what's been given in discovery for every trial you've ever testified in. It doesn't matter. All Jessup needed was access to the Internet and he could've —"

"Jessup's been in prison for twenty-four years. He knows less about the Internet than I do. He had to have help and I'm betting it came from Royce."

"Look, we don't know that."

Bosch looked pointedly at me, a darkness crossing his eyes.

"You're defending *him* now?"

"No, I'm not defending anybody. I'm just saying we shouldn't rush to any conclusions here. Jessup's got a roommate and is a minor celebrity. Celebrities get people to do things for them, okay? So why don't you calm down and let's back up a little bit. Tell me what happened at your house."

Bosch seemed to take it down a notch but he was still anything but calm. I half expected him to get up and take a swing at a lamp or punch a hole in a wall. Thankfully, Maggie was the one who told the story.

"We were with the SIS, watching him. We thought he was going to go up to one of the parks he's been visiting. Instead, he drove right by them all and kept going on Mulholland. When we got to Harry's street we had to hang back so he wouldn't see us. The SIS has a bike car. Two of them saddled up and rode down. They found Jessup sitting in his car in front of Harry's house."

"Goddamn it!" Bosch said. "I have my daughter living with me. If this prick is —"

"Harry, not so loud and watch what you say," I said. "My daughter's on the other side of that wall. Now, please, go back to the story. What did Jessup do?"

Bosch hesitated. Maggie didn't.

"He just sat there," Maggie said. "For about a half hour. And he lit a candle."

"A candle? In the car?"

"Yeah, on the dashboard."

"What the hell does that mean?"

"Who knows?"

Bosch couldn't remain sitting. He jumped up from the couch and started pacing.

"And after a half hour he drove off and went home," Maggie said. "That was it. We just came from Venice."

Now I stood up and started to pace, but in a pattern clear of Bosch's orbit.

"Okay, let's think about this. Let's think about what he was doing."

"No shit, Sherlock," Bosch said. "That's the question."

I nodded. I had that coming.

"Is there any reason to think that he knows or suspects he's being followed?" I asked.

"No, no way," Bosch said immediately.

"Wait a minute, not so fast on that," Maggie said. "I've been thinking about it. There was a near-miss earlier in the night. You remember, Harry? On Breeze Avenue?"

Bosch nodded. Maggie explained it to me.

"They thought they lost him on a walk street in Venice. The lieutenant sent a guy in with a pizza box. Jessup came out from between two houses after taking a leak. It was a close call."

I spread my hands.

"Well, maybe that was it. Maybe that planted suspicion and he decided to see if he was being followed. You show up outside the lead investigator's house and it's a good way to draw out the flies if you've got them on you."

"You mean like a test?" Bosch asked.

"Exactly. Nobody approached him out there, right?"

"No, we left him alone," Maggie said. "If he had gotten out of his car I think it would've been a different story."

I nodded.

"Okay, so it was either a test or he's got something planned. In that case, it would've been a reconnaissance mission. He wanted to see where you live."

Bosch stopped and stared out the window. The sky was fully lit now.

"But one thing you have to keep in mind is that what he did was not illegal," I said. "It's a public street and the OR put no restrictions on travel within Los Angeles County. So no matter what he was up to, it's a good thing you didn't stop him and reveal yourself."

Bosch stayed at the window, his back to us. I didn't know what he was thinking.

"Harry," I said. "I know your concerns and I agree with them. But we can't let this be a distraction. The trial is coming up quick and we have work to do. If we convict this guy, he goes away forever and it won't matter if he knows where you live."

"So what do I do till then, sit on my front porch every night with a shotgun?"

"The SIS is on him twenty-four/seven, right?" Maggie said. "Do you trust them?"

Bosch didn't answer for a long moment.

"They won't lose him," he finally said.

Maggie looked at me and I could see the concern in her eyes. Each of us had a daughter. It would be hard to put your trust in anybody else, even an elite surveillance squad. I thought for a moment about something I had been considering since the conversation began.

"What about you moving in here? With your daughter. She can use Hayley's room because Hayley's going back to her mother's today. And you can use the office. It's got a sleeper sofa that I've spent more than a few nights on. It's actually comfortable."

Bosch turned from the window and looked at me.

"What, stay here through the whole trial?"

"Why not? Our daughters will finally get a chance to meet when Hayley comes over."

"It's a good idea," Maggie said.

I didn't know if she was referring to the daughters meeting or the idea of Bosch and child staying with me.

"And look, I'm here every night," I said. "If you have to go out with the SIS, I got you covered with your daughter, especially when Hayley's here."

Bosch thought about it for a few moments but then shook his head.

"I can't do that," he said.

"Why not?" I asked.

"Because it's my house. My home. I'm not going to run from this guy. He's going to run from me."

"What about your daughter?" Maggie asked.

"I'll take care of my daughter."

"Harry, think about it," she said. "Think about your daughter. You don't want her in harm's way."

"Look, if Jessup has my address, then he probably has this address, too. Moving in here isn't the answer. It's just...just running from him. Maybe that's his test—to see what I do. So I'm not doing anything. I'm not moving. I've got the SIS, and if he comes back and so much as crosses the curb out front, I'll be waiting for him."

"I don't like this," Maggie said.

I thought about what Bosch had said about Jessup having my address.

"Neither do I," I said.

24

Wednesday, March 31, 9:00 A.M.

Bosch didn't need to be in court. In fact, he wouldn't be needed until after jury selection and the actual trial began. But he wanted to get a close look at the man he had been shadowing from a distance with the SIS. He wanted to see if Jessup would show any reaction to seeing him in return. It had been a month and a half since they had spent the long day in the car driving down from San Quentin. Bosch felt the need to get closer than the surveillance allowed him to. It would help him keep the fire burning.

It was billed as a status conference. The judge wanted to deal with all final motions and issues before beginning jury selection the next day and then moving seamlessly into the trial. There were scheduling and jury issues to discuss and each side's list of exhibits were to be handed in as well.

The prosecution team was locked and loaded. In the last two weeks Haller and McPherson had sharpened and streamlined the case, run through mock witness examinations and reconsidered every piece of evidence. They had carefully choreographed the ways in which they would bring the twenty-four-year-old evidence forward. They were ready. The bow had been pulled taut and the arrow was ready to fly.

Even the decision on the death penalty had been made — or rather, announced. Haller had officially withdrawn it, even though Bosch assumed all along that his use of it to threaten Jessup had merely been a pose. He was a defense attorney by nature, and there was no getting him across that line. A conviction on the charges would bring Jessup a sentence of life in prison without the possibility of parole, and that would have to be enough justice for Melissa Landy.

Bosch was ready as well. He had diligently reinvestigated the case and located the witnesses who would be called to testify. All the while, he was still out riding with the SIS as often as possible — nights that his daughter stayed at the homes of friends or with Sue Bambrough, the assistant principal. He was prepared for his part and had helped Haller and McPherson get ready for theirs. Confidence was high and that was another reason for Bosch to be in the courtroom. He wanted to see this thing get started.

Judge Breitman entered and the courtroom was brought to order at a few minutes after nine. Bosch was in a chair against the railing directly behind the prosecution table where Haller and McPherson sat side by side. They had told him to pull the chair up to the table but Harry wanted to hang back. He wanted to be able to watch Jessup from behind, and besides, there was too much anxiety coming from the two prosecutors. The judge was going to make a ruling on whether Sarah Ann Gleason would be allowed to testify against Jessup. As Haller had said the night before, nothing else mattered. If they lost Sarah as a witness, they would surely lose the case.

"On the record with *California versus Jessup* again," the judge said upon taking the bench. "Good morning to all."

After a chorus of good mornings fired back to her, the judge got right down to business.

"Tomorrow we begin jury selection in this case and then we proceed to trial. Therefore today is the day that we're going to clean out the garage, so to speak, so that we can finally bring the car in. Any last motions, any pending motions, anything anybody wants to talk about in regard to exhibits or evidence or anything else, now is the time. We have a number of motions pending and I will get to them first. The prosecution's request to redress the issue of the defendant's use of makeup to cover certain body tattoos is dismissed. We argued that at length already and I do not see the need to go at it further."

Bosch checked Jessup. He was at a sharp angle to him, so he could not see the defendant's face. But he did see Jessup nod his head in approval of the judge's first ruling of the day.

Breitman then went through a housekeeping list of minor motions from both sides. She seemed to want to accommodate all so neither side emerged as a clear favorite. Bosch saw that McPherson was meticulously keeping notes on each decision on a yellow legal pad.

It was all part of the buildup to the ruling of the day. Since Sarah was to be McPherson's witness to question during trial, she had handled the oral arguments on the defense motion two days earlier. Though Bosch had not attended that hearing, Haller had told him that Maggie had held forth for nearly an hour in a well-prepared response to the motion to disqualify. She had then backed it with an eighteen-page written response. The prosecution team was confident in the argument but neither member of the team knew Breitman well enough to be confident in how she would rule.

"Now," the judge said, "we come to the defense motion to disqualify Sarah Ann Gleason as a witness for the prosecution. The question has been argued and submitted by both sides and the court is ready to make a ruling."

"Your Honor, could I be heard?" Royce said, standing up at the defense table.

"Mr. Royce," the judge said, "I don't see the need for further argument. You made the motion and I allowed you to respond to the prosecution's submission. What more needs to be said?"

"Yes, Your Honor."

Royce sat back down, leaving whatever he was going to add to his attack on Sarah Gleason a secret.

"The defense's motion is dismissed," the judge said immediately. "I will be allowing the defense wide latitude in its examination of the prosecution's witness as well as in the production of its own witnesses to address Ms. Gleason's credibility before the jury. But I believe that this witness's credibility and reliability is indeed something that jurors will need to decide."

A momentary silence enveloped the courtroom, as if everyone collectively had drawn in a breath. No response followed from either the prosecution or defense table. It was another down-the-middle ruling, Bosch knew, and both sides were probably pleased to have gotten something. Gleason would be allowed to testify, so the prosecution's case was secured, but the judge was going to let Royce go after her with all he had. It would come down to whether Sarah was strong enough to take it.

"Now, I would like to move on," the judge said. "Let's talk about jury selection and scheduling first, and then we'll get to the exhibits."

The judge proceeded to outline how she wanted voir dire to proceed. Though each side would be allowed to question prospective jurors, she said she would strictly limit the time for each side. She wanted to start a momentum that would carry into the trial. She also limited each side to only twelve peremptory challenges — juror rejections without cause — and said she wanted to pick six alternates because it was her practice to be quick with the hook on jurors who misbehaved, were chronically late or had the audacity to fall asleep during testimony.

"I like a good supply of alternates because we usually need them," she said.

The low number of peremptory challenges and the high number of alternates brought objections from both the prosecution and the defense. The judge grudgingly gave each side two more challenges but warned that she would not allow voir dire to get bogged down.

"I want jury selection completed by the end of the day Friday. If you slow me down, then I will slow you down. I will hold the panel and every lawyer in here until Friday night if I have to. I want opening statements first thing Monday. Any objection to that?"

Both sides seemed properly cowed by the judge. She was clearly exerting command of her own courtroom. She next outlined the trial schedule, stating that testimony would begin each morning at nine sharp and continue until five with a ninety-minute lunch and morning and afternoon breaks of fifteen minutes each.

"That leaves a solid six hours a day of testimony," she said. "Any more and I find the jurors start losing interest. So I keep it to six a day. It will be up to you to be in here and ready to go each morning when I step through the door at nine. Any questions?"

There were none. Breitman then asked each side for estimates on how long their case would take to present. Haller said he would need no more than four days, depending on the length of the cross-examinations of his witnesses. This was already a shot directed at Royce and his plans to attack Sarah Ann Gleason.

For his part, Royce said he needed only two days. The judge then did her own math, adding four and two and coming up with five.

"Well, I'm thinking an hour each for opening statements on Monday morning. I think that means we'll finish Friday afternoon and go right to closing arguments the following Monday."

Neither side objected to her math. The point was clear. Keep it moving. Find ways to cut time. Of course a trial was a fluid thing and there were many unknowns. Neither side would be held to what was said at this hearing, but each lawyer knew that there might be consequences from the judge if they didn't keep a continuous velocity to their presentations.

"Finally, we come to exhibits and electronics," Breitman said. "I trust that everyone has looked over each other's lists. Any objections to these?"

Both Haller and Royce stood up. The judge nodded at Royce.

"You first, Mr. Royce."

"Yes, Judge, the defense has an objection to the prosecution's plans to project numerous images of Melissa Landy's body on the courtroom's overhead screens. This practice is not only barbaric but exploitative and prejudicial."

The judge swiveled in her seat and looked at Haller, who was still standing.

"Your Honor, it is the prosecution's duty to produce the body. To show the crime that brings us here. The last thing we want to do is be exploitative or prejudicial. I will grant Mr. Royce that it is a fine line, but we do not plan to step across it."

Royce came back with one more shot.

"This case is twenty-four years old. In nineteen eighty-six there were no overhead screens, none of this Hollywood stuff. I think it infringes on my client's right to a fair trial."

Haller was ready with his own comeback.

"The age of the case has nothing to do with this issue, but the defense is perfectly willing to present these exhibits the way they would've —"

McPherson had grabbed his sleeve to interrupt him. He bent down and she whispered in his ear. He then quickly straightened up.

"Excuse me, Your Honor, I misspoke. The *prosecution* is more than willing to present these exhibits in the manner they would have been presented to the jury in nineteen eighty-six. We would be happy to hand out color photographs to the jurors. But in earlier conversation the court indicated that she did not like this practice."

"Yes, I find that handing these sorts of photos directly to the jurors to be possibly more exploitative and prejudicial," Breitman said. "Is that what you wish, Mr. Royce?"

Royce had walked himself into a jam.

"No, Judge, I would agree with the court on this point. The defense was simply trying to limit the scope and use of these photographs. Mr. Haller lists more than thirty photographs that he wants to put on the big screen. It seems over-the-top. That is all."

"Judge Breitman, these are photographs of the body in the place it was found as well as during autopsy. Each one is —"

"Mr. Haller," the judge intoned, "let me just stop you right there. Crime scene photographs are acceptable, as long as they come with appropriate foundation and testimony. But I see no need to show our jurors this poor girl's autopsy shots. We're not going to do that."

"Yes, Your Honor," Haller said.

He remained standing while Royce sat down with his partial victory. Breitman spoke while writing something.

"And you have an objection to Mr. Royce's exhibit list, Mr. Haller?"

"Yes, Your Honor, the defense has a variety of drug paraphernalia alleged to have once been owned by Ms. Gleason on its exhibit list. It also lists photos and videos of Ms. Gleason. The prosecution has not been given the opportunity to examine these materials but we believe they only go to the point that we will be conceding at trial and eliciting in direct examination of this witness. That is that at one time in her life she used drugs on a regular basis. We do not see the need to show photos of her using drugs or the pipes through which she ingested drugs. It's inflammatory and prejudicial. It is not needed based on the concessions of the prosecution."

Royce stood back up and was ready to go. The judge gave him the floor.

"Judge, these exhibits are vitally important to the defense case. The prosecution of Mr. Jessup hinges on the testimony of a longtime drug addict who cannot be relied upon to remember the truth, let alone tell it. These exhibits will help the jury understand the depth and breadth of this witness's use of illegal substances over a lengthy period of time."

Royce was finished but the judge was silent as she studied the defense exhibit list.

"All right," she finally said, putting the document aside. "You both make cogent arguments. So what we are going to do is take these exhibits one at a time. When the defense would like to proffer an exhibit, we will discuss it first out of earshot of the jury. I'll make a decision then."

The lawyers sat down. Bosch almost shook his head but didn't want to draw the judge's attention. Still, it burned him that she had not slapped the defense down on this one. Twenty-four years after seeing her little sister abducted from the front yard, Sarah Ann Gleason was willing to testify about the awful, nightmarish moment that had changed her life forever. And for her sacrifice and efforts, the judge was actually going to entertain the defense's request to attack her with the glass pipes and accoutrements she had once used to escape what she had been through. It didn't seem fair to Bosch. It didn't seem like anything that approached justice.

The hearing ended soon after that and all parties packed their briefcases and moved through the doors of the courtroom en masse. Bosch hung back and then insinuated himself into the group right behind Jessup. He said nothing but Jessup soon enough felt the presence behind him and turned around.

He smirked when he saw it was Bosch.

"Well, Detective Bosch, are you following me?"

"Should I be?"

"Oh, you never know. How's your investigation going?"

"You'll find out soon enough."

"Yes, I can't—"

"Don't talk to him!"

It was Royce. He had turned and noticed.

"And don't *you* talk to him," he added, pointing a finger at Bosch. "If you continue to harass him, I'll complain to the judge."

Bosch held his hands out in a no-touching gesture.

"We're cool, Counselor. Just making small talk."

"There is no such thing when it comes to the police."

He reached out and put his hand on Jessup's shoulder and shepherded him away from Bosch.

In the hallway outside they moved directly to the waiting huddle of reporters and cameras. Bosch moved past but looked back in time to see Jessup's face change. His eyes went from the steely glare of a predator to the wounded look of a victim.

The reporters quickly gathered around him.

PART THREE

—To Seek a True and Just Verdict

25

Monday, April 5, 9:00 A.M.

I watched the jury file in and take their assigned seats in the box. I watched them closely, keying on their eyes mostly. Checking for how they looked at the defendant. You can learn a lot from that; a furtive glance or a strong judgmental stare.

Jury selection had gone as scheduled. We went through the first panel of ninety prospective jurors in a day but had sat only eleven after most were eliminated because of their media knowledge of the case. The second panel was just as difficult to choose from and it wasn't until Friday evening at five-forty that we had our final eighteen.

I had my jury chart in front of me, and my eyes were jumping between the faces in the box and the names on my Post-its, trying to memorize who was who. I already had a good handle on most of them but I wanted the names to become second nature to me. I wanted to be able to look at them and address them as if they were friends and neighbors.

The judge was on the bench and ready to go at nine sharp. She first asked the attorneys if there was any new or unfinished business to address. Upon learning there was not, she called in the jurors.

"Okay, we are all here," she said. "I want to thank all of the jurors and other parties for being on time. We begin the trial with opening statements from the attorneys. These are not to be construed as evidence but merely —"

The judge stopped, her eyes fixed on the back row of the jury box. A woman had timidly raised her hand. The judge stared for a long moment and then checked her own seating chart before responding.

"Ms. Tucci? Do you have a question?"

I checked my chart. Number ten, Carla Tucci. She was one of the jurors I had not yet committed to memory. A mousy brunette from East Hollywood. She was thirty-two years old, unmarried and she worked as a receptionist at a medical clinic. According to my color-coded chart, I had her down as a juror who could be swayed by stronger personalities on the panel. This was not a bad thing. It just depended on whether those personalities were for a guilty verdict or not.

"I think I saw something I wasn't supposed to see," she said in a frightened voice.

Judge Breitman hung her head for a moment and I knew why. She couldn't get the wheels out of the mud. We were ready to go and now the trial would be delayed before opening statements were even in the record.

"Okay, let's try to take care of this quickly. I want the jury to stay in place. Everyone else stay in place and Ms. Tucci and the attorneys and I will go quickly back to chambers to find out what this is about."

As we got up I checked my jury chart. There were six alternates. I had three of them pegged as pro-prosecution, two in the middle and one siding with the defense. If Tucci was ejected for whatever misconduct she was about to reveal, her replacement would be chosen randomly from the alternates. This meant that I had a better-than-even chance of seeing her replaced with a juror who was partial to the prosecution and only a one in six chance of getting a juror who was pro-defense. As I followed the entourage into chambers I decided that I liked my chances and I would do what I could to have Tucci ejected from the panel.

In chambers, the judge didn't even go behind her desk, perhaps hoping this was only going to be a minor question and delay. We stood in a group in the middle of her office. All except the court reporter, who sat on the edge of a side chair so she could type.

"Okay, on the record," the judge said. "Ms. Tucci, please tell us what you saw and what is bothering you."

The juror looked down at the ground and held her hands in front of her.

"I was riding on the Metro this morning and the man sitting across from me was reading the newspaper. He was holding it up and I saw the front page. I didn't mean to look but I saw a photo of the man on trial and I saw the headline."

The judge nodded.

"You are talking about Jason Jessup, correct?"

"Yes."

"What newspaper?"

"I think it was the *Times*."

"What did the headline say, Ms. Tucci?"

"New trial, old evidence for Jessup."

I hadn't seen the actual *L.A. Times* that morning but had read the story online. Citing an unnamed source close to the prosecution, the story said the case against Jason Jessup was expected to be comprised entirely of evidence from the first trial and leaning heavily on the identification provided by the victim's sister. Kate Salters had the byline on it.

"Did you read the story, Ms. Tucci?" Breitman asked.

"No, Judge, I just saw it for a second and when I saw his picture I looked away. You told us not to read anything about the case. It just kind of popped up in front of me."

The judge nodded thoughtfully.

"Okay, Ms. Tucci, can you step back into the hallway for a moment?"

The juror stepped out and the judge closed the door.

"The headline tells the story, doesn't it?" she said.

She looked at Royce and then me, seeing if either of us was going to make a motion or a suggestion. Royce said nothing. My guess was that he had juror number ten pegged the same way that I did. But he might not have considered the leanings of the six alternates.

"I think the damage is done here, Judge," I said. "She knows there was a previous trial. Anybody with any basic knowledge of the court system knows they don't retry you if you get a not-guilty. So she'll know Jessup went down on a guilty before. As much as that prejudices things in the prosecution's favor, I think to be fair she has to go."

Breitman nodded.

"Mr. Royce?"

"I would agree with Mr. Haller's assessment of the prejudice, not his so-called desire to be fair. He simply wants her off the jury and one of those churchgoing alternates on it."

I smiled and shook my head.

"I won't dignify that with a response. You don't want to kick her off, that's fine with me."

"But it's not counsel's choice," the judge said.

She opened the door and invited the juror back in.

"Ms. Tucci, thank you for your honesty. You can go back to the jury room and gather your things. You are dismissed and can report back to the juror assembly room to check with them."

Tucci hesitated.

"Does that mean —?"

"Yes, unfortunately, you are dismissed. That headline gives you knowledge of the case you should not have. For you to know that Mr. Jessup was previously tried for these crimes is prejudicial. Therefore, I cannot keep you on the jury. You may go now."

"I'm sorry, Judge."

"Yes, so am I."

Tucci left the chambers with her shoulders slumped and with the hesitant walk of someone who has been accused of a crime. After the door closed, the judge looked at us.

"If nothing else, this will send the right message to the rest of the jury. We're now down to five alternates and we haven't even started. But we now clearly see how the media can impact our trial. I have not read this story but I will. And if I see anyone in this room quoted in it I am going to be very disappointed. There are usually consequences for those who disappoint me."

"Judge," Royce said. "I read the story this morning and no one here is quoted by name but it does attribute information to a source close to the prosecution. I was planning to bring this to your attention."

I shook my head.

"And that's the oldest defense trick in the book. Cut a deal with a reporter to hide behind the story. A source close to the prosecution? He's sitting four feet across the aisle from me. That was probably close enough for the reporter."

"Your Honor!" Royce blurted. "I had nothing to —"

"We're holding up the trial," Breitman said, cutting him off. "Let's get back to court."

We trudged back. As we went back into the courtroom I scanned the gallery and saw Salters, the reporter, in the second row. I quickly looked away, hoping my brief eye contact had not revealed anything. I had been her source. My goal was to manipulate the story—the *scene setter*, as the reporter had called it—into being something that gave the defense false confidence. I hadn't intended it as a means of changing the makeup of the jury.

Back on the bench, the judge wrote something on a pad and then turned and addressed the jury, once again warning the panelists about reading the newspaper or watching television news programs. She then turned to her clerk.

"Audrey, the candy bowl, please."

The clerk then took the bowl of individually wrapped sourballs off the counter in front of her desk, dumped the candy into a drawer, and took the bowl to the judge. The judge tore a page from her notebook, tore it again into six pieces and wrote on each piece.

"I have written the numbers one through six on pieces of paper and I will now randomly select an alternate to take juror number ten's seat on the panel."

She folded the pieces of paper and dropped them into the bowl. She then swirled the bowl in her hand and raised it over her head. With her other hand she withdrew one piece of paper, unfolded it and read it out loud.

"Alternate number six," Breitman said. "Would you please move with any belongings you might have to seat number ten in the jury box. Thank you."

I could do nothing but sit and watch. The new juror number ten was a thirty-six-year-old film and television extra named Philip Kirns. Being an extra probably meant that he was an actor who had not yet been successful. He took jobs as a background extra to make ends meet. That meant that every day, he went to work and stood around and watched those who had made it. This put him on the bitter side of the gulf between the haves and have-nots. And this would make him partial to the defense—the underdog facing off against the Man. I had him down as a red juror and now I was stuck with him.

Maggie whispered into my ear at the prosecution table as we watched Kirns take his new seat.

"I hope you didn't have anything to do with that story, Haller. Because I think we just lost a vote."

I raised my hands in a *not me* gesture but it didn't look like she was buying it.

The judge turned her chair fully toward the jury.

"Finally, I believe we are ready to start," she said. "We begin with the opening statements from the attorneys. These statements are not to be taken as evidence. These statements are merely an opportunity for the prosecution and defense to tell the jury what they expect the evidence will show. It is an outline of what you can expect to see and hear during the trial. And it is incumbent upon counsel to then present evidence and testimony that you will later weigh during deliberations. We start with the prosecution statement. Mr. Haller?"

I stood up and went to the lectern that was positioned between the prosecution table and the jury box. I took no legal pad, 3 × 5 cards or anything else with me. I believed that it was important first to sell myself to the jury, then my case. To do that I could not look away from them. I needed to be direct, open and honest the whole time. Besides, my statement was going to be brief and to the point. I didn't need notes.

I started by introducing myself and then Maggie. I next pointed to Harry Bosch who was seated against the rail behind the prosecution table and introduced him as the case investigator. Then I got down to business.

"We are here today about one thing. To speak for someone who can no longer speak for herself. Twelve-year-old Melissa Landy was abducted from her front yard in nineteen eighty-six. Her body was found just a few hours later, discarded in a Dumpster like a bag of trash. She had been strangled. The man accused of this horrible crime sits there at the defense table."

I pointed the finger of accusation at Jessup, just as I had seen prosecutor after prosecutor point it at my clients over the years. It felt falsely righteous of me to point a finger at anyone, even a murderer. But that didn't stop me. Not only did I point at Jessup but I pointed again and again as I summarized the case, telling the jury of the witnesses I would call and what they would say and show. I moved along quickly, making sure to mention the eyewitness who identified Melissa's abductor and the finding of the victim's hair in Jessup's tow truck. I then brought it around to a big finish.

"Jason Jessup took the life of Melissa Landy," I said. "He grabbed her in the front yard and took her away from her family and this world forever. He put his hand around this beautiful little girl's throat and choked the life out of her. He robbed her of her past and of her future. He robbed her of everything. And the state will prove this to you beyond a reasonable doubt."

I nodded once to underline the promise and then returned to my seat. The judge had told us the day before to be brief in our openers, but even she seemed surprised by my brevity. It took her a moment to realize I was finished. She then told Royce he was up.

As I expected he would, Royce deferred to the second half, meaning he reserved his opening statement until the start of the defense's case. That put the judge's focus back on me.

"Very well, then. Mr. Haller, call your first witness."

I went back to the lectern, this time carrying notes and printouts. I had spent most of the previous week before jury selection preparing the questions I would ask my witnesses. As a defense attorney I am used to cross-examining the state's witnesses and picking at the testimony brought forward by the prosecutor. It's a task quite different from direct examination and building the foundation for the introduction of evidence and exhibits. I fully acknowledge that it is easier to knock something down than to build it in the first place. But in this case I would be the builder and I came prepared.

"The People call William Johnson."

I turned to the back of the courtroom. As I had gone to the lectern Bosch had left the courtroom to retrieve Johnson from a witness waiting room. He now returned with the man in tow. Johnson was small and thin with a dark mahogany complexion. He was fifty-nine but his pure white hair made him look older. Bosch walked him through the gate and then pointed him in the direction of the witness stand. He was quickly sworn in by the court clerk.

I had to admit to myself that I was nervous. I felt what Maggie had tried to describe to me on more than one occasion when we were married. She always called it the *burden of proof.* Not the legal burden. But the psychic burden of knowing that you stood as representative of all the people. I had always dismissed her explanations as self-serving. The prosecutor was always the overdog. The Man. There was no burden in that, at least nothing compared to the burden of the defense attorney, who stands all alone and holds someone's freedom in his hands. I never understood what she was trying to tell me.

Until now.

Now I got it. I felt it. I was about to question my first witness in front of the jury and I was as nervous as I had been at my first trial out of law school.

"Good morning, Mr. Johnson," I said. "How are you, sir?"

"I am good, yes."

"That's good. Can you tell me, sir, what you do for a living?"

"Yes, sir. I am head of operations for the El Rey Theatre on Wilshire Boulevard."

"'Head of operations,' what does that mean?"

"I make sure everything works right and runs—from the stage lights to the toilets, it's all part of my job. Mind you, I have electricians work on the lights and plumbers work on the toilets."

His answer was greeted with polite smiles and modest laughter. He spoke with a slight Caribbean accent but his words were clear and understandable.

"How long have you worked at the El Rey, Mr. Johnson?"

"For going on thirty-six years now. I started in nineteen seventy-four."

"Wow, that's an achievement. Congratulations. Have you been head of operations for all that time?"

"No, I worked my way up. I started as a janitor."

"I would like to draw your attention back to nineteen eighty-six. You were working there then, correct?"

"Yes, sir. I was a janitor back then."

"Okay, and do you remember the date of February sixteenth of that year in particular?"

"Yes, I do."

"It was a Sunday."

"Yes, I remember."

"Can you tell the court why?"

"That was the day I found the body of a little girl in the trash bin out back of the El Rey. That was a terrible day."

I checked the jury. All eyes were on my witness. So far so good.

"I can imagine that being a terrible day, Mr. Johnson. Now, can you tell us what it was that brought you to discover the body of the little girl?"

"We were working on a project in the theater. We were putting new drywall into the ladies' room on account of a leak. So I took a wheelbarrow full of the stuff we had demoed — the old wall and some rotting wood and such — and wheeled it out to put in the Dumpster. I opened the top and there this poor little girl was."

"She was on top of the debris already in the trash bin?"

"That's right."

"Was she covered at all with any trash or debris?"

"No, sir, not at all."

"As if whoever threw her in there had been in a hurry and didn't have time to cover —"

"Objection!"

Royce had jumped to his feet. I knew he would object. But I had almost gotten the whole sentence — and its suggestion — to the jury.

"Mr. Haller is leading the witness and asking for conclusions for which he would have no expertise," Royce said.

I withdrew the question before the judge could sustain the objection. There was no sense in having the judge side with the defense in front of the jury.

"Mr. Johnson, was that the first trip you had made to the trash bin that day?"

"No, sir. I had been out there two times before."

"Before the trip during which you found the body, when had you last been to the trash bin?"

"About ninety minutes before."

"Did you see a body on top of the trash in the bin that time?"

"No, there was no body there."

"So it had to have been placed in that bin in the ninety minutes prior to you finding it, correct?"

"Yes, that's right."

"Okay, Mr. Johnson, if I could draw your attention to the screen."

The courtroom was equipped with two large flat-screen monitors mounted high on the wall opposite the jury box. One screen was slightly angled toward the gallery to allow courtroom observers to see the digital presentations as well. Maggie controlled what appeared on the screens through a PowerPoint program on her laptop computer. She had constructed the presentation over the last two weeks and weekends as we choreographed the prosecution's case. All of the old photos from the case files had been scanned and loaded into the program. She now put up the trial's first photo exhibit. A shot of the trash bin Melissa Landy's body had been found in.

"Does that look like the trash bin in which you found the little girl's body, Mr. Johnson?"

"That's it."

"What makes you so sure, sir?"

"The address—fifty-five fifteen—spray-painted on the side like that. I did that. That's the address. And I can tell that's the back of the El Rey. I've worked there a long time."

"Okay, and is this what you saw when you raised the top and looked inside?"

Maggie moved to the next photo. The courtroom was already quiet but it seemed to me that it grew absolutely silent when the photo of Melissa Landy's body in the trash bin went up on the screens. Under the existing rules of evidence as carved by a recent ruling by the Ninth District, I had to find ways of bringing old evidence and exhibits to the present jury. I could not rely on investigative records. I had to find people who were bridges to the past and Johnson was the first bridge.

Johnson didn't answer my question at first. He just stared like everyone else in the courtroom. Then, unexpectedly, a tear rolled down his dark cheek. It was perfect. If I had been at the defense table I would have viewed it with cynicism. But I knew Johnson's response was heartfelt and it was why I had made him my first witness.

"That's her," he finally said. "That's what I saw."

I nodded as Johnson blessed himself.

"And what did you do when you saw her?"

"We didn't have no cell phones back then, you see. So I ran back inside and I called nine-one-one on the stage phone."

"And the police came quickly?"

"They came real quick, like they were already looking for her."

"One final question, Mr. Johnson. Could you see that trash bin from Wilshire Boulevard?"

Johnson shook his head emphatically.

"No, it was behind the theater and you could only see it if you drove back there and down the little alley."

I hesitated here. I had more to bring out from this witness. Information not presented in the first trial but gathered by Bosch during his reinvestigation. It was information that Royce might not be aware of. I could just ask the question that would draw it out or I could roll the dice and see if the defense opened a door on cross-examination. The information would be the same either way, but it would have greater weight if the jury believed the defense had tried to hide it.

"Thank you, Mr. Johnson," I finally said. "I have no further questions."

The witness was turned over to Royce, who went to the lectern as I sat down.

"Just a few questions," he said. "Did you see who put the victim's body in the bin?"

"No, I did not," Johnson said.

"So when you called nine-one-one you had no idea who did it, is that correct?"

"Correct."

"Before that day, had you ever seen the defendant before?"

"No, I don't think so."

"Thank you."

And that was it. Royce had performed a typical cross of a witness who had little value to the defense. Johnson couldn't identify the murderer, so Royce got that on the record. But he should have just let Johnson pass. By asking if Johnson had ever seen Jessup before the murder, he opened a door. I stood back up so I could go through it.

"Redirect, Mr. Haller?" the judge asked.

"Briefly, Your Honor. Mr. Johnson, back during this period that we're talking about, did you often work on Sundays?"

"No, it was my day off usually. But if we had some special projects I would be told to come in."

Royce objected on the grounds that I was opening up a line of questioning that was outside the scope of his cross-examination. I promised the judge that it was within the scope and that it would become apparent soon. She indulged me and overruled the objection. I went back to Mr. Johnson. I had hoped Royce would object because in a few moments it would look like he had been trying to stop me from getting to information damaging to Jessup.

"You mentioned that the trash bin where you found the body was at the end of an alley. Is there no parking lot behind the El Rey Theatre?"

"There is a parking lot but it does not belong to the El Rey Theatre. We have the alley that gives us access to the back doors and the bins."

"Who does the parking lot belong to?"

"A company that has lots all over the city. It's called City Park."

"Is there a wall or a fence separating this parking lot from the alley?"

Royce stood again.

"Your Honor, this is going on and on and it has nothing to do with what I asked Mr. Johnson."

"Your Honor," I said. "I will get there in two more questions."

"You may answer, Mr. Johnson," Breitman said.

"There is a fence," Johnson said.

"So," I said, "from the El Rey's alley and the location of its trash bin, you can see into the adjoining parking lot, and anyone in the adjoining parking lot could see the trash bin, correct?"

"Yes."

"And prior to the day you discovered the body, did you have occasion to be at work on a Sunday and to notice that the parking lot behind the theater was being used?"

"Yes, like a month previously, I came to work and in the back there were many cars and I saw tow trucks towing them in."

I couldn't help myself. I had to glance over at Royce and Jessup to see if they were squirming yet. I was about to draw the first blood of the trial. They thought Johnson was going to be a noncritical witness, meaning he would establish the murder and its location and nothing else.

They were wrong.

"Did you inquire as to what was going on?" I asked.

"Yes," Johnson said. "I asked what they were doing and one of the drivers said that they were towing cars from the neighborhood down the street and holding them there so people could come and pay and get their cars."

"So it was being used like a temporary holding lot, is that what you mean?"

"Yes."

"And did you know what the name of the towing company was?"

"It was on the trucks. It was called Aardvark Towing."

"You said trucks. You saw more than one truck there?"

"Yeah, there were two or three trucks when I saw them."

"What did you tell them after you were informed what they were doing there?"

"I told my boss and he called City Park to see if they knew about it. He thought there could be an insurance concern, especially with people being mad about being towed and all. And it turned out Aardvark wasn't supposed to be there. It wasn't authorized."

"What happened?"

"They had to stop using the lot and my boss told me to keep an eye out if I worked on weekends to see if they kept using it."

"So they stopped using the lot behind the theater?"

"That's right."

"And this was the same lot from which you could see the trash bin in which you would later find the body of Melissa Landy?"

"Yes, sir."

"When Mr. Royce asked you if you had ever seen the defendant before the day of the murder, you answered that you didn't think so, correct?"

"Correct."

"You don't think so? Why are you not sure?"

"Because I think he could've been one of the Aardvark drivers I saw using that lot. So I can't be sure I didn't see him before."

"Thank you, Mr. Johnson. I have no further questions."

26

Monday, April 5, 10:20 A.M.

For the first time since he had been brought into the case Bosch felt as though Melissa Landy was in good hands. He had just watched Mickey Haller score the first points of the trial. He had taken a small piece of the puzzle Bosch had come up with and used it to land the first punch. It wasn't a knockout by any means but it had connected solidly. It was the first step down the path of proving Jason Jessup's familiarity with the parking lot and trash bin behind the El Rey Theatre. Before the trial would end, its importance would be made clear to the jury. But what was even more significant to Bosch at the moment was the way Haller had used the information Harry had provided. He had hung it on the defense, made it look as though it had been their attempt to obfuscate the facts of the case that drew the information out. It was a smooth move and it gave Bosch a big boost in his confidence in Haller as a prosecutor.

He met Johnson at the gate and walked him out of the courtroom to the hallway, where he shook his hand.

"You did real good in there, Mr. Johnson. We can't thank you enough."

"You already have. Convicting that man of killing that little girl."

"Well, we're not quite there yet but that's the plan. Except most people who read the paper think we're going after an innocent man."

"No, you got the right man. I can tell."

Bosch nodded and felt awkward.

"You take care, Mr. Johnson."

"Detective, your music is jazz, right?"

Bosch had already turned to go back to the courtroom. Now he looked back at Johnson.

"How'd you know that?"

"Just a guess. We got jazz acts that come through. New Orleans jazz. You ever want tickets to a show at the El Rey, you look me up."

"Yeah, I'll do that. Thanks."

Bosch pushed through the doors leading back into the courtroom. He was smiling, thinking about Johnson's guess about his music. If he was right about that, then maybe he would be right about the jury convicting Jessup. As he moved down the aisle, he heard the judge telling Haller to call his next witness.

"The state calls Regina Landy."

Bosch knew he was on. This part had been choreographed a week earlier by the judge and over the objection of the defense. Regina Landy was unavailable to testify because she was dead, but she had testified in the first trial and the judge had ruled that her testimony could be read to the current jurors.

Breitman now turned to the jurors to offer the explanation, guarding against revealing any hint that there had been an earlier trial.

"Ladies and gentlemen, the state has called a witness who is no longer available to testify. However, previously she gave sworn testimony that we will read to you today. You are not to consider why this witness is unable to testify or where this previous sworn testimony is from. Your concern is the testimony itself. I should add that I have decided to allow this over the objection of the defense. The U.S. Constitution holds that the accused is entitled to question his accusers. However, as you will see, this witness was indeed questioned by an attorney who previously represented Mr. Jessup."

She turned back to the court.

"You may proceed, Mr. Haller."

Haller called Bosch to the stand. He was sworn in and then took the seat, pulling the microphone into position. He opened the blue binder he had carried with him and Haller began.

"Detective Bosch, can you tell us a little bit about your experience as a law enforcement officer?"

Bosch turned toward the jury box and moved his eyes over the faces of the jurors as he answered. He did not leave the alternates out.

"I have been a sworn officer for thirty-six years. I have spent more than twenty-five of those years working homicides. I have been the lead investigator in more than two hundred murder investigations in that time."

"And you are the lead investigator on this case?"

"Yes, I am now. I did not take part in the original investigation, however. I came into this case in February of this year."

"Thank you, Detective. We will be talking about your investigation later in the trial. Are you prepared to read the sworn testimony of Regina Landy taken on October seventh, nineteen eighty-six?"

"I am."

"Okay, I will read the questions that were posed at the time by Deputy District Attorney Gary Lintz and defense counsel Charles Barnard and you will read the responses from the witness. We start with direct examination from Mr. Lintz."

Haller paused and studied the transcript in front of him. Bosch wondered if there would be any confusion from his reading the responses of a woman. In deciding to allow the testimony the week before, the judge had disallowed any reference to emotions described as having been exhibited by Regina Landy. Bosch knew from the transcript that she was crying throughout her testimony. But he would not be able to communicate that to the present jurors.

"Here we go," Haller said. " 'Mrs. Landy, can you please describe your relationship with the victim, Melissa Landy.' "

" 'I am her mother,' " Bosch read. " 'She was my daughter . . . until she was taken away from me.' "

27

≈≈≈

Monday, April 5, 1:45 P.M.

The reading of Regina Landy's testimony from the first trial took us right up to lunch. The testimony was needed to establish who the victim was and who had identified her. But without the incumbent emotion of a parent's testimony, the reading by Bosch was largely procedural, and while the first witness of the day brought reason to be hopeful, the second witness was about as anticlimactic as a voice from the grave could possibly be. I imagined that Bosch's reading of Regina Landy's words was confusing to the jurors when they were not provided with any explanation for her absence from the trial of her daughter's alleged killer.

The prosecution team had lunch at Duffy's, which was close enough to the CCB to be convenient but far enough away that we wouldn't have to worry about jurors finding the same place to eat. Nobody was ecstatic about the start of the trial but that was to be expected. I had planned the presentation of evidence like the unfolding of *Scheherazade*, the symphonic suite that starts slow and quiet and builds to an all-encompassing crescendo of sound and music and emotion.

The first day was about the proof of facts. I had to bring forward the body. I had to establish that there was a victim, that she had been taken from her home and later found dead and that she had been murdered. I had hit two of those facts with the first witnesses, and now the afternoon witness, the medical examiner, would complete the proof. The prosecution's case would then shift toward the accused and the evidence that tied him to the crime. That would be when my case would really come to life.

Only Bosch and I came back from lunch. Maggie had gone over to the Checkers Hotel to spend the afternoon with our star witness, Sarah Ann Gleason. Bosch had gone up to Washington on Saturday and flown down with her Sunday morning. She wasn't scheduled to testify until Wednesday morning but I had wanted her close and I had wanted Maggie to spend as much time as possible prepping her for her part in the trial. Maggie had already been up to Washington twice to spend time with her but I believed that any time they could spend together would continue to promote the bond I wanted them to have and the jury to see.

Maggie left us reluctantly. She was concerned that I would make a misstep in court without her there watching over me as my second. I assured her that I could handle the direct examination of a medical examiner and would call her if I ran into trouble. Little did I know how important this witness's testimony would come to be.

The afternoon session got off to a late start while we waited ten minutes for a juror who did not return from lunch on time. Once the panel was assembled and returned to court, Judge Breitman lectured the jurors again on timeliness and ordered them to eat as a group for the remainder of the trial. She also ordered the courtroom deputy to escort them to lunch. This way no one would stray from the pack and no one would be late.

Finished with the lunch business, the judge gruffly ordered me to call my next witness. I nodded to Bosch and he headed to the witness room to retrieve David Eisenbach.

The judge grew impatient as we waited but it took Eisenbach a few minutes longer than most witnesses to make his way into the courtroom and to the witness stand. Eisenbach was seventy-nine years old and walked with a cane. He also carried a pillow with a handle on it, as if he were going to a USC football game at the Coliseum. After being sworn in he placed the pillow on the hard wood of the witness chair and then sat down.

"Dr. Eisenbach," I began, "can you tell the jury what you do for a living?"

"Currently I am semiretired and derive an income from being an autopsy consultant. A *gun for hire*, you lawyers like to call it. I review autopsies for a living and then tell lawyers and juries what the medical examiner did right and did wrong."

"And before you were semiretired, what did you do?"

"I was assistant medical examiner for the county of Los Angeles. Had that job for thirty years."

"As such you conducted autopsies?"

"Yes, sir, I did. In thirty years I conducted over twenty thousand autopsies. That's a lot of dead people."

"That is a lot, Dr. Eisenbach. Do you remember them all?"

"Of course not. I remember a handful off the top of my head. The rest of them I would need my notes to remember."

After receiving permission from the judge I approached the witness stand and put down a forty-page document.

"I draw your attention to the document I have placed before you. Can you identify it?"

"Yes, it's an autopsy protocol dated February eighteenth, nineteen eighty-six. The deceased is listed as Melissa Theresa Landy. My name is also on it. It is one of mine."

"Meaning you conducted the autopsy?"

"Yes, that is what I said."

I followed this with a series of questions that established the autopsy procedures and the general health of the victim prior to death. Royce objected several times to what he termed leading questions. Few of these were sustained by the judge but that was not the point. Royce had adopted the tactic of attempting to get me out of rhythm by incessantly interrupting, whether such interruptions were valid or not.

Working around these interruptions, Eisenbach was able to testify that Melissa Landy was in perfect health until the moment of her violent death. He said she had not been sexually attacked in any determinable way. He said there was no indication of prior sexual activity — she was a virgin. He said the cause of her death was asphyxiation. He said the evidence of crushed bones in her neck and throat indicated she had been choked by a powerful force — a man's single hand.

Using a laser pointer to mark locations on photographs of the body taken at autopsy, Eisenbach identified a bruise pattern on the victim's neck that was indicative of a one-handed choke hold. With the laser point he delineated a thumb mark on the right side of the girl's neck and the larger, four-finger mark on the left side.

"Doctor, did you make a determination of which hand the killer used to choke the victim to death?"

"Yes, it was quite simple to determine the killer had used the right hand to choke this girl to death."

"Just one hand?"

"That is correct."

"Was there any determination of how this was done? Had the girl been suspended while she was choked?"

"No, the injuries, particularly the crushed bones, indicated that the killer put his hand on her neck and pressed her against a surface that offered resistance."

"Could that have been the seat of a vehicle?"

"Yes."

"How about a man's leg?"

Royce objected, saying the question called for pure speculation. The judge agreed and told me to move on.

"Doctor, you mentioned twenty thousand autopsies. I assume that many of these were homicides involving asphyxiation. Was it unusual to come across a case where only one hand was used to choke a victim to death?"

Royce objected again, this time saying the question asked for an answer outside the witness's expertise. But the judge went my way.

"The man has conducted twenty thousand autopsies," she said. "I'm inclined to think that gives him a lot of expertise. I'm going to allow the question."

"You can answer, Doctor," I said. "Was this unusual?"

"Not necessarily. Many homicides occur during struggles and other circumstances. I've seen it before. If one hand is otherwise occupied, the other must suffice. We are talking about a twelve-year-old girl who weighed ninety-one pounds. She could have been subdued with one hand if the killer needed the left hand for something else."

"Would driving a vehicle fall into that category?"

"Objection," Royce said. "Same argument."

"And same ruling," Breitman said. "You may answer, Doctor."

"Yes," Eisenbach said. "If one hand was being used to maintain control of a vehicle the other hand could be used to choke the victim. That is one possibility."

At this point I believed I had gotten all that there was to get from Eisenbach. I ended direct examination and handed the witness over to Royce. Unfortunately for me, Eisenbach was a witness who had something for everybody. And Royce went after it.

"'One possibility,' is that what you called it, Dr. Eisenbach?"

"Excuse me?"

"You said the scenario Mr. Haller described — one hand on the wheel, one hand on the neck — was one possibility. Is that correct?"

"Yes, that is a possibility."

"But you weren't there, so you can't know for sure. Isn't that right, Doctor?"

"Yes, that is right."

"You said one possibility. What are some of the other possibilities?"

"Well...I wouldn't know. I was responding to the question from the prosecutor."

"How about a cigarette?"

"What?"

"Could the killer have been holding a cigarette in his left hand while he choked the girl with his right?"

"Yes, I suppose so. Yes."

"And how about his penis?"

"His..."

"His penis, Doctor. Could the killer have choked this girl with his right hand while holding his penis with his left?"

"I would have to...yes, that is a possibility, too."

"He could have been masturbating with one hand while he choked her with the other, correct, Doctor?"

"Anything is possible but there is no indication in the autopsy report that supports this."

"What about what is not in the file, Doctor?"

"I'm not aware of anything."

"Is this what you meant about being a hired gun, Doctor? You take the prosecution's side no matter what the facts are?"

"I don't always work for prosecutors."

"I'm happy for you."

I stood up.

"Your Honor, he's badgering the witness with —"

"Mr. Royce," the judge said. "Please keep it civil. And on point."

"Yes, Your Honor. Doctor, of the twenty thousand autopsies you have performed, how many of them were on victims of sexually motivated violence?"

Eisenbach looked across the floor to me, but there was nothing I could do for him. Bosch had taken Maggie's place at the prosecution table. He leaned over to me and whispered.

"What's he doing? Trying to make our case?"

I held up my hand so I would not be distracted from the back-and-forth between Royce and Eisenbach.

"No, he's making their case," I whispered back.

Eisenbach still hadn't answered.

"Doctor," the judge said, "please answer the question."

"I don't have a count but many of them were sexually motivated crimes."

"Was this one?"

"Based on the autopsy findings I could not make that conclusion. But whenever you have a young child, particularly a female, and there is a stranger abduction, then you are almost always —"

"Move to strike the answer as nonresponsive," Royce said, cutting the witness off. "The witness is assuming facts not in evidence."

The judge considered the objection. I stood up, ready to respond but said nothing.

"Doctor, please answer only the question you are asked," the judge said.

"I thought I was," Eisenbach said.

"Then let me be more specific," Royce said. "You found no indications of sexual assault or abuse on the body of Melissa Landy, is that correct, Doctor?"

"That is correct."

"What about on the victim's clothing?"

"The body is my jurisdiction. The clothing is analyzed by forensics."

"Of course."

Royce hesitated and looked down at his notes. I could tell he was trying to decide how far to take something. It was a case of "so far, so good—do I risk going further?"

Finally, he decided.

"Now, Doctor, a moment ago when I objected to your answer, you called this a stranger abduction. What evidence from the autopsy supported that claim?"

Eisenbach thought for a long moment and even looked down at the autopsy report in front of him.

"Doctor?"

"Uh, there is nothing I recall from the autopsy alone that supports this."

"Actually, the autopsy supports a conclusion quite the opposite, doesn't it?"

Eisenbach looked genuinely confused.

"I am not sure what you mean."

"Can I draw your attention to page eight of the autopsy protocol? The preliminary examination of the body."

Royce waited a moment until Eisenbach turned to the page. I did as well but didn't need to. I knew where Royce was going and couldn't stop him. I just needed to be ready to object at the right moment.

"Doctor, the report states that scrapings of the victim's fingernails were negative for blood and tissue. Do you see that on page eight?"

"Yes, I scraped her nails but they were clean."

"This indicates she did not scratch her attacker, her killer. Correct?"

"That would be the indication, yes."

"And this would also indicate that she knew her attack—"

"Objection!"

I was on my feet but not quick enough. Royce had gotten the suggestion out and to the jury.

"Assumes facts not in evidence," I said. "Your Honor, defense counsel is clearly attempting to plant seeds with the jury that do not exist."

"Sustained. Mr. Royce, a warning."

"Yes, Your Honor. The defense has no further questions for this prosecution witness."

28

Monday, April 5, 4:45 P.M.

Bosch knocked on the door of room 804 and looked directly at the peephole. The door was quickly opened by McPherson, who was checking her watch as she stood back to let him enter.

"Why aren't you in court with Mickey?" she asked.

Bosch entered. The room was a suite with a decent view of Grand Avenue and the back of the Biltmore. There was a couch and two chairs, one of them occupied by Sarah Ann Gleason. Bosch nodded his hello.

"Because he doesn't need me there. I'm needed here."

"What's going on?"

"Royce tipped his hand on the defense's case. I need to talk to Sarah about it."

He started toward the couch but McPherson put her hand on his arm and stopped him.

"Wait a minute. Before you talk to Sarah you talk to me. What's going on?"

Bosch nodded. She was right. He looked around but there was no place for private conversation in the suite.

"Let's take a walk."

McPherson went to the coffee table and grabbed a key card.

"We'll be right back, Sarah. Do you need anything?"

"No, I'm fine. I'll be here."

She held up a sketchpad. It would keep her company.

Bosch and McPherson left the room and took the elevator down to the lobby. There was a bar crowded with pre–happy hour drinkers but they found a private spot in a sitting area by the front door.

"Okay, how did Royce tip his hand?" McPherson asked.

"When he was cross-examining Eisenbach, he riffed off of Mickey's question about the killer using only his right hand to choke her."

"Right, while he was driving. He panicked when he heard the call on the police radio and killed her."

"Right, that's the prosecution theory. Well, Royce is already setting up a defense theory. On cross he asked whether it was possible that the killer was choking her with one hand while masturbating with the other."

She was silent as she computed this.

"This is the old prosecution theory," she said. "From the first trial. That it was murder in the commission of a sex act. Mickey and I sort of figured that once Royce got all the discovery material and learned that the DNA came from the stepfather, the defense would play it this way. They're setting up the stepfather as the straw man. They'll say he killed her and the DNA proves it."

McPherson folded her arms as she worked it out further.

"It's good but there are two things wrong with it. Sarah and the hair evidence. So we're missing something. Royce has got to have something or someone who discredits Sarah's ID."

"That's why I'm here. I brought Royce's witness list. These people have been playing hide-and-seek with me and I haven't run them all down. Sarah's got to look at this list and tell me which one I need to focus on."

"How the hell will she know?"

"She's got to. These are her people. Boyfriends, husbands, fellow tweakers. All of them have records. They're the people she hung out with before she got straight. Every address is a last-known and worthless. Royce has got to be hiding them."

McPherson nodded.

"That's why they call him Clever Clive. Okay, let's talk to her. Let me try first, okay?"

She stood up.

"Wait a minute," Bosch said.

She looked at him.

"What is it?"

"What if the defense theory is the right one?"

"Are you kidding me?"

He didn't answer and she didn't wait long. She headed back toward the elevator. He got up and followed.

They went back to the room. Bosch noticed that Gleason had sketched a tulip on her pad while they had been gone. He sat down on the couch across from her, and McPherson took the chair right next to her.

"Sarah," McPherson said. "We need to talk. We think that somebody you used to know during those lost years we were talking about is going to try to help the defense. We need to figure out who it is and what they are going to say."

"I don't understand," Sarah said. "But I was thirteen years old when this happened to us. What does it matter who my friends were after?"

"It matters because they can testify about things you might have done. Or said."

"What things?"

McPherson shook her head.

"That's what is so frustrating. We don't really know. We only know that today in court the defense made it clear that they are going to try to put the blame for your sister's death on your stepfather."

Sarah raised her hands as if warding off a blow.

"That's crazy. I was there. I saw that man take her!"

"We know that, Sarah. But it's a matter of what is conveyed to the jury and what and who the jurors believe. Now, Detective Bosch has a list of the defense's witnesses. I want you to take a look at it and tell us what the names mean to you."

Bosch pulled the list from his briefcase. He handed it to McPherson, who handed it to Sarah.

"Sorry, all those notes are things I added," Bosch said, "when I was trying to track them down. Just look at the names."

Bosch watched her lips move slightly as she started to read. Then they stopped moving and she just stared at the paper. He saw tears in her eyes.

"Sarah?" McPherson prompted.

"These people," Gleason said in a whisper. "I thought I'd never see them again."

"You may never see them again," McPherson said. "Just because they're on that list, it doesn't mean they'll be called. They pull names out of the records and load up the list to confuse us, Sarah. It's called *haystacking*. They hide the real witnesses, and our investigator—Detective Bosch—wastes his time checking out the wrong people. But there's got to be at least one name on there that counts. Who is it, Sarah? Help us."

She stared at the list without responding.

"Someone who will be able to say you two were close. Who you spent time with and told secrets to."

"I thought a husband couldn't testify against a wife."

"One spouse can't be forced to testify against the other. But what are you talking about, Sarah?"

"This one."

She pointed to a name on the list. Bosch leaned over to read it. Edward Roman. Bosch had traced him to a lockdown rehab center in North Hollywood where Sarah had spent nine months after her last incarceration. The only thing Bosch had guessed was that they'd had contact in group therapy. The last known address provided by Royce was a motel in Van Nuys but Roman was long gone from there. Bosch had gotten no further with it and had dismissed the name as part of Royce's haystack.

"Roman," he said. "You were with him in rehab, right?"

"Yes," Gleason said. "Then we got married."

"When?" McPherson said. "We have no record of that marriage."

"After we got out. He knew a minister. We got married on the beach. But it didn't last very long."

"Did you get divorced?" McPherson asked.

"No...I never really cared. Then when I got straight I just didn't want to go back there. It was one of those things you block out. Like it didn't happen."

McPherson looked at Bosch.

"It might not have been a legal marriage," he said. "There's nothing in the county records."

"Doesn't matter if it was a legal marriage or not," she said. "He is obviously a volunteer witness, so he can testify against her. What matters is what his testimony is going to be. What's he going to say, Sarah?"

Sarah slowly shook her head.

"I don't know."

"Well, what did you tell him about your sister and your stepfather?"

"I don't know. Those years... I can hardly remember anything from back then."

There was a silence and then McPherson asked Sarah to look at the rest of the names on the list. She did and shook her head.

"I don't know who some of these people are. Some people in the life, I just knew them by street names."

"But Edward Roman you know?"

"Yes. We were together."

"How long?"

Gleason shook her head in embarrassment.

"Not long. Inside rehab we thought we were made for each other. Once we were out, it didn't work. It lasted maybe three months. I got arrested again and when I got out of jail, he was gone."

"Is it possible that it wasn't a legitimate marriage?"

Gleason thought for a moment and halfheartedly shrugged.

"Anything is possible, I guess."

"Okay, Sarah, I'm going to step out with Detective Bosch again for a few minutes. I want you to think about Edward Roman. Anything you can remember will be helpful. I'll be right back."

McPherson took the witness list from her and handed it back to Bosch. They left the room but just took a few paces down the hallway before stopping and talking in whispers.

"I guess you'd better find him," she said.

"It won't matter," Bosch said. "If he's Royce's star witness he won't talk to me."

"Then find out everything you can about him. So when the time comes we can destroy him."

"Got it."

Bosch turned and headed down the hall toward the elevators. McPherson called after him. He stopped and looked back.

"Did you mean it?" McPherson asked.

"Mean what?"

"What you said down in the lobby. What you asked. You think twenty-four years ago she made it all up?"

Bosch looked at her for a long moment, then shrugged.

"I don't know."

"Well, what about the hair in the truck? Doesn't that tie her story in?"

Bosch held a hand up empty.

"It's circumstantial. And I wasn't there when they found it."

"What's that supposed to mean?"

"It means sometimes things happen when the victim is a child. And that I wasn't there when they found it."

"Boy, maybe you should be working for the defense."

Bosch dropped his hand to his side.

"I'm sure they've thought of all of this already."

He turned back toward the elevators and headed down the hallway.

29

Tuesday, April 6, 9:00 A.M.

Sometimes the wheels of justice roll smoothly. The second day of trial started exactly as scheduled. The full jury was in the box, the judge was on the bench and Jason Jessup and his attorney were seated at the defense table. I stood and called my first witness of what I hoped would be a productive day for the prosecution. Harry Bosch even had Izzy Gordon in the courtroom ready to go. By five minutes after the hour, she was sworn in and seated. She was a small woman with black-framed glasses that magnified her eyes. My records said she was fifty years old but she looked older.

"Ms. Gordon, can you tell the jury what you do for a living?"

"Yes. I am a forensic technician and crime scene supervisor for the Los Angeles Police Department. I have been so employed in the forensics unit since nineteen eighty-six."

"Were you so employed on February sixteenth of that year?"

"Yes, I was. It was my first day of work."

"And what was your assignment on that day?"

"My job was to learn. I was assigned to a crime scene supervisor and I was to get on-the-job training."

Izzy Gordon was a major find for the prosecution. Two technicians and a supervisor had worked the three separate crime scenes relating to the Melissa Landy case — the home on Windsor, the trash bin behind the El Rey and the tow truck driven by Jessup. Gordon had been assigned to be at the supervisor's side and therefore had been in attendance at all three crime scenes. The supervisor was long since dead and the other techs were retired and unable to offer testimony about all three locations. Finding

Gordon allowed me to streamline the introduction of crime scene evidence.

"Who was that supervisor?"

"That was Art Donovan."

"And you got a call out with him that day?"

"Yes, we did. An abduction that turned into a homicide. We ended up going from scene to scene to scene that day. Three related locations."

"Okay, let's take those scenes one at a time."

Over the next ninety minutes I walked Gordon through her Sunday tour of crime scenes on February 16, 1986. Using her as the conduit, I could deliver crime scene photographs, videos and evidence reports. Royce continued his tack of objecting at will in an effort to prevent the unimpeded flow of information to the jury. But he was scoreless and getting under the judge's skin. I could tell, and so I did not complain. I wanted that annoyance to fester. It might come in handy later.

Gordon's testimony was fairly pedestrian as she first discussed the unsuccessful efforts to find shoe prints and other trace evidence on the front lawn of the Landy's house. It turned more dramatic when she recalled being urgently called to a new crime scene—the trash bin behind the El Rey.

"We were called when they found the body. It was handled in whispers because the family was there in the house and we did not want to upset them until it was confirmed that there was a body and that it was the little girl."

"You and Donovan went to the El Rey Theatre?"

"Yes, along with Detective Kloster. We met the assistant medical examiner there. We now had a homicide, so more technicians were called in, too."

The El Rey portion of Gordon's testimony was largely an opportunity for me to show more video footage and photographs of the victim on the overhead screens. If nothing else, I wanted every juror in the box to be incensed by what they saw. I wanted to light the fire of one of the basic instincts. Vengeance.

I counted on Royce to object and he did, but by then he had exhausted his welcome with the judge, and his argument that the images were graphic and cumulatively excessive fell on deaf ears. They were allowed.

Finally, Izzy Gordon brought us to the last crime scene—the tow truck— and she described how she had spotted three long hairs caught in the crack that split the bench seat and pointed them out to Donovan for collection.

"What happened to those hairs?" I asked.

"They were individually bagged and tagged and then taken to the Scientific Investigation Division for comparison and analysis."

Gordon's testimony was smooth and efficient. When I turned her over to the defense, Royce did the best he could. He did not bother to assail the collection of evidence but merely attempted once again to gain a foothold for the defense theory. In doing so he skipped the first two crime scenes and zeroed in on the tow truck.

"Ms. Gordon, when you got to the Aardvark towing yard, were there police officers already there?"

"Yes, of course."

"How many?"

"I didn't count but there were several."

"What about detectives?"

"Yes, there were detectives conducting a search of the whole business under the authority of a search warrant."

"And were these detectives you had seen earlier at the previous crime scenes?"

"I think so, yes. I would assume so but I do not remember specifically."

"But you seem to remember other things specifically. Why don't you remember which detectives you were working with?"

"There were several people working this case. Detective Kloster was the lead investigator but he was dealing with three different locations as well as the girl who was the witness. I don't remember if he was at the tow yard when I first arrived but he was there at some point. I think that if you refer to the crime scene attendance logs, you will be able to determine who was at what scene and when."

"Ah, then we shall do just that."

Royce approached the witness stand and gave Gordon three documents and a pencil. He then returned to the lectern.

"What are those three documents, Ms. Gordon?"

"These are crime scene attendance logs."

"And which scenes are they from?"

"The three I worked in regard to the Landy case."

"Can you please take a moment to study those logs and use the pencil I have given you to circle any name that appears on all three lists."

It took Gordon less than a minute to complete the task.

"Finished?" Royce asked.

"Yes, there are four names."

"Can you tell us?"

"Yes, myself and my supervisor, Art Donovan, and then Detective Kloster and his partner, Chad Steiner."

"You were the only four who were at all three crime scenes that day, correct?"

"That is correct."

Maggie leaned into me and whispered.

"Cross-scene contamination."

I shook my head slightly and whispered back.

"That suggests accidental contamination. I think he's going for intentional planting of evidence."

Maggie nodded and leaned away. Royce asked his next question.

"Being one of only four who were at all four scenes, you had a keen understanding of this crime and what it meant, isn't that correct?"

"I'm not sure what you mean."

"Among police personnel, were emotions high at these crime scenes?"

"Well, everyone was very professional."

"You mean nobody cared that this was a twelve-year-old girl?"

"No, we cared and you could say things were at least tense at the first two scenes. We had the family at one and the dead little girl at the other. I don't really remember things being emotional at the tow yard."

Wrong answer, I thought. She had opened a door for the defense.

"Okay," Royce said, "but you are saying that at the first two scenes the emotions were high, correct?"

I stood up, just to give Royce a dose of his own medicine.

"Objection. Asked and answered already, Your Honor."

"Sustained."

Royce was undaunted.

"Then how did these emotions display themselves?" he asked.

"Well, we talked. Art Donovan told me to keep professional detachment. He said we had to do our best work because this had been just a little girl."

"What about detectives Kloster and Steiner?"

"They said the same thing. That we couldn't leave any stone unturned, that we had to do it for Melissa."

"He called the victim by her name?"

"Yes, I remember that."

"How angry and upset would you say Detective Kloster was?"

I stood and objected.

"Assumes facts not in evidence or testimony."

The judge sustained it and told Royce to move on.

"Ms. Gordon, can you refer to the crime scene attendance logs still in front of you and tell us if the arrival and departure of law enforcement personnel is kept by time?"

"Yes, it is. There are arrival and departure times listed after each name."

"You have previously stated that detectives Kloster and Steiner were the only two investigators besides yourself and your supervisor to appear at all three scenes."

"Yes, they were the lead investigators on the case."

"Did they arrive at each of the scenes before you and Mr. Donovan?"

It took Gordon a moment to confirm the information on the lists.

"Yes, they did."

"So they would have had access to the victim's body before you ever arrived at the El Rey Theatre, correct?"

"I don't know what you mean by 'access' but, yes, they were on scene first."

"And so they would have also had access to the tow truck before you got there and saw the three strands of hair conveniently caught in the seat crack, correct?"

I objected, saying the question required the witness to speculate on things she would not have witnessed and was argumentative because of the use of the word "conveniently." Royce was obviously playing to the jury. The judge told Royce to rephrase the question without taking editorial license.

"The detectives would have had access to the tow truck before you got there and before you were the first to see the three strands of hair lodged in the seat crack, correct?"

Gordon took the hint from my objection and answered the way I wanted her to.

"I don't know because I wasn't there."

Still, Royce had gotten his point across to the jury. He had also gotten the point of his case across to me. It was now fair to assume that the defense would put forth the theory that the police—in the person of Kloster and/ or his partner, Steiner—had planted the hair evidence to secure a conviction of Jessup after he had been identified by the thirteen-year-old Sarah. Further to this, the defense would posit that Sarah's wrongful identification of Jessup was intentional and part of the Landy family's effort to hide the fact that Melissa had died either accidentally or intentionally at the hands of her stepfather.

It would be a tough road to take. To be successful it would take at least one person on the jury buying into what amounted to two conspiracies working independently of one another and yet in concert. But I could think of only two defense attorneys in town who could pull it off, and Royce was one of them. I had to be prepared.

"What happened after you noticed the hair on the tow truck's seat, do you remember?" Royce asked the witness.

"I pointed it out to Art because he was doing the actual collection of evidence. I was just there to observe and gather experience."

"Were detectives Kloster and Steiner called over to take a look?"

"Yes, I believe so."

"Do you recall what if anything they did then?"

"I don't recall them doing anything in relation to the hair evidence. It was their case and so they were notified of the evidence find and that was it."

"Were you happy with yourself?"

"I don't think I understand."

"It was your first day on the job—your first case. Were you pleased with yourself after spotting the hair evidence? Were you proud?"

Gordon hesitated before answering, as if trying to figure out if the question was a trap.

"I was pleased that I had contributed, yes."

"And did you ever wonder why you, the rookie, spotted the hair in the seat crack before your supervisor or the two lead investigators?"

Gordon hesitated again and then said no. Royce said he had no further questions. It had been an excellent cross, planting multiple seeds that could later bloom into something larger in the defense case.

I did what I could on redirect, asking Gordon to recite the names of the six uniformed police officers and two other detectives who were listed as arriving ahead of Kloster and Steiner on the crime scene attendance log kept at the location where Melissa Landy's body was found.

"So, hypothetically, if Detective Kloster or Steiner had wanted to take hair from the victim to plant elsewhere, they would have had to do it under the noses of eight other officers or enlist them in allowing them to do it. Is that correct?"

"Yes, it would seem so."

I thanked the witness and sat down. Royce then went back to the lectern for recross.

"Also hypothetically, if Kloster or Steiner wanted to plant hair from the victim at the third crime scene, it would not have been necessary to take it directly from the victim's head if there were other sources for it, correct?"

"I guess not if there were other sources."

"For example, a hairbrush in the victim's home could have provided hair to them, correct?"

"I guess so."

"They were in the victim's home, weren't they?"

"Yes, that was one of the locations where they signed in."

"Nothing further."

Royce had nailed me and I decided not to pursue this any further. Royce would have a comeback no matter what I brought forward from the witness.

Gordon was dismissed and the judge broke for lunch. I told Bosch that he would be on the stand after the break, reading Kloster's testimony into the record. I asked if he wanted to grab lunch together to talk about the defense's theory but he said he couldn't, that he had something to do.

Maggie was heading over to the hotel to have lunch with Sarah Ann Gleason, so that left me on my own.

Or so I thought.

As I headed down the center aisle to the rear door of the courtroom, an attractive woman stepped out of the back row in front of me. She smiled and stepped up to me.

"Mr. Haller, I'm Rachel Walling with the FBI."

At first it didn't compute but then the name caught on a memory prompt somewhere inside.

"Yes, the profiler. You distracted my investigator with your theory that Jason Jessup is a serial killer."

"Well, I hope it was more help than distraction."

"I guess that remains to be seen. What can I do for you, Agent Walling?"

"I was going to ask if you might have time for lunch. But since you consider me a distraction, then maybe I should just..."

"Guess what, Agent Walling. You're in luck. I'm free. Let's have lunch."

I pointed to the door and we headed out.

30

Tuesday, April 6, 1:15 P.M.

This time it was the judge who was late returning to court. The prosecution and defense teams were seated at the appointed time and ready to go but there was no sign of Breitman. And there had been no indication from the clerk as to whether the delay was because of personal business or some sort of trial issue. Bosch got up from his seat at the railing and approached Haller, tapping him on the back.

"Harry, we're about to start. You ready?"

"I'm ready, but we need to talk."

"What's wrong?"

Bosch turned his body so his back was to the defense table and lowered his voice into a barely audible whisper.

"I went to see the SIS guys at lunch. They showed me some stuff you need to know about."

He was being overly cryptic. But the photos Lieutenant Wright had showed him from the surveillance the night before were troubling. Jessup was up to something and whatever it might be, it was going to go down soon.

Before Haller could respond, the background hubbub of the courtroom ceased as the judge took the bench.

"After court," Haller whispered.

He then turned back to the front of the courtroom and Bosch returned to his seat at the railing. The judge told the deputy to seat the jury and soon everyone was in place.

"I want to apologize," Breitman said. "This delay was my responsibility. I had a personal matter come up and it took far longer than I expected it would. Mr. Haller, please call your next witness."

Haller stood and called for Doral Kloster. Bosch stood and headed for the witness stand while the judge once again explained to the jury that the witness called by the prosecution was unavailable and that prior sworn testimony would be read by Bosch and Haller. Though all of this had been worked out in a pretrial hearing and over the objection of the defense, Royce stood once again and objected.

"Mr. Royce, we've already argued this issue," the judge responded.

"I would ask that the court reconsider its ruling as this form of testimony entirely undercuts Mr. Jessup's Constitutional right to confront his accusers. Detective Kloster was not asked the questions I would want to ask him based on the defense's current view of the case."

"Again, Mr. Royce, this issue has been settled and I do not wish to rehash it in front of the jury."

"But, *Your Honor*, I am being inhibited from presenting a full defense."

"Mr. Royce, I have been very generous in allowing you to posture in front of the jury. My patience is now growing thin. You may sit down."

Royce stared the judge down. Bosch knew what he was doing. Playing to the jury. He wanted them to see him and Jessup as the underdogs. He wanted them to understand that it was not just the prosecution against Jessup but the judge as well. When he had drawn out the stare as long as he dared, he spoke again.

"Judge, I cannot sit down when my client's freedom is at stake. This is an egregious—"

Breitman angrily slammed her hand down, making a sound as loud as a shot.

"We're not going to do this in front of the jury, Mr. Royce. Will the jurors please return to the assembly room."

Wide-eyed and alert to the tension that had engulfed the courtroom, the jurors filed out, to a person glancing back over their shoulders to check the action behind them. The whole time, Royce held his glare on the judge. And Bosch knew it was mostly an act. This was exactly what Royce wanted, for the jury to see him being persecuted and prevented from bringing his case forward. It didn't matter that they would be sequestered in the jury room. They all knew that Royce was about to get slapped down hard by the judge.

Once the door to the jury assembly room was closed, the judge turned back to Royce. In the thirty seconds it had taken the jury to leave the courtroom, she had obviously calmed down.

"Mr. Royce, at the end of the trial we will be holding a contempt hearing during which your actions today will be examined and penalized. Until then, if I ever order you to sit down and you refuse that order, I will have the courtroom deputy forcibly place you in your seat. And it will not matter to me if the jury is present or not. Do you understand?"

"Yes, Your Honor. And I would like to apologize for allowing the emotions of the moment to get the best of me."

"Very well, Mr. Royce. You will now sit down and we'll bring the jury back in."

They held each other's eyes for a long moment until Royce finally and slowly sat down. The judge then told the courtroom deputy to retrieve the jury.

Bosch glanced at the jurors as they returned. They all had their eyes on Royce, and Harry could see the defense attorney's gambit had worked. He saw sympathy in their eyes, as if they all knew that at any moment they might cross the judge and be similarly rebuked. They didn't know what happened while they were behind the closed door, but Royce was like the kid who had been sent to the principal's office and had returned to tell everyone about it at recess.

The judge addressed the jury before continuing the trial.

"I want the members of the jury to understand that in a trial of this nature emotions sometimes run high. Mr. Royce and I have discussed the issue and it is resolved. You are to pay it no mind. So, let's proceed with the reading of prior sworn testimony. Mr. Haller?"

"Yes, Your Honor."

Haller stood and went to the lectern with his printout of Doral Kloster's testimony.

"Detective Bosch, you are still under oath. Do you have the transcript of sworn testimony provided by Detective Doral Kloster on October eighth, nineteen eighty-six?"

"Yes, I do."

Bosch placed the transcript on the stand and took a pair of reading glasses out of his jacket's inside pocket.

"Okay, then once again I will read the questions that were posed to Detective Kloster under oath by Deputy District Attorney Gary Lintz, and you will read the responses from the witness."

After a series of questions used to elicit basic information about Kloster, the testimony moved quickly into the investigation of the murder of Melissa Landy.

" 'Now, Detective, you are assigned to the detective squad at Wilshire Division, correct?' "

" 'Yes, I am on the Homicide and Major Crimes table.' "

" 'And this case did not start out as a homicide.' "

" 'No, it did not. My partner and I were called in from home after patrol units were dispatched to the Landy house and a preliminary investigation determined that it appeared to be a stranger abduction. That made it a major crime and we were called out.' "

" 'What happened when you got to the Landy house?' "

" 'We initially separated the individuals there—the mother, father and Sarah, the sister—and conducted interviews. We then brought the family together and conducted a joint interview. It often works best that way and it did this time. In the joint interview we found our investigative direction.' "

" 'Tell us about that. How did you find this direction?' "

" 'In the individual interview, Sarah revealed that the girls had been playing a hide-and-seek game and that she was hiding behind some bushes at the front corner of her house. These bushes blocked her view of the street. She said she heard a trash truck and saw a trashman cross the yard and grab her sister. These events occurred on a Sunday, so we knew there was no city trash pickup. But when I had Sarah recount this story in front of her parents, her father quickly said that on Sunday mornings several tow trucks patrol the neighborhood and that the drivers wear overalls like the city sanitation workers do. And that became our first lead.' "

" 'And how did you follow that lead?' "

" 'We were able to obtain a list of city-licensed tow truck companies that operated in the Wilshire District. By this time I had called in more detectives and we split the list up. There were only three companies that were operating on that day. Each pair of detectives took one. My partner and I went to a tow yard on La Brea Boulevard that was operated by a business called Aardvark Towing.' "

" 'And what happened when you got there?' "

" 'We found that they were about to shut down for the day because they essentially worked no-parking zones around churches. By noon they were done. There were three drivers and they were securing things and about to head out when we got there. They all voluntarily agreed to identify themselves and answer our questions. While my partner asked preliminary questions I went back to our car and called their names into central dispatch so they could check them for criminal records.' "

" 'Who were these men, Detective Kloster?' "

" 'Their names were William Clinton, Jason Jessup and Derek Wilbern.' "

" 'And what was the result of your records search?' "

" 'Only Wilbern had an arrest record. It was an attempted rape with no conviction. The case, as I recall, was four years old.' "

" 'Did this make him a suspect in the Melissa Landy abduction?' "

" 'Yes, it did. He generally fit the description we had gotten from Sarah. He drove a large truck and wore overalls. And he had an arrest record involving a sex crime. That made him a strong suspect in my mind.' "

" 'What did you do next?' "

" 'I returned to my partner and he was still interviewing the men in a group setting. I knew that time was of the essence. This little girl was still missing. She was still out there somewhere and usually in a case like this, the longer the individual is missing, the less chance you have of a good ending.' "

" 'So you made some decisions, didn't you?' "

" 'Yes, I decided that Sarah Landy ought to see Derek Wilbern to see if she could identify him as the abductor.' "

" 'So did you set up a lineup for her to view?' "

" 'No, I didn't.' "

" 'No?' "

" 'No. I didn't feel there was time. I had to keep things moving. We had to try to find that girl. So what I did was ask if the three men would agree to go to a separate location where we could continue the interview. They each said yes.' "

" 'No hesitation?' "

" 'No, none. They agreed.' "

" 'By the way, what happened when the other detectives visited the other towing companies that worked in the Wilshire District?' "

" 'They did not find or interview anyone who rose to the level of suspect.' "

" 'You mean no one with a criminal record?' "

" 'No criminal records and no flags came up during interviews.' "

" 'So you were concentrating on Derek Wilbern?' "

" 'That's right.' "

" 'So when Wilbern and the other two men agreed to be interviewed at another location, what did you do?' "

" 'We called for a couple of patrol cruisers and we put Jessup and Clinton in the back of one car and Wilbern in the back of the other. We then closed and locked the Aardvark tow yard and drove ahead in our car.' "

" 'So you got back to the Landy house first?' "

" 'By design. We had told the patrol officers to take a circuitous route to the Landy house on Windsor so we could get there first. When we arrived back at the house I took Sarah upstairs to her bedroom, which was located at the front and was overlooking the front yard and street. I closed the blinds and had her look through just a crack so she would not be visibly exposed to the tow truck drivers.' "

" 'What happened next?' "

" 'My partner had stayed out front. When the patrol cruisers arrived, I had him take the three men out of the cars and have them stand together on the sidewalk. I asked Sarah if she recognized any of them.' "

" 'Did she?' "

" 'Not at first. But one of the men — Jessup — was wearing a baseball hat and he was looking down, using the brim to guard his face.' "

Bosch flipped over two pages of the testimony at this point. The pages had been X-ed out. They contained several questions about Jessup's demeanor and attempt to use his hat to hide his face. These questions were objected to by Jessup's then-defense counsel, sustained by the trial judge, then resculpted and reasked, and objected to again. In the pretrial hearing, Breitman had agreed with Royce's contention that the current jury should not even hear them. It was one of the only points Royce had won.

Haller picked up the reading at the point the skirmish had ended.

" 'Okay, Detective, why don't you tell the jury what happened next?' "

" 'Sarah asked me if I could ask the man with the hat to remove it. I radioed my partner and he told Jessup to take off the hat. Almost immediately, Sarah said it was him.' "

" 'The man who abducted her sister?' "

" 'Yes.' "

" 'Wait a minute. You said Derek Wilbern was your suspect.' "

" 'Yes, based on his having a record of a prior arrest for a sex crime, I thought he was the most likely suspect.' "

" 'Was Sarah sure of her identification?' "

" 'I asked her several times to confirm the identification. She did.' "

" 'What did you do next?' "

" 'I left Sarah in her room and went back downstairs. When I got outside I placed Jason Jessup under arrest, handcuffed him and put him in the back of a patrol car. I told other officers to put Wilbern and Clinton in another car and take them down to Wilshire Division for questioning.' "

" 'Did you question Jason Jessup at this point?' "

" 'Yes, I did. Again, time was of the essence. I didn't feel that I had the time to take him to Wilshire Division and set up a formal interview. Instead, I got in the car with him, read him the Miranda warning and asked if he would talk to me. He said yes.' "

" 'Did you record this?' "

" 'No, I did not. Frankly, I forgot. Things were moving so quickly and all I could think about was finding that little girl. I had a recorder in my pocket but I forgot to record this conversation.' "

" 'Okay, so you questioned Jessup anyway?' "

" 'I asked questions but he gave very few answers. He denied any involvement in the abduction. He acknowledged that he had been on tow patrol in the neighborhood that morning and could have driven by the Landy house but that he did not remember specifically driving on Windsor. I asked him if he remembered seeing the Hollywood sign, because if you are on Windsor you have a straight view of it up the street and on top of the hill. He said he didn't remember seeing the Hollywood sign.' "

" 'How long did this questioning go on?' "

" 'Not long. Maybe five minutes. We were interrupted.' "

" 'By what, Detective?' "

" 'My partner knocked on the car's window and I could tell by his face that whatever he had was important. I got out of the car and that's when he told me. They had found her. A girl's body had been found in a Dumpster down on Wilshire.' "

" 'That changed everything?' "

" 'Yes, everything. I had Jessup transported downtown and booked while I proceeded to the location of the body.' "

" 'What did you discover when you got there?' "

" 'There was a body of a girl approximately twelve or thirteen years old discarded in the Dumpster. She was unidentified at that time but she appeared to be Melissa Landy. I had her photograph. I was pretty sure it was her.'"

"'And you moved the focus of your investigation to this location?'"

"'Absolutely. My partner and I started conducting interviews while the crime scene people and coroner's people dealt with the body. We soon learned that the parking lot adjacent to the rear yard of the theater had previously been used as a temporary auto storage point by a towing company. We learned that company was Aardvark Towing.'"

"'What did that mean to you?'"

"'To me it meant there was now a second connection between the murder of this girl and Aardvark. We had the lone witness, Sarah Landy, identifying one of the Aardvark drivers as the abductor, and now we had the victim found in a Dumpster next to a parking lot used by Aardvark drivers. To me the case was coming together.'"

"'What was your next step?'"

"'At that point my partner and I split up. He stayed with the crime scene and I went back to Wilshire Division to work on search warrants.'"

"'Search warrants for what?'"

"'One for the entire premises at Aardvark Towing. One for the tow truck Jessup was driving that day. And two more for Jessup's home and personal car.'"

"'And did you receive these search warrants?'"

"'Yes, I did. Judge Richard Pittman was on call and he happened to be playing golf at Wilshire Country Club. I brought him the warrants and he signed them on the ninth hole. We then began the searches, starting at Aardvark.'"

"'Were you present at this search?'"

"'Yes, I was. My partner and I were in charge of it.'"

"'And at some point did you become aware of any particular evidence being found that you deemed important to the case?'"

"'Yes. At one point the forensics team leader, a man named Art Donovan, informed me that they had recovered three hairs that were brown in color and over a foot in length each from the tow truck that Jason Jessup was driving that day.'"

"'Did Donovan tell you specifically where in the truck these hair specimens were found?'"

"'Yes, he said they were caught in the crack between the lower and upper parts of the truck's bench seat.'"

Bosch closed the transcript there. Kloster's testimony continued but they had reached the point where Haller had said he would stop because he would have all he needed on the record.

The judge then asked Royce if he wished to have any of the defense's cross-examination read into the record. Royce stood to respond, holding two paper-clipped documents in his hand.

"For the record, I am reluctant to participate in a procedure I object to but since the court is calling the game, I shall play along. I have two brief read-backs of Detective Kloster's cross-examination. May I give a high-lighted printout to Detective Bosch? I think it will make this much easier."

"Very well," the judge said.

The courtroom deputy took one of the documents from Royce and deliv-ered it to Bosch, who quickly scanned it. It was only two pages of testi-mony transcriptions. Two exchanges were highlighted in yellow. As Bosch read them over, the judge explained to the jury that Royce would read questions posed by Jessup's previous defense attorney, Charles Barnard, while Bosch would continue to read the responses of Detective Doral Kloster.

"You may proceed, Mr. Royce."

"Thank you, Your Honor. Now reading from the transcript, 'Detective, how long was it from when you closed and locked Aardvark Towing and took the three drivers over to Windsor, and returned with the search warrant?'"

"'May I refer to the case chronology?'"

"'You may.'"

"'It was about two hours and thirty-five minutes.'"

"'And when you left Aardvark Towing, how did you secure those premises?'"

"'We closed the garages, and one of the drivers—I believe, Mr. Clin-ton—had a key to the door. I borrowed it to lock the door.'"

"'Did you return the key to him after?'"

"'No, I asked if I could keep it for the time being and he said that was okay.'"

"'So when you went back with the signed search warrant, you had the key and you simply unlocked the door to enter.'"

"'That is correct.'"

Royce flipped the page on his copy and told Bosch to do likewise.

"Okay, now reading from another point in the cross-examination. 'Detective Kloster, what did you conclude when you were told about the hair specimens found in the tow truck Mr. Jessup had been driving that day?'"

"'Nothing. The specimens had not been identified yet.'"

"'At what later point were they identified?'"

"'Two days later I got a call from SID. A hair-and-fiber tech told me that the hairs had been examined and that they closely matched samples taken from the victim. She said that she could not exclude the victim as a source.'"

"'So then what did that tell you?'"

"'That it was likely that Melissa Landy had been in that tow truck.'"

"'What other evidence in that truck linked the victim to it or Mr. Jessup to the victim?'"

"'There was no other evidence.'"

" 'No blood or other bodily fluids?' "

" 'No.' "

" 'No fibers from the victim's dress?' "

" 'No.' "

" 'Nothing else?' "

" 'Nothing.' "

" 'With the lack of other corroborating evidence in the truck, did you ever consider that the hair evidence was planted in the truck?' "

" 'Well, I considered it in the way I considered all aspects of the case. But I dismissed it because the witness to the abduction had identified Jessup, and that was the truck he was driving. I didn't think the evidence was planted. I mean, by who? No one was trying to set him up. He was identified by the victim's sister.' "

That ended the read-back. Bosch glanced over at the jury box and saw that it appeared that everyone had remained attentive during what was most likely the most boring stage of the trial.

"Anything further, Mr. Royce?" the judge asked.

"Nothing further, Judge," Royce responded.

"Very well," Breitman said. "I think this brings us to our afternoon break. I will see everyone back in place — and I will admonish myself to be on time — in fifteen minutes."

The courtroom started to clear and Bosch stepped down from the witness stand. He went directly to Haller, who was huddled with McPherson. Bosch butted into their whispered conversation.

"Atwater, right?"

Haller looked up at him.

"Yes, right. Have her ready in fifteen minutes."

"And you have time to talk after court?"

"I'll make time. I had an interesting conversation at lunch, as well. I need to tell you."

Bosch left them and headed out to the hall. He knew the line at the coffee urn in the little concession stand near the elevators would be long and full of jurors from the case. He decided he would hit the stairwell and find coffee on another floor. But first he ducked into the restroom.

As he entered he saw Jessup at one of the sinks. He was leaning over and washing his hands. His eyes were below the mirror line and he didn't realize Bosch was behind him.

Bosch stood still and waited for the moment, thinking about what he would say when he and Jessup locked eyes.

But just as Jessup raised his head and saw Bosch in the mirror, the door to a stall to the left opened and juror number ten stepped out. It was an awkward moment as all three men said nothing.

Finally, Jessup grabbed a paper towel out of the dispenser, dried his hands and tossed it into the wastebasket. He headed to the door while the juror took his place at the sink. Bosch moved silently to a urinal but looked back at Jessup as he was pushing through the door.

Bosch shot him in the back with his finger. Jessup never saw it coming.

31

≋

Tuesday, April 6, 3:05 P.M.

During the break I checked on my next witness and made sure she was good to go. I had a few spare minutes, so I tracked Bosch down in the line at the coffee concession one floor down. Juror number six was two spots in front of him. I took Bosch by the elbow and led him away.

"You can get your coffee later. There's no time to drink it anyway. I wanted you to know that I had lunch with your girlfriend from the bureau."

"What? Who?"

"Agent Walling."

"She's not my girlfriend. Why did she have lunch with you?"

I led him to the stairwell and we headed back upstairs as we talked.

"Well, I think she wanted to have lunch with you but you split out of here too fast so she settled for me. She wanted to give us a warning. She said she's been watching and reading the reports on the trial and she thinks if Jessup is going to blow, it's going to be soon. She said he reacts to pressure and he's probably never been under more than he is right now."

Bosch nodded.

"That's sort of what I wanted to talk to you about before."

He looked around to make sure that no one was in earshot.

"The SIS says Jessup's nighttime activities have increased since the start of the trial. He's going out every night now."

"Has he gone down your street?"

"No, he hasn't been back there or to any of the other spots off Mulholland in a week. But over the last two nights he's done things that are new."

"Like what, Harry?"

"Like on Sunday they followed him down the beach from Venice and he went into the old storage area under the Santa Monica Pier."

"What storage area? What's this mean?"

"It's an old city storage facility but it got flooded by high tides so many times it's locked up and abandoned. Jessup dug underneath one of the old wood sidings and crawled in."

"Why?"

"Who knows? They couldn't go in or they would risk exposing the sur-veillance. But that's not the real news. The real news is, last night he met with a couple of guys at the Townhouse in Venice and then went out to a car in one of the beach lots. One of the guys took something wrapped in a towel out of the trunk and gave it to him."

"A gun?"

Bosch shrugged.

"Whatever it was, they never saw, but through the car's plates they IDed one of the two guys. Marshall Daniels. He was in San Quentin in the nine-ties — same time as Jessup."

I was now catching some of the tension and urgency that was coming off Bosch.

"They could've known each other. What was Daniels up there for?"

"Drugs and weapons."

I checked my watch. I needed to be back in court.

"Then we have to assume Jessup has a weapon. We could violate his OR right now for associating with a convicted felon. Do they have pictures of Jessup and Daniels together?"

"They have photos but I am not sure we want to do that."

"If he's got a gun...Do you trust the SIS to stop him before he makes a move or does some damage?"

"I do, but it would help if we knew what the move was."

We stepped out into the hallway and saw no sign of any jurors or anyone else from the trial. Everybody was back in court but me.

"We'll talk about this later. I have to get back into court or the judge will jump on my ass next. I'm not like Royce. I can't afford a contempt hearing just to make a point with the jury. Go get Atwater and bring her in."

I hurried back to Department 112 and rudely pushed around a couple of the courthouse gadflies who were moving slowly through the door. Judge Breitman had not waited for me. I saw everyone but me in place and the jury was being seated. I moved up the aisle and through the gate and slipped into the seat next to Maggie.

"That was close," she whispered. "I think the judge was hoping to even things up by holding *you* in contempt."

"Yeah, well, she may still."

The judge turned away from the jurors and noticed me at the prosecu-tion table.

"Well, thank you for joining us this afternoon, Mr. Haller. Did you have a nice excursion?"

I stood.

"My apologies, Your Honor. I had a personal matter come up and it took far longer than I expected it would."

She opened her mouth to deliver a rebuke but then paused as she realized I had thrown her words from the morning's delay — her delay — right back at her.

"Just call your next witness, Counselor," she said curtly.

I called Lisa Atwater to the stand and glanced to the back of the courtroom to see Bosch leading the DNA lab technician down the aisle to the gate. I checked the clock up on the rear wall. My goal was to use up the rest of the day with Atwater's testimony, bringing her to the nuts and bolts just before we recessed for the day. That might give Royce a whole night to prepare his cross-examination, but I would happily trade that for what I would get out of the deal — every juror going home with knowledge of the unimpeachable evidence that linked Jason Jessup to the murder of Melissa Landy.

As I had asked her to, Atwater had kept her lab coat on when she walked over from the LAPD lab. The light blue jacket gave her a look of competence and professionalism that the rest of her didn't convey. Atwater was very young — only thirty-one — and had blond hair with a pink stripe down one side, modeling her look after a supercool lab tech on one of the TV crime shows. After meeting her for the first time, I tried to get her to think about losing the pink, but she told me she wouldn't give up her individuality. The jurors, she said, would have to accept her for who and what she was.

At least the lab coat wasn't pink.

Atwater identified herself and was sworn in. After she took the witness seat I started asking questions about her educational pedigree and work experience. I spent at least ten more minutes on this than I normally would have, but I kept seeing that ribbon of pink hair and thought I had to do all I could to turn it into a badge of professionalism and accomplishment.

Finally, I got to the crux of her testimony. With me carefully asking the questions, she testified that she had conducted DNA typing and comparison on two completely different evidence samples from the Landy case. I went with the more problematic analysis first.

"Ms. Atwater, can you describe the first DNA assignment you received on the Landy case?"

"Yes, on February fourth I was given a swatch of fabric that had been cut from the dress that the victim had been wearing at the time of her murder."

"Where did you receive this from?"

"It came from the LAPD's Property Division, where it had been kept in controlled evidence storage."

Her answers were carefully rehearsed. She could give no indication that there had been a previous trial in the case or that Jessup had been in prison for the past twenty-four years. To do so would create prejudice against Jessup and trigger a mistrial.

"Why were you sent this swatch of fabric?"

"There was a stain on the fabric that twenty-four years ago had been identified by the LAPD forensics unit as semen. My assignment was to extract DNA and identify it if possible."

"When you examined this swatch, was there any degradation of the genetic material on it?"

"No, sir. It had been properly preserved."

"Okay, so you got this swatch of material from Melissa Landy's dress and you extracted DNA from it. Do I have that right so far?"

"That's right."

"What did you do next?"

"I turned the DNA profile into a code and entered it into the CODIS database."

"What is CODIS?"

"It's the FBI's Combined DNA Index System. Think of it as a national clearinghouse of DNA records. All DNA signatures gathered by law enforcement end up here and are available for comparison."

"So you entered the DNA signature obtained from semen on the dress Melissa Landy wore on the day she was murdered, correct?"

"Correct."

"Did you get a hit?"

"I did. The profile belonged to her stepfather, Kensington Landy."

A courtroom is a big space. There is always a low-level current of sound and energy. You can feel it even if you can't really hear it. People whisper in the gallery, the clerk and deputy handle phone calls, the court reporter touches the keys on her steno machine. But the sound and air went completely out of Department 112 after Lisa Atwater said what she said. I let it ride for a few moments. I knew this would be the lowest point of the case. With that one answer I had, in fact, revealed Jason Jessup's case. But from this point on, it would all be my case. And Melissa Landy's case. I wouldn't forget about her.

"Why was Kensington Landy's DNA in the CODIS database?" I asked.

"Because California has a law that requires all felony arrest suspects to submit a DNA sample. In two thousand four Mr. Landy was arrested for a hit-and-run accident causing injury. Though he eventually pleaded to lesser charges, it was originally charged as a felony, thus triggering the DNA law upon his booking. His DNA was entered into the system."

"Okay. Now getting back to the victim's dress and the semen that was on it. How did you determine that the semen was deposited on the day that Melissa Landy was murdered?"

Atwater seemed confused by the question at first. It was a skilled act.

"I didn't," she said. "It is impossible to know exactly when that deposit was made."

"You mean it could have been on the dress for a week before her death?"

"Yes. There's no way of knowing."

"What about a month?"

"It's possible because there is —"

"What about a year?"

"Again, it is —"

"Objection!"

Royce stood. About time, I thought.

"Your Honor, how long does this have to go on past the point?"

"Withdrawn, Judge. Mr. Royce is right. We're well past the point."

I paused for a moment to underline that Atwater and I would now be moving in a new direction.

"Ms. Atwater, you recently handled a second DNA analysis in regard to the Melissa Landy case, correct?"

"Yes, I did."

"Can you describe what that entailed?"

Before answering she secured the pink band of hair behind her ear.

"Yes, it was a DNA extraction and comparison of hair specimens. Hair from the victim, Melissa Landy, which was contained in a kit taken at the time of her autopsy and hair recovered from a tow truck operated by the defendant, Jason Jessup."

"How many hair specimens are we talking about?"

"Ultimately, one of each. Our objective was to extract nuclear DNA, which is available only in the root of a hair sample. Of the specimens we had, there was only one suitable extraction from the hairs recovered from the tow truck. So we compared DNA from the root of that hair to DNA from a hair sample taken from the autopsy kit."

I walked her through the process, trying to keep the explanations as simple as possible. Just enough to get by, like on TV. I kept one eye on my witness and one on the jury box, making sure everybody was staying plugged in and happy.

Finally, we came out the other end of the techno-genetic tunnel and arrived at Lisa Atwater's conclusions. She put several color-coded charts and graphs up on the screens and thoroughly explained them. But the bottom line was always the same thing; to feel it, jurors had to hear it. The most important thing a witness brings into a courtroom is her word. After all the charts were displayed, it came down to Atwater's words.

I turned and looked back at the clock. I was right on schedule. In less than twenty minutes the judge would recess for the evening. I turned back and moved in for the kill.

"Ms. Atwater, do you have any hesitation or doubt at all about the genetic match you have just testified about?"

"No, none whatsoever."

"Do you believe beyond a doubt that the hair from Melissa Landy is a unique match to the hair specimen obtained from the tow truck the defendant was operating on February sixteenth, nineteen eighty-six?"

"Yes, I do."

"Is there a quantifiable way of illustrating this match?"

"Yes, as I illustrated earlier, we matched nine out of the thirteen genetic markers in the CODIS protocol. The combination of these nine particular genetic markers occurs in one in one-point-six trillion individuals."

"Are you saying it is a one-in-one-point-six-trillion chance that the hair found in the tow truck operated by the defendant belonged to someone other than Melissa Landy?"

"You could say it that way, yes."

"Ms. Atwater, do you happen to know the current population of the world?"

"It's approaching seven billion."

"Thank you, Ms. Atwater. I have no further questions at this time."

I moved to my seat and sat down. Immediately I started stacking files and documents, getting it all ready for the briefcase and the ride home. This day was in the books and I had a long night ahead of me preparing for the next one. The judge didn't seem to begrudge me finishing ten minutes early. She was shutting down herself and sending the jury home.

"We will continue with the cross-examination of this witness tomorrow. I would like to thank all of you for paying such close attention to today's testimony. We will be adjourned until nine o'clock sharp tomorrow morning and I once again admonish you not to watch any news program or—"

"Your Honor?"

I looked up from the files. Royce was on his feet.

"Yes, Mr. Royce?"

"My apologies, Judge Breitman, for interrupting. But by my watch, it is only four-fifty and I know that you prefer to get as much testimony as possible in each day. I would like to cross-examine this witness now."

The judge looked at Atwater, who was still on the witness stand, and then back to Royce.

"Mr. Royce, I would rather you begin your cross tomorrow morning rather than start and then interrupt it after only ten minutes. We don't go past five o'clock with the jury. That is a rule I will not break."

"I understand, Judge. But I am not planning to interrupt it. I will be finished with this witness by five o'clock and then she will not be required to return tomorrow."

The judge stared at Royce for a long moment, a disbelieving look on her face.

"Mr. Royce, Ms. Atwater is one of the prosecution's key witnesses. Are you telling me you only need five minutes for cross-examination?"

"Well, of course it depends on the length of her answers, but I have only a few questions, Your Honor."

"Very well, then. You may proceed. Ms. Atwater, you remain under oath."

Royce moved to the lectern and I was as confused as the judge about the defense's maneuver. I had expected Royce to take most of the next morning on cross. This had to be a trick. He had a DNA expert on his own witness list but I would never give up a shot at the prosecution's witness.

"Ms. Atwater," Royce said, "did all of the testing and typing and extracting you conducted on the hair specimen from the tow truck tell you how the specimen got inside that truck?"

To buy time Atwater asked Royce to repeat the question. But even upon hearing it a second time, she did not answer until the judge intervened.

"Ms. Atwater, can you answer the question?" Breitman asked.

"Uh, yes, I'm sorry. My answer is no, the lab work I conducted had nothing to do with determining how the hair specimen found its way into the tow truck. That was not my responsibility."

"Thank you," Royce said. "So to make it crystal clear, you cannot tell the jury how that hair — which you have capably identified as belonging to the victim — got inside the truck or who put it there, isn't that right?"

I stood.

"Objection. Assumes facts not in evidence."

"Sustained. Would you like to rephrase, Mr. Royce?"

"Thank you, Your Honor. Ms. Atwater, you have no idea — other than what you were perhaps told — how the hair you tested found its way into the tow truck, correct?"

"That would be correct, yes."

"So you can identify the hair as Melissa Landy's but you cannot testify with the same sureness as to how it ended up in the tow truck, correct?"

I stood up again.

"Objection," I said. "Asked and answered."

"I think I will let the witness answer," Breitman said. "Ms. Atwater?"

"Yes, that is correct," Atwater said. "I cannot testify about anything regarding how the hair happened to end up in the truck."

"Then I have no further questions. Thank you."

I turned back and looked at the clock. I had two minutes. If I wanted to get the jury back on track I had to think of something quick.

"Any redirect, Mr. Haller?" the judge asked.

"One moment, Your Honor."

I turned and leaned toward Maggie to whisper.

"What do I do?"

"Nothing," she whispered back. "Let it go or you might make it worse. You made your points. He made his. Yours are more important — you put Melissa inside his truck. Leave it there."

Something told me not to leave it as is but my mind was a blank. I couldn't think of a question derived from Royce's cross that would get the jury off his point and back onto mine.

"Mr. Haller?" the judge said impatiently.

I gave it up.

"No further questions at this time, Your Honor."

"Very well, then, we will adjourn for the day. Court will reconvene at nine A.M. tomorrow and I admonish the jurors not to read newspaper accounts about this trial or view television reports or talk to family or friends about the case. I hope everyone has a good night."

With that the jury stood and began to file out of the box. I casually glanced over at the defense table and saw Royce being congratulated by Jessup. They were all smiles. I felt a hollow in my stomach the size of a baseball. It was as though I had played it to near perfection all day long—for almost six hours of testimony—and then in the last five minutes managed to let the last out in the ninth go right between my legs.

I sat still and waited until Royce and Jessup and everybody else had left the courtroom.

"You coming?" Maggie said from behind me.

"In a minute. How about I meet you back at the office?"

"Let's walk back together."

"I'm not good company, Mags."

"Haller, get over it. You had a great day. *We* had a great day. He was good for five minutes and the jury knows that."

"Okay. I'll meet you there in a little bit."

She gave up and I heard her leave. After a few minutes I reached over to the top file on the stack in front of me and opened it up halfway. A school photo of Melissa Landy was clipped inside the folder. Smiling at the camera. She looked nothing like my daughter but she made me think of Hayley.

I made a silent vow not to let Royce outsmart me again.

A few moments later, someone turned out the lights.

32

≈

Tuesday, April 6, 10:15 P.M.

Bosch stood by the swing set planted in the sand a quarter mile south of the Santa Monica Pier. The black water of the Pacific to his left was alive with the dancing reflection of light and color from the Ferris wheel at the end of the boardwalk. The amusement park had closed fifteen minutes earlier but the light show would go on through the night, an electronic display of ever-changing patterns on the big wheel that was mesmerizing in the cold darkness.

Harry raised his phone and called the SIS dispatcher. He had checked in earlier and set things up.

"It's Bosch again. How's our boy?"

"He appears to be tucked in for the night. You must've worn him out in court today, Bosch. On the way home from the CCB he went to Ralphs to pick up some groceries and then straight home, where he's been ever since. First night in five he hasn't been out and about at this time."

"Yeah, well, don't count on it staying that way. They've got the back door covered, right?"

"And the windows and the car and the bicycle. We got him, Detective. Don't worry."

"Then I won't. You've got my number. Call me if he moves."

"Will do."

Bosch put the phone away and headed toward the pier. The wind was strong off the water and a fine mist of sand stung his face and eyes as he approached the huge structure. The pier was like a beached aircraft carrier. It was long and wide. It had a large parking lot and an assortment of restaurants and souvenir shops on top. At its midpoint it had a full amusement park with a roller coaster and the signature Ferris wheel. And at its furthest extension into the sea it was a traditional fishing pier with a bait shop, management office and yet another restaurant. All of it was supported on a thick forest of wood pilings that started landside and carried seven hundred feet out beyond the wave break and to the cold depths.

Landside, the pilings were enclosed with a wooden siding that created a semi-secure storage facility for the city of Santa Monica. Only semi-secure for two reasons: The storage area was vulnerable to extreme high tides, which came on rare occasion during offshore earthquakes. Also, the pier spanned a hundred yards of beach, which entailed anchoring the wood siding in moist sand. The wood was always in the process of rotting and was easily compromised. The result was that the storage facility had become an unofficial homeless shelter that had to be periodically cleared out by the city.

The SIS observers had reported that Jason Jessup had slipped underneath the south wall the night before and had spent thirty-one minutes inside the storage area.

Bosch reached the pier and started walking its length, looking for the spot in the wood siding where Jessup had crawled under. He carried a mini Maglite and quickly found a depression where the sand had been dug out at the wall's base and partially filled back in. He crouched down, put the light into the hole and determined that it was too small for him to fit through. He put the light down to the side, reached down and started digging like a dog trying to escape the yard.

Soon the hole seemed big enough and he crawled through. He was dressed for the effort. Old black jeans and work boots, and a long-sleeved

T-shirt beneath a plastic raid jacket he wore inside out to hide the luminescent yellow LAPD across the front and back.

He came up inside to a dark, cavernous space with slashes of light filtering down between the planks of the parking lot above. He stood up and brushed the sand off his clothes, then swept the area with the flashlight. It had been made for close-in work, so its beam did little to illuminate the far reaches of the space.

There was a damp smell and the sound of waves crashing through the pilings only twenty-five yards away echoed loudly in the enclosed space. Bosch pointed the light up and saw fungus caked on the pier's crossbeams. He moved forward into the gloom and quickly came upon a boat covered by a tarp. He lifted up a loose end and saw that it was an old lifeguard boat. He moved on and came upon stacks of buoys and then stacks of traffic barricades and mobile barriers, all of them stenciled with CITY OF SANTA MONICA.

He next came to three stacks of scaffolding used for paint and repair projects on the pier. They looked long untouched and were slowly sinking in the sand.

Across the rear was a line of enclosed storage rooms, but the wood sidings had cracked and split over time, making storage in them porous at best.

The doors were unlocked and Bosch went down the line, finding each one empty until the second to the last. Here the door was secured with a shiny new padlock. He put the beam of his light into one of the cracks between the planks of the siding and tried to look in. He saw what appeared to be the edge of a blanket but that was all.

Bosch moved back to the door and knelt down in front of the lock. He held the light with his mouth and extracted two lock picks from his wallet. He went to work on the padlock and quickly determined that it had only four tumblers. He got it open in less than five minutes.

He entered the storage corral and found it largely empty. There was a folded blanket on the ground with a pillow on top of it. Nothing else. The SIS surveillance report had said that the night before, Jessup had walked down the beach carrying a blanket. It did not say that he had left it behind under the pier, and there had been nothing in the report about a pillow.

Harry wasn't even sure he was in the same spot that Jessup had come to. He moved the light over the wall and then up to the underside of the pier, where he held it. He could clearly see the outline of a door. A trapdoor. It was locked from underneath with another new padlock.

Bosch was pretty sure that he was standing beneath the pier's parking lot. He had occasionally heard the sound of vehicles up above as the pier crowd went home. He guessed that the trapdoor had been used as some sort of loading door for materials to be stored. He knew he could grab one of the scaffolds and climb up to examine the second lock but decided not to bother. He retreated from the corral.

As he was relocking the door with the padlock he felt his phone begin to vibrate in his pocket. He quickly pulled it out, expecting to learn from SIS dispatch that Jessup was on the move. But the caller ID told him the call was from his daughter. He opened the phone.

"Hey, Maddie."

"Dad? Are you there?"

Her voice was low and the sound of crashing waves was loud. Bosch yelled.

"I'm here. What's wrong?"

"Well, when are you coming home?"

"Soon, baby. I've got a little bit more work to do."

She dropped her voice even lower and Bosch had to clamp a hand over his other ear to hear her. In the background he could hear the freeway on her end. He knew she was on the rear deck.

"Dad, she's making me do homework that isn't even due until next week."

Bosch had once again left her with Sue Bambrough, the assistant principal.

"So next week you'll be thanking her when everybody else is doing it and you'll be all done."

"Dad, I've been doing homework all night!"

"You want me to tell her to let you take a break?"

His daughter didn't respond and Bosch understood. She had called because she wanted him to know the misery she was suffering. But she didn't want him to do anything about it.

"I'll tell you what," he said. "When I get back I will remind Mrs. Bambrough that you are not in school when you are at home and you don't need to be working the whole time. Okay?"

"I guess. Why can't I just stay at Rory's? This isn't fair."

"Maybe next time. I need to get back to work, Mads. Can we talk about it tomorrow? I want you in bed by the time I get home."

"Whatever."

"Good night, Madeline. Make sure all the doors are locked, including on the deck, and I'll see you tomorrow."

"Good night."

The disapproval in her voice was hard to miss. She disconnected the call ahead of Bosch. He closed his phone and just as he slid it into his pocket he heard a noise, like a banging of metal parts, coming from the direction of the hole he had slid through into the storage area. He immediately killed his flashlight and moved toward the tarp that covered the boat.

Crouching behind the boat, he saw a human figure stand up by the wall and start moving in the darkness without a flashlight. The figure moved without hesitation toward the storage corral with the new lock on it.

There were streetlights over the parking lot above. They sent slivers of illumination down through the cracks formed by retreating planks in the boardwalk. As the figure moved through these, Bosch saw that it was Jessup.

Harry dropped lower and instinctively reached his hand to his belt just to make sure his gun was there. With his other hand he pulled his phone and hit the mute button. He didn't want the SIS dispatcher to suddenly remember to call him to alert him that Jessup was moving.

Bosch noticed that Jessup was carrying a bag that appeared to be heavily weighted. He went directly to the locked storage room and soon swung the door open. He obviously had a key to the padlock.

Jessup stepped back and Bosch saw a slash of light cross his face as he turned and scanned the entire storage area, making sure he was alone. He then went inside the room.

For several seconds, there was no sound or movement, then Jessup reappeared in the doorway. He stepped out and closed the door, relocking it. He then stepped back into the light and did a 180-degree scan of the larger storage area. Bosch lowered his body even further. He guessed that Jessup was suspicious because he had found the hole under the wall freshly dug out.

"Who's there?" he called out.

Bosch didn't move. He didn't even breathe.

"Show yourself!"

Bosch snaked his hand under the raid jacket and closed his hand on his gun's grips. He knew the indications were that Jessup had obtained a weapon. If he made even a feint in Bosch's direction, Harry was going to pull his own weapon and be ready to fire first.

But it never happened. Jessup started moving quickly back to the entrance hole and soon he disappeared in the darkness. Bosch listened but all he could hear was the crashing of the waves. He waited another thirty seconds and then started moving toward the opening in the wall. He didn't turn on the light. He wasn't sure Jessup had actually left.

As he moved around the stack of scaffolding frames, he banged his shin hard on a metal pipe that was extending out from the pile. It sent a sudden burst of pain up his left leg and shifted the balance of metal frames. The top two loudly slid off stack, clattering to the sand. Bosch threw himself to the sand next to the pile and waited.

But Jessup didn't appear. He was gone.

Bosch slowly got up. He was in pain and he was angry. He pulled his phone and called SIS dispatch.

"You were supposed to call me when Jessup moved!" he whispered angrily.

"I know that," said the dispatcher. "He hasn't moved."

"What? Are you — patch me through to whoever's in charge out there."

"I'm sorry, Detective, but that's not how —"

"Look, shithead, Jessup is not *tucked in* for the night. I just saw him. And it almost turned bad. Now let me talk to somebody out there or my next call is to Lieutenant Wright at home."

While he waited Bosch moved to the sidewall so he could get out of the storage area. His leg hurt badly and he was walking with a limp.

In the darkness he couldn't find the spot where he could slip under the wall. Finally, he put the light on, holding it low to the ground. He found the spot but saw that Jessup had pushed sand into the hole, just as he had the night before.

A voice finally came to him over the phone.

"Bosch? This is Jacquez. You claim you just saw our subject?"

"I don't claim I saw him. I did see him. Where are your people?"

"We're sitting on his zero, man. He hasn't left."

Zero was a surveillance subject's home location.

"Bullshit, I just saw him under the Santa Monica pier. Get your people up here. Now."

"We got his zero down tight, Bosch. There's no —"

"Listen, Jackass, Jessup is my case. I know him and he almost just crawled up my ass. Now call your men and find out which one went off post because —"

"I'll get back to you," Jacquez said curtly and the line went dead.

Bosch turned the phone's ringer back on and put it in his pocket. Once again he dropped to his knees and quickly dug out the hole, using his hands as a scoop. He then pushed his body through, half expecting Jessup to be waiting for him when he came up on the other side.

But there was no sign of him. Bosch got up, gazed south down the beach in the direction of Venice and saw no one in the light from the Ferris wheel. He then turned and looked up toward the hotels and apartment buildings that ran along the beach. Several people were on the beach walk that fronted the buildings but he didn't recognize any of the figures as Jessup.

Twenty-five yards up the pier was a set of stairs leading topside and directly to the pier's parking lot. Bosch headed that way, still limping badly. He was halfway up the stairs when his phone rang. It was Jacquez.

"All right, where is he? We're on our way."

"That's the thing. I lost him. I had to hide and I thought you people were on him. I'm going to the top of the pier now. What the hell happened, Jacquez?"

"We had a guy step out to drop a deuce. Said his stomach was giving him trouble. I don't think he'll be in the unit after tonight."

"Jesus Christ!"

Bosch got to the top of the steps and walked out onto the empty parking lot. There was no sign of Jessup.

"Okay, I'm up on the pier. I don't see him. He's in the wind."

"Okay, Bosch, we're two minutes out. We're going to spread. We'll find him. He didn't take the car or the bike, so he's on foot."

"He could've grabbed a cab at any one of the hotels over here. The bottom line is we don't know where —"

Bosch suddenly realized something.

"I gotta go. Call me as soon as you have him, Jacquez. You got that?"

"Got it."

Bosch ended the call and then immediately called his home on the speed dial. He checked his watch and expected Sue Bambrough to answer, since it was after eleven.

But his daughter picked up the call.

"Dad?"

"Hey, baby, why are you still up?"

"Because I had to do all that homework. I wanted a little break before I went to sleep."

"That's fine. Listen, can you put Mrs. Bambrough on the line?"

"Dad, I'm in my bedroom and I'm in my pajamas."

"That's okay. Just go to the door and tell her to pick up the phone in the kitchen. I need to talk to her. And meantime, you have to get dressed. You're leaving the house."

"What? Dad, I have—"

"Madeline, listen to me. This is important. I am going to tell Mrs. Bambrough to take you to her house until I can get there. I want you out of the house."

"Why?"

"You don't need to know that. You just need to do what I ask. Now, please, get Mrs. Bambrough on the phone."

She didn't respond but he heard the door of her room open. Then he heard his daughter say, "It's for you."

A few moments later the extension was picked up in the kitchen.

"Hello?"

"Sue, it's Harry. I need you to do something. I need you to take Maddie to your house. Right now. I will be there in less than an hour to get her."

"I don't understand."

"Sue, listen, we've been watching a guy tonight who knows where I live. And we lost him. Now, there is no reason to panic or to believe he is heading that way but I want to take all precautions. So I want you to take Maddie and get out of the house. Right now. Go to your place and I will see you there. Can you do this, Sue?"

"We're leaving right now."

He liked the strength in her voice and realized it probably came with the territory of being a teacher and assistant principal in the public school system.

"Okay, I'm on my way. Call me back as soon as you get to your place."

But Bosch wasn't really on his way. After the call, he put the phone away and went back down the steps to the beach. He returned to the hole he had dug under the storage area wall. He crawled back under and this time used his flashlight to find his way to the locked storage room. He used his picks again on the padlock and the whole time he worked he was distracted by thoughts of Jessup's escape from the surveillance. Had it just been a coincidence that he had left his apartment at the same time the SIS watcher had left his post, or was he aware of the surveillance and did he break free when he saw the opportunity?

At the moment, there was no way to know.

Finally, he got the lock open, taking longer than he had the first time. He entered the storage room and moved the light to the blanket and pillow on the ground. The bag Jessup had carried was there. It said *Ralphs* on its side. Bosch dropped to his knees and was about to open it when his phone buzzed. It was Jacquez.

"We got him. He's on Nielson at Ocean Park. It looks like he's walking home."

"Then try not to lose him this time, Jacquez. I gotta go."

He disconnected before Jacquez could reply. He quickly called his daughter's cell. She was in the car with Sue Bambrough. Bosch told her they could turn around and go back home. This news was not received with a thankful release of tension. His daughter was left upset and angry over the scare. Bosch couldn't blame her but he couldn't stay on the line.

"I'll be home in less than an hour. We can talk about it then if you're still awake. I'll see you soon."

He disconnected the call and focused on the bag. He opened it without moving it from its spot next to the blanket.

The bag contained a dozen single-serving-size cans of fruit. There were diced peaches in heavy syrup, chopped pineapple and something called fruit medley. Also in the bag was a package of plastic spoons. Bosch stared at the contents for a long moment and then his eyes moved up the wall to the crossbeams and the locked trapdoor above.

"Who are you bringing here, Jessup?" he whispered.

33

Wednesday, April 7, 1:05 P.M.

All eyes were on the back of the courtroom. It was time for the main event, and while I had ringside seats, I was still going to be just a spectator like everybody else. That didn't sit very well with me but it was a choice I could live with and trust. The door opened and Harry Bosch led our main witness into the courtroom. Sarah Ann Gleason told us she didn't own any dresses and didn't want to buy one to testify in. She wore black jeans and a purple silk blouse. She looked pretty and she looked confident. We didn't need a dress.

Bosch stayed on her right side and when opening the gate for her positioned his body between her and Jessup, who sat at the defense table, turned like everybody else toward his main accuser's entrance.

Bosch let her go the rest of the way by herself. Maggie McFierce was already at the lectern and she smiled warmly at her witness as she went by. This was Maggie's moment, too, and I read her smile as one of hope for both women.

We'd had a good morning, with testimony from Bill Clinton, the former tow truck driver, and then Bosch taking the case through to lunch. Clinton told his story about the day of the murder and Jessup borrowing his Dodgers cap just before they became part of the impromptu lineup outside the house on Windsor Boulevard. He also testified to the Aardvark drivers' frequent use of and familiarity with the parking lot behind the El Rey Theatre, and Jessup's claim to Windsor Boulevard on the morning of the murder. These were good, solid points for the prosecution, and Clinton gave no quarter to Royce on cross.

Then Bosch took the stand for a third time in the trial. Rather than read previous testimony, this time he testified about his own recent investigation of the case and produced the Dodgers cap — with the initials *BC* under the brim — from property that had been seized from Jessup during his arrest twenty-four years earlier. We were forced to dance around the fact that the hat as well as Jessup's other belongings had been in the property room at San Quentin for the past twenty-four years. To bring that information out would be to reveal that Jessup had previously been convicted of Melissa Landy's murder.

And now Sarah Gleason would be the prosecution's final witness. Through her the case would come together in the emotional crescendo I was counting on. One sister standing for a long-lost sister. I leaned back in my seat to watch my ex-wife — the best prosecutor I had ever encountered — take us home.

Gleason was sworn in and then took her seat on the stand. She was small and required the microphone to be lowered by the courtroom deputy. Maggie cleared her voice and began.

"Good morning, Ms. Gleason. How are you today?"

"I'm doing pretty good."

"Can you please tell the jury a little bit about yourself?"

"Um, I'm thirty-seven years old. Not married. I live in Port Townsend, Washington, and I've been there about seven years now."

"What do you do for a living?"

"I'm a glass artist."

"And what was your relationship to Melissa Landy?"

"She was my younger sister."

"How much younger was she than you?"

"Thirteen months."

Maggie put a photograph of the two sisters up on the overhead screen as a prosecution exhibit. It showed two smiling girls standing in front of a Christmas tree.

"Can you identify this photo?"

"That was me and Melissa at the last Christmas. Right before she was taken."

"So that would be Christmas nineteen eighty-five?"

"Yes."

"I notice that she and you are about the same size."

"Yes, she wasn't really my little sister anymore. She had caught up to me."

"Did you share the same clothes?"

"We shared some things but we also had our favorite things that we didn't share. That could cause a fight."

She smiled and Maggie nodded that she understood.

"Now, you said she was taken. Were you referring to February sixteenth of the following year, the date of your sister's abduction and murder?"

"Yes, I was."

"Okay, Sarah, I know it will be difficult for you but I would like you to tell the jury what you saw and did on that day."

Gleason nodded as if steeling herself for what was ahead. I checked the jury and saw every eye holding on her. I then turned and glanced at the defense table and locked eyes with Jessup. I did not look away. I held his defiant stare and tried to send back my own message. That two women — one asking the questions, the other answering them — were going to take him down.

Finally, it was Jessup who looked away.

"Well, it was a Sunday," Gleason said. "We were going to go to church. My whole family. Melissa and I were in our dresses so my mother told us to go out front."

"Why couldn't you use the backyard?"

"My stepfather was building a pool and there was a lot of mud in the back and a big hole. My mother was worried we might fall down and get our dresses dirty."

"So you went out to the front yard."

"Yes."

"And where were your parents at this time, Sarah?"

"My mother was still upstairs getting ready and my stepfather was in the TV room. He was watching sports."

"Where was the TV room in the house?"

"In the back next to the kitchen."

"Okay, Sarah, I am going to show you a photo called 'People's prosecution exhibit eleven.' Is this the front of the house where you lived on Windsor Boulevard?"

All eyes went to the overhead screen. The yellow-brick house spread across the screen. It was a long shot from the street, showing a deep front yard with ten-foot hedges running down both sides. There was a front porch that ran the width of the house and that was largely hidden behind ornamental vegetation. There was a paved walkway extending from the sidewalk, across the lawn and to the steps of the front porch. I had reviewed our photo exhibits several times in preparation for the trial. But for the first time, I noticed that the walkway had a crack running down the center of its entire length from sidewalk to front steps. It somehow seemed appropriate, considering what had happened at the home.

"Yes, that was our house."

"Tell us what happened that day in the front yard, Sarah."

"Well, we decided to play hide-and-seek while we waited for our parents. I was It first and I found Melissa hiding behind that bush on the right side of the porch."

She pointed to the exhibit photo that was still on the screen. I realized we had forgotten to give Gleason the laser pointer we had prepared her testimony with. I quickly opened Maggie's briefcase and found it. I stood and handed it to her. With the judge's permission, she gave it to the witness.

"Okay, Sarah, could you use the laser to show us?" Maggie asked.

Gleason moved the red laser dot in a circle around a thick bush at the north corner of the front porch.

"So she hid there and you found her?"

"Yes, and then when it was her turn to be It, I decided to hide in the same spot because I didn't think she would look there at first. When she was finished counting she came down the steps and stood in the middle of the yard."

"You could see her from your hiding place?"

"Yes, through the bush I could see her. She was sort of turning in a half circle, looking for me."

"Then what happened?"

"Well, first I heard a truck go by and—"

"Let me just stop you right there, Sarah. You say you heard a truck. You didn't see it?"

"No, not from where I was hiding."

"How do you know that it was a truck?"

"It was very loud and heavy. I could feel it in the ground, like a little earthquake."

"Okay, what happened after you heard the truck?"

"Suddenly I saw a man in the yard...and he went right up to my sister and grabbed her by her wrist."

Gleason cast her eyes down and held her hands together on the dais in front of her seat.

"Sarah, did you know this man?"

"No, I did not."

"Had you ever seen him before?"

"No, I had not."

"Did he say anything?"

"Yes, I heard him say, 'You have to come with me.' And my sister said...she said, 'Are you sure?' And that was it. I think he said something else but I didn't hear it. He led her away. To the street."

"And you stayed in hiding?"

"Yes, I couldn't...for some reason I couldn't move. I couldn't call for help, I couldn't do anything. I was very scared."

It was one of those solemn moments in the courtroom when there was absolute silence except for the voices of the prosecutor and the witness.

"Did you see or hear anything else, Sarah?"

"I heard a door close and then I heard the truck drive away."

I saw the tears on Sarah Gleason's cheeks. I thought the courtroom deputy had noticed as well because he took a box of tissues from a drawer in his desk and crossed the courtroom with them. But instead of taking them to Sarah he handed the box to juror number two, who had tears on her cheeks as well. This was okay with me. I wanted the tears to stay on Sarah's face.

"Sarah, how long was it before you came out from behind the bush where you were hiding and told your parents that your sister had been taken?"

"I think it was less than a minute but it was too late. She was gone."

The silence that followed that statement was the kind of void that lives can disappear into. Forever.

Maggie spent the next half hour walking Gleason through her memory of what came after. Her stepfather's desperate 9-1-1 call to the police, the interview she gave to the detectives, and then the lineup she viewed from her bedroom window and her identifying Jason Jessup as the man she saw lead her sister away.

Maggie had to be very careful here. We had used sworn testimony of witnesses from the first trial. The record of that entire trial was available to Royce as well, and I knew without a doubt that he had his assistant counsel, who was sitting on the other side of Jessup, comparing everything Sarah Gleason was saying now with the testimony she gave at the first trial. If she changed one nuance of her story, Royce would be all over her on it during his cross-examination, using the discrepancy to try to cast her as a liar.

To me the testimony came off as fresh and not rehearsed. This was a testament to the prep work of the two women. Maggie smoothly and efficiently brought her witness to the vital moment when Sarah reconfirmed her identification of Jessup.

"Was there any doubt at all in your mind when you identified Jason Jessup in nineteen eighty-six as the man who took your sister?"

"No, none at all."

"It has been a long time, Sarah, but I ask you to look around the courtroom and tell the jury whether you see the man who abducted your sister on February sixteenth, nineteen eighty-six?"

"Yes, him."

She spoke without hesitation and pointed her finger at Jessup.

"Would you tell us where he is seated and describe an article of clothing he is wearing?"

"He's sitting next to Mr. Royce and he has a dark blue tie and a light blue shirt."

She paused and looked at Judge Breitman.

"Let the record show that the witness has identified the defendant," she said.

She went right back to Sarah.

"After all these years, do you have any doubt that he is the man who took your sister?"

"None at all."

Maggie turned and looked at the judge.

"Your Honor, it may be a bit early but I think now would be a good time to take the afternoon break. I am going to go in a different direction with this witness at this point."

"Very well," Breitman said. "We will adjourn for fifteen minutes and I will expect to see everyone back here at two-thirty-five. Thank you."

Sarah said she wanted to use the restroom and left the courtroom with Bosch running interference and making sure she would not cross paths with Jessup in the hallway. Maggie sat down at the table and we huddled.

"You have 'em, Maggie. This is what they've been waiting all week to hear and it's better than they thought it was going to be."

She knew I was talking about the jury. She didn't need my approval or encouragement but I had to give it.

"Now comes the hard part," she said. "I hope she holds up."

"She's doing great. And I'm sure Harry's telling her that right now."

Maggie didn't respond. She started flipping through the legal pad that had her notes and the rough script of the examination. Soon she was immersed in the next hour's work.

34

Wednesday, April 7, 2:30 P.M.

Bosch had to shoo away the reporters when Sarah Gleason came out of the restroom. Using his body as a shield against the cameras he walked her back to the courtroom.

"Sarah, you're doing really well," he said. "You keep it up and this guy's going right back to where he belongs."

"Thanks, but that was the easy part. It's going to get hard now."

"Don't kid yourself, Sarah. There is no easy part. Just keep thinking about your sister, Melissa. Somebody has to stand up for her. And right now that's you."

As they got to the courtroom door, he realized that she had smoked a cigarette in the restroom. He could smell it on her.

Inside, he walked her down the center aisle and delivered her to Maggie McFierce, who was waiting at the gate. Bosch gave the prosecutor the nod. She was doing really well herself.

"Finish the job," he said.

"We will," Maggie said.

After passing the witness off, Bosch doubled back up the center aisle to the sixth row. He had spotted Rachel Walling sitting in the middle of the row. He now squeezed around several reporters and observers to get to her. The space next to her was open and he sat down.

"Harry."

"Rachel."

"I think the man who was in that space was planning on coming back."

"That's okay. Once court starts, I have to move back up. You should've told me you were coming. Mickey said you were here the other day."

"When I have some time I like to come by. It's a fascinating case so far."

"Well, let's hope the jury thinks it's more than fascinating. I want this guy back in San Quentin so bad I can taste it."

"Mickey told me Jessup was moonlighting. Is that still —"

She lowered her voice to a whisper when she saw Jessup walking down the aisle and back to his seat at the defense table.

"—happening?"

Bosch matched her whisper.

"Yeah, and last night it almost went completely south on us. The SIS lost him."

"Oh, no."

The judge's door opened and she stepped out and headed up to the bench. Everyone stood. Bosch knew he had to get back to the prosecution table in case he was needed.

"But I found him," he whispered. "I have to go, but are you sticking around this afternoon?"

"No, I have to go back to the office. I'm just on a break right now."

"Okay, Rachel, thanks for coming by. I'll talk to you."

As people started sitting back down he worked his way out of the row and then quickly went back down the aisle and through the gate to take a seat in the row of chairs directly behind the prosecution table.

McPherson continued her direct examination of Sarah Ann Gleason. Bosch thought that both prosecutor and witness had been doing an exceptional job so far, but he also knew that they were moving into new territory now and soon everything said before wouldn't matter if what was said now wasn't delivered in a believable and unassailable fashion.

"Sarah," McPherson began, "when did your mother marry Kensington Landy?"

"When I was six."

"Did you like Ken Landy?"

"No, not really. At first things were okay but then everything changed."

"You, in fact, attempted to run away from home just a few months before your sister's death, isn't that right?"

"Yes."

"I show you People's exhibit twelve, a police report dated November thirtieth, nineteen eighty-five. Can you tell the jury what that is?"

McPherson delivered copies of the report to the witness, the judge and the defense table. Bosch had found the report during his record search on the case. It had been a lucky break.

"It's a missing persons report," Gleason said. "My mother reported me missing."

"And did the police find you?"

"No, I just came home. I didn't have anyplace to go."

"Why did you run away, Sarah?"

"Because my stepfather...was having sex with me."

McPherson nodded and let the answer hang out there in the courtroom for a long moment. Three days ago Bosch would have expected Royce to jump all over this part of the testimony but now he knew that this played to the defense's case as well. Kensington Landy was the straw man and any testimony that supported that would be welcomed.

"When did this start?" McPherson finally asked.

"The summer before I ran away," Gleason responded. "The summer before Melissa got taken."

"Sarah, I am sorry to put you through these bad memories. You testified earlier that you and Melissa shared some of each other's clothes, correct?"

"Yes."

"The dress she wore on the day she was taken, that was your dress, wasn't it?"

"Yes."

McPherson then introduced the dress as the state's next exhibit and Bosch set it up for display to the jury on a headless manikin he placed in front of the jury box.

"Is this the dress, Sarah?"

"Yes, it is."

"Now, you notice that there is a square of material removed from the bottom front hem of the dress. You see that, Sarah?"

"Yes."

"Do you know why that was removed?"

"Yes, because they found semen on the dress there."

"You mean forensic investigators?"

"Yes."

"Now, is this something you knew back at the time of your sister's death?"

"I know it now. I wasn't told about it back then."

"Do you know who the semen was genetically identified as belonging to?"

"Yes, I was told it came from my stepfather."

"Did that surprise you?"

"No, unfortunately."

"Do you have any explanation for how it could have gotten on your dress?"

Now Royce objected, saying that the question called for speculation. It also called for the witness to diverge from the defense theory, but he didn't mention that. Breitman sustained the objection and McPherson had to find another way of getting there.

"Sarah, prior to your sister borrowing your dress on the morning she was abducted, when was the last time you wore it?"

Royce stood and objected again.

"Same objection. We're speculating about events twenty-four years old and when this witness was only thirteen years old."

"Your Honor," McPherson rejoined, "Mr. Royce was fine with this so-called speculation when it fit with the defense's scheme of things. But now he objects as we get to the heart of the matter. This is not speculation. Ms. Gleason is testifying truthfully about the darkest, saddest days of her life and I don't think—"

"Objection overruled," Breitman said. "The witness may answer."

"Thank you, Your Honor."

As McPherson repeated the question Bosch studied the jury. He wanted to see if they saw what he saw—a defense attorney attempting to stop the forward progression of truth. Bosch had found Sarah Gleason's testimony to be fully convincing up to this point. He wanted to hear what she had to say and his hope was that the jury was in the same boat and would look unkindly upon defense efforts to stop her.

"I wore it two nights before," Gleason said.

"That would have been Friday night, the fourteenth. Valentine's Day."

"Yes."

"Why did you wear the dress?"

"My mother was making a nice dinner for Valentine's Day and my stepfather said we should get dressed up for it."

Gleason was looking down again, losing all eye contact with the jurors.

"Did your stepfather engage in a sexual act with you on that night?"

"Yes."

"Were you wearing the dress at the time?"

"Yes."

"Sarah, do you know if your father ejac—"

"*He wasn't my father!*"

She yelled it and her voice echoed in the courtroom, reverberating around a hundred people who now knew her darkest secret. Bosch looked at McPherson and saw her checking out the jury's reaction. It was then Bosch knew that the mistake had been intentional.

"I am sorry, Sarah. I meant your stepfather. Do you know, did he ejaculate in the course of this moment with you?"

"Yes, and some of it got on my dress."

McPherson studied her notes, flipping over several pages of her yellow pad. She wanted that last answer to hang out there as long as possible.

"Sarah, who did the laundry at your house?"

"A lady came. Her name was Abby."

"After that Valentine's Day, did you put your dress in the laundry?"

"No, I didn't."

"Why not?"

"Because I was afraid Abby would find it and know what happened. I thought she might tell my mother or call the police."

"Why would that have been a bad thing, Sarah?"

"I...my mother was happy and I didn't want to ruin things for her."

"So what did you do with the dress that night?"

"I cleaned off the spot and hung it in my closet. I didn't know my sister was going to wear it."

"So two days later when she wanted to put it on, what did you say?"

"She already had it on when I saw her. I told her that I wanted to wear it but she said it was too late because it wasn't on my list of clothes I didn't share with her."

"Could you see the stain on the dress?"

"No, I looked and because it was down at the hem I didn't see any stain."

McPherson paused again. Bosch knew from the prep work that she had covered all the points she wanted to in this line of questioning. She had sufficiently explained the DNA that was the cause of everyone's being here. She now had to take Gleason further down the road of her dark journey. Because if she didn't, Royce certainly would.

"Sarah, did your relationship with your stepfather change after your sister's death?"

"Yes."

"How so?"

"He never touched me again."

"Do you know why? Did you talk to him about it?"

"I don't know why. I never talked to him about it. It just never happened again and he tried to act like it had never happened in the first place."

"But for you, all of this — your stepfather, your sister's death — it took a toll, didn't it?"

"Yes."

"In what way, Sarah?"

"Uh, well, I started getting into drugs and I ran away again. I ran away a lot, actually. I didn't care about sex. It was something I used to get what I needed."

"And were you ever arrested?"

"Yes, a bunch of times."

"For what?"

"Drugs mostly. I got arrested once for soliciting an undercover, too. And for stealing."

"You were arrested six times as a juvenile and five more times as an adult, is that correct?"

"I didn't keep count."

"What drugs were you taking?"

"Crystal meth mostly. But if there was something else available, I would probably take it. That was the way I was."

"Did you ever receive counseling and rehabilitation?"

"A lot of times. It didn't work at first and then it did. I got clean."

"When was that?"

"About seven years ago. When I was thirty."

"You've been clean for seven years?"

"Yes, totally. My life is different now."

"I want to show you People's exhibit thirteen, which is an intake and evaluation form from a private rehab center in Los Angeles called the Pines. Do you remember going there?"

"Yes, my mother sent me there when I was sixteen."

"Was that when you first started getting into trouble?"

"Yes."

McPherson distributed copies of the evaluation form to the judge, clerk and defense table.

"Okay, Sarah, I want to draw your attention to the paragraph I have outlined in yellow in the evaluation section of the intake form. Can you please read it out loud to the jury?"

"Candidate reports PTSD in regard to the murder of her younger sister three years ago. Suffers unresolved guilt associated with murder and also evinces behavior typical of sexual abuse. Full psych and physical evaluation is recommended."

"Thank you, Sarah. Do you know what PTSD means?"

"Post-traumatic stress disorder."

"Did you undergo these recommended evaluations at the Pines?"

"Yes."

"Did discussion of your stepfather's sexual abuse come up?"

"No, because I lied."

"How so?"

"By then I'd had sex with other men, so I never mentioned my stepfather."

"Before revealing what you have today in court, did you ever talk about your stepfather and his having sex with you with anyone?"

"Just you and Detective Bosch. Nobody else."

"Have you been married?"

"Yes."

"More than once?"

"Yes."

"And you didn't even tell your husbands about this?"

"No. It's not the kind of thing you want to tell anybody. You keep it to yourself."

"Thank you, Sarah. I have no further questions."

McPherson took her pad and returned to her seat, where she was greeted with a squeeze on the arm by Haller. It was a gesture designed for the jury to see but by then all eyes were on Royce. It was his turn and Bosch's measure of the room was that Sarah Gleason had everybody riding with her. Any effort by Royce to destroy her ran the strong risk of backfiring against his client.

Royce did the smart thing. He decided to let emotions cool for a night. He stood and told the judge that he reserved the right to recall Gleason as a witness during the defense phase of the trial. In effect he put off her cross-examination. He then retook his seat.

Bosch checked his watch. It was four-fifteen. The judge told Haller to call his next witness but Bosch knew there were no more witnesses. Haller looked at McPherson and in unison they nodded. Haller then stood up.

"Your Honor," he said. "The People rest."

35

The prosecution team convened for dinner at Casa Haller. I made a thick Bolognese using a store-bought sauce for a base and boiled a box of bow tie pasta. Maggie chipped in with her own recipe for Caesar salad that I had always loved when we were married but hadn't had in years. Bosch and his daughter were the last to arrive, as Harry first took Sarah Ann Gleason back to her hotel room following court and made sure she was secure for the night.

Our daughters were shy upon meeting and embarrassed by how obvious their parents were about watching the long-awaited moment. They instinctively knew to move away from us and convened in the back office, ostensibly to do their homework. Pretty soon after, we started to hear laughter from down the hall.

I put the pasta and sauce into a big bowl and mixed it all together. I then called the girls out first to serve themselves and take their dishes back to the office.

"How's it going back there, anyway?" I asked them while they were making their plates. "Any homework getting done?"

"Dad," Hayley said dismissively, as if my question were a great invasion of privacy.

So I tried the cousin.

"Maddie?"

"Um, I'm almost finished with mine."

Both girls looked at each other and laughed, as if either the question or its answer were cause for great glee. They scurried out of the kitchen then and back to the office.

I put everything out on the table, where the adults were sitting. The last thing I did was make sure the door to the office was closed so the girls would not hear our conversation and we would not hear theirs.

"Well," I said as I passed the pasta to Bosch. "We're finished with our part. Now comes the hard part."

"The defense," Maggie said. "What do we think they have in store for Sarah?"

I thought for a moment before answering and tried my first bow tie. It was good. I was proud of my dish.

"We know they'll throw everything they can at her," I finally said. "She's the case."

Bosch reached inside his jacket and brought out a folded piece of paper. He opened it on the table. I could see that it was the defense's witness list.

"At the end of court today Royce told the judge he would complete the defense's case in one day," he said. "He said he's calling only four witnesses but he's got twenty-three listed on here."

"Well, we knew all along that most of that list was subterfuge," Maggie said. "He was hiding his case."

"Okay, so we have Sarah coming back," I said, holding up one finger. "Then we have Jessup himself. My guess is that Royce knows he has to put him on. That's two. Who else?"

Maggie waited until she finished a mouthful of food before speaking.

"Hey, this is good, Haller. When did you learn to make this?"

"It's a little thing I like to call Newman's Own."

"No, you added to it. You made it better. How come you never cooked like this when we were married?"

"I guess it came out of necessity. Being a single father. What about you, Harry? What do you cook?"

Bosch looked at us both like we were crazy.

"I can fry an egg," he said. "That's about it."

"Let's get back to the trial," Maggie said. "I think Royce has got Jessup and Sarah. Then I think he's got the secret witness we haven't found. The guy from the last rehab center."

"Edward Roman," Bosch said.

"Right. Roman. That makes three and the fourth one could be his investigator or maybe his meth expert but is probably just bullshit. There is no fourth. So much of what Royce does is misdirection. He doesn't want anybody's eyes on the prize. Wants them looking anywhere but right at the truth."

"What about Roman?" I said. "We haven't found him, but have we figured out his testimony?"

"Not by a long shot," Maggie said. "I've gone over and over this with Sarah and she has no idea what he's going to say. She couldn't remember ever talking about her sister with him."

"The summary Royce provided in discovery says he will testify about Sarah's 'revelations' about her childhood," Bosch said. "Nothing more specific than that and, of course, Royce claims he didn't take any notes during the interview."

"Look," I said, "we have his record and we know exactly what kind of guy we're dealing with here. He's going to say whatever Royce wants him to say. It's that simple. Whatever works for the defense. So we should be less concerned by what he says—because we know it will be lies—and more concerned with knocking him out of the box. What do we have that can help us there?"

Maggie and I both looked at Bosch and he was ready for us.

"I think I might have something. I'm going to go see somebody tonight. If it pans out we'll have it in the morning. I'll tell you then."

My frustrations with Bosch's methods of investigation and communication boiled over at that point.

"Harry, come on. We're part of a team here. This secret agent stuff doesn't really work when we're in that courtroom every day with our asses on the line."

Bosch looked down at his plate and I saw the slow burn. His face grew as dark as the sauce.

"*Your* asses on the line?" he said. "I didn't see anywhere in the surveillance reports that Jessup was hanging around outside your house, Haller, so don't tell me about your ass being on the line. Your job is in that courtroom. It's nice and safe and sometimes you win and sometimes you lose. But no matter what happens, you're back in court the next day. You want your ass on the line, try working out there."

He pointed out the window toward the view of the city.

"Hey, guys, let's just calm down here," Maggie said quickly. "Harry, what's the matter? Has Jessup gone back to Woodrow Wilson? Maybe we should just revoke this guy and put him back in lockup."

Bosch shook his head.

"Not to my street. He hasn't been back there since that first night and he hasn't been up to Mulholland in more than a week."

"Then what is it?"

Bosch put his fork down and pushed his plate back.

"We already know there's a good chance that Jessup has a gun from that meeting the SIS saw him have with a convicted gun dealer. They didn't see what he got from the guy, but since it came wrapped in a towel, it doesn't take a lot to figure it out. And then, you want to know what happened last night? Some bright guy on the surveillance decides to leave his post to use the john without telling anybody and Jessup walked right out of the net."

"They lost him?" Maggie asked.

"Yeah, until I found him right before he found me, which might not have turned out so well. And you know what he's up to? He's building a dungeon for somebody and for all I know—"

He leaned forward over the table and finished in an urgent whisper.

"—might be for my kid!"

"Whoa, wait, Harry," Maggie said. "Back up. He's building a dungeon? Where?"

"Under the pier. There's like a storage room. He put a lock on the door and dropped canned food off there last night. Like he's getting it ready for somebody."

"Okay, that's scary," Maggie said. "But your daughter? We don't know that. You said he went by your place only the one time. What makes you think—?"

"Because I can't afford not to think it. You understand?"

She nodded.

"Yes, I do. Then I come back to what I just said. We violate him for associating with a known criminal — the gun dealer — and pull his OR release. There's only a few days left in the trial and he obviously didn't act out or make the mistake we thought he would. Let's be safe and put him back inside until this is over."

"And what if we don't get the conviction?" Bosch said. "What happens then? This guy walks and that'll also be the end of the surveillance. He'll be out there without any eyes on him."

That brought a silence to the table. I stared at Bosch and understood the pressure he was under. The case, the threat to his daughter, and no wife or ex-wife to help him out at home.

Bosch finally broke the uneasy silence.

"Maggie, are you taking Hayley home with you tonight?"

Maggie nodded.

"Yes, when we're finished here."

"Can Maddie stay with you two tonight? She brought a change of clothes in her backpack. I'd come by in the morning in time to take her to school."

The request seemed to take Maggie by surprise, especially since the girls had just met. Bosch pressed her.

"I need to meet somebody tonight and I don't know where it will take me," Bosch said. "It might even lead to Roman. I need to be able to move without worrying about Maddie."

She nodded.

"Okay, that's fine. It sounds like they're becoming fast friends. I just hope they don't stay up all night."

"Thank you, Maggie."

About thirty seconds of silence went by before I spoke.

"Tell us about this dungeon, Harry."

"I was standing in it last night."

"Why the Santa Monica pier?"

"My guess is that it's because of the proximity to what's on top of the pier."

"Prey."

Bosch nodded.

"But what about noise? You're saying this place is directly below the pier?"

"There are ways of controlling human sound. And last night the sound of waves crashing against the pilings under there was so loud you could've screamed all night and nobody would've heard you. You probably wouldn't even hear a gunshot from down there."

Bosch spoke with a certain authority of the dark places of the world and the evil they held. I lost my appetite then and pushed my plate away. I felt dread come inside me.

Dread for Melissa Landy and all the other victims in the world.

36

~~~~~

Gilbert and Sullivan were waiting for him in a car parked on Lankershim Boulevard near its northern terminus at San Fernando Road. It was a blighted area populated primarily with used-car lots and repair shops. In the midst of all of this low-rent industry was a run-down motel advertising rooms for fifty dollars a week. The motel had no name on display. Just the lighted sign that said MOTEL.

Gilbert and Sullivan were Gilberto Reyes and John Sullivan, a pair of narcs assigned to the Valley Enforcement Team, a street-level drug unit. When Bosch was looking for Edward Roman he put the word out in all such units in the department. His assumption from Roman's record was that he had never gotten away from the life as Sarah Gleason had. There had to be somebody in the department's narco units with a line on him.

It paid off with a call from Reyes. He and his partner didn't have a bead on Roman but they knew him from past interactions on the street and knew where his current trick partner was holed up and apparently awaiting his return. Long-term drug addicts often partnered with a prostitute, offering her protection in exchange for a share of the drugs her earnings bought.

Bosch pulled his car up behind the narcs' UC car and parked. He got out and moved up to their car, getting in the back after checking the seat to make sure it was clean of vomit and any other detritus from the people they had transported lately.

"Detective Bosch, I presume?" said the driver, whom Bosch guessed was Reyes.

"Yeah, how are you guys?"

He offered his fist over the seat and they both gave him a bump while identifying themselves. Bosch had it wrong. The one who looked to be of Latin origin was Sullivan and the one who looked like a bag of white bread was Reyes.

"Gilbert and Sullivan, huh?"

"That's what they called us when we got partnered," Sullivan said. "Kind of stuck."

Bosch nodded. That was enough for the meet-and-greet. Everybody had a nickname and a story to go with it. These guys together didn't add up to

how old Bosch was and they probably had no clue who Gilbert and Sullivan were, anyway.

"So you know Eddie Roman?"

"We've had the pleasure," Reyes said. "Just another piece of human shit
that floats around out here."

"But like I told you on the phone, we ain't seen him in a month or so,"
Sullivan added. "So we got you his next best thing. His onion. She's over
there in room three."

"What's her name?"

Sullivan laughed and Bosch didn't get it.

"Her name is Sonia Reyes," said Reyes. "No relation."

"That he knows of," Sullivan added.

He burst into laughter, which Bosch ignored.

"Spell it for me," he said.

He took out his notebook and wrote it down.

"And you're sure she's in the room?"

"We're sure," Reyes said.

"Okay, anything else I should know before I go in?"

"No," Reyes said, "but we were planning on goin' in with you. She might
get squirrelly with you."

Bosch reached forward and clapped him on the shoulder.

"No, I got this. I don't want a crowd in the room."

Reyes nodded. Message delivered. Bosch did not want any witnesses to
what he might need to do here.

"But thanks for the help. It will be noted."

"An important case, huh?" Sullivan said.

Bosch opened the door and got out.

"They all are," he said.

He closed the door, slapped the roof twice and walked away.

The hotel had an eight-foot security fence around it. Bosch had to press a
buzzer and hold his badge up to a camera. He was buzzed into the com-
pound but walked right by the office and down a breezeway leading to the
rooms.

"Hey!" a voice called from behind.

Bosch turned and saw a man with an unbuttoned shirt leaning out the
door of the motel's office.

"Where the fuck you goin', dude?"

"Go back inside and shut the door. This is police business."

"Don't matter, man. I let you in but this is private property. You can't just
come through the—"

Bosch started quickly moving back up the breezeway toward the man.
The man took his measure and backed down without Bosch saying a word.

"Never mind, man. You're good."

He quickly stepped back inside and closed the door. Bosch turned back and found room three without a further problem. He leaned close to the jamb to see if he could pick up any sound. He heard nothing.

There was a peephole. He put his finger over it and knocked. He waited and then knocked again.

"Sonia, open up. Eddie sent me."

"Who are you?"

The voice was female, ragged and suspicious. Bosch used the universal pass code.

"Doesn't matter. Eddie sent me with somethin' to hold you over till he's done."

No response.

"Okay, Sonia, I'll tell him you weren't interested. I've got someone else who wants it."

He took his finger off the peep and started walking away. Almost immediately the door opened behind him.

"Wait."

Bosch turned back. The door was open six inches. He saw a set of hollow eyes looking out at him, a dim light behind them.

"Let me see."

Bosch looked around.

"What, out here?" he said. "They got cameras all over the place."

"Eddie tol' me not to open the door for strangers. You look like a cop to me."

"Well, maybe I am, but that doesn't change that Eddie sent me."

Bosch started to turn again.

"Like I said, I'll tell him I tried. Have a nice night."

"Okay, okay. You can come in but only to make the drop. Nothing else."

Bosch walked back toward the door. She moved behind it and opened it. He entered and turned to her and saw the gun. It was an old revolver and he saw no bullets in the exposed chambers. Bosch raised his hands chest high. He could tell she was hurting. She'd been waiting too long for somebody, putting blind junkie trust in something that wouldn't pay off.

"That's not necessary, Sonia. Besides, I don't think Eddie left you with any bullets."

"I got one left. You want to try it?"

Probably the one she was saving for herself. She was skin and bones and close to the end of the line. No junkie went the distance.

"Give it to me," she ordered. "Now."

"Okay, take it easy. I have it right here."

He reached his right hand into his coat pocket and pulled out a balled piece of aluminum foil he had taken from a roll in Mickey Haller's kitchen. He held it out to the right of his body and he knew her desperate eyes would follow it. He shot his left hand out and snatched the gun out of her hand. He then stepped forward and roughly shoved her onto the bed.

"Shut up and don't move," he commanded.

"What is —?"

"I said shut up!"

He popped the gun's barrel out and checked it. She had been right. There was one bullet left. He slid it out into his palm and then put it in his pocket. He hooked the gun into his belt. Then he pulled his badge wallet and opened it for her to see.

"You had that right," he said.

"What do you want?"

"We'll get to that."

Bosch moved around the bed, looking about the threadbare room. It smelled like cigarettes and body odor. There were several plastic grocery bags on the floor containing her belongings. Shoes in one, clothing in a few others. On the bed's lone side table was an overloaded ashtray and a glass pipe.

"What are you hurting for, Sonia. Crack? Heroin? Or is it meth?"

She didn't answer.

"I can help you better if I know what you need."

"I don't want your help."

Bosch turned and looked at her. So far things were going exactly as he predicted they would.

"Really?" he said. "Don't need my help? You think Eddie Roman is going to come back for you?"

"He's coming back."

"I got news for you. He's already gone. I'm guessing they got him cleaned up nice and neat and he won't be coming back up here once he does what they want him to do. He'll take the paycheck and when that runs out he'll just find himself a new trick partner."

He paused and looked at her.

"Somebody who still has something somebody would want to buy."

Her eyes took on the distant look of someone who knows the truth when she hears it.

"Leave me alone," she said in a hoarse whisper.

"I know I'm not telling you anything you don't already know. You've been waiting for Eddie longer than you thought you would, huh? How many days you have left on the room?"

He read the answer in her eyes.

"Already past, huh? Probably giving the guy in the office blowjobs to let you stay. How long's that going to last? Pretty soon he'll just want the money."

"I said go away."

"I will. But you come with me, Sonia. Right now."

"What do you want?"

"I want to know everything you know about Eddie Roman."

PART FOUR

— The Silent Witness

37

Thursday, April 8, 9:01 A.M.

Before the judge called for the jury, Clive Royce stood and asked the court for a directed verdict of acquittal. He argued that the state had failed to live up to its duty in carrying the burden of proof. He said that the evidence presented by the prosecutors failed to cross the threshold of guilt beyond a reasonable doubt. I was ready to stand to argue the state's side, but the judge held up her hand to signal me to stay in place. She then quickly dispensed with Royce's motion.

"Motion denied," Breitman said. "The court holds that the evidence presented by the prosecution is sufficient for the jury to consider. Mr. Royce, are you ready to proceed with the defense?"

"I am, Your Honor."

"Okay, sir, then we will recall the jury now. Will you have an opening statement?"

"A brief one, Your Honor."

"Very well, I am going to hold you to that."

The jurors filed in and took their assigned places. On many of them I saw expressions of anticipation. I took this as a good sign, as if they were wondering how in the hell the defense would be able to dig its way out of all the evidence the state had dumped on it. It was probably all wishful thinking on my part, but I had been studying juries for most of my adult life and I liked what I saw.

After welcoming the jury back, the judge turned the courtroom over to Royce, reminded the jurors that this was an opening statement, not a listing of facts unless backed up later with testimony and evidence. Royce strode with full confidence to the lectern without a note or file in his hand. I knew he had the same philosophy as I did when it came to making opening statements. Look them in the eyes and don't flinch and don't back down from your theory, no matter how far-fetched or unbelievable. Sell it. If they don't think you believe it, they never will.

His strategy of deferring his opener until the start of the defense's case would now pay dividends. He would begin the day and his case by delivering to the jury a statement that didn't have to be true, that could be as outlandish as anything ever heard in the courtroom. As long as he kept the jury riding along, nothing else really mattered.

"Ladies and gentlemen of the jury, good morning. Today begins a new phase of the trial. The defense phase. This is when we start to tell you our side of the story, and believe me, we have another side to almost everything the prosecution has offered you over the past three days.

"I am not going to take a lot of your time here because I am very eager, and Jason Jessup is very eager, to get to the evidence that the prosecution has either failed to find or chosen not to present to you. It doesn't matter which, at this point; the only things that matter are that you hear it and that it allows you to see the full picture of what transpired on Windsor Boulevard on February sixteenth, nineteen eighty-six. I urge you to listen closely, to watch closely. If you do that, you will see the truth emerge."

I looked over at the legal pad on which Maggie had been doodling while Royce spoke. In large letters she had written *WINDBAG!* I thought, She hasn't seen anything yet.

"This case," Royce continued, "is about one thing. A family's darkest secrets. You got only a glimpse of them during the prosecution's presentation. You got the tip of the iceberg from the prosecution, but today you will get the whole iceberg. Today you will get the cold hard truth. That being that Jason Jessup is the true victim here today. The victim of a family's desire to hide their darkest secret."

Maggie leaned toward me and whispered, "Brace yourself."

I nodded. I knew exactly where we were going.

"This trial is about a monster who killed a child. A monster who defiled one young girl and was going to move on to the next when something went wrong and he killed that child. This trial is about the family that was so fearful of that monster that they went along with the plan to cover up the crime and point the finger elsewhere. At an innocent man."

Royce pointed righteously at Jessup as he said this last line. Maggie shook her head in disgust, a calculated move for the jury.

"Jason, would you please stand up?" Royce said.

His client did as instructed and turned fully to the jury, his eyes boldly scanning from face to face, not flinching or looking away.

"Jason Jessup is an innocent man," Royce said with the requisite outrage in his voice. "He was the fall guy. An innocent man caught in an impromptu plan to cover up the worst kind of crime, the taking of a child's life."

Jessup sat down and Royce paused so his words would burn into every juror's conscience. It was highly theatrical and planned that way.

"There are two victims here," he finally said. "Melissa Landy is a victim. She lost her life. Jason Jessup is also a victim because they are trying to take his life. The family conspired against him and then the police followed their lead. They ignored the evidence and planted their own. And now after twenty-four years, after witnesses are gone and memories have dimmed, they've come calling for him..."

Royce cast his head down as if tremendously burdened by the truth. I knew he would now wrap things up.

"Ladies and gentlemen of the jury, we are here for only one reason. To seek the truth. Before the end of this day, you will know the truth about Windsor Boulevard. You will know that Jason Jessup is an innocent man."

Royce paused again, then thanked the jury and moved back to his seat. In what I was sure was a well-rehearsed moment, Jessup put his arm around his lawyer's shoulders, gave him a squeeze and thanked him.

But the judge gave Royce little time to savor the moment or the slick delivery of his opening statement. She told him to call his first witness. I turned in my seat and saw Bosch standing in the back of the courtroom. He gave me the nod. I had sent him to get Sarah Ann Gleason from the hotel as soon as Royce had informed me upon arriving at court that she would be his first witness.

"The *defense* calls Sarah Ann Gleason to the stand," Royce said, putting the accent on defense in a way that suggested that this was an unexpected turnabout.

Bosch stepped out of the courtroom and quickly returned with Gleason. He walked her down the aisle and through the gate. She went the rest of the way on her own. She again was dressed for court informally, wearing a white peasant blouse and a pair of jeans.

Gleason was reminded by the judge that she was still under oath and turned over to Royce. This time when he went to the lectern he carried a thick file and a legal pad. Probably most of it — the file, at least — was just an attempt to intimidate Gleason, to make her think he had a big fat file on everything she had ever done wrong in life.

"Good morning, Ms. Gleason."

"Good morning."

"Now, you testified yesterday that you were the victim of sexual abuse at the hands of your stepfather, Kensington Landy, is that correct?"

"Yes."

With the first word of her testimony I detected trepidation. She hadn't been allowed to hear Royce's opening statement but we had prepared Gleason for the way we thought the defense case would go. She was exhibiting fear already and this never played well with the jury. There was little Maggie and I could do. Sarah was up there on her own.

"At what point in your life did this abuse start?"

"When I was twelve."

"And it ended when?"

"When I was thirteen. Right after my sister's death."

"I notice you didn't call it your sister's murder. You called it her death. Is there a reason for that?"

"I'm not sure what you mean."

"Well, your sister was murdered, correct? It wasn't an accident, was it?"

"No, it was murder."

"Then why did you refer to it as her death just a moment ago?"

"I'm not sure."

"Are you confused about what happened to your sister?"

Maggie was on her feet objecting before Gleason could answer.

"Counsel is badgering the witness," she said. "He's more interested in eliciting an emotional response than an answer."

"Your Honor, I simply am trying to learn how and why this witness views this crime the way she does. It goes to state of mind of the witness. I am not interested in eliciting anything other than an answer to the question I asked."

The judge weighed things for a moment before ruling.

"I'm going to allow it. The witness may answer the question."

"I'll repeat it," Royce said. "Ms. Gleason, are you confused about what happened to your sister?"

During the exchange between lawyers and the judge, Gleason had found some resolve. She answered forcefully while hitting Royce with a hard stare of defiance.

"No, I'm not confused about what happened. I was there. She was kidnapped by your client and after that I never saw her again. There is no confusion about that at all."

I wanted to stand and clap. Instead, I just nodded to myself. It was a fine, fine answer. But Royce moved on, acting as though he had not been hit with the tomato.

"There have been times in your life when you were confused, however, correct?"

"About my sister and what happened and who took her? Never."

"I'm talking about times you were incarcerated in mental health facilities and the psych wards of jails and prisons."

Gleason lowered her head in full realization that she would not escape this trial without a full airing of the lost years of her life. I just had to hope she would respond in the way Maggie had told her to.

"After the murder of my sister, many things went wrong in my life," she said.

She then looked up directly at Royce as she continued.

"Yes, I spent some time in those kinds of places. I think, and my counselors agreed, that it was because of what happened to Melissa."

Good answer, I thought. She was fighting.

"We'll get back into that later on," Royce said. "But getting back to your sister, she was twelve at the time of her murder, correct?"

"That's right."

"This would have been the same age you were when your stepfather began to sexually abuse you. Am I right?"

"About the same, yes."

"Did you warn your sister about him?"

There was a long pause as Gleason considered her answer. This was because there was no good answer.

"Ms. Gleason?" the judge prompted. "Please answer the question."

"No, I didn't warn her. I was afraid to."

"Afraid of what?" Royce asked.

"Him. As you've already pointed out, I've been through a lot of therapy in my life. I know that it is not unusual for a child to be unable to tell anyone. You get trapped in the behavior. Trapped by fear. I've been told that many times."

"In other words, you go along to get along."

"Sort of. But that is a simplification. It was more—"

"But you did live with a lot of fear in your life back then?"

"Yes, I—"

"Did your stepfather tell you not to tell anyone about what he was doing to you?"

"Yes, he said—"

"Did he threaten you?"

"He said that if I told anyone I would be taken away from my mother and sister. He said he would make sure that the state would think my mother knew about it and they would consider her unfit. They would take Melissa and me away. Then we would get split up because foster homes couldn't always take two at a time."

"Did you believe him?"

"Yes, I was twelve. I believed him."

"And it scared you, didn't it?"

"Yes. I wanted to stay with my fam—"

"Wasn't it that same fear and control that your stepfather had over you that made you go along to get along after he killed your sister?"

Again Maggie jumped up to object, stating that the question was leading and assumed facts not in evidence. The judge agreed and sustained the objection.

Undeterred, Royce went at Gleason relentlessly.

"Isn't it true that you and your mother did and said exactly what your stepfather told you to in the cover-up of Melissa's murder?"

"No, that's not—"

"He told you to say it was a tow truck driver and that you were to pick one of the men the police brought to the house."

"No! He didn't—"

"Objection!"

"There was no hide-and-seek game outside the house, was there? Your sister was murdered inside the house by Kensington Landy. Isn't that true!"

"Your Honor!"

Maggie was now shouting.

"Counsel is badgering the witness with these leading questions. He doesn't want her answers. He just wants to deliver his lies to the jury!"

The judge looked from Maggie to Royce.

"All right, everyone just calm down. The objection is sustained. Mr. Royce, ask the witness one question at a time and allow her the time to answer. And you will not ask leading questions. Need I remind you, you called her as a witness. If you wanted to lead her you should've conducted a cross-examination when you had the opportunity."

Royce put on his best look of contrition. It must've been difficult.

"I apologize for getting carried away, Your Honor," he said. "It won't happen again."

It didn't matter if it happened again. Royce had already gotten his point across. His purpose was not to get an admission from Gleason. In fact, he expected none. His purpose was to get his alternate theory to the jury. In that, he was being very successful.

"Okay, let's move on," Royce said. "You mentioned earlier that you spent a considerable part of your adult life in counseling and drug rehab, not to mention incarceration. Is that correct?"

"To a point," Gleason said. "I have been clean and sober and a —"

"Just answer the question that was asked," Royce quickly interjected.

"Objection," Maggie said. "She is trying to answer the question he asked, but Mr. Royce doesn't like the full answer and is trying to cut her off."

"Let her answer the question, Mr. Royce," Breitman said tiredly. "Go ahead, Ms. Gleason."

"I was just saying that I have been clean for seven years and a productive member of society."

"Thank you, Ms. Gleason."

Royce then led her through a tragic and sordid history, literally going arrest by arrest and revealing all the details of the depravity Sarah wallowed in for so long. Maggie objected often, arguing that it had little to do with Sarah's identification of Jessup, but Breitman allowed most of the questioning to continue.

Finally, Royce wrapped up his examination by setting up his next witness.

"Getting back to the rehabilitation center in North Hollywood, you were there for five months in nineteen ninety-nine, correct?"

"I don't remember exactly when or for how long. You obviously have the records there."

"But you do remember meeting another client, named Edward Roman, known as Eddie?"

"Yes, I do."

"And you got to know him well?"

"Yes."

"How did you meet him?"

"We were in group counseling together."

"How would you describe the relationship you had with Eddie Roman back then?"

"Well, in counseling we sort of realized that we knew some of the same people and liked doing the same things — meaning drugs. So we started hanging out and it continued after we were both released."

"Was this a romantic relationship?"

Gleason laughed in a way that was not supposed to impart humor.

"What passed for romance between two drug addicts," she said. "I think the term is *enablers*. By being together we were enabling each other. But *romance* is not a word I would use. We had sex on occasion — when he was able to. But there was no romance, Mr. Royce."

"But didn't you in fact believe at one point that you two were married?"

"Eddie set something up on the beach with a man he said was a minister. But it wasn't real. It wasn't legal."

"But at the time you thought it was, didn't you?"

"Yes."

"So were you in love with him?"

"No, I wasn't in love with him. I just thought he could protect me."

"So you were married, or at least thought you were. Did you live together?"

"Yes."

"Where?"

"In different motels in the Valley."

"All this time you were together, you must've confided in Eddie, yes?"

"About some things, yes."

"Did you ever confide in him about your sister's murder?"

"I am sure I did. I didn't keep it a secret. I would have talked about it in group therapy in North Hollywood and he was sitting right there."

"Did you ever tell him that your stepfather killed your sister?"

"No, because that didn't happen."

"So if Eddie Roman were to come to this courtroom and testify that you did indeed tell him that, then he would be lying."

"Yes."

"But you have already testified yesterday and today that you have lied to counselors and police. You have stolen and committed many crimes in your life. But you're not lying here. Is that what we are to believe?"

"I'm not lying. You are talking about a period of my life when I did those things. I don't deny that. I was human trash, okay? But I am past that now and have been past it for a long time. I'm not lying now."

"Okay, Ms. Gleason, no further questions."

As Royce returned to his seat, Maggie and I put our heads together and whispered.

"She held up really well," Maggie said. "I think we should let it stand and I'll just hit a couple high notes."

"Sounds good."

"Ms. McPherson?" the judge prompted.

Maggie stood.

"Yes, Your Honor. Just a few questions."

She went to the lectern with her trusty legal pad. She skipped the buildup and got right to the matters she wanted to cover.

"Sarah, this man Eddie Roman and the phony marriage — whose idea was it to get married?"

"Eddie asked me to get married. He said we would work together as a team and share everything, that he would protect me and that we could never be forced to testify against each other if we got arrested."

"And what did working together as a team mean in that circumstance?"

"Well, I...he wanted me to sell myself so we would have money to buy drugs and to have a motel room."

"Did you do that for Eddie?"

"For a little bit of time. And then I got arrested."

"Did Eddie bail you out?"

"No."

"Did he come to court?"

"No."

"Your record shows you pleaded guilty to soliciting and were sentenced to time served, is that correct?"

"Yes."

"How long was that?"

"I think it was thirteen days."

"And was Eddie there waiting when you got out of jail?"

"No."

"Did you ever see him again?"

"No, I didn't."

Maggie checked her notes, flipped up a couple pages and found what she was looking for.

"Okay, Sarah, you mentioned several times during your testimony earlier today that you did not remember specific dates and occurrences that Mr. Royce asked you about during the time you were a drug user. Is that a fair characterization?"

"Yes, that's true."

"During all of those years of drug abuse and counseling and incarceration, were you ever able to forget what happened to your sister, Melissa?"

"No, never. I thought about it every day. I still do."

"Were you ever able to forget about the man who crossed your front yard and grabbed your sister while you watched from the bushes?"

"No, never. I thought about him every day and still do."

"Have you ever had a moment of doubt about the man you identified as your sister's abductor?"

"No."

Maggie turned and pointedly looked at Jessup, who was looking down at a legal pad and writing what were probably meaningless notes. Her eyes held on him and she waited. Just as Jessup looked up to see what was holding up the testimony she asked her last question.

"Never a single doubt, Sarah?"

"No, never."

"Thank you, Sarah. No further questions."

38

Thursday, April 8, 10:35 A.M.

The judge followed Sarah Gleason's testimony by announcing the mid-morning break. Bosch waited in his seat at the railing until Royce and Jessup got up and started to file out. He then stood and moved against the grain to get to his witness. As he passed by Jessup he clapped him hard on the arm.

"I think your makeup's starting to run, Jason."

He said it with a smile as he went by.

Jessup stopped and turned and was about to respond to the taunt when Royce grabbed him by the other arm and kept him going.

Bosch moved forward to collect Gleason from the witness stand. After parts of two days on the stand, she looked like she was both emotionally and physically drained. Like she might need help just getting up from the chair.

"Sarah, you did great," he told her.

"Thank you. I couldn't tell if anybody believed me."

"They all did, Sarah. They all did."

He walked her back to the prosecution table, where Haller and McPherson had similar reviews of her testimony. McPherson got up out of her seat and hugged her.

"You stood up to Jessup and you stood up for your sister," she said. "You can be proud of that for the rest of your life."

Gleason suddenly burst into tears and held her hand over her eyes. McPherson quickly pulled her back into the hug.

"I know, I know. You've held it together and stayed strong. It's okay to let it go now."

Bosch walked over to the jury box and grabbed the box of tissues. He brought them to Gleason and she wiped away her tears.

"You're almost done," Haller said to her. "You've totally finished testifying so now all we want you to do is sit in court and observe the trial. We want you to sit up here in the front row when Eddie Roman testifies. After that, we can put you on a plane home this afternoon."

"Okay, but why?"

"Because he's going to tell lies about you. And if he is going to do that, then he's going to have to tell them to your face."

"I don't think he's going to have a problem with that. He never did."

"Well, then, the jury will want to see how you react. And how he'll react. And don't worry, we've got something else cooking that'll make Eddie feel some heat."

At that, Haller turned to Bosch.

"You ready with this?"

"Just give me the sign."

"Can I ask something?" Gleason said.

"Sure," Haller said.

"What if I don't want to get on a plane today? What if I want to be here for the verdict? For my sister."

"We would love that, Sarah," Maggie said. "You are welcome and can stay as long as you like."

Bosch stood in the hallway outside the courtroom. He had his phone out and was slowly typing a text to his daughter with one finger. His efforts were interrupted when he received a text. It was from Haller and was only one word.

NOW

He put his phone away and walked to the witness waiting room. Sonia Reyes was slumped in a chair with her head down, two empty coffee cups on the table in front of her.

"Okay, Sonia, rise and shine. We're going to go do this. You okay? You ready?"

She looked up at him with tired eyes.

"That's too many questions, po-liceman."

"Okay, I'll settle for one. How're you feeling?"

"About how I look. You got any more of that stuff they gave me at the clinic?"

"That was it. But I'm going to have someone take you right back there as soon as we're finished here."

"Whatever you say, po-liceman. I don't think I've been up this early since the last time I was in county lockup."

"Yeah, well, it's not that early. Let's go."

He helped her up and they headed toward Department 112. Reyes was what they called a *silent witness*. She wouldn't be testifying in the trial. She was in no condition to. But by walking her down the aisle and putting her in the front row, Bosch would make sure she would be noticed by Edward Roman. The hope was that she'd knock Roman off his game, maybe even make him change it up. They were banking on his not knowing the rules of evidence and therefore not understanding that her appearance in the gallery precluded her from testifying at the trial and exposing his lies.

Harry hit the door with a fist as he pushed it open because he knew it would draw attention inside the court. He then ushered Reyes in and walked her down the aisle. Edward Roman was already on the stand, sworn in and testifying. He wore an ill-fitting suit borrowed from Royce's client closet and was clean-shaven with short, neat hair. He stumbled verbally when he saw Sonia in the courtroom.

"We had group counseling twice..."

"Only twice?" Royce asked, unaware of the distraction in the aisle behind him.

"What?"

"You said you only had group counseling with Sarah Gleason twice?"

"Nah, man, I meant twice a day."

Bosch escorted Reyes to a seat with a reserved sign on it. He then sat down next to her.

"And approximately how long did this last?" Royce asked.

"Each one was fifty minutes, I think," Roman answered, his eyes holding on Reyes in the audience.

"I mean how long were you both in counseling? A month, a year, how long?"

"Oh, it was for five months."

"And did you become lovers while you were in the center?"

Roman lowered his eyes.

"Uh... yeah, that's right."

"How did you manage that? I assume there are rules against that."

"Well, if there's a will, there's always a way, you know? We found time. We found places."

"Did this relationship continue after you two were released from the center?"

"Yes. She got out a couple weeks ahead of me. Then I got out and we hooked up."

"Did you live together?"

"Uh-huh."

"Is that a yes?"

"Yes. Can I ask a question?"

Royce paused. He hadn't expected this.

"No, Mr. Roman," the judge said. "You can't ask a question. You are a witness in these proceedings."

"But how can they bring her in here like that?"

"Who, Mr. Roman?"

Roman pointed out to the gallery and right at Reyes.

"Her."

The judge looked at Reyes and then at Bosch sitting next to her. A look of deep suspicion crossed her face.

"I'm going to ask the jury to step back into the jury room for a few moments. This should not take long."

The jurors filed back into the jury room. The moment the last one in closed the door, the judge zeroed in on Bosch.

"Detective Bosch."

Harry stood up.

"Who is the woman sitting to your left?"

"Your Honor," Haller said. "Can I answer that question?"

"Please do."

"Detective Bosch is sitting with Sonia Reyes, who has agreed to help the prosecution as a witness consultant."

The judge looked from Haller to Reyes and back to Haller.

"You want to run that by me again, Mr. Haller?"

"Judge, Ms. Reyes is acquainted with the witness. Because the defense did not make Mr. Roman available to us prior to his testimony here, we have asked Ms. Reyes to give us advice on how to proceed with our cross-examination."

Haller's explanation had done nothing to change the look of suspicion on Breitman's face.

"Are you paying her for this advice?"

"We have agreed to help her get into a clinic."

"I should hope so."

"Your Honor," Royce said. "May I be heard?"

"Go ahead, Mr. Royce."

"I think it is quite obvious that the prosecution is attempting to intimidate Mr. Roman. This is a gangster move, Judge. Not something I would expect to see from the District Attorney's Office."

"Well, I strongly object to that characterization," Haller said. "It is perfectly acceptable within the canon of courtroom procedure and ethics to hire and use consultants. Mr. Royce employed a jury consultant last week and that was perfectly acceptable. But now that the prosecution has a consultant that he knows will help expose his witness as a liar and someone who preys on women, he objects. With all due respect, I would call that the gangster move."

"Okay, we're not going to debate this now," Breitman said. "I find that the prosecution is certainly within bounds in using Ms. Reyes as a consultant. Let's bring the jury back."

"Thank you, Judge," Haller said as he sat down.

As the jurors filed back into the box, Haller turned and looked back at Bosch. He gave a slight nod and Bosch knew that he was happy. The exchange with the judge could not have worked better in delivering a message to Roman. The message being that we know your game, and come our turn to ask the questions, so will the jury. Roman now had a choice. He could stick with the defense or start playing for the prosecution.

Testimony continued once the jury was back in place. Royce quickly established through Roman that he and Sarah Gleason had a relationship that lasted nearly a year and involved the sharing of personal stories as well as drugs. But when it came to revealing those personal stories, Roman did a cut and run, leaving Royce hanging in the wind.

"Now, did there come a time when she spoke about her sister's murder?"

"A time? There were lots of times. She talked about it a lot, man."

"And did she ever tell you in detail what she called the 'real story'?"

"Yes, she did."

"Can you tell the court what she told you?"

Roman hesitated and scratched his chin before answering. Bosch knew this was the moment that his work either paid off or went for naught.

"She told me that they were playing hide-and-seek in the yard and a guy came and grabbed her sister and that she saw the whole thing."

Bosch's eyes made a circuit of the room. First he checked the jurors and it seemed that even they had been expecting Roman to say something else. Then the prosecution table. He saw that McPherson had grabbed Haller by the back of his arm and was squeezing it. And lastly Royce, who was now the one hesitating. He stood at the lectern looking down at his notes, one armed cocked with his fist on his hip like a frustrated teacher who could not draw the correct answer from a student.

"That is the story you heard Sarah Gleason tell in group counseling at the rehabilitation center, correct?" he finally asked.

"That's right."

"But isn't it true that she told you a different version of events — what she called the 'real story' — when you were in more private settings?"

"Uh, no. She pretty much stuck to the same story all the time."

Bosch saw McPherson squeeze Haller's arm again. This was the whole case right here.

Royce was like a man left behind in the water by a dive boat. He was treading water but he was in the open sea and it was only a matter of time before he went down. He tried to do what he could.

"Now, Mr. Roman, on March second of this year, did you not contact my office and offer your services as a witness for the defense?"

"I don't know about the date but I called there, yeah."

"And did you speak to my investigator, Karen Revelle?"

"I spoke to a woman but I can't remember her name."

"And didn't you tell her a story that is quite different from the one you just recounted?"

"But I wasn't under oath or nothin' then."

"That's right, sir, but you did tell Karen a different story, true?"

"I might've. I can't remember."

"Didn't you tell Karen at that time that Ms. Gleason had told you that her stepfather had killed her sister?"

Haller was up with the objection, arguing that not only was Royce leading the witness but that there was no foundation for the question and that counsel was trying to get testimony to the jury that the witness was not willing to give. The judge sustained the objection.

"Your Honor," Royce said, "the defense would like to request a short break to confer with its witness."

Before Haller could object the judge denied the request.

"By this witness's own testimony this morning, you have had since March second to prepare for this moment. We go to lunch in thirty-five minutes. You can confer with him then, Mr. Royce. Ask your next question."

"Thank you, Your Honor."

Royce looked down at his legal pad. From Bosch's angle he could tell he was looking at a blank page.

"Mr. Royce?" the judge prompted.

"Yes, Your Honor, just rechecking a date. Mr. Roman, why did you call my office on March second?"

"Well, I seen something about the case on the TV. In fact, it was you. I seen you talking about it. And I knew something about it from knowing Sarah like I did. So I called up to see if I was needed."

"And then you came to my offices, correct?"

"Yeah, that's right. You sent that lady to pick me up."

"And when you came to my office, you told me a different story than you are telling the jury now, isn't that right?"

"Like I said, I don't remember exactly what I said then. I'm a drug addict, sir. I say a lot of things I don't remember and don't really mean. All I remember is that the woman who came said she'd put me up in a nicer hotel and I had no money for a place at that time. So I sort of said what she told me to say."

Bosch made a fist and bounced it once on his thigh. This was an unmitigated disaster for the defense. He looked over at Jessup to see if he realized how bad things had just turned for him. And Jessup seemed to sense it. He turned and looked back at Bosch, his eyes dark with growing anger and realization. Bosch leaned forward and slowly raised a finger. He dragged it across his throat.

Jessup turned away.

39

Thursday, April 8, 11:30 A.M.

I have had many good moments in court. I've stood next to men at the moment they knew that they were going free because of my good work. I have stood in the well in front of a jury and felt the tingle of truth and righteousness roll down my spine. And I have destroyed liars without mercy on the witness stand. These are the moments I live for in my professional life. But few of them measured up to the moment I watched Jason Jessup's defense unravel with the testimony of Edward Roman.

As Roman crashed and burned on the stand, my ex-wife and prosecution partner squeezed my arm to the point of pain. She couldn't help it. She knew it, too. This was not something Royce was going to recover from. A key part of what was already going to be a fragile defense was crumbling before his eyes. It wasn't so much that his witness had pulled a one-eighty on him. It was the jury seeing a defense that was now obviously built upon a liar. The jury would not forgive this. It was over and I believed everyone in the courtroom — from the judge to the gadflies in the back row of the gallery — knew it. Jessup was going down.

I turned and looked back to share the moment with Bosch. After all, the silent witness maneuver had been his idea. And I caught him giving Jessup the throat slash — the internationally recognized sign that it was over.

I looked back to the front of the court.

"Mr. Royce," the judge said. "Are you continuing with this witness?"

"A moment, Your Honor," Royce said.

It was a valid question. Royce had few ways with which to go with Roman at this point. He could cut his losses and simply end the questioning. Or he could ask the judge to declare Roman to be a hostile witness — a move that was always professionally embarrassing when the hostile witness is one you called to the stand. But it was a move that would allow Royce more latitude in asking leading questions that explored what Roman had initially said to the defense investigator and why he was dissembling now. But this was fraught with danger, especially since this initial interview had not been recorded or documented in an effort to hide Roman during the discovery process.

"Mr. Royce!" the judge barked. "I consider the court's time quite valuable. Please ask your next question or I will turn the witness over to Mr. Haller for cross-examination."

Royce nodded to himself as he came to a decision.

"I'm sorry, Your Honor. But no further questions at this time."

Royce walked dejectedly back to his seat and a waiting client who was visibly upset with the turnabout. I stood up and started moving to the lectern even before the judge turned the witness over to me.

"Mr. Roman," I said, "your testimony has been somewhat confusing to me. So let me get this straight. Are you telling this jury that Sarah Ann Gleason did or did not tell you that her stepfather murdered her sister?"

"She didn't. That's just what they wanted me to say."

"Who is 'they,' sir?"

"The defense. The lady investigator and Royce."

"Besides a hotel room, were you to receive anything else if you testified to such a story today?"

"They just said they'd take care of me. That a lot of money was at—"

"Objection!" Royce yelled.

He jumped to his feet.

"Your Honor, the witness is clearly hostile and acting out a vindictive fantasy."

"He's your witness, Mr. Royce. He can answer the question. Go ahead, sir."

"They said there was a lot of money at stake and they would take care of me," Roman said.

It just kept getting better for me and worse for Jessup. But I had to make sure I didn't come off to the jury as gleeful or vindictive myself. I recalibrated and focused on what was important.

"What was the story that Sarah told you all those years ago, Mr. Roman?"

"Like I said, that she was in the yard and she was hiding and she saw the guy who grabbed her sister."

"Did she ever tell you she identified the wrong man?"

"No."

"Did she ever tell you that the police told her who to identify?"

"No."

"Did she ever once tell you that the wrong man was charged with her sister's murder?"

"No."

"No further questions."

I checked the clock as I returned to my seat. We still had twenty minutes before the lunch break. Rather than break early, the judge asked Royce to call his next witness. He called his investigator, Karen Revelle. I knew what he was doing and I was going to be ready.

Revelle was a mannish-looking woman who wore slacks and a sport jacket. She had ex-cop written all over her dour expression. After she was sworn in, Royce got right to the point, probably hoping to stem the flow of blood from his case before the jurors went to lunch.

"What do you do for a living, Ms. Revelle?"

"I am an investigator for the law firm of Royce and Associates."

"You work for me, correct?"

"That is correct."

"On March second of this year, did you conduct a telephone interview with an individual named Edward Roman?"

"I did."

"What did he tell you in that call?"

I stood and objected. I asked the judge if I could discuss my objection at a sidebar conference.

"Come on up," she said.

Maggie and I followed Royce to the side of the bench. The judge told me to state my objection.

"My first objection is that anything this witness states about a conversation with Roman is clearly hearsay and not allowed. But the larger objection is to Mr. Royce trying to impeach his own witness. He's going to use Revelle to impeach Roman, and you can't do that, Judge. It's damn near suborning perjury on Mr. Royce's part, because one of these two people is lying under oath and he called them both!"

"I strongly object to Mr. Haller's last characterization," Royce said, leaning over the sidebar and moving in closer to the judge. "Suborning perjury? I have been practicing law for more than —"

"First of all, back up, Mr. Royce, you're in my space," Breitman said sternly. "And second, you can save your self-serving objection for some other time. Mr. Haller is correct on all counts. If I allow this witness to continue her testimony, you are not only going to go into hearsay but we will have a situation where one of your witnesses has lied under oath. You can't have it both ways and you can't put a liar on the stand. So this is what we're going to do. You are going to get your investigator off the stand, Mr. Haller is going to make a motion to strike what little testimony she has already given and I will agree to that motion. Then we're going to lunch. During that time, you and your client can get together and decide what to do next. But it's looking to me like your options got really limited in the last half hour. That's all."

She didn't wait for any of us to respond. She simply rolled her chair away from the sidebar.

Royce followed the judge's advice and ended his questioning of Revelle. I moved to strike and that was that. A half hour later I was sitting with Maggie and Sarah Gleason at a table at the Water Grill, the place where the case had started for me. We had decided to go high-end because we were celebrating what appeared to be the beginning of the end for Jason Jessup's case, and because the Water Grill was just across the street from Sarah's hotel. The only one missing at the table was Bosch, and he was on his way after dropping our silent witness, Sonia Reyes, at the drug rehab facility at County-USC Medical Center.

"Wow," I said after the three of us were seated. "I don't think I've ever seen anything like that before in a courtroom."

"Me, neither," Maggie said.

"Well, I've been in a few courtrooms but I don't know enough to know what it all means," said Gleason.

"It means the end is near," Maggie said.

"It means the entire defense imploded," I added. "See, the defense's case was sort of simple. Stepfather killed the girl and the family concocted a cover-up. They came up with the story about hide-and-seek and the man on the lawn to throw the authorities off of stepdad. Then sister—that's you—made a false identification of Jessup. Just sort of randomly set him up for a murder he did not commit."

"But what about Melissa's hair in the tow truck?" Gleason asked.

"The defense claims it was planted," I said. "Either in conspiracy or independent of the family's cover-up. The police realized they didn't have much of a case. They had a thirteen-year-old girl's ID of a suspect and almost nothing else. So they took hair from the body or a hairbrush and planted it in the tow truck. After lunch—if Royce is foolish enough to continue this—he will present investigative chronology reports and time logs that will show Detective Kloster had enough access and time to make the plant in the tow truck before a search warrant was obtained and forensics opened the truck."

"But that's crazy," Gleason said.

"Maybe so," Maggie said, "but that was their case and Eddie Roman was the linchpin because he was supposed to testify that you told him your stepfather did it. He was supposed to plant the seed of doubt. That's all it takes, Sarah. One little doubt. Only he took one look at who was in the audience—namely Sonia Reyes—and thought he was in trouble. You see Eddie did the same thing with Sonia as he did with you. Met her, got close and turned her out to keep him in meth. When he saw her in court, he knew he was in trouble. Because he knew if Sonia got on the stand and told the same story about him as you did, then the jury would know what he was—a liar and predator—and wouldn't trust a single thing he said. He also had no idea what Sonia might have told us about crimes they committed together. So he decided up there that his best out was the truth. To screw the defense and make the prosecution happy. He changed his story."

Gleason nodded as she began to understand.

"Do you think Mr. Royce really told him what to say and was going to pay him off for his lies?"

"Of course," Maggie said.

"I don't know," I said quickly. "I've known Clive a long time. I don't think that's how he operates."

"What?" Maggie said. "You think Eddie Roman just made it all up on his own?"

"No, but he spoke to the investigator before he ever got to Clive."

"Plausible denial. You're just being charitable, Haller. They don't call him Clever Clive for no reason."

Sarah seemed to sense that she had pushed us into a zone of contention that had existed long before this trial. She tried to move us on.

"Do you really think it's over?" she asked.

I thought for a moment about it and then nodded.

"I think if I was Clever Clive I'd be thinking of what's best for my client and that would be not to let this go to a verdict. I'd start thinking about a deal. Maybe he'll even call during lunch."

I pulled my phone out and put it down on the table, as if being ready for Royce's call would make it happen. Just as I did so, Bosch showed up and took the seat next to Maggie. I grabbed my water glass and raised it to him.

"Cheers, Harry. Smooth move today. I think Jessup's house of cards is falling down."

Bosch raised a water glass and clinked it off mine.

"Royce was right, you know," he said. "It was a gangster move. Saw it in one of the *Godfather* movies way back."

He then held his water glass up to the two women.

"Anyway, cheers," he said. "You two are the real stars. Great work yesterday and today."

We all clinked glasses but Sarah hesitated.

"What's wrong, Sarah?" I asked. "Don't tell me you're afraid of clinking glass."

I smiled, proud of my own humor.

"It's nothing," she said. "I think it's supposed to be bad luck to toast with water."

"Well," I said, quickly recovering, "it's going to take more than bad luck to change things now."

Bosch switched subjects.

"What happens next?" he asked.

"I was just telling Sarah that I don't think this will go to a jury. Clive has to be thinking disposition. They really don't have any other choice."

Bosch turned serious.

"I know there's money on the line and your boss probably thinks that's the priority," he said, "but this guy has got to go back to prison."

"Absolutely," Maggie said.

"Of course," I added. "And after what happened this morning, we have all the leverage. Jessup has to take what we offer or we —"

My phone started to buzz. The ID screen said UNKNOWN.

"Speak of the devil," Maggie said.

I looked at Sarah.

"You might be on that plane home tonight after all."

I opened the phone and said my name.

"Mickey, District Attorney Williams here. How are you?"

I shook my head at the others. It wasn't Royce.

"I'm doing fine, Gabe. How are you?"

My informality didn't seem to faze him.

"I'm hearing good things out of court this morning."

His statement confirmed what I had thought all along. While Williams had never once showed his face in the courtroom, he had a plant in the gallery watching.

"Well, I hope so. I think we'll know more about which way this will go after lunch."

"Are you considering a disposition?"

"Well, not yet. I haven't heard from opposing counsel, but I assume that we may soon enter into discussions. He's probably talking to his client about it right now. I would be if I were him."

"Well, keep me in the loop on that before you sign off on anything."

I paused as I weighed this last statement. I saw Bosch put his hand inside his jacket and pull out his own phone to take a call.

"Tell you what, Gabe. As independent counsel I prefer to stay independent. I'll inform you of a disposition if and when I have an agreement."

"I want to be part of that conversation," Williams insisted.

I saw some sort of darkness move into Bosch's eyes. Instinctively, I knew it was time to get off my call.

"I'll get back to you on that, Mr. District Attorney. I've got another call coming in here. It could be Clive Royce."

I closed the phone just as Bosch closed his and started to stand up.

"What is it?" Maggie asked.

Bosch's face looked ashen.

"There's been a shooting over at Royce's office. There's four on the floor over there."

"Is Jessup one of them?" I asked.

"No . . . Jessup's gone."

40

Thursday, April 8, 1:05 P.M.

Bosch drove and McPherson insisted on riding with him. Haller had split off with Gleason to head back to court. Bosch pulled a card out of his wallet and got Lieutenant Stephen Wright's number off it. He handed the card and his phone to McPherson and told her to punch in the number.

"It's ringing," she said.

He took the phone and got it to his ear just as Wright answered.

"It's Bosch. Tell me your people are on Jessup."

"I wish."

"Damn it! What the hell happened? Why wasn't SIS on him?"

"Hold your horses, Bosch. We *were* on him. That's one of my people on the floor in Royce's office."

That hit like a punch. Bosch hadn't realized a cop was one of the victims.

"Where are you?" he asked Wright.

"On my way there. I'm three minutes out."

"What do you know so far?"

"Not a hell of a lot. We had a light tail on him during court hours. You knew that. One team during court and full coverage before and after. Today they followed him from the courthouse to Royce's office at lunchtime. Jessup and Royce's team walked over. After they were in there a few minutes my guys heard gunshots. They called it in and then went in. One was knocked down, the other pinned down. Jessup went out the back and my guy stayed to try CPR on his partner. He had to let Jessup go."

Bosch shook his head. The thought of his daughter pushed through everything. She was at school for the next ninety minutes. He felt that she would be safe. For now.

"Who else was hit?" he asked.

"As far as I know," Wright said, "it was Royce and his investigator and then another lawyer. A female. They were lucky it was lunchtime. Everybody else in the office was gone."

Bosch didn't see much that was lucky about a quadruple murder and Jessup out there somewhere with a gun. Wright kept talking.

"I'm not going to shed a tear over a couple of defense lawyers but my guy on the floor in there's got two little kids at home, Bosch. This is not a good goddamn thing at all."

Bosch turned onto First, and up ahead he could see the flashing lights. Royce's office was in a storefront on a dead-end street that ran behind the Kyoto Grand Hotel on the edge of Japantown. Easy walking distance to the courthouse.

"Did you get Jessup's car out on a broadcast?"

"Yes, everybody has it. Somebody will see it."

"Where's the rest of your crew?"

"Everybody's heading to the scene."

"No, send them out looking for Jessup. At all the places he's been. The parks, everywhere, even my house. There's no use for them at the scene."

"We'll meet there and I'll send them out."

"You're wasting time, Lieutenant."

"You think I can stop them from coming to the scene first?"

Bosch understood the impossibility of Wright's situation.

"I'm pulling up now," he said. "I'll see you when you get here."

"Two minutes."

Bosch closed the phone. McPherson asked him what Wright had said and he quickly filled her in as he pulled the car to a stop behind a patrol car.

Bosch badged his way under the yellow tape and McPherson did the same. Because the shooting had occurred only twenty-five minutes earlier, the crime scene was largely inhabited by uniformed officers — the first responders — and was chaotic. Bosch found a patrol sergeant issuing orders regarding crime scene protection and went to him.

"Sergeant, Harry Bosch, RHD. Who is taking this investigation?"

"Isn't it you?"

"No, I'm on a related case. But this one won't be mine."

"Then I don't know, Bosch. I was told RHD will handle."

"Okay, then they're still on their way. Who's inside?"

"Couple guys from Central Division. Roche and Stout."

Babysitters, Bosch thought. As soon as RHD moved in, they would be moved out. He pulled his phone and called his lieutenant.

"Gandle."

"Lieutenant, who's taking the four on the floor by the Kyoto?"

"Bosch? Where are you?"

"At the scene. It was my guy from the trial. Jessup."

"Shit, what went wrong?"

"I don't know. Who are you sending and where the hell are they?"

"I'm sending four. Penzler, Kirshbaum, Krikorian and Russell. But they were all at lunch up at Birds. I'm coming over, too, but you don't have to be there, Harry."

"I know. I'm not staying long."

Bosch closed the phone and looked around for McPherson. He had lost her in the confusion of the crime scene. He spotted her crouching down next to a man sitting on the sidewalk curb in front of the bail-bonds shop next door to Royce's office. Bosch recognized him from the night he and McPherson rode on the surveillance of Jessup. There was blood on his hands and shirt from his efforts to save his partner. Bosch went to them.

"...he went to his car when they got back here. For just a minute. Got in and then got out. He then went into the office. Right away we heard shots. We moved and Manny got hit as soon as we opened the door. I got off a couple rounds but I had to try to help Manny..."

"So Jessup must've gotten the gun from his car, right?"

"Must've. They've got the metal detectors at the courthouse. He didn't have it in court today."

"But you never saw it?"

"No, never saw the weapon. If we had seen it, we would've done something."

Bosch left them there and went to the door of Royce and Associates. He got there just as Lieutenant Wright did. Together they entered.

"Oh, my God," Wright said when he saw his man on the floor just inside the front door.

"What was his name?" Bosch asked.

"Manuel Branson. He's got two kids and I have to go tell his wife."

Branson was on his back. He had bullet entry wounds on the left side of his neck and upper left cheek. There had been a lot of blood. The neck shot appeared to have sliced through the carotid artery.

Bosch left Wright there and moved past a reception desk and down a hallway on the right side. There was a wall of glass that looked into a boardroom with doors on both ends. The rest of the victims were in here, along with two detectives who wore gloves and booties and were taking notes on clipboards. Roche and Stout. Bosch stood in the first doorway of the room but did not enter. The two detectives looked at him.

"Who are you?" one asked.

"Bosch, RHD."

"You taking this?"

"Not exactly. I'm on something related. The others are coming."

"Christ, we're only two blocks from the PAB."

"They weren't there. They were at lunch up in Hollywood. But don't worry, they'll get here. It's not like these people are going anywhere."

Bosch looked at the bodies. Clive Royce sat dead in a chair at the head of a long board table. His head was snapped back as if he were looking at the ceiling. There was a bloodless bullet hole in the center of his forehead. Blood from the exit wound at the back of his head had poured down the back of his jacket and chair.

The investigator, Karen Revelle, was on the floor on the other side of the room near the other door. It appeared that she had tried to make a run for it before being hit by gunfire. She was facedown and Bosch could not see where or how many times she had been hit.

Royce's pretty associate counsel, whose name Bosch could not remember, was no longer pretty. Her body was in a seat diagonal to Royce, her upper body down on the table, an entry wound at the back of her head. The bullet had exited below her right eye and destroyed her face. There was always more damage coming out than going in.

"What do you think?" asked one of the Central guys.

"Looks like he came in shooting. Hit these two first and then tagged the other as she made a run for the door. Then backed into the hall and opened up on the SIS guys as they came in."

"Yeah. Looks that way."

"I'm going to check the rest of the place out."

Bosch continued down the hall and looked through open doors into empty offices. There were nameplates on the wall outside the doors and he was reminded that Royce's associate was named Denise Graydon.

The hallway ended at a break room, where there was a kitchenette with a refrigerator and a microwave. There was another communal table here. And an exit door that was three inches ajar.

Bosch used his elbow to push the door open. He stepped into an alley lined with trash bins. He looked both ways and saw a pay parking lot a half block down to his right. He assumed it was the lot where Jessup had parked his car and had gone to retrieve the gun.

He went back inside and this time took a longer look in each of the offices. He knew from experience that he was treading in a gray area here. This was a law office, and whether the lawyers were dead or not, their clients were still entitled to privacy and attorney-client privilege. Bosch touched nothing and opened no drawer or file. He simply moved his eyes over the surface of things, seeing and reading what was in plain sight.

When he was in Revelle's office he was joined by McPherson.

"What are you doing?"

"Just looking."

"We might have a problem going into any of their offices. As an officer of the court I can't—"

"Then wait outside. Like I said, I'm just looking. I am making sure the premises are secure."

"Whatever. I'll be out front. The media's all over the place out there now. It's a circus."

Bosch was leaning over Revelle's desk. He didn't look up.

"Good for them."

McPherson left the room at the same moment Bosch read something off a legal pad that was on top of a stack of files on the side of the desk near the phone.

"Maggie? Come back here."

She returned.

"Take a look at this."

McPherson came around the desk and bent over to read the notes on the top page of the pad. The page was covered with what looked like random notes, phone numbers and names. Some were circled, others scratched out. It looked like a pad Revelle jotted on while on the phone.

"What?" McPherson asked.

Without touching the pad, Bosch pointed to a notation in the bottom right corner. All it said was *Checkers — 804*. But that was enough.

"Shit!" McPherson said. "Sarah isn't even registered under her name. How did Revelle get this?"

"She must've followed us back after court, paid somebody for the room number. We have to assume that Jessup has this information."

Bosch pulled his phone and called Mickey Haller on speed dial.

"It's Bosch. You still have Sarah with you?"

"Yes, she's here in court. We're waiting for the judge."

"Look, don't scare her but she can't go back to the hotel."

"All right. How come?"

"Because there's an indication here that Jessup has that location. We'll be setting up on it."

"What do I do, then?"

"I'll be sending a protection team to the court — for both of you. They'll know what to do."

"They can cover her. I don't need it."

"That'll be your choice. My advice is you take it."

He closed the phone and looked at McPherson.

"I gotta get a protection team over there. I want you to take my car and get my daughter and your daughter and go somewhere safe. You call me then and I'll send a team to you, too."

"My car's two blocks from here. I can just —"

"That'll waste too much time. Take mine and go now. I'll call the school and tell them you're coming for Maddie."

"Okay."

"Thank you. Call me when you have —"

They heard shouting from the front of the office suite. Angry male voices. Bosch knew they came from the friends of Manny Branson. They were seeing their fallen comrade on the floor and getting fueled with outrage and the scent of blood for the hunt.

"Let's go," he said.

They moved back through the suite to the front. Bosch saw Wright standing just outside the front door, consoling two SIS men with angry, tear-streaked faces. Bosch made his way around Branson's body and out the door. He tapped Wright on the elbow.

"I need a moment, Lieutenant."

Wright broke away from his two men and followed. Bosch walked a few yards to where they could speak privately. But he need not have worried about being overheard. In the sky above, there were at least four media choppers circling over the crime scene and laying down a layer of camouflage sound that would make any conversation on the block private.

"I need two of your best men," Bosch said, leaning toward Wright's ear.

"Okay. What do you have going?"

"There's a note on the desk of one of the victims. It's the hotel and room number of our prime witness. We have to assume our shooter has that information. The slaughter inside there indicates he's taking out the people associated with the trial. The people he thinks did him wrong. That's a long list but I think our witness would be at the top of it."

"Got it. You want to set up at the hotel."

Bosch nodded.

"Yeah. One man outside, one inside and me in the room. We wait and see if he shows."

Wright shook his head.

"We use four. Two inside and two outside. But forget waiting in the room, because Jessup will never get by the surveillance. Instead, you and I find a viewpoint up high and set up the command post. That's the right way to do it."

Bosch nodded.

"Okay, let's go."

"Except there's one thing."

"What's that?"

"If I bring you in on this, then you stay back. My people take him down."

Bosch studied him for a moment, trying to read everything hidden in what he was saying.

"There are questions," Bosch said. "About Franklin Canyon and the other places. I need to talk to Jessup."

Wright looked over Bosch's shoulder and back toward the front door of Royce and Associates.

"Detective, one of my best people is dead on the floor in there. I'm not guaranteeing you anything. You understand?"

Bosch paused and then nodded.

"I understand."

41

Thursday, April 8, 1:50 P.M.

There was more media in the courtroom than there had been at any other point of the trial. The first two rows of the gallery were shoulder-to-shoulder with reporters and cameramen. The rest of the rows were filled with courthouse personnel and lawyers who had heard what had happened to Clive Royce.

Sarah Gleason sat in a row by the courtroom deputy's desk. It was marked as reserved for law enforcement officers but the deputy put her there so the reporters couldn't get to her. Meantime, I sat at the prosecution table waiting for the judge like a man on a desert island. No Maggie. No Bosch. Nobody at the defense table. I was alone.

"Mickey," someone whispered from behind me.

I turned to see Kate Salters from the *Times* leaning across the railing.

"I can't talk now. I have to figure out what to say here."

"But do you think your total destruction of this morning's witness is what could have —?"

I was saved by the judge. Breitman entered the courtroom and bounded up to the bench and took her seat. Salters took hers and the question I wanted to avoid for the rest of my life remained unasked — at least for the moment.

"We are back on the record in *California versus Jessup*. Michael Haller is present for the People. But the jury is not present, nor is defense counsel or the defendant. I am aware through unconfirmed media reports of what has transpired in the last ninety minutes at Mr. Royce's office. Can you add anything to what I have seen and heard on television, Mr. Haller?"

I stood up to address the court.

"Your Honor, I don't know what they are putting out to the media at the moment, but I can confirm that Mr. Royce and his cocounsel on this case, Ms. Graydon, were shot and killed in their offices at lunchtime. Karen Revelle is also dead, as well as a police officer who responded to the shooting. The suspect in the shooting has been identified as Jason Jessup. He remains at large."

Judging by the murmur from the gallery behind me, those basic facts had probably been speculated upon but not yet confirmed to the media.

"This is, indeed, very sad news," Breitman said.

"Yes, Your Honor," I said. "Very sad."

"But I think at this moment we need to put aside our emotions and act carefully here. The issue is, how do we proceed with this case? I am pretty sure I know the answer to that question but am willing to listen to counsel before ruling. Do you wish to be heard, Mr. Haller?"

"Yes, I do, Judge. I ask the court to recess the trial for the remainder of the day and sequester the jury while we await further information. I also ask that you revoke Mr. Jessup's pretrial release and issue a capias for his arrest."

The judge considered these requests for a long moment before responding.

"I will grant the motion revoking the defendant's release and issue the capias. But I don't see the need to sequester the jury. Regrettably, I see no alternative to a mistrial here, Mr. Haller."

I knew that would be her first thought. I had been considering my response since the moment I had returned to the courthouse.

"The People object to a mistrial, Judge. The law is clear that Mr. Jessup waives his right to be present at these proceedings by voluntarily absenting himself from them. According to what the defense represented earlier, he was scheduled to be the last witness today. But he has obviously decided not to testify. So, taking all of this into —"

"Mr. Haller, I am going to have to stop you right there. I think you are missing one part of the equation and I am afraid the horse is already out of the barn. You may recall that Deputy Solantz was assigned lunch duty with our jurors after we had the issue of tardiness on Monday."

"Yes."

"Well, lunch for eighteen in downtown Los Angeles is a tall order. Deputy Solantz arranged for the group to travel by bus together and eat each day at Clifton's Cafeteria. There are TVs in the restaurant but Deputy Solantz always keeps them off the local channels. Unfortunately, one TV was on CNN today when the network chose to go live with what was occurring at Mr. Royce's office. Several jurors saw the live report and got the gist of what was happening before Deputy Solantz managed to kill the feed. As you can imagine, Deputy Solantz is not very happy with himself at the moment, and neither am I."

I turned and looked over at the courtroom deputy's desk. Solantz had his eyes down in humiliation. I looked back at the judge and I knew I was dead in the water.

"Needless to say, your suggestion of sequestering the jury was a good one, just a little late. Therefore, and after taking all things into consideration, I find that the jury in this trial has been prejudiced by events which have occurred outside of the court. I intend to declare a mistrial and continue this case until such time as Mr. Jessup has been brought again before this court."

She paused for a moment to see if I had an objection but I had nothing. I knew what she was doing was right and inevitable.

"Let's bring in the jury now," she said.

Soon the jurors were filing into the box, many of them glancing over at the empty defense table.

When everyone was in place, the judge went on the record and turned her chair directly to the jurors. In a subdued tone she addressed them.

"Ladies and gentlemen of the jury, I must inform you that because of factors that are not fully clear to you but will soon become so, I have declared a mistrial in the case of *California versus Jason Jessup*. I do this with great regret because all of us here have invested a great deal of time and effort in these proceedings."

She paused and studied the confused faces in front of her.

"No one likes to invest so much time without seeing the case through to a result. I am sorry for this. But I do thank you for your duty. You were all dependable and for the most part on time every day. I also watched you closely during the testimony and you were all attentive. The court cannot thank you enough. You are dismissed now from this courtroom and discharged from jury duty. You may all go home."

The jurors slowly filed back into the jury room, many taking a last look back at the courtroom. Once they were gone the judge turned back to me.

"Mr. Haller, for what it's worth, I thought you acquitted yourself quite well as a prosecutor. I am sorry it ended this way but you are welcome back to this court anytime and on either side of the aisle."

"Thank you, Judge. I appreciate that. I had a lot of help."

"Then I commend your whole team as well."

With that, the judge stood and left the bench. I sat there for a long time,

listening to the gallery clear out behind me and thinking about what Breitman had said at the end. I wondered how and why such a good job in court
had resulted in such a horrible thing happening in Clive Royce's office.

"Mr. Haller?"

I turned, expecting it to be a reporter. But it was two uniformed police
officers.

"Detective Bosch sent us. We are here to take you and Ms. Gleason into
protective custody."

"Only Ms. Gleason and she's right here."

Sarah was waiting on the bench next to Deputy Solantz's desk.

"Sarah, these officers are going to take care of you until Jason Jessup is in
custody or..."

I didn't need to finish. Sarah got up and walked over to us.

"So there's no more trial?" she asked.

"Right. The judge declared a mistrial. That means if Jessup is caught, we
would have to start over. With a new jury."

She nodded and looked a little dumbfounded. I had seen the look on the
faces of many people who venture naively into the justice system. They
leave the courthouse wondering what just happened. Sarah Gleason would
be no different.

"You should go with these men now, Sarah. We'll be in touch as soon as
we know what happens next."

She just nodded and they headed for the door.

I waited a while, alone in the courtroom, and then headed out to the
hallway myself. I saw several of the jurors being interviewed by the reporters. I could've watched but at the moment I wasn't interested in what anybody had to say about the case. Not anymore.

Kate Salters saw me and broke away from one of the clusters.

"Mickey, can we talk now?"

"I don't feel like talking. Call me tomorrow."

"The story's today, Mick."

"I don't care."

I pushed by her in the direction of the elevators.

"Where are you going?"

I didn't answer. I got to the elevators and jumped through the open
doors of a waiting car. I moved into the rear corner and saw a woman
standing by the panel. She asked me the same question as Salters.

"Where are you going?"

"Home," I said.

She pushed the button marked G and we went down.

PART FIVE

—The Takedown

42

Thursday, April 8, 4:40 P.M.

Bosch was stationed with Wright in a borrowed office across the street from the Checkers Hotel. It was the command post, and although no one thought Jessup would be stupid enough to walk in the front door of the hotel, the position gave them a good view of the entire property as well as two of the other surveillance positions.

"I don't know," Wright said, staring out the window. "This guy is smart, right?"

"I guess so," Bosch said.

"Then I don't see him making this move, you know? He'd have already been here if he was. He's probably halfway to Mexico by now and we're sitting here watching a hotel."

"Maybe."

"If I were him, I'd get down there and lie low. Try to spend as many days on the beach as I could before they found me and put me back in the Q."

Bosch's phone began to buzz and he saw that it was his daughter.

"I'm going to step out to take this," he said to Wright. "You got it covered here?"

"I've got it."

Bosch answered the phone as he left the office for the hallway.

"Hey, Mads. Everything all right?"

"There's a police car outside now."

"Yeah, I know. I sent it there. Just an added precaution."

They had talked an hour earlier after Maggie McPherson had gotten them safely to a friend's home in Porter Ranch. He had told his daughter about Jessup being out there and what had happened at Royce's office. She didn't know about Jessup's nocturnal visit to their house two weeks earlier.

"So they didn't catch that guy yet?"

"We're working on it and I'm in the middle of stuff here. Stay close to Aunt Maggie and stay safe. I'll come get you as soon as this is over."

"Okay. Here, Aunt Maggie wants to talk to you."

McPherson took the phone.

"Harry, what's the latest?"

"Same as before. We're out looking for him and sitting on all the known locations. I'm with Wright at Sarah's hotel."

"Be careful."

"Speaking of that, where's Mickey? He turned down protection."

"He's at home right now but said he's coming up here."

"Okay, sounds good. I'll talk to you later."

"Keep us posted."

"I will."

Bosch closed the phone and went back into the office. Wright was still at the window.

"I think we're wasting our time and should shut this down," he said.

"Why? What's going on?"

"Just came over the radio. They found the car Jessup was using. In Venice. He's nowhere near here, Bosch."

Bosch knew that dumping the car in Venice could merely be a misdirection. Drive out to the beach, leave the car and then double back in a cab to downtown. Nonetheless, he found himself reluctantly agreeing with Wright. They were spinning their wheels here.

"Damn it," he said.

"Don't worry. We'll get him. I'm keeping one team here and one on your house. Everybody else I'm moving down into Venice."

"And the Santa Monica Pier?"

"Already covered. Got a couple teams on the beach and nobody's gone in or out of that location."

Wright went on the SIS band on the radio and started redeploying his men. As Bosch listened he paced the room, trying to figure Jessup out. After a while he stepped back out to the hallway so as not to disturb Wright's radio choreography and called Larry Gandle, his boss at RHD.

"It's Bosch. Just checking in."

"You still at the hotel?"

"Yeah, but we're about to clear and head to the beach. I guess you heard they found the car."

"Yeah, I was just there."

Bosch was surprised. With four victims at Royce's office, he thought Gandle would still be at the murder scene.

"The car's clean," Gandle said. "Jessup still has the weapon."

"Where are you now?" Bosch asked.

"On Speedway," Gandle said. "We just hit the room Jessup was using. Took a while to get the search warrant."

"Anything there?"

"Not so far. This fucking guy, you see him in court wearing a suit and you think...I don't know what you think, but the reality was, he was living like an animal."

"What do you mean?"

"There are empty cans all over the place, food still rotting in them. Food rotting on the counter, trash everywhere. He hung blankets over the windows to black it out like a cave. He made it like a prison cell. He was even writing on the walls."

All at once it hit him. Bosch knew who Jessup had prepared the dungeon under the pier for.

"What kind of food?" he asked.

"What?" Gandle asked.

"The canned food. What kind of food?"

"I don't know, fruits and peaches — all kinds of stuff you can get fresh in any store you walk into. But he had it in cans. Like prison."

"Thanks, Lieutenant."

Bosch closed the phone and walked quickly back into the office. Wright was off the radio now.

"Did your people go under the pier and check the storage room or just set up surveillance?"

"It's a loose surveillance."

"Meaning they didn't check it out?"

"They checked the perimeter. There was no sign that anybody went under the wall. So they backed out and set up."

"Jessup's there. They missed him."

"How do you know?"

"I just know. Let's go."

43

≋

Thursday, April 8, 6:35 P.M.

I stood at the picture window at the end of my living room and looked out at the city with the sun dropping behind it. Jessup was out there someplace. Like a rabid animal he would be hunted, cornered and, I had no doubt, put down. It was the inevitable conclusion to his play.

Jessup was legally to blame but I couldn't help but think about my own culpability in these dark matters. Not in any legal sense, but in a private, internal sense. I had to question whether consciously or not I had set all of this in motion on the day I sat with Gabriel Williams and agreed to cross a line in the courtroom as well as within myself. Maybe by allowing Jessup his freedom I had determined his fate as well as that of Royce and the others. I was a defense attorney, not a prosecutor. I stood for the underdog, not for the state. Maybe I had taken the steps and made the maneuvers so that there would never be a verdict and I would not have to live with it on my record and conscience.

Such were the musings of a guilty man. But they didn't last long. My phone buzzed and I pulled it from my pocket without looking away from my view of the city.

"Haller."

"It's me. I thought you were coming up here."

Maggie McFierce.

"Soon. I'm just finishing up here. Everything all right?"

"For me, yes. But probably not for Jessup. Are you watching the TV news?"

"No, what are they showing?"

"They've evacuated the Santa Monica Pier. Channel Five has a chopper over it. They're not confirming that it's related to Jessup but they said that LAPD's SIS unit sought an okay from SMPD to conduct a fugitive apprehension. They're on the beach moving in."

"The dungeon? Did Jessup grab somebody?"

"If he did, they're not saying."

"Did you call Harry?"

"I just tried but he didn't pick up. I think he's probably down there on the beach."

I broke away from the window and grabbed the television remote off the coffee table. I snapped on the TV and punched in Channel 5.

"I have it on here," I told Maggie.

On the screen was an aerial view of the pier and the surrounding beach. It looked like there were men on the beach and they were advancing on the pier's underside from both the north and south.

"I think you're right," I said. "It's gotta be him. The dungeon he made down there was actually for himself. Like a safe house he could run to."

"Like the prison cell he was used to. I wonder if he knows they're coming in on him. Maybe he hears the helicopters."

"Harry said the waves under there are so loud you couldn't even hear a gunshot."

"Well, we might be about to find that out."

We watched in silence for a few moments before I spoke.

"Maggie, are the girls watching this?"

"God, no! They're playing video games in the other room."

"Good."

They watched in silence. The newscaster's voice echoing over the line as he inanely described what was on the screen. After a while Maggie asked the question that had probably been on her mind all afternoon.

"Did you think it would come to this, Haller?"

"No, did you?"

"No, never. I guess I thought everything would sort of be contained in the courtroom. Like it always is."

"Yeah."

"At least Jessup saved us the indignity of the verdict."

"What do you mean? We had him and he knew it."

"You didn't watch any of the juror interviews, did you?"

"What, on TV?"

"Yeah, juror number ten is on every channel saying he would've voted not guilty."

"You mean Kirns?"

"Yeah, the alternate that got moved into the box. Everybody else interviewed said guilty, guilty, guilty. But Kirns said not guilty, that we hadn't convinced him. He would've hung the jury, Haller, and you know Williams wouldn't have signed on for round two. Jessup would've walked."

I considered this and could only shake my head. Everything was for nothing. All it took was one juror with a grudge against society, and Jessup would've walked. I looked up from the TV screen and out toward the western horizon to the distance, where I knew Santa Monica hugged the edge of the Pacific. I thought I could see the media choppers circling.

"I wonder if Jessup will ever know that," I said.

44

Thursday, April 8, 6:55 P.M.

The sun was dropping low over the Pacific and burning a brilliant green path across the surface. Bosch stood close to Wright on the beach, a hundred yards south of the pier. They were both looking down at the 5 × 5 video screen contained in a front pack strapped to Wright's chest. He was commanding the SIS takedown of Jason Jessup. On the screen was a murky image of the dimly lit storage facility under the pier. Bosch had been given ears but no mike. He could hear the operation's communications but could not contribute to them. Anything he had to say would have to go through Wright.

The voices over the com were hard to hear because of the background sound of waves crashing beneath the pier.

"This is Five, we're in."

"Steady the visual," Wright commanded.

The focus on the video tightened and Bosch could see that the camera was aimed at the individual storage rooms at the rear of the pier facility.

"This one."

He pointed to the door he had seen Jessup go through.

"Okay," Wright said. "Our target is the second door from the right. Repeat, second door from the right. Move in and take positions."

The video moved in a herky-jerky fashion to a new position. Now the camera was even closer.

"Three and Four are—"

The rest was wiped out by the sound of a crashing wave.

"Three and Four, say again," Wright said.

"Three, Four in position."

"Hold until my go. Topside, you ready?"

"Topside ready."

On the upper level of the evacuated pier there was another team, which had placed small explosives at the corners of the trapdoor above the storage corral where they believed Jessup was holed up. On Wright's command the SIS teams would blow the trapdoor and move in from above and below.

Wright wrapped his hand around the mike that ran along his jawline and looked at Bosch.

"You ready for this?"

"Ready."

Wright released his grip and gave the command to his teams.

"Okay, let's give him a chance," he said. "Three, you have the speaker up?"

"That's a go on the speaker. You're hot in three, two...one."

Wright spoke, trying to convince a man hidden in a dark room a hundred yards away to give himself up.

"Jason Jessup. This is Lieutenant Stephen Wright of the Los Angeles Police Department. Your position is surrounded top and bottom. Step out with your hands behind your head, fingers laced. Move forward to the waiting officers. If you deviate from this order you will be shot."

Bosch pulled his earplugs out and listened. He could hear the muffled sound of Wright's words coming from under the pier. There was no doubt that Jessup could hear the order if he was under there.

"You have one minute," Wright said as his final communication to Jessup.

The lieutenant checked his watch and they waited. At the thirty-second mark Wright checked with his men under the pier.

"Anything?"

"This is Three. I got nothing."

"Four, clear."

Wright gave Bosch a wishful look, like he had hoped it wouldn't come to this.

"Okay, on my mark we go. Keep tight and no cross-fire. Topside, if you shoot, you make sure you know who you—"

There was movement on the video screen. A door to one of the storage corrals flung open, but not the door they were focused on. The camera made a jerking motion left as it redirected its aim. Bosch saw Jessup emerge from the darkness behind the open door. His arms came up and together as he dropped into a combat pose.

"Gun!" Wright yelled.

The barrage of gunfire that followed lasted no more than ten seconds. But in that time at least four officers under the pier emptied their weapons. The crescendo was punctuated by the unneeded detonation from the top-side. By then Bosch had already seen Jessup go down in the gunfire. Like a man in front of a firing squad, his body seemed at first to be held upright by the force of multiple impacts from multiple angles. Then gravity set in and he fell to the sand.

After a few moments of silence, Wright was back on the com.

"Everybody safe? Count off."

All officers under and on top of the pier reported in safe.

"Check the suspect."

In the video Bosch saw two officers approach Jessup's body. One checked for a pulse while the other held his aim on the dead man.

"He's ten-seven."

"Secure the weapon."

"Got it."

Wright killed the video and looked at Bosch.

"And that's that," he said.

"Yeah."

"I'm sorry you didn't get your answers."

"Me, too."

They started walking up the beach to the pier. Wright checked his watch and went on the com, announcing the official time of the shooting as 7:18 P.M.

Bosch looked off across the ocean to his left. The sun was now gone.

PART SIX

—All That Remains

45

Friday, April 9, 2:20 P.M.

Harry Bosch and I sat on opposite sides of a picnic table, watching the ME's disinterment team dig. They were on the third excavation, working beneath the tree where Jason Jessup had lit a candle in Franklin Canyon.

I didn't have to be there but wanted to be. I was hoping for further evidence of Jason Jessup's villainy, as though that might make it easier to accept what had happened.

But so far, in three excavations, they had found nothing. The team moved slowly, stripping away the dirt one inch at a time and sifting and analyzing every ounce of soil they removed. We had been here all morning and my hope had waned into a cold cynicism about what Jessup had been doing up here on the nights he was followed.

A white canvas sheet had been strung from the tree to two poles planted outside the search zone. This shielded the diggers from the sun as well as from the view of the media helicopters above. Someone had leaked word of the search.

Bosch had the stack of files from the missing persons cases on the table. He was ready to go with records and descriptors of the missing girls should any human remains be found. I had simply come armed with the morning's newspaper and I read the front-page story now for a second time. The report on the events of the day before was the lead story in the *Times* and was accompanied by a color photo of two SIS officers pointing their weapons into the open trapdoor on the Santa Monica Pier. The story was also accompanied by a front-page sidebar story on the SIS. Headline: ANOTHER CASE, ANOTHER SHOOTING, SIS's BLOODY HISTORY.

I had the feeling this would be a story with legs. So far, no one in the media had found out that the SIS knew Jessup had obtained a gun. When that got out—and I was sure it would—there would no doubt be a firestorm of controversy, further investigations and police commission inquiries. The chief question being: Once it was established that it was likely that this man had a weapon, why was he allowed to remain free?

It all made me glad I was no longer even temporarily in the employ of the state. In the bureaucratic arena, those kinds of questions and their answers have the tendency to separate people from their jobs.

I needed not worry about the outcome of such inquiries for my livelihood.

I would be returning to my office — the backseat of my Lincoln Town Car. I was going back to being private counsel for the defense. The lines were cleaner there, the mission clearer.

"Is Maggie McFierce coming?" Bosch asked.

I put the paper down on the table.

"No, Williams sent her back to Van Nuys. Her part in the case is over."

"Why isn't Williams moving her downtown?"

"The deal was that we had to get a conviction for her to get downtown. We didn't."

I gestured to the newspaper.

"And we weren't going to get one. This one holdout juror is telling any-body who'll listen that he would've voted not guilty. So I guess you can say Gabriel Williams is a man who keeps his word. Maggie's going nowhere fast."

That's how it worked in the nexus of politics and jurisprudence. And that's why I couldn't wait to go back to defending the damned.

We sat in silence for a while after that and I thought about my ex-wife and how my efforts to help her and promote her had failed so miserably. I wondered if she would begrudge me the effort. I surely hoped not. It would be hard for me to live in a world where Maggie McFierce despised me.

"They found something," Bosch said.

I looked up from my thoughts and focused. One of the diggers was using a pair of tweezers to put something from the dirt into a plastic evidence bag. Soon she stood up and headed toward us with the bag. She was Kathy Kohl, the ME's forensic archaeologist.

She handed Bosch the bag and he held it up to look. I could see that it contained a silver bracelet.

"No bones," Kohl said. "Just that. We're at thirty-two inches down and it's rare that you find a murder interment much further down than that. So this one's looking like the other two. You want us to keep digging?"

Bosch glanced at the bracelet in the bag and looked up at Kohl.

"How about another foot? That going to be a problem?"

"A day in the field beats a day in the lab anytime. You want us to keep digging, we'll keep digging."

"Thanks, Doc."

"You got it."

She went back to the excavation pit and Bosch handed the evidence bag to me to examine. It contained a charm bracelet. There were clots of dirt in the links and its charms. I could make out a tennis racket and an airplane.

"Do you recognize it?" I asked. "From one of the missing girls?"

He gestured to the stack of files on the table.

"No. I don't remember anything about a charm bracelet in the lists."

"It could've just been lost up here by somebody."

"Thirty-two inches down in the dirt?"

"So you think Jessup buried it, then?"

"Maybe. I'd hate to come away from this empty-handed. The guy had to have come up here for a reason. If he didn't bury them here, then maybe this was the kill spot. I don't know."

I handed the bag back to him.

"I think you're being too optimistic, Harry. That's not like you."

"Well, then what the hell do you think Jessup was doing up here all those nights?"

"I think he and Royce were playing us."

"Royce? What are you talking about?"

"We were had, Harry. Face it."

Bosch held the evidence bag up again and shook it to loosen the dirt.

"It was a classic misdirection," I said. "The first rule of a good defense is a good offense. You attack your own case before you ever get to court. You find its weaknesses and if you can't fix them, then you find ways of deflecting attention away from them."

"Okay."

"The biggest weakness to the defense's case was Eddie Roman. Royce was going to put a liar and a drug addict on the stand. He knew that given enough time, you would either find Roman or find out things about him or both. He needed to deflect. Keep you occupied with things outside the case at hand."

"You're saying he knew we were following Jessup?"

"He could've easily guessed it. I put up no real opposition to his request for an OR release. That was unusual and probably got Royce thinking. So he sent Jessup out at night to see if there was a tail. As we already considered before, he probably even sent Jessup to your house to see if he would engage a response and confirm surveillance. When it didn't, when it got no response, Royce probably thought he was wrong and dropped it. After that, Jessup stopped coming up here at night."

"And he probably thought he was in the clear to go build his dungeon under the pier."

"It makes sense. Doesn't it?"

Bosch took a long time to answer. He put his hand on top of the stack of files.

"So what about all these missing girls?" he asked. "It's all just coincidence?"

"I don't know," I said. "We may never know now. All we know is that they're still missing and if Jessup was involved, then that secret probably died with him yesterday."

Bosch stood up, a troubled look on his face. He was still holding the evidence bag.

"I'm sorry, Harry."

"Yeah, me, too."

"Where do you go from here?"

Bosch shrugged.

"The next case. My name goes back into the rotation. What about you?"

I splayed my hands and smiled.

"You know what I do."

"You sure about that? You made a damn good prosecutor."

"Yeah, well, thanks for that, but you gotta do what you gotta do. Besides, they'd never let me back on that side of the aisle. Not after this."

"What do you mean?"

"They're going to need somebody to blame for all of this and it's going to be me. I was the one who let Jessup out. You watch. The cops, the *Times*, even Gabriel Williams will eventually bring it around to me. But that's okay, as long as they leave Maggie alone. I know my place in the world and I'm going to go back to it."

Bosch nodded because there was nothing else to say. He shook the bag with the charm bracelet again and worked it with his fingers, removing more dirt from its surfaces. He then held it up to study closely and I could tell he saw something.

"What is it?"

His face changed. He was keying on one of the charms, rubbing dirt off it through the plastic bag. He then handed it to me.

"Take a look. What is that?"

The charm was still tarnished and dirty. It was a square piece of silver less than a half inch wide. On one side there was a tiny swivel at center and on the other what looked like a bowl or a cup.

"Looks like a teacup on a square plate," I suggested. "I don't know."

"No, turn it over. That's the bottom."

I did and I saw what he saw.

"It's one of those...a mortarboard. A graduation cap and this swivel on the top was for the tassel."

"Yeah. The tassel's missing, probably still in the dirt."

"Okay, so what's it mean?"

Bosch sat back down and quickly started looking through the files.

"You don't remember? The first girl I showed you and Maggie. Valerie Schlicter. She disappeared a month after graduating from Riverside High."

"Okay, so you think..."

Bosch found the file and opened it. It was thin. There were three photos of Valerie Schlicter, including one of her in her graduation cap and gown. He quickly scanned the few documents that were in the file.

"Nothing here about a charm bracelet," he said.

"Because it probably wasn't hers," I said. "This is a long shot, don't you think?"

He acted as though I had said nothing, his mind shutting out any opposing response.

"I'm going to have to go out there. She had a mother and a brother. See who's still around and can look at this thing."

"Harry, you sure you—"

"You think I have a choice?"

He stood back up, took the evidence bag back from me and gathered up the files. I could almost hear the adrenaline buzzing through his veins. A dog with a bone. It was time for Bosch to go. He had a long shot in his hand but it was better than no shot. It would keep him moving.

I got up, too, and followed him to the excavation. He told Kohl that he had to go check out the bracelet. He told her to call him if anything else was found in the hole.

We moved to the gravel parking lot, Bosch walking quickly and not looking back to see if I was still with him. We had driven separately to the dig.

"Hey," I called to him. "Wait up!"

He stopped in the middle of the lot.

"What?"

"Technically, I'm still the prosecutor assigned to Jessup. So before you go rushing off, tell me what the thinking is here. He buried the bracelet here but not her? Does that even make sense?"

"Nothing makes sense until I ID the bracelet. If somebody tells me it was hers, then we try to figure it out. Remember, when Jessup was up here, we couldn't get close to him. It was too risky. So we don't know exactly what he was doing. He could've been looking for this."

"Okay, I can maybe see that."

"I gotta go."

He continued on to his car. It was parked next to my Lincoln. I called after him.

"Let me know, okay?"

He looked back at me when he got to his car.

"Yeah," he said. "I will."

He then dropped into the car and I heard it roar to life. Bosch drove like he walked, pulling out quickly and throwing dust and gravel into the air. A man on a mission. I got in the Lincoln and followed him out of the park and up to Mulholland Drive. After that, I lost him on the curving road ahead.

About the author

Michael Connelly is the author of the recent #1 *New York Times* bestsellers *The Fifth Witness*, *The Reversal*, *The Scarecrow*, *The Brass Verdict*, and *The Lincoln Lawyer*, as well as the bestselling Harry Bosch series of novels. He is a former newspaper reporter who has won numerous awards for his journalism and his novels. He spends his time in California and Florida.

And for the next Mickey Haller novel…

Please turn the page for a preview of *The Fifth Witness*, available in bookstores, as an ebook, and as an audiobook.

1

Mrs. Pena looked across the seat at me and held her hands up in a beseeching manner. She spoke in a heavy accent, choosing English to make her final pitch directly to me.

"Please, you help me, Mr. Mickey?"

I looked at Rojas, who was turned around in the front seat even though I didn't need him to translate. I then looked past Mrs. Pena, over her shoulder and through the car window, to the home she desperately wanted to hold on to. It was a bleached pink, two-bedroom house with a hardscrabble yard behind a wire fence. The concrete step to the front stoop had graffiti sprayed across it, indecipherable except for the number 13. It wasn't the address. It was a pledge of allegiance.

My eyes finally came back to her. She was forty-four years old and attractive in a worn sort of way. She was the single mother of three teenage boys and had not paid her mortgage in nine months. Now the bank had foreclosed and was moving in to sell the house out from under her.

The auction would take place in three days. It didn't matter that the house was worth little or that it sat in a gang-infested neighborhood in South L.A. Somebody would buy it, and Mrs. Pena would become a renter instead of an owner—that is, if the new owner didn't evict her. For years she had relied on the protection of the Florencia 13. But times were different. No gang allegiance could help her now. She needed a lawyer. She needed me.

"Tell her I will try my best," I said. "Tell her I am pretty certain I will be able to stop the auction and challenge the validity of the foreclosure. It will at least slow things down. It will give us time to work up a long-range plan. Maybe get her back on her feet."

I nodded and waited while Rojas translated. I had been using Rojas as my driver and interpreter ever since I had bought the advertising package on the Spanish radio stations.

I felt the cell phone in my pocket vibrate. My upper thigh read this as a text message as opposed to an actual phone call, which had a longer vibration. Either way I ignored it. When Rojas completed the translation, I jumped in before Mrs. Pena could respond.

"Tell her that she has to understand that this isn't a solution to her problems. I can delay things and we can negotiate with her bank. But I am not promising that she won't lose the house. In fact, she's already lost the house. I'm going to get it back but then she'll still have to face the bank."

Rojas translated, making hand gestures where I had not. The truth was that Mrs. Pena would have to leave eventually. It was just a question of how far she wanted me to take it. Personal bankruptcy would tack another year onto foreclosure defense. But she didn't have to decide that now.

"Now tell her that I also need to be paid for my work. Give her the schedule. A thousand up front and the monthly payment plan."

"How much on the monthly and how long?"

I looked out at the house again. Mrs. Pena had invited me inside but I preferred meeting in the car. This was drive-by territory and I was in my Lincoln Town Car BPS. That stood for Ballistic Protection Series. I bought it used from the widow of a murdered enforcer with the Sinaloa cartel. There was armored plating in the doors, and the windows were constructed of three layers of laminated glass. They were bulletproof. The windows in Mrs. Pena's pink house were not. The lesson learned from the Sinaloa man was that you don't leave the car unless you have to.

Mrs. Pena had explained earlier that the mortgage payments she had stopped making nine months ago had been seven hundred a month. She would continue to withhold any payments to the bank while I worked the case. She would have a free ride for as long as I kept the bank at bay, so there was money to be made here.

"Make it two-fifty a month. I'll give her the cut-rate plan. Make sure she knows she's getting a deal and that she can never be late with the payments. We can take a credit card if she has one with any juice on it. Just make sure it doesn't expire until at least twenty twelve."

Rojas translated, with more gestures and many more words than I had used, while I pulled my phone. The text had come from Lorna Taylor.

CALL ME ASAP.

I'd have to get back to her after the client conference. A typical law practice would have an office manager and receptionist. But I didn't have an office other than the backseat of my Lincoln, so Lorna ran the business end of things and answered the phones at the West Hollywood condo she shared with my chief investigator.

My mother was Mexican born and I understood her native language better than I ever let on. When Mrs. Pena responded, I knew what she said — the gist of it, at least. But I let Rojas translate it all back to me anyway. She promised to go inside the house to get the thousand-dollar cash retainer and to dutifully make the monthly payments. To me, not the bank. I figured that if I could extend her stay in the house to a year my take would be four grand total. Not bad for what was entailed. I would probably never see Mrs. Pena again. I would file a suit challenging the foreclosure and stretch things out. The chances were I wouldn't even make a court appearance. My young associate would do the courthouse legwork. Mrs. Pena would be happy and so would I. Eventually, though, the hammer would come down. It always does.

I thought I had a workable case even though Mrs. Pena would not be a sympathetic client. Most of my clients stop making payments to the bank after losing a job or experiencing a medical catastrophe. Mrs. Pena stopped when her three sons went to jail for selling drugs and their weekly financial support abruptly ended. Not a lot of goodwill to be had with that story. But the bank had played dirty. I had looked up her file on my laptop. It was all there: a record of her being served with notices involving demands for payment and then foreclosure. Only Mrs. Pena said she had never received these notices. And I believed her. It wasn't the kind of neighborhood where process servers were known to roam freely. I suspected that the notifications had ended up in the trash and the server had simply lied about it. If I could make that case, then I could back the bank off Mrs. Pena with the leverage it would give me.

That would be my defense. That the poor woman was never given proper notice of the peril she was in. The bank took advantage of her, foreclosed on her without allowing her the opportunity to make up the arrears, and should be rebuked by the court for doing so.

"Okay, we have a deal," I said. "Tell her to go in and get her money while I print out a contract and receipt. We'll get going on this today."

I smiled and nodded at Mrs. Pena. Rojas translated and then jumped out of the car to go around and open her door.

Once Mrs. Pena left the car I opened the Spanish contract template on my laptop and typed in the necessary names and numbers. I sent it to the printer that sat on an electronics platform on the front passenger seat. I then went to work on the receipt for funds to be deposited into my client trust account. Everything was aboveboard. Always. It was the best way to keep the California Bar off my ass. I might have a bulletproof car but it was the bar I most often checked for over my shoulder.

It had been a rough year for Michael Haller and Associates, Attorneys-at-Law. Criminal defense had virtually dried up in the down economy. Of course crime wasn't down. In Los Angeles, crime marched on through any economy. But the paying customers were few and far between. It seemed as though nobody had money to pay a lawyer. Consequently, the public defender's office was busting at the seams with cases and clients while guys like me were left starving.

I had expenses and a fourteen-year-old kid in private school who talked about USC whenever the subject of colleges came up. I had to do something and so I did what I had once held as unthinkable. I went civil. The only growth industry in the law business was foreclosure defense. I attended a few bar seminars, got up to speed on it and started running new ads in two languages. I built a few websites and started buying the lists of foreclosure filings from the county clerk's office. That's how I got Mrs. Pena as a client. Direct mail. Her name was on the list and I had sent her a letter—in Spanish—offering my services. She told me that my letter happened to be the first indication she had ever received that she was in foreclosure.

The saying goes that if you build it, they will come. It was true. I was getting more work than I could handle—six more appointments after Mrs. Pena today—and had even hired an actual associate to Michael Haller and Associates for the first time ever. The national epidemic of real estate foreclosure was slowing but by no means abating. In Los Angeles County I could be feeding at the trough for years to come.

The cases went for only four or five grand a pop but this was a quantity-over-quality period in my professional life. I currently had more than ninety foreclosure clients on my docket. No doubt my kid could start planning on USC. Hell, she could start thinking about staying for a master's degree.

There were those who believed I was part of the problem, that I was merely helping the deadbeats game the system while delaying the economic recovery of the whole. That description fit some of my clients for sure. But I viewed most of them as repeat victims. Initially scammed with the American dream of home ownership when lured into mortgages they had no business even qualifying for. And then victimized again when the bubble burst and unscrupulous lenders ran roughshod over them in the subsequent foreclosure frenzy. Most of these once-proud home owners didn't stand a chance under California's streamlined foreclosure regulations. A bank didn't even need a judge's approval to take away someone's house. The great financial minds thought this was the way to go. Just keep it moving. The sooner the crisis hit bottom, the sooner the recovery would begin. I say, Tell that to Mrs. Pena.

There was a theory out there that this was all part of a conspiracy among the top banks in the country to undermine property laws, sabotage the judicial system and create a perpetually cycling foreclosure industry that had them profiting from both ends of the process. Me, I wasn't exactly buying into that. But during my short time in this area of the law, I had seen enough predatory and unethical acts by so-called legitimate businessmen to make me miss good old-fashioned criminal law.

Rojas was waiting outside the car for Mrs. Pena to return with the money. I checked my watch and noted we were running late on my next appointment—a commercial foreclosure over in Compton. I tried to bunch my new client consultations geographically to save time and gas and mileage on the car. Today I worked the south end. Tomorrow I would hit East L.A. Two days a week I was in the car, signing up new clients. The rest of the time I worked the cases.

"Let's go, Mrs. Pena," I said. "We gotta roll."

I decided to use the waiting time to call Lorna. Three months earlier I had started blocking the ID on my phone. I never did that when I practiced criminal, but in my brave new world of foreclosure defense, I usually didn't want people having my direct number. And that included the lender attorneys as well as my own clients.

"Law offices of Michael Haller and Associates," Lorna said when she picked up. "How can I —"

"It's me. What's up?"

"Mickey, you have to get over to Van Nuys Division right away."

There was a strong urgency in her voice. Van Nuys Division was the LAPD's central command for operations in the sprawling San Fernando Valley, on the north side of the city.

"I'm working the south end today. What's going on?"

"They have Lisa Trammel there. She called."

Lisa Trammel was a client. In fact, my very first foreclosure client. I had kept her in her home for going on eight months and was confident I could take it at least another year further before we dropped the bankruptcy bomb. But she was consumed by the frustrations and inequities of her life and could not be calmed or controlled. She'd taken to marching in front of the bank with a placard decrying its fraudulent practices and heartless actions. That is, until the bank got a temporary restraining order against her.

"Did she violate the TRO? Are they holding her?"

"Mickey, they're holding her for murder."

That wasn't what I was expecting to hear.

"Murder? Who's the victim?"

"She said they're charging her with killing Mitchell Bondurant."

That gave me another great big pause. I looked out the window and saw Mrs. Pena coming out through her front door. She held a wad of cash in her hand.

"All right, get on the phone and reschedule the rest of today's appointments. And tell Cisco to head up to Van Nuys. I'll meet him there."

"You got it. Do you want Bullocks to take the afternoon appointments?"

"Bullocks" was what we called Jennifer Aronson, the associate I had hired out of Southwestern, a law school housed in the old Bullocks department store building on Wilshire.

"No, I don't want her doing intake. Just reschedule them. And listen, I think I have the Trammel file with me, but you have the call list. Track down her sister. Lisa's got a kid. He's probably in school and somebody's going to have to take him if Lisa can't."

We made every client fill out an extensive contact list because sometimes it was hard to find them for court hearings — and to get them to pay for my work.

"I'll start on that," Lorna said. "Good luck, Mickey."

"Same to you."

I closed the phone and thought about Lisa Trammel. Somehow I wasn't surprised that she had been arrested for killing the man who was trying to take her home away from her. It's not that I had thought it would come to this. Not even close. But deep down, I had known it was going to come to something.

2

I quickly took Mrs. Pena's cash and gave her a receipt. We both signed the contract and she got a copy for her own records. I took a credit card number from her and she promised it would withstand a $250-a-month hit while I was working for her. I then thanked her, shook her hand and had Rojas walk her back to her front door.

While he did that I popped the trunk with the remote I carried, and got out. The Lincoln's trunk was spacious enough to hold three cardboard file boxes as well as all my office supplies. I found the Trammel file in the third box and pulled it. I also grabbed the fancy briefcase I used for police station visits. When I closed the trunk I saw the stylized 13 spray-painted in silver on the lid's black paint.

"Son of a bitch."

I looked around. Three front yards down, a couple of kids were playing in the dirt but they looked too young to be graffiti artists. The rest of the street was deserted. I was baffled. Not only had I not heard or noticed the assault on my car that had taken place while I was having a client conference inside it, but it was barely past one and I knew most gangbangers didn't get up and embrace the day and all its possibilities until late afternoon. They were night creatures.

I headed back to my open door with the file. I noticed Rojas was standing at the front stoop, chatting with Mrs. Pena. I whistled and signaled him back to the car. We had to get going.

I got in. Message received, Rojas trotted back to the car and jumped in himself.

"Compton?" he asked.

"No, change of plans. We've got to get up to Van Nuys. Fast."

"Okay, Boss."

He pulled away from the curb and started making his way back to the 110 Freeway. There was no direct freeway route to Van Nuys. We would have to take the 110 into downtown where we'd pick up the 101 north. We couldn't have been starting off from a worse position in the city.

"What was she saying at the front door?" I asked Rojas.

"She was asking about you."

"What do you mean?"

"She said you looked like you shouldn't need a translator, you know?"

I nodded. I got that a lot. My mother's genes made me look more south of the border than north.

"She also wanted to know if you were married, Boss. I told her you were. But if you want to circle back and tap that, it'll be there. She'd probably want a discount on the fees, though."

"Thanks, Rojas," I said dryly. "She already got a discount but I'll keep it in mind."

Before opening the file I scrolled through the contacts list on my phone. I was looking for the name of someone in the Van Nuys detective squad who might share some information with me. But there was nobody. I was going in blind on a murder case. Not a good starting point either.

I closed the phone and put it into its charger, then opened the file. Lisa Trammel had become my client after responding to the generic letter I sent to the owners of all homes in foreclosure. I assumed I wasn't the only lawyer in Los Angeles who did this. But for some reason Lisa answered my letter and not theirs.

As an attorney in private practice you get to choose your own clients most of the time. Sometimes you choose wrong. Lisa was one of those times with me. I was eager to start the new line of work. I was looking for clients who were in jams or who had been taken advantage of. People who were too naive to know their rights or options. I was looking for underdogs and thought I had found one in Lisa. No doubt she fit the bill. She was losing her house because of a set of circumstances that had fallen like dominoes out of her control. And her lender had turned her case over to a foreclosure mill that had cut corners and even violated the rules. I signed Lisa up, put her on a payment plan and started to fight her fight. It was a good case and I was excited. It was only after this that Lisa became a nuisance client.

Lisa Trammel was thirty-five years old. She was the married mother of a nine-year-old boy named Tyler and their house was on Melba in Woodland Hills. At the time she and her husband, Jeffrey, bought the house in 2005, Lisa taught social studies at Grant High while Jeffrey sold BMWs at the dealership in Calabasas.

Their three-bedroom house carried a $750,000 mortgage against an appraised value of $900,000. The market was strong then and mortgages were plentiful and easy to get. They used an independent mortgage broker who shopped their file around and got them into a low-interest loan that carried a balloon payment at the five-year mark. The loan was then folded into an investment block of mortgages and reassigned twice before finding its permanent home at WestLand Financial, a subsidiary of WestLand National, the Los Angeles–based bank headquartered in Sherman Oaks.

All was well and good for the family of three until Jeff Trammel decided he didn't want to be a husband and father anymore. A few months before the $750,000 note on the house was due, Jeff took off, leaving his BMW M3 demo in the parking lot at Union Station and Lisa holding the balloon.

Down to a single income and a child to care for, Lisa looked at the reality of her situation and made choices. By now the economy had stalled out like a plane lumbering into the sky without enough airspeed. Given her teacher's income, no institution was going to refinance the balloon. She stopped making payments on the loan and ignored all communications from the bank. When the note came due, the property went into foreclosure and that was when I came onto the scene. I sent Jeff and Lisa a letter, not realizing Jeff was no longer in the picture.

Lisa answered it.

I define a nuisance client as one who does not understand the bounds of our relationship, even after I clearly and sometimes repeatedly delineate them. Lisa came to me with her first notice of foreclosure. I took the case and told her to sit back and wait while I went to work. But Lisa couldn't sit back. She couldn't wait. She called me every day. After I filed a lawsuit putting the foreclosure before a judge, she showed up at court for routine filings and continuances. She had to be there and she had to know every move I made, see every letter I sent and be summarized on every call I received. She often called me and yelled when she perceived that I was not giving her case my fullest attention. I began to understand why her husband had hightailed it. He had to get away from her.

I began to wonder about Lisa's mental health and suspected a bipolar affliction. The incessant calls and activities were cyclical. There were weeks when I heard nothing, alternating with weeks where she would call daily and repeatedly until she got me on the line.

Three months into the case she told me she had lost her job with the L.A. County School District because of unexcused absences. It was then that she talked about seeking damages from the bank that was foreclosing on her home. A sense of entitlement moved into the discourse. The bank was responsible for everything: the abandonment by her husband, the loss of her job, the taking of her home.

I made a mistake in revealing to her some of my case intelligence and strategy. I did it to appease her, to get her off the line. Our examination of the loan record had turned up inconsistencies and issues in the mortgage's repeated reassignment to various holding companies. There were indications of fraud that I thought I could use to swing leverage to Lisa's side when it came time to negotiate an out.

But the information only galvanized Lisa's belief in her victimization at the hands of the bank. Never did she acknowledge the fact that she had signed for a loan and was obliged to repay it. She saw the bank only as the source of her woes.

The first thing she did was register a website. She used www.california-foreclosurefighters.com to launch an organization called Foreclosure Litigants Against Greed. It worked better as an acronym — FLAG — and she effectively made use of the American flag on her protest signs. The message being that fighting foreclosure was as American as apple pie.

She then took to marching in front of WestLand's corporate headquarters on Ventura Boulevard. Sometimes by herself, sometimes with her young son, and sometimes with people she had attracted to the cause. She carried signs that decried the bank's involvement in illegal foreclosures and in putting families out of their homes and onto the streets.

Lisa was quick to alert local media outlets to her activities. She got on TV repeatedly and was always ready with a sound bite that gave voice to people in her situation, casting them as victims of the foreclosure epidemic, not garden-variety deadbeats. I had noticed that on Channel 5 she had even become part of the stock footage thrown up on the screen whenever there was an update on nationwide foreclosure issues or statistics. California was the third leading state in the country for foreclosures and Los Angeles was the hotbed. As these facts were reported, there would be Lisa and her group on the screen carrying their signs — DON'T TAKE MY HOME! STOP ILLEGAL FORECLOSURE NOW!

Alleging that her protests were illegal gatherings that impeded traffic and endangered pedestrians, WestLand sought and received a restraining order that kept Lisa one hundred yards from any bank facility and its employees. Undaunted, she took her signs and her fellow protestors to the county courthouse, where foreclosures were fought every day.

Mitchell Bondurant was a senior vice president at WestLand. He headed up the mortgage loan division. His name was on the loan documents relating to Lisa Trammel's house. As such his name was on all of my filings. I had also written him a letter, outlining what I described as indications of fraudulent practices by the foreclosure mill WestLand had contracted with to carry out the dirty work of taking the homes and other properties of their default customers.

Lisa was entitled to see all documents arising from her case. She was copied on the letter and everything else. Despite being the human face of the effort to take her home away, Bondurant remained above the fray, hiding behind the bank's legal team. He never responded to my letter and I never met him. I had no knowledge that Lisa Trammel had ever met or spoken with him either. But now he was dead and the police had Lisa in custody.

We exited the 101 at Van Nuys Boulevard and headed north. The civic center was a plaza surrounded by two courthouses, a library, City Hall North and the Valley Bureau police complex, which included the Van Nuys Division. Various other government agencies and buildings were clustered around the main grouping. Parking was always a problem but it wasn't my worry. I pulled my phone and called my investigator, Dennis Wojciechowski.

"Cisco, it's me. You close?"

In his early years Wojciechowski was associated with the Road Saints motorcycle club but there was already a member named Dennis. Nobody could pronounce Wojciechowski so they called him the Cisco Kid because of his dark looks and mustache. The mustache was now gone but the name had stuck.

"Already here. I'll meet you on the bench by the front stairs to the PD."

"I'll be there in five. Have you talked to anyone yet? I've got nothing."

"Yeah, your old pal Kurlen's running lead on this. The victim, Mitchell Bondurant, was found in the parking garage at WestLand's headquarters on Ventura about nine this morning. He was on the ground between two cars. Not clear how long he was down but he was dead on scene."

"Do we know the cause yet?"

"There it gets a little hinky. At first they put out that he'd been shot because an employee who was on another level of the garage told responding police she had heard two popping sounds, like shots. But when they examined the body on the scene it looked like he had been beaten to death. Hit with something."

"Was Lisa Trammel arrested there?"

"No, from what I understand, she was picked up at her home in Woodland Hills. I still have some calls out but that's about the extent of what I've got so far. Sorry, Mick."

"Don't worry about it. We'll know everything soon enough. Is Kurlen at the scene or with the suspect?"

"I was told he and his partner picked up Trammel and took her in. The partner's a female named Cynthia Longstreth. She's a D-one. I've never heard of her."

I had never heard of her either but since she was a detective one, my guess was that she was new to the homicide beat and paired with the veteran Kurlen, a D-3, to get some seasoning. I looked out the window. We were passing a BMW dealership and it made me think of the missing husband who had sold Beemers before pulling the plug on the marriage and disappearing. I wondered if Jeff Trammel would show up now that his wife was arrested for murder. Would he take custody of the son he had abandoned?

"You want me to get Valenzuela over here?" Cisco asked. "He's only a block away."

Fernando Valenzuela was a bail bondsman I used on Valley cases. But I knew he wouldn't be needed this time.

"I'd wait on that. If they've tagged her with murder she isn't going to make bail."

"Right, yeah."

"Do you know if a DA's been assigned yet?"

I was thinking about my ex-wife who worked for the district attorney's office in Van Nuys. She might be a useful source of back-channel information — unless she had been put on the case. Then there would be a conflict of interest. It had happened before. Maggie McPherson wouldn't like that.

"I've got nothing on that."

I considered what little we knew and what might be the best way to proceed. My feeling was that once the police understood what they had in this case — a murder that could draw wide attention to one of the great financial catastrophes of the time — they would quickly go to lockdown, putting a lid on all sources of information. The time to make moves was now.

"Cisco, I changed my mind. Don't wait for me. Go over to the scene and see what you can find out. Talk to people before they get locked down."

"You sure?"

"Yeah. I'll handle the PD and I'll call if I need anything."

"Got it. Good luck."

"You too."

I closed the phone and looked at the back of my driver's head.

"Rojas, turn right at Delano and take me up Sylmar."

"No problem."

"I don't know how long I'll be. I want you to drop me and then go back up Van Nuys Boulevard and find a body shop. See if they can get the paint off the back of the car."

Rojas looked at me in the rearview mirror.

"What paint?"

The Van Nuys police building is a four-story structure serving many purposes. It houses the Van Nuys police division as well as the Valley Bureau command offices and the main jail facility serving the northern part of the city. I had been here before on cases and knew that as with most LAPD stations large or small, there would be multiple obstacles standing between my client and me.

I have always had the suspicion that officers assigned to front desk duty were chosen by cunning supervisors because of their skills in obfuscation and disinformation. If you doubt this, walk into any police station in the city and tell the desk officer who greets you that you wish to make a complaint against a police officer. See how long it takes him to find the proper form. Desk cops are usually young and dumb and unintentionally ignorant, or old and obdurate and completely deliberate in their actions.

At the front desk at Van Nuys station I was met by an officer with the name CRIMMINS printed on his crisp uniform. He was a silver-haired veteran and therefore highly accomplished when it came to the dead-eyed stare. He showed this to me when I identified myself as a defense attorney with a client waiting to see me in the detective squad. His response consisted of pursing his lips and pointing to a row of plastic chairs where I was supposed to meekly go to wait until he deemed it time to call upstairs.

Guys like Crimmins are used to a cowering public: people who do exactly as he says because they are too intimidated to do anything else. I wasn't part of that public.

"No, that's not how this works," I said.

Crimmins squinted. He hadn't been challenged by anybody all day, let alone a criminal defense attorney — emphasis on *criminal*. His first move was to fire up the sarcasm responders.

"Is that right?"

"Yes, that's right. So pick up the phone and call upstairs to Detective Kurlen. Tell him Mickey Haller is on the way up and that if I don't see my client in the next ten minutes I'll just walk across the plaza to the courthouse and go see Judge Mills."

I paused to let the name register.

"I'm sure you know of Judge Roger Mills. Lucky for me, he used to be a criminal defense attorney before he got elected to the bench. He didn't like being jacked around by the police back then and doesn't like it much when he hears about it now. He'll drag both you and Kurlen into court and make you explain why you were playing this same old game of stopping a citizen from exercising her constitutional rights to consult an attorney. Last time it went down like that Judge Mills didn't like the answers he got and fined the guy who was sitting where you are five hundred bucks."

Crimmins looked like he'd had a hard time following my words. He was a short-sentence man, I guessed. He blinked twice and reached for the phone. I heard him confer directly with Kurlen. He then hung up.

"You know the way, smart guy?"

"I know the way. Thank you for your help, Officer Crimmins."

"Catch you later."

He pointed his finger at me like it was a gun, getting the last shot in so he could tell himself that he had handled that son-of-a-bitch lawyer. I left the desk and headed into the nearby alcove where I knew the elevator was located.

On the third floor Detective Howard Kurlen was waiting for me with a smile on his face. It wasn't a friendly smile. He looked like the cat who just ate the canary.

"Have fun down there, Counselor?"

"Oh, yeah."

"Well, you're too late up here."

"How's that? You booked her?"

He spread his hands in a phony *Sorry about that* gesture.

"It's funny. My partner took her out of here just before I got the call from downstairs."

"Wow, what a coincidence. I still want to talk to her."

"You'll have to go through the jail."

This would probably take me an extra hour of waiting. And this was why Kurlen was smiling.

"You sure you can't have your partner turn around and bring her down? I won't be long with her."

I said it even though I thought I was spitting into the wind. But Kurlen surprised me and pulled his phone off his belt. He hit a speed-dial button. It was either an elaborate hoax or he was actually doing what I asked. Kurlen and I had a history. We had squared off against each other on prior cases. I had attempted on more than one occasion to destroy his credibility on the witness stand. I was never very successful at it but the experience still made it hard to be cordial afterward. But now he was doing me a good turn and I wasn't sure why.

"It's me," Kurlen said into the phone. "Bring her back here."

He listened for a moment.

"Because I told you to. Now bring her back."

He closed the phone without another word to his partner and looked at me.

"You owe me one, Haller. I could've hung you up for a couple hours. In the old days, I would've."

"I know. I appreciate it."

He headed back toward the squad room and signaled me to follow. He spoke casually as he walked.

"So, when she told us to call you she said you were handling her foreclosure."

"That's right."

"My sister got divorced and now she's in a mess like that."

There it was. The quid pro quo.

"You want me to talk to her?"

"No, I just want to know if it's best to fight these things or just get it over with."

The squad room looked like it was in a time warp. It was vintage 1970s, with a linoleum floor, two-tone yellow walls and gray government-issue desks with rubber stripping around the edges. Kurlen remained standing while waiting for his partner to come back with my client.

I pulled a card out of my pocket and handed it to him.

"You're talking to a fighter, so that's my answer. I couldn't handle her case because of conflict of interest between you and me. But have her call the office and we'll get her hooked up with somebody good. Make sure she mentions your name."

Kurlen nodded and picked a DVD case off his desk and handed it to me.

"Might as well give you this now."

I looked at the disc.

"What's this?"

"Our interview with your client. You will clearly see that we stopped talking to her as soon as she said the magic words: I want a lawyer."

"I'll be sure to check that out, Detective. You want to tell me why she's your suspect?"

"Sure. She's our suspect and we're charging her because she did it and she made admissions about it before asking to call her lawyer. Sorry about that, Counselor, but we played by the rules."

I held the disc up as if it were my client.

"You're telling me she admitted killing Bondurant?"

"Not in so many words. But she made admissions and contradictions. I'll leave it at that."

"Did she by any chance say in so many words why she did it?"

"She didn't have to. The victim was in the process of taking away her house. That's plenty enough motive right there. We're as good as gold on motive."

I could've told him that he had that wrong, that I was in the process of stopping the foreclosure. But I kept my mouth shut about that. My job was to gather information here, not give it away.

"What else you got, Detective?"

"Nothing that I care to share with you at the moment. You'll have to wait to get the rest through discovery."

"I'll do that. Has a DA been assigned yet?"

"Not that I heard."

Kurlen nodded toward the back of the room and I turned to see Lisa Trammel being walked toward the door of an interrogation room. She had the classic deer-in-the-headlights look in her eyes.

"You've got fifteen minutes," Kurlen said. "And that's only because I'm being nice. I figure there's no need to start a war."

Not yet, at least, I thought as I headed toward the interrogation room.

"Hey, wait a minute," Kurlen called to my back. "I have to check the briefcase. Rules, you know."

He was referring to the leather-over-aluminum attaché I was carrying. I could've made an argument about the search infringing on attorney-client privilege but I wanted to talk to my client. I stepped back toward him and swung the case up onto a counter, then popped it open. All it contained was the Lisa Trammel file, a fresh legal pad and the new contracts and power-of-attorney form I had printed out while driving up. I figured I needed Lisa to re-sign since my representation was crossing from civil to criminal.

Kurlen gave it a quick once-over and signaled me to close it.

"Hand-tooled Italian leather," he said. "Looks like a fancy drug dealer's case. You haven't been associating with the wrong people, have you, Haller?"

He put on that canary smile again. Cop humor was truly unique in all the world.

"As a matter of fact, it did belong to a courier," I said. "A client. But where he was going he wasn't going to need it anymore so I took it in trade. You want to see the secret compartment? It's kind of a pain to open."

"I think I'll pass. You're good."

I closed the case and headed back to the interrogation room.

"And it's Colombian leather," I said.

Kurlen's partner was waiting at the room's door. I didn't know her but didn't bother to introduce myself. We were never going to be friendly and I guessed she would be the type to stiff me on the handshake in order to impress Kurlen.

She held the door open and I stopped at the threshold.

"All listening and recording devices in this room are off, correct?"

"You got it."

"If they're not that would be a violation of my client's —"

"We know the drill."

"Yeah, but sometimes you conveniently forget it, don't you?"

"You've got fourteen minutes now, sir. You want to talk to her or keep talking to me?"

"Right."

I went in and the door was closed behind me. It was a nine-by-six room. I looked at Lisa and put a finger to my lips.

"What?" she asked.

"That means don't say a word, Lisa, until I tell you to."

Her response was to break down in a cascade of tears and a loud and long wail that tailed off into a sentence that was completely unintelligible. She was sitting at a square table with a chair opposite her. I quickly took the open chair and put my case up on the table. I knew she would be positioned to face the room's hidden camera, so I didn't bother to look around for it. I snapped open the case and pulled it close to my body, hoping that my back would act as a blind to the camera. I had to assume that Kurlen and his partner were listening and watching. One more reason for his being "nice."

While one by one I took out the legal pad and documents with my right hand, I used the left to open the case's secret compartment. I hit the engage button on the Paquin 2000 acoustic jammer. The device emitted a low-frequency RF signal that clogged any listening device within twenty-five feet with electronic disinformation. If Kurlen and his partner were illegally listening in, they were now hearing white noise.

The case and its hidden device were almost ten years old and as far as I knew, the original owner was still in federal prison. I'd taken it in trade at least seven years ago, back when drug cases were my bread and butter. I knew law enforcement was always trying to build a better mousetrap, and in ten years the electronic eavesdropping business must have undergone at least two revolutions. So I was not completely put at ease. I would still need to exercise caution in what I said and hoped my client would as well.

"Lisa, we're not going to talk a whole lot here because we don't know who may be listening. You understand?"

"I think so. But what is happening here? I don't understand what's *happening!*"

Her voice had risen progressively through the sentence until she was screaming the last word. This was an emotional speaking pattern she had used several times on the phone with me when I was handling only her foreclosure. Now the stakes were higher and I had to draw the line.

"None of that, Lisa," I said firmly. "You do not scream at me. You understand? If I'm going to represent you on this you do not scream at me."

"Okay, sorry, but they're saying I did something I didn't do."

"I know and we're going to fight it. But no screaming."

Because they had pulled her back before the booking process had begun, Lisa was still in her own clothes. She was wearing a white T-shirt with a flower pattern on the front. I saw no blood on it or anywhere else. Her face was streaked with tears and her brown curly hair was unkempt. She was a small woman and seemed even more so in the harsh light of the room.

"I need to ask you some questions," I said. "Where were you when the police found you?"

"I was home. *Why are they doing this to me?*"

"Lisa, listen to me. You have to calm down and let me ask the questions. This is very important."

"But what's going on? No one tells me anything. They said I was under arrest for murdering Mitchell Bondurant. When? How? I didn't go near that man. I didn't break the TRO."

I realized that it would have been better if I had viewed Kurlen's DVD before speaking with her. But it was par for the course to come into a case at a disadvantage.

"Lisa, you are indeed under arrest for the murder of Mitchell Bondurant. Detective Kurlen — he's the older one — told me that you made admissions to them in re—"

She shrieked and brought her hands to her face. I saw that she was cuffed at the wrists. A new round of tears started.

"I didn't admit anything! *I didn't do anything!*"

"Calm down, Lisa. That's why I'm here. To defend you. But we don't have a lot of time right now. They're giving me ten minutes and then they're going to book you. I need to—"

"I'm going to jail?"

I nodded reluctantly.

"Well, what about bail?"

"It is very hard to get bail on a murder charge. And even if I could get something set, you don't have the—"

Another piercing wail filled the tiny room. I lost my patience.

"*Lisa! Stop doing that!* Now listen, your life is at stake here, okay? You have to calm down and listen to me. I am your attorney and I will do my best to get you out of here but it's going to take some time. Now listen to my questions and answer them without all the—"

"What about my son? What about Tyler?"

"Someone from my office is making contact with your sister and we will arrange for him to be with her until we can get you out."

I was very careful not to introduce a hard time line for her release. *Until we can get you out.* As far as I was concerned, that might be days, weeks or even years. It might never happen. But I did not need to get specific.

Lisa nodded as if there was some relief in knowing her son would be with her sister.

"What about your husband? You have a contact number for him?"

"No, I don't know where he is and I don't want you contacting him anyway."

"Not even for your son?"

"Especially not for my son. My sister will take care of him."

I nodded and let it go. Now was not the time to ask about her failed marriage.

"Okay, calmly now, let's talk about this morning. I have the disc from the detectives but I want to go over this myself. You said you were home when Detective Kurlen and his partner arrived. What were you doing?"

"I was...I was on the computer. I was sending e-mails."

"Okay, to who?"

"To my friends. To people in FLAG. I was telling them that we were going to meet tomorrow at the courthouse at ten and to bring the placards."

"Okay, and when the detectives showed up, what exactly did they say?"

"The man did all the talking. He—"

"Kurlen."

"Yes. They came in and he asked me some things. Then he asked if I wouldn't mind coming to the station to answer questions. I said about what and he said Mitch Bondurant. He didn't say anything about him being dead or killed. So I said yes. I thought maybe they were finally investigating him. I didn't know they were investigating me."

"Well, did he tell you that you had certain rights not to speak to him and to contact a lawyer?"

"Yes, like on TV. He told me my rights."

"When exactly?"

"When we were already here, when he said I was under arrest."

"Did you ride with him here?"

"Yes."

"And did you speak in the car?"

"No, he was on his cell phone almost the whole time. I heard him say things like 'I have her with me' and like that."

"Were you handcuffed?"

"In the car? No."

Smart Kurlen. He risked riding in the car with an uncuffed murder suspect in order to keep her suspicions down and to lull her into agreeing to speak with him. You can't build a better mousetrap than that. It would also allow the prosecution to argue that Lisa was not under arrest yet and therefore her statements were voluntary.

"So you were brought here and you agreed to talk to him?"

"Yes. I had no idea they were going to arrest me. I thought I was helping them with a case."

"But Kurlen didn't say what the case was."

"No, never. Not until he said I was under arrest and that I could make a call. And that's when they handcuffed me, too."

Kurlen had used some of the oldest tricks in the book but they were still in the book because they worked. I had to watch the DVD to know exactly what Lisa had admitted to, if anything. Asking her about it while she was upset was not the best use of my limited time. As if to underscore this, there was a sudden and sharp knock on the door followed by a muffled voice saying I had two minutes.

"Okay, I am going to go to work on this, Lisa. I need you to sign a couple of documents first, though. This first one is a new contract that covers criminal defense."

I slid the one-page document over to her and put a pen on top of it. She started to scan it.

"All these fees," she said. "A hundred fifty thousand dollars for a trial? I can't pay you this. I don't have it."

"That's a standard fee and that's only if we go to trial. And as far as what you can pay, that's what these other documents are for. This one gives me your power of attorney, allowing me to solicit book and movie deals, things like that, coming from the case. I have an agent I work with on this stuff. If there's a deal out there he'll get it. The last document puts a lien on any of those funds so that the defense gets paid first."

I knew this case was going to draw attention. The foreclosure epidemic was the country's biggest ongoing financial catastrophe. There could be a book in this, maybe even a film, and I could end up getting paid.

She picked up the pen and signed the documents without reading further. I took them back and put them away.

"Okay, Lisa, what I am about to tell you now is the most important piece of advice in the world. So I want you to listen and then tell me you understand."

"Okay."

"Do not talk about this case with anyone other than me. Do not talk to detectives, jailers, other jail inmates, don't even talk to your sister or son about it. Whenever anyone asks — and believe me, they will — you simply tell them that you cannot talk about your case."

"But I didn't do anything wrong. I'm innocent! It's people who are guilty who don't talk."

I held my finger up to admonish her.

"No, you're wrong, and it sounds to me like you are not taking what I say seriously, Lisa."

"No, I am, I am."

"Then do what I am telling you. Talk to no one. And that includes the phone in the jail. All calls are recorded, Lisa. Don't talk on the phone about your case, even to me."

"Okay, okay. I got it."

"If it makes you feel any better, you can answer all questions by saying 'I am innocent of the charges but on the advice of my attorney I am not going to talk about the case.' Okay, how's that?"

"Good, I guess."

The door opened and Kurlen was standing there. He was giving me the squint of suspicion, which told me it was a good thing I had brought the Paquin jammer with me. I looked back at Lisa.

"Okay, Lisa, it gets bad before it gets good. Hang in there and remember the golden rule. Talk to no one."

I stood up.

"The next time you'll see me will be at first appearance and we'll be able to talk then. Now go with Detective Kurlen."